Closer scrutiny w

Had this pair been more so have seen the mostly unmarked skin beneath the grime and the rangy but sturdy frame of a well-fed lad beneath the rags. Keener eyes and a fraction more time would also have discerned the small bulge of the knife beneath my threadbare jerkin. But these unfortunates lacked the required keenness of vision, and they were out of time. It had only been moments since I had stumbled into their path, but the distraction had been enough to bring their entire party to a halt. Over the course of an eventful and perilous life, I have found that it is in these small, confused interludes that death is most likely to arrive.

For the soldier on the right it arrived in the form of a crow-fletched arrow with a barbed steel head. The shaft came streaking from the trees to enter his neck just behind the ear before erupting from his mouth in a cloud of blood and shredded tongue. As he toppled from the saddle, his whip-bearing comrade proved his veteran status by immediately dropping the whip and reaching for his longsword. He was quick, but so was I. Snatching my knife from its sheath I put my bandaged foot beneath me and launched myself up, latching my free hand to his horse's bridle. The animal reared in instinctive alarm, raising me the additional foot I required to sink my knife into the soldier's throat before he could fully draw his sword. I was proud of the thrust, it being something I'd practised as much as my witless expression, the blade opening the required veins at the first slice.

I kept hold of the horse's reins as my feet met the ground, the beast threatening to tip me over with all its wheeling about. Watching the soldier tumble to the road and gurgle out his last few breaths, I felt a pang of regret for the briefness of his end. Surely this fellow with his well-worn whip had earned a more prolonged passing in his time. However, my regret was muted as one of many lessons in outlaw craft drummed into me over the years came to mind: *When the task is a killing, be quick and make sure of it. Torment is an indulgence. Save it for only the most deserving.*

By Anthony Ryan

THE RAVEN'S SHADOW
Blood Song
Tower Lord
Queen of Fire

THE DRACONIS MEMORIA
The Waking Fire
The Legion of Flame
The Empire of Ashes

THE RAVEN'S BLADE
The Wolf's Call
The Black Song

THE COVENANT OF STEEL
The Pariah

THE
PARIAH

BOOK ONE OF
THE COVENANT OF STEEL

ANTHONY RYAN

orbit

orbitbooks.net

Copyright © 2021 by Anthony Ryan
Excerpt from *Son of the Storm* copyright © 2021 by Suyi Davies Okungbowa
Excerpt from *The Jasmine Throne* copyright © 2021 by Natasha Suri

Cover design by Lauren Panepinto
Cover illustration by Jaime Jones
Cover copyright © 2021 by Hachette Book Group, Inc.
Map by Anthony Ryan
Author photograph by Ellie Grace Photography

Orbit
Hachette Book Group
1290 Avenue of the Americas
New York, NY 10104
orbitbooks.net

First Edition: August 2021
Simultaneously published in Great Britain by Orbit

Orbit is an imprint of Hachette Book Group.
The Orbit name and logo are trademarks of Little, Brown Book Group Limited.

The publisher is not responsible for websites (or their content) that are not owned by the publisher.

The Hachette Speakers Bureau provides a wide range of authors for speaking events. To find out more, go to www.hachettespeakersbureau.com or call (866) 376-6591.

Library of Congress Control Number: 2021933401

ISBNs: 978-0-316-43076-0 (trade paperback), 978-0-316-43077-7 (ebook)

Printed in the United States of America

LSC-C

Printing 1, 2021

Dedicated to the memory of George MacDonald Fraser, author of the Flashman books, who first taught me the joy of seeing the world through caddish eyes

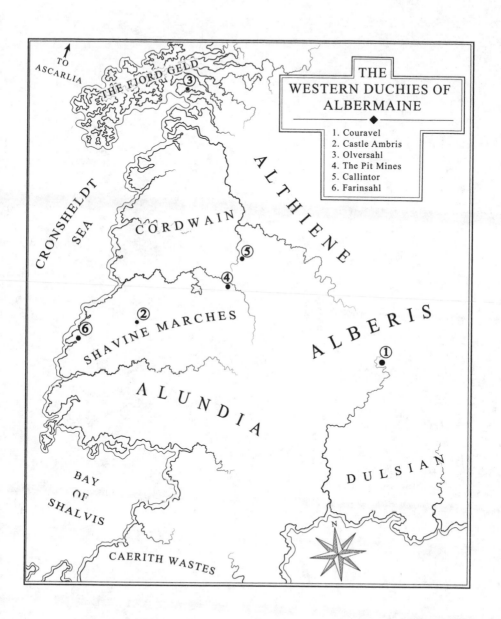

TO
ASCARLIA

THE FJORD GELD

③

THE
WESTERN DUCHIES OF
ALBERMAINE
◆

1. Couravel
2. Castle Ambris
3. Olversahl
4. The Pit Mines
5. Callintor
6. Farinsahl

CRONSHELDT
SEA

CORDWAIN

ALTHIENE

⑤

④

②

⑥

SHAVINE MARCHES

ALBERIS

①

ALUNDIA

DULSIAN

BAY
OF
SHALVIS

N

CAERITH WASTES

DRAMATIS PERSONAE

Alwyn Scribe – Outlaw, scribe and later Supplicant Blade in Covenant Company

Evadine Courlain – Noble-born captain of Covenant Company, Communicant and later Aspirant cleric in the Covenant of Martyrs

Deckin Scarl – Outlaw leader and bastard son of Duke Rouphon Ambris of the Shavine Marches

Elbyn Blousset – Appointed Duke of the Shavine Marches by King Tomas upon the condemnation of Duke Rouphon

Lorine D'Ambrille – Chief lieutenant and lover of Deckin

Raith – Outlaw and Caerith charm worker

Gerthe – Outlaw, whore and linguist, member of Deckin's band

Erchel – Outlaw of vile inclinations

Shilva Sahken – Outlaw leader and friend of Deckin

Todman – Outlaw, member of Deckin's band

Hostler – Outlaw of devout leanings, member of Deckin's band

King Tomas Algathinet – First of his name, monarch of Albermaine

Ehlbert Bauldry – Knight of famed martial abilities, champion to King Tomas

Princess Leannor Algathinet – Sister of King Tomas

The Chainsman – Caerith pedlar of captive outlaws

Toria – Outlaw, inmate of the Pit Mines, friend of Alwyn

Sihlda Doisselle – Former senior Covenant cleric and inmate of the Pit Mines, tutor of Alwyn

Brewer – Inmate in the Pit Mines, congregant of Sihlda

Hedgeman – Inmate in the Pit Mines, congregant of Sihlda

Magnis Lochlain – Pretender to the Throne of Albermaine, also known as the 'True King'

Althus Levalle – Knight Commander of Crown Company

Eldurm Gulatte – Lord Warden of the King's Mines

Ascendant Hilbert – Senior cleric of the Shrine to Martyr Callin in the sanctuary town of Callintor

Arnild – Master illuminator in the scriptorium of the Shrine to Martyr Callin in the sanctuary town of Callintor

Albyrn Swain – Supplicant Sergeant of Covenant Company

Ofihla Barrow – Supplicant Blade of Covenant Company

Delric Cleymount – Supplicant and healer of Covenant Company

The Sack Witch – Caerith spell worker and healer, said to be of hideous appearance beneath the sackcloth mask she wears

Wilhum Dornmahl – Disgraced turncoat knight formerly in service to the Pretender, soldier in Covenant Company and childhood friend of Evadine

Berrine Jurest – Fjord Gelder, servant of the Library of King Aeric in Olversahl

Maritz Fohlvast – Fjord Gelder, Lord Elderman of Olversahl, merchant and intriguer

Margnus Gruinskard – Ascarlian warband leader and Tielwald sworn to the Sister Queens

PART I

"You say my claim to the throne was false, that I began a war that spilled the blood of thousands for nothing. I ask you, Scribe, what meaning is there in truth or lies in this world? As for blood, I have heard of you. I know your tale. History may judge me as monstrous, but you are a far bloodier man than I."

From *The Testament of the Pretender Magnis Lochlain,*
as recorded by Sir Alwyn Scribe

CHAPTER ONE

Before killing a man, I always found it calming to regard the trees. Lying on my back in the long grass fringing the King's Road and gazing at the green and brown matrix above, branches creaking and leaves whispering in the late-morning breeze, brought a welcome serenity. I had found this to be true ever since my first faltering steps into this forest as a boy ten years before. When the heart began to thud and sweat beaded my brow, the simple act of looking up at the trees brought a respite, one made sweeter by the knowledge that it would be short lived.

Hearing the clomp of iron-shod hooves upon earth, accompanied by the grinding squeal of a poorly greased axle, I closed my eyes to the trees and rolled onto my belly. Shorn of the soothing distraction, my heart's excited labour increased in pitch, but I was well schooled in not letting it show. Also, the sweat dampening my armpits and trickling down my back would only add to my stench, adding garnish for the particular guise I adopted that day. Lamed outcasts are rarely fragrant.

Raising my head just enough to glimpse the approaching party through the grass, I was obliged to take a deep breath at the sight of the two mounted men-at-arms riding at the head of the caravan. More concerning still were the two soldiers perched on the cart that followed, both armed with crossbows, eyes scanning the forest on either side of the road in a worrying display of hard-learned vigilance. Although not within the chartered bounds of the Shavine Forest, this stretch of the King's Road described a long arc through its northern fringes. Sparse in comparison to the deep forest, it was still a place of bountiful cover and not one to be travelled by the unwary in such troubled times.

As the company drew closer, I saw a tall lance bobbing above the small throng, the pennant affixed beneath its blade fluttering in the breeze with too much energy to make out the crest it bore. However, its gold and red hues told the tale clearly: royal colours. Deckin's intelligence had, as ever, been proven correct: this lot were the escort for a Crown messenger.

I waited until the full party had revealed itself, counting another four mounted men-at-arms in the rearguard. I took some comfort from the earthy brown and green of their livery. These were not kingsmen but ducal levies from Cordwain, taken far from home by the demands of war and not so well trained or steadfast as Crown soldiery. However, their justified caution and overall impression of martial orderliness was less reassuring. I judged them unlikely to run when the time came, which was unfortunate for all concerned.

I rose when the leading horsemen were a dozen paces off, reaching for the gnarled, rag-wrapped tree branch that served as my crutch and levering myself upright. I was careful to blink a good deal and furrow my brow in the manner of a soul just roused from slumber. As I hobbled towards the verge, keeping the blackened bulb of my bandaged foot clear of the ground, my features slipped easily into the gape-mouthed, emptied-eyed visage of a crippled dullard. Reaching the road, I allowed the foot to brush the churned mud at the edge. Letting out an agonised groan of appropriate volume, I stumbled forwards, collapsing onto all fours in the middle of the rutted fairway.

It should not be imagined that I fully expected the soldiers' horses to rear, for many a warhorse is trained to trample a prone man. Fortunately, these beasts had not been bred for knightly service and they both came to a gratifyingly untidy halt, much to the profane annoyance of their riders.

"Get out of the fucking road, churl!" the soldier on the right snarled, dragging on his reins as his mount wheeled in alarm. Beyond him, the cart and, more importantly, the bobbing lance of the Crown messenger also stopped. The crossbowmen sank lower on the mound of cargo affixed to the cart-bed, both reaching for the bolts in their quivers. Crossbowmen are always wary of leaving their weapons primed for long intervals, for it wears down the stave and the string. However, failing to do so this day would soon prove a fatal miscalculation.

I didn't allow my sight to linger on the cart, however, instead gaping up at the mounted soldier with wide, fearful eyes that betrayed little comprehension. It was an expression I had practised extensively, for it is not easy to mask one's intellect.

"Shift your arse!" his companion instructed, his voice marginally less angry and speaking as if addressing a dull-witted dog. When I continued to stare up at him from the ground he cursed and reached for the whip on his saddle.

"Please!" I whimpered, crutch raised protectively over my head. "Y-your pardon, good sirs!"

I had noticed on many occasions that such cringing will invariably stoke rather than quell the violent urges of the brutishly inclined, and so it proved now. The soldier's face darkened as he unhooked the whip, letting it unfurl so its barbed tip dangled onto the road a few inches from my cowering form. Looking up, I saw his hand tighten on the diamond-etched pattern of the handle. The leather was well worn, marking this as a man who greatly enjoyed opportunities to use this weapon.

However, as he raised the lash he paused, features bunching in disgust. "Martyrs' guts, but you're a stinker!"

"Sorry, sir!" I quailed. "Can't help it. Me foot, see? It's gone all rotten since me master's cart landed on it. I'm on the Trail of Shrines. Going to beseech Martyr Stevanos to put me right. Y'wouldn't hurt a faithful fellow, would you?"

In fact, my foot was a fine and healthy appendage to an equally healthy leg. The stench that so assailed the soldier's nose came from a pungent mix of wild garlic, bird shit and mulched-up leaves. For a guise to be convincing, one must never neglect the power of scent. It was important that these two see no threat in me. A lamed youth happened upon while traversing a notoriously treacherous road could well be faking. But one with a face lacking all wit and a foot exuding an odour carefully crafted to match the festering wounds this pair had surely encountered before was another matter.

Closer scrutiny would surely have undone me. Had this pair been more scrupulous in their appraisal they would have seen the mostly unmarked skin beneath the grime and the rangy but sturdy frame of a well-fed lad beneath the rags. Keener eyes and a fraction more time would also have discerned the small bulge of the knife beneath my threadbare jerkin. But these unfortunates lacked the required keenness of vision, and they were out of time. It had only been moments since I had stumbled into their path, but the distraction had been enough to bring their entire party to a halt. Over the course of an eventful and perilous life, I have found that it is in these small, confused interludes that death is most likely to arrive.

For the soldier on the right it arrived in the form of a crow-fletched arrow with a barbed steel head. The shaft came streaking from the trees to enter his neck just behind the ear before erupting from his mouth in a cloud of blood and shredded tongue. As he toppled from the saddle, his whip-bearing comrade proved his veteran status by immediately dropping the whip and reaching for his longsword. He was quick, but so was I. Snatching my knife from its sheath I put my bandaged foot beneath me and launched myself up, latching my free hand to his horse's bridle. The animal reared in instinctive alarm, raising me the additional foot I required to sink my knife into the soldier's throat before he could fully draw his sword. I was proud of the thrust, it being something I'd practised as much as my witless expression, the blade opening the required veins at the first slice.

I kept hold of the horse's reins as my feet met the ground, the beast threatening to tip me over with all its wheeling about. Watching the soldier tumble to the road and gurgle out his last few breaths, I felt a pang of regret for the briefness of his end. Surely this fellow with his well-worn whip had earned a more prolonged passing in his time. However, my regret was muted as one of many lessons in outlaw craft drummed into me over the years came to mind: *When the task is a killing, be quick and make sure of it. Torment is an indulgence. Save it for only the most deserving.*

It was mostly over by the time I calmed the horse. The first volley of arrows had felled all but two of the guards. Both crossbowmen lay dead on the cart, as did its drover. One man-at-arms had the good sense to turn his horse about and gallop off, not that it saved him from the thrown axe that came spinning out of the trees to take him in the back. The last was made of more admirable, if foolhardy stuff. The brief arrow storm had impaled his thigh and skewered his mount, but still he contrived to roll clear of the thrashing beast and rise, drawing his sword to face the two dozen outlaws running from the treeline.

I have heard versions of this tale that would have you believe that, when confronted by this brave and resolute soul, Deckin Scarl himself forbade his band from cutting him down. Instead he and the stalwart engaged in solitary combat. Having mortally wounded the soldier, the famed outlaw sat with him until nightfall as they shared tales of battles fought and ruminated on the capricious mysteries that determine the fates of all.

These days, similarly nonsensical songs and stories abound regarding Deckin Scarl, renowned Outlaw King of the Shavine Marches and, as some would have it, protector of churl and beggar alike. *With one hand he stole and the other he gave,* as one particularly execrable ballad would have it. *Brave Deckin of the woods, strong and kind he stood.*

If, dear reader, you find yourself minded to believe a word of this I have a six-legged donkey to sell you. The Deckin Scarl I knew was certainly strong, standing two inches above six feet with plenty of muscle to match his height, although his belly had begun to swell in recent years. And kind he could be, but it was a rare thing for a man does not rise to the summit of outlawry in the Shavine Forest by dint of kindness.

In fact, the only words I heard Deckin say in regard to that stout soldier was a grunted order to, "Kill that silly fucker and let's get on." Neither did Deckin bother to spare a glance for the fellow's end, sent off to the Martyrs' embrace by a dozen arrows. I watched the outlaw king come stomping from the shadowed woods with his axe in hand, an ugly weapon with a blackened and misshapen double blade that was rarely far from his reach. He paused to regard my handiwork, shrewd eyes bright beneath his heavy brows as they tracked from the soldier's corpse to the horse I had managed to capture. Horses were a prize worth claiming for they fetched a good price, especially in times of war. Even if they couldn't be sold, meat was always welcome in camp.

Grunting in apparent satisfaction, Deckin swiftly turned his attention to the sole survivor of the ambush, an outcome that had not been accidental. "One arrow comes within a yard of the messenger," he had growled at us all that morning, "and I'll have the skin off the hand that loosed it, fingers to wrist." It wasn't an idle threat, for we had all seen him make good on the promise before.

The royal messenger was a thin-faced man clad in finely tailored jerkin and trews with a long cloak dyed to mirror the royal livery. Seated upon a grey stallion, he maintained an expression of disdainful affront even as Deckin moved to grasp the bridle of his horse. For all his rigid dignity and evident outrage, he was wise enough not to lower the lance he held, the royal pennant continuing to stand tall and flutter above this scene of recent slaughter.

"Any violence or obstruction caused to a messenger in Crown service is considered treason," the thin-faced fellow stated, his voice betraying a creditably small quaver. He blinked and finally consented to afford Deckin the full force of his imperious gaze. "You should know that, whoever you are."

"Indeed I do, good sir," Deckin replied, inclining his head. "And I believe you know full well who I am, do you not?"

The messenger blinked again and shifted his eyes away once more, not deigning to answer. I had seen Deckin kill for less blatant insults, but now he just laughed. Raising his free hand, he gave a hard, expectant snap of his fingers.

The messenger's face grew yet more rigid, rage and humiliation flushing his skin red. I saw his nostrils flare and lips twitch, no doubt the result of biting down unwise words. The fact that he didn't need to be asked twice before reaching for the leather scroll tube on his belt made it plain that he certainly knew the name of the man before him.

"Lorine!" Deckin barked, taking the scroll from the messenger's reluctant hand and holding it out to the slim, copper-haired woman who strode forwards to take it.

The balladeers would have it that Lorine D'Ambrille was the famously fair daughter of a distant lordling who fled her father's castle rather than suffer an arranged marriage to a noble of ill repute and vile habits. Via many roads and adventures, she made her way to the dark woods of the Shavine Marches where she had the good fortune to be rescued from a pack of ravening wolves by none other than the kindly rogue Deckin Scarl himself. Love soon blossomed betwixt them, a love that, much to my annoyance, has echoed through the years acquiring ever more ridiculous legend in the process.

As far as I have been able to ascertain there was no more noble blood in Lorine's veins than mine, although the origin of her comparatively well-spoken tones and evident education are still something of a mystery. She remained a cypher despite the excessive time I would devote to thinking of her. As with all legends, however, a kernel of truth lingers: she was fair. Her features held a smooth handsomeness that had survived years of forest living and she somehow contrived to keep her lustrous copper hair free of grease and burrs. For one suffering the boundless lust of youth, I couldn't help but stare at her whenever the chance arose.

After removing the cap from the tube to extract the scroll within, Lorine's smooth, lightly freckled brow creased a little as she read its contents. Captured as always by her face, my fascination was dimmed somewhat by the short but obvious spasm of shock that flickered over her features. She hid it well, of course, for she was my tutor in the arts of disguise and even more practised than I in concealing potentially dangerous emotions.

"You have it all?" Deckin asked her.

"Word for word, my love," Lorine assured him, white teeth revealed in a smile as she returned the scroll to the tube and replaced the cap. Although her origins would always remain in shadow, I had gleaned occasional mentions of treading stages and girlhood travels with troupes of players, leading me to conclude that Lorine had once been an actress. Perhaps as a consequence, she possessed the uncanny ability to memorise a large amount of text after only a few moments of reading.

"If I might impose upon your good nature, sir," Deckin told the messenger, taking the tube from Lorine. "I would consider it the greatest favour if you could carry an additional message to King Tomas. As one king to another, please inform him of my deepest and most sincere regrets regarding this unfortunate and unforeseen delay to the journey of his trusted agent, albeit brief."

The messenger stared at the proffered tube as one might a gifted turd, but took it nonetheless. "Such artifice will not save you," he said, the words clipped by his clenched teeth. "And you are not a king, Deckin Scarl."

"Really?" Deckin pursed his lips and raised an eyebrow in apparent surprise. "I am a man who commands armies, guards his borders, punishes transgressions and collects the taxes that are his due. If such a man is not a king, what is he?"

It was clear to me that the messenger had answers aplenty for this question but, being a fellow of wisdom as well as duty, opted to offer no reply.

"And so, I'll bid you good day and safe travels," Deckin said, stepping back to slap a brisk hand to the rump of the messenger's horse. "Keep to the road and don't stop until nightfall. I can't guarantee your safety after sunset."

The messenger's horse spurred into a trot at the slap, one its rider was quick to transform into a gallop. Soon he was a blur of churned mud, his trailing cloak a red and gold flicker among the trees until he rounded a bend and disappeared from view.

"Don't stand gawping!" Deckin barked, casting his glare around the band. "We've got loot to claim and miles to cover before dusk."

They all fell to the task with customary enthusiasm, the archers claiming the soldiers they had felled while the others swarmed the cart. Keen to join them, I looked around for a sapling where I could tether my stolen horse but drew up short as Deckin raised a hand to keep me in place.

"Just one cut," he said, coming closer and nodding his shaggy head at the slain soldier with the whip. "Not bad."

"Like you taught me, Deckin," I said, offering a smile. I felt it falter on my lips as he cast an appraising eye over the horse and gestured for me to pass him the reins.

"Think I'll spare him the stewpot," he said, smoothing a large hand over the animal's grey coat. "Still just a youngster. Plenty of use left in him. Like you, eh, Alwyn?"

He laughed one of his short, grating laughs, a sound I was quick to mimic. I noticed Lorine still stood a short way off, eschewing the frenzied looting to observe our conversation with arms crossed and head cocked. I found her expression strange; the slightly pinched mouth bespoke muted amusement while her narrowed gaze and drawn brows told of restrained concern. Deckin tended to speak to me more than the other youngsters in the band, something that aroused a good deal of envy, but not usually on Lorine's part. Today, however, she apparently saw some additional significance in his favour, making me wonder if it had something to do with the contents of the messenger's scroll.

"Let's play our game, eh?" Deckin said, instantly recapturing my attention. I turned back to see him jerk his chin at the bodies of the two soldiers. "What do you see?"

Stepping closer to the corpses, I spent a short interval surveying them before providing an answer. I tried not to speak too quickly, having learned to my cost how much he disliked it when I gabbled.

"Dried blood on their trews and cuffs," I said. "A day or two old,

I'd say. This one—" I pointed at the soldier with the arrowhead jutting from his mouth "—has a fresh-stitched cut on his brow and that one." My finger shifted to the half-bared blade still clutched in the gloved fist of the one I had stabbed. "His sword has nicks and scratches that haven't yet been ground out."

"What's that tell you?" Deckin enquired.

"They've been in a fight, and recently."

"A fight?" He raised a bushy eyebrow, tone placid as he asked, "You sure it was just that?"

My mind immediately began to race. It was always a worrisome thing when Deckin's tone grew mild. "A battle more like," I said, knowing I was speaking too fast but not quite able to slow the words. "Something big enough or important enough for the king to be told of the outcome. Since they were still breathing, until this morn, I'd guess they'd won."

"What else?" Deckin's eyes narrowed further in the manner that told of potential disappointment; apparently, I had missed something obvious.

"They're Cordwainers," I said, managing not blurt it out. "Riding with a royal messenger, so they were called to the Shavine Marches on Crown business."

"Yes," he said, voice coloured by a small sigh that told of restrained exasperation. "And what is the Crown's principal business in these troubled times?"

"The Pretender's War." I swallowed and smiled again in relieved insight. "The king's host has fought and won a battle with the Pretender's horde."

Deckin lowered his eyebrow and regarded me in silence for a second, keeping his unblinking gaze on me just long enough to make me sweat for the second time that morning. Then he blinked and turned to lead the horse away, muttering to Lorine as she moved to his side. The words were softly spoken but I heard them, as I'm sure he intended I would.

"The message?"

Lorine put a neutral tone to her reply, face carefully void of expression. "You were right, as usual, my love. The daft old bastard turned his coat."

Deckin ordered the bodies cleared from the road and dumped deeper in the forest where the attentions of wolves, bears or foxes would soon ensure all that remained were anonymous bones. The Shavine Forest is a hungry place and fresh meat rarely lasts long when the wind carries its scent through the trees. It had been dispiritingly inevitable that it would be Erchel who found one of them still alive. He was just as hungry as any forest predator, but it was hunger of a different sort.

"Fucker's still breathing!" he exclaimed in surprised delight when the crossbowman we had been dragging through the ferns let out a confused, inquisitive groan. Jarred by the unexpectedness of his survival, I instantly let go of his arm, letting him slump to the ground, where he continued to groan before raising his head. Despite the holes torn into his body by no fewer than five arrows, he resembled a man woken from a strange dream as he gazed up at his captors.

"What's happened, friend?" Erchel enquired, sinking to his haunches, face drawn in an impressive semblance of concern. "Outlaws, was it? My fellows and I found you by the road." His face became grim, voice taking on a hoarse note of despair. "What a terrible thing. They're naught but beasts, Scourge take them. Don't worry—" He set a comforting hand on the crossbowman's lolling head. "—We'll see you right."

"Erchel," I said, voice edged with a forbidding note. His eyes snapped to meet mine, catching a bright, resentful gleam, sharp, pale features scowling. We were much the same age but I was taller than most lads of seventeen, if that was in fact my age. Even today I can only guess my true span of years, for such is the way with bastards shucked from a whorehouse: birthdays are a mystery and names a gift you make to yourself.

"Got no time for your amusements," I told Erchel. The aftertaste of murder tended to birth a restless anger in me and the exchange with Deckin had deepened the well, making my patience short. The band had no formal hierarchy as such. Deckin was our unquestioned and unchallenged leader and Lorine his second, but beneath them the pecking order shifted over time. Erchel, by dint of his manners and habits, foul even by the standards of outlaws, currently stood a good few pegs lower than me. Being as much a pragmatic coward as he was a vicious dog, Erchel could usually be counted on to back down when faced with even marginally greater authority. Today, however, the prospect of indulging his inclinations overrode his pragmatism.

"Get fucked, Alwyn," he muttered, turning back to the crossbowman who, incredibly, had summoned the strength to try and rise. "Don't tax yourself, friend," Erchel advised, his hand slipping to the knife on his belt. "Lay down. Rest a while."

I knew how this would go from here. Erchel would whisper some more comforting endearments to this pitiable man, and then, striking swift like a snake, would stab out one of his eyes. Then there would be more cooing assurances before he took the other. After that it became a game of finding out how long it took the benighted wretch to die as Erchel's knife sliced ever deeper. I had no stomach for it most days, and certainly not today. Also, he had failed to heed me which was justification enough for the kick I delivered to his jaw.

Erchel's teeth clacked as his head recoiled from the impact. The kick was placed to cause the most pain without dislocating his jaw, not that he appreciated my consideration. Just a scant second or two spent blinking in shock before his narrow face mottled in rage and he sprang to his feet, bloodied teeth bared, knife drawn back to deliver a reply. My own knife came free of the sheath in a blur and I crouched, ready to receive him.

In all honesty, the matter might have been decided in favour of either of us, for we were about evenly matched when it came to knife work. Although, I like to think my additional bulk would have tipped the scales in my direction. But it all became moot when Raith dropped the body he had been carrying, strode between us and crouched to drive his own knife into the base of the crossbowman's skull.

"To be wasteful of time is to be wasteful of life," he told us in his strange, melodious accent, straightening and directing a steady, unblinking stare at each of us in turn. Raith possessed a gaze I found hard to meet at the best of times, the overly bright blue eyes piercing in a way that put one in mind of a hawk. Also, he was big, taller and broader even than Deckin but without any sign of a belly. More off-putting still were the livid red marks that formed two diagonal stripes across the light brown skin of his face. Before clapping eyes on him during my first faltering steps into Deckin's camp, I hadn't beheld one of Caerith heritage before. The sense of strangeness and threat he imbued in me that day had never faded.

In those days, tales of the Caerith and their mysterious and reputedly arcane practices abounded. Never a common sight in Albermaine, those who lived among us were subject to the fear and derision common to those viewed as alien or outlandish. Experience would eventually teach us the folly of such denigration, but all that was yet to come. I had heard many a lurid yarn about the Caerith, each filled with allusions to witchy strangeness and dire fates suffered by Covenant missionaries who unwisely crossed the mountains to educate these heathen souls in the Martyrs' example. So, I was quick to avert my eyes while Erchel, ever cunning but rarely clever, was a little slower, prompting Raith to afford him the benefit of his full attention.

"Wouldn't you agree, weasel?" he asked in a murmur, leaning closer, the brown skin of his forehead briefly pressing against Erchel's pale brow. As the bigger man stooped, his charm necklace dangled between them. Although just a simple length of cord adorned with bronze trinkets, each a finely wrought miniature sculpture of some kind, the sight of it unnerved me. I never allowed my gaze to linger on it too long, but my snatched glances revealed facsimiles of the moon, trees and various animals. One in particular always caught my eye more than the others: the bronze skull of a bird I took to be a crow. For reasons unknown, the empty eye sockets of this artefact invoked more fear in me than its owner's unnaturally bright gaze.

Raith waited until Erchel gave a nod, eyes still lowered. "Put it over there," the Caerith said, nodding towards a cluster of elm a dozen paces away as he slowly wiped his bloodied blade on Erchel's jerkin. "And you can carry my bundle on the way back. Best if I don't find anything missing."

"Caerith bastard," Erchel muttered as we heaved the crossbowman's corpse into the midst of the elm. As was often his way, our confrontation now appeared to have been completely forgotten. Reflecting on his eventual fate all these years later I am forced to the conclusion that Erchel, hideous and dreadful soul that he was, possessed a singular skill that has always eluded me: the ability to forgo a grudge.

"They're said to worship trees and rocks," he went on, careful to keep his voice low. "Perform heathen rights in the moonlight and such to bring them to life. My kin would never run with one of his kind. Don't know what Deckin's thinking."

"Mayhap you should ask him," I suggested. "Or I can ask him for you, if you like."

This blandly spoken offer had the intended effect of keeping Erchel's mouth closed for much of the remainder of our journey. However, as we progressed into the closer confines of the deep forest, drawing nearer to camp, his tongue invariably found another reason to wag.

"What did it say?" he asked, once again keeping his voice quiet for Raith and the others weren't far off. "The scroll?"

"How should I know?" I replied, shifting the uncomfortable weight of the loot-filled sack on my shoulder. The bodies had all been stripped clean before I could join in the scavenging, but the cart had yielded half a meal sack, some carrots and, most prized of all, a pair of well-made boots which would fit me near perfectly with a few minor alterations.

"Deckin talks to you. So does Lorine." Erchel's elbow nudged me in demanding insistence. "What could it say that would make him risk so much just to read it?"

I thought of the spasm of shock I had seen on Lorine's face as she read the scroll, as well as her contradictory expression as she stood and watched Deckin coax deductions from me. *The daft old bastard turned his coat,* she had said. My years in this band had given me a keen nose for a shift in the varied winds that guided our path, Deckin always being the principal agent. Never fond of sharing his thoughts, he would issue commands that seemed odd or nonsensical only for their true intent to stand revealed later. So far, his guarded leadership had always led us to profit and clear of the duke's soldiers and sheriffs. *The duke . . .*

My feet began to slow and my eyes to lose focus as my always-busy mind churned up an insight that should have occurred to me back at the road. The messenger's guards were not ducal levies from the Shavine Marches but Cordwainers fresh from another battle in the Pretender's War. Soldiers in service to the king, which begged the question: if his own soldiers couldn't be trusted with escorting a Crown agent, which side had the Duke of the Shavine Marches been fighting on?

"Alwyn?"

Erchel's voice returned the focus to my gaze, which inevitably slipped towards Deckin's bulky form at the head of the column. We had reached the camp now and I watched him wave away the outlaws who came to greet him, instead stomping off to the shelter he shared with Lorine. Instinct told me neither would join us at the communal feast that night, the customary celebration of a successful enterprise. I knew they had much to discuss. I also knew I needed to hear it.

"There's something I feel you should know, Erchel," I said, walking off towards my own shelter. "You talk too fucking much."

Chapter Two

S pillage of blood always made the subsequent celebrations a raucous affair. Deckin took a dim view of persistent drunkenness but usually allowed the ale and brandy to flow following a successful raid. So, once night had fallen and the hog on the spit was roasted to grease-dripping perfection, my bandmates gave vent to their various joys or nurtured grievances. I had come to understand over the years that occasions like these were a necessary aspect of an outlaw's life, a release of laughter, argument and song fuelled by excess drink and whatever intoxicants we could gather.

I often wonder at my capacity for looking back on this collection of reprobates with such fond nostalgia, and yet as my mind's eye drifts from one face to another, I find that I do. There was Gerthe, second only to Lorine as the object of my lust, apple cheeks bulging as she smiled and danced, skirts flaring. Joining her in the dance were Justan and Yelk, the forger and the lock-pick, as devoted a pair of lovers as I would ever meet. Old wrinkled Hulbeth, who could appraise the value of gold or silver with just a bite of her yellow teeth and a dab of her tongue, giggling as she shared a pipe with Raith. The Caerith was not given to exuberance but during occasions like this he would at least take on an affable serenity, puffing away on his ornately carved pipe which he was generous enough to share with the outlaws clustered around him. As the night wore on, they would all drift away into whatever oblivion the weed had crafted in their addled minds.

At the edge of the firelight, Baker and Twine, our best bowmen, were engaged in the glowering and shoving that told of an imminent fight. Violence was inevitable among this bunch when drink loosened tongues and memories of slights bubbled up. However, Deckin's law insisted that all knives and other weapons were to be left in our shelters so severe injuries or killings were rare. Watching the two archers jab fingers into each other's faces as their voices rose in volume, I judged the resultant exchange of punches would be brief but bruising. They would roll around in an ugly clinch for a time until their fracas became irksome enough for Raith or one of the more feared lieutenants to drag them apart. By morning, Baker and Twine would be friends again, exchanging jokes as they compared bruises.

Watching their escalating argument was a stocky man with a balding pate shaved down to stubble, a dearth of hair he made up for with an extensive beard. Todman stood several rungs higher than I did in the band's hierarchy, favoured by Deckin for his judicious use of brutality, which made him good in a fight but better when it came time to dole out some punishment. He was a large man, as those charged with enforcement of rules often are, but didn't quite match the stature of Raith or Deckin. Seeing the keen anticipation in his eyes as Baker and Twine's shoves became punches, I assumed he was hoping this brawl might turn into murder, thereby raising the prospect of a gruesome execution. It is not always easy to divine the source of the hatred one feels for another, but in Todman's case I had little difficulty in doing so. Like Erchel, he enjoyed his cruelty too much. But, unlike Erchel, there was a very sharp brain behind those sadistic eyes.

Some instinct must have warned him of my attention, for his gaze snapped to mine and narrowed considerably. It is the nature of hatred to find its mirror in those you hate, and Todman reflected mine with interest. I should have lowered my gaze as I had with Raith, but didn't. Perhaps the half-cup of brandy I had imbibed made me foolishly brave, but I believe my lack of circumspection had more to do with the growing suspicion, nursed over the preceding few months, that I was capable of killing Todman if it came to it. He had the advantage of strength and size, to be sure, but I was quicker and all it took was one good cut, after all.

I watched Todman's features twitch in response to my lack of fear, taking a step forwards and prompting me to rise. As per Deckin's law, I had no knife, but there was one jabbed into the half-eaten hog on the spit. I knew I could get to it before Todman could get to me. The realisation that I would have to gamble on Deckin forgiving the death of so useful a lieutenant summoned a belated welling of good sense, causing me to grit my teeth and lower my eyes. It was entirely possible that such contrition wouldn't cool Todman's ire, however, and I knew my brandy-fuelled pride would likely cost me a beating tonight. Luckily, before Todman could take another step, Twine attempted to gouge out Baker's eye, the resultant struggle sending them both into the firepit in a blaze of sparks.

Letting out an annoyed curse in the Caerith tongue, Raith got to his feet and pulled the thrashing pair apart. Todman, due to his acknowledged role as enforcer, was obliged to lend a hand, hauling Baker away while Raith wrapped a meaty arm around Twine's neck. With all eyes now fixed on the unfolding drama, I felt it the most opportune moment to slip away. It wouldn't do to attract any more of Todman's notice and I had a mission of my own to pursue.

With the onset of winter, Deckin's band had taken up residence amid the overgrown ruins found in the darkest heart of the Shavine Forest. They consisted mostly of dislodged stone, sometimes indistinguishable from common boulders in their weathered, moss-covered irregularity. But in a few places distinct form and structure protruded from the tangle of bush, root and branch. This was the principal advantage of camping here when the rain turned chill and the frost began to sparkle in the morning light, for these resolute if stunted walls were easy to convert into shelters and provided many a ready-made store for loot and supplies.

I had heard some in the band opine that the ruins had once

comprised a mighty city, raised to greatness only to be cast down amid the fury of the Scourge. If so, I saw little evidence of greatness, or even of civilisation. Surely a mighty city would have had a statue or two, perhaps even some glimmers of ancient treasure among the green and grey jumble. But I saw none. Here and there one could make out the dim, worn indentations that spoke of writing, too faded to fully discern its form and none in this company could have translated it in any case, least of all my own unlettered self.

Naturally, Deckin and Lorine had occupied the largest shelter available, a near-complete chamber of four diminished but thick walls, augmented by a roof crafted from woven branches and piled ferns. It was also positioned in fortuitous proximity to the weathered, moss-covered remnants of a great, tumbled pillar. I assumed it must have been a monument of some kind, standing a hundred feet tall. What or who it commemorated forever an unanswerable mystery. Its segments had only partially shattered when it had fallen. Beneath one of these granite cylinders there lay a small hollow. I had discovered it weeks before when looking for a place to hide my more valuable loot. Stealing within the band was strictly forbidden, but whatever coin or sundry valuables I managed to collect had an irksome tendency to disappear. In truth, this was mostly due to my habit of spending my earnings almost as soon as they fell into my purse, but I was sure a small portion had found its way into the pockets of my untrustworthy bandmates. Closer inspection of my chosen hidey-hole also revealed that it afforded a clear view of the entrance to Deckin and Lorine's shelter while being close enough to hear near every word they spoke.

"'. . . comprising twelve companies in all,'" Lorine was saying in her smooth, flowing tones, eyes closed as she recited the royal message with her typical precision. She and Deckin sat on either side of a blazing fire, he poking at the flames with a blackened branch while she sat in placid recital. "'Nine of foot and three mounted. Henceforth, our number was counted in excess of three thousand, all good and dutiful men sworn to Your Highness's service in sight of Ascendant Durehl Vearist, most senior and revered Covenant Cleric of the

Shavine Marches. In addition, our host was supplemented by no fewer than three score men-at-arms formerly in service to the traitor Duke Rouphon Ambris. I am sure Your Highness will be heartened to learn of the faithfulness of these stout-hearted fellows who chose loyalty to king above oaths sworn to a treasonous noble—'"

Lorine fell silent as Deckin interrupted, his voice low but tone harsh. "Faithless bastards smart enough to gauge which way the wind was blowing, more like." His beard shifted into a chastened grimace as Lorine opened her eyes to afford him a reproachful glare. "Apologies, my love. Please continue."

Sighing, Lorine closed her eyes and resumed her recital. "'Of the Pretender's forces, I judge their number at having exceeded over four thousand under arms, with a near equal number of camp followers. Your Highness will know that this is far below the strength heretofore ascribed to the rebel horde, calling into doubt the honesty of those rewarded for intelligence now revealed as erroneous or outright fraudulent. Addended to this missive is a list of those I humbly suggest be subject to arrest and seizure of property for such shameful injury to Your Highness's trust.

"'However parlous the enemy's numbers, had the Pretender succeeded in joining his horde with Duke Rouphon's companies and levies, numbering well over a thousand, the day may well have gone against us. It is thanks to providence, and mayhap the Martyrs' favour, that the marching route taken by Duke Rouphon was revealed to us when one of his scouts fell into our hands. Having encamped a scant twelve miles from the Pretender's assembly, Duke Rouphon was set upon by our full number come the dawn, his forces slain, captured or scattered.'"

Lorine paused then and I saw the working of her throat as she swallowed to wet a nervous tongue. Still, when she spoke on her tone was its usual, measured self. "'It is also my deepest honour to report that the duke himself is now in the custody of your esteemed champion, Sir Ehlbert Bauldry, having defeated and disarmed the traitor in personal combat.

"'Once order had been restored to my command, I marched with all speed upon the Pretender's encampment, inflicting upon him a severe defeat despite the ferocity of his followers' resistance. I feel it of great significance to report that among the rebel ranks were a number of Ascarlian mercenaries allied with Fjord Geld heretics. The staunchest combat was required to overcome these northern savages, which, to my eternal regret, allowed the Pretender himself to flee along with a retinue numbering perhaps twenty turncoat knights. Your Highness is assured that a rapid pursuit of the rebel leader is under way, and I fully expect to receive word of his capture or just demise within days.

"'My force is now in possession of Castle Ambris where Your Highness's messenger will find me. The other party we discussed before my departure from court has been sent for and is expected to arrive shortly. Intelligence gleaned from patrols and paid informants tells of little unrest among churl, artisan or minor noble regarding the duke's arrest. Nor does there appear to be any widespread sympathy for the Pretender's cause within this duchy. It is my intention, in compliance with Your Highness's injunctions, to subject Duke Rouphon to trial forthwith. A list of those captives of noble birth are also addended to this missive. I await your command regarding execution, mercy or ransom of their persons. Captive men-at-arms, levied churls and camp followers have been put to death under my warrant as Crown agent with Extraordinary Dispensation.

"'I remain, Your Highness, your most faithful and devoted servant, Sir Althus Levalle, Knight Commander of Crown Company.'"

Deckin maintained a mostly unchanging expression as he listened to it all, the only shift in his demeanour coming when Lorine related the fate of the unfortunate Duke Rouphon. The branch in Deckin's hands creaked then snapped as his meaty hands tightened before casting the remnants into the fire. When she concluded her recitation, he said nothing, letting the silence stretch.

"Althus," Deckin murmured finally, clasping his hands together. "Makes sense it would be him. He always did like the messier work. A man who takes pleasure in transforming chaos into order."

"You know the knight commander of Crown Company?" Lorine

asked, I noted the pitch of genuine surprise in her voice. Deckin apparently kept secrets from her too.

His beard twitched in faint irritation and he shook his head. "I used to. A story for another night, my love."

She hid it well, but I could discern the worry that lay beneath Lorine's next statement, blandly phrased though it was. "I assume the 'other party' he refers to is the newly chosen Duke of the Shavine Marches. I wonder who it might be."

"The list of candidates is short." Deckin gave a humourless laugh. "Rouphon's rivals had a tendency towards accidents and unexpected illness." Another laugh, this one carrying an acidic edge. "He was never a man known for excessive kindness to those who shared his blood."

"Mayhap his successor will be of a more accommodating nature. A gift of suitable value might at least facilitate opening an avenue of communication. We'll have to be careful about how we approach him, of course . . . " Lorine trailed off as Deckin waved a disinterested hand.

"Doesn't matter who it is." He got to his feet, groaning and rubbing his back. "It's time, Lorine. Been a good long wait, but now it's time. With Rouphon about to lose his head, the Pretender's War raging and trouble brewing in the north, we'll never get a better chance."

"The Pretender was just defeated. The war is all but over."

"So it appears, or at least that's what Althus would have the king believe. Did you note he failed to give an account of his own losses? Althus is a man of duty above all, but he's also a fucking liar when it suits him. My guess is that he soundly thrashed the duke's forces and captured him as he said, largely due to having Sir Ehlbert on his side. He also probably managed to inflict a defeat on the Pretender, but not the great victory he claims. Even if it is true, as long as the Pretender draws breath there's always a chance he can gather another army. Claiming the throne by dint of royal blood will always hold an allure for the dispossessed or the disgruntled. His rebellion is far from done. When next he raises his standard, it's likely to be far from the Shavine Marches, meaning Sir Althus and, more importantly, the king's dread champion will also soon be far away."

Lorine closed her eyes again, lowering her face. Taking a breath, she spoke words I knew it had taken courage to craft. "The messenger was right, Deckin. Whatever title churl and outlaw might bestow, the fact remains you are not a king."

"I've never deluded myself otherwise, my love." Deckin's tone and bearing betrayed no anger as he stepped towards Lorine, large hand cupping her jaw and raising her face until she consented to open her eyes. His next words were spoken with kind solicitation, but also unwavering certainty. "I am, however, determined to be a duke."

The next morning Deckin had us strike camp and trace a northwards course through the hidden trails known only to poacher and outlaw. As usual, no explanation was given and those who grumbled about their drink-muddled heads and myriad aches were quick to fall silent at the briefest glare from the Outlaw King. We were all expert at reading his changing moods and the band marched under the burden of knowing that one word or glance out of place just now would reap the most severe reprisal.

I volunteered to scout ahead of the band as it wound its way through the green maze of the deep forest. Marching with the others would invariably see me traipsing alongside Erchel and I had currently exhausted my tolerance for his company. It also put me at a decent remove from Todman, which I felt would be a wise precaution for the time being. Deckin's favour afforded me a few additional words of conversation or praise, but it didn't provide protection.

There were four of us in the scouting party. Baker and Twine patrolled the flanks with their bows, their argument, of course, now just a dim memory despite their bruises. In the centre, Hostler, our finest tracker and huntsman, took the lead with me following a dozen paces behind. The rationale for such an arrangement was simple: if an arrow or other missile should come sailing out of the forest and strike the huntsman down, I would be left to raise the alarm.

Although it was rare for sheriff's men or ducal soldiers to venture into the deep forest, neither was it unheard of. I possessed dark memories of the outcome years before, when the band had happened upon a full company of Duke Rouphon's household guards. Luckily, the hour had been late and most of us contrived to escape the subsequent chaotic skirmish. I was still a boy then and the memory of sprinting clear of that vicious exchange of arrows and blades, the closest I had been to an actual battle, left a deep impression.

Scanning the trees to either side of Hostler, moving with a steady fluency at odds with his lanky frame, my mind slipped repeatedly to Deckin and Lorine's conversation the night before. *I am determined to be a duke.* One of the curses suffered by the intelligent is the power of imagination, for a clever mind will explore the dark possibilities with far more dedication than the bright.

What does he lead us into? was the first question that rose to mind that first day, soon followed by a plague of others. *What is he planning? Where are we going? How can he imagine that an outlaw, even an outlaw king, could ever be a duke?*

I hadn't been so foolish as to share what I knew with anyone else, for trust is a luxury young outlaws soon learn to forgo. In other circumstances I would have sought answers from Lorine, having known since our first meeting that she was the only other truly clever soul among this collection of dregs.

Well, here's a lad with a shrewd look to him. Deckin's first words to me that day he had found a dirty and bruised boy lying in the woods ten years before.

When the whoremaster drove me from the meagre shelter of the whorehouse, he had done so with considerable enthusiasm. "Get out of here, you useless little fucker!" had been the last words I could recall him ever speaking to me, and these were among his kindest. The switch left welts on my arse cheeks as I scampered away, running for the thick blanket of ferns fringing the border of the collection of hovels I had, until that point, called home. Usually, when the whoremaster's temper was up, I could hide there until nightfall, wait for him to drink himself insensible, then creep back in. The kindlier whores could be counted on to share some of their supper with me after which I would crawl into the rafters to sleep. But not that day.

Growling, he had chased me through the ferns, switch catching me on the neck and head until I consented to flee for the dark embrace of the forest. The sight of the wall of jagged shadows was enough to bring me to a halt and brave further blows. My childhood had been rich in overheard stories regarding the fate of those foolish enough to venture into the forest proper. Cursing my intransigence, the whore-master crouched to gather stones and proceeded to pelt me, one missile sending a scattering of stars across my vision when it smacked into my forehead. I recall falling before my gaze turned black and, when it cleared, I found myself staring up at a swaying matrix of branches.

It may have been delirium brought on by a hefty blow to the skull, but I felt as if the forest spoke to me then. The rustle of leaves and creak of twisting timbers combined into a voice, not speaking words I could comprehend, but speaking nonetheless. To my boyish and befuddled mind, it sounded like a welcome, one soon swallowed by the sound of Deckin's greeting.

Sitting up, I found myself confronted by a very large man with a copious black beard and a slender woman with copper hair tied into long, neat braids. I could see a glimmer of white teeth in the large man's beard as he smiled, a mix of amusement and interest in his eyes. The woman didn't smile, but neither was her face unkind. I have since ascertained that Lorine couldn't have been more than twenty years old at our first meeting, but even then I felt there to be something ageless and regal in her bearing.

"What's your name, lad?" the bearded man said, striding closer. He reached down to grasp me by the shoulders and lift me up, setting me on my feet. Due to my lingering confusion, or perhaps some deeper instinctive warning, I didn't shy from his touch or attempt to run.

"A-Alwyn," I stuttered back, blinking as the action of speaking opened the cut on my forehead, allowing blood to trickle into my eyes.

"Alwyn, eh?" The bearded man grimaced a little as he thumbed the blood from my brows. "Was it your mother or your father that gave you that name?"

"Didn't know 'em. Gave it to myself," I replied, fear quickening my heart as the singular fact that I was alone in the forest with two strangers began to solidify in the lessening confusion of my brain. "Whoremaster said she died birthing me. My father was just some fucker who fucked her before fucking off, he said."

The copper-haired woman spoke then, moving to the large man's side and sinking to her haunches. "A man with a colourful turn of phrase, this whoremaster," she said. I found my boy's eyes captured by her expression, for it was one I hadn't seen before: a mingling of sympathy and steely anger, albeit part hidden by a warm smile. "And quite a temper too," she added, pulling a rag from the sleeve of her woollen blouse and pressing it to my forehead. "I'd say that man would benefit from a lesson in restraint." She raised one sparse eyebrow and glanced at the bearded man. "Wouldn't you agree, my love?"

"That I would." The large man gave an affable snort, rising to his full height so that I was obliged to crane my neck to meet his gaze. "Best if you stop at our camp for tonight, young Alwyn. There's a whole brace of pigeons stewing in the pot and we'll need help eating it all."

Stooping, he gathered my small hand in his while the woman took the other. I walked along with them, feeling no urge to run, for where could I go? Of course, one night at their camp soon became a week which slipped into months during which I learned many new things. Also, for the first time in my short life I no longer spent every hour suffering hunger or the fear of an unexpected swipe of the switch. As the months became years, dark thoughts regarding the whoremaster grew, only to fade when, having vented my vengeful intent to Lorine, she informed me in an offhandedly cheerful tone that the fellow had been found strangled on the very doorstep of his brothel not long after my departure. My varied paths in life have never led me back to the cluster of hovels where I was raised, and even now I feel not the slightest inclination towards a visit, for there is nothing there to see and no one to kill.

"Hsst!"

The sharp sting of a thrown twig rebounding from my nose

banished my reminiscing and I scowled at Hostler's stern, judgemental frown. "Wake up, heathen," he ordered, voice quiet but pitched with his usual flat curtness. "If you're going to guard my back, do it right, Scourge take you."

I shifted my scowl into as bright and cheerful a smile as I could muster, knowing it would stoke his anger worse than any retort. Hostler was perhaps the most unusual outlaw ever to haunt the Shavine Forest, for he was as fully devout and faithful a follower of the Covenant of Martyrs as any soul I ever met. His resentment for the company of his fellow villains was a constant, burning flame, but seemed to burn brightest for me, perhaps because I never tired of feeding the fire.

Taking a calming breath, he muttered the passage of scripture that typically rose to his lips whenever I tested his patience. "'For it is the fate of the truly faithful to suffer the company of the sinful and profane. To suffer is to be purified in the sight of the Seraphile.'" With that, he turned about and resumed his careful progress through the trees.

We rested a few miles on, perching on the trunk of a fallen ash to eat our ration of salted pork. Winter's grip hadn't yet fully tightened on the woods, but the air had already taken on the edge that would soon deepen to bone-cutting chill. For a lad of my inclinations there were many advantages to living in the forest, but the weather wasn't among them; winters cold enough to kill and summers that would birth clouds of midges and sundry bugs in numbers enough to drive you to distraction. I always preferred the more clement but all-too-brief respites of spring and autumn.

"You ever hear of a knight named Sir Ehlbert Bauldry?" I asked Hostler as we ate, keeping my voice to the soft murmur we adopted when on the move.

"Plague me not with your prattle, heathen," Hostler muttered back. For reasons I never established, Hostler reserved title of "heathen" for me alone. Everyone else was merely a sinner.

"King's Champion, so I hear," I went on blithely. "Thought you might've crossed paths in your soldiering days."

It was a calculated taunt, since I was aware Hostler's time under the banners was a sore subject. In fact, I only knew of it from the sermons he preached to himself for want of another audience. Most evenings he would wander in a circle around his fire with his eyes closed, quoting endless invective from the Martyr Scrolls interspersed with rare but revealing contrition for the many sins that had coloured his life, contrition that didn't prevent him from running with the most infamous outlaw band in the Shavine Forest.

The previous summer I had seen this man split a guardsman's skull fully open with a hatchet, the blow delivered without any hesitation or utterance of scripture. He was as worthless and vicious as any other member of this band, but his faith in his own salvation never faltered. I had long ago concluded his faith was the ardent belief of the mad and stopped pondering the contradiction of it all, except when I found myself the focus of his delusional hypocrisy.

I expected another curt dismissal, so was surprised when Hostler's face took on a cast of grave recollection. Some would have called his features handsome, although the manic light that frequently shone in his gaze tended to negate such an impression. Now though, he appeared almost normal and when he spoke his voice lacked the usual flatness or judgement.

"He wasn't champion when I saw him," he said. "Just a young knight in the service of King Mathis, but even then I doubt there was a fighter of any station in all the duchies who could match him. For so large a man to move with such swiftness seemed . . . unnatural. And to wreak such slaughter, even among rebels, might be seen by some as sinful. But he did not rejoice in it as the other knights did, or partake in the cruelties they inflicted on the captives. When we piled the bodies, he knelt with proper solemnity as the Ascendant gave supplication. A true knight of Covenant and Crown."

It's good that you like him, I quipped inwardly, my thoughts returning to Deckin and Lorine's conversation. *Mayhap we're going to meet him soon.*

"And Sir Althus Levalle," I said. "Ever hear tell of him?"

The abrupt narrowing of Hostler's eyes was a clear sign I had miscalculated. This man may well have been mad as a pox-brained monkey, but he wasn't stupid.

"Why so interested, heathen?" he asked, shifting to face me.

"Heard those Cordwainers talking back at the road," I replied with a shrug, keeping my tone bland. "From the sound of things, they'd fought a battle recently."

Hostler's gaze failed to soften, maintaining a steady enquiry as his instinct for detecting the transgressions of others came to the fore. His next questions might have left me floundering for more explicating lies. Skilled in deceit as I was, it rarely worked on him. Fortunately, I was saved by the faint whiff of smoke sent wafting into our noses by the southerly breeze. Hostler and I blinked in unison and immediately rose to a crouch.

Across the small clearing from us, Baker and Twine were also getting to their feet, each drawing an arrow from their quivers and setting them to the bow stave. No one save a fool would light a fire in this region of the forest. We were still deep in the recognised territory of the Outlaw King and the duke's soldiers and sheriffs knew better than to betray their presence in such a manner.

Hostler held up a hand to hold us in place and spent a short time in stilled silence, eyes closed but nostrils flared. Finally, he opened his eyes and nodded to the north-west where the trees were marginally thinner. We adopted the standard scouting formation, me trailing Hostler with the archers on the flanks. The scent of smoke duly thickened until I could see wisps of it drifting through the branches above. Then came the sound of voices. They were faint and odd sounding, the words impossible to discern, but they led us on better than any beacon.

After another fifty paces, the voices grew loud enough for me to conclude they were speaking a language I didn't know. Casting a baffled glance at Hostler I saw his face grow sour as he mouthed his reply: "Ascarlians."

Halting, he jerked his head at the broad trunk of an aged yew a few paces off. I followed as he climbed, scaling the twisting limbs with the ease that came from years of needful practice. The camp lay revealed when we had ascended perhaps twenty feet from the forest floor. I could make out the source of the smoke easily, a stack of piled timber leaking a pale-grey miasma into the air. The people around the fire were rendered indistinct through the canopy of leaves and branches, but I estimated about a dozen. Two were made more prominent by virtue of constantly wandering back and forth through the smoke. The pitch of their voices told of a heated argument, the words an unintelligible melange of soft vowels and harsh exclamations.

"Any notion of what their saying?" I whispered to Hostler.

"I don't sully myself with heretic speech," he murmured back, eyeing the camp. "But they're northern savages, to be sure." He shifted his gaze to me. "Find Deckin. Tell him we have trespassers."

CHAPTER THREE

Before striding into the trespassers' camp, Deckin had it surrounded. Moving with silent and practised swiftness, the band formed a tightening circle that covered all avenues of escape. There were no sentries or lookouts to warn of our approach, making me wonder at the guileless ignorance of these interlopers. Did they not know where they were?

The argument that had continued to rage as we formed our trap fell to an abrupt silence at the sight of Deckin's bulky form emerging from the trees. Lorine stood to his right and Raith his left while Todman, always keen to remain in range of Deckin's notice, trailed after. I joined the others as we came to a halt at the edge of the small clearing where this strange lot had made their camp. I counted twelve, eight men and four women. During forays into the port towns on the coast, I had encountered a few folk from the Fjord Geld, the northernmost Albermaine duchy seized from the Ascarlians by one of King Tomas's ancestors. These people were similar in appearance, standing an inch or two taller than those of the southern duchies with pale skin and blond or light brown hair. Also, they were all armed and armoured, albeit poorly. Axes and hatchets hung from their belts and many wore leather tunics adorned with iron plates. My eyes picked out many tears and stains on those tunics and noted how their faces were all besmirched with the mixture of sweat, dirt and blood unique to those who have survived a violent confrontation.

Only one carried a sword. He was the tallest of the bunch with a mass of flaxen hair tied in braids, some of which had come adrift to create the impression of a wind-tossed haystack. His expression was no less wild, eyes wide and unblinking as he stared at Deckin, mouth slightly agape. I saw no fear in that countenance, but rather a near manic spasm of relief. The outlaw's life provides a fine education in judging when a meeting will remain amicable or descend into violence. Reading the northman's face left me in no doubt as to how this would go.

To his left stood a girl with hair of a more golden hue than the tousled swordsman. I put her age at much the same as my own, though the pleasing absence of any scars to the skin beneath the grime on her face told of a far more comfortable upbringing. She was the least armed of the group, possessing only a long-bladed dagger, and her clothes, while hardy, were free of armour. The fearful gaze she cast at Deckin, which widened considerably as she surveyed the rest of the band, told me she also possessed a far more rational mind than her companion.

Deckin said nothing, coming to a halt ten paces short of the swordsman and folding his arms. The forest air thickened as the northerner continued to stare at this imposing newcomer with his wide, hungry eyes while Deckin regarded him in arch expectation. Finally, the swordsman spoke, a rapid, harshly accented torrent in his own language that was accompanied by a fair amount of spittle. The fellow crouched into a fighting stance as he spat his words, hand shifting to grasp the handle of his sword. The girl also spoke, the words no more intelligible but the faint and tremulous timbre of her voice marked it as the desperate warning of a terrified soul. The rest of their group were busy exchanging uncertain glances and I saw sweat glistening on the axe handles as they gripped them with nervous hands.

Deckin's beard bunched and his brows furrowed at the swordsman's words. "Gerthe!" he called out, glancing over his shoulder to summon the band's most accomplished linguist. Gerthe was a maiden of many talents, often expensive and carnal in nature, but a remarkable facility for languages was the one Deckin valued most. Having learned her trade in the ports on the Shavine coast, she could speak no fewer than seven different tongues with fluent ease and converse in a half-dozen more.

"Ascarlian, I take it?" Deckin asked as she hurried to his side.

Gerthe bobbed her head in affirmation. "From the southern gelts, I think."

"And what's he saying?"

Gerthe's usually cheerful features took on a reluctant grimace, her eyes flicking between Deckin and the swordsman in apprehension. "It . . . wasn't nice, Deckin," she said.

"Just tell me."

Coughing to smother the quaver in her voice, Gerthe translated in as uninflected a tone as she could manage. "'What scum is this that approaches? Have you come to beg or steal? In either case, I have only death to offer.'"

Deckin let out a small grunt of laughter which gave leave for the rest of the band to follow suit. The mirth caused the northerners to crowd closer together, except for the swordsman who apparently took it as an affront to his manly dignity. Snarling out more words he drew the sword free of its scabbard, brandishing it at Deckin before sweeping the blade around, his voice hoarse and near comical in its stridency.

"'Laugh, you worthless wretches,'" Gerthe related dutifully. "'Laugh as I, Skeinweld, Sword of the Altvar, see you to your graves!'"

This, naturally, only brought forth more merriment and mockery, enraging the northerner such that his face took on a crimson hue. However, our amusement abruptly faded when Deckin raised a hand. His face had taken on the narrow, unsmiling focus we all knew so well. Whatever was about to happen, it wouldn't be funny.

Glancing at Gerthe he said, "Tell this silly little bugger that he's in my forest without leave. Tell him that, by way of a toll, I'll take that fine sword he clearly has no notion of how to use. After that he'll have safe passage to the coast where he and his friends can find a ship to piss off home in."

This was an unusually generous offer; Deckin was rarely so forgiving of trespassers. However, the Ascarlian barely seemed to hear the words Gerthe related to him. When she finished talking, his feature acquired an absurd eagerness and he made a beckoning gesture to Deckin. More words spilled from the Ascarlian's mouth as Deckin moved to stand only a few short paces from him. The northman's voice was softer now, his lips moving more rapidly.

"More insults?" Deckin asked Gerthe.

"Prayers," she said, face tightening as she, Lorine and the others backed away. "His death ode to the Altvar."

A shadow passed over Deckin's face then, too brief for me to fully read the emotion beneath it. I thought at first it might be contempt, but now I think it was more a mingling of regret and pity. But it was gone in an instant, replaced with the same hard, narrow focus. Facing the Ascarlian, he raised his hands, both still empty for his axe was still strapped to his belt.

"Well?" he asked.

The swordsman continued to whisper his prayers for a moment longer, and then, gripping the sword in both hands, he let out a roar and charged. It was over in a heartbeat, as I knew it would be. Deckin was right; even I could tell this Ascarlian was no true swordsman. His grip was too tight and his balance poor. He charged with excessive speed, leaving himself no opportunity to dodge clear as Deckin nimbly danced clear of the blade, wrapped both arms around the northman's neck and bore him to the ground. Deckin emitted a hard grunt as he jerked his arms and I heard the loud crack of the Ascarlian's upper spine being wrenched apart.

Rising from the twitching body, Deckin turned to regard the other northerners. A few were weeping openly at the death of their country-man, but most were too stricken by terror to do more than stare. The golden-haired girl was the sole exception, watching the swordsman's death throes with a face that betrayed only weary disappointment. When he lay still, she drew the long dagger from her belt and tossed it on to the ground. Looking to her companions, she spoke a soft word in Ascarlian and they quickly followed suit, axes and hatchets falling into an untidy heap at Deckin's feet.

"I think we've covered enough miles for today," he said, reaching down to take the sword from the dead northerner's limp hand. It was different from the swords found in the duchies of Albermaine, the blade broader and the handle shorter, made to fit a one-handed grip.

"Gerthe," he went on, "ask our visitors if they'd care to join us for supper. In the morning they can take their weapons and be on their way, their toll having been paid in blood." He paused to squint at the blade's edge as it caught the sun, grunting in appreciation before adding with a faint grin, "And steel."

Come the evening, Deckin bade me join him for supper. Raith, Lorine and Gerthe were also present, as was the northern girl. I saw Todman prowling the shadows beyond the fire, the glow illuminating the stern frown of resentment he directed at me. In response, I raised a cup of ale in his direction while offering a smile of comradely warmth. This brought the expected reward of seeing his frown tighten into a snarl before he stalked off into the gloom. I also noted a less bulky form moving about among the flickering trees, hungry eyes catching a gleam from the firelight. While Todman's baleful gaze had been fixed on me, Erchel's interest was focused entirely on our golden-haired guest.

As he ate, Deckin directed a series of questions at the girl. His demeanour was that of an affable host towards a welcome visitor, but the girl was evidently too clever not to understand the truth of her circumstance. She maintained a downcast gaze for much of the meal, eyes rarely shifting from the fire, and then only to shoot a worried glance at her hosts. The other northerners were clustered together at the neighbouring fire, their position in the heart of the camp making any attempt to run off a pointless and dangerous enterprise.

"Berrine," the girl said when Gerthe translated Deckin's request for her name. Her answers were short and stripped of inflection, from either fear of causing offence or a desire to avoid giving too much away.

"Berrine," Deckin repeated. "A name with a pleasing sound. What does it mean?"

"Daughter of the Sea," Gerthe supplied. "It's a common thing for

Ascarlians to make everything about the sea. Seems like all their songs and stories make mention of it in some way—"

"Just her own words, thank you, Gerthe," Lorine cut in. She smiled kindly as Gerthe faltered to silence. "I think we would all like to know the very interesting tale of how she and her friends came to be here."

I saw the Ascarlian girl's mouth tighten at this, just a fractional movement that all others present missed, but it told me something of singular value. I kept a close watch on her face as she listened to Gerthe relate Lorine's request. The girl's response was as clipped as her previous answers. However, I detected a sour undercurrent that, later in life, I would recognise as youthful idealism confronted by experience.

"She's from the Aldvir Geld, the southernmost province of the lands ruled by the Sister Queens of Ascarlia," Gerthe translated as Berrine spoke. "She and her friends belong to something called the *Skardryken*." Gerthe's brow creased in confusion at the next few sentences. "Not sure what exactly it is, but *skard* means axe and *ryke* is something like a Supplicant or priest."

She hid it well, but Berrine's mouth formed a very small, contemptuous curve in response to this translation. Once again, I opted not to share what it told me.

"Fanatics," Deckin concluded. "Warriors sworn to the Altvar, the Ascarlian gods."

"I think so," Gerthe said, the confusion on her brow fading as Berrine continued. "Months ago, a man came from across the sea, a messenger from one who called himself the True King of the Southlands."

"The Pretender," Lorine surmised. "So, he's been seeking an alliance with the Sister Queens."

"She says the queens wouldn't receive him," Gerthe related a moment later. "But he was permitted to speak to any who would listen. He promised great things to warriors of stout heart who would come and fight the hated southerners. And not just gold: land in the Fjord Geld which would be returned to the Sister Queens when the Pretender gained the throne."

Deckin let out a faint snort of derision. "Her and all these other whelps believed this dung, did they?"

"She says regaining the Fjord Geld is a sacred trust of the *Skard-ryken*. That's what they fought for. They had no interest in gold."

"Which is a shame," Deckin said, favouring Berrine with a sympathetic smile. "Because they'll need some if they're going to buy passage home. I want to know about the battle. How badly did the Pretender lose?"

The Ascarlian's face darkened in response to this question, anger plain in the answer she snapped out. "She says he lost perhaps two dozen men at most, of his own host that is," Berrine explained. "The way she tells it, the Pretender got word of Crown Company's approach and broke camp before they could attack. The Ascarlians held them off while most of the Pretender's mob got away. She and these others are all that's left. They've been running from the king's host for days."

I saw Deckin direct a brief but smug glance at Lorine before turning back to the northerner. "Can't say I'm surprised. If that fool with the sword was any indication, these *Skard-ryken* can't fight worth a fly-covered turd. Don't tell her that," he added in tired admonition when Berrine began to translate his words.

Deckin shifted his gaze from the girl to me, eyebrow raised. "So, Alwyn, is this fanatic devotee of false gods lying, or no?"

I was impressed by the way Berrine managed to endure the weight of my scrutiny while maintaining a confused quirk to her brows. I'm sure it convinced the others that she had no notion that my next words might mean her death. In recent months, Deckin had increasingly called upon my facility for detecting untruths, a gift stemming from what he termed my over-keen eyes and overly busy brain. There was nothing arcane in it, just an instinctive ability for perceiving falsity in the confluence of voice and facial expression. I wasn't always right, which had unfortunate consequences for the unconvincingly truthful. But I was right more than I was wrong, at least I hope so.

It would probably have enhanced my standing a little if I'd shared all of what I'd had seen in Berrine's face, but I didn't. Instead, I turned to Deckin and shook my head. "If she's lying, she's very good at it."

Deckin eyes slipped to Raith. The Caerith didn't look at the girl, or betray any particular interest in what she'd said, instead staring into the fire while he fingered one of the charms on his necklace: a crow skull etched with some form of minuscule writing. Raising his eyes, he gave Deckin a very slight nod before resuming his contemplation of the fire. I saw Lorine shift in discomfort at this wordless exchange. I had divined before how she took a dim view of Deckin's rarely mentioned but obvious reliance on Raith's supposed insights. To be an outlaw is one thing, but to be a heretic would invite the condemnation of the Covenant as well as the law. Such a weight of official disapproval was dangerous even for the Outlaw King.

"Thank her for her candour," Deckin told Gerthe, inclining his head in a sign of dismissal. "Come the morn, she and the others are free to go on their way, as I said. Give her the names of the smuggler captains most likely to carry them home, but warn her the price will be high."

Gerthe began to usher Berrine away from the fire, then paused as Deckin grunted out an order to wait. "This should fetch a decent enough price," he said, hefting the sword he had taken from the slain Ascarlian. "Recompense for her honesty. Besides, I never had much use for swords." He tossed the weapon to a startled Berrine, who caught it by the scabbard, almost dropping it before she clutched it to her breast.

Deckin fell to silence as Gerthe and Berrine departed, apparently ignorant of the weight of Lorine's gaze. Risking a closer look, I saw worry mixed with expectation on her face, emotions she chose not to hide. It was clear to me that something of importance had happened tonight. Berrine's tale had confirmed Deckin's assumptions regarding the Pretender's War being far from over, meaning the course he had set us upon would not be changed. None of which, I felt sure, was at all to Lorine's liking.

"With the Pretender still abroad," she ventured when Deckin's silence grew long, "the country around Ambriside will be thick with patrols."

"There'll be some soldiers about," Deckin conceded, his tone distracted. "But I'd guess most of Althus's horse will be off chasing after the Pretender, wherever he's gone. He won't march his foot away until he's tried the duke. Don't fret, love." His voice took on a slight edge as he said this, eyes flicking to Lorine in clear instruction.

"Tell all to rest well," he said, rising to cast a brief glance around the fire. "We'll be pushing hard tomorrow, making for Castle Ambris, if you hadn't already guessed it."

Turning, he walked off into the gloom. I found it noteworthy that Lorine made no effort to follow him. Instead, she fixed a hard, accusing eye on Raith. "If those trinkets of yours are so powerful," she said, "how is it they haven't warned him against this path?"

The Caerith continued to afford his full attention to the dancing flames, still fingering the etched crow skull. "Some paths have to be walked," he replied, his musical tones now possessed of a dreamy quality that made me wonder if he had partaken of his pipe earlier in the evening. "Regardless of all warnings."

Lorine's lips curled as she let out a disdainful snort. "Known a few like you in my time. Trinket pedlars and charm weavers taking coin from honest folk in return for telling them lies they want to hear. It's all just shit."

"I take no coin, except my due as a member of this band," Raith replied, tone still placid, although he finally consented to return her stare. "And where, pray tell, are the honest folk here?"

Lorine gathered her cloak and rose from the fire, unconcealed dislike writ large on her face. "Oh, fuck a tree, you heretic arsehole," she told the Caerith before turning her glare upon me. "You heard Deckin. Get some sleep."

I watched her storm off into the night, pointedly heading in the opposite direction to Deckin. Discord between them made me uneasy, it being so rare.

"Paths to walk, fates to meet."

I turned back to Raith, finding he had resumed his contemplation of the fire. However, instead of the crow skull, he now held his necklace bunched tight in his fist. His face betrayed only the same serene placidity even though I could see a trickle of blood welling between his fingers, the fist shuddering.

I found the sight fascinating but also too off-putting to endure. Edging back, I slipped into the shadow, thinking it best not to offer a parting word.

Berrine regarded me with unabashed suspicion as I bedded down, choosing the hollow of an ancient oak trunk only a few feet from where she and the other Ascarlians huddled together.

"A fine and dry night," I offered as I unrolled the stitched-together, fur-filled blankets that formed my bedroll. "Something to be thankful for, at least."

She gave no reply, watching me settle myself with an unaltered expression. Her companions, I suspect due to simple exhaustion, were all asleep, some snoring which was a strange sound among our company. Outlaws who snore rarely last long in the forest and the body's instinct for survival tends to quell the impulse.

Resting my back against the oak, I passed time repeatedly tossing a stone into the air. I had gathered it upon leaving Raith's side, a small flat boulder with suitably sharp edges. Berrine's gaze narrowed as it tracked the stone's rise and fall. She continued to sit, the sword resting on her shoulder and arms wrapped around the scabbard. Although she must have been tired, her eyes remained steady and her head didn't loll. I suspected that, if she were to sleep, she wouldn't snore.

I stopped my stone flipping as the surrounding fires dwindled to smoking embers in the dark. Soon the forest adopted its nightly song of creaking branches, wind-twisted leaves and the occasional skitter and scratch of unseen creatures. It required an experienced ear to detect the one sound out of place: a faint scraping of the earth punctuated by the muted snap of fern stems. Luckily, my ear was very practised.

I waited until I caught the sway of a sapling a few paces to my right. It was a marginal movement, but against the breeze. Whipping my arm out, I cast the stone, hearing the thwack of it finding flesh followed by a harsh exclamation and a brief, quickly swallowed outburst of profanity.

"Piss off, Erchel," I said, voice hard and flat. I drew my knife as I spoke, knowing he would see the gleam of the blade despite the meagre moonlight.

This was the most dangerous moment, the interval during which Erchel's base urges vied with his instinct for self-preservation. He could draw his own blade and rush me, but the resultant ruckus would surely wake the camp, not to mention arouse Deckin's ire. Also, if it came to knife work, it was a toss of a coin who would win.

The mingled groan and grunt of vexation from the shadows told me that, for tonight at least, Erchel's better judgement had prevailed. A short pause then I saw his wiry shadow flitting through the trees. I wondered if his aversion to nursing grudges would hold come the morn, given the prize I had denied him. For Erchel, the despoilment of a maiden like Berrine was a thing to be cherished and enjoyed, although I doubted she would have proven an easy victim.

"He won't be back," I told her.

Berrine's face, quarter-lit by the fractured moonlight penetrating the forest canopy, was noticeably more fearful now. When she failed to reply, I shrugged and lay down on my bedroll, pulling up a blanket to cover myself. I knew sleep would come quickly despite the excitements of the day, for outlaws soon learn to grab what rest they can.

The first tendrils of slumber had begun to creep across my mind when Berrine spoke, her words a whisper of precise if accented Albermainish. "What did he want?"

Sighing, I raised myself up, finding she had edged a little closer, still holding tight to the sword. "What do you think he wanted?" I asked.

She darted a glanced into the surrounding shadows, quelling a shudder that told me sleep would be long in coming for her this night. "My thanks," she breathed. "But if you're expecting payment . . . " She fell silent at my soft laugh and the fear lingering on her face caused my mirth to fade.

"I'll take some more information as payment," I said. "If you're offering. You speak Albermainish with more fluency than Ascarlian and your accent is of the Fjord Geld. You're not really one of them, are you?"

"Ascarlian blood runs in my veins," she said, fierce insistence adding a hiss to her voice. "As it does in all true Fjord Gelders, regardless of the southern kings we are forced to bow to." Her voice caught and faltered for a second. When she spoke again it was with a practised cadence, as if reciting scripture. "There are those who hold to the old ways, before our Geld was stolen, before our weakness dishonoured us in the eyes of the Altvar and our blood became corrupted by southern ways and misbegotten faiths."

I noticed how her hands clutched the sword as she spoke, as if trying to draw conviction from the steel beneath the scabbard. I knew then that this was a soul as wedded to her faith as Hostler was to his, albeit shaken by dire events.

"Your friend," I said, nodding at the sword, "the one who wielded that. He wanted to die, didn't he?"

She lowered her face and I heard the working of her throat as she swallowed her sorrow. "Skeinweld," she murmured. "He had the heart of a true Ascarlian warrior, but the skills of a wool merchant. It was his father's trade, you see, on the coast of the Aldvir Geld where things are more settled than elsewhere in Ascarlia. Yet, there it was that the *Skard-ryken* were born, among the young but true sons and daughters of Ascarlia. It was to the Aldvir Geld I fled when I could no longer stomach my family's adherence to your death-worshipping faith. There I met Skeinweld and found my true calling with the *Skard-ryken*. There we heard the words of the True King's emissary."

She paused to let out a bitter sigh. "We thought our time had come. We would fight his war and win freedom for the Geld, but war is not what the sagas would have you believe. War is a life of hardship lived among wretches of the worst habits. War is deceit, and murder."

I didn't prompt her, having keen ears and eyes for those who have more to say. There are things folk will voice to strangers they would never confess to friends or family, for a stranger's judgement matters little.

"This," she said, smoothing a hand over the scabbard, "was Skeinweld's grandfather's sword, once wielded in war against the southern army. He died with this in hand, thus winning his place among the mighty lords and ladies of the Endless Halls. Skeinweld wanted to emulate his forebear, be the warrior he had heard so many stories about. But when the battle came . . . "

Shadows shifted on her face as she lowered her head. This time, I knew a prompt to be in order. "He ran," I said.

"We all did." She raised her face, letting out a thin, humourless laugh, eyes bright and wet. "All of us scions of the Altvar, the *Skard-ryken*. We ran."

"So, it was shame that drove him."

I heard a mix of awe and fear creep into her voice then, like someone recalling a nightmare. "I think it was the sight of that monster they sent against us, a towering man of steel who tore through the True King's men as if they were straw and he a whirlwind. His helm bore a red flame that seemed to burn as he fought. I saw stouter hearts than ours flee the monster's wrath. So why wouldn't we? Once we were deep in the forest, once the fear had gone, then came the shame. Skeinweld raged at us, at me, blaming us for infecting him with our cowardice. In truth, he was the first to take to his heels, and he knew it. If you and your friends hadn't come along, he would have found a way to end himself, with a rope if not a blade."

"You never really know who someone is until the blades start flying," I murmured. It was a pearl of his wisdom Deckin had shared with me back during my earliest days in the band. Two outlaws had opted to settle a dispute with knives, one suffering a cut to the arm and promptly fleeing into the forest. He returned come the evening, hiding his shame behind forced cheerfulness and an acceptance of an argument properly settled. Deckin welcomed him back with a hearty embrace before shattering his skull with a single blow of his misshapen axe.

All men are cowards of one stripe or another, he told me as I stared at the fellow's corpse being dragged away. *But I've no use for a man who runs after just one cut. Two means you're smart; three means you're stubborn.* He crouched to tap a bloodied fingertip to my nose. *Remember that, young Alwyn.*

"I am not a warrior," Berrine said, dispelling the memory. She lowered her gaze to match mine, wiping the tears away with an irritated hand. "I see that now. I have been too weakened by southern ways, made soft by your customs. I must find other means of serving the Altvar. The Sister Queens will return the gods to the Fjord Geld and scour away the pollution of your Covenant. It has been foretold."

Her eyes gleamed with a sudden, fervent zeal that brought a dismayed groan to my lips. Her honesty had made me like her, but this dogged attachment to her gods stirred a doleful recognition. She was another Hostler, just gabbling out different scripture.

"A true believer, eh?" I sighed, settling back into my blankets. "And who foretold this, pray tell? Some filth-covered hermit who spent years starving himself in a cave to summon visions? It usually is."

"'And the ships of the Altvar shall sweep across the sea to bring fire to the defilers. What was stolen will be regained. What was slain will be avenged.'" She raised her head with a triumphant air. "So speaks the *Altvar-Rendi*, most sacred of all texts."

"Old words on old paper." I yawned, closing my eyes. "Didn't stop you running from a battle. Won't stop you running from the next one."

As my mind slipped into sleep she spoke again, the words dull and voiced in Ascarlian, but for some unfathomable reason my memory contrives to retain them even now. The passing years have enabled me to acquire mastery of several languages, Ascarlian among them, so I know the words she spoke were a quote from the *Altvar-Rendi*, the collection of myth and legend that forms the basis of Ascarlian belief.

"'Thus spake Ulthnir, Father of the Altvar: Every battle is a forge, and every soul that survives the flames is made stronger.'"

The events of a long and interesting life have forced me to conclude that Ulthnir, like many a god, was full of shit.

CHAPTER FOUR

Berrine and her friends were gone when I awoke. Ever true to his word, Deckin allowed them to rise with the dawn and set off for the coast with no further obstruction, even providing a few sacks of grain to sustain them through the journey. Naturally, Hostler took a dim view of affording any form of assistance to heretic northerners and I was obliged to suffer a diatribe on the subject as we resumed our trek north.

"All who close their hearts to the Martyrs' example and the Seraphile's grace will suffer for their perfidy, in this world and the next," he told me during one of our pauses for rest. "For in their sin they bring us ever closer to the dawn of the Second Scourge."

We were well into the upper reaches of the Shavine Forest now, where the trees began to open out, creating broad clearings that were best avoided. We had halted at the edge of one glade where a lone apple tree rose from a flower-speckled meadow. Even in late autumn, it was a pleasing sight, not that Hostler seemed to notice.

"A lesson you would do well to learn, young ingrate." Over recent days "ingrate" had gradually replaced "heathen" when he addressed me directly. I assumed it to be a result of my continued resistance to the lessons he imparted as my self-appointed tutor in matters spiritual. I wasn't sure which I resented more, since I hadn't asked for an education.

"Allow these teachings into your soul," he went on. "Follow the example of the Martyrs and know a life of peace and fulfilment."

"*They* didn't," I muttered back. I had learned it was best to still my tongue when he began to preach, since the alternative would invite hours of tedious argument. But sometimes his blindness to his own absurdities overthrew my reticence.

"What?" he demanded, hands pausing in the act of raising an oat cake to his mouth.

"The Martyrs," I said. "I mean, the title itself says it all. They died, all of them. Hundreds, maybe thousands of the poor sods put to death because of words scribbled down thousands of years ago. And, as far as I can tell, none got an easy death for their efforts. If that's the example you want me to follow, my thanks for your concern, but I think I prefer to remain a heathen."

"The blood of martyrs," Hostler grated, "washes away the sins of humanity thereby keeping open the Divine Portals of the Eternal Realm, allowing the grace of the Seraphile to flow. Should their grace ever fade from us the Malecite will rise . . . "

" . . . and the Seraphile will be forced to scourge the earth once again to cleanse it of their corruption," I finished with a disparaging roll of my eyes. "Bit strange, don't you think? All those countless bewinged, magic folk living in a paradise in the sky none of us can see, willing to destroy the world to prove how much they love us. Sounds like a man I knew who took a particular shine to a whore. He loved her so much he used to pay the whoremaster to beat her bloody once a week so no other man would look at her."

"Do not compare the Seraphile's boundless love with some faithless, whore-chasing wretch!" He lurched towards me, the oat cake falling from his grip as he grabbed hold of my arm, voice pitched at an unwise volume.

"Best calm yourself," I advised, staring into his wide, blazing eyes. I placed the knife I had already drawn against his hand as it continued to clutch my sleeve. I had no compunction about severing a vein or two, which Hostler might have understood if I hadn't stoked his righteous anger to an unreasoning boil. His grip tightened on my arm as mine tightened on my knife, the moment speeding towards violent climax until Deckin's hand came to rest on Hostler's shoulder.

He didn't say anything, nor was his touch particularly heavy, but it was still enough to convince Hostler to remove his hand. The zealot stepped back, face pale with anger and nostrils flaring as he drew in chilled air to cool his rage. "I'm done with this ingrate," he told Deckin. He was careful not to raise his voice or colour it with any defiance, but his tone was emphatic. "His vile manners and heresy besmirch my soul too much."

Deckin's gaze slipped to me and I found I couldn't help but retreat a step before forcing myself to stillness. He wasn't happy, and that was never good, but trying to flee this moment would invite worse punishment. So, I stood, bracing myself for the blow. If he was feeling generous it might just be a cuff across the face. If not, I would wake an hour or two later with a spectacular bruise to my jaw and maybe a loosened tooth.

Therefore, it was with gratified surprise that I saw him jerk his head in dismissal. "Fetch Erchel and see Lorine. It's time for a new guise. Best learn it well before we reach Castle Ambris."

"Still too neat," Lorine decided, lips pursed in appraisal as she looked us over. Flicking her scissors, she snipped stitches and cut rents in the woollen jerkin and soft leather trews I wore. Prior to this, she had me roll around in earth and bracken to dirty it up, then added a liberal dousing of wine and ale to create a convincing pattern of stains. She hadn't felt the need to alter Erchel's garb hardly at all since it didn't take much to make him appear an impoverished, dull-witted churl.

"Why were you cast out of your village?" she asked me, sheathing the scissors.

"Got drunk and tupped the ploughman's daughter. She was betrothed to the farrier's son, so I had to run or face the pillory alongside her."

"And the true reason?"

One of Lorine's most valuable lessons in deceit was that it was always advisable to layer one's lies, reserving an embarrassing or criminal secret the sharing of which creates a bond of trust. "I hit the Supplicant 'cause he fondled my balls?" I suggested after a moment's pondering.

"That'll work," she said, nodding in satisfaction. "But make it a full beating rather than a single blow. Soldiers like a bloody tale." She arched an eyebrow at Erchel, raising a hand to still his tongue when he began to offer up his own concoction of lies. For all his cunning, Erchel was a poor liar and his tales were either absurdly convoluted or gruesomely off-putting.

"You're a simpleton who stole a pig," she said. "Keep your eyes wide, mouth agape and leave the talking to Alwyn. You two met on the road. You heard there might be work in Ambriside, or at least some free ale on account of the duke's trial. Where do you find soldiers most likely to talk?"

"The cheapest alehouse or inn," I said.

"That's right." Lorine inclined her head in satisfaction at a lesson well learned. "Remember, avoid Crown Company at all costs. They're too sharp of wit and have no need of recruits. It's duchy men-at-arms you want, the drunker and greedier the better."

Her eyes took on a flinty aspect as she shifted her gaze from me to Erchel. "Deckin wants information, not blood, not loot," she said, speaking with hard precision. "You glean what you can then you get out, hopefully without anyone even recalling you were there. Understand?"

I had rarely seen Lorine afford Erchel such close attention. Ever since his uncle had led him into Deckin's camp five years before, Lorine had regarded him with mostly bland disdain. She taught him, as she taught all the whelps, but it was clear she wouldn't have cared a jot if he disappeared one night. For his part, Erchel was always assiduous in affording her the respect due to Deckin's chief lieutenant. Even in his less guarded moments when he thought no one was looking, his expression when looking upon Lorine was one of suppressed fear rather than the ugly hunger that I would have expected. It is in the nature of predators to fear the more dangerous beast, after all.

"'Course," he muttered now, bobbing his head and avoiding her flinty gaze.

Lorine gave a soft grunt and stepped back. "Names?"

"Ash," I said. "Short and easy to remember. My da' was a charcoal burner, see?" I nodded at Erchel. "I call this one Gabbler, since he hardly ever talks."

"That'll do." Tapped her chin as she gave us a final looking-over. "Both a tad too well fed for my liking, so it'll be half rations until we reach Castle Ambris. Don't grumble; it's only two days."

"He didn't beg, y'know."

The old drover's many-wrinkled brow formed into something I took to be an expression of admiration as he followed my gaze to the top of the castle's south-facing wall. The outer defences were at their lowest point here and the moat at its narrowest: a carefully chosen spot for it afforded a clear view of the grisly objects arrayed atop the wall. The light was fading but it was a clear sky for once and I could make out the features clearly enough. I had only ever seen Duke Rouphon once, a brief, distant glimpse two years before when I'd followed Deckin to a glade in the western woods. We'd crouched in dense bushes and watched this man ride past on a tall horse, a falcon on his wrist and a pack of hounds and huntsmen hurrying in his wake. I recalled how Deckin's hard, unmoving features were an uncanny mirror of the noble on the fine horse. I also recalled the hatred I saw shining in his eyes and wondered how badly Deckin would have wanted to be here to savour this man's end.

Despite the depredations of torture and the sagging quality that comes with death, I was still able to confirm that the head impaled atop the spike was indeed that of Duke Rouphon Ambris, until recently a knight of Albermaine and Overlord of the Shavine Marches. The other heads were rendered anonymous by bloating or wounds, but I took them to be those captured alongside the duke – family retainers or bondsmen obliged to share his treason and his fate.

"Did you see the trial?" I asked the drover, receiving a disparaging tongue-click in response.

"That I did, just this morning, not that there was much of a trial to see. They stood the duke on the scaffold alongside the other traitors. The lord constable read out the charges and asked if any would come forth to bear arms in their defence, like they do. Of course, no one did. Not with the King's Champion standing up there and the full number of Crown Company lined up alongside. Ascendant Durehl came forward to hear the duke's testament and when he was done Sir Ehlbert took his head off with one swipe of that big sword of his. Just the duke's head, mind. As soon as it was done, the big fellow walked off and left those others to the headsman."

"Did you hear the duke's testament?" I asked, aware that Deckin would wish to know.

"Too far away, and I doubt he had much've a voice left after the torments he'd suffered. But, like I said, it was plain he didn't beg." The drover looked back at the head on the wall and clicked his tongue again. "He wasn't the worse sort, for a noble. Fair, for the most part. Generous with alms too when the harvests were poor. But, by all accounts, you wouldn't have wanted to let him near your daughter, and he wasn't a man to cross if you wanted to keep your skin."

The drover gave a final tongue-click and tugged on the reins of his ox, the animal obediently hauling the cart along the moat-side track. "I'd stay out of the town tonight, lads," he advised us over his shoulder. "Lessen you're keen on marching under the banners. Awful lot of soldiers about."

I raised a hand in thanks, turning my attention to the sprawl of buildings rising from the flat ground to the east of the castle's main gate, following the shore of the Leevin River that fed the moat. Years of comparative peace had enabled the town of Ambriside to grow into a large if untidy collection of houses, inns, workshops and stables. Despite having spent my infancy in a similar but smaller clutch of hovels, I found the scent of woodsmoke and dung stirred dislike rather than nostalgia. I much preferred the woods; for all the danger, things were simpler among the trees.

"I know what it was," Erchel said.

"What?"

"His testament." He nodded at the head on the wall, face tilted at an inquisitive angle. As before, any enmity towards me had apparently vanished, even though he surely sported a nasty bruise somewhere from the stone I threw at him.

"I, Duke Rouphon Ambris, seek the Seraphile's pardon for my many sins," he went on in a parody of noble speech. "For years I have sat my fat arse upon horses I didn't raise, eating food I didn't grow and meat I didn't butcher. All the while I fucked any churlish maid I took a fancy to while helping myself to coin and goods not my own in the name of Crown taxes. Every now and then I'd piss off somewhere and slaughter some poor unfortunate sods 'cause the king told me to. Then I turned on him like an ungrateful dog for not making me richer than I already am, so here we are. Now cleanse my soul, you pious bastard, so I get to live in paradise for ever."

He turned to me with a grin. "Tell Deckin that's he what he said. He'd like that."

"No." I recalled Deckin's face the day we spied on the duke's hunting party and spared the grisly parade on the wall a last glance before turning and starting for the town. "He wouldn't. Come on, Gabbler, let's be about it."

In accordance with Lorine's tutelage, we made for the most ill-favoured-looking tavern, reasoning only those soldiers with the deepest thirst would congregate at the place with the cheapest ale. Securing ourselves a table at the rear of the dingy establishment required some judicious intimidation of the two churls already in residence. Both older men with ragged beards and the lean but tired features of those born to the plough or the hoe, the pair stared up at us with wary eyes but didn't consent to rise. One seemed about to sneer a warning but fell silent when Erchel leaned down, taking hold of the fellow's clay tankard and drawing it clear of his hand.

"Fuck off, eh?" he said with a bland smile and a wink. To emphasise the point, he put a twitch on his face and a flare to his nostrils that told of contained violence, evidently with sufficient clarity for both churls to surrender possession of their table and swiftly depart the tavern.

"Sure this is the best place?" Erchel said, sinking onto a stool and setting the tankard down with a disdainful scowl. "Even a drunkard wouldn't soil his tongue with this piss-water."

"A true drunkard comes in search of spirits, not ale." I gestured to the brandy casks visible beyond the bulky form of the tavern-keeper. "The cheaper the better. Don't fret; they'll be along. And still your tongue. You're a simpleton, remember?"

True to my prediction, a half-dozen soldiers from the duchy levies arrived not long after. They entered with none of the boisterous swagger common to those new to their profession, creased and weathered faces uniform in their dourness. A grim morning's work apparently made for a grim mood and a desire to drink it away. War, as I would learn in time, does much to strip youth from the youthful. They had shorn themselves of their armour but kept daggers and swords sheathed at their belts, most more than one. They were all decently washed and trimmed of hair but their clothing – mostly leather jerkins and trews and shirts of wool – had the patched, slightly ragged look common to garments in a permanent state of disrepair.

"Brandy," one called to the tavern-keeper after a scant survey of the shadowed interior. "And best make sure it's the good stuff, friend."

He tossed a few sheks on to the counter and the soldiers moved to occupy a set of tables close to the fireplace. The few townsmen seated there fled with markedly more alacrity than the pair of churls Erchel and I had scared away. We watched the soldiers sit in silence while the tavern-keeper poured each a measure of brandy into a clay cup. When he was done, the one who had paid – a burly fellow with a face more creased than his companions' – solemnly raised his cup and the others followed suit.

"Pray thanks to the Martyrs for a short campaign and beseech them to care for the soul of Duke Rouphon," he said. "A stout heart gone bad who nevertheless deserved a better end."

The other soldiers all murmured agreement before draining their cups whereupon their dourness seemed to evaporate all at once.

"More!" Crease-face called to the tavern keeper, holding his cup aloft. "And don't staunch until we tell you."

As they drank, Erchel and I assumed our roles, huddling close together and barely sipping our ale in a sign that we couldn't afford a second tankard. I shot guarded glances at the soldiers, leaning closer in an apparent effort to hear the stories they began to tell as brandy lightened their mood and loosened their tongues.

"Saw him at Velkin's Ford, I did," one was saying. He was broader than the others, one ear mangled into something that resembled a small pink cabbage. He also seemed to have achieved the required state of inebriation quicker, allowing for a loud recitation of his anecdote. "The duke . . . former duke. Right at the front of the charge he was, Sir Ehlbert alongside. The water turned white when they charged and red when they came trotting back only a quarter-hour later. Martyrs know how many churls they cut down that day, nary a noble among 'em. Worst day's looting I ever had."

"Something interest you, lad?"

My eyes jerked towards Crease-face with a suitably startled blink before I quickly looked away. I knew from experience that one of two things would happen next. Crease-face would either deliver a profane warning to attend to my own business or rise from his table and engage two possible recruits in conversation. It depended on how short of coin this lot might be. Soldiers were usually paid a bounty by their sergeant for any youngsters they could lure to a life beneath the banner. Crease-face clearly had a light purse for he scraped his chair back and sauntered over with a friendly grin.

"Can't say I blame you for eavesdropping. My friend spins a fair tale, though it's not his best. Is it, Pots?"

"Not by half," Pots agreed with a hearty chuckle, though his eyes belied a sudden onset of greed. Plainly he was not so drunk as to miss the opportunity for a share in the sergeant's bounty. "Was there for the storming of the citadel in Couravel, I was. Last day of the Duchy Wars and what a day it was. Hawker—" he winked at Crease-face "—why not stand these lads an ale and I'll tell 'em all about it."

And so it went. Erchel and I sat mostly in wide-eyed, seemingly half-drunk silence as Pots told his tales and Hawker kept the ale coming. As the hours passed stories of battle were leavened by tales of loot and women. "Girls might show favour to a kindly man with a song to sing, but it's the man with scars and a full purse that really stirs them up."

I laughed along dutifully, although this man's broken-nosed, vein-laced features stirred unpleasant memories of the sots who would crowd the whorehouse whenever an army marched through. Such men had scars aplenty, but rarely a full purse, and were far too fond of aiming kicks at small boys who might stray into their path.

"Was the duke at that one too?" Erchel piped up as Pots related another story. I managed to keep the reproachful glare from my face, although the mischievous glint in his eyes made me sorely tempted to launch a punch at him across the table. Erchel had apparently decided the role of wordless simpleton didn't suit him, which would inevitably make this night a far more complicated affair than it needed to be.

"Former duke," Hawker stated, his tone hard enough to make Erchel lower his gaze in wary contrition.

"Not that day, no," Pots said. His story was one I had already heard. The tale of the Battle of the Brothers was well known: a grand clash of armies led by two noble siblings who had chosen different sides in the Duchy Wars. At the battle's end, one brother held the other as he lay dying, weeping piteous tears and beseeching the Martyrs for forgiveness. In truth, I had been assured by Deckin, himself a veteran of the Duchy Wars, that this apparently tragic epic had been little more than a large, inconclusive skirmish after which the surviving brother pissed on his slain kin's corpse, for they had hated each other all their lives.

"In truth, I only ever saw him fight at Velkin's Ford," Pots continued. "But I saw enough to know he was as fine a knight as I was ever likely to clap eyes on." His face clouded as he gulped more brandy, adding in a mutter, "Not like that shit-sack skulking up north. Fine fucking duke he's going to make."

"Shit-sack?" I asked, careful to slur my words and furrow my brow to indicate only slight interest and a diminished capacity to recall anything I might learn.

"Duke Rouphon's second cousin twice removed, or somesuch," Pots replied. "Only noble-arse with any blood-claim to this duchy they could find, Martyrs help them."

"Pots," Hawker said, voice hardening.

Pots, however, was too lost in his cups to heed a cautionary word. "Duke Elbyn Blousset, they made us call him. Like tying a gold ribbon to a dead hog. Caught a few words 'twixt him and Sir Ehlbert when we were billeted in that shitheap castle of his." He burped out a humourless laugh before adopting a high, whiny voice. "'But I am not a man of war, good sir. I leave such things to you . . .'"

I had wanted to enquire as to the exact location of this shitheap castle, but Hawker's hand came down hard on the table along with a stern command to silence. Pots curled his lip but wasn't sufficiently drunk to risk a brawl so fell quiet, leaving the task of regaling his two young friends with the delights of a soldier's life to his companion.

"I reckon you lads are no strangers to toil, as I was once," Hawker observed. "Years I spent apprenticed to a cruel master, my back aching from his cane and the endless slog he set me to. None of that when you swear to the banners."

"Thought soldiers were flogged all the time," Erchel commented in a slow, befuddled drawl, a convincing lack of focus to his eyes. He was enjoying this role, taking delight in the success of his deceit. I found it worrying, for with Erchel deceit was always a prelude to darker acts.

"Only cowards taste the whip in our company," Hawker assured him, jostling our shoulders. "And I can tell two such stout fellows would never run from a battle . . . "

The day wore into night. Pots and Hawker were kind enough to invite us to visit their company where plentiful drink and more stories were to be had. I knew how this went for those unfortunates foolish enough to put their feet in the snare. They would wake with an aching head come the morn, manacled to a cartwheel with a silver sovereign shoved into their mouth. A sergeant-at-arms would relieve them of the sovereign with firm assurances that it would be returned along with another when their five years under the banner were done. With the Pretender's War raging, plus all the camp fevers, poxes and sundry dangers of a soldier's life, the chances of collecting both coins were slim. The days when youths flocked to the banners with visions of glory were long over, hence the need to resort to such villainous tactics to maintain the strength of a company.

There's two types of willing soldier, Deckin had told me once, *the mad and the desperate. All others are no more willing than some poor bastard toiling in the Pit Mines.*

"Need to piss first," I said, getting unsteadily to my feet. The plan was for Erchel and I to stumble to the slurry pit at the rear of the tavern and simply vanish. The soldiers would curse their luck at having let us slip the snare and probably forget us soon enough. By dawn we would be back at camp telling Deckin all we knew.

"We'll piss on the way," Erchel declared loudly, rising to his feet and downing the dregs of his ale. "Ye have brandy, y'say?"

"A whole cask of the stuff," Hawker assured him with a clap to the shoulder, leading him towards the door. "Courtesy of the Pretender himself. The bastard ran off and left us all his grog."

We emerged from the tavern to be greeted by chill air and a freshly frosted ground. It helped to dispel the effects of the night's drink. A hard knot formed in my gut as we sauntered along with Hawker and Pots, born of the knowledge that there was now no chance of avoiding an ugly conclusion to the evening's events. The other soldiers had stayed behind, which was fortunate for us but not these two. While Crown Company had been billeted in Castle Ambris, the duchy companies were encamped on the far side of the river, presumably as a guard against possible trouble from the townsfolk. Erchel waited until we had crossed the narrow wooden bridge to the far bank before coming to a halt. He swayed back and forth, face drawn in the befuddled discomfort of the overly drunk.

"I'm . . . " he muttered before staggering off to the thick blanket of reeds at the river's edge. Soon after there came the sounds of a youth at retch.

"This one needs a little tempering," Pots commented cheerfully as Erchel continued his spewing, loud enough to capture the full attention of both soldiers. "Few years under the banner and you'll have a gut like iron." Fortunately, their captain had neglected to post a guard on the bridge and the pickets patrolling the camp were too distant to take note of what happened next.

My sap was concealed at the small of my back, a tight-wound, six-inch column of leather encasing a ball of melted sheks at one end. No good in a brawl where a knife or a cudgel worked better, but in skilled hands it did very nicely at times like this, and my hands were well practised. The weighted end caught Hawker behind the ear, the blow sending him straight down as if every tendon in his legs had been cut at once. His collapse drew a puzzled grunt from Pots who turned to stare at me with eyes that refused to widen thanks to the liquor in his veins, although they did consent to do so when Erchel thrust a small dagger into the base of his skull.

"What the shitting fuck!?" I demanded in a furious hiss, advancing to grab hold of Erchel's coarse-woven shirt. His face formed a familiar half-contrite, half-smirking mask as I dragged him close, tempting me to plant the sap firmly between his eyes.

"They've seen our faces," he said, thin shoulders shrugging. "Dead men's tongues don't wag."

"We were supposed to have fucked off well before now, you mad bastard." The smug cast to his eyes, resembling a boy caught with his finger in a fresh-baked pie, made me want to exchange my sap for my knife. I could stab him here and be on my way, and I doubted Deckin would mind if I had. I was aware that this was partially my doing. Having cheated Erchel of one murder a few nights before, he had been nursing his need until now. Although resistant to grudges, it seemed he was not fully immune to revenge. It would be me who had to explain things to Deckin. But it was not the awareness of my unwitting complicity that stilled my hand. I had known Erchel from boyhood. For all his awfulness, he was still of the band. Besides, he had a knife too.

"Their whole fucking company will be hunting us come the morn," I grated, shoving him away.

"Waylaid by footpads." Erchel flicked blood from his blade and shrugged. "Woods are thick with outlaws."

"We were seen leaving the tavern with them, you shithead! Soldiers waylaid and robbed by those they're trying to slip the sovereign is one thing – happens all the time. Murder's another. *You* can fucking well tell Deckin and don't expect me to lie for you."

His half-smirk became a weak tremulous smile as he regarded my increasingly hard gaze. Only now the thrill of murder had begun to fade did he begin to contemplate the consequences. The moment stretched then broke when Hawker let out a faint groan, reminding us both that time was short.

"I should see to him," Erchel said.

"No." Stoking his madness with another killing so soon would not be wise. "I'll do it. Search that one and drag him into the river. With luck the current'll carry him off."

I finished Hawker with one of his own daggers, a swift, deep thrust to the neck, holding it and twisting until he shuddered and lay still. He had another knife tucked into his boot which I shoved into my own before rifling his corpse, finding a light purse and a Covenant medallion. It was a roughly hammered bronze sun, the motif of Martyr Hersephone, the first Resurrected Martyr whose blessings were said to bestow good fortune. I gave a faint, bitter laugh as I regarded the trinket, a poorly crafted thing of little worth. I kept it anyway, hooking the chain over my head before taking hold of Hawker's legs and dragging him to the river.

We were obliged to wade into the ball-shrivelling current to make sure it carried them away. We had no time to gather stones to weigh them down; soon their comrades would vacate the tavern and wend their way to camp. Water filled the corpses' pockets and boots, drawing them under the surface before the river took them, but I knew the humours birthed by their dead flesh would soon bring them back up.

Struggling free of the water we set off at a steady run for the trees, fleeing into the dark and welcome embrace of the woods. As we ran, I considered and abandoned different schemes to murder Erchel. There was no time and no surety of success. As you continue to partake of the tale set down in these pages, dear reader, you will fully understand why there hasn't been a day since when I haven't regretted not contriving a means of cutting his throat that night.

CHAPTER FIVE

"So, a killing then?" Deckin asked, voice flat and lacking emotion. "Two killings in fact," he added, unblinking eyes flicking to me. "If one fell the other had to," I replied, trying to match his flat tone with my own. I had said little until now, letting Erchel stumble over his report in the faint hope any blame would fall entirely on his shoulders.

"Right," Deckin said, voice softer now. "Except I don't recall ordering one killing, never mind two. Lorine—" his voice rose a fraction as he glanced at where she stood, leaning against a nearby tree, arms crossed and features grim "—is my recollection at fault? Did I order a killing?"

"No." Lorine's voice was flat and her expression remained dark, either with judgement or disappointment. "I don't believe you did, my love."

"But surely, I must have." Deckin's bushy brows twisted as he frowned in apparent puzzlement. "For a killing has been done by one of this band. So—" he shifted his gaze to address the others, the entire band standing in silence among the surrounding trees "—I must have ordered it, must I not?"

One of his overlarge hands shot out, snake swift, to enclose Erchel's neck. His eyes bulged as the hand squeezed, Deckin's arm stiffening to raise Erchel up so that his toes scraped the earth.

"For those who honour me with their loyalty know better," Deckin continued with barely a pause, voice counterpointed by Erchel's increasingly loud chokes. "Do they not?"

When the monster that was Deckin's rage got loose it was best not to make him repeat a question and the chorus of agreement was quick, my own voice perhaps loudest among it.

"Was I not kindly in allowing you into this band?" His voice took on a quivering, growling quality as he dragged Erchel closer. "A rat-faced, worthless turd dragged to my camp by his own kin who could no longer tolerate his habits? My heart is too soft, is it not, Lorine?"

At first, Erchel had been wise in keeping his hands dangling at his sides, but his air-starved lungs had them clutching at Deckin's wrist, without particular effect. They reminded me of wet leaves clinging to a branch when the wind drives rain through the trees, while the crack that came from within his gullet as something gave way under the pressure recalled a creaking tree limb.

"Your generosity is properly famous, my love." I noticed how Lorine's features had taken on a frown as Deckin's grip tightened yet further. Her gaze slipped from Erchel's feeble struggles to fix on me then flicked towards Deckin's now-snarling face. It was a clear instruction to speak up. I wasn't aware she held any particular fondness for Erchel, none of us did, and put her concern down to a desire to maintain the band's numbers. Her urging was not the only reason I stirred my tongue, however. Once Deckin was done with one unsanctioned killer, what was to stop him turning on the other?

"They said he died well," I said after a hard swallow to quell any treacherous quaver. "The duke, I mean to say."

Deckin's hand stopped its tightening as his small eyes flicked to me, Erchel continuing to choke in his grasp. "Did he now?" Deckin enquired. "And with what fine words did he meet his end?"

"The fellow we spoke to wasn't close enough to hear his testament." I found I had to swallow again but did manage to contain a cough before continuing. "But he was brave. He didn't beg."

Deckin's small eyes narrowed a fraction, nostrils flaring as he drew in a deep breath. Erchel chose this moment to cough a glob of reddened spit onto Deckin's hand, an involuntary consequence of his strangling rather than a gesture of defiance for, even in the face of imminent death, he knew that to be a very poor notion.

Deckin grunted in disgust and cast Erchel away, his slight frame colliding with the trunk of a nearby birch before slipping to the ground. "Gauntlet," Deckin said, casting his voice at the whole band.

Todman and Baker duly came forward to haul Erchel to his feet. After ripping off his clothes they dragged him to the twin lines formed by the rest of the band. They all held cudgels or staffs ready, some eager, some indifferent, but all fully willing and able to do Deckin's bidding.

Todman delivered a hard kick to Erchel's bared arse, propelling him into the lane between the lines. The first blow landed before he took a step, Baker delivering a hefty thwack to his legs with a leather strap he liked to keep for such occasions. To his credit, Erchel contrived to keep upright as he made his stumbling progress through the gauntlet and the blows rained down. His increasingly piteous cries and sobs were not so creditable, loud despite the new rasping quality to his voice. However, my attention was mostly captured by Deckin's lingering stare. I had suffered a few punishments during my years with the band, a few beatings and a caning when my pilfering or acerbic tongue drew Deckin's notice. But I hadn't yet been forced to run the gauntlet, a trial I had seen take the life from others more than once.

Finally, Deckin's small eyes blinked again and he turned to Lorine. "Don't let them kill him," he said, jerking his head at the ongoing spectacle. "Little shit's got his uses, and his uncle's still owed a favour."

She nodded, favouring me with a small curve of her lips as she strode off, calling out in her strident but pleasing tones, "All right, that'll do!" Even in the midst of my fear I couldn't help but take note of the sway of her hips before Deckin's mutter snapped my gaze back to him.

"Let's take a walk, young Alwyn. I would hear more of the duke's courageous end."

*

I followed Deckin to the fallen, moss-shrouded trunk of a tall birch a good distance clear of the camp. Walking in his wake, my eyes continually flicking from his broad back to the surrounding forest, I entertained wild and very brief thoughts of simply fleeing into the trees. Perhaps he wanted to deal with me in private, a secluded murder away from the rest of the band, some of whom actually liked me. Or he may have been intent on a maiming, taking an ear or an eye, which the others would say was in fact a kindness, for hadn't we witnessed him sever a man's cock and balls not so long ago?

But I didn't flee, partly due to the simple fact that I had no refuge to flee to, save the dubious solace of cold and lonely starvation. Dumb loyalty also played its part, for such is the way with boys taken in by rogues; the largesse of the strong breeds a particular form of attachment that doesn't break so easily. But I prefer to think that what kept me trudging along after him like an obedient hound was the recognition that the will to murder had seeped from him now. He walked with a slump to his back and a bow to his head that told of sombre disappointment, a mood that generally stirred him to reflection rather than violence.

His breath blossomed in a cloud as he let out a sigh, sinking down to perch on the fallen birch, nodding for me to do the same before holding up an expectant hand. "Coin."

I quickly handed over the purse I had purloined from Hawker's corpse. Normally he would take half and return the rest, but not today. "That all?" he enquired, tucking the purse into his belt.

"Got these," I said, fumbling for the knives I had looted, which he also took. "And this." I grasped the chain about my neck but Deckin let out a derisive snort when he caught sight of the rough-hewn copper disc it held.

"Hersephone, eh? Keep the bitch. A man makes his own fortune in this world."

I let the chain fall and watched him shift his gaze to the forest. "Why didn't you kill Erchel?" he asked, his voice betraying only a slight note of interest.

"Didn't know if you'd have wanted it. Felt like it though."

"Balls. You didn't do it 'cause you didn't want to. 'Cause you're not like him. Killing's not a pleasure for you, just a chore. All born killers are outlaws but not all outlaws are born killers." His beard bunched as he smiled at his own wit. "For Erchel, killing's as sweet as fucking. You know this; you've seen it. With these." He rested one hand on my head and raised the other, tracing two large, rough fingers over my brows, forcing my eyelids shut.

"These, Alwyn." The fingers exerted a small amount of pressure, just enough to hurt and remind me that he possessed more than enough strength to push them all the way into my brain if he chose. "These are your principal asset to this band, to me. I pegged it right away all those years ago when we found you wandering, a bundle of rag, skin and bone barely hours from the grave, but with such bright eyes. Eyes that saw so much, with a big brain behind them to store it all up in. Lorine's my counsel, Raith my guide to the unseen, Todman my punisher, but you, you're my spy, the one that sees what needs seeing. And I know you see that one day Erchel will need to be put down, and when the time comes it'll be your hand that does it."

The fingers pressed against my eyes once more, fractionally harder this time before he released me with a sigh. "That's your punishment, Alwyn, for not acting on what your eyes showed you. Got any objections, voice them now."

I blinked away tears, not allowing myself a pause before replying, the tremor stripped from my voice. "No objections, Deckin."

"That's good, then. It'll be a few weeks yet so don't dwell on it too much. Erchel's got some blood ties that mean I'll need to do a little bargaining first." He fell to silence, unfocused gaze returning to the trees where it seemed to linger for a long time.

"So," he grunted finally, "you see the duke's end?"

"No, it had been done that morning. We heard how he spoke to the Ascendant for a good while, though. Ascendant Durehl. Seems he wasn't happy about the whole business. Nor . . . " I coughed. "Nor the King's Champion, so we heard."

"Still did his duty though, didn't he? Still swung the sword and took the bastard traitor's head for the king."

I said nothing, wondering if Deckin truly wanted a full description of the tormented remnant now resting on a spike on the wall of Castle Ambris. Fortunately, Deckin spoke on before I could fumble out a response.

"Except he wasn't the bastard," Deckin muttered. "I was. One of many. Do you know, I've no real notion how many brothers and sisters I've got running around this duchy? There's four I know of for sure, a few others with an uncanny resemblance glimpsed over the years. All unacknowledged issue of the duke's loins and poor as dirt, just like I was."

He let the words sit, a secret that wasn't truly a secret since the truth of Deckin's parentage had long been rumoured, if not openly discussed. The resemblance was there for any who cared to see, and he had never denied it, but neither did he want to talk of it. We all knew that speaking of Duke Rouphon in Deckin's presence could have unpredictable consequences.

"If I remember right, you never knew your father, did you?" he asked when I began to wonder if I should say something more.

"No, Deckin." I forced a laugh as I often did when the subject of my childhood came up. "Could've been any one of a thousand wayward cocks trooping through the whorehouse that month."

"Then consider yourself lucky, for I've found fathers are usually a great disappointment to their sons. Who else was there to witness the execution?"

"Besides the Champion and the Ascendant, the lord constable was the only man of note we heard tell of. Just them, Crown Company and a bundle of soldiers from other duchies. I think they were expecting trouble from the townsfolk."

"But there wasn't none, was there?" I saw his lips form a grin under his beard. "They might have tolerated their lord, even liked him a little, but they never loved him. There were few who did."

He angled his head to regard me, voice and gaze sharper now. "What did you learn? Assuming you managed to get something out of those poor sods before you killed them."

I replied promptly, relieved to have shifted to another topic. "The new duke, Elbyn Blousset, they said he's called. The old duke's second cousin twice removed—"

"First cousin," Deckin corrected. "The son of my grandfather's sister. What else?"

"The soldiers said they had been billeted in Blousset's castle for a time. Sir Ehlbert was there. They overheard them talking. Seems Blousset was too cowardly to fight his cousin."

"Cowardice and good sense are often the same thing. What else?"

"That's it, more or less. A whole bundle of tall tales about the battles they'd seen, some gossip about sergeants they hated or captains they liked, usual thing. Couldn't get the name of the castle."

"I know its name. Castle Shelfine, seat of the Blousset family for three generations. A shitpile it may be, but its walls are thick and not easily scaled. But, fortunately, I doubt he'll be in residence much longer." He lapsed into silence once again, though only briefly before inclining his head towards the main camp. "Go eat. Tell Lorine I'll be along shortly. And Alwyn," he added as I got to my feet, "don't tell her any of this." He gave me a thin smile that didn't alter the hard instruction in his gaze. "No matter how sweetly she asks."

"I won't, Deckin."

He turned back to contemplate the forest as I hurried off, compelled by a mingling of fear and relief to seek out a more pleasant diversion.

"That's not even worth my hand, never mind my nethers," Gerthe said, squinting at the proffered medallion in amused contempt.

"It's a gift." I gave her the full measure of my winning smile. I had been practising it for a while, along with what I imagined to be a roguishly charming tone. "A token of my esteem."

"Can't eat your esteem, can I?" Gerthe laughed in professional disdain. "And I ain't gobbling nothing else of yours unless you come up with something better than a pissy little Martyr trinket. Do I strike you as a girl of devout inclination, Alwyn?"

"You have always struck me as a lady of discerning wit, not to mention ineffable beauty."

"Oh, fuck off." She laughed again, and I felt a small surge of optimism at the genuine humour it held. "Ineffable. Collecting words again, eh? Hear that one in Ambriside did you?"

She raised an eyebrow, the healthy sheen of her dimpled cheeks sending a hungry thrill through my lust-ridden body. Deckin had found Gerthe wandering the southern woods a year ago, having been turfed out of her whorehouse when the pimp discovered her light-fingered habits with the customers' coin. Skills like hers, both linguistic and carnal, were always valuable in the band. But Deckin was a fair employer and insisted she receive commensurate reward for her services, usually at prices I found well beyond my reach.

"That merchant we held for ransom last spring talked a lot," I admitted with a shrug.

"That so? Pity you didn't keep hold of your share. Then you wouldn't be wasting my time with a pointless haggle. Now, sod you off, young fellow. I've cooking to do." She returned to the business I had interrupted, stirring a pot of steaming rabbit stew.

"I'll take a bowl of that, if it's all that's on offer," I said, fishing out two sheks, the last of my fortune. Every shek I earned in the band had a tendency to slip through my fingers with annoying alacrity. While I may flatter myself in having acquired numerous skills in life, keeping hold of coin has never been one of them.

She wanted three sheks but on this, at least, was willing to be bargained down. I took the bowl she filled and wandered off. One bite of stew was enough to rekindle my hunger and I was soon gulping it down. I exchanged nods and quiet greetings as I progressed through the camp. Voices were rarely raised in the woods where betraying sounds could echo longer than seemed natural, perhaps drawing unwelcome attention in the process.

Licker, called such on account of his missing tongue, greeted me with his toothless grin, Hulbeth with a saucy wink of her wrinkled, pox-addled face. The inseparable Justan and Yelk waved from the shadowed interior of the shelter where, I assumed, they had spent some time in blissful, enviable intimacy. Todman, Baker and Twine briefly glanced up from their game of sevens. Baker and Twine each gave me a nod while Todman's gaze lingered a mite longer.

"Stew but no fucking, eh?" he asked with a satisfied grin. "Even Gerthe's got standards."

I should have just offered a bland smile and passed by without comment. Instead, I paused, returning his stare in full measure while I ate another spoonful of stew, taking my time over it. Usually, finding myself in this man's company provoked a good deal of fear to match the hatred, but not today. By my reckoning I had probably killed just as many men as Todman by now and, while he was certainly stronger, I felt sure I was faster.

"Something I can help you with, boy?" he asked, stepping closer. He exhibited his contempt and lack of concern by folding his arms, hands well clear of the knife at his belt. In that instant, I knew killing him was definitely within the scope of my skills. He was too incautious, too attached to his displays of superiority. A dangerous fellow by any measure, but still just a bully at heart. Throw the stew in his face, one quick flick of the knife while he wasted time sputtering and raging. No more Todman.

I suppressed the urge, aware that killing so useful a member of the band after such a recent debacle would test Deckin's forgiveness beyond its limits. But neither did I look away. If Todman struck first, I couldn't be blamed for what came next.

But, to my considerable surprise, he didn't.

Instead, he watched me eat my stew as I watched his nostrils flare and skin redden in impotent rage. As I had taken my measure of him, it appeared he had done the same of me. This, I knew, was a man deeply regretting the fact that he hadn't killed me years before.

"Things change, boy," he grated, the words hissed through clenched teeth. "His favour fades every time you fuck things up. And *she* won't be around for ever."

His lips clamped shut as soon as the words were out, his pallor shifting from red to the paleness of fear. In this company, one word out of place could mean death, and he had just said several. Speaking ill of Lorine was just as dangerous as voicing criticism of Deckin's leadership, perhaps more so given her uncanny facility for ferreting out dissent.

I raised an eyebrow in unspoken invitation for Todman to continue, which of course he didn't. "Go and gawp elsewhere," he muttered, turning his back. "This is a game for men." Crouching, he tossed a shek into the circle and promptly lost it with a clumsy, hurried throw of the dice.

I made sure he heard my laugh before moving on.

By the time I'd finished the stew my wanderings had brought me close to Hostler's fire. As was typical, he had established a den for himself a decent remove from the rest of the band. It was a mostly unspoken but mutual agreement that he not inflict his endless prattle on us in return for being spared the sight of our endlessly sinful ways. In consequence, he generally kept to himself until Deckin decided he was needed. Not that solitude ever seemed to staunch the flow of his invective.

"As with sacrifice so with compassion," he was saying as I rounded a broad elm to see him wandering around a small fire near the entrance to his den. His eyes were closed and his head tilted back as he summoned words from the depthless well of his memory. "As with compassion so with courage. With these words did Martyr Lemtuel suffer the arrows of his tormentors, heathens all with black hearts, but one among them was not so black—"

"Wasn't Lemtuel whipped to death?" I enquired, bringing the recitation to an abrupt halt.

Hostler's brows drew into a glower as he opened his eyes and turned their harsh, judgemental gleam upon me. "Whipped with a hundred strokes," he said. "Then pierced with a hundred arrows, all of which failed to kill him, and it fell to the one heathen his words had reached to end his suffering. As with sacrifice, so with compassion."

"Oh, right," I said with a grin that failed to dim the judgement in his gaze.

"You recall me saying I was done with you, ingrate?"

"I do. I also recall not giving much of a stinky shit." Baiting him wasn't smart, for Hostler was probably a good deal more dangerous than Todman. Yet, being in his presence never failed to stir my tongue to taunts.

However, instead of the expected threats or resort to fists, this time Hostler laughed. It was a short, harsh sound, made odd by its sheer rarity. "You think I don't see your soul, ingrate?" he enquired, voice rich in righteous satisfaction. "I see the truth of you. You think your-self clever and yet you are even more stupid than the rest of these scum. They are blind to their fate yet you have the wit to see yours, and choose not to in your indolence and fear. What do you imagine your life will be? You will rise one day to lead this band, be the Outlaw King? No, the Scourge will claim you long before that."

I let out a weary groan and walked on. Hostler's preaching about the Martyrs was tedious but when he started on about the Scourge, he became unbearable. "It draws near, ingrate," he called after me, his passion for his subject making him abandon the outlaw's ingrained tendency towards quiet. "Called forth by the sin and vice of this world of hypocrites! It will not spare you! All will be fire! All will be pain! As it was before, so shall it be again when the Seraphile's grace is denied us once more . . . "

At this juncture, dear reader, you may be expecting an account of my oft-reported Revelation. Was this the very moment of my epiphany? Did the preaching of this addle-brained fanatic open my eyes to the truth of the Covenant and set me on the path to eventual redemption?

In short: no. I didn't believe a word of it, not then as I waved a hand in sardonic farewell and walked away, his voice pursuing me through the trees. All my belief came later, a gift I never wanted nor was grateful to have received. If there is one principal lesson to be garnered from the wayward often chaotic path of my life it's the knowledge that true faith – not the rote hypocrisy of desperate, fearful curs like Hostler – is as more a curse than a blessing. Not that he would ever know that, poor fool that he was. Strangely, I never hated him, and pity vies with contempt when I think of him now, for it is hard to hate a man who has saved your life.

Chapter Six

The Shavine Forest was far larger in the days before the demands of forge and shipyard sent hordes of charcoal burners and woodcutters to ravage it down to its current size. Although this despoilment was well under way when Deckin's band haunted the woods, the forest remains huge in my memory. I often think of it as a beast in its own right, a sprawling leviathan of ancient trees with few clearings and innumerable root-choked gullies where outlaws of craft and experience could evade the duke's sheriffs for months or even years.

So, when the time came to break camp and head for Leffold Glade we did so with a cautious slowness, moving in silent and precise order from one hiding place to another. The old duke was fond of periodically sending companies of soldiers and huntsmen into the darker regions of the forest where, with luck, the hounds might ferret out a miscreant or two for the noose. Whether this newly appointed cousin would prove so diligent remained an open question and Deckin was disinclined towards chancing a rapid march.

His decision was not popular with the band, although no tongue was so foolish as to say so. Travelling at the dawn of winter meant days of miserable traipsing across frosted ground where game was sparse and fires difficult to light come nightfall. The nights were the worst, long hours of shivering darkness alleviated only by Gerthe occasionally consenting to snuggle next to me for warmth. Sadly, snuggling was all she would permit and I was too wary of her small but sharp dagger to risk a wandering hand.

Leffold Glade sat twenty miles to the north amid the thick forest between the duchy's heartland and the wetlands of the north-eastern border. Reaching it required traversing a few miles of open country, something we only ever did in the dead of night and in carefully established order. Bowmen were posted on both flanks a good thirty paces from the central group all bunched close around Deckin and Lorine with daggers and sundry weapons in hand. Lacking any skill with the bow and considered not yet hefty enough to act as a guard, I was sent to scout the ground ahead, ready to let out a piercing whistle at the sight of any patrolling soldiery.

The band moved at a run when we did this chore, covering the ground to the road and beyond at a pace just below a sprint. Although the old duke's men rarely patrolled at night, it wasn't unknown for his sheriffs to lay an ambush at frequently used crossing places. Fortune smiled that night and I reached the safety of the trees without detecting any problems. Still, the forest was alive with the creak of the trees, branches heavy with the first snows of winter. Although well used to life in the woods, time alone in the wild dark was always a disconcerting experience, stirring fears born of an instinctive knowledge that this was neither a place nor a time for people to be abroad.

Therefore, I should have been grateful for the sight of Lorine hurrying towards me, breath pluming white in the gloom, but there was something about the cast of her face that set me on edge. She wore a careful smile, her gaze set in the bright, searching look of one keen to read another's reaction. The artifice of it bothered me, as did the fact that I had spotted it so easily; normally she was a much better actress.

"Thought you'd need another set of eyes," she said. "Since Erchel's not here."

Erchel usually joined me when scouting ahead, but thanks to his punishment he was currently in no condition to do more than stumble along in wincing misery. I responded to Lorine with a nod, blowing air into my hands and rubbing them together. She made a show of looking around before letting out a satisfied sigh. If it hadn't been for her counterfeit smile my lust-ridden mind might have entertained the notion she had orchestrated a little private time for a dalliance, a very special reward for my recent work. A perilous but still enticing fantasy that vanished as soon as it entered my mind. I found myself possessed of a keen desire to move away from her, well-honed instincts warning that we were about to have a very dangerous conversation.

She didn't speak at first, turning and cupping her hands around her mouth to call out the three owl hoots that told the others the path was clear. It wasn't until their shadowy forms began to appear that she murmured, "You know what he intends to do, I assume?"

"'Course not." I blew on my hands again, casting my eyes around so as not to meet hers.

"You're very far from being a stupid lad, Alwyn. I know you spy on us. I know you hear and see more than you're supposed to." I could feel her gaze on me, my skin growing hot despite the chill, a heat that had nothing to do with my many sweaty imaginings of what it might be like to find myself alone with this woman. As ever in life, the reality was a sharp and unpleasant contrast to the dream. "Tell me—" snow crunched as she took a step closer "—what do you think he's planning?"

"Something to do with the new duke." I risked a glance at her face, finding the smile vanished and her expression one of intent scrutiny. "He'd fetch a hefty ransom. We've done it before. We'll snatch him and the king'll have to cough up a whole cartful of gold to get him back."

"Merchants and a noble or two – that's who we've ransomed before. This is different. And what makes you so sure it's just ransom Deckin's after?"

I am determined to make myself a duke. I didn't repeat what Deckin said that night, although I was fairly sure she knew I had heard them. This entire conversation felt like being trapped in a pit with hissing snakes all around. "What else is there?" I regretted the question as soon as it was out of my mouth, for it gave her leave to draw closer.

"He talks to you," she said, voice quiet. "Says things to you he doesn't say to me. The bond between bastards is strong, eh? You tell me what he's after."

Looking into her searching gaze, I understood that her question wasn't rhetorical. She genuinely thought I knew something she didn't. "We talk, sometimes," I said. "He says a lot, but tells me little."

"He'll tell you more, when he gets maudlin and needs to vent all that sorrow, all that hate and love for the man who fathered him. Once it was me he vented at. Now it's you."

Her hand moved, quick and sharp, causing me to take a step back in expectation of a blade's sting. Instead, something flickered in the air between us, catching the dim moonlight as it spun and fell into my palm. One skill life had taught me early was to never let a falling coin touch the ground for there were always plenty of other hands ready to claim it. The silver sovereign weighed no more than a couple of sheks, but felt heavy in my hand, heavier still when she added another alongside it.

"He'll tell you things," she began, "things I'll need to hear, for all our sakes . . . "

She fell to an abrupt silence as I upended my hand, both coins making small holes in the snow as they fell.

"Always liked you, Lorine," I told her. Her face suddenly lacked all expression, but also, I fancied, had grown a shade paler. I glanced over her shoulder at the shadowy forms of the band hurrying towards the trees, Deckin's bulk looming largest among them.

"So," I added, turning away from her blank mask of a face, "I'll forget this. Best if you do too."

Leffold Glade was perhaps the best-kept secret among the varied outlaw bands that once ranged the Shavine Forest, a ready-made and conveniently situated meeting place where disparate packs of miscreants came to agree alliances or settle disputes. For reasons unknown it had never been discovered by any duke or sheriff, making it something of a pilgrimage site for folk of our persuasion; you weren't truly an outlaw until you'd seen the glade.

At this point in my life the word "amphitheatre" had yet to enter my lexicon but that's certainly what this place had once been. Descending rows of tiered steps created a bowl around a flat circle some forty paces wide. The whole thing was overgrown with roots and weeds, of course, but the granite and marble visible beneath the blanket of snow-dusted green made it clear that it was not a natural feature of the landscape. Despite the cracked and mossed-over appearance of the stonework, the grandeur of the place lingered, my youthful mind conjuring varied and surely fanciful imaginings every time we came here.

I envisioned a great mass of people crowding these tiers, all cheering or jeering at whatever spectacle unfolded in the arena below. In fact, I remain uncertain that it was in fact an arena. Pre-Scourge writings are rarer than gold and while some allude to combat as a form of entertainment others speak of a people as passionately fond of plays and poetry as they were bloody spectacle. In those days such conjecture was beyond my imagination, however, and I continued to envisage lurid battles between ancient slave warriors after which the victors would surely enjoy the amorous adulations of a female admirer or two, their lust stoked to insatiability by the sight of blood . . .

"Alwyn."

I turned in time to receive the corpse of a white-pelted hare in the face, much to Justan's amusement. "Cooking time!" he told me, still laughing and holding up a brace of recently snared beasts.

He was a slight fellow and it wouldn't have been beyond my strength to administer a beating, but, despite a fondness for pranks, was also the least malicious of any member of this band and consequently hard to dislike. He was also a precisely vicious hand with a knife, which tended to discourage any unwise notions regarding petty revenge.

"Get one of the whelps to help," I said, referring to the dozen or so youngsters in our company. With my recent success I felt such chores should be beneath me.

"Deckin's orders." He stepped back, moving his head in an authoritative jerk at the cluster of youngsters assembling a firepit near the edge of the arena. "Wants a proper tasty feast for our visitors and with my dearest Yelk gone on his travels, you're the next best cook we have."

We had been at the glade for close on three weeks now. Upon arrival, Deckin had chosen the messengers. To my surprise, Erchel had been among them. "Be sure to tell your uncle how you got that limp and all those scrapes," Deckin instructed, handing him what less-educated eyes would have taken as a bundle of frayed cord. In fact, it consisted of four different lengths of rope all tied in a particular knot beyond the ken of most hands to craft. Few outlaws can read, but any worth their salt in the Shavine Marches knew the meaning of those knots: a summons from the Outlaw King.

Erchel, as thoroughly cowed and reduced to craven obedience as I would ever see him, bobbed his head and duly limped off towards the east. Twine, Baker and Yelk were entrusted with the other knots and dispatched to the remaining points of the compass. While we waited for Deckin's summons to be answered we built shelters against the deepening chill and increasingly heavy snow, reaping what game we could from the surrounding woods. The previous evening the outlying scouts had reported back with news of other bands approaching from east and west, meaning this place would soon witness the largest gathering of outlaws for many years, all of whom would be expecting a decent measure of hospitality from their host.

Sighing, I swallowed further protest and moved towards the firepit. "We'll need more wood than that, and a lot more water."

The most impressive prizes from our hunting efforts were a pair of full-grown boars, which were duly gutted, spitted and set to roasting over the fire for the many hours it would take to render them ready for table. I marshalled my company of underlings with the efficiency of a sergeant-at-arms, setting them to the myriad tasks required when feeding a large number of people. Steam billowed in clouds from the many pots and cauldrons holding soup flavoured with wild herbs and the marrow of butchered bones. The band had a decent stock of salt to draw upon and Deckin gave me leave to use all of it. True spices were rarer, though we had plenty of garlic and thyme. A glower from

Deckin had sufficed to compel the others to give up their private hoards of pepper or sugar, Gerthe even handing over a small wrap of saffron.

"Was gonna sell this in the spring," she muttered with a sullen reluctance that made me want to hand it back, albeit in exchange for a special favour. But with Deckin looking on I confined my response to an apologetic smile and went about adding the precious scarlet fronds to a bowl of groundnut oil.

My young workforce attended to their various tasks with a mostly silent and industrious diligence, free of complaint or bickering. It was one of the contradictions of outlaw life that those called to it at a young age were often better behaved than seemed natural for children, but then fear is a great disciplinarian. That being said, they were never reduced to complete subservience and the need for occasional correction was inevitable.

"Oi!" I said, delivering a hard cuff to the back of Uffel's head when his hands, which should have been engaged in chopping up bones for the broth, strayed to the skirts of the girl next to him. Besides Lorine, Elga was the prettiest face in our band and, though thirteen, could still pass for younger which made her useful during cutpurse excursions to the larger towns. Uffel was a year her junior but the lusts of manhood had arrived early, along with a growing spatter of pus-filled pimples that covered his face from brow to neck.

"Back to work," I growled with a baleful eye, an order with which he complied after daring a scowl in my direction. Elga, ever a bright soul, gave a small giggle and blew a kiss at him which only made his blotched features scowl more. She pouted at him and turned away to offer me a curtsy of practised daintiness.

"My thanks for protecting my honour, good sir."

"I'm no more a sir than you're a lady." The knife in my hand blurred as I rendered a horseradish into shavings. Reaching for another, I found my gaze caught by the sight of Todman talking to Lorine. It was only a few words exchanged in passing but rare enough to draw my eye for they rarely spoke. For the most part Lorine seemed to regard Todman with only marginally less disdain than I, and I would have expected any interaction between them to be short and sharp. But this was different, the unheard words uttered without any obvious resentment but rather a cautious, clipped brevity.

"I bet you'd like to call her lady," Elga said. "And more besides." I looked down to regard her impish grin, then jabbed a finger at the half-ground garlic in her pestle.

"If you don't get that done you can call me 'sir' every time I stroke your hide with a hickory rod."

She pouted again but duly returned to her work while I watched Lorine and Todman walk in opposite directions, recalling the weight of the two silver sovereigns she had placed my palm. The questions this raised were obvious and troubling in the quandary they presented. *How many did she put in his palm? What did she expect in return?* And, most troubling of all: *Do I tell Deckin?*

I have heard it is common in other parts of the world for outlaw bands to name themselves, but in the Shavine Forest we tended not to bother with such formality. Groups came together and split apart with a frequency that made keeping track of them all a pointless task. Deckin's band was a singular exception in having remained a more or less cohesive body under one leader for more than a decade. Loosely affiliated gangs, often born out of familial ties, were much more the norm. These criminal fraternities conformed to a vague, constantly shifting territorial patchwork.

Although Deckin enjoyed an unchallenged ascendancy over the whole forest, his absolute authority covered the heart and south of the forest. The various factions of the Sakhel family kept mostly to the western reaches where they preyed on caravans carrying goods from the coastal ports. The less prosperous north was the province of a scattering of smaller bands under the control of the Thessil brothers, whom it's said were once both sergeants under the old duke's household banner but had fallen out of favour after pillaging one village too many without ducal leave.

It was in the east where a sense of order among thieves was least discernible. Here disparate families of old outlaw standing pursued feuds of indistinct origin and vied endlessly, and unsuccessfully, for dominion. It was from one of these tribes, the Cutters, that Erchel had been exiled when still a whelp when his tendencies became intolerable even for his own villainous kin. Deckin had taken him in as a favour, after payment of a decent fee of course. It had been hoped that Deckin's brand of discipline would straighten Erchel's twisted soul into something useful in time. As it transpired, his principal use was now as a conduit to his family.

Erchel's folk were the first to arrive, a band some thirty strong, all sharing various degrees of rattish resemblance. Their fellow easterners were not long in following them into the glade, six different gangs of differing strength who eyed each other with a feral enmity that would normally escalate to violence in short order. However, old custom dictated that no blood was ever spilled in the glade and, for all their myriad faults, these scoundrels were fiercely attached to tradition.

I watched Erchel stand by as Drenk Cutter, his uncle, exchanged greetings with Deckin, all hearty laughs and comradely backslapping. Erchel's eyes were downcast and his back stooped, no doubt fearful of attracting too much notice. I wondered if he knew that one of the many discussions about to take place in this refuge would concern his own imminent murder, but doubted it. Although possessed of an enviable cunning and nose for trouble, Erchel was not truly a schemer. His instincts were tuned towards immediate survival and I considered him incapable of thinking much beyond the next day.

The Thessil brothers came next, both brawny men in their late thirties leading a sixty-strong retinue. Deckin's welcome was of a much more formal kind than that offered to Erchel's folk, a respectful half-bow followed by an extended hand. The brothers were not twins but shared a uniformity of stature and dress, both accepting the proffered hand with the same stiff caution. They carried themselves with a soldierly bearing and neatness of grooming and attire that set them apart from most of the outlaws crowding this place. Watching the contempt they tried, mostly without success, to keep from their blocky features as they surveyed the gathering, I judged them as men who would much rather have remained under the banner.

The Sakhels were the last to arrive and, next to Deckin's band, proved to be the largest in number, over a hundred men and women resolving out of the trees at twilight. Their clan had fractured and reformed many times over the years but retained a uniformity of garb and facial decoration. I had heard they were descended from warriors exiled from the frosty wastes of the northern Fjord Geld generations ago, a legend I found increasingly credible upon viewing a plethora of tattooed faces rich in studded noses and ears. They were also the most well-armed group in attendance, every one bearing a sword or an axe, some inlaid with engraved runes that told of ancient origin.

Their leader was a tall woman with blonde hair that deepened to gold in the fading light. It snaked in a long braid from the centre of her otherwise bald scalp, the shaved pate covered in a dense tattoo of runic lettering. She and Deckin stood at much the same height and I took note of the fact that they both inclined their heads at the same time.

"You aged quickly," the woman observed with a grin. "Grey in your beard, I see."

"A little." Deckin gave her a grin of his own. "Whereas, Shilva, you seem to have gotten younger."

"Oh, piss off." She laughed and they both moved into a tight embrace. "Missed you, you old rogue!" she told him, moving back to grasp a hand to his neck, their foreheads touching. "Turns out Father was wrong. You did last more than a summer on your own."

"He was nearly right. Came close to losing my head the first week, never mind the summer. Come on." He put an arm around her shoulders and guided her towards the glade. "Got hogs roasting and ale in need of drinking."

As might be expected when the worst scum of an entire duchy are gathered together and provided with copious food and liquor, the night proved to be a raucous affair. My carefully prepared feast disappeared in a brief and gluttonous frenzy. All was gobbled down without, I must say, much in the way of appreciation or the basic courtesy of a thank you. My subtly crafted flavours were smothered in a tide of ale and brandy that soon had many a voice raised in song. The handful of musicians among us brought out flutes and mandolins to add to the half-melodious din and soon a dance of sorts began to unfold in the arena. There was plenty of jostling but no brawling, the rule of the glade and the threat of Deckin's disfavour sufficing to ensure old vendettas were set aside, at least for this one night.

Having kept back a good portion of my most carefully prepared pork stew, I took a bowl and went in search of Gerthe, hoping her strict adherence to commerce had been eased by the flow of drink. Such hopes were alas dashed when I saw her disappearing into the gloom beyond the glade with two tattooed ruffians from the Sakhel clan. From her loud giggles I discerned that she had in fact set business aside tonight, just not to my benefit.

I consoled myself by eating the stew and downing a cup of brandy, my gaze roving the various female guests in search of a likely prospect. The only one to return my gaze was a thin-faced girl nestled among the ranks of Erchel's kin. I began to formulate some stratagem for extracting her from their suspicious huddle when Deckin's voice rang out, loud and strong.

"Do you like this feast, my friends?!"

The music and song faded, replaced by an appreciative cheer from the assembled villainy.

"Are your bellies full?" Deckin asked, teeth bared in jocular humour, drawing forth another louder cheer. "Do your spirits lift with this ale I have provided? Are your hearts lightened?"

More cheers, goblets and tankards raised high, the tumult of gratitude dying to abrupt silence with Deckin's face darkened to a snarl.

"You're all a bunch of witless cunts!"

His gaze roved over the suddenly blank or baffled faces, mouth twisting in a sneer of harsh judgement. I noted that only Shilva Sakhel seemed unsurprised by this abrupt shift in mood, hiding a smile as she lowered her face to her tankard. I had heard Deckin speak of her on occasion, usually in gruff but respectful terms, and now understood their association to be far deeper and longer than previously suspected. She, like me, knew the furious diatribe we were about to receive was all theatre, a carefully prepared performance geared towards a specific outcome.

"How easy it would be to have killed you all this night," Deckin growled. "I could've slit the throat of every fucking one of you. Slipped hemlock into the liquor you've dulled your senses with and you'd never even have tasted it, you utter fools. You think you're safe here in this place?" He swept his hand around at the tiered steps of this ancient ruin. "This is just a pile of old stones. You think this forest is our protection? You're wrong. It's our prison. The old duke rolled the dice on treachery and died for it. The new duke is the king's creature and you can wager your soul the first thing Tomas will order his creature to do is deal, finally and for ever, with us."

He paused, turning to beckon Hostler from the crowd. "Many of you know this man," he said, resting a hand on Hostler's shoulder. "And you know him as a man who, though he plights his troth with those who live outside the tyranny of the law, never lies. Hostler of the truthful tongue, they call him. Tell them, Truth Tongue, tell them of the captive we took on the King's Road and what he told us before he perished."

Hostler, whom I had never once heard referred to as Truth Tongue before now, coughed and raised his eyes to the throng. Usually, when given the rare opportunity to speak to an audience of more than one, his voice was strong, a preacher's voice, declaiming scripture for as long as you could stand to hear it. Now it was decidedly thinner. Although still loud enough to reach every ear present, to those who knew him, it was the voice of a liar.

"The soldier we took was grievously wounded and soon to depart the world," he said. "Desperate for a Supplicant to hear his testament, he unburdened his soul to me for he could tell I am a true devotee of the Covenant of Martyrs." He stopped, just for a second, but I saw how his throat worked to swallow away a sudden dryness. "This man was captain of a company from Cordwain and knew a good deal of the king's instructions to the new duke. He spoke of a thousand kingsmen and a hundred knights to be spared from the war with the Pretender. 'They will join with the ducal levies to sweep that cursed forest from end to end,' he said. 'Every cur caught will not be spared the noose. If need be, they'll burn the forest down to the bare earth to find the last one. Come the spring there will be no more outlaws alive to curse the Shavine Marches. The king has commanded it and so shall it be.'" He swallowed again but his features remained the hard, purposeful mask of a truthful man. "That is what I heard from the lips of a dying man with no reason to lie."

"And this is not all!" Deckin added, and I felt a sudden plummeting in the gut as his hand swung towards me, fingers beckoning. "Some of you know this young rogue, I'm sure." Laughter greeted me as I rose and moved to his side, forcing a sheepish grin. "The Fox of the Shavine Forest, they call him. He has the keenest eyes and ears in all the duchy and, though he's a renowned liar—" his hand landed on my shoulder, resting lightly but possessing much the same weight as Lorine's sovereigns "—he never lies to me, not if he values keeping those keen eyes of his." More laughter, the hand on my shoulder tightening a fraction. "Tell them, Alwyn."

I didn't cough. I didn't swallow. Instead I put a frown of grim reluctance on my face and raised clear, honest eyes to rapt faces staring in hushed anticipation. "It's true, all of it," I said. "Recently I was sent to spy in Ambriside. The soldiers there were full of tales about the rewards they've been promised, a silver sovereign for every outlaw's head they bring in. Some were saying how they were going to make sport with any women they caught before hacking their heads off, the young 'uns too. They laughed about it."

A slight tightening of Deckin's fingers told me I'd said enough, perhaps even gilded the lie too much. However, the burgeoning growl of anger from all around indicated it had struck the required note.

"So, you see, my friends." Deckin's hand slipped from my shoulder as he stepped away, arms raised in a manner that was both commanding and beseeching. "You see that I did not call you here to plan some grand theft merely to fatten our purses. I called you here so that we may plan for our very survival."

He let the murmur of angry agreement swirl around for a bit before speaking on, voice harsher now, more demanding. "These woods are ours. By right of any natural law or justice, this forest belongs to us, for we won it, with blood. Now an upstart duke of no family, a mere licker of the king's arse who's never once raised a blade in defence of home or family, wants to take it from us. I mean to stop him. I mean to put an end to the days of skulking and freezing as we run from lesser souls. I mean to defy this king, this Tomas the Good, who all know rightly as Tomas the Pincher, this liar, this thief of all who has mired this land in blood and poverty and still demands loyalty from those he has beggared. He calls for heads, let's give him some. Let's give him a hundred. A thousand if need be. As many as it takes to make him see that this forest is not his and never will be. And we'll start with that arse-licker he's set against us. Who's with me?"

The growl became a shout that soon built to a roar, all the thieves, cut-throats, rustlers, cardsharps and whores on their feet and calling out their willing submission to Deckin Scarl's newborn feud. However, I saw their leaders cheer along with markedly less enthusiasm.

The Thessil brothers clapped their hands and exchanged eager grins with their followers but I could tell it was mummery. Erchel's uncle Drenk was the most effusive, spilling ale as he snarled his agreement along with his wildly celebrating kin, but even his beady, drunken eyes held a glimmer of worry. For reasons I couldn't fathom, I found Shilva Sakhel's reaction the most troubling, for she just laughed while her folk whooped and screamed in hungry anticipation. Hers was not the laughter of celebration, more the surprised, hearty peals of one who has heard a new and especially amusing joke.

Deckin's arm circled my shoulders as the cheering wore on, drawing me into a hug. "Nicely done, lad," he said quietly, still grinning to the crowd. "You always lie best when you're put on the spot. Don't think it needed mention of the young 'uns though."

"Sorry, Deckin."

"Oh," he patted my chest, "no harm done. This lot would eat all the shit I shovel and ask for seconds." I glanced up to see his gaze darken a fraction as it settled on Shilva, still giving full vent to her mirth. "On the morrow," he sighed, "comes the hard part."

Chapter Seven

"This is not an army." Danick Thessil was the elder of the two brothers and did most of their talking. As I'd suspected, their apparent enthusiasm for Deckin's scheme had evaporated come the morn and his sibling, Rubin, maintained a stern and mostly silent visage for much of the unfolding conversation. "And these are not soldiers." Danick gestured towards the glade where smoke rose in thickening clouds as the collection of rogues woke to suffer the effects of the previous night.

Deckin had called these outlaw captains together at a small clearing some distance from the glade. My inclusion in this august assembly had been a surprise. Less so was Deckin's instruction to stay on the fringe and say nothing unless given leave by him alone. Danick Thessil was the first to offer his shek's worth of wisdom concerning the proposed enterprise and the expressions worn by others present told of a similar attachment to realism. Drenk Cutter was clearly suffering the effects of too much ale, but a bright glimmer of shrewdness remained in his reddened eyes. Like his nephew, he possessed a sharp instinct for survival, regardless of what passions Deckin might have stirred in his kin. Shilva Sahken wore a half-grin throughout it all which sometimes quirked into a suppressed laugh. Evidently, the amusement born of Deckin's speech hadn't faded.

"It's not yet an army, no," Deckin conceded. I had often admired his capacity for switching moods as the need arose. The rageful inspiration of the previous night had now been replaced by intent, calm persuasion. "But it will be. All revolts begin with a spark that births a flame. We prey on the nobles and the merchants, not the churls. They know who their true enemies are. How many died last winter because their stores had been raided to fill the king's taxes? How many face this winter with empty bellies and sickened children?"

"We prey on nobles and merchants because they have money," Shilva said, her smile still in place. "Churls don't. Neither do they have weapons, armour or horses. Not that we have much of that either."

"A scythe or a wood-axe can kill just as well as a sword," Deckin returned. "And armour is only useful when worn. I do not intend to strike when our enemy is girded for battle."

"So, we kill this new duke, the churls rise in support and the duchy's ours, is that it?" Shilva looked as if she were about to start laughing again.

"What alternative do we have?" Deckin nodded to where I loitered, leaning against a tree with what I hoped to be nonchalant confidence. In fact, my head ached from the unwise mixing of ale and brandy and my guts were riven by a persistent, queasy roil that had as much to do with fear as excess. "You heard what the lad said. They will be coming for us, Shilva. Have no doubt of it."

The blonde woman's gaze slid towards me, her humour subsiding into narrow scrutiny. I tried to return her stare in full measure, keeping my features blank, but there was a surety to this woman that couldn't help but provoke a blink or two.

"Would you gull me into a war, old friend?" she asked Deckin, keeping her eyes on me. My stomach chose this inopportune moment to voice a liquid growl while I felt a treacherous trickle of sweat begin to trace its way from my scalp to my forehead.

"You know me better," Deckin said. "And I know you'd only ever fight one if there was profit to be had. And there will be. As he tours the duchy, Elbyn carries with him a chest full of gold crown sovereigns to be doled out to his fellow nobles as the king ordains. When we take him it's yours to split." He spread his hands to ensure the brothers and Drenk knew they were included in his largesse. "I'll not take a single coin of it. When it's done you can join me in securing our future in this duchy or return to your dens with no insult suffered on my part." He paused to let the bait dangle a little. One-third of a chest crammed with gold crown sovereigns was worth a good deal of risk to any outlaw, for it presented the chance to fulfil the fabled and rarely achieved ambition of us all: comfortable retirement.

"Did your lad see this chest, also?" Shilva enquired, eyes flicking between me and Deckin. For a panicked moment I assumed I would be required to voice another lie, one certain to be detected by this woman's overly keen insight. Fortunately, Deckin had another tale to tell.

"You imagine I have but one spy?" He arched an eyebrow at Shilva. "I have worked towards this moment for years. There are many in this duchy who owe me far more fealty than they owe a distant king they've never seen or a cowardly fop risen to dukedom through mere chance of blood." His gaze tracked across each of them as he spoke with hard, inarguable authority. "You have my word the gold will be there, and you all know my word is never given lightly and never broken."

This, at least, was true. As to the rest of it, who can say? My many researches and endless pondering on successive events have unearthed neither confirmation nor denial of the fabled sovereigns supposedly carted about by the newly minted duke. All I can attest to with any certainty is that in this moment, all present, even the clearly dubious Shilva Sahken, believed Deckin Scarl's unbreakable word.

"Where?" the blonde woman asked after a short, thoughtful interval. "When?"

"Castle Duhbos," Deckin told her. "Seat of Lord Duhbos, the most famed and respected knight in the Shavine Marches, who also happens to be married to our new duke's sister. Elbyn will want to secure his support early if he's to govern this duchy. I doubt Duhbos was pleased with the manner of Duke Rouphon's demise; they rode together in the Duchy Wars.

"The duke's retinue has most likely already reached it, but he'll be obliged to linger until the High Moon feast. Leaving sooner would insult his brother-in-law, who will also be expecting a bundle of expensive gifts."

"A killing during the High Moon is an ill-starred thing," Drenk Cutter said in his high, raspy voice. "Said to raise up the Malecite to perform foul deeds upon the earth." He stared at Deckin for a second before letting out a harsh, barking laugh. "Not that I give a weasel's cock. For that many sovereigns I'd let the Malecite fuck my grand-mother. My folk are with you in this, Deckin. Count on it, but—" his thin face took on a serious aspect "—I'll need you to forget that favour you asked of me."

Deckin shrugged and waved a dismissive hand. "Done. But I won't have your nephew in my band a day longer. You want the little shit alive, you take him and best of luck to you."

The Thessil brothers exchanged a long glance. Although a few notches higher on the thinking scale than was usual for outlaws, they were still as driven by greed and the desire for a comfortable old age. Also, they probably worried over the reaction of their gangmates should they fail to heed Deckin's call to arms.

"One-third of the gold," Danick said, "and we want first pick of the castle armoury."

"Take it," Deckin told them before turning to Shilva with an expectant eye. "Your father always dreamed of building his own merchant house in Farinsahl," he prompted. "With your share you could buy your own fleet."

"My father had a head full of dreams," she returned. Her humour had disappeared now and if she still considered this whole notion a joke, it was a poor one. "Dreams are what killed him in the end, for dreams have a tendency to overcome sense." She sat back, letting out a deep sigh of resignation. "But many of my lot are straining at their leash over your fine words and will surely follow you on their own account, with or without my blessing. I'll be with you in this, Deckin, but know that I'll be heading home the moment I have my share."

"Why, my lady—" Deckin lowered his head in a courteous bow "—I would expect nothing else."

"Castle Duhbos is a stout fortress," Danick pointed out. "And its owner a renowned soldier. Besieging it is out of the question."

"Nor will we do so," Deckin assured him. "I know Castle Duhbos. As a boy I worked the stables there and learned well its secrets. There's a way in, hidden and difficult, but with the revels of the High Moon feast to mask our entry, we'll be in and about our business before they hear the first alarm."

"We'll need a list," Shilva said. "Who to kill, who to spare."

"No list." Deckin's features took on a grim certainty, his voice soft but implacable. "No sparing. They all fall, every noble, soldier and servant within the walls, else this enterprise will be doomed before it's begun."

"Lord Duhbos is well liked in the duchy," Danick said. "By both commons and nobles. And his bride is not yet eighteen summers old."

"With a womb that may already be quickened with the old man's seed." Deckin's voice grew softer still, but no less commanding. "The Ambris bloodline has to end. They all have to fall. No sparing."

"Something to tell me, young Alwyn?"

For a large man, Deckin had a disconcerting facility for appearing at one's back without warning. I'm sure it was something he took great delight in, almost as much as he did in voicing unexpected and unwelcome questions.

One glance at his placid but insistent expression told me obfuscation or bluster would be pointless, also dangerous. We had begun the march to the Lake Marsh the day after his palaver with the other leaders, the four groups heading for the rally point in Moss Mill village, moving separately for fear of attracting too much notice. Even so, such a large if disconnected migration of villainy was sure to attract attention and scouts had orders to ensure the silence of any forest wardens or other duchy servants they might encounter. Leave was also given to deal with any churls who seemed either overly inquisitive or likely to run off to the nearest sheriff with a valuable tale to tell. In effect, this meant Deckin had granted permission for almost all the outlaws in the Shavine Forest to murder and rob their way north. For a fabled champion of the churls, he seemed remarkably unperturbed by what he had unleashed upon them, for his ability to read my moods remained as sharp as ever.

"You've guts aplenty when the fists and the blades start flying," he added, moving to stride alongside me, "but in between times that brain of yours starts to working up all manner of fears, especially when you've got reason to worry. Out with it, then."

In point of fact, there were two nagging worries bothering my brain and I opted to voice what I reasoned to be the least dangerous. "The duke's chest full of sovereigns," I said, voice stripped of inflection save faint curiosity.

"What of it?"

"It strikes me that, if we're to be soldiers rather than outlaws, seizing this duchy is likely to be an expensive business. If we give all those sovereigns away to the other bands, what's left for us? Outlaws can always go off and do some more stealing if they have to, but soldiers need paying if they're to stay on the march."

Deckin's eye twinkled as he gave me a sidelong glance, his beard bunching in the manner that told of amused satisfaction. "Only a day since my grand address and already you're no longer thinking like a thief." He laughed, delivering a good-natured shove to my shoulder. "And it's a point worth pondering, to be sure. One of the reasons I held off on commencing this scheme for so long was the question of how to pay for it. Because you're right, young Alwyn, soldiers need to be paid. Suffice to say, the matter is well in hand." He paused, his humour fading as he added in a mutter, "Or it will be shortly, now I know where the Hound laid his head."

"Hound?" I asked, the unfamiliarity of the name overcoming my usual caution. It was never a good idea to ask questions of Deckin, not without leave to do so.

"Best if you don't bother your busy head about that," he told me, the twinkle in his eye hardening into a warning gleam.

I was quick to lower my head to a suitably contrite angle. "Sorry, Deckin."

He let out a soft grunt, but I felt his gaze lingering. "What else,

Alwyn? I've a sense it's more than just a decent share of loot that's got you fretting."

I should have known he would ferret out both sources of worry, the second being by far the most perilous to voice. However, once he'd fixed that steely, demanding gaze on you, silence was not an option. Taking a deep breath, I glanced around to ensure there were no others within earshot. "Lorine—" I began, only for him to cut me off with a loud laugh.

"Been at you too, has she?" he enquired when his mirth subsided. "Wanting to know the details of our little chats, I assume? What did she offer? A silver sovereign?"

"Two," I said, which provoked another laugh.

"She only offered Todman one, as if I'd tell him anything worth a rat's turd."

"He told you?"

"'Course he did. Not a man to fret over winning favour, Todman. Unlike you, eh?"

A sudden lurch to my heart had me gabbling out a contrite explanation, which he silenced with a shake of his head. "Calm y'self, lad. Not the first time Lorine's gone squirrelling where she shouldn't. Won't be the last either. Scheming is what she does best, next to vexing me with her fretful botheration." His brow creased into a sombre frown. "When this is done, I'll confess I'm not sure what's to be done with her. Making her a duchess could cause all manner of complications down the road."

"Duchess?" The word escaped my lips before I could staunch it, driven by a mingling of surprise and realisation. I had heard him avow his ambitions but to hear it spoken so plainly was still jarring. *So, he really means to do it*, I thought, suffering a spasm of worry that he might take offence, but he just laughed again.

"What did you think I was about with this grand design, Alwyn? Can't have a duchy without a duke now, can you?"

This time I managed not to voice the torrent of baffled questions bubbling up inside, confining my response to a slack-mouthed gape worthy of the lamed beggar I often pretended to be.

"You want to know how a mere bastard could dare to sit the duke's chair?" Deckin enquired. "You're thinking that surely the king would never tolerate such an outrage. Let me share with you some lessons I learned from my father. You probably think I hated him, and you'd be right. Why would I not hate a man who refused to legitimise my birth? A man who condemned his son, his eldest son I might add, to a life of hunger and villainy. But hate is not born of indifference, but experience. I hated him because I knew him.

"My mother may not have been his favourite among the several women he kept in various houses and castles, all given the title of housekeeper and paid a reasonable stipend, for he was ever a generous whore-chaser. She had herself a sharp tongue, my mother, one her famed comeliness didn't always make up for, but it was sharp enough to nag him into making a place for me when I tottered from infant-hood to scampering, annoying childhood.

"At first, I turned spits in kitchens, sweating in the fire's glare for hours on end and wondering if I'd roast along with the meat. Later I shovelled dung from stables, dug weeds from gardens and did all other sundry chores his stewards beat me to. They all knew my blood, of course – it was no particular secret, but also nothing ever to be spoken of, least of all by me. I was spared neither rod nor fist, given the slops to eat and required to bed down among the hounds. My father liked his hounds. Great were his kindnesses to them and he knew all their names. They would flock around him, yelping and fawning as he doled out treats and kind words, words he never once spoke to me. Years under his roof, dragged along as part of his retinue from one castle to another, and not one word spoken to me throughout it all. But that's not why I hated him, though I'd contend it's reason enough.

"My mother died when I was a month past my thirteenth birthday. Some sickness born of a swelling in her womb, they told me, or rather they told him as I stood by shuffling and trying not to weep. I think it was the sound of my sniffling that drew his eye, the only time I remember receiving his full regard. He looked me up and down, just for a moment. 'He's sturdy enough now,' he told the steward. 'Take him to the sergeant.'"

Deckin fell to silence, a distance creeping into his gaze as we walked along. From the reluctant recollection I saw in his face I understood this to be a rarely, perhaps never spoken tale.

When he continued it was with the clipped, studied lightness of a lifelong cynic. "Six years under the banner. I had the fortune to become a soldier just as the Duchy Wars sprang back into life. If any fucker ever tells you battle is a glorious thing, you have my leave to cut his lying tongue out. Still, it taught me a whole host of valuable skills. The best way to slit a man's throat when he lies wounded; you have to clamp a hand on their mouth and hunch over them so others think you're easing their final moments with kind words. I learned how soldiers will often keep their most valuable trinkets in their boots. Remember that if you ever get chance to scour a battlefield for loot. Most of all, it taught me nobles care nothing for the lives of those they set themselves over. All they truly care about are the twinned lusts of wealth and power. Y'see, I began to learn more about my family by marching around outside my father's castle than I ever did within its walls. Turns out that not more than twelve decades ago my father's kin were barely a notch above common churls themselves.

"The Rouphon claim on this duchy rose when the previous duke got on the wrong side of some king or other regarding disputed water rights or somesuch. It doesn't matter. What does matter is that it all resulted in a bloody massacre after which the impoverished Ambris family found themselves with a tenuous claim to dukeship, one the king decided to endorse because poor folk are always easier to win over than rich folk. A full belly after a life of hunger buys a great deal of loyalty. What's more, the first duke of the Ambris line, Sir Miltram, was himself a bastard, just like you and me. It's all there in the histories if you care to go looking. What's also there, but not so easily found, is that Sir Miltram, having gained the duke's seat, spent the next year hunting down and murdering any unfortunate with the slightest drop of the old duke's blood. A willingness to do the necessary thing, regardless of scruple, has long been one of my family's traits.

"The first duke, for all his mean ways and meaner origins, understood something very important as regards power: it can be inherited through right of blood, but can only be truly won and held by spilling it. The Pretender is a man without a drop of royal blood, despite his claims, with a whole army at his back and a decent chance of seizing the throne from the Algathinets. Bastards have risen high in this kingdom before, and will do so again."

"They all have to fall," I said, voice as faint and bland as I dared. "No sparing."

"Yes." His lips formed a grim smile, coming to a halt and obliging me to do the same. "Here," he said, fishing inside his bearskin cloak. "Reward for your performance back at the glade. Didn't want you squandering it just yet, is all."

He took my wrist and extended his spade-sized hand, dropping a silver sovereign into my palm. "I told Gerthe to forgo other customers when we get to Moss Mill," Deckin said, putting an arm around my shoulders as we resumed our trudge through the snow. "There'll be a room set aside for you at the inn. When you speak of me in years to come, young Alwyn, regardless of what others might say, be sure to speak well."

We walked together for much of the remaining day as he spoke of the battles he had seen as a soldier, the sergeant he'd murdered when he deserted the banner and all his many adventures since. I like to think I learned more from Deckin Scarl that day than I did throughout the preceding years of our association. However, the principal lesson he would teach me in very short order would be this: all ambition is folly when it fails to be matched by reason.

CHAPTER EIGHT

Moss Mill was the only settlement of any appreciable size to sprout within the confines of the northern sprawl of the Shavine Forest. There were other hamlets and clusters of mean cottages scattered about the fringes of the great green expanse, but only Moss Mill could be said to be a true village.

Its legal standing remained a permanently unsettled question, for all villages within the duchy were supposed to receive a charter from the duke, mainly to facilitate the collection of taxes. However, since settlement within the forest was expressly forbidden, the village technically didn't exist as far as the ducal accounts were concerned. Despite this, the Mill's occupants would hand over a substantial portion of their yearly income to the forest wardens, who could be counted among the most valuable customers for its inns and whorehouses. The wardens would duly ensure the duke got his share and so Moss Mill was permitted to continue its secluded existence as a useful way station for outlaw and forester alike. Although it didn't enjoy the same traditional immunity from discord as Leffold Glade, it was still generally accepted as neutral ground between the duke's sheriffs and the villainous fraternity, provided both contrived to avoid appearing at the same time and in overly large numbers.

Many of Shilva Sahken's folk had already turned up by the time we arrived, along with a dozen or so of the Thessils' cut-throats. They pitched camp around the village's borders or along the riverbank close to the mill that gave the place its name, the huge wheel stilled by the ice covering the stream that curved around the settlement from north to south.

"Where'd all these fuckers come from, Deckin?" Izzie the Clutch demanded from the stoop of her inn. "A whole horde of western savages yesterday, and now you lot turn up."

Izzie was a woman of meaty proportions, standing almost as tall as Deckin and matching his stature ounce for ounce. The item from which she derived her name hung around her neck on a thick leather strap, a heavy satchel said to be filled with coin that was never far from the touch of her hand. The largest inn, the trading post and the mill were all owned by her or her many children. They were a close-knit clan and not people to cross lightly for those who caused trouble in the Mill had a tendency towards quiet vanishment. Normally, I would have expected Deckin to utter some jovial and placatory words but today he met Izzie's glower with one of his own.

"Got business brewing to the north," he said, voice hard. "And it's not for discussion, Iz." He took a heavy purse from his belt and tossed it to her. "For the inconvenience. We'll be on our way in two days. Till then we'll be as quiet as you like. All goods and ale will be paid for, but I'll need your folk to stay home and not go wandering."

Izzie's broad, crease-rich features tensed in resentful frustration and she took her time in examining the purse's contents. She was certainly a power in the forest but also wise enough to recognise a greater one, especially when he came bearing coin.

"Want no part of it." She sniffed, drawing the purse strings tight and consigning it to her satchel. "Whatever it is. Sheriffs come looking, I can't stand surety none of my folk'll talk."

"They won't," Deckin assured her. "In fact, I reckon it'll be a good long while before you see a sheriff again."

Izzie sniffed again, eyes narrowing in a sign of piqued curiosity, but she was a woman for whom caution always won out over greed and asked no more. "S'pose you'll be wanting the big room," she said.

"I will." Deckin's hand thumped me on the back, drawing a snicker from the others present. "But not for me."

"Y'know, Alwyn," Gerthe sighed, the mattress bouncing as she shifted, removing her head from my lap to rest it on my shoulder, "I must say I was expecting a mite more enthusiasm."

I wiped a finger across my brow to clear the sweat-matted hair from my eyes, voicing a somewhat breathless reply. "Three goes seems fairly enthusiastic to me."

"It's not bad, I'll grant you." Gerthe's teeth nibbled at my ear, teasingly delightful but not enough to rouse me to further ardour. "A young fellow like y'self, though." She tutted. "Once got hired to tutor a young lordling in Farinsahl. He managed it five times that first night. I could hardly walk the next day." She gave a half-nostalgic, half-enticing giggle as her fingers danced across my damp belly, sliding a leg over my thighs. "Got standards, y'see, and a whole sovereign buys a great deal. Don't want you running off to Deckin with tales of disappointment, do I?"

"I'm not disappointed." I pressed a conciliatory and very grateful kiss to her forehead. "Just . . . tired."

She sighed again, abandoning her teasing to settle against me in companionable entanglement. I felt her eyes on me in the dark, eyes that saw almost as much as mine did when the mood took her. "It's not that," she murmured. "You're thinking again. Poor Alwyn." She poked a finger to my temple. "Always far too much going on up here. What is it, then? Something you forgot to tell Deckin? Or scheming as to how you're finally going to settle with Todman?" She giggled again as I tensed. "It's all right. I don't like him much either. So—" she bounced the mattress again in insistence "—which is it?"

"You know what Deckin's planning?"

"I was a little distracted when he gave his big speech but I gathered the gist from the others. He's going to take the duchy."

"And how is he going to take it? Did you gather that?"

"The same way we take everything else, I suppose."

"He's going to have us kill everyone in that castle. Every noble, every servant. Even . . . " I trailed off, visions of Lord Duhbos' pregnant young bride looming large, as they had with irksome clarity during our recent exertions. I had never set eyes on this woman, nor could I know if the old goat had actually managed to get her with child, but this didn't prevent my ever-busy mind conjuring images of a swollen-bellied, porcelain-faced beauty lying dead amid a mound of slain kin. *They all have to fall.*

"You've killed before," Gerthe said. "So have I, for that matter. It's the fate of those of us who choose not to die in the gutter we were born to. Don't weep for nobles, Alwyn. They'll never weep for you."

She snuggled closer, resuming her enticements with impatient insistence until she reached down and gave a soft groan of satisfaction. "That's better. Now then."

She had begun to straddle me when I heard a sudden, harsh shout from beyond the shuttered window. The burgeoning gathering of outlaws had produced a growing murmur of conversation throughout the night, interspersed by the occasional song or burst of raucous laughter. But this was different, a shout born of pained surprise rather than banter. Gerthe ignored it, lowering herself with a groan, then stopping at my lack of response. "For fuck's sake, Alwyn—"

"Quiet!" I said, straining to hear as another shout came from outside. At first, I assumed it to be some of Shilva's people engaged in a brawl, as villains are like to do when the nights grow long or boring. But there was an additional harshness to this cry, a piercing quality that told of real, perhaps mortal injury. More troubling still was the faint but discernible ring of steel meeting steel. I felt Gerthe stiffen at the next sound, a hard, dry snap we both recognised. *Crossbow.*

"Shit!" She was off me in a trice, gathering her clothes as I hurried to do the same. I pulled on my trews and shirt before dragging on my boots, scraping nails across my flesh in my haste as the tumult outside grew into the unmistakable, chaotic chorus of many folk engaged in combat.

"Wait!" I hissed as Gerthe, far more practised than I at dressing quickly, made for the door. I finished lacing my boots and pulled on my jerkin before donning the belt that held my knives, drawing the longest of the two. I saw Gerthe had armed herself with the small but wickedly sharp crescent blade she kept in case of trouble.

"Discord or the sheriff, d'you think?" she asked, wincing at the ongoing cacophony, which was counterpointed by a plethora of hard snaps.

"Too many crossbows for discord," I said, reaching for her hand and leading her out onto the landing. "Forget about fighting, run for the trees. If we get separated, make for the Glade."

We descended the stairs at a run, drawing up short at the sight of the bodies lying across the inn's doorway. They lay atop one another, a woman who appeared to be one of Shilva's people from her tattooed arms, lying under the twitching form of a man. He had been hacked across the face and it took me a moment to recognise Baker under the gore. His sundered lips moved as he tried to speak, but his eyes held the emptiness unique to fast-approaching death.

Fresh shouts and the thunder of hooves drew my gaze from the dying archer to the gloom beyond the doorway. The fleet forms of several running men flitted across the dark rectangle followed swiftly by the larger bulk of a horse at full gallop. It was only a brief glimpse but I saw the gleam of firelight on armour that told of a knight rather than a sheriff's man who typically wore hardened leather. The implications were obvious. It was possible that a passing sheriff's patrol could have blundered into Deckin's makeshift army, but no knight would ever come to Moss Mill except on very specific business.

"The back way," I said, turning and dragging Gerthe through the empty but disordered inn, shoving aside upset tables and skidding on spilled ale. The back entrance was thankfully free of more corpses, but not so the street beyond. Several bodies littered the ground, blood dark on the frosted ruts of the dirt road. Only half were outlaws, the rest villagers cut down without distinction. My eyes tracked over each until they fixed on a bulky corpse I recognised. Even in death, Izzie had contrived to keep hold of her satchel, the contents spilled out to lie in untidy piles among her pooling blood. More troubling were the two smaller bodies lying nearby. Gerthe letting out a sob as we drew nearer.

Death tends to rob faces of beauty, but Elga's pale, oval features remained pretty as they stared sightlessly up at the sky. Uffel's body lay on top of her. From the ragged tears to his clothing and unnatural twist to their limbs, I concluded he had thrown himself across her in a vain effort to protect her from the trampling hooves of a charging horse.

Tearing my gaze away, I darted a glance to either side before tugging on Gerthe's hand, moving across the road at a sprint. We rounded a cottage and, hearing the snort and jingle of galloping horses, clambered over a wall into a sty. Crouching, we listened to the horses speeding by and the ongoing discordance of combat and murder. Soon the protesting squeals of the pigs forced us to move on. A few more moments of frantic dodging from one hiding place to another brought us to a narrow gap between a shed and a cottage. Only twenty yards away lay the welcoming haven of the forest.

The treeline was lit by a flickering glow from the village that told of many dwellings set ablaze. The chorus of screams at our back also indicated a battle rapidly turning into a massacre, one I had no desire to witness.

"Come on," I whispered, taking a firmer hold of Gerthe's hand and starting for the trees. I only covered a few steps before her grip abruptly slackened and she let out a sharp gasp. Normally, well-honed instinct would have compelled me to let go and keep running, but it's a hard thing to abandon a woman you've just spent several hours fucking.

Stumbling to a halt, I turned, feeling a blossoming of relief at finding Gerthe still upright. However, the lifeless slump of her shoulders and lolling head told a different tale. It took me a second to notice the feathers of a fletching protruding from the centre of her chest. The crossbow bolt had pinned her to the wooden wall of the shed behind. Why I hadn't heard the bowstring's snap would forever remain a mystery, but the years since have taught me that the senses miss a great deal in the midst of carnage.

The rattle of a windlass drew my sight from the limp rag doll of Gerthe's corpse to a man a dozen yards away. He was clad in old, poorly kept mail, the red-brown rust of which contrasted with his freshly polished breastplate. His face, beardless and sweaty despite the chill, was a pale thing beneath his ill-fitting helm. Our eyes met as he continued to turn the windlass of his crossbow and I saw how bright and fearful they were, eyes that told of a youth scarcely older than I. A youth who, despite his fear, had already killed at least once this night. He had also, I saw upon shifting my gaze, succeeded in drawing the string of his crossbow halfway to the lock.

Gerthe's hand slipped from mine and I began my charge, raising a cloud of snow in my wake, feral rage emerging from my throat in a guttural snarl. A more experienced fellow would have dropped the crossbow and drawn a dagger. But this soldier, I saw as I closed on him, was just a scared boy with even fewer years than I'd initially thought. To his credit he did manage to get the bowstring into the lock before I reached him, but the bolt he drew from the quiver went spinning away as I ducked low then surged up, driving my knife into the flesh below his chin. I leapt, wrapping my arm around him to bear him down, keeping the knife in place then pushing it deeper as we fell, the impact providing the final ounce of pressure to drive the blade into his brain.

He jerked beneath me, coughing a spatter of blood into my face before lying still. Heaving myself off him, I quickly cast around for any more soldiers and, finding none, took hold of the dead boy's legs and dragged him to the shed. I wasn't familiar with the various straps and fastenings required to remove and then don a breastplate so it took several feverish minutes of fumbling before I encased my chest in the heavy contraption. The helm was easier and, I fancied, fit me rather better than its owner. Not knowing how much time I had, I left the dead boy's other accoutrements, apart from a purse holding a paltry eight sheks and his quiver and crossbow which I scooped up from the snow upon emerging from my refuge.

Don't run, I told myself, adopting what I hoped to be a soldierly bearing as I sauntered through the snow, describing a deliberately wayward course towards the dark wall of the forest. There were others about now, halberdiers clad in red and gold livery I had last seen at the old duke's execution: kingsmen. They prowled the fringes of the village, pausing now and again to spear any prone unfortunate they noticed twitching.

This end of Moss Mill featured a slight rise as it neared the woods, offering a vantage point for the centre of the village. Much of it was shrouded in smoke from the blazing houses. Apart from a few outlying buildings, every dwelling in the place was now aflame, making for a garish spectacle of shifting shadows playing over scenes of varying horror.

I saw one of Shilva's tribe stumbling about, flailing with an axe at a surrounding circle of armoured tormentors. A great, shaggy-haired fellow of impressive stature, he shouted challenges in the Fjord Geld dialect with every ineffectual swing of his axe, shouts that turned to screams when one of the soldiers darted forward to drive the point of his halberd into his leg. Laughter joined with screams as the others closed in, halberds and billhooks rising and falling.

"Don't stand and gawp, idiot boy!"

My gaze snapped to the sight of a stocky halberdier running through the snow close by. I experienced a spasm of grateful relief for the dead crossbowman's final cough, for the blood must have obscured my features enough for his comrade to mistake me in the dark.

"Drop that fucker!" he shouted, pointing towards something near the trees.

Following the line of his arm I made out a running shape against the swaying shadows of the woods, a long-legged figure moving at an impressively fast pace. There were few among the band who possessed such height and I had seen him run often enough to recognise Hostler's fleeing form.

I will not claim any hesitancy as regards my next action. I will not, dear reader, insult your insight by pretending anguish or reluctance, for I sense you know the manner of my soul at this turn of our story. However, I should like it known that I felt no pleasure in taking a bolt from my quiver and setting it to the stock. Nor did I relish raising and sighting the weapon, the gleaming line of the bolt's barbed head tracking across the snow until it met Hostler's fleeing shadow. For all his faults, his tiresome beliefs and endless sermons, he had been one of us and it pained me to loose that bolt. Not, of course, as much as it pained him.

I was not particularly skilled or experienced with a crossbow, but Erchel and I had played around with a stolen one often enough to know the basics. Also, I find the proximity of certain death will always sharpen one's skills if one can master one's fear enough to quell shaking hands.

The bolt described a shallow arc through the air, catching Hostler in the shoulder and spinning him to the ground, much to my new comrade's satisfaction. "A good eye, for once. Come on." His hand thumped my shoulder as he sped past. "I'll let you have halves on whatever loot he's got."

I followed his track through the snow at a slower pace, head turning continually to check on the proximity of the other soldiers. Fortunately, the closest were more than a hundred paces off by the time I reached Hostler.

"Still some fight in you, eh?" the halberdier noted cheerfully, dodging a kick from one of Hostler's long legs. He stared up at us, face riven with fury and pain, the reddened bolt-head protruding from his shoulder and one arm dangling limp and useless. He clutched a knife in the other and tried repeatedly to rise, lunging at the soldier before his pain caused him to collapse.

"Martyrs, I implore you," I heard him gasp, "grant me the strength to smite the faithless."

"A devout outlaw!" the soldier exclaimed in surprised delight. "Sorry, friend." He sidestepped another lunge and slammed the butt of his halberd into the side of Hostler's head. "The Martyrs aren't here this night. It's just us come to deal out rightful justice."

The humour abruptly slipped from his face and he delivered another blow, this time to Hostler's hunched back, hard enough to crack a rib from the sound of it. "And you can't claim it's not deserved now, can you?" His features bunched into a grin of malicious enjoyment and he brought the halberd's haft down again, birthing another dull crack of breaking bone.

"Here," he said, handing his halberd to me and drawing the falchion from the scabbard on his belt. "Save us the trouble of dragging his carcass back." He planted a booted foot on Hostler's back, forcing him flat, then hefted the falchion in a two-handed grip. "Any last prayers, friend, now's the time."

He turned to me with a conspiratorial wink, clearly intending to hack Hostler's head from his shoulders the instant he began to speak. However, the soldier's features took on a puzzled blankness when a fresh burst of flame from the village cast enough light to reveal my face in full.

"Did they capture Deckin Scarl yet?" I asked. The soldier blinked and I saw comprehension flood in. He managed to half turn towards me, but not swift enough to avoid my thrust as I drove the halberd's spiked blade into his face. I took pride in that thrust, one heave sufficing to send the steel point through bone and cartilage, deep enough to sever the spine. The soldier sagged on the end of the weapon, his weight dragging it from my grip while my eyes darted about to ensure none of his comrades had witnessed his demise.

"Ingrate," said a thin, pain-wracked voice.

Hostler lay slumped on his back, crimson-hued breath pluming from his mouth, the snow beneath turning dark with the blood leaking from his wound. Despite his pains he regarded me with a disconcertingly steady gaze. Matching his stare, I thought of offering an explanation, even an apology, but knew they would be insults gabbled to a dying man. Instead I bent to retrieve the soldier's falchion before crouching at Hostler's side.

"Did they take him?" I asked. "Deckin."

He groaned out a sigh and nodded, his words emerging in halting, pain-filled grunts. "Took down the pickets . . . first, silently . . . Didn't know what . . . was happening until the crossbows started up . . . Then they were . . . everywhere. Too many to fight . . . "

He sagged, eyes losing focus until I reached out to shake him. "Deckin," I insisted.

"He fought . . . killed a few . . . then, the tall knight . . . the champion . . . he came."

I darted another look at the village, searching the drifting smoke and glowing haze for a tall, armoured figure. "Bauldry," I breathed. "He's here?"

"With his knights . . . and a good deal more. He beat Deckin down . . . with a staff. Didn't even bother . . . drawing his sword. Then had his men . . . rope him up. Everyone else . . . " Hostler sagged again, eyes dimming further.

"Justan?" I shook him. "Lorine?"

"Didn't see. I ran . . . " I saw a glimmer of shame in his fading gaze. I felt the strength go out of him, his head lolling onto the snow. "I shamed the Martyrs . . . in my fear . . . " His hands flapped, but weakly, like injured birds trying to take flight. "I beseech thee . . . holy Martyrs . . . blessed Seraphile in thy grace . . . see my contrition and accept my soul . . . Do not deny me the portal . . . "

He continued to babble out his prayers, hands flapping with increased animation and voice gaining volume. I had seen this before, those close to death finding a last well of strength before it claimed them. He might rant on for another minute or two, drawing attention in the process. There was also the chance that, should I leave him alive, a soldier might wring from him the knowledge that not all of Deckin Scarl's band had died this night.

"Hush," I said, putting a hand on Hostler's forehead, holding him in place. "The Martyrs, the Seraphile, they'll know what's in your heart."

I think it was the smile I offered that betrayed my intention, for when had I ever smiled at him except in scorn? Hostler's features hardened into the expression I had seen most often – cold, disappointed judgement. "Ingrate," he said, softly but with careful precision.

I put the edge of the falchion's blade to his neck, the smile slipping from my lips. "Yes," I said.

CHAPTER NINE

I threw the crossbow away upon reaching the woods, quickly followed by the breastplate and the helm. I had miles to flee before dawn and couldn't do so carrying such a weight. I did keep the falchion. The weapon had a pleasing heft to it and, judging by the ease with which it had opened Hostler's neck, a keen edge I might well be glad of later. I strapped the soldier's belt across my chest so the falchion rested on my back, leaving my legs unencumbered, and began to run. The snow started to fall soon after, heavy enough to penetrate the trees and blanket the ground. It made for hard going but did provide some comfort in knowing my tracks would soon be covered and any pursuit slowed. Even so I ran with my ears straining for the distant yelp of hounds. My footsteps might be gone but not the scent of a sweaty, bloodstained youth.

I had learned at an early age that the key to evading a pursuit is to surrender to your fears. When death seems a certainty the body will respond with all manner of ingrained instincts, lending strength and speed normally beyond the reach of mere mortals. I made no effort to maintain a steady pace, allowing my panic to force me to a sprint, recent scenes of slaughter playing undimmed in my mind. The feel of Gerthe's suddenly limp hand in mine, the tall axeman's torment, Hostler's final, blood-choked gasp as the falchion's edge bit deep.

Added to this were the horrors I hadn't witnessed but knew to have taken place amid that blazing ruin of a village. Successive years would do much to educate me on the truth of what occurred during the Moss Mill Massacre, as history would record it, and they would prove worse even than the fevered conjurings of my terrorised brain.

In time I would learn that the Thessil brothers had been cornered in a barn and fought it out bravely for a time. When the barn was set alight they charged out fighting, clothes and hair burning. Rubin died quickly but Danick had been captured and forced to watch while the soldiers inflicted a great many indignities on his brother's corpse. Stories vary but most agree Danick met his end when they hanged him from the mill's sails using Rubin's intestines as a rope.

Shilva Sahken was not among the many victims that night. Most of her savage tribe, however, were not so fortunate, nor were the villagers of Moss Mill. Those not felled in the initial bout of slaughter were either cut down attempting to flee or herded into a fenced pasture. Come the morn a sheriff read out the ducal proclamation naming them as squatters on noble lands and thereby subject to indentured service.

Notable among the survivors that night were the disordered eastern contingent. After departing Leffold Glade, Erchel's kin apparently made a laggardly progress towards the Mill and, having been spared death by their laziness, soon melted back into the woods and returned to their more familiar hunting grounds. At least, that's how the story went.

As for Deckin, well, dear reader, you will learn his fate in due course, for it was ever bound up with mine.

All this unpleasantness I would discover later, but it was my fertile imagination that kept me running that night. My lungs burned like fire, my legs ached and my feet and hands turned blue and numb with cold, but still I ran. Exhaustion finally forced a collapse when the snow at last abated and the sky I glimpsed through the trees turned a slightly less dark shade of grey. My legs folded beneath me and I pitched headlong into a snow drift, my skin too chilled to feel the scrape of it against my face. For a second I was completely incapable of movement, raising fears that I might suffocate until I gathered enough resolve to flop onto my back. Gazing up at the overlapping chaos of snow-burdened branches, I watched my breath rise like steam from an over-boiled kettle.

With rest inevitably came pain as feeling returned to benumbed limbs and the strain of the run took its toll. The mingled force of it was enough to make me cry out but I was grateful nonetheless, for pain gives strength. I knew I had to get up. I knew that to lie there would mean death. Still, the temptation was strong, the pain diminished quickly in concert with clouding vision and fading terrors, for no mind can stay fearful for ever. Soon the icy mound of snow I lay on would start to feel like a warm mattress, like the one I had shared with Gerthe only hours ago . . .

My last glimpse of Gerthe's rag-doll corpse hanging from the shed wall was enough to get me moving, for it added anger to the fading pain. *She didn't deserve that*, I thought, heaving myself over, hands digging into the snow as I pushed myself upright. This may have been a debatable point. Gerthe was an accomplished and enthusiastic thief as well as a whore and not shy with the knife if the need arose. But still, she had possessed her own brand of kindness. More than that she had been family, or as much family as one such as I could claim. So had Baker, Twine, Lorine, even Todman who I planned to kill one day. Now they were all most likely corpses, if they were lucky.

Shouting with the effort, I pushed myself upright and stumbled on. Running was now impossible but I did manage a hurried shuffle. The journey that followed was full of hungry days and fearful, shivering nights during which I didn't dare light a fire. There would be rabbits or hares to snare even in winter, but you can't move through a forest and live off it at the same time. What food I ate consisted of roots clawed from the hard earth or the occasional cache of nuts left by an unlucky squirrel. It was meagre, stomach-straining fare but kept me from true starvation until I finally reached Leffold Glade.

It had long been habit of passing outlaws to leave a cache of supplies at the glade, insurance against circumstances much like this one. The goods lay behind a large but moveable stone amid the ruins scattered through the trees on the amphitheatre's west-facing side. Usually, shifting the stone would have been the work of a moment or two, but in my weakened state it required what felt like an hour or more of effort. Inch by torturous inch, the stone scraped over the frosted ground in response to my pitiful heaves until, finally, I created enough of a gap to reach for the treasure within. The stores were not copious: some dried beef and clay pots of pickled onions and berries and a small cask of ale. Altogether it wouldn't have fed the whole band for more than a day. That day, however, it was a bounteous feast into which I threw myself with ravening abandon.

Starvation has a curious effect on the body, causing the stomach to rebel when provided with plentiful nourishment. Consequently, I was soon obliged to spew up a large portion of what I had eaten. Afterwards, I spent a long time slumped next to the hiding place, groaning in my gut-aching misery while occasionally letting out a shrill laugh at the unexpected novelty of my survival. It would please me to report that this was the only occasion on which I experienced profound surprise at finding myself still alive, but that, as you will see, would be very far from the truth.

That night the cold descended with such breath-stealing force that I allowed myself the danger of a fire. Making camp in the oval centre of the ancient stone bowl, I struck my flint to a small stack of stripped kindling and branches, hoping the enclosing tiers would conceal the glow. Leffold Glade was a well-kept secret but who knew what had been wrung from those captured at Moss Mill? I found I had to resist the temptation to linger, surrender to the notion that this ancient place offered some form of preternatural protection. But Deckin had been right: it was just a pile of old stones, the location of which may well have already been betrayed to the sheriff's men, or the dread Sir Ehlbert Bauldry.

The towering champion had begun to loom ever larger in my fear-stoked mind throughout my flight, taking on monstrous proportions and stirring unwelcome dreams during my brief snatches of sleep. *Who will bear arms in this traitor's defence?* he demanded from behind his visor, holding up a dripping head, except instead of being Duke

Rouphon's it was the head of his unacknowledged bastard who twitched and dripped gore. Of course, this wasn't how it had been the day the duke died. I had never at this point seen Sir Ehlbert or heard his voice and had no way of knowing if it matched the harsh, barely human rasp that emerged from the helm. But my imagination was ever an inventive sadist. That night in Leffold Glade as I huddled close to my dwindling fire and surrendered to sleep, it was Deckin's head that spoke.

You ran, Deckin said. He regarded me with a corpse's eyes, grey pupils in milky-white orbs that somehow retained the piercing quality they had possessed in life. His tone held a note of regretful injury rather than accusation. *Why did you run, Alwyn? Was I not always fair to you? You would have perished if not for me, and yet you killed Hostler and just ran away . . .*

I woke to a bone-deep chill that was only partly due to my camp-fire dwindling into a charred black circle overnight. Sitting up, I rested my back against the arena wall, looking around the large, empty bowl of my refuge only recently filled with celebrating villainy. It seemed bigger now, and a great deal colder. Even so, once again I felt the temptation to linger here. If I had escaped, then others could have too. Perhaps they were hurrying here and we would meet in sombre but relieved companionship. If enough of them turned up then a new band would be born, Alwyn's band, the scions of Deckin's legacy . . .

My absurd imaginings died as I let out a bitter laugh, shaking my head. "No one's coming," I told myself, speaking aloud because why wouldn't I? "If any managed to run, they ran somewhere else."

I recalled that Erchel's folk hadn't been there for the slaughter, meaning possible refuge awaited me in the eastern woods. The pros-pect of enlisting in a gang composed of those who might share Erchel's blood was far from enticing, but so was a lonely death from hunger or cold in the depths of the forest. As I sat in doleful resignation, another thought occurred, one surely born of the nightmare I had just endured. *They took Deckin alive.*

Castle Duhbos lay within reach if I rationed my provisions and kept clear of roads and settlements. Castle Duhbos where surely the King's Champion would have taken his prize to face the duke's justice.

"And what," I enquired, voice rich in self-mockery, "will you do when you get there?"

There's a way in, came the response from some traitorous idiot, deep inside. *The one Deckin told us about.*

"No!" I got to my feet, teeth gritted, shaking my head fast enough to dizzy my sight. "Not a fucking chance!"

Why did you run? the traitor asked, pushing Deckin's twitching, dripping head to the forefront of my thoughts. *Was I not always fair to you?*

I clamped my eyes closed, folding my arms tight against my chest as the compulsion built. I have often reflected on the fact that one of the banes of a human existence is the tendency towards addiction. Some go through life a slave to drink, intoxicating weeds, the entice-ments of the flesh or the illusory promise of dice or cards. My principal addiction has ever been the urge towards unwise action, the lust for the dramatic course, an unquenchable appetite for doing the unexpected. I spent an hour or more wrestling with the traitorous voice that insisted on recalling every kind or encouraging word Deckin had ever uttered in my direction, while ignoring the cuffs, threats and infrequent beatings, all to no avail.

Even as I gathered my bundle for the journey, I told myself this was a mission born of curious sentiment and no more. I wanted to know Deckin's fate – that was all. Did he not at least deserve a witness to his end? Rescue was a fantasy, a deadly one at that. But, days of weary travel and lonely nights inevitably led to speculation which in turn gave birth to scheming. *He'll be locked in a dungeon, so even if I make it within the walls, how to free him? Dungeons have locks, so you need keys. Who holds those keys? The gaoler, who is perhaps a fellow prone to drink or, even better, not averse to bribery. But how to bribe a man when I have no coin? Steal some, you fuckwit . . .*

And so it went. Throughout the long trudge to Castle Duhbos, my outlaw's mind evolved and discounted myriad plans for the liberation of Deckin Scarl. I knew as I plotted that it was folly of the worst kind, the kind that would in short order see a lad of promise and no small ability strung up alongside his mentor. Despite the endless whispering of the traitor's voice and the ever more intricate stratagems it gave rise to, I knew with hard certainty that I walked towards my doom and would in truth never set eyes on Deckin Scarl again.

I was wrong on both counts.

Chapter Ten

"Will any come forth to bear arms in this traitor's defence?" The lord constable's voice sang clear in the chill morning air, rousing only a small murmur from the assembled mass of churls and townsfolk. I heard a modicum of anger among the muttering and whispering, even a few prayers to the Martyrs, but no open shouts of defiance and certainly no strident acceptance of the constable's challenge. Among the several score of gawpers who clustered before the scaffold that day, not one stepped forwards to raise a weapon in defence of Deckin Scarl. He knelt at the edge of the platform, bedraggled and bleeding in his brace of tight, heavy chains. His beard and hair had been shaved, rendering his features an arresting exhibition of scars, scabs and multi-hued bruising. At his back stood a knight of impressive stature, clad in a full suit of armour that glimmered bright, as did the brass eagle emblazoned on his breastplate.

An eagle, not a flame, I thought, looking the knight over. This then was not the famed Sir Ehlbert Bauldry. A glance around the platform confirmed the presence of a quartet of kingsmen in Crown Company livery, but no other knights. For reasons unknown, the King's Champion was not present this day.

I had arrived at Castle Duhbos that very morning, straggling along the icy, wheel-rutted road to find a great many people already gathered for the coming spectacle. There was no need to ferret out information or linger in the vicinity of gossiping strangers. The reason for their attendance was on every set of lips: today they would witness the death of the Outlaw King himself.

Like Castle Ambris, Castle Duhbos had its own collection of hovels outside its walls, the scaffold having been erected on the expanse of grass that separated the two. From the shortness of the grass I assumed it to be a space normally reserved for tourneys or fairs. The number of onlookers present told of far more people than could have been drawn from the hovels or the castle itself. From the cloaks they wore and bundles they carried, I judged most had walked several miles to witness the judgment of Deckin Scarl, in the midst of winter too.

"Doesn't look much like a king now, does he?" I heard one fellow in the crowd mutter to his neighbour. The air had been thick with such whispered commentary as I worked my way through the throng. Some made jokes or voiced caustic observations. Others murmured of past encounters with Deckin Scarl, their voices coloured by keen satisfaction. Not once did I hear a word of sympathy or the sound of tears being shed. For all his fame, and his occasional, purely pragmatic largesse, Deckin remained an outlaw. This fate was the deserved end of his kind, as it always had been and always would be.

I kept pushing forward until the press of bodies grew too dense to allow further progress. However, I was close enough to see the faces of those on the platform and hear all words spoken.

"Witness this, traitor!" the lord constable called out, turning to point at the prisoner's bowed head. The constable, a thin, spindly limbed fellow despite his voluminous voice, would have seemed comical on a less ominous occasion. The way his long coat flapped, and the tassels of his skullcap flailed, resembled a jackanapes's capering at the fair. "See how well the people of this duchy recognise your treason," he railed, "for not one will raise a hand to preserve your miserable life!"

His stridency and near manic expression bespoke a man clearly enjoying both his task and the notoriety that came with it. He adopted a melodramatic pose at this juncture, head raised and arm outflung to the crowd. Had Lorine been here to witness it she would surely have laughed in professional disdain.

I looked for her on the platform, but there were no captives present save Deckin. There were, however, a long line of heads impaled on stakes on the battlement above the castle gate. I hadn't had the opportunity for more than a cursory glance, finding them all too degraded by corruption to make out any recognisable features. I did espy one with long hair that straggled in the wind, but it was too distant to discern if those fluttering tresses held a copper sheen.

"Long has this man been a terror to the good folk of this duchy," the constable continued. "For he stands convicted in the sight of Commons, Crown and Covenant of so many foul deeds that to list them would require a full day and night. But, good people, know that today the manner of his punishment is determined not by his mere criminality, but by his treachery. For let it be known that this—" the constable's lip curled as he swung his outstretched hand towards Deckin, finger pointed in unwavering accusation "—worthless cur, not content with base thievery and bloody murder, has further condemned himself through vile treason against the Crown. This man, with deliberate intent, did molest and steal from a Crown agent, a royal messenger no less. Also, sound evidence has been provided that he did conspire with the traitorous rebel Magnis Lochlain, known commonly as the Pretender, to foment violent revolt in this duchy. This he did to avenge the just execution of his father, the traitor and false Duke Rouphon Ambris. I ask you, good folk of the Shavine Marches, has there ever been a man more deserving of just execution?"

The constable threw his arms wide as he asked this, no doubt expecting some uproar of bloodthirsty agreement. Instead, the response was more a combination of murmured assent and growling anticipation, punctuated by a few coughs and impatient mutterings. I saw the constable's face twitch with angry embarrassment, a pink flush creeping into his cheeks that soon took on a deeper shade of red as another sound came from the platform.

As his head jerked, Deckin's wounds scattered blood onto those at the front of the crowd. At first, I thought him possessed of a coughing fit, or, as the grunts coming from his throat grew, some manner of hysterics. Then he raised his head fully, revealing features riven by cuts and charred by burns, but also set in a mask of genuine merriment. Deckin Scarl was laughing.

"Silence this swine!" the constable snapped, casting an imperious hand at the knight who stood behind Deckin. However, instead of delivering the expected blow to the captive's head, the knight merely altered the angle of his visored face to hold the constable in silent regard. I saw the pallor of the constable's face pale, although his narrow features took on an enraged aspect. This, I knew, was a man at war with his own pride. As the senior agent of Crown law present, authority over these proceedings rested with him, but he had just been openly defied. His status required that he voice a rebuke, but the prospect of delivering one to this knight was clearly far from appealing. Fortunately, he was spared the decision when Deckin's laughter gave way to speech.

"Kill me for the truth, if you must," he told the constable, the words emerging from swollen and cracked lips in a rasp that still managed to carry to my ears. "I'll not deny I deserve it. But don't kill me for a lie, you worthless shitstain."

The constable's gaze wavered between Deckin and the recalcitrant knight for a prolonged interval. Finally, the growing chorus of coughs and irked mutterings from the crowd reminded him that he had an execution to conclude.

Taking a deep breath, the constable swung back to address the crowd, tassels flailing afresh. "Let it be known that our sovereign, Great King Tomas, First of this name and most deserving of the Seraphile's grace, is a man of mercy and compassion, even unto the most vile. No subject, be they of noble or mean blood, will be put to death without the chance to cleanse their soul." He paused to wave a hand to the rear of the scaffold. "Let Communicant Ancred, Appointed Chaplain of Castle Duhbos, come forward so that he may hear the traitor's testament."

Communicant Ancred was a tall, aged man with a long grey beard, who approached Deckin on faltering and hesitant legs. He moved with his back bent and it seemed to me he kept upright only by virtue of the staff he clutched in his spotted hands. I saw little enthusiasm for his task in the sagging creases of his face, even a glimmer of fear in those watery eyes. When he halted to stoop at Deckin's side, the voice that emerged was a thin, piping trill most present couldn't hope to catch.

"Speak now of your transgressions and voice no lie," the old cleric intoned. "For the Seraphile know all that resides in your soul. Honour the Martyrs' example with truth and receive their cleansing grace."

Despite the ruin inflicted on Deckin's face, I could still discern the expression of sour contempt he turned upon the communicant. "My father got an Ascendant," Deckin said with a weary shake of his head. "All I get is a piss-smelling old goat."

The laugh that rippled through the crowd wasn't particularly loud, but it did suffice to earn a hard glare from the constable. He opened his mouth to utter some words of castigation only for Deckin to interrupt him.

"I'll make testament," he said, voice strained but still loud enough to reach all ears present. "But not to this Martyr-bothering loon. My words are for them." Deckin jerked his head at the throng.

"You have no rights here, traitor!" the constable snarled, advancing towards Deckin. "No rights to speak! No rights to do anything other than die for your crimes . . . "

His voice faded when the knight stepped into his path. Where before the constable's fear had been muted by his pride, now it blossomed into full, wide-eyed terror as a few short words emerged from the knight's visor. Neither I nor any other soul in the crowd heard the words the knight spoke then, for they were too faint and distorted by his helm. However, the constable heard them very clearly.

Swallowing, he stepped back from the knight, flustered hands wiping at his long coat before he clasped them together. Taking a moment to master himself, he addressed the crowd once more. "In observance of custom and Covenant law, the traitor is permitted to make testament."

Deckin spared the constable a short, pitying glance before hunching as he struggled to get his feet under him. He rose with a noticeable sway, legs trembling and chains rattling on the platform's timbers. His wrists were confined by manacles and I thought he had clasped them into fists until I saw that his fingers had been severed down to the second knuckle. Although the words he spoke would never fade from my memory, I think it was the sight of his hands that set me on the course that would dominate my life for years to come. While those hands had left me bruised and cowed on many occasions, looking at them now I could only recall the times they had rested on my shoulder in affection or comfort. That first day in the forest loomed largest of all, the knowledge of deliverance that came from his touch. Whatever else he had done, Deckin Scarl had once saved my life.

"I seek no pardon from the Seraphile," Deckin began, voice hoarse at first but gathering strength as he winced and managed to straighten his back. "They'll make of me what they will, and a pox on them if they don't like what they see."

This drew a muted thrum of mirth from the throng, as well as an appalled gape from Communicant Ancred. The old man came close to toppling over as he made a tottering effort to retreat from this heretical outlaw with all haste, something that stoked the crowd's amusement to a yet higher pitch.

"As for treason," Deckin continued, "I'll make no bones about my intent to take this duchy, but I didn't plan to do so for my father's sake. The king took his head with cause and he's welcome to it. No, I planned to take this duchy because it's mine, by right of strength and will if not blood. All duchies and all kingdoms are won in the same way, and don't let these noble fuckers tell you otherwise. If that's treason, then so be it, and I'll seek no pardon for it. As regards the Pretender, I never met or had any truck with the bastard, so no pardon needed there either. But . . . " His voice dwindled and his head lolled a little and he was forced to steady himself as the tremble of his legs threatened to tip him over.

"But, I do seek pardon from you," Deckin went on. "I stand convicted as a thief and a killer, for that is what I've been. I can claim reasons, but they're lies and you've heard them all before. I could claim that I stole to eat and I killed to keep what I stole. But the truth is I stole and I killed for ambition. I'll suffer no shame for the nobles I robbed, or for those I killed, but I will suffer it for stealing from you. For killing your kin and your kind. Those are my true crimes, and for that I seek your pardon."

He paused again, lowering his gaze, the battered, scabbed and stained features taking on a sorrowful cast. It was then that he saw me. Deckin had always possessed unusually sharp eyes capable of spotting ambush or prey in the shifting green of the forest with what I felt to be unnatural swiftness. Now those eyes picked my face out of the assembly with much the same ease, widening only slightly while he kept any sign of recognition from his distorted visage save for the smallest curve to his lips. He held my gaze for only a heartbeat before looking away, but I saw enough even in that brief interval to know that Deckin Scarl would die this day with at least one morsel of comfort.

"My band, those that followed me, are all dead now," he said, voice growing yet more hoarse. "But if their souls linger to witness this testament, I would have them know that I valued their service and their company more than they knew. We fought and we bickered, but we also suffered hunger and cold together, as families do, and family is to be cherished, as is life." His eyes flicked back to me, just for the briefest instant. "And life should not be wasted on pointless feuds or hopeless endeavours. This much I've learned."

Blinking, he glanced at the knight and nodded. "My thanks, old friend."

The knight gave no reply, at least not one I could hear. Setting a gauntleted hand on Deckin's shoulder, he guided him to his knees. I didn't want to see what came next. I wanted to flee and find a corner to weep in. But I didn't. Escaping the sight of Deckin's end would have been a betrayal. As far as I knew, I was all that remained of the band of miscreants he called family. The only one to stand witness to his end and know grief rather than jubilation.

The knight with the eagle breastplate went about his business with swift and unhesitant efficiency; no final pause to twist the crowd's tension tighter, no flourish to the rise and fall of his longsword. Nor, as may have been his intention, did he allow any delay in which Deckin could call out any last declamations. I stood in frozen observance as Deckin's head parted from his body with the first stroke. It made a faint thud as it met the planking, the body slumping into a pile of bones and flesh with blood jetting from the stump, thick at first, then subsiding to a trickle.

I had never seen a traitor's execution before so only learned later that it was custom for the executioner to hold the severed head up and proclaim justice done in the king's name. This knight, however, had little regard for custom that morning. As soon as the deed was done, he turned smartly about and strode to his former position, resuming the same posture, bloodied sword pointed down. His head failed to turn as silence descended, refusing to regard the constable's expectant stare.

To my surprise, there were no shouts or cheers from the crowd. The decapitation had been met with a sharp inhalation but none of the wild celebration I'd expected. Usually the air was thick with cheers when an outlaw dangled from the rope or a heretic suffered a public whipping. It may have been his testament, or the unexpected swiftness of his end, but that day the crowd saw no reason to celebrate the death of the Outlaw King of the Shavine Forest.

I watched the constable stiffen in annoyance at the knight's continued indifference, face flushing in mingled disgust and resignation, he bent to grasp the fallen head, gripping it with both hands.

"Behold," he said, straightening to raise the slack-faced, dripping thing up for all to see. His voice was hoarse and he had to cough before recovering his former stridency. "Behold! The head of Deckin Scarl, traitor and outlaw. Let his name be spoken no more. All hail King Tomas!"

He unwisely chose to shake Deckin's head in concert with his final declaration, sending a copious spatter of gore over his coat which rather spoiled the moment. The constable was unable to conceal his spasm of revulsion quickly followed by a retching which saw lordly vomit mix with outlaw blood on the planking. The crowd's response was equally unedifying, a murmur of grudging subservience rather than an outpouring of fervent loyalty.

"All hail King Tomas," I muttered along with everyone else.

The crowd began to thin immediately, heading for the village where the taverns were sure to be busy. I contrived to linger, watching the knight wait until the constable and attendant functionaries had left before shifting from his stance. A few castle servants climbed the steps to gather up the corpse but were soon sent scurrying by a barked command and dismissive wave from the knight. "Away!"

He raised a hand and gestured to the kingsmen below, summoning a half-dozen to the platform where they went about carefully wrapping the body and head in a muslin shroud. Once done they raised the burden on to their shoulders, carrying it down the steps and away towards the dark bulk of the castle.

Chapter Eleven

I kept to the most shadowed corner of the alehouse, having no desire to draw the eye of the soldiers that crowded its mean confines. Those who had gathered for the execution had drifted away by now, hefting their bundles and embarking on the long trek back to their farm or village. In their wake, the soldiers came for their grog. I began the evening with a clear intent: I would sit quietly and garner all details I could regarding the demise of Deckin and the others. I was particularly keen to learn the name of the knight who wore the brass eagle on his breastplate.

I have learned much more than I care to about revenge and its myriad complexities, but perhaps the principal lesson to heed is that it begins as a small thing, a seed destined to sprout monstrous branches. Feuds are an intrinsic and, in some way, necessary part of the outlaw's life, for they ensure a certain order among the chaos of those required to live beyond legal stricture. Betrayal inevitably results in death or the promise of such, as does the murder of one you call leader.

So, as I sat and listened to the soldiers' gossip, finding little of interest in truth, my busy mind began its plotting once again. Instead of outlandish schemes of rescue it now evolved equally absurd stratagems for the murder of the eagle-bearing knight, whoever he may be. There was a morose quality to my plotting, the sight of Deckin's head rolling on the platform adding to my malaise. As is the way with misery when visited upon young men, it stirred an unwise thirst for ale, which in this establishment was not as watered down as one might expect.

"Another, good sir," I told the innkeeper with forced humour and a slight slur, setting my tankard down. He waited until I slid a shek across the uneven timber before consenting to provide a refill. Sudden weariness gripped me then and I leaned heavily on the counter, feeling a welling of sorrow that, incredibly, brought tears to my eyes. The inescapable knowledge that I was now utterly alone brought forth memories of that first night in the woods as a boy. I recalled the sting of the bruises left by the beating the pimp had given me. How I had whimpered as I stumbled about until Deckin and Lorine found me.

A small metallic glimmer shone in my unfocused gaze as I slumped lower on the serving table and I blinked moisture away to see the Covenant medallion dangling before my eyes. It was such a light, inconsequential thing I had forgotten it lay about my neck.

Keep the bitch, I thought, recalling Deckin's words regarding the luck afforded by Martyrs. *A man makes his own fortune.* I took hold of the tiny bronze disc, my lips twisting into a smile at the thought of this small token serving as a protective charm throughout my recent travails. How Hostler would have raged at me for voicing that particular notion.

"A devotee of Martyr Hersephone, is it?"

I blinked and wiped my eyes again before turning to regard the man at my side. I knew him as a soldier instantly, but not of the type I was accustomed to. His features were lean and clean shaven and his tunic dyed in the colours of a kingsman. A dagger with a garnet pommel sat in a scabbard at his belt alongside a sword, the handle of which was enmeshed in wire. The dagger might be for show, but the sword certainly wasn't. He wore a friendly expression but there was a keenness to his gaze that would have sounded more of a warning bell if I hadn't partaken of so much under-watered ale.

"'And lo,'" I quoted raising my tankard to the soldier, "'when her kin laid her in the earth her body had been ravaged and her breath stilled, but she did rise come the morning sun and no sign of injury marred her beauty.'" I smiled and took a deep draught from my tankard. "Thus speak the scrolls, anyhow."

"So young and yet already a scholar of Covenant lore." The soldier laughed, settling beside me and waving the innkeeper over. "A brandy, and one for my devoted friend."

"Not a scholar," I muttered, fingers turning the medallion. "But I had a . . . teacher. A man who knew much of the Martyrs, though his principal area of study was the Scourge."

"Supplicant, was he?" the soldier enquired.

"Hardly." I laughed again, the sound grating in its cynicism. However, my humour faded quickly as the memory of Hostler's demise flared bright and ugly in my head.

"Don't be sad, friend." The soldier's hand, light but strong, jostled my arm. "We've much to celebrate, after all. Deckin Scarl's head finally rests on a spike, as well it should. Drink to that—" he pushed the brandy cup into my hand "—if nothing else."

"He did his share of bad, to be sure," I mumbled, raising the cup towards my lips, then pausing in suspicion. "Did you put a sovereign in this?"

The soldier laughed again, clapping me on the back. "I'm Crown Company, friend. Those that march under the Crown banner have no need for tricks when we need fresh blood. I've seen men fight for the privilege." He lowered his voice to a conspiratorial whisper. "And the pay. Three times what any duke'll cough up, plus a share of the ransom whenever we snag ourselves a noble. Rewards too, on occasion. Each of us got two silver sovs for our part in snaring that shit-eater Scarl."

There was a precision to this statement that should have made me wary, a prod to the words and a weight to his gaze that told of a man seeking a reaction. Once again, to my shame, my faculties were too degraded to take proper heed.

"You were there?" I asked. "At . . . when he got took?"

"Surely. Bit more of a fight than we were expecting, if I'm honest. Lost three men from our company and another twenty-odd from the duchy-men and sheriff's lot. Those buggers with the tattoos were the worst. But we got 'em all in the end, bar a few runners. Cowardly rats scampering off to the woods to let their kin be slaughtered like hogs." He raised his cup to his lips, eyes never straying from me as he drank, steady enough to finally set me on edge.

Slowly, I let my gaze wander the tavern, finding two more soldiers standing at the door. They held no tankards, hands resting on the hilts of their swords. A half-glance to my left revealed another leaning against the counter. He was taller than the others by several inches and alongside the sword on his belt there sat a coiled length of strong rope. None of them looked directly at me, which told the tale clear enough.

There's nothing quite like fear to sober a man. It floods through you from head to toe, returning clarity with an instancy beyond any physic or potion. It also adds a tremble to your hands and treacherous quaver to your voice which, fortunately, I was skilled in quelling. However, before speaking on, I was unable to choke down a cough. Just a small noise, but one men such as these would take as proof their snare had found some prey.

"Must've been quite a fight," I said, putting a dull, disinterested note to my voice and taking a hefty swig of brandy.

"That it was," the soldier agreed. "One I confess I'll take greater pride in than even our worst battle with the Pretender's mob. Y'see, lad—" he inched closer to me, speaking with soft, earnest sincerity "—I had m'self a grudge to settle. Just recently I've nourished a great hatred for outlaws. War is always an ugly thing, but it gets uglier still when there's blood to settle. Family blood, I mean to say."

His hand snaked over my shoulders as he continued in companionable confidence. "Not a rich family, my folk, but not full churl either. Da was a farmer but he owned his own plot so we did better than most. But he had three sons, all of whom lived to manhood by the Seraphile's grace, and only the eldest can inherit. I was youngest and Ralf second in line. We could've stayed, I suppose, but it's not an easy thing to work as a mere servant to your own brother, so when the banners came marching by it seemed a decent choice.

"Wasn't quite so much war about then so the sergeants were a mite more picky. But we were strong lads, well fed and muscled through all the labour we did, and they took us. In time I got chosen to try for Crown Company. Ralf, Martyrs bless him, was always a little too fond of his drink and his brawling so would remain a duchy man-at-arms. Time and marching orders meant we hardly set eyes on one another for years, till recently when duty called me back to the Shavine Marches. Except, the brother I set eyes on this time was dead. Some fucker put a knife in him, and his friend."

The soldier paused to raise his brandy cup again, taking his time over it, his arm tightening about my shoulders. "If I'm honest I wouldn't have known him if his sergeant hadn't assured me of it. His face was all swollen and nibbled by fish. Seems whoever killed him shoved him in the river afterwards. Took three days before he washed up downstream. His company thought he'd deserted, which is a shameful thing. For all his faults, Ralf was no coward.

"I had the Supplicant pen a letter home about it all. My ma can't read it but my sister-in-law knows her letters. When I sent it, I wanted to return the keepsake she gave him the day we marched off under the banners. Gave me one too. She's like you, y'see, devout in her faith with a particular fondness for Martyr Hersephone. 'You'll need luck,' she told us." The soldier's hand disappeared into the collar of his tunic, emerging with a small bronze disc on a chain. "'And *she* brings luck.'"

He set his hand down on the counter alongside mine and I saw his medallion to be a near identical version of the one still dangling from my fingers. "She's skilled with trinkets, my ma," the soldier continued. "Sells 'em at the fairs and such. Made one medallion for me and another for Ralf. Not that you'd've known him by that name. Y'see, he had a gift for taming birds so folk called him Hawker. Curious thing: when they fished him out of the water, his medallion was nowhere to be found."

The soldier sighed and pulled me closer still, voice little more than a whisper now. "Hate's not a good thing, lad. It eats at a man, like a maggot feeding on your soul from within. So strong was my hate that, after all the killing I did at Moss Mill, I took myself off to the Supplicant in search of guidance. 'Will the Martyrs forgive a man who revels in so much blood?' I asked him. You want to know what he told me? 'The Martyrs' example is one to aspire to, but the Seraphile's grace is only denied to those who make no effort towards aspiration.'"

His lips brushed my ear, brandy tinged breath hot on my skin. "And how hard do you aspire, you little shi—?"

The years have taught me many ways to slip from a clinch, most dependent on correctly calculating the size and abilities of your opponent. This fellow had another inch in height on me and a fair deal more weight and muscle. Also, I had few illusions about his skill with a blade. But, he was a soldier, not an outlaw. Soldiers know how to fight, while outlaws know tricks.

I had kept most of the brandy in my mouth throughout his tragic tale and now, turning my head a fraction, I squirted it directly into his eyes. However strong or capable a man might be, his body will always react with pure instinct when suffering an unexpected sting. He jerked back with a startled snarl, arm loosening about my shoulders just enough to allow me to drive my elbow into his mouth, a hard jab mashing his lips against his teeth.

I ducked as the soldier's head snapped back, trailing blood. Going to my knees, I rolled away as the big bastard at my back made his lunge, grabbing at my legs but failing to gain purchase as I scrambled clear. I ignored the doorway where the other two were already charging towards me, instead hopping onto a table and barrelling for the nearest window, arms raised to cover my head. Fortunately, the shutters were old and rotted, giving way at the first impact, albeit leaving a few splinters in my hands and face.

I landed with a grunt on the hard-packed snow outside, barely feeling the shock of the suddenly icy air as I surged to my feet and sprinted away. I covered only a dozen yards before something came spinning out of the dark. It was an expertly aimed throw, slipping a quarterstaff between my pumping legs at precisely the right moment to send me into an untidy tumble. Shouting, I kicked the staff away and regained my feet, only to suffer a stunning blow to the head. Like the thrown staff, this was delivered with great accuracy to my temple with just enough force to render me senseless. I caught a glimpse of the man who had delivered it as I fell – a short, hatchet-faced fellow in Crown Company livery who hadn't been present in the tavern. He might not be an outlaw, but this soldier knew plenty of tricks too.

As I lay too stunned to move, I heard the crunch of multiple boots on snow, provoking a surge of fear-born strength that enabled me to stand, albeit briefly before a rope looped over my head. I gulped air as it pulled taut, jerking me off my feet and dragging me across the ground, legs flailing.

And thus, dear reader, was I caught.

Chapter Twelve

"A fighter, eh?" a voice asked before a kick drove a boot into my belly, my struggles ceasing as I doubled over. "Did my brother fight? I'd bet you never gave him the chance!" Another kick, this time to the head, sending a heaven's worth of stars into my eyes but, sadly, not sufficiently forceful to render me unconscious or immune to pain, for there were many more kicks to come. I would have covered my head and nethers with my hands if they hadn't been engaged in grasping at the rope about my neck.

"All right, get him up."

The kicking stopped and I found myself hauled upright and dragged, sagging and bleeding, away from the tavern. Through my red-tinged, clouded eyes I could make out the shape of a large oak in the centre of the village, one with a branch hanging low enough to catch a thrown rope.

"You should be proud, boy," the soldier told me, grinning despite his swelling lips and reddened teeth. "Dying on the same day as your famed leader." He drew his garnet-pommel dagger as his comrades dumped me beneath the branches, holding the blade close to my face while they gave vent to an anticipatory laugh. "Don't worry," he told me with a wink. "I keep it clean, so the wound won't fester. Not that it'll have time to. But first things first."

I heard a scrape of rope on wood, then the coil about my neck drew tight once more. I managed to get my fingers between the rope and the skin of my neck, meaning I didn't choke right away, not that my tormentors wanted me to. They heaved on the rope, dragging me clear of the ground as I continued to fight the noose, jerking in the unreasoning panic unique to imminent death.

"That's it, lad!" one called out, to much raucous laughter "Dance for us!"

The pounding pulse in my head soon swallowed their taunts, vision dimming once more as the rope pressed my fingers into my neck. Froth bubbled from my mouth as I bucked, feeling my eyes bulge so large I wondered they hadn't been squeezed from my skull. But a body starved of air cannot struggle for ever and, though I willed it otherwise, my hands slackened on the rope and the flailing of my legs faded to a twitch. My vision went from red to grey, and then, quicker than expected, became utterly and completely black.

If you are of devout leanings you may, at this juncture, be expecting a florid description of the Divine Portals, shining bright and glorious in the heavens, flanked by Seraphile guards while a chorus of Martyrs sang a welcome. Or, given the course of my life up until this event, you would be forgiven for imagining my endless screams as the Malecite dragged me into their fiery domain, claiming my wretched soul for their own. In either case, I regret to disappoint you.

It is true that I died that night, just for a moment, for as the blackness closed in, I felt my heart stop. Despite the plethora of nonsense since penned by unworthy tale spinners who pretend to the title of scholar or chronicler, this foray into the realm of death was not the moment of my revelation. All that would come much later. No, dear reader. It pains me to tell you that, as I felt the last faltering beat of my heart fade away, I saw nothing. I felt nothing. It all just . . . stopped.

"You've killed him, you clumsy fucks!"

The aggrieved sputter of the soldier's voice was loud in my ears, painful even. So too was the icy kiss of frosted ground against my cheek. More painful still, even though it was an exultant form of agony, was the great gasp of chilled air I drew into my lungs, for it heralded a good deal of retching and outpouring of bile-tinged spit.

"See?" another voice said. "Told you he wasn't gone yet."

The chill vanished from my cheek as a hand gripped my face, drawing it up. A few hard slaps and my vision swam back into focus, revealing the soldier from the tavern. His face no longer held any vestige of affable pretence. Now it was the bloodied, savage visage of a man fully consumed by vengeance.

"Good," he grunted, shoving me onto my back. "Hold him!" he snapped to his friends. "He's sure to buck hard."

I tried to struggle again but could manage only a feeble spasm or two before a dozen hands pressed down and the soldier went about ripping my clothes away, using his dagger to slice through my jerkin and trews, exposing me from chest to groin.

"I should warn you," he hissed, looming close, eyes wide and hungry, "I was never much good at gutting hogs on the farm." He reversed his grip on the dagger, lowering the point until it touched my skin, pressing hard enough to draw forth a small bead of blood. "They always squealed longest and loudest—"

"What's all this palaver about?"

The voice came from beyond the enclosing circle of soldiers, not overly loud but infused with a peerless authority that sufficed to have them all abandon their hold on me and rise to their feet. The bloody-faced soldier lingered a fraction longer, features bunching in frustration before withdrawing the dagger and rising to stand at stiff-backed attention.

"Caught ourselves another villain, Sir Althus," he said in clipped, respectful tones. "One of Scarl's lot, I'd swear. Also—" his baleful gaze slipped back to me for an instant "—the murderer of my own brother."

"Oh. One of those fellows we dragged out of the river back in Ambriside, wasn't it?"

"Yes, my lord."

"Mmm." The circle of soldiers lowered their heads, snow crunching as they retreated. The man who appeared to stare down at me was somewhere north of thirty years in age, tall and well built with dark close-cropped hair and a short, neatly groomed beard. He wore a fine cotton and fur jerkin, one side of which featured an eagle embroidered in gold thread. His gaze was commanding but it was the eagle that captured my eye.

This knight, this Sir Althus, stared at my face for what felt like a long time, gaze narrowed in what I might have thought to be recognition if I wasn't certain he had never clapped eyes on me before. "What's your proof?" he grunted, glancing at the soldier.

"Here, my lord." The soldier crouched, reaching down to tear the medallion from my neck, holding it up alongside his own. "You see how they match. One made for me, one for my brother. There's only one way this wretch could've claimed it."

Sir Althus merely raised an eyebrow at that. Taking the medallion from the soldier he stepped closer and sank to his haunches at my side. Once again, his eyes lingered on my face longer than seemed normal for a noble regarding a snared outlaw. "What's your name, boy?"

I had to engage in a bout of coughing and swallowing before my throat consented to gasp out a response. "Gab . . . m'lord."

"Gab." His face remained mostly impassive, but I detected a small curl to his lips that told me this was a man with a keen ear for lies. "So, tell me, Gab—" he dangled the medallion before my eyes "—how did you come by this precious family heirloom?"

"W-won . . . it, m'lord. Playing . . . sevens."

"Lying little shit!"

The soldier turned, raising his leg in order to deliver a stamp to my chest, but stopped at a hard glance from the crouching knight. "Who gambles for a Martyr medallion, my lord?" he asked instead. Lowering his boot, he held up the two trinkets once more. "Besides, these aren't worth a single shek."

"I've seen men gamble for all manner of things when the mood takes them," Sir Althus replied in a placid tone, his gaze still mostly focused on me. "Once saw a fellow wager his own arse for a buggering, so sure was he of his luck." He gave a small chuckle. "Turns out he was wrong. That's the way of things with dice: they don't play favourites. Fall one way and they make you rich; fall another—" he raised an eyebrow at me, lips forming a faint grin that I felt to be somewhat inappropriate in the circumstances "—and you find yourself fucked."

"He . . . " the soldier faltered, clearly struggling to quell the fury that would certainly have coloured his voice had he been addressing a lesser personage. "He's not local, my lord. Turns up here the day of Scarl's beheading, all alone in the middle of winter. Where's he come from if it's not some outlaw den?"

"That is a curious thing," Sir Althus admitted, angling his head at me. "This is hardly fine," he added, reaching out to finger the hem of my coat, "but not churl's cloth either."

"My master's parting gift, my lord," I said, voice no longer hesitant but possessed of a rasp that has never fully faded in all the long years since. "Couldn't keep me on, see? Not enough work. Been walking the roads ever since, trying to find another place. Heard there might be work for a wright in Lord Duhbos' castle."

"More shit from the sewer!" the soldier hissed, teeth clenched and air steaming from his nostrils. "He's a villain, my lord. I can smell it on him."

"Your nose does not constitute evidence, Kingsman." The knight's voice had an edge of curt dismissal to it, one that evidently instilled a good portion of fear. Every man-at-arms present immediately stood to even more rigid attention, including the grieving, bloody-faced brother. Vengeance is a potent brew, but even it couldn't press a man to test the authority enjoyed by Sir Althus.

"Did you do that to him?" he asked me, inclining his head at the soldier's dripping features.

"Panicked, milord," I gabbled, attempting a smile that most likely resembled a many-hued gargoyle thanks to the beating I'd taken. "Don't know my own strength sometimes . . . "

"Strength is it?" he cut in rising to his feet. "We'll see how strong you are."

He turned to the surrounding circle of soldiers. "The king's edict of urgent justice extended only to those found in concert with Deckin Scarl. In accordance with Crown law this boy's guilt will be determined by Duke Elbyn after due hearing wherein claims of outlawry can be evidenced and any plea he makes to the contrary heard. In the meantime, it is certain he has done injury to a kingsman of Crown Company and will suffer for it."

He made a sharp beckoning gesture and another group of soldiers came forward. Like my erstwhile executioners they were dressed in the king's livery but had a neater appearance and, like the knight, bore a gold eagle on their tunics. The other soldiers quickly stepped aside at their approach, though not without a resentful glare or two.

"One day in the pillory should be sufficient accounting," Sir Althus said as the new arrivals hauled me to my feet. I was still too weak to walk so they draped my arms over their shoulders as they bore me away, pausing when the knight held up a hand.

"You were a fool to come here," he told me, leaning close and keeping his voice too soft for the others to hear. Had the injuries done by their attentions not begun to dull my wits now my panic had abated, my head might have jerked up in surprise at the word he spoke next. As it was, all I could manage was a sideways loll to regard his sad grimace as he said, "Alwyn."

While most churls can expect to spend their often truncated span of days labouring in the fields with scant interruption to the monotony of toil, townsfolk are typically afforded considerably more in the way of amusements. Bands of musicians and sundry players will tour the towns of most duchies, even in times of war, their arrival often coinciding with the principal feast days of the Martyrs. Similarly, the hawkers, tinkers and purveyors of dubious remedies that comprise the travelling fairs will find much custom amid the hovels that cluster around a castle, port or frequently trafficked bridge. However, despite these sundry distractions, I have often pondered the fact that there is no entertainment or spectacle more enjoyed by townsfolk than the opportunity to visit torment and degradation upon any poor sod so unfortunate as to find himself locked into the pillory.

Like children with a snared fox, I mused as something soft and rotten splattered against my cheek. The chance to indulge cruelty without consequence is often irresistible, especially to those born to the daily struggle for subsistence. Thus it was not the artisans or tradespeople of the town that assembled to cast their filth at me but their servants or apprentices, also the drunks and beggars who lurked on the fringes of town life. These were by far the worst, scraping stones from the earth to add to the continual torrent of rotting vegetation or dog-chewed bones. For folk who suffered so much from the cold or the effects of lifelong drunkenness, they seemed to possess a uniform keenness of eye and strength of arm. As one stone after another rebounded from my brow, nose or chin, I found myself grateful for the foul-smelling dung and other filth with which I had already been spattered; the miasma it birthed was sure to keep away any foul humours which might otherwise cause my numerous cuts to fester.

As was expected of such occasions, a hail of insults accompanied the cascade of projectiles. Once again it was the town dregs who had the most colourful turn of phrase. Much of it was lost to my stunned and diminished awareness but a few choice gems remain in my memory even now.

"Pig-fucking, baby-stealing son of a whore!" screeched a woman with a nose so reddened by liquor my befuddled brain wondered if she hadn't strapped an apple to her face.

"Have this, you shit-eater!" grunted out a stick-thin man, his bare feet dancing on the frosted earth as he cast a broken pot at me. Fortunately, he was not so keen of eye as his fellow wretches and the pot's jagged edges merely scraped over the crown of my head before shattering on the thick timbers of the pillory.

It should not be thought that this was an entirely unruly affair. The soldiers waited until the sun had fully risen before forcing me to my knees then pressing my head and wrists into the three semicircular channels carved into the heavy iron-braced beam forming the lower half of the pillory. As they locked the upper beam into place their sergeant proclaimed my punishment to the growing crowd of townsfolk, a short statement that did not neglect to mention my potential status of a member of Deckin's band. Perhaps as a consequence, the crowd were already gathering their missiles before the sergeant's proclamation ended.

Furling the scroll, the sergeant took his halberd and scraped out a curving line in the icy ground, creating a barrier about twenty paces from the pillory beyond which none of my tormentors were permitted to step. It wasn't unknown for folk to die in the pillory when the mob's zealous pursuit of justice was permitted to get out of hand. The subsequent shower of refuse, stones and abuse wore on for most of the day with occasional lulls in which my gaggle of punishers went off to gather more missiles or revive themselves with drink. I found I dreaded these intervals more than the assaults, for they brought a return of sensation to my battered features along with a semblance of reason.

I knew I was caught and I knew my fate. Everything I suffered now would be as nothing to what came next. I would be paraded before the duke for what I expected to be a short hearing. Though I possessed a way with words, no amount of mummery or story spinning would loosen this particular trap – not that I expected to be capable of speech come the morn. My lips were swollen and split and my neck throbbed with the ache of my near hanging. Added to that was the sense of my reason slipping away as the day's torment wore on. Every stone thudding against my now-lolling head, every slap of filth against my skin, even the unending taunts, combined to push me back from the world. I retreated from it all like a turtle withdrawing into its shell, finding refuge in garbled memories and dreams of things that never were and never would be.

So complete was my surrender to delirium that when a blast of shocking cold brought me back to the world, I found myself regarding a darkened and mostly empty town square. The sky was clear and bright with stars and the surrounding houses dark save for the faint glimmer of a candle behind the shutters. A few drunks lingered in shadowed corners but daren't come any closer thanks to the dozen kingsmen posted around the pillory.

"Still in there, are you?" a voice enquired as Sir Althus's bearded face loomed into view. He peered into my bleary eyes before grunting and stepping back, tossing aside the bucket he had used to douse my head in icy water. "Of course you are. He said you weren't an easy lad to kill."

He pulled a clay pipe from his tunic and fingered leaf into the bowl, watching without expression as I blinked and sputtered my way back to full consciousness. While I could no longer feel my hands, or much of the rest of my body, my head and face felt like they were aflame. It was scant surprise to find I was unable to draw breath through my nose and I spent a long interval gasping in pain as the cold air and the water stung my various injuries.

"Here," Sir Althus grunted around his pipe stem, holding a flask to my lips. Water flooded my mouth, tasting more wonderful than the sweetest nectar to my parched and bruised throat. After I had gulped the flask dry, I strained my neck to peer up at him, watching as he positioned the pipe stem between his teeth. Holding it in place, he struck a flint to the leaf crammed into the bowl. It was a practised, skilful gesture that soon brought forth a musky, floral-tinted cloud of smoke as Sir Althus puffed away.

"Seen worse," he mused, leaning down to survey my battered visage. "But I find it doubtful any maid will ever call you handsome. Try this." He removed the pipe from his mouth and placed it between my swollen lips. "It'll take some of the pain away."

Pipe leaf was a rarity in those days, something shipped across the sea from far away that commanded a correspondingly high price and therefore remained a luxury to be enjoyed only by nobles. My first inhalation set me coughing once again but, after a short interval, as the oddly sweet vapour made its way into my lungs, I felt the fire engulfing my face begin to subside.

"Not too much," he said, removing the pipe before I could draw in more of the blessed smoke. "Wouldn't want you insensible, would I? Not before we've had a little chat."

He wiped the pipe stem on his tunic before holding it to his mouth again, sighing as he sat on the topmost step of the small dais upon which the pillory rested. "I'd apologise for this . . . spectacle if I wasn't possessed of a deep certainty that you deserve it, and more besides." He had positioned himself so I could see his face without straining overmuch and I found myself regarded by a serious, insistent frown. "You did kill that fellow's brother, did you not, Alwyn?"

Various responses rose and fell from my lips, ranging from flat denial to desperate apportioning of blame to one I assumed most likely dead. *It was a terrible, bloodthirsty villain by the name of Erchel. He forced me to a life of outlawry, m'lord, I swear by all the Martyrs.* But all that eventually emerged from my mouth was a weary groan of resignation, one Sir Althus heard enough truth in to let out a grunt of satisfaction.

"Thought so. Deckin's orders, I assume?"

I returned his frown with one of my own then winced as the effort prompted a resurgence of pain and seepage of blood from open cuts.

"No?" The knight raised his eyebrows in surprise. "I'd wager he wasn't happy when you told him. Always was a man to be wary of when his temper started to boil. I once saw him punch the life out of an archer who crowed too loudly about beating him at cards. But he was younger then – perhaps age mellowed him. Or was it just his fondness for you that spared you the knife?"

I fought to keep my features still, fearing both another surge of pain and betrayal of dangerous secrets to this overly perceptive knight. However, mention of his prior association with Deckin brought a small but curious squint to my gaze.

"That's right," he said, smoke shrouding his teeth as he smiled. "I knew him, back when his name was Deckin the Spit. It's what they used to call him in the old duke's castle, on account of all the years he spent turning meat in front of the fire. It wasn't a name he was fond of but that's the one the sergeant used when he marched us under the banner the first time and had us stutter out our oaths. We got sworn on the same day, y'see? Two boys whose balls hadn't yet fully dropped and there we were, soldiers about to march to war."

Sir Althus paused to take a long pull from his pipe, releasing the pale-grey cloud in concert with a laugh that was both rueful and bitter. When he spoke on, I noted how his voice had altered, the soft inflection and precise enunciation of the nobility replaced by the coarse tones and clipped vowels of the commons.

"You'd've thought they might've spared us the worst of it, at least for a bit. Waited until we'd grown some before they shoved us into line clutching halberds that weighed more than we did. But that's not how it was under the banners at the tail end of the Duchy Wars. Whatever the age, whatever the spindliness of your arms or lack of skill with weapons, you fought alongside everyone else and, if the Martyrs lent you luck, you got to live. It also helped if you had a sturdy friend to guard your arse when things got lively. See this?"

Sir Althus drew back the sleeve of his right arm, displaying a patch of pale bare skin among the otherwise hairy skin and muscle. "Crossbow bolt straight through from end to end at the second siege of Ilvertren, or was it the third?" He shrugged. "Doesn't matter. Point is, I came closer to dying that day than I've ever done since, and it was Deckin who bore me away from the walls before some other keen-eyed bastard could finish the job."

Another upsurge of pain pushed a groan from my mouth and he paused to put the pipe to my lips once again, letting me puff away a little longer this time. The smoke brought a notable lessening to my agonies but also added a cloudy befuddlement to my vision. When Sir Althus sat back his face had taken on a vague, distorted quality, although I continued to discern his words with decent clarity.

"Time and the waywardness of war eventually parted Deckin and I," he said with a note of nostalgic regret. "I got a chance at Crown Company and took it while he opted to stay as a duchy man. I suspect he had resolved to take the outlaw's path by then, drawn back to the Shavine Marches by the father he hated. It was his grand obsession all the years I knew him, the great scheme of ultimate revenge. How it must have irked him when Duke Rouphon contrived to put his own head on the block."

The knight shook his head with a soft laugh. He no longer looked at me, his gaze distant and unfocused, leading me to conclude this tale was not in fact for me. I was just a convenient ear for a story he couldn't tell his noble friends.

"So," he went on after a moment of brief, sombre reflection, "Deckin became an outlaw while I, after many travails, became a knight. I won't trouble you with the details of my elevation, Alwyn, for I suspect you couldn't give two shits. Suffice to say that whereas

I once bowed and knuckled my forehead to those born to privilege, now others bow and knuckle to me. Some years ago, King Tomas's father put a sword on my shoulder and named me Sir Althus Levalle, Knight Commander of Crown Company. I have a wife of noble, if not particularly noteworthy blood, a castle of my own and lands and churls to go with it. These can be the rewards of war, if you live long enough to claim them. They could have been Deckin's too, if not for his obsession, for he was always the better soldier, and said as much when I sat at his side in the dungeon not three nights ago, as I now sit beside you. The duke's torturers had been at him but he never spoke a word, not to them. But he would speak to me. 'You would've died a dozen times but for me,' he said, and I can't claim him a liar. 'You owe me a dozen debts, old friend. But I'll only ask for settlement of two.'"

A sudden, deep weariness swept through me then, causing my head to dip and bringing another groan to my lips. Either through the effects of his pipe or the gathering dusk, everything was growing dark. Sir Althus was a distant echo when he spoke again.

"Only two favours, that's what he asked of me. First, that it be me who wielded the sword when he received the King's justice. 'I'd prefer death at the hands of a friend, if you're willing.'

"I've never been a shirker, Alwyn. Duty is duty and it's what I'm sworn to. Something you'd do well to remember: only ever give an oath if you're willing to keep it, even unto death. A false oath has no value and the only reward it brings is the distrust and enmity of others, usually those with more wealth and power than you'll ever have. So, if you give your word, make sure you keep it. As I kept it when I took the head of a man I once loved as a brother. As I'm keeping it now. Y'see, Deckin's second favour was that I keep watch for a youth of his acquaintance, a lad clever enough to have escaped the slaughter at Moss Mill but, he suspected, not so clever as to stay well clear of this place."

Firm hands took hold of my chin, lifting my gaze to regard his shifting, fuzzy-edged face. Despite my growing confusion, I could discern the grim regret in his eyes and voice. "Deckin asked that I get you away from here, find a place for you in my household, but thanks to your adventures last night that's impossible now. I'm afraid it niggles my conscience a mite too much to give safe harbour to one who murders a soldier."

His words stirred a flurry of terror deep inside me, but it was a contained thing, kept small by the pipe and my pain-wracked, starved state. "But don't worry," Sir Althus continued, voice even more distant now so that it seemed he spoke from the far end of a very long tunnel. At the time the words made only slight purchase on my mind, so in penning this account I have been forced to guess much of it. However, I'd lay a good-sized wager as to its accuracy if Sir Althus were in a position to verify it, which, students of history will be aware, he certainly is not.

"Neither will I drag you before the new duke for judgment," is what I believe he told me as I slipped rapidly towards insensibility. "That bitch he's taken a liking to will surely confirm your membership of Deckin's band then there will be nothing I can do for you. No, it's the Pit Mines for you, my lad. By fortunate chance the chainsman was already making his rounds to collect Lord Duhbos' dregs from the dungeons. He gets twenty sheks for every benighted soul he delivers to the Pit, so was easily persuaded to take another. That fellow who was so keen to gut you will kick off something fierce, I'm sure, but a silver sovereign should quiet him, especially when I've told him where you've been sent. After a while in the Pit you might come to reflect that the rope and a gizzard slitting would have been preferable in the end . . ."

I know he said more but it's forever lost to me now. I recall watching boots merging with a fast-descending black cloud as his voice became a mournful, wordless dirge. I wouldn't see Sir Althus Levalle again for several years and when I did, despite the debt I owe him and in contrast to the pity stirred when I think of Deckin, it was with a great welling of anger. It's true that Sir Althus saved me, so I shouldn't hate his memory, but he also damned me, and so I do.

CHAPTER THIRTEEN

I awoke to a song, not particularly tuneful and sung in a language I didn't know, but nonetheless cast forth with an enthusiasm that matched its volume. I blinked blood-encrusted eyes, raising my head only for it to be jerked against something hard as the surface on which I lay gave an abrupt shift. My vision remained blurred and gritted but the swaying floor and creaking squeal of an axle told me I was on a cart of some kind. The stench of sweat and stale shit also told me I wasn't alone.

"The sleeping princess isn't dead after all," a voice commented, and my occluded sight swung towards a pale, blurred oval. The voice was female but somewhat grating, the accent telling of origins beyond the Marches. *One of the southern duchies*, I thought.

"Might be another one gone in the head, though," the voice went on as I continued to regard its owner with a gaping mouth and unfocused gaze. The face loomed closer and I discerned a frowning brow above small, piercing eyes. "Are you simple?" she asked with slow deliberation. "Do you know words?"

"I know fucking words," I muttered as annoyance cut through my confusion. I tried to raise my hand to shove this inquisitor away only to find it constrained by a manacle fixed to a short chain. The sharp pain as the iron band bit into my wrist brought a hiss to my lips and a slight moisture to my eyes which had the fortunate effect of clearing my vision enough to discern my surroundings.

My initial puzzlement at finding the sky cut into a series of uneven squares became sour chagrin as I realised I was peering at it through a cage. The bars were formed of flat iron strips affixed into a box, the joints secured with thick bolts. My experienced gaze quickly sought out patches of rust, finding only a few, which meant this cage wouldn't be easily busted. Woodland passed by on either side of the cart which, I noted with dismay, was escorted by six mounted men-at-arms in unfamiliar livery of grey and black. I found my attention momentarily captured by the woods, finding them composed mostly of tall pines jutting up from a blanket of frosted ferns. This was not the Shavine Forest I knew so well.

I swung my now-clear eyes towards the woman who had greeted my awakening, finding her in fact little more than a girl. Her hair was a mass of matted black spikes framing oval features that might have been pretty, but it was hard to tell under the mask of grime. I found the rest of her too scrawny to pique my lust, not that I was capable of such diversions at that juncture. Beside her lay the source of much of the smell I found so offensive despite my damaged nose – a very large man who seemed to be as wide as he was tall. He lay in filthy and corpulent somnolence, chins and belly wobbling every time the cart traversed a rut. He was clad in a thin covering of thread-bare rags but, judging by the wisps of vapour rising from his slack mouth, had nonetheless contrived to survive the cold.

"I call him the Sleeping Boar," the spiky-haired girl told me in her grating accent. "Wagered Silent Simp here you'd be the first one to wake, not that he took the bet." She inclined her head at the other occupant of the cart, the sight of him causing me to jerk my chains in surprise.

"Raith!"

The Caerith barely seemed to register my greeting, his attention entirely fixed on the bulky figure of the drover of this cage on wheels. His shaggy head lifted as he let out a fresh, even louder outburst of song in a strong but discordant voice that echoed alien words through the trees.

"He does that a lot," the girl said, grimacing as she shifted to alleviate an ache in her back. "You really don't want to tell him to shut it, tempting though it is. He's got a hefty stick and isn't shy about using it."

"Raith," I said again, straining against my manacles to reach out to the Caerith. This time he turned to me and I found myself confronted by a hollowed-cheeked shadow of the man I knew. The crossed pattern of marks across his face appeared more livid now, a crimson contrast to the unhealthy, waxy sheen of his skin. He wore a tattered, sleeveless jerkin, arms that had once been thick with muscle now noticeably thinner.

"Old friends are you?" the girl enquired. "Hope you're more talkative than he is. Just sits there staring at the chainsman all day. Won't eat the scraps we're given neither. It's like he wants to die."

"Deckin . . . " I began, finding I had little more to say, for it was clear Raith either already knew what I had to tell him, or didn't care. I saw only the vaguest semblance of reason in his gaze, but still, with no other sources of information to hand, felt the need to press him.

"Lorine," I said. "Did you see . . . ?"

"She cut him," the Caerith said, his voice a flat monotone. "Opened him all the way up."

"Who?" I squinted at him in bafflement. "Who did she cut?"

Raith, however, no longer felt obliged to provide me answers. Blinking, he turned and resumed his fascinated observance of our drover's broad back. As I grunted in defeat and drew back, I noticed that, for the first time I could remember, Raith was not wearing his necklace of charms.

"How long since Castle Duhbos?" I asked the girl.

She settled her cautious but curious eyes on me for a time before consenting to answer. "Three days since they bundled you into the cart along with Silent Simp and this lard-bucket." She jabbed a toe at the flaccid bulk of the Sleeping Boar. "I've been freezing my arse in this thing for three weeks now. Started to think I'd have no company."

She gave a humourless smile and I glimpsed yellow teeth before her mouth closed quickly and the scrutiny returned. I knew her as an outlaw without hearing a word of her story; she just had that look, the part-feral, barely contained energy common to youthful thieves. I took some gratification from knowing she would want out of this cage as much as I did. It always paid to have help if you wanted to slip a chain.

"Alwyn," I told her, resting my back against the bars and offering a smile I instantly regretted for it opened some of my cuts.

"Alwyn what?" she enquired.

"Just Alwyn."

"So, Alwyn the Just, then?"

She showed her yellow teeth again in a grin as my face took on a withering expression.

"When they pushed you in here, I heard mention of Deckin Scarl," she said, voice lowered a little and casting a wary eye at the fur-covered bulk of the humming chainsman. "Is it true? You ran with him?"

I entertained the notion of lying again, but dishonesty now seemed a pointless indulgence. Deckin and the rest were all dead and Raith and I, the only survivors of that legendary pack of villains, on our way to a short life in the Pit Mines.

"Ran with him," I said. "Stole with him. Killed with him on occasion." I tried to shrug but the gesture just tightened my chain again. It was fixed to the cart's bed by a substantial iron bracket which, like the bars, was mostly rust free. A sudden anger had me delivering a kick to the bracket, hauling hard on the chain in the vain hope I might see it splinter the surrounding wood.

"Don't!" the girl hissed sharply, eyes snapping to the chainsman's bulk in warning. I noticed that the fellow's song had diminished to a hum and he cocked his head a little so I caught a glimpse of a florid, mottled brow. The girl's alarm and my well-honed eye for a threat caused me to abandon my struggles, lowering my head and sitting quiet until the chainsman turned his head and resumed his song.

"When the song stops," the girl advised softly, "that's when you have to worry."

Definitely pretty under all that muck, I decided as my anger seeped away and I took a more discerning look at her face. *And clever with it*, I mused further, seeing the shrewdness in her eyes. Appearing stupid is always the hardest skill for clever people to learn and it seemed to me this one had never bothered to try.

"I introduced myself," I reminded her. "You didn't. That's rude."

She didn't answer straight away, instead sitting in silent contemplation of me with unblinking, clever eyes which, I noticed, were a pale shade of blue. "Toria," she told me finally. "Don't ask me where I'm from or why I'm in this cage." Another bland, yellow-toothed smile. "It's none of your fucking business. Suffice to say, Alwyn the un-Just, I'm not a whore so don't expect anything beyond conversation."

"The thought hadn't occurred," I replied honestly. I bent my knees to inch closer to her, wincing with the effort of working life back into stiff muscle. Lowering my head, I spoke in a murmur so the words would be missed by our singing captor. "I assume, dear lady, you don't much like being chained up in here. Nor do I imagine the Pit Mines offer an appetising prospect as to future longevity."

"That's a nice bit of word-spinning," Toria told me with a half-sneer. "How's about you just say what the fuck is on your mind?"

"I'm saying I've got no desire to end up in the Pits so's I can spend the next few years being worked to death. Between here and there we're bound to find at least one chance to loose these chains. Be easier all round if we take it together." I glanced at Raith before adding in a doubtful mutter, "All three of us."

"For a fellow who's only been awake a few minutes, you seem awful certain about our prospects."

"Time is our friend." I tried a smile of my own, then stopped as it brought forth a bead of blood from my mangled lips. Spitting, I added, "For time brings opportunity. We just have to be ready for it."

"Meaning you don't have a plan, just an intention." She shook her head in faintly amused disdain. "Martyrs save me from ambitious men who think the world will always turn to accommodate their schemes."

"That's some pretty word-spinning of your own. And what's wrong with ambition?"

"Well, for a start, it put you in here with me, didn't it?"

I lowered my gaze, a sudden weariness pulling a sigh from my lips. "No," I muttered in resignation, shuffling back from her. "It was sentiment and folly that did that."

She watched me huddle into myself, hands clamped into fists as I lay on my side to curve my body around them so they wouldn't freeze. I knew it wouldn't be wise to sleep, for I might not wake if the cold grew worse, but fatigue had descended with such sudden, irresistible force I felt myself being dragged inevitably towards slumber.

"Oi!" Toria's foot, a small thing clad in a shoe of thin leather that nevertheless possessed an irksome hardness, jabbed my buttock. "Sleep only when the cart stops. The chainsman lights a fire come nightfall. If you don't beg he might even toss you some food."

A grunt of dismissal rose and faded from my lips, for mention of food will birth hope in any starved soul. But still, the weariness gripped me hard, pulling me towards the black welcome of oblivion.

"The guards," Toria added in a whisper, her tone containing an insistent weight that had me raising my head.

"What about them?"

"They're lazy. He's not." She jerked her head at the chainsman before settling her shrewd gaze on mine. "Hardly seems to sleep. But these guards that follow us, I doubt they'd give a tinker's ball if this cart makes it to the Pits full or empty."

The grunt finally escaped my lips, but it was one of amusement rather than dismissal. "Seems you've been harbouring ambitions of your own."

She snorted a laugh before casting a wary glance at the chainsman. Before settling back, she added in a faint murmur, "You're right. The Pits don't appeal. Not at all." Seeing my head dip as the weariness closed in again, she jabbed her toe to my behind once more. "No sleeping! Wait for nightfall. Rest assured I'll be kicking your arse every minute till then. No need to thank me."

The next few days provided ample evidence for Toria's observations. The guards were notably lax in their duties, riding along at too far a remove from the cart, which I guessed owed much to the stench rising from our corpulent, unwaking companion. They also kept only a desultory watch on the surrounding forest, spending much of the day guiding their horses with heads bowed or engaging each other in dull conversation. I noted how they were all older than most soldiers of my experience, not one with fewer than thirty years under his belt by my estimation. They had the scars and hardened looked of men with a good deal of campaigning behind them but, from the unkempt look of their armour and weapons, I deduced it had been quite some time since they had actually been required to fight.

"Old, tired soldiers are my favourite kind," I muttered to Toria one evening. "Men such as these put great stock in their own survival. Having risked much in their youth, they find their courage has waned along with their illusions of glory."

"So?" Toria enquired, cheek bulging as she chewed on a carrot tossed to us by the chainsman. He squatted before a large fire, positioned close enough to the cart to afford some measure of warmth to its occupants. However, to enjoy its glow we were obliged to strain our chains, pressing against the Sleeping Boar's bulk and suffering his odours in the process. Raith didn't join us in this endeavour, nor did he consent to eat anything despite my urging. Instead, he just continued to stare at the chainsman who, for his part, responded to the scrutiny with complete indifference.

"So," I replied, taking a bite from my half of carrot, a vegetable I had never much cared for that now tasted sweeter than any honey cake, "should they find themselves presented with a choice between risking their person or allowing us to flee, it's odds on they'll choose the former."

The chainsman was sparing in the fare he provided, just enough to keep us living and not enough to build strength. I suspected Toria remained reasonably vital because her frame required comparatively little sustenance. But every day spent in this cart weakened me and made escape an ever more distant dream, albeit one I refused to abandon.

"So we need to present a danger," Toria said with a sceptical frown. "Not much chance of that."

"Danger needn't come from us." I glanced around at the forest, which still consisted of mostly pines, rendered tall, anonymous sentinels in the gloom. Throughout the journey I had heard little beyond a distant wolf howl and the nocturnal scrabble and shriek of badger or fox. It was a wild place, to be sure, but not wild enough. "Any notion of where we are, exactly?" I asked Toria.

"Exactly? No. But I'd guess we're fifty miles from the Pits. They sit at the junction between the duchies of Alberis, Althiene and the Shavine Marches. Makes it a handy place for nobles to dump their undesirables."

I fell to silence, munching my way through the rest of the carrot and trying to dredge up every scrap of knowledge I could about the Marches' eastern regions. I had travelled a fair deal within the duchy but never outside of it and rarely more than a few miles from the security of the forest.

"The Nehlis Swamp," I said when my memory happened upon a fragment of conversation with Klant, another old soldier who had fetched up in Deckin's band after a falling out with his captain. "There was a battle there, early in the Duchy Wars. Lot of men drowned due to their armour or somesuch. It covers the western bank of the Siltern River for many miles. I'd guess anyone making for the Pit Mines will need to either skirt it or trek through it."

"So we run off into the swamp and these lazy bastards are too fearful to follow." Toria's eyes, shining bright and keen in the firelight, fixed on the chainsman's bulky form. "Might be true of them, but not *him*. That's even if we can slip these chains and get out of this cage."

I settled my own gaze on the chainsman. As usual he had his back to us, humming as was his wont. The soldiers never shared his fire, preferring to pitch their own camp several yards away. Nor had I witnessed them exchange a single word with this man throughout the journey. Folk of his profession were typically shunned by churls but I hadn't known they were also despised by soldiers. Noting how they tended to avoid his gaze, I suspected their shunning owed as much to fear as custom. I had gained only a few glimpses of the chainsman's face, finding it an oddly discoloured mask of red blotches and pale, near-white skin. I wondered if he might be victim of some disease but he appeared healthy enough and certainly he didn't want for food, sparing as he was with his scraps. Also, he never spoke. The only sound that escaped his lips came in the form of indecipherable song, which made me ponder the contradiction of his lack of facility for it.

I asked Toria if she had any inkling of the language with which he sang these ear-paining ditties. Her gaze took on a wary cast and she shot the chainsman a brief glance before replying in a faint voice, "Caerith."

"He's Caerith?" I asked, drawing a glare from her as surprise added volume to my voice. I looked at Raith, seeing for the first time how similar the pattern of marks across his face was to the chainsman's disfigurement. I had assumed that, as all Caerith hailed from the same region beyond the southern mountains, they would share the same colouring. Also, the language of the chainsman's song felt very different on the ear than the more melodious tongue I had heard from Raith's lips.

The novelty of finding myself now a captive of one of Raith's kind almost brought a smile to my misshapen lips along with a good deal of conjecture as to how this heathen had contrived to end up a chainsman in the kingdom of Albermaine. Clearly, this was an interesting fellow, but experience has taught me that the more interesting someone is, the more danger they are likely to pose. Even then as I neared the end of my callow youth, I sensed a great deal of danger in this interesting soul.

"There'll be a chance," I insisted, more to myself than Toria. "There always is. Just a second or two, a fleeting thing that may be gone before we see it, so be watchful . . . " I stopped speaking as the chainsman's humming abruptly faded. He cocked his head in the same way he had after my first awakening in the cart. I was certain our plotting had been too softly spoken for him to have any chance of having heard but saw a knowing amusement in the half-smile I glimpsed before the chainsman turned his mottled face away and resumed his humming.

"Alwyn . . . " Toria began in a worried whisper, falling silent as I shot her a glare.

"Watch for the chance," I told her, hissing the words as a command. "It'll come. Just wait."

The next morning, I awoke with a start, roused by the squeal of the cage's door being hauled open. The air was even more chilled than usual and I shuddered as I took in the sight of the landscape beyond the bars. The view had changed now, the trees replaced by the befogged, grass-spiked flatness of a marsh. Just a few hundred paces from the road this marsh would, I knew, become a bog where no sane man in armour would dare tread, but a desperate outlaw surely would.

The longed-for prospect of escape caused my heart to beat faster as I took in the sight of the opened cage, my excitement soon dimmed by the realisation that my chains were still firmly in place. Toria lay next to the Sleeping Boar, her features twisting in the manner that told of an imminent waking. Raith, however, was absent. Also, I could no longer hear the chainsman's song.

"*Caihr teasla?*"

The voice snapped my gaze to the two figures beyond the cage. The chainsman stood over a kneeling Raith. It was jarring to see a man I had feared for years so cowed, head lowered and shoulders hunched, very much like a child expecting a blow from an angry parent. His expression retained the same wide-eyed immobility whereas the chainsman's features were set in a hard mask of contempt. For the first time I could see his face in full. The red marks that discoloured his pale skin were far more extensive than those of his fellow Caerith. They stretched from brow to neck, resembling flame in its chaotic pattern and the stark contrast they made with his skin. I found it hard to age him, seeing wrinkles around his eyes and mouth but no trace of grey in the shaggy black mass of his hair.

Leaning closer to Raith, the captor raised something in his hand that gave a faint rattle as he shook it next to the outlaw's ear: Raith's charm necklace. "*Caihr teusla?*" the chainsman repeated, and I could hear the taunt in his voice. Whatever this question was, it was clear he already knew the answer.

Straightening, the chainsman spoke a jumble of words in this foreign tongue too fast for my ears to catch. They clearly held some meaning for Raith, however, for his expression finally changed. Closing his eyes, he drew in a long shuddering breath before raising his face to the chainsman. When he opened his eyes again they blazed with a bright, unwavering defiance and the words he spoke came from between clenched teeth.

"*Ihs Doenlisch kurihm ihsa gaelihr.*"

The contempt on the chainsman's face slipped abruptly into anger, though not before I saw a spasm of fear pass over it. His fist came down hard, striking Raith's cheek. I heard bone break under the force of the blow as the outlaw reeled then collapsed onto the track. He coughed blood while the chainsman shifted to plant both feet on either side of his head, leaning low to voice a question in the same baffling tongue.

"*Vearath?*"

Raith continued to shudder on the ground for a time, spitting out a couple of teeth until he gathered a few ragged breaths and contrived to lever himself up a fraction.

"*Vearath?!*" the chainsman demanded in a shout.

However, instead of turning to him, Raith craned his neck to regard me. The silent, terror-stricken man he had been for the duration of this journey was gone now and he was once again the Raith I knew, his gaze uncowed and steady.

"Paths to walk . . . " he choked, blood dribbling down his chin. "Fates to meet . . . "

The chainsman let out a feral grunt of rage then, both hands descending to clamp Raith's head in a fierce grip. The veins on the chainsman's hands and wrists bulged as he exerted unrelenting pressure. I had seen many men die in different ways, but none like this. I shut my eyes before the end, but the wet crunch of Raith's skull surrendering to the chainsman's strength sent a convulsive shudder through me. Had there been anything in my stomach to disgorge, I surely would have.

"Fuck me." Opening my eyes, I found Toria staring at the sight beyond the bars in stark fascination. "He hasn't done that before."

I forced myself to watch the chainsman drag Raith's corpse into the marsh grass fringing the road, hearing a dim splash as it was consigned to the bog. When he reappeared, the chainsman paused on the verge, face grim as he looked at the charm necklace in his hand, holding it up to examine the bronze trinkets fastened to the cord. I saw how his attention lingered longest on the crow skull, but not with any great interest. Soon his features tightened into a contemptuous sneer and he cast the necklace into the marsh to join its murdered owner.

As he stomped back to the cart and swung the door closed, I heard him voice a harsh mutter in the unknown tongue: "*Ishlichen.*" It had the timbre of an insult or a curse and the chainsman's features retained a forbidding glower as he moved to the front of the cart, resuming his usual position on the board. Sadly, his apparently soured mood didn't prevent him from quickly resuming his song. As he snapped the reins and set the dray to motion, his voice rose high and more gratingly discordant than ever.

Chapter Fourteen

I t took another three days for our chance to appear, arriving in the form of an unasked-for gift that nonetheless brought a great blossoming of gratitude to my breast.

"He's dead." Toria's toe delivered a series of jabs to the Sleeping Boar's taut belly, drawing forth the foulest and most prolonged fart his otherwise inert bulk had yet produced. We had woken, shivering with the dawn, to find the usual wisps of vapour were no longer rising from our companion's fleshy face. The rise and fall of his mound-like gut had also ceased. His skin certainly had the look of a corpse, pale and veiny at the extremities, dark with pooled blood where it met the cart bed. However, I had seen folk in a similar state who would spring to frightful alertness even as their grave was being dug.

Straining my chains to get a closer look at the Boar's features, lips slack and drawn back from his teeth in the signature grin of death, I took relieved satisfaction in the knowledge that he wouldn't be sitting up again. Had hunger and cold not combined to stoke my desperation, I would surely have taken more heed of Raith's fate and what it said of our captor. However, the necessity of removing the Boar's corpse from this cart presented an opportunity I was determined not to forgo.

"He's dead!" I repeated Toria's declaration, raising my voice to cast it at the chainsman's broad back. He continued to hum, failing to turn as the cart trundled on.

"Oi!" I shouted, paining my not-yet-healed throat to cut through the drone of his humming. "This fucker's dead! You hear me? You can't leave us in here with a dead man!"

This brought a trickle of laughter from our escort, riding closer now that the road had narrowed in the wetlands. "Least you'll have plenty to eat now!" one called back. He was the oldest and therefore most haggard of the group, his craggy face marked by the blossomed veins and sallowness that told of too much drink. For the most part, the soldiers regarded Toria and I with indifference save for a contemptuous glance or two, but this one was fond of assailing us with attempts at wit, usually at night after the brandy bottle had been passed around. He gave a cackle of amusement and started to voice another barb. Whatever gem he had been about to offer would forever remain unknown, for his mouth abruptly clamped shut when the chainsman brought the cart to a halt.

The soldiers quickly trotted their mounts to the verge, putting a good distance between themselves and the cart. They had done the same before Raith's demise, bespeaking a habituation to the chainsman's ways or perhaps dire experience of what might occur if they interfered with them.

The cart swayed and creaked as he climbed down, moving to the rear to work a heavy key in the brick-sized lock that secured the door to this cage. As the door swung open I saw little expression on the chainsman's face beyond the slight frown of a man engaged in an oft-repeated chore. To my surprise, I found the most disconcerting thing about him now was not his face but the fact that all vestige of song had disappeared. Not even the faintest hum came from his lips as he leaned into the cart and took firm hold of Toria's manacles.

I expected some growled warning, or at least a glare, but the chainsman removed the manacles with a quick turn of the key and a few deft flicks of his wrists. Stepping back with the manacles in hand, he gestured for Toria to climb out, which she did with some difficulty, teeth gritted at the effort of shifting a body unused to movement. Her feet had barely touched the ground before the Caerith's hand fell on her shoulder, forcing her to her knees. I lost sight of them as he crouched and heard the rattle of chains being looped through the spokes of a wheel.

Straightening, the chainsman leaned into the cart to remove my manacles. His expression changed as he went about the task, shifting from mostly blank caution to clear if muted amusement. I saw his lips curl as he met my eye, hands working with automatic precision to free my wrists. My confidence slipped several notches as I read his expression as that of a man entertained by his own joke.

Stepping back, he inclined his shaggy head in invitation. I had tried to work my leg and arm muscles during my days of captivity, flexing them whenever our captor's attention was elsewhere, but it still hurt a good deal to clamber free of the cage, as did the feel of frozen earth on my rag-bound feet.

Not yet, I cautioned myself, hunching over as various aches assailed me while I cast brief glances at the surrounding country. It was all the same, however, just grass and fog with nary a tree or hill in sight. At least this made my choice of route easier. *Wait until he tries to put the chain back on. Sit nice and quiet, like a defeated captive, then a swift butt to the nose and I'm away.*

I couldn't stop my gaze settling on Toria, just for an instant. She sat on the cold ground, arms and legs arranged so that it seemed she embraced the cartwheel, staring at me with hard resignation. I took some comfort from that look, the shared knowledge that only one of us would be escaping the cage, for I saw no accusation in her gaze. Still, the flare of guilt at leaving her behind was strong, and unexpected.

"Here."

I started at the sound of the chainsman's voice. It had an odd inflection, the accent lilting and unfamiliar. The shock of hearing him speak Albermainish prevented me from catching the key he tossed me. It evaded my fumbling hands and fell to the rutted road, forcing me to strain my protesting back to retrieve it. Looking up I saw the Caerith pointing a steady finger at the Sleeping Boar's corpse. "You do not want to share with him," the chainsman said in his oddly accented voice, the words spoken with the precision of one employing a language they hadn't been born to. "Then you drag him out."

Having girded myself for violence, this sudden absence of chains or constraining hands left me in a state of baffled indecision. The chainsman stood regarding me with his fire-streaked, faintly amused face cocked at an inquisitive angle. He was a good six paces away, a decent gap for a lad well used to dodging lunging men.

"Yes," he said, the curve of his lips broadening into a full smile, "you can run." He gestured to the surrounding marsh. "I will not follow. Nor will they." He jerked his head at the mounted guards. I noted how their lack of amusement contrasted sharply with his and they made no move to trot their horses closer. I knew these were the kind of men for whom cruelty was recreation, but their demeanour was fearful rather than eager. They sat still in their saddles, regarding this unfolding drama with the wary but unwavering gaze of men unable to look away from an ugly spectacle.

They expect me to die here, I realised, shifting my attention back to the chainsman. He continued to smile, making no effort to come closer. "The swamp is closest in that direction," he said, pointing over my shoulder. "You will reach it after a mile fighting through wet ground. There you will wander the edges of the swamp and slowly freeze. After a time, you will try to return to the road but you will not reach it. The cold will kill you first, unless you choose to drown yourself. Or perhaps not." His mouth twitched as he contained a laugh. "Perhaps you will be found by a kindly fisherman out checking his lines. Perhaps this generous soul will drag you aboard his boat and take you to his nice warm cottage."

The laugh escaped him then, a shrill giggle that brought to mind a half-strangled cat. When the laugh faded, he lowered a hand to Toria's head, her features bunching in fearful disgust as he played gentle fingers through the matted spikes of her hair. The memory of what his hands had done to Raith no doubt burned as bright in her mind as it did in mine.

"But know," the chainsman went on, "that if you do run, she dies.

I will not kill her. But I will not feed her and she will get no water. It is five days to the Pit Mines." The angle of his head grew a little more acute, eyebrows raising in a genuinely curious arch. "Do you think she will survive that long?"

His humour had evaporated now, replaced by an intense focus, his eyes boring into me in a manner that recalled Deckin whenever he fell to pondering his next scheme. The outcome of this test was of great interest to him. Also, the grim familiarity with which the guards regarded this drama told me I was not the first to be so tested. How many bodies littered the marsh flanking this road? How many other desperate fools fled rather than stay to save a companion they barely knew?

There's always a chance, I reminded myself as my eyes inevitably slipped back to Toria. She refused to look at me, head lowered and eyes closed, sparing me the sight of her fear. The fact that this kindness, if kindness it was, left the choice entirely in my own hands sent a brief spasm of resentment through me. But for her I wouldn't have lingered. But for her I would have risked the chilly, near-certain doom of the marsh and the swamp. I would make my own way. I would swim the fucking swamp if I had to and the Scourge take kindly fishermen.

Swallowing a groan, I took a firmer grip on the key the chainsman had tossed to me and moved on wavering legs towards the cart. Hauling the Sleeping Boar's increasingly odorous corpse from the cart to the road was not easy in my reduced state, requiring long minutes of effort with no assistance from the chainsman or his onlooking escort.

"Put it in the marsh," he instructed when the body finally fell free of the cart, birthing another gust of stinking gas as it connected with the hard ground. "This is the king's highway and should not be besmirched with outlaw remains."

I did as he bid, the effort causing me to stumble into a knee-deep bog from which I had to squelch my way free before completing the business of dragging the Sleeping Boar's reeking bulk into the grass. I was destined to never discover his name or what crimes had consigned him to the cart. But whoever he had been, and whatever his misdeeds, I couldn't imagine he deserved to die alongside strangers and be cast on to the side of the road like so much refuse. I had seen dead dogs receive more respect.

My exhaustion was such that I had to crawl back to the cart, hauling myself into the cage with hands I couldn't feel. I fell at the first attempt, drawing another shrill giggle from the chainsman. Now his test had produced a result he seemed more given to amusement, finding a great deal in my wasted state.

Leaning close as I dragged myself level with the cart bed, he put his lips close to my ear, whispering in his overly precise intonations: "They almost always choose to run. Even those with kin chained to the wheel. The outlaw's fear of chains usually wins out. But you stayed."

I felt his hand on my neck as he leaned closer, finding his touch icier than the midwinter air. "This does not redeem you," he told me. "You will find tests aplenty in the Pits, boy. I doubt they will redeem you either. We both know you did not stay for her. You were just too smart to run." He spoke in little more than a whisper, although it felt like a shout when he added, "Hostler wants to know if you are still an ingrate. I think I will tell him you most certainly are."

He shoved me the rest of the way into the cart, pushing Toria in then fixing our manacles in place with swift efficiency and slamming the door closed. I matched stares with him through the bars for an instant, his red and white face impassive now but for the mutual understanding that would in time seal both our fates. I had known bad men before, the vicious, the sadistic, the greedy, but a truly evil soul was, so far, beyond my experience. Now I beheld one and knew what I beheld.

CHAPTER FIFTEEN

I had been hearing tales of the Pit Mines all my life, for outlaws often fear them more than they fear the rope. A century or so ago one of King Tomas's more pragmatic forebears found himself presented with twin dilemmas. A rich seam of iron ore had been discovered on the eastern fringe of the Shavine Marches. Digging such a prize commodity from the earth required shafts of previously unseen depth and many days of dangerous labour certain to rouse the local churls to outright revolt should they be pressed to the task. However, thanks to yet another round of dynastic feuding and accompanying battle, this clever-minded king came into possession of several hundred captives who could be safely condemned as rebels. Killing such a number all at once would forever see his legacy besmirched by the title of butcher, an appellation that troubles some kings more than others. His genius lay in finding a solution to both problems by marrying one to another: the rebels would mine the ore. Over the succeeding years, as the rebels died off, fresh recruits to what soon became known as the Pit Mines were sought out from every duchy in the kingdom. Typically, inmates of the Pits consisted of malcontents and outlaws who lacked sufficient reputation to make their execution a worthy example. Toria and I were therefore perfect candidates.

I hadn't known what to expect upon arriving at the Pit Mines, but the sight of a bland wooden stockade barely twenty feet high was unexpected. It snaked across an undulating, treeless landscape for several hundred paces in either direction, terminating in the south at a stone castle of modest dimensions and grim appearance. The chainsman brought the cart to a halt in front of the tower guarding the castle's outer bailey, dismounting to unlock the cage and undo our chains. The guards who had escorted us throughout the journey all trotted their horses into the castle without a word or a glance at the chainsman, who didn't deign to take note of their departure.

The small flare of opportunity I felt as I followed Toria from the cage proved short-lived when I took note of the dozen or more soldiers standing close by, most bearing halberds but a couple holding cross-bows. A stocky man in sergeant's livery came forward, offering the chainsman the briefest glance of acknowledgement before turning an unimpressed gaze on his cargo.

"Just two?" he asked, voice clipped and impatient. Like the guards on the road he didn't meet the Caerith's eye and stood well clear of his reach.

"I started with four." The chainsman's bulky shoulders moved in a shrug. "Winter brings a poor harvest and the new duke of the Marches is keen on hangings at present."

The sergeant was plainly keen to conclude this business but an appraising glance at Toria and I gave him pause. "Can't give you full price for these," he stated, a grimace to his blunt features. "They won't last a week the state they're in."

"You are wrong," the chainsman replied. He said nothing else, his gaze lingering on the sergeant until the fellow consented to meet his eye. I could tell the sergeant was a man well used to authority and the violence inherent in his role here, but he exhibited much the same response to the chainsman as the guards on the road. Still, either through pride or stupidity he wouldn't allow himself to be cowed, jaw clenching and brow darkening as he asked, "How so?"

The chainsman took no obvious offence at having his word ques-tioned, instead pointing a finger at me and replying in a mild tone, "This one will last years and eventually attempt to escape. You should watch him closely. This one—" his finger shifted to Toria "—is not so . . . significant. But she is stronger than she seems." His hand shifted away from us, extending an open palm to the sergeant. "In either case, their labour here will produce profit for your lord and therefore I require payment in full."

I saw a small war play out on the sergeant's face – muscles twitched and creases deepened as he fought the instinct to escalate this disagreement. Hatred and fear battled each other until the latter, usually the strongest in my experience, won out and the sergeant reached for the purse on his belt.

Upon receiving his forty sheks the chainsman turned back to his cart, then hesitated, turning to me. I wasn't aware of staring at him in a particularly challenging manner. The days since his test on the road had seen me receive even less food than before, leaving little room in my head for more than hunger. However, he must have discerned something in my bearing for he stepped closer, the flame-like marks on his forehead narrowing as he frowned. But for my exhaustion and general lethargy, I might then have recognised his expression as the fear that arises from having made a very serious misjudgement, but that realisation came later. In that moment I could only return his scrutiny with dull-eyed indifference, my mind fixed on the possibility that these new captors might consent to feed me.

"A moment," the chainsman said to the sergeant, hefting his own purse. "I will buy this one back—"

"Can't," the sergeant interrupted with curt but obvious satisfaction. He held up a tally stick sliced with two fresh notches. "Already marked my stick, see? His lordship's a terror for checking the sticks every day."

I saw the chainsman crouch a little, the red marks on his face seeming to take on a deeper hue. "I will pay double," he said, loosening the ties on the purse.

This caused the sergeant to pause, but even the prospect of extra coin wasn't sufficient to deny him the pleasure of frustrating the chainsman. Fear usually wins out over hatred, it's true, but one always breeds more of the other.

"Too late," the sergeant told him with evident relish. "Now," he went on, casting a meaningful glance at the soldiers nearby, "I believe it's time you took your heathen Caerith arse elsewhere. You know my lads don't like it when you linger."

A faint hiss escaped the chainsman's lips as he cast a final, frustrated glare in my direction. He said something then, a short phrase in the same tongue he had exchanged with Raith: "*Eornlisch dien tira.*"

Despite my preoccupation with imminent starvation and the cold that gripped all reaches of my body, and the fact that I had no way of parsing his meaning, these words contrived to send an additional chill through me. Also, the mystery of what he had said in the aftermath of his test added an edge to my fear. *Hostler wants to know if you are still an ingrate.*

I found myself instinctively shying away from the implication contained in those words, much as I retreated from the evil I had seen in the chainsman's gaze when he closed the cage. I had no inkling of how he had learned Hostler's fate, or the term with which he liked to denigrate me, and some primal sense warned me against pondering the strangeness of it all. I could only be sure of one thing: this man's evil and his capacity for knowing things he couldn't know were bound up together in the same ugly, flame-faced package. I wanted no more part of it and, when he finally consented to stalk back to his cart and climb aboard, I actually felt a swell of relief in the knowledge that I would soon be cast into the comparatively safe embrace of the Pit Mines.

"Pay heed to me, boy!" the sergeant snapped, dragging my attention from the sight of the departing chainsman with a hard cuff to the top of my head. The sergeant stood back, looking over this pair of emaciated wretches with a caustic eye. "Forty sheks," he muttered with a shake of his head before coughing and straightening a little to continue in the flat tone of the oft-spoken speech.

"Know this and mark it well for it won't be told to you again," he began. "Under Crown law your person is now indentured for life in the service of Lord Eldurm Gulatte, warden by the king's grace of Castle Loftlin and the Mines Royal, better known as the Pit Mines to scum like you. Lord Eldurm is renowned for his generous spirit and the largesse he shows to those in his charge, provided they obey the very wise rules set down by his esteemed ancestor one hundred years ago. First, work well and you will be fed. Second, cause trouble and you will be flogged. Third, cause trouble for a second time and you will be hanged. Fourth, make any attempt to flee your obligation to honest labour and you will be hanged. Other than that—" he gave an empty smile he had surely offered to countless unfortunates "—you filthy, lawless buggers are free to do what the fuck you like. Now isn't that grand?"

He turned to beckon a pair of guards forward. Like the soldiers on the road they all wore the same grey and black livery, though they were of a markedly less cowed demeanour. The chainsman's presence had muted the habitual brutality of the others but this lot faced no such constraints. Recognising the increased risk, I lowered my gaze to a respectfully subservient angle, nudging Toria to do the same when she continued to let her too-clever eyes roam.

"Put them in the woodshed and take a couple of days to feed them up before you shove them in," the sergeant instructed the two guards. "They won't last the week otherwise and his lordship's been griping about the losses lately."

The shed they pushed us into was small and cramped with piled logs, obliging us to huddle together for warmth. The guards had surprised me by tossing us a couple of blankets along with a decent supply of bread, cheese and water.

"Don't gulp it all at once," I cautioned Toria as the door slammed shut and she began to tear into the bread. "A belly that's been empty for so long needs to be reaccustomed to food. It'll throw it all back up if you eat too quick."

She slowed her chewing accordingly, avoiding my gaze despite the proximity. I had wrapped the blankets around us and our breath mingled in the chill. She hadn't said much after the chainsman's test but had been assiduous in her self-appointed role of keeping me awake during daylight. We had also shared in suffering his increased parsimony in providing food. Despite finding myself pressed close to a young woman, I felt no lust, only hunger and, as the pain of starvation abated, a growing and familiar brand of hatred for our recent captor.

"If it takes me all my remaining years," I said around a mouthful of cheese, "I'll find that heathen bastard."

Toria's eyes flicked to me then away again, leaving me with a sense of something unsaid but of great import.

"What?" I demanded.

"The words he spoke," she said then fell to silence again, stiff with reluctance.

"You speak Caerith?" I said, giving her an insistent nudge when she didn't answer.

"Caerith are a common sight in the southern duchies," she replied in a grudging mutter. "Mostly traders working the roads between the ports. I picked up a few words when I was younger. *Eornlisch* – it means 'fate'. I think he said, 'Fate is a lie.' Didn't sound very convinced of it though."

"What fate?"

"How the fuck should I know? Whatever it was—" she shrugged "—it's fairly certain he regretted not killing you on the road."

This was a point I couldn't argue. In time, I fully intended to ask the chainsman all about his baffling words and might even give him a quick death if he was properly forthcoming.

"You didn't run," Toria said, interrupting the flow of my thoughts as they slipped towards vindictive plotting. "Back in the marsh. Why not?"

"Like he said, I'd've died in fairly short order. Staying was the smart thing to do."

Once again she darted her bright, clear-sighted eyes at my face. "You're lying. That's not good."

The growing ball of food in my belly proved sufficiently restorative to bring a small laugh to my lips. "Why?"

"Because when you didn't run you created a debt, a life debt. That means a lot where I'm from."

"And where is that? You've yet to tell me."

Her oval face twitched in irritation and she took another bite from the loaf. "Doesn't matter. What matters is I'm not allowed to let you die."

"Allowed by who?"

"The Seraphile, of course. You die through a fault of mine and they'll never let me step through the Portals."

Another laugh rose in my throat then died when I saw the seriousness of her expression. It wasn't quite the implacable, devout certainty I had seen in Hostler, but it was the face of a sincerely held belief nonetheless.

"Best not do that, then," I told her. "Though I suspect you'll have your work cut out, for I've no intention of staying in the Pits one hour longer than I have to, and I'll bear any risk in escaping."

"It's never been done. Every outlaw throughout this kingdom knows it: there's no escape from the Pit Mines."

"I should've died a dozen times over the course of the last few weeks, and yet I still draw breath. Don't worry, I'll not leave you behind." I put an arm around her shoulders, the first time I had touched her, feeling just bone and muscle with barely a hint of softness. I half expected her to pull away, but she shuffled closer, compelled by the need for warmth, I assumed.

"I'm still not going to fuck you," she cautioned me. "Whatever the debt between us."

"I shall endeavour to conceal my heartbreak, my lady."

Toria let out a small sound, not quite a laugh, but her next words held no vestige of humour. "It might be best if you put a leash on that word-spinning tongue of yours. I doubt it'll carry much weight with our fellow miners."

The wonder of food and relative warmth soon began to pall into anxious boredom as our two days in the woodshed wore on. Toria and I exchanged our outlaw tales charting various exploits, from amusing failures to unexpected profits. She remained frustratingly vague about her origins but from what I could gather her career had begun in Dulsian, the most southern duchy in Albermaine. She had also stolen or tricked her way through parts of Alundia before moving on to Alberis, most populous and richest duchy in the kingdom. I was particularly interested in her tales of Couravel, the great city where King Tomas held court and, it was said, so many people lived it was impossible to count them all. Judging by her description it seemed a bad place for those of our calling.

"Most of it is just houses piled up on top of each other, making for narrow streets choked with shit, beggars and the nearly dead. The pickings are poor unless you're willing to cut throats for one of the gangs. They run the whores and the alehouses and spend the whole time fighting each other. If we ever do get out of here, I'm not going back there."

She in turn was greatly interested in my time with the legendary Deckin Scarl. I knew he had long been a figure of great renown within the Marches, but it seemed his fame had reached absurd proportions in the wider kingdom.

"So," she asked, pulling the blanket tighter as the night's chill closed in, "he really did give to the poor?"

"When he wanted them to keep their mouths shut or curry favour. But mostly, what we stole, we spent."

"All of it? He must've kept some." She shifted to regard me with a suspicious eye. "You wouldn't be holding back some precious knowledge, now would you? It strikes me there must be a spot deep in the Shavine Forest where Deckin Scarl hoarded his treasure."

"If he had a hoard, I never saw it."

"You're missing the point." She made an exasperated face. "A map pointing the way to Deckin Scarl's buried loot would be sure to fetch a sovereign or three. A dozen such maps would fetch a great deal more, especially when reluctantly sold by the only surviving member of his famous band."

"A very good point." I allowed my outlaw's mind to wander, sparking possibilities with its many turns. "Or, such a map might draw the eye of a guard willing to part with his keys one dark night."

"But first we'd have to draw it, and letter it. I've no hand for either."

"Nor I. But it's something to ponder in the days ahead."

"Or the years."

"Days," I said, voice hardening with a surety that now brings a faint smile to my lips at the folly of my youthful optimism. "I have much to do and it won't get done wasting away in a mine."

My certainty suffered the first of many dispiriting knocks upon beholding the Pit Mines in full for the first time. I hadn't expected much, perhaps a well-guarded tunnel leading to subterranean depths. Instead, as the gates swung open just wide enough to allow the guards to shove Toria and me through, I looked upon a great crater some three hundred paces wide and about a third as many deep. The walls were cut by a single unbroken descending ramp that spiralled down to its arena-like floor. The spiral's passage was marked by several mineshafts, dark rectangles breaking the monotony of grey-brown soil and rock. People entered and emerged from the shafts in a continual stream. Those who emerged walked with backs bent by burdensome sacks while those passing in the opposite direction moved with marginally more energy, backs straighter but heads sagging with fatigue. The sack bearers ascended the spiral ramp to convey their burdens to a large pile near the rim of the crater. Having delivered their cargo, they turned about and began a weary downward trudge.

The grimness of the scene was depressing in itself, but my escape-obsessed mind focused more on the fact that this entire crater could be observed with ease by anyone walking the wooden wall that snaked around it. I saw now that the wall was in fact formed of two barriers, the inner side being far more formidable in its sturdiness than the outer. Also, for every guard looking out, there were three looking in, a fair number of crossbowmen among them.

"Not one in a hundred years, remember?" Toria sighed as the guards swung the gate closed behind us. Upon being roused from a fitful slumber we had made a brief and swiftly punished attempt to engage them in talk of Deckin's mythical treasure.

"Got a map have you?" one enquired before delivering a hard jab of his gloved fist to my ribs. It wasn't forceful enough to double me over but did cause a bout of painful retching. "They've always got a fucking map," he muttered to his companion as they bundled us from the shed. Toria had the good grace to offer me a sheepish shrug before we were shoved through the gate with a cheerful, "Be sure to make friends early on." The guard paused to favour Toria with a leer. "'Specially you, love."

I rubbed bruised ribs and continued to search for any flaw in what I quickly realised was a perfectly constructed trap. Toria was much more concerned with our immediate prospects, slapping a hand to my arm and nodding at the crater. The reaction of our fellow inmates to our arrival consisted of a few weary glances but no attempt to approach. At Deckin's instruction I had once allowed myself to be captured by the sheriff's men and cast into a gaol in some minor castle. It had all been part of a scheme to free an old associate of his who, it transpired, had already succumbed to consumption before my arrival. The inmates there had swarmed upon me like rats presented with a fresh scrap of meat, administering a beating that would surely have descended into worse if I hadn't drawn the small knife hidden in my shoe and jabbed out a couple of eyes. Here, the parade of prisoners continued their labour without interruption until Toria spied two figures, one small, the other large, ascending the spiral ramp towards us.

As they came closer, I saw that the smaller of the two was a woman, hair mostly grey but features, although creased in part, possessed of an odd smoothness that made it hard to guess her age. I estimated the large man at her side to be about forty, though I was soon to learn that even a short time in the Pits could add years to a face and body. His face and scalp were shaved down to grey stubble and he wore a patch over his left eye, the surrounding flesh marked with old scars leaving a pale web in the skin. This, I assumed, must be the leader here. All prisons have them, the one inmate who, through virtue of guile and brute strength, rises to dominate the others. One glance at the man's hands, larger even than Deckin's, left me in no doubt that challenging him was out of the question. From the baleful glint of his one eye as the pair came to a halt a few paces away, I concluded that the lack of overt defiance was unlikely to spare me a ritual demonstration of authority.

It was therefore a surprise when the woman was the first to speak, hcr voice even more surprising in its uninflected, educated fluency. It wasn't quite the voice of a noble, but neither did it come from the fields nor the streets.

"Welcome, friends," she told us with a tight smile, placing a hand on her chest. "I am called Sihlda. This—" she shifted her hand to the one-eyed man's arm "—is Brewer. Who, might we know, are you?"

"Alwyn," I said, matching her courteous tone and adding a bow. "This is Toria. We find ourselves cast into this place due to the most vile injustice—"

"That doesn't matter," Sihlda informed me. Her words were spoken without particular volume but nevertheless possessed enough habitual authority to stop the flow of my lies. "What brought you here is of no consequence," she added. "All that matters now is your conduct within the confines of this sacred place."

The word was so unexpected it prompted me to enquire with quizzical surprise, "Sacred?"

"Yes." Her smile remained in place, conveying a familiar sense of serenity that made her next words less surprising. "You may look upon this great scratch in the earth and see only a place of toil and punishment, but, in truth, you are blessed to find yourselves at the door to the most divine temple to the Martyrs' example and the Seraphile's grace."

"Oh fuck," Toria muttered in disgust, thankfully too softly for this devout woman to hear.

"A temple?" I asked, experiencing the highly unusual sensation of not knowing quite what to say next. "I see."

"No." The woman laughed, an oddly pleasing sound for it was free of malice or judgement. "You do not. But perhaps in time you will." She cocked her head and stepped closer, putting me in mind of a cat eyeing something that may transpire to be food or just inedible detritus. "Tell me, Alwyn, why did Ahlianna refuse King Lemeshill's hand in marriage?"

More tests, I realised. However, unlike the chainsman's little game, thanks to Hostler this was one I knew how to play. Putting a suitably devout expression on my face, I decided a quote would be the most effective response: "'How canst I, one who hath heard the words of the Seraphile and witnessed the truth of the Scourge, surrender her heart and body to one such as thee? For, mighty and brave as thou art, thy heart is mired in cruelty and the uncountable deceits of the Malecite.'"

She gave a placid nod, betraying a worrying lack of delight at my impressive recitation. Instead, she took another step closer to me, unblinking eyes searching deep into mine. "And what became of them both?"

Having memorised only one passage from this particular tale, I was obliged to craft a summation of the story as best as I could recall from Hostler's preaching. "Enraged by her rejection, Lemeshill ordered Ahlianna be executed. Maddened by guilt he swore allegiance to the Covenant and began the first Crusade of the Martyr, laying waste to the armies of those in thrall to the Malecite until he was eventually killed in battle by foul and unnatural means. He and Ahlianna are named in the Covenant Scrolls as the Second and Third Martyrs."

"Yes." The woman's voice had softened but the hard inquisition in her eyes told a different story. Devout she may be, but I could tell her faith hadn't addled her wits as it often did others'. I had little doubt this woman could tell I had no attachment to the words I spoke. "And now they dwell beyond the Divine Portals, do they not? Bound together in their love for all eternity."

This was a trap, but one easily sidestepped. "The Seraphile promise eternal grace to those who follow the Martyrs' example, but only they can know what lies beyond the Portals. The rewards we receive when our time upon this earth comes to an end are not for us to know, for in the knowing we may falter." I gave her a serious, slightly offended frown. "To speculate on such things is heresy."

"Indeed it is." She retreated a little, switching her attention to Toria. "Are you also so well versed in the Covenant, my dear?"

"As versed as I need to be," Toria replied in a flat tone. As usual, her cleverness hadn't extended to concealing her feelings and a scowl of deep suspicion creased her brow. For one who attached otherworldly connotations to the debt she felt she owed me, I found her reaction to this devout woman strange.

"Her devotion differs from mine in some respects," I cut in. "But rest assured it is faith that binds us. She has an obligation to me, you see, one she fears will draw the ire of the Seraphile should she fail to meet it."

Sihlda arched an eyebrow at Toria who replied with a shrug of agreement. "He saved me," she said. "A life debt not settled will anger the Seraphile."

"Anger?" Sihlda's brow arched a little higher. "The Covenant does not ascribe such base feeling to the Seraphile, at least not the true Covenant."

Toria's face darkened in response, lips forming a sneer of defiance. "Your truth, not mine."

I expected this truculence to rouse some anger in Sihlda but she merely laughed and turned away. "Fear not, my friends, for all who endeavour to follow the Martyrs' example are welcome in our temple, regardless of what schisms may have riven the faith beyond our walls." She waved a beckoning hand and started down the spiral slope. "Come, let me show you our place of worship."

Toria and I were quick to follow but came to an abrupt halt when Brewer stepped into our path. His eye tracked over us, bright with mingled suspicion and warning. "They're both too clever," he growled in a coarse Marches accent, his words clearly addressed to Sihlda even though his eye remained locked on us. "Lies come too easy, especially for this one." He jabbed a large finger into my chest. "I don't like it."

"I heard no lies," Sihlda said, a statement I found highly revealing. Apparently, her brand of devotion didn't exclude dishonesty for I knew she had seen through my words as easily as finely made glass. "Besides," she added, "we have need of cleverness, do we not?"

Brewer's mouth twitched and I could tell he was fighting the urge to argue. This was a very odd prison, for it was clear to me now that power resided not in this man's brute strength and criminal guile, but in the word of a small devout woman.

"Don't mistake me, boy," Brewer said, looming close enough so that the foulness of his breath gusted across my face. "Devout I am, but I'll wring every drop of blood from your broken carcass if you do or say anything to harm Ascendant Sihlda."

"Ascendant?" I looked at the small woman descending the slope, noting how she favoured the other inmates with a kindly smile as she passed by. Most either averted their gaze or responded with a half-bow, one hand placed over their chest, the customary show of respect to a senior Covenant cleric. It made me wonder if the title of Ascendant was one she had given herself or, even though it seemed incredible, she truly was a high member of the clergy. If so, what could possibly have caused her to be cast into this pit?

"Best come on then," Brewer said, turning to follow in Sihlda's wake. As we passed the other inmates, I saw that none felt obliged to offer any bows, but every pair of eyes was quick to look away. Sihlda might command respect here, but Brewer commanded fear. As we traversed the shuffling line of weary souls, I caught a few glares directed at Brewer's safely turned back. Most were just the dark grimace of resentment of the weak towards the strong, but others were the more rigid but bright-eyed stare that rose from true hate or long-nursed grudges. There were also a few leers of naked lust, directed at Toria for the most part but a few also focused on me.

"What the fuck are you looking at, weasel face?" Toria snarled at one overly interested inmate with unusually narrow features and a prominent nose. He shrank back a step but seemed unable to turn his gaze away, obliging me to restrain Toria as she began an instinctive lunge, fists balled.

"Leave it," I said, keeping my tone and face expressionless as I tugged her along.

"Don't like gawpers," she griped, pulling her arm free of my hand.

"You might want to get used to it." I surveyed the passing array of unwashed bodies clad in earth-stained clothes that weren't quite rags. "Don't seem to be many women here."

We followed Brewer down the curving ramp all the way to the crater floor. There were people at work here too, two dozen prisoners carrying sacks from a shaft and piling them up at the base of the slope. They contrasted with the other inmates in being not quite so thin with less threadbare clothes. They were also more inclined to offer a friendly countenance.

"I am pleased to welcome our new brother and sister to the temple," Sihlda said, extending a hand to beckon us forward. "Alwyn and Toria."

The prisoners all paused in their labours to offer a nod, some placing their hands over their chests in the greeting of the devout Covenanter to their own kind. While I was quick to don an expression of appropriate solemnity and return the gesture, Toria crossed her arms and confined any greeting to a terse jerk of her head. Although this group differed from those at the upper portions of the crater by including several women among their number, their presence failed to alleviate Toria's guarded suspicion.

"Come," Sihlda went on, moving to the dark portal of the mineshaft. "I'm sure you will wish to pay observance to the Martyr shrine before we attend to other business."

I kept the obvious question from reaching my lips but Toria was not so circumspect. "What business?"

"All in good time, young sister," Sihlda told her with mild amusement, her voice taking on an echo as her small form faded into the blackness of the shaft.

Toria came to a halt, turning to me in trepidation. I gave a meaningful glance at Brewer, standing next to the shaft entrance in pointed expectation. When she continued to hesitate, I put an arm around her shoulders and guided her forwards, feeling her tremble and stifle a gasp as the shadow enveloped us.

Chapter Sixteen

During our time on the road I had assessed Toria as a mostly fearless soul, or at least well practised in the art of concealing such things. However, her gasp as we entered the tunnel told a different story.

"Is it the dark or the confinement?" I asked in a low murmur.

"Both," she whispered back. Her eyes were bright, catching a small gleam from a torch burning somewhere in the depths ahead. I knew Brewer's hulking presence at our back added to her apprehension. "Don't like being so far from the sight of the sky."

"I'm here," I said, hoping she found some reassurance in a statement of the obvious. "Besides, I doubt these folk wish us ill."

"They're *too* friendly." The gleam of her eyes flickered as they darted about. "What kind of gaol is this?"

I lowered my voice as much as I dared, putting my lips close to her ear. "One with a shrine. Which means there are people here willing to believe in hope. That's something we can use."

She fell silent for a short while before swallowing hard and replying with a forced laugh, words emerging in a rapid tumble. "Or we could sell them a map to Deckin's treasure."

"Yes," I laughed in return, squeezing her shoulders. "There's always that."

The torchlight was soon joined by others as we ventured deeper, revealing rough-hewn stone walls and a surprisingly smooth floor. My feet detected a gentle but definite downward slant while my skin flushed at an unexpected warmth to the air. The shaft had a musty smell that mingled damp stone with a faint whiff of rot, but it wasn't unbearable and held no trace of excrement. Those who toiled here at least had the good sense to find somewhere to dispose of their filth.

A hundred or so paces brought us to a junction where the shaft met several others. The sound of pick and hammer echoed up from the other tunnels and we were obliged to stand aside for an inmate making his way to the surface bearing a sack of freshly mined ore.

"Work is the price we pay to serve at this shrine," Sihlda explained. She stood beside the narrowest tunnel, the only one from which I could detect no sound. "Brewer, be so good as to show Toria her quarters and provide her the tools she will need. Alwyn—" she gestured to the silent tunnel "—please come with me."

Toria tensed in my grip as the outlaw's instinct towards flight or struggle took hold. "It's all right," I whispered to her. "This is all just another cage. Be patient."

Grunting a sigh, she straightened, shrugging my arm from her shoulders, and followed Brewer's large form into the maw of the widest shaft.

Sihlda waited by the tunnel entrance with an expectant smile until I consented to step into its confines. It stretched away in front of me, its terminus lost to a blackness so absolute it seemed to swallow the light from the torch she held. Sensing that further query would not be welcome I started forward whereupon Sihlda began to voice questions of her own.

"Do you have no other name than Alwyn?"

"In truth, no," I replied, biting down on an expletive laden curse as my head connected with the tunnel's low and irregular ceiling. "As is the way with bastards."

"But not outlaws. For instance, beyond these walls Brewer was known as Brewer the Butcher. Perhaps you heard of him?"

"Can't say as I have." This was true, which seemed odd since outlaws of any repute were usually known to Deckin's band. It made me wonder if Brewer might have exaggerated his reputation somewhat.

"No matter," Sihlda said. "So, if he was the Butcher, what, pray tell, were you?"

"I had many names hurled at me over the years, most far too coarse and profane for the ears of an Ascendant. Though, an outlaw of some repute once named me the Fox of Shavine Forest. This was all before what I like to call my enlightenment—"

I heard her make a small, restrained noise which it took me a moment to recognise as a smothered laugh. "How well you speak," she said. "Have you had schooling?"

"Only in the truth of the Covenant. I was fortunate in my teacher. A fellow who, through his kind heart and deep knowledge of the scrolls, steered me from the outlaw's life and opened my soul to the Seraphile's grace."

"A commendable fellow indeed. How came you by him?"

"On the Trail of Shrines. A few companions and I were pursuing our trade on the King's Road, without much success it must be said, when we found him. Just one man, a humble hostler to trade, making his own pilgrimage to the Shrine to Martyr Stevanos, unworried by fear for he knew his faith would preserve him. And so it did. As my friends began to assail him he raised no hand in his defence, instead giving voice to Covenant scripture. My friends were deaf to its message but not I . . ."

I fell silent, coming to a halt with a wistful shake of my head. "Truth cuts worse than any knife, and it cut me that day, Ascendant Sihlda, all the way to my core. I gave all my accumulated loot to my fellow outlaws in return for leaving the hostler alone and together we made pilgrimage to the shrine. There I did look upon the relics of Martyr Stevanos himself and felt the Seraphile's grace fill my soul and wash clean my sins. Sadly—" I gave a rueful huff as I resumed walking "—when the sheriff's men caught up with me my sins had not been washed from his ledger and so I find myself here."

"A tale both beautiful and sad. Is a single word of it true?"

I came to a halt, turning to find Sihlda's face had lost all trace of humour. Instead, she regarded me with a hard, unwavering query, features composed with the confident expectation of one who harbours no doubts regarding their own authority. This, I knew, was truly the face of an Ascendant of the Covenant of Martyrs. I had never seriously entertained the more outlandish notions regarding the insights supposedly afforded those who rise high in the faith: their unerring facility for discerning truth, their capacity for infallible judgement in matters of law or disagreement. However, the peerless ease with which this woman had seen through my veneer of lies made me wonder for the first time if there might be something to all the superstition.

I briefly entertained the notion of continuing the lie, perhaps even embellishing it further with jocular protestations that my redemption at the Shrine to Martyr Stevanos had left me incapable of deceit. But an outlaw with any modicum of wisdom knows when his mask has slipped. I had little doubt that my future prospects of survival and eventual escape rested solely with whatever favour I could garner from this woman.

"The man who taught me Covenant lore truly was a hostler," I said. I tried to offer a weak smile of apology but, for reasons I couldn't fathom, succeeded only in putting an ugly twist on lips already permanently misshapen thanks to my tenure in the pillory. "Or had been in his previous life," I added with a cough, finding I had to swallow before speaking on. "But he was devout in his faith in the Covenant, despite being as much a villain as any who ran with Deckin Scarl."

"And where is he now, this devout villain?"

"Dead." To this day I don't know why I continued to speak, but the words flowed as freely and easily as ale from a tapped barrel. "I killed him. I had to. The rest of the band were taken or dead. He was hurt and would have slowed me down. I wanted to pretend it was a kindness to spare him pain but in truth I worried what he might tell the soldiers if they took him alive."

"Then—" she took a step closer to me, a sudden sweat beading my brow as the torch came within an inch of my face "—would it not be

fair to say, Alwyn, that you deserve to be here? You deserve punishment, do you not? For the murder you did? For your other sins, which
are surely many?"

Her eyes captured me, holding me in place despite the uncomfortable proximity of her torch. The familiar refrain of denial common
to all outlaws rose within me: *what choice did a whore's bastard with
no home have? What other scraps do the nobles leave us? Would you
not have done the same?* But this chorus of excuses was a small, wailing
creature now, diminished, I had no doubt, by her.

"Yes," I replied, voice flat with acceptance. "I deserve to be here. I
deserved my time in the pillory and I deserved the hanging they were
going to give me. I deserved all of it and more."

Sihlda blinked slowly and stepped back, a faintly sorrowful smile
of satisfaction curving her lips. "Most think the Martyrs' example
consists of naught but suffering and sacrifice," she said, moving
around me, her slight form making it easy even in the confines of
the tunnel. "But most are wrong, for it is in the power of knowledge
that their true lesson lies. Every Martyr who died to form the
Covenant did so in the certain knowledge of who they were and
what their faith required them to do. Come and I will show you what
the Covenant requires of you."

She started along the tunnel and I followed, drawn with all the
urgent need of a dog trailing its master. I couldn't say how long I
followed her, ears alive for any word she might utter. Even in my most
servile moments in Deckin's company I hadn't experienced such a
desperate need for approval, or, more accurately, as I would understand
later, absolution.

The shaft eventually led us to a chamber, its dimensions hidden in
total darkness until Sihlda's torch cast its glow over granite walls. They
ascended to a height of at least twenty feet before fading into the
gloom above while the long echo of our footfalls told of a truly
impressive space.

"Welcome to the Shrine to Martyr Callin," Sihlda said, touching
her torch to another set into the wall by means of a crude iron bracket.

"Callin?" I asked. The name struck a chime in my memory but

summoned scant details. I recalled Hostler muttering this a few times, usually when the hour was late and he sat weary and angered by his ungrateful, unreceptive audience.

"You don't know his story?" Sihlda asked, giving a wry shake of her head as she moved to touch flame to a second torch. "I always find it odd that those most ignorant of Martyr Callin are those who would benefit most from his example."

She moved on, lighting three more torches, the accumulated glow revealing much of the surrounding chamber. Walls of both smooth and rough stone rose on either side of us, arcing up into the anonymous void in a manner that reminded me of the more ornate Covenant shrines. The walls bracketed a floor covering a space at least fifty paces wide, its limits lost to the dark.

"Yes," the Ascendant agreed, once again revealing her uncanny insight into my thoughts as she added, "Strange that such a perfect cathedral should be crafted by the random hand of nature, if anything in this world can truly be called random. Look here, if you would."

She strode towards one of the smooth patches of stone where shadows flickered about what I initially took to be an impractically small doorway. Moving closer, I saw it was in fact an alcove carved into the rock. Even to my unskilled eye I could tell there had been real artistry in the hands that crafted this, the perfectly flat base and sides that curved to an elegant point. Sitting on the base was a small, lidded clay jar.

"The clerics of other shrines will festoon their altars with every relic they can lay hands upon," Sihlda said. "Many, if not most of them, fakes fashioned to gull clerics greedy for more pilgrims. Here, however, we find we need but one relic for our altar, for Martyr Callin was a man who had learned to shun the treachery of riches."

Placing her torch in an empty stanchion next to the alcove, she lifted the lid from the pot. "Behold, Alwyn," she said, retreating a step and beckoning me forward. "The holy relic of Martyr Callin."

I had never seen a true relic before. My visits to the varied shrines found in the Shavine Marches had been undertaken purely for purposes of thievery. Had I actually entered the Shrine to Martyr

Stevanos then the dozen or more bones, strips of flayed skin and blackened vestments adorning the altar would surely have made more of an impression than what I beheld now.

"A shek?" I asked, casting a dubious glance at the Ascendant before returning my gaze to the single copper coin sitting in the jar.

"Quite so," she said. "You may examine it if you wish."

I hesitated before reaching for the jar. Faithless as I was, a lifetime of exposure to Covenant lore made the prospect of actually touching a true relic a daunting one. But, when I tipped the coin into my palm, no visions of the Seraphile came upon me and my soul was not flooded with their grace. I felt only the chill of metal and looked upon a small coin much like the countless others I had allowed to slip through my fingers over the course of an eventful and unwise life. Holding it up to the light, I saw that the head stamped onto one side differed from typical Crown coinage. Sheks used today bore either the head of King Tomas or that of his late father, the reputedly more formidable King Mathis the Fourth. More unusual still was that it was the head of a woman.

"Queen Lisselle," Sihlda said, watching me peer at the coin. "The only woman of the Algathinet dynasty to sit on the throne. In her day, the churls were wont to call her Bloody Liss, for she had not been blessed with a merciful heart."

"How old is this?" I asked, turning the coin in the torchlight. There were numbers stamped onto the reverse but too faint to make out.

"I'd guess it's been almost two centuries since that coin was minted and eventually found its way into Callin's purse. He said it was the only coin he had earned through honest labour and so would be the only one he would keep. Callin, you see, was like you, an outlaw for much of his life. The story of his redemption varies greatly for his scroll was penned in a poor hand and those that copied it were even less skilled. But, it is known that having received a vision of the Second Scourge he gave up his villainous ways and walked the length and breadth of Albermaine preaching his warning. 'For it is certain that the Scourge will claim the wealthy but spare the poor if they open their hearts to the Covenant,' he said. 'To know salvation, you must know poverty.'"

Even though I found Sihlda's words were as commanding as her gaze, my tendency towards cynicism remained. "I doubt that went down well," I said with a tight grin. The Ascendant, however, merely smiled a little broader.

"On the contrary, Callin gathered many adherents during his travels," she said. "More than two thousand people were trailing after him at one point. Two thousand churls, to be clear. Those of noble blood were uniformly deaf to his message and less than pleased that so many of their tenants were abandoning their farms to follow a shoeless thief who never washed and preached that ownership of land was an abomination in the sight of the Seraphile.

"Queen Lisselle was always gruesomely efficient in putting a stop to anything that roused discord in her realm. Callin was seized and his followers scattered. One of the more garbled passages in his scroll alludes to a private meeting with the queen, but what passed between them remains forever lost. She did, however, grant him the mercy of a beheading rather than the death normally afforded a heretic, much to the annoyance, it must be said, of senior Covenant clergy. They found his preaching just as alarming as did the nobility. As Callin was led to the block he gave this coin, his only remaining possession, to the axeman in payment for his labour."

Sihlda took the jar from me and held it out until I dropped the coin into it. "It came into my hands a long time ago, but that is a story for another time." She set the jar back into position in its finely carved alcove and replaced the lid. "A humble relic for a man who valued humility above all things. For he saw that when we humble ourselves, we are redeemed."

Shifting her gaze from the jar she captured me once again, her eyes snaring me as easily as the manacles that had so recently bound me to the chainsman's cart. "Are you willing to humble yourself, Alwyn? Are you willing to be redeemed by Martyr Callin's example?"

A faint, forlorn chorus of lies rose and died within me. Telling this imprisoned luminary of the Covenant all she wanted to hear was certainly a good strategy, but I found I had no desire to spin yet more lies. Not for her.

"I don't know," I said with simple honesty. "Deserving as I am of my place here, still I lust only for escape, for freedom."

"Freedom." The word brought an amused lilt to her tone, though her gaze remained implacably serious. "And what would you do with it?"

More honesty, spilling from my mouth in a torrent, surprising myself with the passion in my voice. "I have scales to balance. Accounts to settle." My jaw ached as unbidden fury put a clench to my teeth. "I have people to kill! Though I know this condemns me in your eyes, I'll not deny it."

"Who?" she enquired with a curious arch to her brow. "And why?"

So I told her. All of it. Every detail of my sordid life of villainy. Of the crimes I had visited upon others and those visited upon me. I listed every one of my intended victims. My still festering grudge against Todman, should he still somehow draw breath. The brother of the soldier I had murdered, and all of his comrades, for trying to hang and fillet me. Lord Althus Levalle for his hypocritical brand of mercy. The chainsman, whose murder of Raith and test on the road had left the most recent and raw marks on my growing tally of vengeance.

Finally falling silent, rendered flushed and breathless by my diatribe, I expected soothing words from the Ascendant. She would, I knew, seek to counsel me in the folly of vindictiveness. Lecture me in the emptiness of revenge for it was sure to just bring more violence into my already brutalised life.

Instead she thought for a short interval, lips and brow drawn in contemplation, then said, "It strikes me there are several names missing from your list."

I straightened, looking at her in bafflement. "Missing?"

"Yes. If you truly wish to balance the crimes committed against you, then it seems most of them result from the attack at Moss Mill, do they not?"

I gave a dumb nod and she paused again for brief reflection before continuing, "Deckin Scarl's reputation made itself known even here. It occurs to me that he was far too wily an outlaw to blithely place himself in a trap. Unless you imagined that Crown Company happened upon your band by mere chance that night?"

"I know we must have been betrayed," I said, "but couldn't fathom by who. Perhaps one of the villagers ran off to tell the sheriff's men—"

"And somehow the king's own soldiers managed to launch a well-planned attack that very night? No, they were waiting for Deckin's arrival and probably had been for several days, if not weeks. Meaning they had been told of his plans far in advance. I imagine there is a very short list of people who knew enough to lay such a trap. Also, it might be worth pondering not just who died at Moss Mill, but who wasn't there to die that night."

It took only a few seconds for my mind to churn up the answer, the words bubbling forth in a cloud of angry spit. "Erchel's kin! They weren't fucking there."

"Alwyn!" She spoke the admonition in a curt snap, giving a meaningful glance at the relic in the alcove.

"Sorry," I said in automatic contrition.

Sihlda inclined her head in forgiveness and said, "You might also want to consider the people you didn't see die that night and whose head was not impaled atop the castle wall. The absence of knowledge can often tell you a great deal."

The people I didn't see die . . . There was Todman for a start, and not just him. In fact, for the first time it occurred to me that beyond Hostler and Gerthe, the tally of gangmates I knew for sure had been slain at the mill was fairly short. The fates of many remained unknown. It was a long list of potential traitors and parsing the guilty from the innocent was not something I could do while toiling my life away in a mine.

"I can see your frustration," Sihlda said, breaking the increasingly busy stream of my thoughts. "Your desire for recompense. Tell me—" she angled her head, a genuine curiosity colouring her voice "—why should a man like Deckin Scarl inspire such passion for justice?"

My anger settled to a low boil then, the bland inquisitiveness of her question bringing a reflective calm. For a second I was a lost boy in the forest again, staring up at a large bearded stranger through teary, desperate eyes.

"Because . . . " I began, finding I had to swallow before I could push the words past a choked throat. "Because no one else ever cared about me."

"Ah," was her only response before her face once again took on the intent and sincere face of a true Ascendant. "The freedom you lust for, I can give it to you."

"How?"

Her features took on the same hard inquisition I had seen when she quizzed me on Covenant lore, head angling with catlike appraisal once more. I knew there to be considerable intellect at work as she stood in silent calculation, as well as a certain ruthlessness. Ascendant or not, wise and kind or not, one did not survive a place like this on such things alone.

"Should my trust in you prove misplaced," she said, retrieving her torch and turning away, "I will not be able to protect you from Brewer's wrath. He is a true and devout servant of the Covenant, but his . . . lapses can be both spectacular and ugly."

Gesturing for me to follow, she strode away into the most shadowed depths of this naturally formed cathedral. "Your freedom will, of course, be won through your acceptance of the Covenant," she lectured as I trailed after the bobbing course of her torch. "But also through a great deal of learning and bodily effort. More of the latter than the former, I'm afraid, but even the faithful need to eat. Much of your labour will be spent hewing ore from rock and carrying it aloft in return for the food that sustains us. As our group is more productive than the others, we receive more and better food than those unfortunate souls who choose to shun our devout ways. That food, and our adherence to the Covenant, provide the strength needed for this."

She came to a sudden halt, obliging me to draw up short lest I collide with her. We had ventured at least a hundred paces from the glow of the other torches, birthing a sense of being adrift in a formless void, so absolute was the gloom. But it was far from silent. Water cascaded in a rapid torrent somewhere, enough of it to leave a fine misting on my skin. As Sihlda raised and extended her torch, the light played over a curtain of water rushing through a fissure in the rock overhead.

"The Siltern River passes directly above this spot," Sihlda told me, pointing at the gloom beyond the cascading water. "Its eastern bank lies fifty yards in that direction. When I first came to this place years ago this waterfall did not exist. The cascade that formed it was concealed within many tons of rock. You see, Alwyn, what the faithful can do if their devotion is sincere and sustained?"

I saw it then, the odd regularity of the rock visible through the falling water, the straight edges and sharp gouges that told of stone subjected to pick and chisel over many years. The wall took on a deep curve beyond the cascade, creating a funnel of sorts that ended in a small dark opening. Stepping closer I let out a breath, rich in hopeful excitement at what I saw. The tunnel was small, just large enough to allow a full-grown man to crawl on hands and knees, but it was unmistakably a tunnel.

"How far does it go?" I asked, crouching to step through the curtain of water, heedless of the chill.

"Not far enough," Sihlda replied. "Yet. Carver, the only skilled mason among us and the architect of this tunnel for much of its existence, tells me we should reach the other side of the river within four years. He advises another six months' digging after that before crafting an upward channel, to be sure we don't emerge in waterlogged ground."

"Four and a half years," I murmured, my excitement dwindling. It is the curse of the young to experience time as the glacial turn of seasons. To my youthful, vengeance-hungry heart four and a half years seemed a veritable eternity.

"I will not attempt to compel you to this," Sihlda told me with calm reassurance. "If you wish, you and your friend can make your own way within these walls. But, whatever schemes you may have hatched, I assure you they won't work. The guards here are too well paid and too fearful of their lord to be bribed and his ancestor designed a perfect cage. The only route to freedom is here."

She paused to offer another faintly sorrowful smile before turning away and starting back towards the exit. "Come now, you have time to settle into your quarters and share a small meal before the evening shift. At mealtimes it is our habit to read from the few scrolls we possess. Perhaps you would care to take a turn."

"I can't read," I told her, following with much the same doglike devotion as before and would, in truth, maintain for the next four years.

Ascendant Sihlda came to a halt then, letting out a faintly disgusted sigh. "Well that," she said, glancing back at me, "simply won't do."

PART II

"Don't you ever ask of yourself, Scribe, 'Why do I serve the Covenant and the king? What rewards do they bring me? What in life have they provided that I did not provide myself?' The Covenant claims to preserve your soul while the king calls himself the protector of your body. Both are liars and your worst sin resides in your service to those lies."

From *The Testament of the Pretender Magnis Lochlain*, as recorded by Sir Alwyn Scribe

Chapter Seventeen

I've often pondered the human capacity for forming attachments to people with whom one has almost nothing in common and Sir Eldurm Gulatte stands as a singularly fitting example of this enigma. I was born to a whorehouse, he to a castle. I inherited nothing except, so the pimp told me, my mother's incautious tongue, while upon the death of his father Sir Eldurm found himself the owner of both said castle and the Pit Mines it had been constructed to guard. He was therefore one of the wealthier nobles in all of Albermaine while I, at the juncture of our first meeting, remained a penniless outlaw condemned to a life of back-breaking, underground toil. Perhaps the only thing Sir Eldurm and I had in common, thanks to Ascendant Sihlda's patient tutelage, was the ability to read. However, yet another point of difference arose in the fact that, after nigh on four years in the Pits, I could both read and write very well, whereas he, affable dullard that he was, remained a decidedly poor hand at both.

"'You set my loins afire,'" I read, trying not to stumble over the imprecise, blotchy scrawl on the parchment he handed me. "'Your lips are like . . .'" I paused as my eyes tracked over several words which had been scratched into obscurity by a frustrated quill "'. . . two delicious red morsels of the finest meat.'"

I lowered the parchment to raise an eyebrow at Lord Eldurm. He

stood at the window to his upper chamber, the highest point in the
castle, arms crossed and one finger pensively scratching his anvil-like
jaw. He may have had all the wit and charm of the outhouse he resembled, but the flowing blond locks and well-sculpted features were
certainly a match for the knightly hero he longed to be. His attempts
at wooing fair maidens, however, fell far short of a balladeer's ideal.

"Too . . . ?" he began, fumbling for the right word.

"Florid," I supplied. "Perhaps, my lord, 'rubies set upon a satin
cushion' would work better."

"Yes!" He nodded, moving to thump a large and enthusiastic hand
to the table. "By the Martyrs, Scribe, Ascendant Sihlda was right in
speaking so well of you. Outlaw you may be in the sight of the Crown,
but you're the finest poet in all the realm to me."

He laughed, loud and hearty, something he did a lot in those days.
For a fellow who had spent his entire adult life overseeing one of the
most wretched and despised places in all Albermaine, he was an oddly
cheerful soul. Sometimes it pains me to think of his eventual fate,
but then I recall the consistently tall pile of corpses waiting at the
gate to be carted away every month, and his fate pains me less.

"I am gratified to be of service, my lord," I said, setting the parchment down and reaching for a quill. "Might I enquire as to the young
lady's full form of address?"

"Lady Evadine Courlain," Lord Eldurm said, his earnest expression
softening into wistful longing. "The Rose of Couravel."

"A formal title, my lord?"

"Not as such. But her family crest is a black rose, so I think she'll
find it duly flattering, don't you?"

Even a brainless bull manages to find the right hole once in a while,
I thought, inclining my head in approval. "Indeed I do, my lord." I
dipped the quill and began to set out the letters, smooth flowing lines
appearing on the parchment with swift precision.

"My word, Scribe," his lordship said, "you've a prettier hand even
than the Ascendant."

"She has been my most excellent tutor, my lord," I replied, not
lifting my focus from the task at hand. This was my first visit to this

chamber, my first time within the castle walls in fact, although my skills had enabled a few brief sojourns beyond the gates before today. Few of the guards could read and those that did had little skill in writing. Taking on scribing duties for the garrison had been Ascendant Sihlda's first stratagem in winning preferential treatment for her congregation. Now, with her knees protesting more and more at the climb to the gate, the duty fell to me, along with a new name. To Sihlda, Toria and others I was still Alwyn, redeemed former associate of the legendary Deckin Scarl. To the guards, and now this noble lackwit, I was simply Scribe.

"If I might suggest, my lord," I said upon completing the letter's formal opening, "'Know that you have stoked a fire in my heart' might be more . . . seemly than the mention of loins."

"True," he agreed, face darkening a little. "And probably wise. Her dread father is sure to read it before it gets anywhere near her dainty hand. And the lady herself is of a distinctly devout character."

Although my ears were always greedy for any information that might offer an advantage, I resisted the impulse to ask about this dread father and his feelings towards his would-be son-in-law. *A servant*, Sihlda had cautioned me more than once, *must know their place, Alwyn. And that is what you are now, at least until our day of deliverance arrives.*

I was not the only servant drawn from the ranks of those who laboured in the Pits. Most of the maids, stewards and cooks who saw to the endless needs of a working castle were inmates, spending their days aboveground but always pushed back through the gates come nightfall. I had heard a great deal about the cruelties of Sir Eldurm's father whose reign of terror had included regular, often fatal, floggings and compelling the more attractive prisoners to whore for the guards. His son had instigated a far less harsh regime, influenced to no small degree by Ascendant Sihlda who had known him since childhood. His comparatively enlightened attitude, however, didn't accommodate any slackening in the ritualised strictures that governed life in the Pit Mines, both for the prisoners and the guards. It was the most salient point of honour to the Gulatte family that they had never allowed an

These were commonly referred to as the Shunned, those whose lack of devotion and uncivil manners made them unfit for Sihlda's congregation or acceptance into the other groups that occupied the middle tiers. Their position of proximity to the gate enabled a short journey with their burdensome sacks but they also had the poorest seams to work. Digging the required amount of ore from the upper shafts required twice the labour than those below, meaning the rations of the Shunned were often cut for failing to make quota. Since my elevation to scribe status I had found walking past their staring, resentful faces a less than pleasant daily chore.

"So, Alwyn," Sihlda said to me later as the congregants gathered for the evening meal, "what news from the outside?"

Evenings among the congregants consisted of a meal followed by two hours' toil in the tunnel. I, like most of us, itched to spend more time on our avenue of escape but Sihlda insisted we conserve enough strength to maintain the flow of ore. The congregation was by far the most productive group in the Pit which, along with the scribing duties now undertaken by me, ensured Sir Eldurm's good graces and better rations. The sacks I had carried down the slope had been evenly distributed among the other congregants, helping to sustain our collective efforts but also ensuring my comparatively favourable status didn't engender any resentment.

"The Pretender's still abroad," I said, recalling what scraps of information I had been able to glean from the guard's gossip and the correspondence littering Sir Eldurm's desk. "Ranging the border between Cordwain and the Fjord Geld, so they say. He either has ten thousand men or barely three depending who you listen to. Rumour is the king is about to call another muster to deal with him for once and all."

"Just like the last five musters," Brewer grunted, face soured by remembrance of his own service under the banners. "He can have the throne, for all I care, and a pox on it."

"War is never just," Sihlda told him, "whatever the outcome." She raised a questioning eyebrow at me. "Anything else of note?"

"The usual." I shrugged. "Riots here and there. Folk are awful tired of paying taxes towards the war. And it's not just the nobles they're angry at. I heard tell of an Aspirant in Couravel getting pulled from his litter by a mob of churls. Supposedly they stripped him bare and pelted him with shit all the way back to the cathedral."

"Heresy," muttered Hedgeman. A relatively new arrival with only a year in the Pit, he had nevertheless earned Sihlda's regard with the depth of his devotional zeal.

"'The rich despise the poor for their wretchedness and condemn them for their envy,'" Sihlda recited in a mild tone, a passage from the Scroll of Martyr Callin. I noticed she rarely quoted from anything else these days. "'Yet they never seem to comprehend that a rich man is just a poor man with better luck.' Those who serve in the senior ranks of the Covenant grow richer and so the poor grow more envious. It seems to me that the remedy for the latter lies in the former, wouldn't you say?"

I concealed a smirk at Hedgeman's contrite lowering of his head. Zealous he was, and more practised in quoting Covenant lore than all of us save Sihlda, but true thought and agency were beyond him. If any soul was more suited to life as a congregant than Hedgeman, I never met them.

"And the king's sister's husband died," I added. "Lord Alferd someone or other."

"Died how?" Sihlda asked, her interest for some reason piqued by this nugget of news.

"Not in battle, that much I could gather. Some sickness so the guards said. Most seemed to think it the Vehlman's pox, as his dead lordship liked his whores, though a few muttered about poison, but they always do when someone of importance dies all unexpected."

"His name was Lord Alferd Keville," Sihlda said, voice soft and gaze distant. She rarely succumbed to reveries of her life before the Pit, but when she did they were usually provoked by the death of a prior acquaintance. "And he was good man, in his way, deserving of a better fate." She paused, her voice lowering to just a whisper that I doubted anyone other than Brewer and I could hear. "And a better bride."

CHAPTER EIGHTEEN

"Hand me the smallest chisel!" Toria's voice sounded from the tunnel's black depths, the irritated urgency of it given additional emphasis thanks to the echo.

A year ago, the escape tunnel we had worked on for so long had intersected with a number of broad chambers with peculiar effects on the passage of sound. The first would transform a high voice into a near perfect baritone while this one, the largest yet encountered, made the smallest whisper last for what seemed an age. At first, we had welcomed this discovery, for the hollows were ready-made passages through the rock. However, Carver, the former mason and overseer of this grand design, soon pointed out that, far from aiding our escape, these chambers endangered it. Our tunnelling had weakened the natural structures that created them, threatening the most feared of all events in the Pit: a cave-in.

Buttressing the various cracks and fissures we had created was the only solution, a tedious business due to the need to limit our requests for additional beams from the guards. Replacing old props was a constant task but a sudden increase in the supply of timber would surely have aroused suspicion. Lord Eldurm might be a dullard in many ways, but he remained a keen-eyed gaoler nonetheless.

The delay added months to our already extended schedule, although in truth Sihlda had never set a precise date for our escape. As ever, she seemed content in ministering to her congregation in her subterranean cathedral, maintaining a daily ritual of supplications interspersed with observance of yearly feast days in memory of the principal Martyrs. Although she had won my devotion, if not my soul, at our first meeting, the Ascendant's placidity set my ever-suspicious mind to pondering. Could it be that this whole scheme might be some form of trick? A way to keep us quiescent and servile with the always unfulfilled promise of liberation while she filled our souls with Covenant dogma?

The suspicion dimmed when the buttressing was finally completed and we resumed digging, but the feeling that Sihlda had no real interest in escaping the Pit lingered. I knew this distrustful inclination grew from the task that had filled my mind in rare moments of idleness over the course of the last four years. Endless conjecture on betrayal will breed suspicion of all.

Erchel's kin, I thought, the small knife I carried carving a perfect flourish into the buttress I crouched beside. As I had countless times before, I ran through every face glimpsed at Leffold Glade, every name heard, every mention Erchel had ever uttered to me about his folk. *Uncle Drenk's got the reins these days,* he told me once. *Had to kill Cousin Frell to get 'em. Some dispute about a whore's dues that was most likely made up to excuse the fight. He's an awful clever fellow, Uncle Drenk . . .*

"Chisel!"

Toria's foot jabbed my shoulder, breaking through the stream of calculation which I knew would probably have led nowhere in any case. After four long years, there were only so many answers I could divine, producing a great many more questions in the process.

"Any diamonds and I get equal share, remember," I said, retrieving the required implement from the sack at my feet and leaning into the tunnel to place it in her hand.

"Fuck—" she grunted with the effort of shoving the chisel into an unseen crack in the rock "—off. It's all mine. And all the gold and rubies too."

Squabbling over unfound treasure had been a shared joke between us since taking our first turn in the tunnel, but lately I found it growing thin. Although escape may finally be within reach, talk of riches reminded me that beyond the confines of this mine we would be penniless. It made me wish the fabled map to Deckin's treasure had some basis in fact. Sadly, although possessed of a boundless desire for the riches of others, Deckin had never been one to hoard his wealth.

"We'll need it all," I said, slipping into a more serious tone. "When we get out of here."

"The Covenant will provide once we reach Callintor, at least for a time." Toria paused and the tunnel filled with the sound of her hammer pounding the chisel. Time had made us both somewhat expert miners, but she possessed the keener eye for the best way to dislodge stubborn stone. Also, her slight dimensions made her capable of squirming into crevices denied the rest of us. "Mind out," she said, and I stood aside as a hefty boulder rolled clear of the tunnel. Recently it had taken on an upward slant after Carver decided it was now safe to start angling for the surface.

"Callintor is a twelve-mile stretch from the river," I reminded her. "That's a lot of ground to cover on foot with mounted men on your trail."

"To get clear of this place I'd run a hundred miles in half a day, never mind twelve. Besides—" she huffed a little as she struggled clear of the tunnel to sit at the entrance, tired but still lively enough to regard me with a smile of faux sincerity "—has not our Seraphile-graced Ascendant decreed the sanctuary city as our destination?" Her smile disappeared as she gave an apparently appalled gasp, speaking on in a whisper. "Would you," she began, clutching her chest, "go against the Ascendant's wishes, Alwyn?"

"Piss off," I muttered, sinking down at her side to unstopper a small bottle. "Here." I took a sip, savouring the burn of brandy on my tongue before handing her the bottle. "Drown your blasphemy."

"It'll take more than this." She drank, gulping rather than sipping, a worryingly typical trait on the rare occasions when drink came within reach. I resisted the impulse to pull the bottle away. Life had been hard for both of us here, but she wore it worse.

Despite everything I had somehow grown taller and broader with the years while Toria retained much the same diminutive stature, albeit with more wiriness to her arms. Her size made her a target for the more foolhardy non-congregants, especially the newcomers who hadn't yet learned the deadly consequences of transgressing the unwritten but stringent rules of the Pit. Only a few months before she had been dragged into a mineshaft by a recently arrived trio of footpads from Althiene. Her deft hand with the inch-long blade she carried had stabbed out an eye and lopped off a finger or two, keeping them at bay until Brewer and I came running to investigate the commotion. After a short interval there were two dead footpads from Althiene lying in the shaft and a third left alive as a warning, deprived of both eyes to emphasise the point. The other inmates left him to wander and wail until hunger added another corpse to the monthly toll. As usual, the guards were disinclined to ask questions.

"Good stuff," she said, wiping her mouth. "Steal it from his lordship, did you?"

"There's a maid works the kitchens who likes me."

"Whore." She grinned as she handed back the much-lightened bottle.

"She's old enough to be my mother. Just likes the odd smile and a kind word or two, is all."

"Offer her more and perhaps you'll get two bottles next time." Toria glanced over her shoulder at the small dark maw of the tunnel. "Carver says another year," she murmured. "At least."

"If that's what it takes, that's what it takes."

"And when we're free we dutifully follow the Ascendant to Callintor, right?"

I said nothing. We had spoken about this little so far and my responses had been carefully phrased evasions, but this time Toria was intent on a proper answer. "Right?" She nudged me with her shoulder. "We traipse around after her as she preaches, faithful congregants that we are."

"Brewer will, and Carver." I grunted a laugh. "Hedgeman certainly. You and me can go where we wish."

"To find the long list of folk you want to kill, you mean?"

"It's my list. You don't have to follow."

"Balls I don't. You know that." She paused, reaching for the brandy bottle, which I released after some taunting reluctance. "I'll follow you and help you kill whoever needs killing. I'm just not convinced that's your course any more. I see the way you hang on her words. The way you look at her when she's teaching you. It's not love; it's worse. You think she's going to be happy with you abandoning her holy mission so's you can go off and drench yourself in blood? You know she won't. And I know one word from her and you'll follow her like I'll follow you."

I said nothing, feeling Toria's eyes on me as she took another long drink. "We both know what she thinks she is," she said, voice a little slurred now. "What she wants to be. Fuck, maybe she's right. The Covenant must have had their reasons for shoving her in here in the first place. Reasons she's yet to tell us about. My guess is she scared them, all those grasping hypocrites, and they were right to be scared. Did you know there hasn't been a new Martyr for three hundred years? The Covenant might love the old Martyrs but you can wager your arse they'd hate any new ones. A new Martyr means change, means fucking up all they've built, all they've stolen."

She drank some more then muttered a curse. I watched her upend the bottle to let the last few drops fall before casting it away. It shattered somewhere beyond the reach of the glow cast by our small candle, heralding a brief but thick silence.

"To be a true Martyr she has to die," Toria stated. "When Martyrs die they usually take all their followers with them. It's in all the scrolls even though the Supplicants don't talk about it much. Bloody is the dawn when a Martyr rises. That's what the old folk say back home."

"You hate her because she's an apostate to your people," I said. "Her brand of lore doesn't match yours—"

"I don't hate her at all," Toria cut in. "That's the worst of it. She has the gift of making folk love her even when they can see the doom she brings. But, love her or not, there's no point escaping this place only to find ourselves burning in a heretic's fire before the year's out . . . " She trailed off in annoyance as I turned to the tunnel, frowning at a faint echo that didn't chime with her diatribe. "You listening?" she demanded with a hard shove.

"Quiet!" I snapped, eyes narrowed to peer into the tunnel's gloomy interior, straining to detect an odd and unfamiliar sound combining a sibilant hiss with a clacking rattle. "You hear that?"

"Hear what . . . ?" Toria fell silent as the echo abruptly increased in volume, the rattle and hiss becoming a thunderous cascade we both recognised with awful clarity.

"Cave-in!"

I reached for her arm but Toria, never one to hesitate in times of urgency, was already scrambling ahead of me on all fours, worming her way through the narrow crevice into the next chamber. I followed, scraping my hands in the feverish need to get clear, feeling the first displaced boulders thump against my kicking legs. The last four years had made us witness to several tunnel collapses and the ghastly fate of those who found themselves entombed, bones crushed but still clinging to life in the certain knowledge that there would be no rescue.

"Come on!" Toria shouted as I continued to struggle through the crevice. She grabbed my arm and hauled, cursing through clenched teeth. "Why'd you have to grow so fucking big?"

I came free of the crevice with an explosive yell of relief, falling on to Toria as a thick miasma of dust and grit filled the chamber. Clamping our mouths closed, we pinched our noses and groped blindly for the buttressed passage to the next chamber. Breathing in a lungful of this stuff would be just as deadly as being buried under a ton or more of rock.

I crawled until my free hand found a wooden beam. Toria latched her hand onto my belt and we stumbled through the passage to the far larger, cavernous chamber some twenty yards on. My lungs felt like fire by the time we reached it and I was unable to suppress the instinct to breathe. The dust had reached this far but wasn't so thick, meaning the sudden intake of air failed to kill me, but it did leave me coughing and retching until the pall finally began to settle.

I cleared tearful eyes to see Toria doubled over, disgorging a mix of brandy and grit, before my gaze swung to the passage. The only light came from the single torch in a stanchion hammered into the wall. Its light was too weak to discern anything in the depths of the tunnel, but from the continuing clatter and hiss of falling stone, I divined that our discussion of a few moments ago was now probably irrelevant. Escape was now as distant as the stars on a clear night. However, on this occasion, for once my pessimism was to prove unfounded.

"What a remarkable thing." Carver stood in the vertical shaft, staring at the inky blackness above, fingers teasing his thick beard in contemplation. It had taken a week of arduous toil to clear the dislodged stone from the tunnel, some of the larger boulders having to be broken up before they could be dragged away. It had all been piled up in the Shrine to Martyr Callin. So much displaced rock appearing above ground all at once would be sure to arouse the suspicion of the sentries on the wall. We had expected to find the tunnel itself choked with yet more debris but instead discovered it now intersected yet another chamber, narrower than the others but extending to a much greater height than any so far found.

"Any notion of how high it goes?" Brewer asked, raising his torch, which only illuminated yet more damp rock with no sign of a ceiling.

"Difficult to say," Carver said, stroking his beard for a moment longer before throwing his head back and casting a hearty shout into the gloom. His voice echoed but not for as long as I expected, the shout rebounding at us with an eerie clarity and swiftness.

"Sounds like it narrows a good deal after thirty feet or so," Carver concluded. "And I reckon we're only fifty feet belowground here."

Besides Carver, Brewer and myself, Sihlda was the only other congregant present and I noted that she failed to partake in the resultant sharing of meaningful glances. Instead, she stood with her arms crossed, head lowered and a deep frown on her brow, her features betraying none of the surprised joy I saw on Brewer's craggy visage.

"Scaling this won't be easy," Carver went on, running a hand over the chamber's moist wall. "Still, it's possible with a good supply of timber to craft ladders. If we can get hold of more nails, I can craft them into brackets to secure them to the stone—"

"How long?" Sihlda cut in, her frown still in place.

"That all depends on supplies, Ascendant." Carver spread his hands in apology. "If we have everything we need it could be done in a couple of weeks."

"Weeks," Brewer repeated with a laugh, the smile abruptly slipping from his lips at a sharp glance from Sihlda.

"Calculate what is required," she told Carver. "Be exact and as sparing as you can." She stared hard at him and then Brewer, her voice taking on a rare note of command. "Say nothing of this to the others. If they ask, tell them work on the tunnel is halted for now, until we know it's safe."

She continued to stare until both men responded with grave expressions of agreement. "Alwyn," Sihlda said, turning away. "Come with me."

Ascendant Sihlda's chamber sat close to the shrine's entrance, a cramped alcove furnished only with a sackcloth mattress and a small writing desk. The desk had been crafted for her by a carpenter consigned to the Pit by virtue of having done bloody murder to both his wife and his lord's son after discovering them mid-tryst. One of Sihlda's early congregants, he had, before expiring from black lung, fashioned various items of impressive craftsmanship from what spare wood he could gather. The desk was by far his greatest and most cherished achievement, one I appreciated just as much as the Ascendant for it was at this desk that she had taught me letters.

"Fetch some water, and all the ink you have left," she told me as we made our way to her chamber. "I have an account to dictate and it may take some time."

With the requisite items gathered I sat on the mattress and assembled the desk, feeling the habitual pulse of delight at the ingenuity of its design. At first glance it appeared just a plain, varnished box,

the place capable of scrubbing the floor. I, as is ever my wont, had more in mind than mere drudgery.

"There were many sick and infirm folk about the town and the surrounding farms and I took it upon myself to visit them, ministering to their souls while also providing sustenance and comfort to their bodies. At first the Aspirant took a dim view of my largesse with the shrine's accumulated tithes but became mollified by the gratitude shown by the townsfolk and the churls. Gratitude will bring in yet more tithes than merely allowing adherents to grovel before the altar once a week. But it wasn't just that I ministered to the sick. I could speak, you see. Speak in a way that will command the ear and the eye, and hold them for hours if the words flowed well. And flow they did. From the scrolls to my heart and then out through my mouth. I spoke and many listened.

"Usually the Martyrs' Day supplications were reasonably well attended affairs, but dull and as brief as the Aspirant could make them, for no one likes to stand before a bored audience impatient for release. But after my first sermon the shrine became notably fuller. The following week they were lining the walls and crowding the door. After that, I began preaching in the field outside and soon that proved too small, so large were the crowds come to hear the word of Supplicant Sihlda."

She stopped talking, her forehead creasing in both remembrance and puzzlement. "In truth, I have never truly understood it, their need to flock around me so. At the time, I liked to think it simply the truth of the Covenant's message, ancient and unaltered but now spoken by a new voice. Also, fear of the Second Scourge is ever a potent draw. But now, after many years of pondering, I'm not so sure. It saddens me to say it, but I think some are bestowed with the gift of snaring the souls of others with words alone. Don't mistake me, Alwyn. I see nothing . . . unnatural in this gift. Think on all the history I have taught you and I'm sure you can identify several luminaries who surely possessed the same ability. I would also wager, if it were not beneath an Ascendant's dignity, that the Pretender must possess some similar facility, else how could a man of such low station have gathered so many to his banner?"

She smiled tightly, shaking her head. "No matter. You must stop me if I stray into conjecture again. To return to my tale it will suffice, for the sake of brevity, to relate that within two summers of taking orders as a Supplicant, my increasing following saw me raised to Aspirant and given my own parish. The fact that this new parish was quite some distance from my current one should have raised some suspicions in my mind, but harbouring ill thoughts towards the Covenant was beyond me in those days. So, off I went, travelling difficult roads and traversing marsh and bog until I found myself at the Shrine to Martyr Lemtuel. You recall his tale, I hope?"

"The first Martyr of the northern shore," I replied dutifully. "Flayed to death for preaching Covenant lore to heathens who worshipped the Ascarlian gods."

"Quite so. And, having flayed him, the heathens threw his body into a bog in the duchy of Cordwain. It was eventually recovered many years later and found to be in a remarkably preserved state and a shrine duly constructed to house it. This was where the Covenant chose to send me, a holy place to be sure, but also a place beset by swarms of ravenous bugs in the summer and thick blankets of freezing fog in the winter.

"I realised later that my parish had been selected on the assumption that few of my growing flock would choose to follow me there, an assumption that proved to be mostly correct. Some followed, of course, a few dozen out of the many who had previously clustered in rapt multitudes to catch my every word. The Shrine to Martyr Lemtuel should have been my prison, a handily chosen spot where an overly popular upstart Aspirant could be counted on to waste her days in isolation, if not fall victim to a fortuitous fever. Instead, I turned a prison into a haven, with a good deal of help from the curiously unrotted corpse of Martyr Lemtuel.

"It is common for the lame and sick to drag themselves along the Trail of Shrines hoping to be healed by the mere sight of divine remains, a practice I have always found both mercenary and disgusting. The notion that the bones of Martyrs possess healing properties is found nowhere in the scrolls and, while the Covenant offers guidance for the leading of a good and healthy life, its province lies primarily with the soul, not the body. My preaching on such matters was surely one of the things that saw me consigned to such a remote parish. Due to its remoteness Lemtuel's shrine is one of the least visited places on the Trail, but even so every so often a few pilgrims would wend their weary, stumbling way to our door. I learned from the Supplicants that almost all tended to leave disappointed, their various maladies uncured and their spirits denuded by disappointment and the prospect of a return journey through the bog. Some would inevitably drown in the fog-shrouded waterways after losing their way or succumbing to exhaustion.

"Unable to tolerate their plight, I instituted a rule whereby no pilgrim could leave until I was satisfied they were strong enough to make the return journey. I had a healing house built next to the shrine which soon attracted more than just pilgrims. Although remote, the Cordwain boglands are not without people – peat cutters and fisher-folk who harvest the channels near the coast. Hardy they are but, like all folk, not immune to sickness or injury. So they too came seeking help and, as is the role of the Covenant, I gave it to them. I had some healing knowledge and learned a great deal as the years passed, but I was always more than a healer and my capacity for winning over an audience had never faded.

"It took the better part of a decade but the Shrine to Martyr Lemtuel eventually became a decent-sized village under Covenant governance, a place where those sick in either soul or body came for healing, while others . . . " Sihlda's voice trailed off at this point. Letting out a sigh, she leaned against the doorway to her chamber, head sagging. Suddenly she appeared far older, all the vitality that belied the creases in her face and grey in her hair seeping away to reveal just a tired woman, aged beyond her years.

When she resumed her narrative, her voice took on a new and unfamiliar depth of sadness. "Others," she said, "came for redemption, the absolution that only the Seraphile's grace can offer after making true and unstinting testament of our worst sins. One chilly morn at the turn of autumn to winter, there came three souls – two youthful knights escorting a young woman of fine and noble appearance and a belly swollen with child. Her mission was two-fold: the safe delivery of her babe, and the testament of her sins."

Her eyes flicked towards me and she straightened, the weariness slipping from her as quickly as it had descended. "You can start writing now."

And so I wrote as she talked, for the next hour my quill hardly ceased its track across the page. The resultant document stirs a shameful note in me when I think of it now for it does not resemble the work of a true scribe. There are frequent errors, many scratched-out words and much spattering of ink, for the tale she told caused my hand to twitch often, even tremble at times. When it was done, I had learned that my belief in the deserved fates of all inmates in the Pit Mines had been dreadfully naive.

"My thanks for your dedicated and diligent attention, Alwyn," she said when I dotted the terminus of the final line. "I entrust this account to you alone. You will carry it from here and, when the time comes, make its contents known."

"When?" I asked, eyeing the stacked pages as one might a coiled and hissing snake. "Make it known to who?" I had no doubts at all regarding the veracity of Sihlda's testament and, thanks in part to her tutelage, had a fair notion of the consequences should it become common knowledge. She was handing me something of great power but also dire consequence.

"You will know," she assured me. "Now," she went on with a familiar briskness, "we must contrive a very special lie to convince Lord Eldurm to provide additional timber."

CHAPTER NINETEEN

I found Lord Eldurm sunk into a mood that was both forlorn and, fortuitously for my purposes, highly distracted. He sat slumped behind his desk, which was littered with a more than usual number of sealed letters. All but one remained unopened, a short note from what I could glimpse of it as reading the inverted contents was difficult. Also, the script had the jagged, spiky quality that indicated a quickly scrawled missive, making decipherment tricky. I was, however, able to read the last line and the oddly clear signature: 'Your eternal friend, Evadine.'

Lord Eldurm, it appeared, had received an answer to his declaration and found it severely disappointing.

"Timber?" he said, voice betraying only the slightest interest and gaze barely rising from the note.

"Yes, my lord," I replied with restrained keenness. "So as to fully explore the newly discovered seam." I nodded to the rock I had placed on his desk, a gnarled, ugly thing with patches of brown possessed of a metallic sheen. "Carver thinks there may well be a good deal more like this to find."

Lord Eldurm blinked and found the energy to focus on the rock for a second. "Copper, eh?"

"Indeed, my lord."

In fact, this lump of copper ore was the only one ever dug out of the Pit, unearthed by Brewer's pick over six years ago and never reported to his lordship on Sihlda's instruction. Carver opined that there was surely more to be found but there was no true means of discovering where except by chance or a greatly increased amount of digging. Given that copper fetched a far higher price than iron, Sihlda knew the discovery of a viable seam in the Pit would soon see an influx of additional inmates. Lords would send hordes of their dregs to win a share in such a prize rather than just the worst miscreants.

Half-raising an eyebrow, Lord Eldurm pursed his lips in consideration. "Father always thought there might be more riches to be found here, should we ever dig deep enough."

"Clearly a man of keen foresight, my lord."

"No." Lord Eldurm sighed and returned his attention to the note, reaching out a hand to trace a finger along the well-crafted signature. It was a small gesture but it told me clearly that, whatever the dispiriting contents of Lady Evadine's reply, this remained a man snared by a hopeless longing.

"My father," he went on in a dull mutter, "was a brute who never once opened a book, took great pleasure in voicing the foulest blasphemies against the Covenant and found his principal joy in cruelty. The day he died my main regret was that my beloved mother wasn't alive to relish the sight of his suffering. Perhaps . . . " His voice dwindled as his brows furrowed and eyes widened in a rush of realisation. Leaning forward, animation returned to his gaze as he took a firmer hold of the letter. "Perhaps that is why I am unworthy. She sees the sin in me, the sin of hating my own father."

You poor pitiable bastard, I thought, careful to keep any emotion from my face. I had by now developed a keen sense of when best to keep silent. Next to scribing, it was probably the most valuable lesson I learned during my time in the Pit.

"I require an unburdening," Lord Eldurm continued. His eyes scanned the letter in rapt realisation, reminding me of the rare occasions when Hostler convinced himself he had discerned some new and important insight into Covenant lore. The thought summoned another of Sihlda's favourite quotations from the Scroll of Martyr Callin: *Every man is a liar, but the worst lie is the one he tells himself.* I also found it odd that it didn't occur to this lovelorn fool that the pious Lady Evadine might see a greater sin in enslaving unfortunates in a mine rather than detesting the memory of a man who surely deserved it in full measure.

"'My path and yours are destined to follow different courses,'" Lord Eldurm read in a whisper, the single page trembling in his hand. "It's clear to me now what must be done. My path must alter to meet hers." He let out a short laugh, lowering the letter to address me. "Tomorrow, you will bring Ascendant Sihlda to me. If there is one soul who can unburden mine of sin, it is her."

I swallowed the reminder about the Ascendant's failing knees before it reached my lips. His lordship's delusion offered an opportunity, one I knew Sihlda would willingly suffer some pain to secure.

"I shall, my lord," I replied, bowing in grave obedience, adding as I straightened, "And . . . the timber?"

"Yes, very well." He waved a hand towards the door. "Tell Sergeant Lebas to give you whatever is required. And the Ascendant's congregation will receive three more sacks this week in recognition of this find."

"For which the congregants offer the most heartfelt thanks, my lord." I bowed again, but I had already slipped beneath his attention. As I left, he had taken up position at the window, gazing off into the distance with his hands clasped behind his back, clenching repeatedly in what I knew to be an expression of desperate hope. In later years I have often felt that my contempt for him would be greater but for the fact that in time I would, in many respects, become his mirror image.

"It's well this shaft doesn't have to last for any length of time," Carver said, smoothing a hand over the wet rock. "We're far too close to the river for my liking."

Hooking an arm over a rung of the ladder, I looked up to see him casting a critical eye over the upper reaches of the shaft. As it narrowed and soil began to appear among the rocks, so did an increasing amount of water. Sometimes it formed mere trickles that dampened the stone; in other places energetic springs sent a constant glittering arc into the gloom. More worrying to me wasn't the sight of the water but the scrapes and groans given off by the surrounding stone, sometimes accompanied by a tremor as unseen fissures collapsed or the water carved a new and possibly dangerous channel.

"But it'll hold, right?" I asked, blinking in irritation as a fat droplet of water exploded on my forehead.

"For now." The damp tendrils of Carver's beard, normally a bushy thing of badgerlike dimensions, sent another spatter of drops onto my face as he shook his head. "But not for long. Rivers don't end at the banks, see? Some can spread their waters underground for miles around, and water will always win against stone in the end."

My gaze slipped to the iron bracket securing the ladder to the shaft wall. A crude thing of part-melted nails and scrap, one of many hammered into the rock with brute force alone over the course of the past four weeks. Without mortar to secure the brackets in place they were certain to slip free sooner or later. The congregants' normally fulsome production of iron ore had dwindled as we focused all our efforts on the shaft. Lord Eldurm accepted the shortfall as a price worth paying for our excavation of the mythical copper seam. But his forbearance wouldn't last for ever, regardless of how many days he spent unburdening his soul to Ascendant Sihlda.

"We'll break ground in three days, give or take," Carver said. "When we do, we can't wait. You need to tell her that."

He looked down, meeting my gaze. Although he was perhaps the most placid soul among the congregants, as the day of our escape loomed ever closer, I could see the desperation in him. Sihlda's followers remained devout but witnessing their growing hunger for release from the Pit made me wonder how long such devotion would last.

"I'll tell her," I said, clambering down into the shadows and trying to deafen myself to the protesting squeals of the brackets.

*

I found Sihlda poring over the latest copy of Martyr Callin's scroll. Pride forbids me from describing it as the finest ever rendition of his tale, but other scribes have called it so and those that haven't can be counted as just a gaggle of jealous scratchers unworthy of their title.

The redeemed thief's story had been the principal means by which Sihlda had taught me letters and my first attempt at setting it down resembles the work of the clumsiest child. I kept at it, nevertheless. Other works of perhaps greater import I have lost or discarded over the years but not that first faltering step on the scribe's path. It was not just the learning of letters, you see; it was the understanding behind all those malformed words, for in guiding my hand Sihlda had also guided my mind. The history of this benighted realm. The familial ties of blood and kinship that bound it together. The compact between Covenant and Crown that she dubbed 'the dire necessity'. All this I had learned via the martyrdom of Callin, the thief who had stolen her heart three centuries after his death.

"Found a flaw?" I asked, pausing in the doorway to her chamber. "Another inelegant flourish perhaps?"

"No." She smiled, glancing up from the scroll. "It is, as much as any marriage of ink and parchment can be, as fine and perfect a document as I have ever seen. Your skills may not be complete, Alwyn, but they are considerable."

I resisted the impulse to indulge in smug acknowledgement, instead replying with a humble "My thanks, Ascendant."

Gifted as ever in seeing through my facade, she snorted. "Pride and conceit will undo you in the end," she chided with a sigh. "Out with it, then. You're only so respectful when you have something to say you know I won't like."

"The shaft will be finished in three days," I said. "Carver says it won't last beyond that."

"I see." Setting the scroll aside she sat back and gestured for me to take my usual seat. "It occurs to me that we haven't discussed your calculations for some time. What conclusions have you arrived at recently?"

I frowned in consternation, hesitating in the doorway. "The shaft . . . "

"I heard you, Alwyn." She pointed insistently at the folded desk until I consented to take my customary seat. "Now," she said with an expectant smile, "calculations."

"I've been thinking a lot about Erchel's kin," I began. "Trying to remember as many names as I can. I made a list – cousins, uncles, aunties and such. Erchel had a lot of kin but they weren't memorable folk, beyond the odd tale of well-executed thievery or unusually vicious murder. His uncle was the only notable among them and, while he may have had a hand in it, I can't see him as possessing enough brain to conceive a trap. At least, not a trap that Deckin wouldn't have seen through in a trice."

I couldn't recall how many times we had engaged in this curious ritual. I would relate whatever I had managed to dredge from my memory and she would guide me in an attempt to arrive at previously hidden meanings. It was a frustrating but sometimes fruitful exercise, revealing much that had evaded my notice before. For instance, I now understood that Todman's accent was all artifice and he in fact hailed from one of the southern duchies. It was also apparent that Gerthe had been as practised a thief as she had been a linguist and whore. Thanks to some deft sleight of hand, she was the principal reason why my purse was always too light to pay for her services. Then there was Deckin himself.

Much of the conclusions Sihlda guided me to were small things, like the now-obvious fact that Deckin had no more understanding of letters than I'd once had. Other revelations required a greater depth of reasoning. With Sihlda's aid I began to see clearly the obsession that had led Deckin and his followers to their doom, an obsession that had blossomed into madness by the end. *The man you describe wanted only one thing in life*, she told me, *to finally gain the notice of his father, either through fame as an outlaw or outright assassination. When the King's Champion took his head, Deckin was forever deprived of the goal he had lusted for since boyhood. People have been known to lose their minds over lesser things.*

Victim of betrayal he was, but I knew now that Deckin had placed his own head on the spike long before we ever took the first step towards Moss Mill.

"We've discussed Erchel's kin before," Sihlda said. "With similar conclusions. Which leads us where?"

"To pondering who did have the brain to orchestrate such a trap." Impatient as I was to return to the subject of our hopefully imminent escape, ruminating on this conundrum never failed to capture my full attention. "And that's a short list we've covered before."

"Cover it again, short or not."

"Todman, a brute to be sure but not short of guile, though I always felt him too much a follower to act against Deckin, not alone anyway. Hostler could have done it if he hadn't been so mired . . . so preoccupied with his devotion to the Covenant. Raith was smart enough, but didn't seem to care a whit for ambition. And . . . " I trailed off with a shrug. "The only other head clever and wilful enough to do it was probably sitting on a spike on the wall of Castle Duhbos, last I saw."

"Yes, the lovely Lorine. Tell me, Alwyn, what exactly did you see when you looked upon those heads on the wall? How close did you look?"

In truth it was a memory I had scoured with less attention than the others, it being so ugly. Also, Sihlda's guiding hand tended to lead me down other avenues, until now. "Dead folk," I said, grimacing at the memory. "Too far away and rotted to recognise, but I'm sure one was a woman . . . "

I fell silent as my mind's eye lingered on the long hair that had trailed from that head like a ragged pennant. I often felt that it held a coppery sheen, but that could have just been a trick of the morning sun. "It had to be her," I said, though my voice was coloured by a new uncertainty, stoked to a greater pitch by Sihlda's next words.

"Why?" she asked. "Because you assumed it? Have you not learned by now that the world does not always conform to our assumptions? You have told me a good deal about Lorine over the years, though I suspect your regard for her went deeper than you admit. Such is the way with the lusts and follies of youth: they shame us to self-deceit in later life. Remember what I taught you: cut through the deceit and see the truth."

My eyes lost focus as I followed the lessons she had imparted regarding purposeful cogitation. *Summon the oldest memory first. Follow the trail it sets.* My first sight of Lorine had been of her face drawn in an expression somewhere between a smile and a grimace as she beheld the ragged, sniffling boy in the woods. *You're in luck, young fellow*, she had said when we got to camp, leading me to the shelter she shared with Deckin. *We encountered a very generous cloth merchant only the other day. Best get you properly clothed, hadn't we? You can't go about looking like that. All the others would talk.*

This had drawn a laugh from the rest of the band, and it occurred to me just how skilled Lorine had been at stoking their humour, often as a counter to Deckin's less than jovial moods. Other memories stirred, following the same track, recollections of how much the others liked her, how adept she had been at winning the friendship of newcomers. The women became like sisters, the men brothers or fond but eternally disappointed suitors, for none dare let a hand stray towards Deckin's woman. They feared him, some even loved him the way heathens love a vengeful god, but they liked Lorine, they listened to her and accepted her counsel. The band, I knew now, had been as much hers as his.

Eventually the trail of memory led me to Deckin's mad plan to seize the duchy by means of bloody massacre. Skilled actress though she was, it was clear Lorine had wanted no part of it. Hence the sovereigns she had dropped into my palm, sovereigns I had refused, but there had been other palms, like Todman's.

"Perhaps some sovereigns dropped into hers before they dropped into mine," I muttered aloud as thoughts proceeded along roads yet unexplored.

"Whose sovereigns?" Sihlda asked, voice soft and intent as it always was when we performed this ritual. "When and where?"

"There were times she could have slipped away," I said. "She must have had some inkling of what Deckin planned even before the sword cleaved his father's neck. We first got word that the duke had turned his coat in the autumn. It was always a busy time. She would have had ample opportunity to seek out a sheriff's man or a forest warden, pay a bribe to pass a note, a promise of betrayal in return for a reward or guarantee of release once Deckin's scheme had led us all to disaster. But still, she would have had to receive a reply and send another message to ensure the ambush was laid at Moss Mill."

I felt my features take on a familiar blankness as the churn in my brain began to spit out conclusions. "Erchel," I said. "When Deckin sent him off to gather his kin at Leffold Glade, Lorine must have given the message to him, and a promise for his uncle if he played along. With Deckin gone, the eastern gangs would surely get richer and soon perhaps there would be a new king in the forest. But—" my becalmed features twitched in frustration "—the head on the wall . . . "

Thoughts of Castle Duhbos dragged my mind towards the tavern and the soldiers. From there it was only a few ugly steps to the pillory.

"No," Sihlda said, reading the reluctance on my face, the instinctive shying away from suffering and the unreasoning rage it provoked. "Your thoughts led you there for a reason. Follow them."

They led, of course, to pain, humiliation, the sting of shit in a freshly opened wound, the chafing of wrists bound by iron as I itched to claw at my tormentors, and Lord Althus . . . The torrent of thoughts slowed as he loomed into view, the tone of jocular disdain with which he told his tale, a tale that contained a brief morsel of great import, the words seeping up from the morass of fatigue and agony that had drowned them, but not completely. *Neither will I drag you before the new duke for judgement*, he had told me. *That bitch he's taken a liking to will surely confirm your membership of Deckin's band . . .*

"That bitch he's taken a liking to," I murmured. "That bitch . . . It wasn't Lorine on the wall."

"No," Sihlda said. "I don't believe it was."

The calm surety of her voice caused me to blink at her in realisation. "You knew."

She replied with a small shrug that put a spark to a familiar anger. "All this time," I said, unable to keep the resentment from my voice.

"Not quite. Certainly from the first time you related your tale in its entirety."

"Then why not just tell me?"

"You accepted me as your teacher. What lesson would there have been in telling you the answer before you knew how to properly ask the question?"

I bit down a retort and looked away, trying to redirect my anger to more deserving targets. *Lorine. Todman. Erchel and all his filthy kin. Lord Althus. An ever-growing list. And I'll strike off every fucking name.* The burgeoning rage must have shown on my face for Sihlda reached out to press a hand to my cheek, her touch cool and calming.

"Understanding should bring wisdom," she told me. "But it will be drowned if you surrender to the indulgence of wrath."

"She sold him out," I grated. "The man she loved . . . "

"The man who, you told me yourself, would surely have led you all to ruin."

"We were ruined anyway. They killed dozens at Moss Mill. If she wanted to survive Deckin's scheme she could simply have disappeared. Taken Todman and whichever other easily led prick she was teasing and pissed off one dark night. Deckin might have searched for her, but not for long. Not when he had a massacre to plan."

"Then why?" Sihlda asked, smoothing her hand over my forehead. "What did she gain through betrayal."

My anger lingered but this additional rush of insight brought it to a low simmer. "Money, for a start. Deckin used to say his head was worth ten times its weight in gold given the price on it, and he wasn't wrong. But I doubt it was just that. Lorine was ever an ambitious soul. Seems to me she swapped an outlaw for a duke. Quite a bargain if you're able to strike it."

For some reason my voice caught on the last word and found myself once again averting my gaze, Sihlda's hand slipping from my forehead as I turned from her, swallowing hard.

"I often wonder," she said, "if I have damned you or saved you. In honing your mind have I crafted a better man or just a better outlaw?

You know I have a mission beyond these walls, Alwyn. Can you tell me truly that you wish to be part of it?"

I took a moment to blink the hateful moisture from my eyes and cough away the dryness in my throat. When I turned to meet her gaze once more it was with a steady eye and voice. "I can tell you that I'll follow as long as you command it, for there's too great a debt between us to ever settle. But the moment your mission ends, for whatever reason, I'll begin my own."

She regarded me with a thoughtful but otherwise blank expression and, though I searched for some sign of disappointment or reproach, I couldn't find either. "Then it seems," she said, "you have struck a fair bargain of your own."

She gave a brisk sniff and got to her feet. "Be so good as to gather the others in the shrine," she told me. "We have an escape to plan after all."

CHAPTER TWENTY

"Of course, it had to be raining." Toria grimaced, blinking the spatter of moisture from her eyes as she stared up into the blackness of the shaft. I assumed she shared my growing concern that the thing was about to collapse at any moment. We couldn't see the opening Carver had created that morning, but the constant rain and occasional cascade of mud was both reassuring and frightening. At Sihlda's insistence the moment of our escape had been set at a good stretch past sunset when the guards would be tired and darkness would provide cover for so many fleeing souls.

Each of us carried a full skin of water and a small sack of food, enough for two days. The burdens were deliberately light to allow for a speedy dash to the promised sanctuary of Callintor. In addition to the sacks, many of us had chosen to arm ourselves. Besides our knives, Toria and I carried cudgels fashioned from shortened pickaxe handles. Brewer had contrived to build a crossbow, a task requiring many months, skilled attention that he had somehow managed to keep hidden. It was an enviably well-made thing with a thick stave and cleverly crafted lock, indicating that Brewer was a more accomplished fellow than I previously realised. Besides the crossbow, he also had a modified pickaxe strapped to his back, the blade hammered into a broad, wickedly sharp crescent. From the way he hovered close to

Sihlda as we crouched in the tunnel, I knew these weapons were not for his benefit and felt a small spasm of pity for any pursuers who came close to laying a hand on the Ascendant this night.

The preceding day had passed in an agony of anticipation as we readied our supplies and girded ourselves for what lay ahead. Sihlda spent longer than usual in communion with Lord Eldurm, apparently keen to complete his unburdening before we departed the Pit. I found it curious that so uncomplicated a fellow as our lordly gaoler could possess a soul in need of so much cleansing, but ascribed it to a well-hidden empathy for the plight of his toiling captives. As the day wore on, I grew increasingly worried about the reaction of our fellow inmates. The congregants made some effort to adhere to the expected routine, but with the need to complete the shaft and prepare supplies, far fewer of us had made the journey to the top of the slope than was typical. It was bound to be noticed, surely by the other prisoners and possibly a sharp-eyed guard or two.

Then, with the sky darkened and rain beginning to fall, Sihlda finally appeared in the shrine, a tired but satisfied smile on her face as she scanned the array of tense, expectant faces. "It is good to bid farewell to an unburdened soul," she said.

"Let's hope it cools his rage when he discovers our absence," I said.

To my surprise, Sihlda laughed, a distinctly odd sound in an atmosphere so thickened by fearful suspense. "Some things are beyond even the Martyrs' example." She took a breath and started towards the tunnel. "Shall we?"

"Don't you want to rest for a while?" I asked. "The flight to Callintor will be hard—"

"Not with the Seraphile's grace to sustain me," she said with an airy wave of her hand. "And I feel they are surely with us this night."

Sihlda had been wise in choosing the four most dangerous congregants to be first up the ladder. Toria would take the lead, being the swiftest among us while also possessing the keenest eyes at night. Brewer would follow with his crossbow ready to dispatch any unfortunate glimpsed by her eyes. Hedgeman would be next with his slingshot. Having lived most of his life in the wilds, he was skilled with the weapon and, like Hostler, his devotional zeal didn't prevent him from being a dab hand when the need for violence arose. I would go next and assist Sihlda as she crawled free of the shaft. With the exit secured, the other congregants would follow, forming into ten small groups and following different courses to Callintor. Moving in one great mass might have provided an illusion of protection but was surely an invitation to discovery and subsequent slaughter. Whatever makeshift weapons we had fashioned, this group would be no match for armoured men on horseback, no matter how favourably the Seraphile might view this enterprise.

Carver advised the ladder could tolerate only five bodies at once. As I climbed in Hedgeman's wake, I felt even that was too much, suppressing a flinch at the squeal of the brackets and the groans and creaks of the timbers. The climb seemed to take far longer than necessary, time stretching as it often does in the interval before momentous and irreversible events. I found myself battling a perverse reluctance with each passing rung of the ladder. Tonight would see me either dead or free. Once I climbed out of this shaft there could be no backward step. The last four years had been a miserable trial in many ways but also had been a far safer and more enlightening refuge than any I had known as an outlaw. My mind and skills had expanded greatly under Sihlda's guidance and the congregants, while a dull lot for the most part, were far less fractious and prone to arousing my vindictive streak than the members of Deckin's doomed band. I had also found in Toria the only soul I could truly call a friend. Tonight it could all end, along with everything else.

A chilly and painful slap of mud falling onto my forehead was enough to banish my introspection, along with any reluctant impulse. This course had been set years ago and couldn't just be abandoned on a cowardly whim. Besides, what manner of man would ever think of the Pit as home? Sihlda had her mission and I had mine. Neither would be fulfilled by wasting away digging ore to fatten the purses of nobles.

The rain grew heavier as we neared the top of the shaft, the protests of the ladder drowned by a loud rumble of thunder. Looking up, I saw the opening revealed in full by a flash of lightning, Toria's slight silhouette resembling a scurrying spider as she crawled through, lost to darkness as the lightning flickered and died. I felt the ladder shift and sway to an alarming degree as Brewer heaved his considerable bulk into the open. I swallowed a curse as Hedgeman's shoe made brief but painful contact with my scalp then another burst of lightning revealed he had also clambered out.

I paused to let the lingering smear of colour fade from my eyes then climbed the last few rungs to the surface. I waited at the lip of the hole, feeling the caress of damp, wind-tossed grass on my face as I glanced down, expecting Sihlda to follow. Instead the shaft remained dark and empty.

"Ascendant!" I hissed in impatience, lowering myself to peer into the gloom. As I did so I heard something new, a fresh concordance of sound that had been swallowed by the tumult of the storm above. Shouting. Screams. Some angry. Some pained. Also, dim but detectable to my practised ear, the clash and clatter of metal on metal.

"Sihlda!" I called out, descending several rungs as panic seized me, then stopped when a flicker of lightning revealed the small pale oval of her face. It was gone in an instant, but in that brief glimpse I had seen more emotion in her features than ever before. She was weeping but also smiling, the same serene smile I knew so well, the smile that told all who saw it that she knew everything worth knowing. But there was sadness too, a great deal of it shining in the wet orbs of her eyes. In later years, I would sometimes try to convince myself that guilt had also been present in that stricken yet content face and know it to be just a comforting lie. A soul possessed of so much certainty is incapable of guilt.

"We all deserve to be here, Alwyn," she told me, voice rendered faint by the storm and the din of combat below. "But a few deserve another chance, one I do not require for this is my parish where I am content to remain."

"Don't be fucking stupid!" I said, panic stripping away all formality as I descended further, reaching down to clutch at where I imagined her hand to be. "We're nearly there. Your mission! Remember your mission!"

"You are my mission, Alwyn. The testament I gave you. Martyr Callin's scroll. They and you are my gifts to a world I failed. I know you do not yet know the truth of the Covenant in your heart, but you will, in time. Of that, I am certain."

"Come with me and see for yourself!" I flailed about, grasping for the slightest touch of her but all I felt was the faint heat of a breath on my fingers as she spoke the last ever words I would hear from her.

"I left a note for Lord Eldurm, with instructions he not read it until midnight. I told him it contained the final step in his unburdening. For a soul to be free of sin, it must know itself, know its true nature. He is a gaoler of souls deserving of punishment. You are a man in search of a reckoning that will lead to far better things." A brief pause as her lips kissed my hand before her fingers pressed something into my grasp. "Goodbye, Alwyn."

A short pause, then from far below a thud sounded amid the chaotic chorus of voices. It heralded a brief interruption in the cacophony followed by a sudden and savage resurgence. Sihlda's name was screamed out from desperate throats, the thud and clatter of weapons echoing loud for a few frenzied moments, then slowly diminishing. Defiant cries choked into gurgling death rattles interspersed with hard, wet thwacks familiar to any butcher's shop.

I hung there, staring into the blackness as rain pelted from above, then the ladder began to shake more violently than before, juddering and squealing as a dozen or more bodies began to climb.

"Alwyn!" Toria's shout filled the shaft, shrill and desperate. "Where the fuck are you?!"

A familiar sense of purpose gripped me then, outlaw's instinct reasserting itself with a cold implacability. *She's dead. Save yourself.*

I scrambled the remaining distance to the opening in a few frenzied seconds, emerging into a rain-lashed meadow of tall grass whipped into chaos by the storm. "The Ascendant!" Brewer demanded, gripping my arm hard. I tore myself free, staring at the coin resting in my palm: Martyr Callin's only relic, the Ascendant's final gift. Consigning it to my pocket I rushed to crouch at the opening, fixing my hands on the ladder's topmost bracket and hauling hard.

"Where is she?" Brewer shouted, large hands clamping onto my shoulder. I glanced up to regard a man beset by forlorn desperation rather than rage. I could tell the next words I spoke held no surprise, but still they wounded him worse than any blade.

"Dead!" I yelled into his face, his hands falling limp at his side. "The guards found the tunnel! She gave her life to stall them! If you don't want to join her," I grunted, as I continued to try to work the bracket loose from the shaft wall, "then help me!"

He continued to stare in slack-mouthed shock, barely shifting as Toria pushed past him. Crouching, she jabbed her knife at the bracket in an effort to work it loose, the ladder flexing with greater animation as the guards climbing it drew closer to the top. Its stubborn resistance to destruction caused me to reflect that Carver should have had more faith in his own craftsmanship.

"Won't . . . fucking . . . budge!" Toria cursed, words part swallowed by another crash of thunder as she continued to worry at the bracket. I looked around to see Hedgeman standing in slumped, blank-eyed indifference, barely stirring at my profane command to help.

"Forget it!" I told Toria, pulling her back from the hole and getting to my feet. "We need to run. Now, or we've got no chance—"

I flinched as something fast and heavy cut the air an inch from my nose. Brewer's roar as he brought the modified pickaxe down on the ladder was loud enough to contend with the thunder, also painful to hear in its sheer animalistic pain and fury. Lightning flashed as he raised the pickaxe, revealing a murderous visage before he brought it down again. The upper rungs of the ladder disappeared into splinters then the stone surrounding the bracket turned to powder under the force of a half-dozen blows. Dust rose briefly from the hole, accompanied by a chorus of short, quickly smothered screams. I felt the ground tremble beneath my feet as the shaft collapsed, several tons of rock colliding and subsiding to crush the unfortunate guards to pulp.

As the tremble faded from the earth, Brewer continued to stand over the rubble-filled hole, I assumed in the manic hope that he might get to smash the skull of any guard who had miraculously survived to poke his head out. I knew there was every chance Brewer and the still silent and unmoving Hedgeman would continue to stand vigil over the site of Sihlda's death until pursuers arrived from the Pit, probably in just a few short hours if not sooner. However, I felt I owed both her and them some last show of comradeship. We had been congregants of the same shrine after all.

"She wanted us to live," I told Brewer, moving closer but not near enough to place me within reach of his pickaxe. The storm had lessened somewhat so I didn't have to shout, but the rain continued to fall in thick, chilling sheets. "If you die tonight you betray her."

His one eye flicked up at me, glimmering now with suspicion rather than rage. "How did they know?" he said, his voice possessed of a worryingly calm note. Looking into that narrow orb I had little doubt speaking the truth at this juncture would invite a dire and possibly fatal response. I might be closer to his height these days but had no hope of matching him in brute strength, especially when he was filled with a maddened rage.

"We aroused suspicion somehow," I replied with a helpless shrug. "The Shunned. One of the guards. Who can say?"

"No." Hedgeman's voice was thin and grating, the words choked out as he stumbled towards us. I was sorely tempted to punch some reason back into him but his next words tumbled forth before I could raise a fist. "No. It was treachery. No one outside the congregation knew." He sank to his knees with a piteous sob, hands clutching at the rocks sealing the shaft. "Martyr Sihlda has fallen to a traitor's hand!"

"Something to reckon out at another time," I said, turning away and gathering up my sack of food and sundry valuables. The folded writing desk was by far the heaviest item but I felt no temptation to abandon it, not then and not at any point since. "We're going to Callintor," I added, jerking my head at Toria and striding off towards the dark irregular wall of woodland to the east. "Come or don't. Just remember, you let yourselves die here you'll be dishonouring the Ascendant's memory."

"It was you!" Hedgeman's words were barely coherent, gabbled out in a rapid, spittle-flecked torrent. He rushed to bar my path, a brief flash of lightning revealing the knife in his hand. "You were never her true disciple. I saw it. I saw how you remained deaf to her truths. You sold her to the lord!"

"You're off your fucking head," I said, trying to go around him but coming to a halt as he lurched to my front once more. His eyes were wide and lacking all reason, but he held the knife with a practised hand. I would realise later that this man had surrendered himself entirely to Sihlda's teachings, gifted to her every ounce of faith that remained him. With her divine mission ended before it had even begun he had nothing, a soul emptied of purpose and desperate to fill the void with what he saw as holy retribution.

"She is a Martyr now!" Hedgeman gabbled, crouching in readiness. "And you her slayer. Those who spill Martyr's blood can know but one end. Every scroll that forms the Covenant speaks thus."

I let my sack fall from my shoulder and mirrored his pose, knife in one hand and cudgel in the other. Toria moved to my right, doing the same. This, I knew, would be quick and ugly. We had no time for any more talk, and, disordered of mind or not, Hedgeman was a lethal fighter. If I escaped this with only a cut or two, I would count myself lucky.

A dull snap sounded to my rear, accompanied by the thrum of a vibrating cord. Hedgeman jerked upright, standing in rigid immobility before embarking upon a chaotic dance through the swaying grass, stumbling about on stiff, spasming legs while strange, guttural grunts gibbered from his lips. The cause of his distress was concealed by the gloom until a distant shimmer of lightning outlined the fletching of a crossbow bolt jutting from his forehead. His shadowed form slumped abruptly to the ground, coughed and farted out a truly noxious odour which was to stand as Hedgeman's last testament to a world that wouldn't miss him.

I turned to watch Brewer cast his crossbow away and shoulder his own sack. "Too heavy to carry," he said, striding past us towards the distant woods. "You coming?" he added, spurring to a run as Toria and I continued to stare at his fast-receding form.

CHAPTER TWENTY-ONE

For a big man, Brewer proved capable of maintaining a fast pace through the meadow and the woods, so much so that Toria and I found ourselves straining to keep up. We had all memorised the route to Callintor before climbing the shaft, repeating it word for word at Sihlda's instruction. It had been formulated by a select few congregants with knowledge of the local country, a winding, at times aggravatingly wayward course that avoided the principal roads.

Through the woods east of the river, I recounted inwardly as I ran, checking constantly to ensure Toria was still close by. *Keep going until you reach the stream. Follow it north to the old ruined mill.* From there it was a supposedly straight run north over open country to Callintor, a prospect I viewed with a distinct lack of anticipation. The woods felt like home, my outlaw's eye for hiding places and ambush sites returning as the storm abated and the burgeoning sun revealed our surroundings. It birthed a temptation to abandon this increasingly taxing flight and seek out a refuge among the trees, an impulse I crushed with ruthless insistence. I had not escaped the worst prison in all of Albermaine to return to a life of skulking in the woods.

We rested only briefly, pausing in the lee of the largest trees just long enough to gulp water and force down a mouthful or two of food. Nothing was said as words would be an indulgence now, but I felt a nagging desire to question Brewer regarding his murder of Hedgeman. The only sentiment we shared was a devotion to Sihlda and with her gone I found his actions hard to fathom, especially since his face betrayed nothing beyond the strain of exertion and the distant gaze that comes from grief.

I resisted voicing the question throughout the day, following his untiring course along the stream bank. As we ran, I kept one ear cocked for the rhythmic thud of hooves or baying of hounds. I indulged some hope that Lord Eldurm would assume the shaft's collapse had claimed all the escapees along with several luckless guards but knew such optimism to be dangerous. Agreeable idiot he may have been, but by merely attempting an escape we had besmirched his family honour. No noble, however steeped in hopeless longing for a woman who didn't give a whit for his existence, could simply accept such an injury. He would at least search for the shaft's opening and, having found it, discover a corpse with a bolt through the head. His hounds would also be quick in sniffing out a trail leading to the woods. We had at least a three-hour head start by my reckoning, but men on horseback would eat that up fairly soon.

We allowed ourselves the longest rest upon reaching the ruined mill, an ancient place that must have stood during the days of the first Tri-Reign. Some semblance of its former purpose lingered in the shape of its moss-covered stones, but all that remained of its once mighty wheel was an iron hub rusted to abstraction.

We secluded ourselves in a nook formed of three stunted walls, Toria collapsing onto all fours as soon as she came to a halt. She quickly retched up the sparse food she had eaten, before slumping onto her back, chest heaving and sweaty face staring up at the sky through the overlapping branches. Speech was beyond her but she did manage to force a scowl when I panted, "Can I have your knife if you die?"

I tossed my sack to the ground and rested my back against the wall, intending to brace myself against it until my exhaustion faded. My legs, however, had ideas of their own and promptly folded beneath me. I lay stunned and numb by the strain and fear of it all until I recovered enough strength to heave myself into a sitting position.

Brewer had succeeded in propping himself against the wall without falling over. I sat and watched as bugs swarmed about his sweaty face, marvelling at the fact that he still carried the pickaxe on his back.

"Why?" I asked him. The question brought focus to his still-distant gaze for a moment, though I couldn't tell whether it was anger or just grief.

"Because she told me to," he said. "When we began her mission my role would be to keep you safe. I didn't understand her meaning, but she made me promise I would abide, whatever might befall us."

"When we get to Callintor," I said, groaning with the effort of reaching for my sack, "you can forget that promise. Feel at liberty to consider yourself released now, if you like."

"It's not for you to release me."

I looked up from rummaging to find his eye still on me, even more focused and set with purpose. "I don't a need a protector," I said, which drew a caustic laugh.

"Truly you were deaf to the Martyr Sihlda's truths," Brewer said. "'Know yourself above all others', remember? You, Alwyn Scribe, are a man people will always want to kill. I'd have done it myself years ago if she hadn't forbidden it."

"No." I returned my attention to the sack, extracting the sole apple I had secured for the journey. "You would have tried."

The bite I took from the apple was a wonderful thing, flooding my mouth with liquid sweetness. I took another bite and looked to see Toria rising from her slump. "Here," I said, tossing her the half-eaten fruit. "An empty belly will do you no good today."

"Another gift from his lordship?" she asked, eyeing the apple doubtfully before forcing herself to take a bite. Her sagging face and bowed back worried me and her gaze held the dullness that told of a body nearing its limits. She was strong and lithe to be sure, with muscle honed by years of labour, but no one could run for ever.

"From a guard," I said. "For writing him a letter to his sweetheart. Eat up and drink well."

I hoped this interval might last until evening set in, providing sufficient rest for Toria to complete the final run to Callintor without undue difficulty. Of course, fate is rarely so generous.

It was just a faint sound carried by the easterly wind and would have been easily missed among rustle and birdsong of the forest, but my outlaw's ear remained as keen as my eye. *Still a good way off*, I surmised, cocking an ear to gauge the direction of the distant yipping. *But they have our trail.*

"Hounds," I said, wincing as I dragged myself upright.

"Can't hear fuck all," Toria protested as I reached down to haul her up.

"Then it's lucky for you I can, isn't it? Lose that." I tugged the sack from her hand and tossed it away. "We can't stop again." My concern deepened at what I saw in her face. True exhaustion is a treacherous thing; it lies to its victim, whispers promises it can't keep, pretends danger doesn't exist and all will be right with the world if you just lie here one more minute. I could see these notions flitting through Toria's mind, leading me to an obvious but highly risky course.

The slap was hard, my hand smacking across her jaw and cheek with sufficient force to bruise the flesh. Her response, however, was gratifyingly swift.

"Bastard!"

I dodged the knife before it could open my throat, then sidestepped the next two thrusts she jabbed at my chest.

"I'll feed you your own cock, you shit!" She lowered herself into a fighting crouch, knife blade turning this way and that, a standard tactic intended to confuse an opponent. Her face burned red except for the pale mark left by my hand, eyes shining bright with little sign of exhaustion.

"Kill me later," I said, taking one last gulp from my water skin before throwing it away. "For now, all we need do is run."

We cleared the forest within the hour, pitching headlong into the wheat field beyond. The descending sun painted the swaying crop a reddish gold hue that would have been pleasing to less frantic eyes.

Fortunately for us, the wheat was tall and near ready for harvest, meaning we could run at a crouch and perhaps evade the gaze of our pursuers. However, there was no hiding from the noses of their hounds.

The distant yipping had grown into a recurrent chorus of barks and howls as the day wore on. These, I knew, would be wolfhounds bred specially for the purpose of hunting people rather than game. Such dogs stood tall at the shoulder and one was usually strong enough to bring down a fully grown man. I feared their fangs well enough but feared their masters' whips and blades more. The dogs would be trained to hold rather than kill us, except through over-enthusiasm. Lord Eldurm, I had little doubt, would want his escaped charges alive. Three corpses would make scant impression on the other inmates at the Pit, so inured were they to the sight of death. But three living souls subjected to prolonged torment before being strung up in front of the gate would provide a long-lasting example.

Such thoughts kept me running despite the pain that now seemed to throb in every muscle I possessed. It must also have had an equally fortifying effect on Toria for she managed to keep pace with me for much of the run, despite a few stumbles. I had a faint hope her renewed energy wouldn't transform into retribution when we reached our destination, but that was a worry for another time.

As before, Brewer led the way, although even he was starting to sag. Inevitably, his fatigued feet happened upon a molehill, sending him into an untidy tumble. "No!" I heard him grunt in furious self-recrimination, using his pickaxe to push himself to his feet. "Do this one thing, you miserable cur!"

About halfway across the field the strain of the run became so all-consuming that I felt the moment of collapse approaching, the point at which my body would simply surrender. It would surely have claimed me within seconds if my eyes hadn't alighted upon the spires. There were four of them, one for each of the Martyr shrines in Callintor, rising above the wheat like dark spearpoints against the reddening evening sky.

At my side Toria fell again, emitting a piteous groan as she collided with the ground. "Come on!" I looped an arm around her slim waist and dragged her upright, pointing to the spires. "Look! We're nearly there!"

Some frenzied dragging and pushing finally brought us clear of the field, the tall wheat parting to reveal Brewer staggering in near exhaustion, feet tripping over the ruts of a cart track. A dozen yards on lay the bank of a narrow but deep river. On the far side rose the wooden walls of the sanctuary city of Callintor. A swift survey of our surroundings revealed that the track we stood on traced the unusually straight course of the river to either side with no sign of a bridge or a gatehouse.

"Seems we're a mite off course," I gasped, allowing Toria to slip from my grip. She slumped to her knees, head thrown back as she dragged air into her lungs.

"The main gate's this way." Brewer jerked a thumb over his shoulder towards the east. "Just a bit further on . . . "

I would learn later that certain breeds of wolfhound are trained to fall silent when approaching their prey. The barks and howls emitted while following a trail are for the benefit of their human masters and abandoned when the prospect of capture looms. The beast that erupted from the wheat to land on Brewer's back would have matched him in height if stood on its hind legs, the long shaggy body possessing enough weight to bear its bulky victim to the ground in a trice. It coiled its neck and spread its jaws with a snakelike speed and precision, aiming to latch its fangs onto Brewer's upraised arm.

I leapt without thinking, sinking my knife into the tendons behind the hound's jaw, my right arm and legs wrapping around its body to drag it clear as I rolled away. My back connected painfully with the ground, but I maintained my grip with a savage strength born of survival. The hound thrashed at me with desperate ferocity as I drew the knife clear to deliver two more stabs to its neck, hoping to find a decently large vein. I was fortunate in the accuracy of my first blow for the hound's jaws flapped at me without effect, my knife bringing forth plenty of blood but failing to land a killing blow.

There was a whoosh of air then the hound stiffened with a whimper before all animation fled its body. Scrambling clear, I watched Brewer plant a foot on the fallen beast's ribcage and drag the pickaxe's spike free.

A rustle of disturbed wheat had him whirling, another hound springing forth in a blur of grey then rearing up with an aggrieved howl as something small but very fast impacted on its eye. A glance to my right revealed Toria fitting another stone to the sling she had taken from Hedgeman's body. She gave a practised flick of her arm and the second stone flew free, striking the still-confused hound on the rump. It immediately switched attention from Brewer to her, lips quivering around bared fangs as it crouched for a lunge. However, this proved a grave mistake for it gave Brewer enough time to raise his pickaxe and bring the curved blade down on the beast's neck. Blood jetted as its head fell clear of the body, which twitched and scrabbled in an obscene dance.

The shrill pealing of a horn drew my gaze to the field, the wheat thrashing as several long shapes loped their way towards us. Beyond them I saw the more worrying sight of fading sunlight gleaming on the armour of a dozen mounted men. Lord Eldurm hadn't bothered to bring his family banner but I recognised him easily as the tall figure in front. The bared sword in his hand led me to a conclude that recapture and prolonged torture might not be his intent after all.

"Forget the gate," I said, getting to my feet and turning back to the river. "We'll swim for it."

I took a firm grip of the sack containing my writing desk, the leather-bound treasures of Sihlda's testament and the Scroll of Martyr Callin and hurled it with all the energy I could muster. Before plunging into the water, I saw the sack land amid the reeds on the far side of the river. It was a slow-flowing channel, the water foul with scum and the telltale stink of effluent, both human and animal. I barely noticed, churning my way across in a few strokes as the thunder of fast-approaching hooves summoned my last reserves of strength.

Flopping among the reeds fringing the far bank, I flailed about until I recovered the sack. Crawling free, I struggled to my feet and staggered to the old, mortar-buttressed timbers that formed the walls of Callintoɩ. As I collapsed against the rough barrier, it occurred to me I had no means of attracting the attention of those inside. Sihlda had patiently educated all of us in the correct phrasing to employ when appealing for sanctuary, but what use was it when there was no one to hear it?

Droplets spattered my face as Brewer stumbled to the wall, sinking down beside me with a great huff of air that told me his strength had finally given out. A mingling of splashes and high-pitched grunts drew my gaze to the river where Toria was dragging herself clear of the water. Once free, she crawled towards us, slumping against me to deliver a feeble slap to my cheek.

"Paid y'back . . . " she groaned. "Bastard . . . "

The three of us lay there, too spent to move as the dozen armed and armoured men reined their horses to a halt on the other side of the river. A cluster of wolfhounds milled about in confusion, evidently put off by the stink and depth of the water. Another rider, clearly identifiable as the huntsman by his lack of armour and rough leather garb, dismounted and went about gathering his pack. His gaze, reddened with grief and recrimination, shifted constantly between us and the slaughtered corpses of his hounds. However, my principal concern lay with Lord Eldurm rather than his bereft huntsman.

Levering back the visor of his helm he revealed the dark, mottled visage of a man beset by the twin torments of rage and betrayal. I had no way of knowing the contents of the letter Sihlda had left him, but the murderous fury I saw in his gaze made it clear they hadn't been welcome. *She told him the truth*, I decided with a weary groan, watching the noble flick an impatient hand at one of his men-at-arms. *It's never easy to hear.*

The sight of the primed and loaded crossbow the soldier placed in Lord Eldurm's hands stirred a faint trill of fear in my drained body. But still, I was unable to do more than twitch as the noble raised the crossbow, settling the butt on his shoulder as he sighted along the stave.

"At least he's man enough to do his own killing," Brewer observed in a listless mutter.

"He's not so bad a sort, in truth," I muttered back.

"Fuck him in his noble arse," Toria put in, too exhausted to colour her voice with the usual venom. "Still going to kill us, isn't he?"

In fact, Lord Eldurm's first attempt succeeded only in sending a crossbow bolt into the wall at least a foot above our heads. Watching him furiously demand another from the soldier then climb down from his horse while attempting to reload the weapon stirred me to an unexpected burst of laughter. It was clear he had no notion of how the crossbow worked, tugging ineffectually at the cord instead of turning the windlass. After a bout of fruitless fumbling, he was forced to hand it back to the soldier, snapping at him to hurry up as he wound the handles and drew the cord into the lock. Throughout it all my mirth increased, becoming loud enough to reach across the river.

His rage stoked to yet greater heights, his lordship snatched the loaded crossbow from the soldier, raising and loosing without pausing to aim. The bolt sank into the ground a clear yard short of us which only made me laugh all the harder.

"It seems, my lord," I called to him, finding amusement had enabled me to recover a modicum of strength, "you are as accomplished in archery as you are in love!"

"Shut your filthy churl's mouth, Scribe!" he shouted back, voice made shrill by consuming fury. Casting the crossbow aside, he lurched back to his horse, dragging his longsword free of its scabbard. His anger had evidently unseated his reason for he began to wade into the river despite the certainty that his armour would soon see him drown in its shit-clouded depths. His men-at-arms were quick to rush forward and drag him clear, despite his voluble protests, the clanking mass of them all collapsing in a shiny heap as he vainly tried to struggle free.

This time I laughed so much I discovered it was actually possible to piss oneself in sheer amusement.

"Stop this disgraceful display at once!"

The voice came from above, a harsh, grating rasp that nevertheless held sufficient volume and authority to bring an abrupt end to both

Lord Eldurm's struggles and my hilarity. Looking up, I found myself confronted by what I at first took to be the face of an owl peering down at me from atop the wall. Two overlarge eyes blinked above a narrow, pointed chin. I stared in confused silence for a second until the owl's face shifted and I saw a bony hand holding some form of wooden frame surrounding a pair of thick lenses. The too-large eyes narrowed as their owner focused his gaze on the jumble of armoured men across the river.

"This is the holiest place in all Albermaine save the Cathedral of Martyr Althinor!" the narrow-faced man stated in his outraged rasp. "How dare you offend its divinity with violence!"

"I—" Lord Eldurm's voice faltered as he attempted to disentangle himself from his men-at-arms, finally breaking free after much scraping and grinding of metal. "I am Sir Eldurm Gulatte," he said, straightening into as dignified a pose as his undimmed anger would allow. "Lord Warden of the King's Mines. And these wretches—" he pointed a quivering finger at the three miscreants at the base of the wall "—are my prisoners, deserving of immediate execution for escaping lawful servitude—"

"Ascendant!" I called out, dragging myself upright and staggering away from the wall. "You are an Ascendant here, are you not?"

I had recognised the man's rank by virtue of the red trim on the cowl of his habit. Also, I doubted a cleric of lesser rank could summon so commanding a voice. Thanks to Sihlda I knew that four Ascendants were always installed in Callintor, one for each of the shrines.

The narrow face and magnified eyes swung back to me as I ploughed on without waiting for an answer, raising the sack in my hand. "I am in possession of the finest ever copy of the Scroll of Martyr Callin for whom this holy city is named. I also carry the Martyr's only known relic, and . . . " I allowed a very brief pause for emphasis " . . . the last testament of Ascendant Sihlda Doisselle. As true adherents of the Covenant of Martyrs myself and my companions beseech the servants of this holy place for sanctuary."

The eyes had remained free of emotion as I spoke, but narrowed at mention of the relic, then even more upon hearing Sihlda's name.

They continued to regard me after I fell silent, returning the scrutiny with a gaze filled by desperate entreaty. Sihlda had warned me not to beg, for those who held authority here were rarely moved by such things. Sanctuary was within the gift of the Covenant, but it was not a right and often afforded on a whim, if not a bribe, and I had just spent the only coin we had.

"That man is a liar and a murderer!" Lord Eldurm cried out, voice more shrill than ever. However, behind their lenses, the Ascendant's eyes barely flickered.

"Petition for sanctuary is granted," he proclaimed, lowering the framed lenses to reveal his face in full. He was not an impressive man at first glance, his features sallow and distinctive only in their ordinariness. But his squinting gaze told of much the same intelligence I had seen in Sihlda's, but with none of the compassion. This, I knew instantly, to be a very calculating man.

"Make your way to the gate," he told us, waving towards the east before glancing in the direction of Lord Eldurm's party. "My lord, if you have objections you are free to submit them in writing to the Council of Luminants in Couravel. As for now, I remind you that I am witness to this event and any violence done in the precincts of this city carries both the penalty of excommunication from the Covenant and Crown sentence of death."

I looked at Ascendant Hilbert's outstretched hand, still too tired to muster the will to conceal my trepidation. Also, I found the sight of it macabrely fascinating, the knuckles swollen to the size of chestnuts and the flesh traced with a matrix of bulging veins. The ink that had stained the fingertips a permanent dark blue also left little doubt that this hand belonged to a man who had spent much of his days toiling over parchment with a quill. The stains on my own fingers were not so dark but, if I somehow contrived to continue as a scribe, would surely one day match his.

Whatever the state of Hilbert's hands, they evidently retained a good deal of dexterity judging by the loud and impatient snap of his finger and thumb. It echoed long in the chamber I had been led to, a place of narrow confines but tall vaulted ceilings positioned to the rear of the Shrine to Martyr Callin. We were alone, Toria and Brewer waiting in the hallway outside in company with a half-dozen burly laymen wearing the black tunics of Covenant custodians.

Our journey through the gate had been surprisingly swift, the custodians who greeted us paying little heed to civility as they hustled us along an oddly straight avenue to the shrine. There were a few onlookers about but our arrival aroused no particular commotion, meaning I was able to hear Lord Eldurn's pursuing diatribe with dispiriting clarity. He and his cohort had tracked us along the bank to the gate, every step we took dogged by the expectation that another crossbow bolt would come our way. Strangely, with deliverance at hand, his lordship's anger no longer struck me as amusing.

"You impugned my honour, Scribe!" he raged as we hurried through the gate. "You cast your churl's piss on my generosity. Don't think this rathole will hide you for ever! One day I'll make you a gift, Scribe! A necklace, fashioned from your own guts . . . "

"The relic." The narrow-faced Ascendant snapped his fingers again. "And the testament. I'll have no argument, unless you would like to walk back through the gate and beseech Lord Eldurm for mercy. Sanctuary can be denied as well as given."

When the time comes, Sihlda had told me, *you will know.* And I did know. I knew that placing the full and unexpurgated version of her testament in this man's hands would be a very large, possibly deadly, mistake. It's the thinkers rather than the sadists you have to be wary of in life, and it was clear to me that Ascendant Hilbert was a man who did a great deal of thinking. I had imagined Sihlda's revelations would be occasioned by meeting a soul of peerless wisdom and piety, some old, sage cleric or other luminary who would know best what to do with such dangerous knowledge. If so, this wasn't it. Still, that didn't mean I had no testament to give him.

"It's a remarkable story." I swallowed, fighting a well of emotion that was only partially faked as I handed him the coin from my pocket before extracting the testament from the sack. "Sure to move the hearts of all who hear it."

Hilbert took a second to turn the coin over, holding it close to his evidently weak eyes then grunting in satisfaction upon confirming its age. However, his principal interest clearly lay with the bundle of bound parchment.

"You have read this?" he asked, making no move to undo the binding, instead tapping one of his ink-stained fingers on it. The movement was tentative, like one testing the heat of a pot.

"She dictated to me." I wiped moisture from my eyes and attempted a smile. I held my pack at my side, hoping his interest in the document in hand would prevent him insisting I empty the entire contents. Had he done so he would have discovered another, longer version of Sihlda's testament, albeit one he would have had difficulty reading. "I am a scribe, you see."

Ascendant Hilbert gave a vague nod at this, his attention still fixed on the testament. "It is, you would say, a fulsome account?"

"To the best of my knowledge." I put a frown on my brow that combined puzzlement with a small impression of offence. "She was not a woman to tolerate dishonesty, in herself or others."

"No," he agreed with a faint shrug. "At least not when I knew her, although our acquaintance was brief. When did she die?"

I saw no utility in lying at this juncture. Hilbert was fully aware of my outlaw status and my most recent crime. However, I felt it best not to enlighten him as to Sihlda's role in her own demise. The Covenant had no official strictures against suicide, but it was still frowned upon by clergy. "Two days ago, Ascendant. We dug a tunnel to escape the Pit. It collapsed before she could get out. They all died, all her congregation, save for myself and my companions."

His gaze finally slid towards me. "She formed a congregation in the Pit Mines?"

"Indeed, Ascendant, and much loved she was."

"Meaning the unlawful escape was her idea."

"It was. But I believe her intent was to place this testament in Covenant hands, along with the copy of Martyr Callin's scroll."

Without waiting for his leave I pulled the scroll from the sack, freeing it from the sealed leather tube that had protected it throughout our flight from the Pit. The Ascendant regarded the proffered scroll without particular interest before consenting to take it. Unfurling the first few inches, his brows rose in surprised interest.

"This is your work?" he asked, not making any attempt to keep the doubt from his voice.

"It is. Ascendant Sihlda was the finest of teachers."

His face clouded a little and he turned away, moving to a large oak writing desk where he set down both documents. "You shouldn't use her title," he told me. "Not within the hearing of other clergy, at least. She was stripped of it when King Mathis pronounced her sentence. You know the nature of her crime, I assume? Since you took down her testament."

"I do, Ascendant." I hesitated and he turned back to me, holding my gaze until I provided the answer. "Murder."

"Yes." He shifted his attention back to the scroll, unfurling more of it on the tilted surface of the desk. "Murder of a fellow cleric, in fact. Some might say the worst crime a servant of the Covenant can commit." He peered closely at the scroll, lips pursed in what I hoped was admiration. "It's a pity this wasn't set down on vellum," he mused. "Parchment is an irksomely short-lived material. Still, I suspect you'll be with us a while, will you not, Alwyn Scribe?"

I bowed, swallowing a sigh of relief. "I should be happy to make another copy, Ascendant."

"Yes." For the first time some animation came into his face, just a very small curling of lips I doubted smiled much at all. "You will. All who receive sanctuary within our walls are required to earn their keep. Housing and food will be provided as long as you work for it. Money is not used in Callintor and none of the vices that arise from it are tolerated. Games, drink, profanity, indulgence in the base lusts of the flesh and any form of criminality large or small are forbidden here. Transgression has but one punishment: expulsion. Supplications take place at first light and sunset and are obligatory. The choice of shrine is left to you but—" he gestured to the scroll "—since you are so well acquainted with the story of our own Martyr, I can't imagine why you would wish to worship anywhere else."

I bowed again, knowing an instruction when I heard it. "Of course, Ascendant."

His impassive expression returned as he looked again at the testament sitting alongside the scroll. "How many copies of this have you made?"

"None, as instructed by Asc—" I choked off the honorific, finding to my surprise it annoyed me more than I expected. If any soul deserved the title it was surely her. "Mistress Sihlda," I finished.

"Good. Keep it that way." He glanced at me once more, the calculation behind his gaze plain to see although I suspected it might not be so obvious to eyes less attuned to reading the moods of others. His offhand tone also indicated an attempt to conceal a deeper interest in the answer to his next question. "What was your crime, incidentally? The one that consigned you to the Pit."

I replied with uninflected candour, once again seeing no reason to lie. "Thievery, trespass and taking of game within the duke's forest, and association with the outlaw Deckin Scarl."

"The Outlaw King himself, eh?" His lips betrayed another almost imperceptible curve. "Tell me, was he really seven feet tall and capable of strangling a man with just one hand?"

"He was a big fellow, Ascendant, but not that big. And I only saw him use two hands whenever he strangled a man."

The Ascendant's lips straightened and a shadow passed across his calculating brow before he turned his attention back to the scroll. "The custodians will show you and your fellow congregants to suitable quarters," he said, waving me to the door. "We expelled a few miscreants for running a dice and drink den last week so there should be a house free. Be sure to return for evening supplications. After supplication tomorrow morning you will report here for duties in the scriptorium. Unless your friends share your skills, they can find honest work in the gardens or the pens."

I gave him a final bow, far lower than before to indicate the depth of my gratitude. Ascendant Hilbert, however, failed to notice, his attention now fully fixed on the testament, one hand caressing the binding in a manner that told me it would be ripped away as soon as the door closed behind me.

CHAPTER TWENTY-TWO

As you will have discerned by now, cherished reader, I have had plentiful acquaintance with prisons. In so doing, I have often found occasion to reflect on the curious fact that a state of imprisonment, regardless of how genteel it may be, will inevitably become intolerable. It had taken four years of hard yet surreptitious toil to escape the hardships of the Pit, but after only three months within the walls of Callintor, I found my thoughts turning once again to liberation.

But why? you may well wonder. Were you not fed? Were you not sheltered? Were your days not filled with fruitful and important labour? Did you not learn a great deal from your fellow scribes in the scriptorium? In answer to all, I say a firm yes, and yet by the dawning of the Feast Day of Martyr Ahlianna, I yearned to be free of Callintor with as much fervour as I ever longed to claw my way out of the Pit. The reason was not mysterious, or difficult to articulate, although I feel Toria put it most eloquently.

"I am so *fucking* bored!"

Her knife sank into the central beam of our dwelling with a loud thunk, the timber splintering as she worked it free and stalked back to the far side of the room. The beam was marked all over with the evidence of her unending practice. Weapons were, of course, forbidden within the confines of the city but she had procured herself a blade via some careful thievery during her regular stint at the butcher's yard. A small triangular blade kept wickedly sharp and, it turned out, perfectly balanced for throwing. The broad, mostly unfurnished space that comprised the lower floor of our house gave her plenty of room for practice.

The capacious size of our new home was one of several comfortable aspects to this novel form of incarceration. The house we shared with Brewer would have been considered luxurious in comparison to the hovels of my childhood village. We each had our own room on the upper floor and Toria would often bring home a portion of meat at the end of the day to roast in front of the large fireplace. Brewer had found himself a place at the orchard, so the fireplace was often stocked with sweet-smelling apple wood and evening meals washed down with a cup or two of cider. Strong liquor was strictly forbidden in Callintor but cider and ale were allowed due to the flux that invariably arose from drinking plain water, provided one didn't become too obviously intoxicated.

Toria's knife thunked into the beam once more and I resisted the urge to shoot her an annoyed glare. Although I spent at least ten hours of every day writing, I always found time after returning from the scriptorium to decode at least a few lines of Sihlda's original testament. On her instruction I had encrypted the text in a code it had taken me a year to learn, a complex double-substitution cypher that required as much knowledge of numbers as it did letters. It was a code known only to Sihlda and myself, rendering her account into a facsimile of ancient Danehric, the language of the Sacred Lands as spoken a thousand years ago. As such it was unreadable by anyone save the most learned scholars and even they would have pronounced it as gibberish.

I had been tempted to leave it alone and negate the risk of discovery by the custodians. These devout ruffians were typically men of little brain but considerable brawn whose favourite entertainment consisted of randomly searching dwellings in hopes of finding evidence for expulsion. The list of proscribed items that would see an unfortunate pushed through the gates was long and often nonsensical. Last month

I had watched them expel an aged woman who spent the better part of a decade evading the noose after murdering her punch-happy husband. Her crime consisted of weaving a tapestry that depicted Martyr Melliah with a half-exposed breast.

The custodians' zeal in pursuing miscreants made me wonder if they weren't paid some form of bounty for every unfortunate they forced through the gates. But still, as my thoughts turned ever more towards departing this place, the prospect of Sihlda's precious words being lost for ever if some misfortune befell me was unbearable.

"Don't tell me you're not bored, either." Toria's knife thudded into the beam again. "You hate this place. I can tell. You're not so good an actor as you think you are."

"Yes I am," I replied, my focus still on the part-decoded testament. "You're just more practised at sniffing out lies than most."

A sigh then the scrape of a stool on the hay-covered floor as she took a place at the table. When she spoke her tone was serious and insistent. "I'm tired of circling around this. When are we leaving?"

"When the time is right."

"When you've finished that, you mean." Toria shifted closer, angling her head to view the words inscribed on the sheet of vellum I had stolen from the scriptorium's stores. "What's it say that's so important anyway?"

I didn't bother to conceal the deciphered words. Despite numerous offers, Toria had never consented to allow Sihlda to teach her letters. "The formula for turning base metal into gold," I muttered.

"Oh, piss off." She gave an annoyed huff and planted her elbows on the table, chin resting on the upraised palms. "She's dead yet you and that bear-sized fool are as much her slaves as you ever were."

"Debt is owed, by all of us. I thought you understood such things."

"I understand I'm going to go mad if I have to stick this place for one more week."

"If four years in the Pit didn't kill you, a few more months here won't either."

"It's not my body I worry over." Her voice lowered a notch or two. "It's my soul. This place sullies it."

This was enough to bring my pen to a halt. She didn't speak much of the southern brand of devotion to the Covenant and I had scant knowledge of the details. I knew that it featured what seemed to me only a few minor differences to the orthodox faith. However, just because she rarely spoke of her beliefs, the weight of misery I saw in her bunched features told me she still held to it with all the fervour Brewer held to his.

"Sullies it how?" I asked, making her shift a little in discomfort.

"The supplications," she muttered.

"Your people don't have supplications?"

"Not like these. At home, we gather to pay homage to the Martyrs but all are allowed to speak our devotion. Our supplications mean more than just clerics gabbling out scripture they learned by rote. In the south there is but one rank of cleric; all are humble Supplicants who stand as a link to the Seraphile's grace, not a barrier, not gate-keepers demanding payment for salvation."

Her voice had risen to an unusually loud pitch, causing me to press a finger to her lips while casting a worried glance at the shuttered window. There were few misdeeds more certain to see us expelled than voicing heresy. She jerked her face away from my hand with a scowl, folding her arms tight. At times like these I wondered if her true age might not be what she claimed, so like a sulky child did she appear.

"We needed a plan to escape the Pit," I said after summoning some patience. "We'll need one to escape Callintor too."

"I have one: we walk through the gate, then we're free."

"No. The moment we walk through the gate some bastard greedy for a reward is certain to run off and tell Lord Eldurm. Then how far do you think we'll get?"

"Couravel's less than a hundred miles from here. That's five or six days' travel, seven at most if we push hard. Even less if we can grab ourselves some horses. It's an easy city to get lost in."

"And easy to never find your way out again, from what I heard. And since when do you know how to ride a horse? I surely don't."

She gave a frustrated grimace. "Then we head for the coast, find a ship. There are other kingdoms than this."

"Ships require coin for passage. Do you happen to have any?"

"There's bound to be a cache here somewhere. Northern clerics always have money, despite their claims to poverty."

I paused at this, finding some truth in it, and the nugget of a plan. I had been pondering various ways to extricate us from this holy snare of a city and basic lack of coin had always been the stumbling block. "A notion worth thinking on," I admitted. "There's plenty of locked doors in the Shrine to Martyr Callin. Why lock a door if not to protect something of value?"

A small grin appeared on her lips and she leaned a little closer, jabbing a fist against my shoulder. "And I worried you'd surrendered your soul to these fuckers—"

She fell silent as someone pounded an urgent fist to the rickety planks that comprised our door. The shrines might have sturdy doors complete with locks but the houses of the sanctuary seekers did not, all the better for the custodians to kick them in.

"Hide that," I hissed at Toria, nodding to the knife still embedded in the beam as I gathered up the ink and parchment. "Have you got anything else?"

She shook her head, working the knife loose before crouching to lift the flagstone where we hid our contraband. "Was going to trade Smythes some meat for a pinch of pipe-leaf," she whispered. "Lucky I didn't."

I waited until she'd replaced the stone and kicked some hay over it before opening the door. Instead of the expected trio of men in black tunics, I found myself regarding the wide eyes and narrow, moistened face of Nucklin, our neighbour. He was a fellow given to much fidgeting and even more sweating, which left him enshrouded by a rancid odour. While a wise man knows that a healthy miasma is needed to ward off the worst illnesses, Nucklin's stench was something far beyond the norm. It made his company difficult to tolerate for long, although it did mean he had the house next to ours all to himself. I assumed it was basic loneliness that compelled him to call round with irksome frequency, but the brief but hungry glances he often shot at Toria indicated a deeper, firmly unreciprocated interest.

"What do you want, stinkman?" she demanded, lips curled with habitual disdain.

Nucklin shied from her curtness and instead addressed his answer to me, speaking in his dolorous Alundian accent of broad vowels and soft sibilants. "Your brother's preaching again."

So as to discourage his interest Toria had told him that Brewer and I were her brothers, and possessed of aggressively protective instincts. It was a measure of the man's lack of insight that he had accepted this despite the fact none of us looked remotely alike. It also failed to prevent him finding excuses to knock on our door, although at least today he had a good reason.

"Where?" I asked with a sigh of mixed anger and annoyance.

"Over by the graveyard. Custodians was already gathering when I came to tell you."

"My thanks." I forced a smile and resisted the urge to pat his shoulder. "Stay here," I instructed Toria as she made to follow me through the door. There was almost certain to be some form of altercation and her inherent aggression had a tendency to escalate tense moments into violence.

I started off at a fast walk as running was sure to attract unwanted attention. Behind me Nucklin stuttered to Toria, "I-I got a jar of fresh tea today. Iffen you'd like some . . . "

I heard the door slam as I rounded a corner, hurrying through a succession of narrow alleys towards the graveyard. I shortened the journey by vaulting a wall and picking a fast but careful path through the pig pens. I had to dodge the charge of a grumpy boar before climbing another wall which placed me at the western corner of the graveyard. I had little trouble finding Brewer's tall form, standing atop a crate near the gate as he gave his sermon to a crowd consisting of a half-dozen townsfolk and the same number of custodians. The townsfolk seemed either puzzled or amused by his preaching, the custodians notably less so.

"To know the scrolls by heart is a good thing," Brewer intoned as I drew closer, casting wary glances at the stern-faced custodians. Brewer spoke in a loud but mostly flat monotone, his shoulders hunched and face flushed, the words forced out rather than proclaimed. It was strange that a man with seemingly no fear of physical danger should be reduced to such a state by the mere act of speaking in public. Nevertheless, here he was, facing his fears as Sihlda had taught us despite the indifference or scorn of his audience.

"But to speak them without knowledge is not," he went on after pausing to swallow, the sweat beading his skin catching the late-evening sun. "The scrolls are not mere incantations. They are not prayers to the Seraphile like the meaningless odes northern heathens gabble to their false gods. Just repeating words set down on a page is meaningless. To truly be part of the Covenant you must know their meaning; you must read them for yourself."

"Shit," I muttered, seeing several custodians bridle at this. More concerning, however, was the surprising fact that one among the sparse group of onlookers seemed to have actually been listening.

"Liar!" a spindly woman of advanced years stepped forward, shaking a bony fist. Despite her slight form, her voice held much of the stridency that Brewer's lacked. "That's the southern creed!"

"No, sister," Brewer said. He attempted to mould his features into a semblance of Sihlda's honest solicitation, the raised eyebrows and open smile that captured so many. On his face, however, it looked more like a leering grimace. "This creed is for everyone. All must read the scrolls, not just the nobles. Not just the clerics—"

"And those of us that can't?" the old woman broke in. "What're we s'posed to do?"

"Learn of course." Brewer's face took on a faintly mocking cast that told of a man engaged in an argument rather than a sermon. Sihlda never argued; she only persuaded. "Stop allowing yourself to be mired in ignorance—"

"Who you calling ignorant?" another onlooker shouted, a beefy fellow I recognised as one of the labourers from the smithy. To my dismay, I saw several more people drift closer at the sound of raised voices. What had been a small cluster of bemused spectators was about to become a crowd, and an angry one at that.

"The Supplicants teach me the scrolls and I'm grateful for it," the labourer went on, face reddening and voice heated. The brief sideways glance he cast towards the custodians made me doubt the veracity of his outrage. In Callintor it always paid to curry favour with orthodox authority.

"As a beggar is grateful for the scraps he receives?" Brewer shot back, his anger suddenly making his voice considerably more compelling. "Are you an adherent or a slave?"

"Heretic!" the old woman yelled, a cry that I have learned is almost certain to be taken up by at least a few others in any crowd of sufficient size. "Heresy will bring the Second Scourge down upon us!"

The resultant chorus of denunciation was loud and possessed of sufficient genuine anger to finally stir the custodians into action. Seeing them begin to push their way through the crowd, I hurried towards Brewer as he vainly attempted to shout above the clamour of faithful anger.

"Had enough?" I asked, moving into his eyeline and casting a glance over my shoulder at the fast-approaching custodians.

The sight of me brought some reason back to Brewer's gaze, shoulders slumping and fervour diminishing into dismay. He made no move to step down from the crate, however.

"Come on," I said, moving to grab his sleeve. "We have to go."

"You, seeker!" the lead custodian said, pointing an imperious finger at Brewer as he and his companions pushed the nearest onlookers aside. "Who gave you leave to preach?"

Seeing a defiant glower blossom in Brewer's eye, I turned to the custodians, attempting a tone of neutral persuasion. "There's no stricture against preaching in Callintor."

I took a small mite of comfort in recognising the foremost custodian as a fellow servant at the Shrine to Martyr Callin, although he had to squint at my face for a moment before consenting to recall our association. "But there's plenty of strictures against heresy," he growled. "I would've thought a scribe would know that."

"I do. I also know my brother has spoken nothing that transgresses the strictures or the scrolls. He only speaks the sermons taught to us by Ascendant Sihlda, she whom Ascendant Hilbert himself has named among the redeemed."

Recent weeks had seen Hilbert make liberal use of Sihlda's testament in his sermons, sometimes crediting her for the many insights, but not always. The increasing frequency with which he quoted her, and the popularity his sermons were garnering, put me in mind of one of Deckin's favourite aphorisms: *Only a fool risks his neck to steal something of no value.*

Mention of Ascendant Hilbert's name had more of an effect than did Sihlda's, the custodian falling silent while his companions dithered. Fortunately, their intervention had served to quell the crowd's discontent, most of whom looked on in lively curiosity rather than anger. Entertainment was always hard to come by in Callintor.

"He's your brother, is he?" the custodian asked, gaze switching doubtfully between Brewer and myself

"My brother in devotion to the Covenant," I said, turning to give Brewer an insistent jerk of my head, concealing a sigh of relief as he climbed down from his perch without further protest.

"Then teach him the true nature of devotion," the custodian said. "Obedience to the Covenant will be blessed by the Seraphile's grace above all virtues."

"Quite so," I agreed cheerfully, clamping a hand on Brewer's arm and tugging him away before he could bridle. Luckily, his sense of defeat outweighed any urge to argument, at least for now. He allowed me to lead him towards the main thoroughfare, not even turning when the custodian called after us.

"Best keep him muzzled," he shouted, drawing some laughter from the thinning crowd. "Not all dogs are bred to bark."

Brewer was silent for much of the journey to our house, head bowed and face set in a frown of both defeat and bafflement.

"Do this again and I'll leave you to custodians," I told him, which only succeeded in bringing a small shift to his shoulders. "I mean it," I added. "Get yourself expelled if you want, but we're not ready to leave. Not yet."

Brewer barely seemed to hear, maintaining his silence for a few steps before muttering, "Her words. Her truth. Why won't they hear it?"

"Because it's not her saying it," I said. I softened my voice a little, trying to match Sihlda's persuasive tones as I went on. "It was never just her words; it was her voice too. It was her . . . " I trailed off, unable to properly articulate Sihlda's gift for capturing hearts. "It was just her. And she's gone. Now it's just us."

"She's a Martyr," Brewer stated, recovering some of his previous passion. "And should be proclaimed as such."

"And will be." My voice held more conviction than I felt on this particular issue, but Brewer was not a man who responded well to uncertainty. "One day. We've planted the seed here. In time it'll grow. Ascendant Hilbert speaks her truth in almost every sermon now."

A dark, resentful shadow passed over Brewer's face at the mention of the plagiaristic Ascendant. "As if it were his own," he said in an aggrieved mutter.

"They're still her words from her testament. We're her witnesses. It's up to us to keep her story alive, but we can't do that if we end up dragged back to the Pit for Lord Eldurm to string up."

I had more lecturing to impart but my voice died abruptly as we rounded the corner where the thoroughfare joined with the gate road. A fresh group of sanctuary seekers were thronging the wooden arch that formed Callintor's main gate. They were about a dozen strong, an unusually large group at most times but increasingly common in recent weeks. Rumour had it the Pretender had once again gathered an army of sufficient size to menace the middle duchies, inevitably stirring King Tomas to raise his standard and muster a force to meet the threat. So many armed men marching about had a tendency to flush outlaws from their dens like rabbits fleeing a ferret.

But it wasn't the size of the group that stilled my tongue and brought me to a sudden halt; it was the sight of one of their number. Their bedraggled appearance was typical, all torn, threadbare clothes and most lacking shoes. Three women and nine men, one of whom captured my attention with all the force of a bear trap snapping shut. He stood taller than the others, but was just as thin as ever, cheeks and eyes hollowed from privation, but still possessed of a predatory danger if you were attuned to such things.

Brewer gave a puzzled grunt as I sidestepped into the shadowed alley between the bakery and the chandlers. I was pretty sure the tall newcomer hadn't seen me but daren't risk the smallest glimpse. The sight of him had lit an ugly fire in me that banished all other concerns in an instant.

"What is it?" Brewer asked, as I flattened myself against the bakery wall.

"The new lot at the gate," I said. "Watch and tell me how many are let in."

Brewer's heavy brow creased in suspicion but he consented to spend a moment observing the sanctuary-seeking ritual play out. "Sent two of the men off pretty quickly," he reported. "Rough-looking types, as you'd expect, stupid with it. Probably couldn't recall a line of scripture between them." He watched for a little longer. "The rest they're leading off to the Shrine to Martyr Athil. I heard their Ascendant complaining about a lack of workers in their turnip field last week."

"The tallest," I said. "A skinny bastard who looks like he might know how to handle himself."

"They let him in." Brewer's eye formed a squint as it slid towards me. "Friend of yours?"

I didn't answer, head filling with all manner of calculations as I poked it out for a cautious glance. The group had mostly disappeared from view so I stepped from the shadows, intending to follow until Brewer moved into my path. "Someone we need to worry about?" he asked in tones that told me he required an answer.

"He was part of Deckin's band," I said. "Witness to some things it's better the clerics don't know."

Brewer's frown deepened. "That's not a worried look I see on your face." He angled his head in scrutiny, looming closer. "It's the look you used to get when there was hard work to do."

Back in the Pit, "hard work" had been our shared euphemism for those occasions when a troublesome inmate would mysteriously find themselves atop the pile of bodies by the gate. We employed it as a sop to Sihlda's sensibilities although I had little doubt she understood the meaning full well.

"Heresy might get us expelled," Brewer said. "Murder'll get us hung."

"Me and Toria happened upon a scheme to get us out of here today," I told him, deciding a little subterfuge was in order. "With pockets full enough to take us to all corners of this land. Places where the word of Martyr Sihlda might find more receptive ears. But it won't work if I have to keep a constant watch on my back."

He relaxed a little, mollified by the prospect of fertile ground for Sihlda's teachings. "If it needs doing I can do it," he said. However transformed his soul might have been through long association with a newly minted Martyr, Brewer would always remain an outlaw at heart. Besides, the scrolls held many allusions to the rightness of killing done in a good cause, and what better cause was there than this?

"No offence," I said, edging round him, "but you're not the quietest hand when it comes to hard work. I'll see you at the house."

I hastened on my way before he could protest, making for the southern quarter where the Shrine to Martyr Athil lay among a surrounding patchwork of enclosed fields. Each shrine in Callintor was responsible for meeting a different aspect of the city's needs. Martyr Callin's shrine was the principal centre of administration by dint of the fact that it was the only one with a scriptorium. The Shrine to Martyr Melliah oversaw the workshops of wrights, potters and smiths. The seekers who found themselves allotted to Martyr Ihlander's shrine spent their time tending livestock in the pigpens or chicken coops. However, sanctuary seekers foolish enough to proclaim their souls attuned to the example of Martyr Athil would face months of back-breaking labour in the fields.

Callintor was not a place where one simply wandered without reason, so I moved with a purposeful stride that didn't invite questions from prowling custodians. Lingering in the vicinity of the fields presented more of a problem but I was fortunate in finding an unpruned bramble bush to hide in. I had to suffer the chirping protests of a nesting goldfinch as I crouched and waited, my gaze fixed on the shrine's rear entrance. It took a gratingly long time for the new arrivals to appear, all bearing hoes or spades as one of the shrine's Supplicants hectored them to their first day of work. The tall, hollow-cheeked figure stood out easily and, as he drew marginally closer, I felt my heart take on a heavy thud as it became apparent my first glimpse hadn't been mistaken.

It was the way he moved rather than his face that clinched it: the half-slumped shoulders, the way his gaze slithered about constantly, lingering most, I noted, on the younger labourers. Seeing the way he stared at one in particular – a lissome girl of bright manners but little brain known to all as Smiling Ayin – I deduced his inclinations had worsened with age.

The thought summoned an unexpected smile to my lips, for I had been experiencing a curious sense of regret for the task ahead. We had grown up together after all. Also, what proof beyond my own endless pondering did I have of his culpability in Deckin's demise? But, seeing the dark need in his gaze, all my scruples faded away and with grim anticipation I whispered a greeting he couldn't hear. "Hello, Erchel."

CHAPTER TWENTY-THREE

I didn't kill him that night. Nor any of the five nights that followed. Of all the lessons Sihlda had imparted, patience had taken the most time and effort and I put it to good use now. Brewer was right about the consequences of murder in this place. Violence was a rarity in Callintor; in all our time here I had seen but one scuffle. A pair of fieldworkers had overindulged in cider and found reason to pummel one another outside the very door to Martyr Athil's shrine. Not content with mere expulsion, the custodians had subjected both to a prolonged caning before shoving them, stumbling and bleeding, through the gate. If a mere brawl merited such punishment, murder was certain to attract the severest penalty.

Killing Erchel was also just one aspect of my intent. I also needed to extract what he knew about Lorine's schemes and, I hoped, some indication of where she might be found. Such a thing would take time and privacy, both rare commodities in a place of endless toil and constant scrutiny. Then there was the matter of our escape and the means with which to fund it.

I remained diligent in my work at the scriptorium, completing the first copy of my version of Martyr Callin's scroll with a rapidity that stirred both the admiration and envy of my fellow scribes. They were all old, or appeared so to my youthful eyes. Bent-backed, wrinkle-faced squinters with permanently stained fingers. Most had found their way here through forgery, penning false wills or sundry official documents regarding land or titles – something that appeared to be a lucrative sideline for most scribes in the outside world judging by the stories they told.

They talked a good deal, these aged scribblers, creating an oddly convivial atmosphere in a place that had been built for quiet reflection. I made efforts to befriend them all, or at least win some measure of trust, with varying success for these were not stupid men and could tell when they were being gulled. For the most part, I was treated with a wary condescension due to my youth, matched by a restrained resentment provoked by my flair with the quill and the speed with which I worked. In return, I felt little for them beyond the mingled pity and contempt the young reserve for the old, with one notable exception.

"Gently now," Arnild cautioned, using a small ball of polished glass to apply the gold leaf to the vellum. "This stuff takes flight at the barest breath."

He was a small man, his head barely reaching my shoulder, the bald, liver-spotted dome encircled by a bush of grey hair. It also sprouted in unkempt tangles from his ears and chops, although he would shave his chin every day, I assumed to prevent any tendrils besmirching his work. His was a craft requiring an additional tier of skill that set him apart in the scriptorium, for Arnild was an illuminator.

"And you don't want to press too hard either," he added, tongue poking through his lips as he applied the glass ball to the leaf. The decoration had been added to the first letter of the opening page to what would eventually become a bound book – the only actual book to reproduce Martyr Callin's scroll in fact. Whereas I had penned every word in the volume, it was Arnild's task to illustrate and garnish the text with various shiny embellishments. Given Martyr Callin's love of thrift, I wondered if he would have approved of so much expense being lavished upon the story of his life. More interesting still was the source of the gold and silver with which Arnild crafted his admittedly marvellous creations, not to mention the garnets and amethysts that would in time decorate the engraved leather covering.

"You try," Arnild said, setting down the tweezers and glass ball on a nearby tray and gesturing for me to take them up. The first character had been almost surrounded by gold but a small patch remained at the base.

"Are you sure?" I asked. "I wouldn't wish to despoil your work."

"We learn through action, Alwyn." He smiled and inclined his head at the tray. "Besides, someone's going to have to do all this when I'm called to the Seraphile's bosom." He paused to rub at his back, face set in a grimace of true pain. "Which I suspect may not be long in coming."

"Nonsense," I said, taking up the tweezers. I managed to place the gold leaf in the correct spot but not without overlapping the edge a little.

"Not to worry," Arnild said. Picking up a sable brush he carefully teased away the excess gold, being careful to guide the small fragments into a jar. "Too precious to waste," he added with a wink as he corked the jar. Sniffing he stepped back from the tilted podium where the finished page sat in its freshly crafted glory.

"Perfect," I whispered in genuine admiration, something that drew a small tut from Arnild.

"Do this for long enough, my young friend, and you'll discover that perfection is an endlessly elusive spectre." He used the tip of his brush to point out the intricate rose-bush motif that covered the left side of the page. "The line is a little uneven here, and the colours not as vibrant as I would like. But still, it stands well alongside the quality of work produced in this scriptorium."

His voice held a very slight edge that inevitably tweaked my curiosity. "The quality here is not," I ventured in a low voice, casting a careful glance at the other scribes bent over their podiums, "exceptional, then?"

Always careful in his choice of words, Arnild twitched a bushy eyebrow at me in admonition. "It is in fact the finest scriptorium in all Albermaine," he told me before stepping closer and dropping his voice, "but I have travelled far in this world, far enough to set eyes upon books that make everything produced here seem like the daubings of a clumsy child."

"And where are these marvellous books to be found?"

His gaze clouded a little and he drew back, turning his attention to the tray containing his various jars and tools. "Heathen lands are always best avoided, lad. Hand me that knife, will you?"

"Heathen lands?" My voice held a little too much volume for he shot me a warning glance. Luckily, none of our fellow scribes seemed to have noticed, I assumed due to the deafness of age.

"Here." Arnild placed the jars containing gold and silver leaf in a leather satchel. "Best get these under lock and key before the evening service. You know where to go?"

"I do."

His expression became more serious as he handed me the satchel. "The Ascendant is scrupulous in weighing each jar at the end of every month. Just so you know."

Before starting for the door I put my hand over my heart in mock offence, drawing a reluctant laugh from Arnild. If not for an excessive liking for dice and its attendant debts, he would never have found himself confined within these walls. By any measure of justice, Master Arnild should be celebrated the world over as a prince of illuminators. Instead, there are few scholars alive now who can name him even as they caress the pages he crafted with such devotion.

The storeroom where the shrine kept its supplies of gold leaf, and other enticing valuables, lay in the heart of the building behind a thick, iron-braced door. Usually there were two custodians standing guard over it, but today there was only one, a typically beefy fellow named Halk who possessed no more life in his soul than the door he guarded.

He grunted in response to my cheerful greeting and ordered me to stand back another yard before consenting to turn and unlock the door. My outlaw's instinct for opportunity flared as he worked the key. He was big, but also slow and it wouldn't have been too arduous a task to slam his head against one of the door's iron braces. Two or three blows to put him down and, obviously, I couldn't leave him alive. I would drag the body into the storeroom, help myself to the most valuable and portable treasures I could find, lock it up and be on my way. I required a few hours to settle things with Erchel but reckoned it might be a good while before anyone thought to check on the absent Halk or unlock the door he had been guarding. All in all, I calculated, it was entirely possible I could attend to my business, collect Brewer and Toria and get clear of the city before midnight. Just one small murder to set me free . . .

"Haven't got all fuckin' day," Halk growled, pointedly jangling his keys as he stood in the open doorway.

"Profanity contravenes the strictures," I advised with a look of stern admonition. Judging by the way the custodian flushed and averted his gaze, it must have been quite convincing.

Proceeding into the store with a haughty sniff, I resisted the impulse to scan the shelves, instead focusing a short but intense scrutiny on the lock. It was a dispiritingly sturdy contrivance far beyond my abilities to pick. Toria, however, had a good deal more skill in this area and might be able to tinker her way past it with the required swiftness. My briefer survey of the store itself yielded mostly shelves crammed with anonymous jars lacking any useful markings. I did, however, espy a substantial chest in the shadowed recesses of the room. The fact that it was secured with a lock of its own instantly marked it as the object of most interest.

"May the Martyrs guide you," I told a sullen Halk as I left, surmising that Brewer could probably choke him unconscious without the need for killing.

With my scribing chores done for the day I had a clear two hours before evening supplications. As I made my way to the shrine's north-facing exit I was obliged to make obsequious progress past Ascendant Hilbert who was engaged in animated conversation with a Supplicant I didn't know. The mud on his boots and cloak told of a recent arrival. He was a well-built fellow with a good deal more lean hardiness to him than was normal for a low-ranking servant of the Covenant. More unusual still was the mace that hung from his belt and the studded leather tunic I glimpsed beneath his cloak. While the dark grey of his garb bespoke a Supplicant, it was clear he was also a soldier and, judging by the old scars marking the crown of his grey stubbled head, one with some experience. He spoke in low, respectful tones I couldn't quite make out, but Hilbert's response was easily discerned, not least because of the restrained alarm I heard in it.

"*She's* coming here?"

As I edged around the pair, I managed to catch the Supplicant's soft reply, his voice kept to a carefully toneless pitch. "Yes, Ascendant. She will arrive tomorrow before noon and asks that all the faithful of this holy city be gathered to hear her words."

"On whose authority?"

Knowing it would be unwise to linger, I rounded a corner before coming to a halt. Flattening myself against the wall, I cocked an ear to detect the rustle of parchment and fabric, followed by the harsher sound of a broken seal and a swiftly unfurled letter.

"You will find it signed by all members of the council," the Supplicant said in his toneless voice.

There came a pause during which Hilbert let out an ill-mannered huff. "She'll find scant pickings here," he said in an aggrieved mutter.

I detected a shift in the soldier-Supplicant's tone as he replied, a judgemental edge unique to true adherents. "The Pretender comes not just for the crown, Ascendant. Should he triumph, the Covenant will be perverted beyond recognition. My communicant captain assured me you were wise enough to know this."

A short, tense silence as Hilbert tried, and failed to master his anger. "Your communicant should remember her rank, and so should you!" he snapped in the curtness common to petty tyrants who find their authority threatened.

The soldier said nothing but I could picture the blank expression of an unimpressed man as Hilbert let out a long sigh. "The seekers will be gathered," he said. "And you're welcome to drag away any foolish enough to step forward. They'll require a good deal of convincing, however."

"Those whose hearts are truly with the Covenant," the Supplicant replied evenly, "will always answer the call when spoken by Communicant Captain Evadine Courlain."

This name brought a puzzled crease to my brow, it being so

familiar. *Evadine Courlain?* Surely it couldn't be Lord Eldurm's uncaring love.

The echo of Hilbert's strident footfalls had me scurrying for the exit before I could ponder the question further. It would have been prudent to go home and explain my plan to Brewer and Toria but the lure of Martyr Athil's shrine was too great. It had become my habit to spend the hours before evening supplications crouched in my bramble bush from where I could observe Erchel. As I watched him form the habits and small rituals that all labourers adopt, the various pieces of my scheme were slowly coming together. Subduing, concealing and questioning a man in a place like Callintor presented a host of problems, some of which I had resolved, others I hadn't. But, as my eavesdropping had revealed, the morrow would bring some manner of significant distraction. All eyes would be on the mysterious Communicant Evadine and not on the small woodshed near the eastern wall that few seekers visited more than once a week.

I'll need a rope, I decided, watching Erchel hoe the soil of the turnip field with all the energy one might expect of a man who had rarely done a day's honest toil. Binding him would be tricky, but I knew getting the truth out of him presented an altogether more arduous task. It wouldn't be easy to sort honesty from deceit when uttered by an accomplished liar desperate to save his own skin. Deckin had always possessed the ability to straighten a captive's tongue through sheer weight of terror but that gift wasn't mine. Getting Erchel to tell me the truth would require a good deal of judiciously applied pain, a prospect I found to my surprise I didn't relish.

"Gerthe," I whispered as I peered through the bramble thorns, buttressing my resolve with the memory of her hand slipping from mine as the bolt pinned her to the wall. "Justan, Hostler . . . Deckin. And me." I filled my head with images of the pillory, the pain and the stink of it, the jeers of the crowd and the dread knowledge that this was nothing compared to the torments to come. "You'll tell me all of it, Erchel," I breathed. "Or I'll feed you your fingers, one by one."

As was so often the case throughout our youth, however, Erchel contrived to despoil my careful scheming with his vile appetites. I had noticed how his interest in Smiling Ayin increased since his arrival, his gaze tracking her giggling, skipping form as she carried baskets hither and yon. She was a decidedly odd soul to find in Callintor, always so bright of face and lacking in guile. It seemed hard to credit that she could have committed any act that merited seeking sanctuary within these walls, and yet here she was. Mostly, folk treated her with an indulgent affection but afforded little in the way of company. Ayin, it should be noted, was capable of scant conversation beyond giggles, the utterance of baffling nonsense and the naming of various creatures which she would run towards in the apparent hope of making friends.

"Hello, Master Wagtail!" she called out now, waving at a bird that had alighted atop a fencepost. It flew off with an irritated chirp as she scampered closer, bringing her within a few yards of where Erchel stood unenthusiastically tilling the earth.

I couldn't hear what he said to her but it sufficed to swiftly capture her interest. She made no move towards prudent retreat as Erchel sidled closer to her, my straining ears detecting the word "cubs". This brought a delighted laugh from Ayin who exhibited only eager excitement as Erchel rested his hoe against the fence, paused for a careful glance around to ensure no one had witnessed this interaction, then led her away.

Go home, I told myself, staring at the rapidly retreating pair. Erchel led Ayin towards the livestock pens, where the snorts and oinks of pigs and the honking of geese was sure to mask any commotion. *The plan is a good one and you do not know this girl. Go home, tell Toria and Brewer their parts, and wait for the morrow.*

As I slipped from the bramble bush and turned towards home a singular memory forced its way to the forefront of my mind: the time Erchel had brought a cat back to camp. He had found the beast skulking near an inn during a scouting trip, a piteous, mewling bundle of damp fur. After carrying it to camp he fed it and nursed it for weeks until it returned to health, transforming into as fine and sleek a cat as you would ever see. One day he took it into the forest and the sounds he drew from the beast as he tormented it to death had never fully faded from my ears. He made it last so long that Deckin finally ordered Todman to go and finish the thing off so we could get some sleep.

Just a cat. Just a mad girl you don't know. Go home.

All undoubtedly true. Why then did my feet turn towards the livestock pens? Why follow, keeping to the long shadows cast by the fading sun? Why crouch and take the small, cloth-wrapped knife from my shoe when I saw Erchel lead Ayin inside an old brick-built hut with a part-collapsed roof? Some questions we can never answer. Perhaps it was Sihlda's teachings, years of patient tutelage having pushed a crumb of conscience into my soul. Or was it something deeper and less admirable?

As I watched Erchel guide his victim into that hut I knew he must have sought this place out with much the same careful diligence as I had the woodshed where I intended to torture the truth from him. Was his hunger so very different from mine? He was as much a slave to his cruelty as I was to my vengeance. The sense of recognition was almost painful in the discomfiting questions it raised, and, more than any other provocation, it was always pain that stirred me to violence.

The hut's door closed as I rose from my concealment behind a pig pen. I kept low as I rushed towards it, slamming my shoulder against the old, part-rotted planks then reeling back as they failed to give way. The door was barred. The sounds of a scuffle and a muffled cry of pain from inside stoked my anger to rage and I threw myself against the door once again. Wood splintered and aged hinges squealed but still it refused to give. Hearing a sharp, agonised screech from within, I retreated a step and drove a series of kicks against the planks, aiming for the protesting hinges. This time it gave way, falling aside as I pushed my way into the hut, breath catching in my throat as I came to a sudden, horrified halt.

"He's a bad man," Ayin told me, her blood-smeared features drawn in a frown that was more annoyed than angry. Something dark and wet dripped red as she held it up, tilting her head at a curious angle. It was then that I noticed the discarded basket at her feet before my eyes tracked to the small, crescent-bladed sickle she held in her other hand, the steel gleaming where it wasn't slick with blood. "Ma told me how to treat bad men."

A thin, shrill cry sounded to my right and I whirled, knife at the ready, finding Erchel in the corner. His features were bleached white in shock and pain, feet scrabbling on the floor while his hands clutched at the dark stain between his legs. The sounds emanating from his gaping mouth were rapidly losing their shrill, breathless quality and would soon build to a full-throated scream.

I hurried to grab hold of the dislodged but mostly still intact door, using it to seal the entrance as best I could before scrambling to Erchel's side and clamping my hand over his mouth, leaving his nose clear.

"He said there were fox cubs here," Ayin went on, her voice a light, breezy contrast to the hard grunts I caged in Erchel's mouth. "Said he thought their ma had gone off and left them and maybe I could be their ma. Little bundles of red fur, he said." A sulky note crept into her voice then. "That wasn't true. He's a bad man."

"Yes, Ayin," I agreed, putting a knee on Erchel's chest as he tried to rise. He was filled with the strength of a terrorised soul and it wasn't easy to force him down, but so much blood lost so quickly inevitably overcame his panic. "A bad man he is."

I continued to restrain Erchel, my hand smothering his cries until I felt him sag, looking down to see the red stain spreading across the dusty floor. Seeing his eyes begin to dim, I shifted my grip to his jaw and shook it, causing them to flare in mingled pain and, I saw with a small chime of satisfaction, recognition.

"You can put that down now," I told Ayin, nodding to the dripping item she continued to examine with guileless scrutiny. All of a sudden, her presence in Callintor made a great deal more sense.

"Just one quick cut." Blood spattered my face as she flicked the sickle she held, her gaze still rapt by her gory prize. "And bad men stop being bad men, just like Ma said."

"Clearly a woman of wisdom and insight," I grunted as Erchel gave a final convulsive heave beneath me before subsiding with a muffled, despairing sob.

The sound brought a small frown of distress to Ayin's brow, her lips curling in vague disgust. "It's getting dark now," she said, casting the dripping object away to land in the corner with a wet thud. "Ascendant Kolaus gets awful tetchy if I'm not there to sweep the dais before supplications."

"Best if you go, then. Ayin," I added, as she retrieved her basket and started towards the door. "There's a trough at the end of the lane. Make sure you wash up well and good, and change your clothes before you go to the shrine. Ascendant Kolaus will get even tetchier if you turn up looking like that, won't he?"

I thought of warning her to keep silent about this incident but doubted she would take any heed. She plainly saw no crime in this, nor, most likely, in any other similar incidents in her past, so why keep it secret? I took some solace in the general lack of interest in her conversation among our fellow seekers. Even so she was sure to smilingly blurt it out to a custodian or cleric at some point.

I watched Ayin's gaze darken as she surveyed the blood staining her arms and ankle-length robe of coarse wool. "Bad man made me dirty," she said, sticking her tongue out at Erchel before hefting the door aside and making her exit.

"That's the problem with cats, Erchel," I said, finally removing my hand from his mouth. "They have claws." He tried to shout as I rose to replace the door but it emerged as just a long, whining groan.

I sank to my haunches in front of him, keeping clear of the expanding blood. His eyes slipped continually from mine to the knife I still held in my hand.

"Oh, don't worry about this," I said, wrapping the small blade in cloth before consigning it to a hidden pocket sewn into the folds of my sackcloth jerkin. "Don't really need it now, do I?" I gave a meaningful glance at his hands trembling amid the blood pooled in his lap.

"There's . . ." he began, voice a thin, reedy croak that choked into a hiss of pain before he tried again. "There's healers here . . ."

I stared into his eyes, seeing a desperate plea. "Yes, there are. Did they have healers at Moss Mill too? I didn't wait around long enough to find out."

His eyes closed and a forlorn sigh escaped his lips. The words that followed were choked out between grating rasps as he sought to fill lungs that were rapidly losing the will to maintain their efforts. "Always were a . . . vindictive fucker . . . Alwyn."

I shrugged and grinned. "Can't argue with you there." Noting how his twitching had begun to abate, I shuffled closer to deliver a slap to his face, which succeeded in opening his eyes. "I've got questions in need of answers, Erchel. Do me the courtesy of not dying just yet."

A semblance of the old familiar sneer curled his lips as he sighed, "Questions? 'Bout what?"

"All sorts of things. But we'll start with the obvious. It was Lorine's scheme, wasn't it? You carried her message to your uncle and he told the duke's men to await us at Moss Mill. Right?"

A harsh, coughing sound emerged from his lips and I realised he was attempting to laugh. "You're not . . . here . . . are you, Alwyn?" Another coughing laugh. "Just a . . . ghost . . . come to torment me."

"I'm here, you depraved fuck. Answer my question. Was it Lorine?"

"Lorine . . . " A parody of a mocking smile passed over his face. "Still pining . . . for that bitch? Even though you're . . . a ghost. We all saw . . . how you mooned over her. You pitiful . . . bastard . . . As if . . . she ever looked . . . at you . . . as more than—" he bared pitted yellow teeth "—a useful . . . dog."

"Dog, eh?" I raised an eyebrow. "But at least I'm a dog who's still got his balls." My humour evaporated in a sudden swell of rage, my hand clamping onto his throat, squeezing hard. "You know where she is. Tell me."

He coughed red spit onto my wrist, summoning enough strength to glare as he choked out a response. "If you're really . . . here . . . get me a healer . . . and I'll tell you . . . every fucking thing!"

My anger cooled, perhaps in faint admiration for his fortitude. Dreadful, warped creature that he was, even in the face of death he found the gumption to bargain.

"It's too late for that," I said, withdrawing my hand to gesture at the blood that had now spread far enough to reach the far wall. "There's no stitching this."

I found it curious that Erchel managed only a meagre response to the certainty of his death, letting out a faint moan and allowing his head to slump to the side. Seeing the light begin to dim from his eyes I tried slapping him again, receiving scant response.

"Let's say you're right," I told him, clenching a fist in the greasy locks of his hair to keep his head from lolling further. "I am a ghost. I died at the Mill. The soldiers slaughtered me and Gerthe before we could even get out of bed. She's here too. She wants to know why you betrayed us. Don't die with a burdened soul, Erchel, lest the Malecite claim it. Make testament and find your way to the Portals."

I had never taken Erchel for a devout character, but some measure of life did return to his features then, for hope will find purchase in even the most wretched heart. "Testament . . . " he whispered. "That's what you're . . . here for?"

"Yes." I leaned closer, attempting the serene, knowing tones a ghost might possess. "Unburden yourself. Despite it all, we ran together in the forest, like—" I nearly choked on the next word but swallowed hard and forced it out "—like brothers. It will pain me to think of your soul lost to eternal torment. Cleanse it. Tell me, why did you do it?"

His eyebrow gave a very small twitch and his head moved in a fractional shrug. "Treasure . . . she promised treasure . . . "

"Treasure?" I repeated, baffled. "What treasure?"

"Lachlan's hoard . . . She knew where to find it."

"Really?" I released his hair with a hard shove and shuffled back to wipe the grease from my jerkin. Lachlan's hoard was an old tale, one that would normally have brought a caustic laugh to my lips. However, proximity to a gelded and dying man will tend to dampen one's humour.

Lachlan Dreol was one of the legends of the Shavine Forest, having once been what Deckin would later become: a king among outlaws. However, Lachlan harboured no pretensions towards nobility and contented himself by amassing a great pile of loot. Another aspect of his story that distinguished him from Deckin was that he felt no inclination towards sharing a single bean of it. No alms to the poor were ever given out by Lachlan. The story went that his greed eventually drove him to murderously suspicious ways. Enemies, real and imagined, were hunted down and slain as he became ever more obsessed with keeping hold of every bauble he had ever stolen. Eventually, even his own brothers fell victim to a massacre when Lachlan slipped over the edge into outright madness. It was said he hid his great hoard somewhere amid the crags and caves of the western coast and sealed himself away with it, dying among riches as he raved in the darkness.

An interesting tale and, like all such legends of lost riches, one I felt could be easily discounted. Yet Erchel and his vile kin had apparently sold Deckin out on the promise of this absurd myth. "Drew you a map, did she?" I asked in disgust.

"It's real, I swear!" Erchel rasped, shuddering with the effort of speaking. Apparently, he was willing to use up his last reserves of strength to make this testament, ridiculous though it was. "Uncle said so . . . Family secret, y'see . . . the Hound's lair, that's where to find it . . . "

Hound? The word chimed with something deep in my memory, words spoken by Deckin years before. *Where the Hound lays his head.* "What hound?" I said. "What lair?"

"Old story Uncle . . . used to tell us," Erchel said in a grating whisper. "'One day . . . we'll find the Hound's lair. Then . . . we'll own the whole fucking . . . forest . . . ' Our forebears ran with Lachlan . . . They just didn't know where he hid it. But . . . Deckin did, Deckin found the Hound's lair . . . It was how he was going to pay . . . for his great rebellion. He knew . . . so did *she*. Except . . . when it was all done, she kept it . . . the secret. Deceitful, murdering bitch."

I took a calming breath, still unconvinced by talk of treasure, but keen to hear more of Lorine's deceit. "So," I said, resuming my ghostly intonation, "she betrayed you, like she betrayed us all?"

Erchel's lips curled again, the sneer angry now. "Was all fine . . . and good, for a time. We had the whole forest . . . to ourselves. Then . . . " He bared his teeth, trembling with the effort. "She had her pet, the duke, set his trap. Called Uncle . . . and all our kin, to a meeting. Said she was going to . . . finally tell us where it was . . . the hoard." Erchel's features slackened again, his head slumping against the wall. His breath came in short gasps now and I could tell he had only moments left. "All a lie . . . " he murmured. "Must've been . . . a thousand of the fuckers, Alwyn. Duke's men, Crown soldiers . . . Had to leave Uncle behind . . . Had to leave them all behind . . . "

"Lorine," I pressed, putting my ear close to Erchel's lips, fighting the mingled stink of loosened bowels and rancid sweat. "She's with the duke? She sits at his side?"

Erchel's mouth twisted into the last smile that would ever appear on his face. "In his . . . bed. But . . . he's more her whore than she . . . is his . . . "

His words ended in a sudden convulsion, Erchel doubling over to heave a foul-smelling mess from his guts. The stench of it all was enough to force me to my feet and back away, watching him shudder into death. He had a few more words to gabble out, mostly gibberish laced with fearful profanity and a good deal of pitiful begging. I should have enjoyed watching him suffer his way towards a richly deserved death, but I didn't. Satisfaction, I realised later, was notably absent from my soul at that point. Watching him twitch and jabber all I felt was mounting disgust and impatience for it to be over.

It was only when he neared the end that I discerned some meaning among the babble, a last sibilant rasp almost too faint to hear. "Deckin . . . told you . . . to kill me . . . Didn't he, Alwyn? That was . . . why . . . "

Then he was done. Staring at his limp, wasted form, besmirched by lashings of blood and filth, my disgust gave way to a blossoming of sorrow, like a small treacherous bird chirping away somewhere deep inside. I crushed it with anger, putting a mask of grim relish on my face even though there was no one to see it. The words that came from my mouth were strained, forced into the angry, mocking jibe this vile sadist and murderer so deserved.

"I bet the pigs choke on your poisonous carcass, you worthless fuck."

CHAPTER TWENTY-FOUR

She was tall, taller than many men in truth. You will no doubt have heard a great deal about how her skin, as pure white as a marble statue, contrasted with the satin blackness of her hair. Also, you will have heard much of the finely sculpted lines of her face, how the sharpness of her cheekbones was softened by the curve of her jaw and fullness of her lips. But this is all a sop intended to please those who demand aesthetic perfection of their idols. Her hair was a deep shade of brown, but it wasn't fully black, and her skin was certainly fair but not without colour, especially in times of great emotion when it could resemble heated steel. But, upon my first sight of Evadine Courlain, it was not her undoubted beauty that struck me, but the aura of peerless strength she exuded, and her voice, of course. That most wondrous gift required of all true Martyrs.

"Do not imagine that I come with the offer of reward," she told the assembled sanctuary seekers of Callintor that fine mid-morning. The sky was a cloudless blue and a welcome breeze banished much of the stink common to all cities but did nothing to diminish her voice. It carried to all ears, ringing clear and true, implacably commanding. It was in many ways the strident mirror of Sihlda's quiet but addictive solicitation. But, whereas Sihlda had a way of leading you on a path to your own devotion, Evadine thrust open the door and demanded you enter.

"Do not delude yourselves that I offer anything but strife and blood," she went on. "For that is war and war is what the Martyrs demand of us now."

The stiff breeze added a pinkness to her cheeks that I found very pleasing. It also banished any doubts that this Evadine was not the recipient of Lord Eldurm's lovelorn correspondence. Seeing her now, I understood my judgement of him as just a heartsick fool had been overly harsh; he had been captured by a woman who had surely done the same to many others without ever trying.

Evadine Courlain turned slowly to cast her gaze over the crowd entire, the low sun gleaming on the armour she wore. Even my inexpert eye could discern the expensive craftsmanship of it, each plate a perfectly shaped steel leaf. Such a suit would surely be the envy of every knight who clapped eyes upon it, even though it possessed none of the ornamentation, embossed finery or enamelled colour so beloved of many a noble. Her armour was entirely functional, its elegance a result of its precision and the form it had been crafted to protect.

"Although we who hold to the Covenant love peace above all," she continued, her voice taking on a very slight catch, a rawness that bespoke a soul compelled to regretted but inescapable action. "no soul who follows the Martyrs' example would ever wish harm upon another, but, brothers and sisters, know that we stand now upon the precipice of destruction. Know that the Pretender and his horde of villains are at our throats and will spare none in their greed and their cruelty. So, if you will not fight to protect the innocents they will slaughter, fight at least to protect the divine Covenant that has sheltered you for so long."

"As long as we work our arses off in return," Toria muttered at my side. We stood with Brewer near the front of the crowd, a position chosen as a result of the worries that had beset me throughout the night. I had waited until the sky was fully dark before dragging Erchel's corpse from the hut. This necessitated missing evening supplications, but that couldn't be helped. My absence would be noted and some form of punishment applied, but expulsion was unlikely given my value to the scriptorium.

Conveying Erchel's half-stiff, half-flaccid vessel to the largest and most populous pig pen required bundling him over a succession of walls, an arduous and odorous business that raised a considerable ruckus among the porcine inhabitants. I dumped Erchel in the lee of a west-facing wall close to the roofed enclosure where the pigs slumbered, knowing the rising sun wouldn't reveal him until midday. By then, with any luck the always ravenous hogs would have done much to reduce him to just another pile of bones among the scraps. It was a far from thorough job but I had little alternative, there being no axe at hand to render Erchel into more easily concealed portions.

I hadn't told Brewer or Toria about my adventure, although they read my mood with ease. I sat in brooding, nervous silence throughout the night, thoughts returning continually to Smiling Ayin and the tale that was sure to spill from her heedless mouth. *Deckin would have killed her too.* A dark thought, but a true one. But then I would have had two bodies to feed to the pigs and even they might not be that hungry.

In the morning the custodians came to hector us all to hear the words of the Lady Evadine Courlain, Communicant Captain of the newly raised Covenant Company. The nature of her mission swiftly became obvious and, perhaps, opportune. So, as she spoke that day I felt no great surge of devotion. Not for the Covenant nor, as you might have expected, for her beauteous and magnetic person. I only half listened, my eyes constantly roving the crowd as I fought the outlaw's instinct to run from imminent trouble. There was always the possibility that Ayin, loon that she was, had forgotten the previous day's events. Perhaps it would still be possible to resume my original plan: a quick, efficient looting of the chest in the shrine's storeroom then a simple walk through the gate and on to pastures new. It is, after all, in the nature of fools to hope.

Evadine Courlain spoke on, voice increasing in fervour and volume. "The King and the Council of Luminants have decreed that those who swear fealty to Covenant Company and march under its banner are forgiven all crimes under Crown decree. Once their service is complete, they will no longer be required to seek sanctuary within this holy place. But that is not reward; it is merely recognition of service owed. Your reward has already been paid, my friends, in your service to these cherished shrines. All I ask is that you repay some small measure of the boundless gift that is the Seraphile's grace and the Martyrs' example with the sweat of your brow and the blood of your bodies which are mere vessels for redeemed souls. Join with me!"

She extended a gauntleted hand to the crowd, her face riven with something that would have resembled desperation but for the strength of her bearing. "Join this fight and banish the Pretender to the heretic's grave he deserves! Battle is at hand; his horde approaches the border to Alberis as we speak. But with your help, my cherished brothers and sisters in this divine Covenant, we will turn him back! With fire, with blood!"

For all the compelling fierceness of her rhetoric, her words made scant purchase on my heart at that juncture, nor on Toria's. "Well," she sniffed, "that all sounds fucking horrible."

Predictably, Brewer was a different matter, as were many in the crowd. Evadine Courlain's final invocation had been followed by a loud murmur of concordance, even a few ardent shouts. A dozen or more men and women had already stepped forwards to fall to their knees at the base of the cart she stood on, voices and arms raised in acclamation. One look at Brewer's face and I could tell he was itching to join them, his eyes wide and moist, face stricken with much the same open-mouthed fascination as when he listened to Sihlda's more insightful sermons.

"Getting a little stiff in the britches, are you?" Toria asked him. "Didn't take you long to forget our new Martyr, did it?"

I would normally have expected some snarling rejoinder from Brewer but he merely spared her an indifferent glance before turning to me. "We are called," he said. "The Covenant calls us and we must answer."

"No," Toria said, folding her arms tight. "Some bitch we don't know calls us to fight the nobles' battles for them." Her face was dark and eyes lowered in the manner that I knew indicated suppressed emotion. However, much we bickered, the Pit and the shared frenzy of our escape had bound the three of us together much as shared blood binds a family. Brewer's willingness to prostrate himself before this ardent noblewoman was, as far as Toria was concerned, a betrayal.

"Sod off then, if you're going," she said, jerking her head at the growing number of volunteers thronging the cart. "More fodder for the threshing."

Brewer tried to bargain with her, appealing to her criminal instincts by speaking of the loot to be scavenged from a battlefield, receiving only a scathing rejoinder. "Can't scavenge if you're dead."

I took no part in their increasingly heated argument, my wary and constantly roving gaze having been captured by the sight of Ascendants Hilbert and Kolaus making a purposeful progress along the gate road with a dozen custodians at their backs. Kolaus was the elder of the two but enjoyed less status, trailing along after Hilbert with an expression of worried shock. Hilbert's visage was much more serious and determined, becoming even more so when he alighted on me. The continued murmuring of the crowd and the loud acclaim called out to the Communicant captain muted the Ascendant's words a good deal, but nevertheless I heard them with gut-plummeting clarity.

"Alwyn Scribe! You will surrender to Covenant justice!" There was a keen urgency to Hilbert's demeanour, the source of which wasn't hard to divine. With me gone it would be all the easier for him to claim Sihlda's testament as his own.

I let out a heavy sigh and turned to regard a bemused Brewer and Toria, their argument abruptly forgotten. "Sorry," I told Toria, brushing past her to hurry towards the vocal mob of volunteers. "Consider your debt paid. There's a chest in the shrine storeroom with a lock worth picking, if you're so minded."

"Alwyn Scribe!" Hilbert's voice rose higher as I jostled my way forwards. "Stand where you are! You have a body to account for! Another former associate of Deckin Scarl, by strange coincidence . . . "

I ignored him and continued to push through the press of sack-cloth-clad bodies, his words, filled with righteous judgement, continuing to chase me. "I can abide a few transgressions from a skilled hand, but not murder! Stand still, you villain!"

I skirted the kneeling volunteers surrounding Evadine Courlain's cart, instead making for the scar-headed, mace-bearing Supplicant who stood to the rear alongside a score of similarly garbed and hardy-looking figures. They all wore the same dark grey cloaks over plain armour and each bore some form of weapon, ranging from swords to crossbows. Having recognised the mace bearer as the same man I had seen speaking to Hilbert the day before, I judged him likely to hold the most authority besides the Lady Evadine. Seeing him at close quarters, I noted how the irregular scar on his close-cropped head resembled a pale, three-pronged fork of lightning engraved into his skin. It crinkled as he raised an unimpressed eyebrow at my approach, nor did he betray a particular interest when I went to one knee before him.

"Supplicant—" I began, only for him to cut me off.

"Supplicant Sergeant Swain to you," he snapped in a curt rasp.

"Supplicant Sergeant," I repeated bowing my head. "Please accept my most humble service—"

"Stop that!"

I didn't look up as a slightly breathless Ascendant Hilbert came to a halt close by. I endeavoured to maintain a servile, hopefully devout aspect as the cleric addressed the sergeant. "This man is bound by Covenant law on charges of murder, and clearly unfit for service in a company ordained under council auspices."

"Murder, eh?" The sergeant's voice held a curious note that had me raising my gaze. He stared down at me with a critical eye, one I had seen on Deckin's face many times when he considered the uses or detriments of a prospective band member.

"Murder most vile," the Ascendant confirmed, gesturing to the custodians. "Bind him and take him to the shrine—"

"Stop!" Supplicant Sergeant Swain's voice was not particularly loud but held the kind of authority that was sure to bring any dutiful soul to a halt. The custodians were not true soldiers but knew well the sound of a superior's voice. I saw a red hue of frustration creep over Ascendant Hilbert's face as the custodians dithered. He began to speak again but the sergeant didn't afford him the chance.

"Who did you kill?" he demanded, still staring down at me. "Don't lie."

This presented a dilemma. If I told the truth, there was the chance it would be Ayin who found herself swinging from a noose by nightfall. However, given Hilbert's interest in securing my demise, I reasoned he would swiftly dismiss the messy and unvarnished facts as lies. Fortunately, at this juncture, he was not the man I needed to convince of anything.

"Someone I used to run with," I told Sergeant Swain. "He betrayed me, years ago. Did a lot of other bad too, but that's beside the point."

Swain gave a brief grunt of acknowledgement. "How'd you do it?"

I risked a glance at Hilbert, seeing a grim triumph on his face. This particular detail would not paint me in the best colours but I saw no alternative.

"Cut his cock and balls off," I said with an empty smile. "It was Deckin Scarl's favourite punishment for tattlers, back in the forest."

"You see," Hilbert said. "This creature will besmirch your banner—"

"It's the Covenant's banner, Ascendant," Swain told him, the hard dismissal of his tone sufficing to stem Hilbert's invective. The sergeant's gaze swung back to me, lingering in consideration then shifting to the sight of Toria and Brewer sinking to their knees at my side.

"You two ball-cutters as well?" he enquired.

"Never, Supplicant," Brewer assured him with a bow.

"Stabbed a few nethers in my time," Toria said. "Never quite managed to slice one off, though."

I saw a mingling of disgust and satisfaction pass across Sergeant Swain's face before he turned to Hilbert, inclining his head in an empty gesture of respect. "I regret to inform you, Ascendant, but this man—" he pointed at me "—had already been accepted into the company before your intervention."

Ignoring Hilbert's stuttering, rage-filled protests Sergeant Swain turned to beckon one of his grey-cloaked comrades forward, a hefty, heavy-jawed figure standing almost as tall as Brewer.

"Supplicant Blade Ofihla, escort these three to the camp. They'll make up the numbers in your troop. And keep a close guard." He stepped into my path as the soldier began to lead us away, staring hard into my eyes. "You just gave an oath, ball-cutter," he said softly. "Break it and what you did to your old friend will be a gentle tickle compared to what I'll do to you. You belong to Covenant Company until *she*—" he jerked his head at Evadine Courlain, smiling as she lowered her hands to the upraised fingers of the worshipful volunteers "—decides you've discharged your obligation. Or—" he gave a smile that was just as empty as the one I had given him "—one of the Pretender's scum guts you, which I'd wager is by far the more likely outcome. Just try to redeem your worthless existence by taking one with you, eh?"

CHAPTER TWENTY-FIVE

"You stand behind him." Supplicant Blade Ofihla's meaty hands shoved me into position, thrusting me far closer to Brewer's sweat-stinking bulk than I would have liked. "And you," she said, shifting Toria into place at my rear, "stand behind him."

I felt Toria bridle at the large woman's touch and took a hand from the haft of my billhook to calm her with a pat to the arm. Three days of soldierly discipline was starting to chafe on her naturally rebellious spirit and we couldn't afford any trouble, at least not while Covenant Company was still encamped within sight of Callintor.

In all, over three hundred seekers had stepped forwards to answer the call to arms proclaimed by the Lady Evadine, who was now being referred to as either the Anointed Lady or the Holy Captain. This had had the effect of emptying the sanctuary town of a large part of its workers, compelling the four Ascendants to request that the company linger for at least a week to ensure the harvesting of the latest crop lest they starve come the autumn. Consequently, the company spent half its day working the fields and the other half at drill. This required hours of enduring the frustrated tempers of experienced soldiers attempting to teach the basics of their craft to novice students, most of whom had spent their prior lives in conscientious avoidance of war and its numerous miseries.

"Head lower," Ofihla said, pushing Toria's head down until it pressed into my back. "Unless you want an arrow in the eye. The Pretender's hired himself a whole company of heretic archers and you can be sure they know their business."

"What about my eyes, Supplicant?" I enquired, nodding at Brewer. "Carthorse though he is, he's not quite big enough to shield me."

"Best learn to duck then, hadn't you?" Ofihla muttered. I had noted how most of her more useful and detailed advice seemed to be directed at Toria while the rest of us were afforded only basic instruction.

I winced as Brewer raised the butt of his seven-foot pike to jab it against my shin. "Carthorse," he growled.

"Stop that grizzling!" Ofihla snapped. "Eyes to your front!"

She nudged us a few more times before letting out a small grunt of satisfaction and stepping back to address the dozen other volunteers standing close by in untidy assembly. "You lot, form up alongside these three in the same fashion. Pikes in front, billhooks second, daggers third. Faster than that! Don't imagine the Pretender's scum will allow you time to dawdle."

It took a tediously prolonged interval of shoving and shouting to get us all into a semblance of order. From the look on Ofihla's face I discerned her grave dismay was no mere act intended to spur us to greater efforts. Simply put, we were not soldiers but a mob of criminals, some willing servants of the Covenant cause, many not, although we pretended otherwise. She and the other real soldiers in this company knew there was little prospect of this clutch of amateurs standing their ground in the face of determined assault by veterans. This was all of only passing interest to me, of course, since I had no intention of getting within smelling distance of a battlefield, but I did feel a mite of sympathy for her justified concern.

"This is known as the hedge," she told us, spreading her arms to encompass the breadth of our uneven ranks. The tallest were placed in the front row with their pikes, a fate I had avoided by contriving to always stand at the rear of any crowd while stooping and bending my knees. However, I couldn't avoid the second rank and the billhook they pushed into my hands, a sturdy but unedifying weapon consisting of a roughly hammered broad steel blade affixed to a four-foot length of ash. Toria and the others of less impressive stature formed the third rank. They had all been armed with an assortment of knives, cleavers and daggers, also a number of wooden mallets the purpose of which escaped me.

"When I shout 'form hedge', this is the formation you make," Ofihla went on. "Make it well and it'll keep you alive. No horse will charge a well-made hedge and no man is strong enough to hack a way through it."

She then had us return to our previous uneven line before shouting her order: "Form hedge!" As might be expected, our first attempt was poor and subsequent efforts throughout an increasingly tiresome day showed only marginal improvement. Ofihla's broad, strong-jawed face shifted its hue from dark red to a pale pink of despair as she went about her duties with a creditable doggedness, and also a curious absence of the profanity I had come to expect of soldiers. The casual brutality I also expected, however, was fully present.

Ofihla's fist made a hard, dry thudding sound as it connected with the cheekbone of a particularly laggardly fellow I vaguely recognised as a potter in service to the Shrine to Martyr Melliah. Not content with always being last to shuffle into place in the second rank, this time he also contrived to fumble his billhook, leaving a nasty cut on the arm of the pikeman to his front.

As she stepped over the potter's insensible form lying face down in the churned mud, Ofihla came the closest I ever saw to voicing an obscenity. "Understand this you f—" She bit down on the word and took a deep breath. I found myself fascinated by the shifting colours of her face as she strove for calm, wondering just how much rage this woman kept caged within herself.

"This is not some mummers' farce," she told us finally, speaking in a slow growl. "You will either learn this or you will die, and a corpse is of no use to the Covenant."

The potter let out a faint groan then, which apparently served to soften the blaze in Ofihla's breast. Blinking, she glanced down at him and let out a thin sigh. "Enough for today. You," she told the injured pikeman, "take yourself to the healer's tent and get that stitched. You, you and you." Her finger flicked at Brewer, Toria and me before she jabbed the toe of her boot to the fallen potter's arse. "Take this one along."

As the three of us came forwards to gather up the limp and groaning artisan, Ofihla added in a quieter voice, "Tell Supplicant Delric I think it best if he finds reason to excuse him from further service in this company."

Supplicant Delric was the only cleric in Covenant Company not to wear armour or carry a weapon. He stood just as tall as Brewer but with none of the bulk and was a good deal older than most folk in this camp with deep lines on his face and pale grey hair to show for it. A naturally taciturn fellow he spoke in short, clipped sentences and, throughout the many years that I would know him, never used a single word more than he had to.

"Sting," he warned the pikeman with the cut arm before dabbing a vinegar-and-lime-dampened cloth to his cut, the man clenching his teeth and hissing in pain. He began to jerk away but stopped at a bark from Supplicant Delric. "Still."

We set the mostly insensate potter down on one of the free beds in the tent and waited while Delric went about his cleaning and stitching of the pikeman's wound. His hands moved with a deftness I had rarely seen as they sealed the lips of the cut in precise but rapid loops of thread and needle. He said nothing on completing his task, sending the pikeman off after downing half a cup of brandy to banish his ache.

"Ofihla," Delric said as he stooped to examine the livid bruise covering the potter's cheek. Apparently, this particular blow was something of a signature for the Supplicant Blade, one I resolved never to allow inscribed upon my face.

"Yes, Supplicant," I told him. "She said to tell you she thinks he's not best suited to soldiering."

Delric made a soft humming sound then rolled up the potter's sackcloth sleeves and trews to examine his joints. "Bone ague," he said after a cursory glance. "Can't fight. Can't march. I'll send him off. Tell her."

"We will, Supplicant. We, ah—" I shared a glance with Toria and Brewer "—also took a few knocks today. Nothing a drop or two of brandy won't cure . . . "

"Out." Delric pointed to the tent flap, moving towards the table that held his mortar and pestle, not sparing us another glance and certainly not another word.

"Miserly old bastard," Toria grumbled once we made our way outside. "Been years since I had a drop of the good stuff. All they've got in town is piss-water."

"And yet," I said, "I'd still welcome a bottle or two of cider once you're done with your evening's work."

She glowered at my grin. As a scribe who was emphatically no longer welcome in either Ascendant Hilbert's scriptorium or within the bounds of the city walls, I had been excused the daily round of fieldwork. Consequently, my evenings were spent avoiding the numerous chores required to keep a soldiers' camp in good order. Instead, I would seek out a secluded spot to continue my transcription of Sihlda's testament.

After Toria and Brewer joined the tired mob traipsing towards the town gates, some judicious scouting led me to the west-facing trunk of an aged willow, its branches arcing down into a busy stream. It was as I settled down to unfold the writing desk that I espied a familiar figure of slender proportions further along the bank. For once Ayin had lost her childlike aspect, her face rendered into a hard frown of focused concentration as she waded slowly into the stream. She had gathered her robe up around her waist and I couldn't help my gaze lingering on the pale flesh of her thighs. After wading several yards into the water she stopped, her form taking on a frozen stillness as she stared into the churning current. She maintained the pose for quite some time, apparently immune to any chill, then suddenly plunged into the stream with catlike swiftness, emerging in sputtering triumph a heartbeat later with a large wriggling trout clutched in both hands.

"He's a big one!" she exclaimed to me, her smile bright amid the water cascading over her face. I had made my way along the bank and stood regarding her happy visage with decidedly mixed emotions.

"That he is," I said, looking around for some fallen timber. "You gut him and I'll make us a fire."

"I heard the Holy Captain speak," Ayin said, her words garbled as she sucked flesh from the trout's roasted head. "Wanted to hear her speak some more. It made my belly go all funny. She's very pretty. D'you think she'll let me kiss her?"

I blinked at her, my eyes stinging a little in the smoke from the small fire I had crafted on the riverbank. Ayin had gutted the trout with a speedy efficiency that told of habitual skill, spitting the splayed carcass on a forked stick before roasting it over the fire. She turned it at regular intervals, ensuring it cooked evenly, seasoning the flesh with some salt from a pouch on her belt. Whatever maladies affected her mind, Ayin certainly possessed some agreeable skills.

"I very much doubt it," I said.

"Just touch her hair then. That's all right, isn't it?"

"It truly isn't. And it would be best if you didn't ask."

"Oh." Ayin pouted a little before shrugging and returning her attention to the fish head. I watched her for a time before venturing a question.

"The bad man – did you tell anyone about him?"

"Oh yes." Having denuded the head of all flesh, including its eyes, which she popped into her mouth, chewing and swallowing as if they were berries, Ayin tossed the bony remnant into the fire and licked grease from her fingers. "Ascendant Kolaus was cross about me being late for supplications and asked me about it next morning. I told him about the bad man and then I told Ascendant Hilbert."

"Hilbert?"

"Oh yes. Ascendant Kolaus took me to him right away and said I had to tell him too."

I grimaced and prodded at the fire with a long twig. "And Ascendant Hilbert was very interested, I'm sure."

"Yes." Ayin burped. "He gave me a whole bag of chestnuts for being so . . ." her smooth brow creased a little as she frowned " . . . forth-right, whatever that is."

"Honest and fulsome in your words. A trait that often does you credit, Ayin. But not always."

"The strictures say to always tell the truth." She angled her head in to regard me with a prim expression. "So I never lie. And you shouldn't either."

"You don't have to lie. Just not tell everyone everything that happens. Especially not here."

"Why?"

I teased a burning branch with the twig, struggling to compose an explanation she might understand. "What happened to the bad man, you've done it before, haven't you?"

"Sometimes." Her primness faded into a sullen reluctance. "But they were all bad, even though their wives said they weren't. They were all liars. Lying is bad."

Her voice took on a good deal more heat as she spoke, her eyes losing focus. I decided a change of tack would be appropriate.

"You cooked that fish very well," I said, which had the fortuitous effect of instantly returning the smile to her face.

"Ma taught me. Ma was a great cook. Everyone said so. She could cook all manner of things and so can I."

"That's . . . good to know, Ayin. Come on." I got to my feet, resisting the urge to offer her a hand as I wasn't entirely sure she wouldn't take it into her head to deprive me of a finger or two. "There's a man we need to talk to."

I found Supplicant Sergeant Swain engaged in conversation with the captain outside a small tent pitched just within the picket line at the camp's northern edge. The unremarkable tent and absence of a servile retinue set the Lady Evadine apart from other nobility. She even groomed and tended her two warhorses herself. Unlike her plain canvas tent, these beasts were clear evidence of wealth, one black with a white patch on its forehead, the other a dappled grey with a hide the colour of polished steel. Embodiments of martial power, they both stood at least eighteen hands at the shoulder and would become aggressive with teeth and hoof if anyone but their owner came near.

I stood with Ayin at a respectful distance as sergeant and captain continued their discussion. Ayin stared at the Lady Evadine with unabashed fascination the whole time while I kept my gaze averted, trying not to betray the fact that I strained to hear every word. I could catch only a few sentences, mostly from Swain rather than the more softly spoken noblewoman.

" . . . a month, at least," he was saying, voice clipped to denude it of emotion but I could hear the concerned edge it held.

I discerned little of Lady Evadine's response beyond mention of "the Shalewell" and a reference to "thirty miles". To this Swain gave a grim response: "I'm not sure this lot could march thirty yards in good order . . . "

The Shalewell, I knew, was the river that formed much of the border between the duchies of Alberis and Althiene. Lady Evadine's speech in Callintor had made it clear the Pretender's horde was encroaching upon the realm's heartland, presumably with the intention of striking at Couravel, capital of Albermaine and ancestral seat of the Algathinet dynasty. I doubted King Tomas and his court would allow themselves to be besieged and, as befits royalty in a time of crisis, could be counted on to hastily decamp for safer environs. Not that this would dissuade the Pretender. With Couravel and its royal palaces, warehouses and moneylenders in his grasp his claims to kingship would finally have some credibility.

"What do you want, ball-cutter?"

Swain's harsh demand broke through my calculations, causing me to bob my head lower before risking a glance at his stern, dismissive features.

"A matter of some importance, Supplicant Sergeant," I said, glancing at Ayin who was now idly twirling a finger through her hair, her gaze still rapt by the sight of the Lady Evadine.

"Supplicant Blade Ofihla commands your troop," Swain snapped, waving us away. "Speak to her."

"It's all right, Sergeant," Lady Evadine said, offering me a smile and beckoning me forward. "Come, good soldier. What name do you go by?"

It is not often the case, dear reader, that I find myself rendered abashed or hesitant in noble company. This moment was a singular exception. The Lady Evadine Courlain had a very direct gaze many described as piercing. Added to that was the disconcerting sense that arose when in proximity to a human being gifted with the kind of beauty normally confined to a statue or painting. Although shorn of her armour today and clad in a plain shirt and trews, she still made an inescapable impression. I entertained few doubts regarding this woman's awareness of her own appearance, or the effect it had on others. Like Lorine, it was another weapon in her armoury, albeit employed to very different ends. In time, I would also come to understand that the disconcertingly penetrating gaze she directed at those she met was a very deliberate ploy, for their reaction told her a great deal.

In my case I simply stared back, meeting her gaze in full, but also momentarily unable to form an answer. Her face captured me, just for an instant, long enough to take some measure of this woman as she took measure of me. In that instant I gained only a marginal insight, but it was enough to convince me of two important facts: she could not be lied to and nor would she lie.

I bowed again, breaking the shared scrutiny. "Alwyn, my lady. Alwyn Scribe."

"It's 'Captain', you ignorant wretch," Swain growled.

The Lady Evadine, however, took no offence. "Scribe?" she asked. "Is that a family name or your profession?"

"My profession . . . Captain. I have no family name."

"He worked in Hilbert's scriptorium, apparently," Swain told her. "Until he murdered a man in the most depraved manner, not one week ago. Also, one of the few members of Deckin Scarl's pack of cut-throats still living. A most bloody man, to be sure."

"All sins are forgiven those who follow our banner," the noblewoman said, her tone possessing a light, chiding note. "Now then—" I shied again as she turned her piercing gaze back to me "—Alwyn Scribe, what brings you to my tent?"

I risked another glance at her face, seeing only honest interest and none of the disgust or judgement I expected. Swallowing a cough, I turned and gestured to Ayin. "She can't be here, Captain."

In response to their attention Ayin clasped her hands behind her back, looking away as a flush crept over her cheeks. This, of course, gave a very misleading impression. I watched Swain give Ayin a long look of appraisal, detecting a faint glimmer of something in his expression. Lust perhaps, or just an echo of feelings long suppressed and rarely summoned.

"Any soldier who lays a hand on another," he said, deliberately shifting his gaze from the girl, "be it in anger or carnal interest, will be flogged and dismissed from this company. Rapists will be hung. You and every other miscreant heard this on the first day of your enlistment."

"With respect, Sergeant, it's not the hands that might be laid upon her that is of concern." I risked another raised glance, seeing shared bemusement on their faces. "I know how she appears. It is not who she is, not entirely."

I steeled myself and looked Evadine Courlain in the eye, keeping my voice to a respectful pitch but also filling it with hard conviction. "Captain, it is my belief that Sergeant Swain let me into this company because you have need of dangerous souls who don't hesitate in the shedding of blood when needed. A bloody man he calls me, and so I've been in my time. So, please trust the word of this bloody man when I say that Ayin requires no protection. This company requires protection from her. For our sake, and hers, she should be sent back to Callintor."

"What manner of danger, exactly?" Swain enquired, the many creases of his forehead bunched in mingled doubt and amusement.

I faltered, unwilling to give a full account of our shared crime and trying to formulate the most effective lie. Ayin, however, possessed both very keen ears and a desire to be helpful.

"I cut a bad man's knackers off," she piped up cheerfully. She twisted a little as she spoke, casting a bashful glance at the Lady Evadine, for all the world a little girl expecting a reward for a well-done chore.

"Oh," Swain grunted, his face softening into scornful realisation. "So she's the real ball-cutter, is she?"

I let out a sigh of annoyed discomfort. With the captain's gaze still fixed on my face I found my usual facility for deceit had treacherously deserted me.

"Out with it man!" Swain demanded. "I've heard enough lies from you."

"She cut him," I said. "I held him down and smothered his screams so he would bleed to death. The other things I told you were true. There was a debt between us, so it was a . . . fortuitous happenstance."

I attempted a smile, but the unyielding judgement on the sergeant's face banished it quickly. The Lady Evadine, by contrast, appeared more saddened than disapproving, shaking her head with a frown before asking, "This girl is kin to you?"

"No, Captain. Just a . . . recently acquired friend."

She angled her head, eyes narrowing as the piercing gaze stabbed a little deeper. I knew there was a question behind those eyes, one that bespoke this woman's lack of naivety and her estimation of my character. *Why didn't you just kill her?* It would have been a relatively easy task. Despite her lethality, Ayin was also a trusting soul and I had given her no reason to fear me. I could have distracted her by pointing excitedly at a bird or a squirrel and swiftly cut her throat when she turned to look. A few rocks to weigh down the body and let the stream be her grave. I could have, so easily. But I hadn't.

A thin line appeared in Evadine Courlain's brow, either puzzlement or satisfaction, I couldn't tell. It vanished as she blinked and shifted her focus to Ayin, smiling and extending a hand. "Come here, child."

Ayin's bashfulness changed as she trotted closer, first into the eager, happy face of a girl receiving sought-for attention, then shifting into something very different. It happened when she came within arm's reach of the captain, her girlish aspect falling away and leaving behind an expression of blank, enraptured devotion. The muddy ground squelched as she sank unbidden to her knees, reaching up with tremulous hands to touch the fingers the lady extended to trace through the soft brown tresses of her hair.

"You," Evadine said, "are a very beautiful soul, my sister."

And Ayin wept. The storm of tears came upon her without warning, welling in her eyes and streaming down features abruptly contorted into a rictus of grief and pain. Ayin collapsed into herself, huddling with hands covering her face, letting out a series of hard, convulsive sobs. The captain crouched at her side, smoothing her hands over the girl's shuddering back.

The change in Ayin had been so jarring I found myself retreating from it, my mind filled with a sensation I hadn't felt for years. The seed of it took a moment to come to me: that moment on the road when the chainsman made mention of Hostler. I knew then I witnessed something far beyond the bounds of normality, and I knew it now.

"Yes," Sergeant Swain murmured, "it's quite something to see."

I turned to find him regarding the lady and the weeping girl with the eyes of a man who had witnessed this before but would never tire of the sight.

"Shhh," the lady said, gentle hands clasping Ayin's shoulders, raising her up.

"I didn't wanna . . . " Ayin wept, her eyes wide as she stared into Evadine's face. "Ma said I had to, else I'd be like her . . . I'd be all *dirty* like her . . . "

"Your soul is clean," Evadine assured her. "I can see it. It shines so brightly."

Ayin spluttered, a desperate smile coming to her lips. "Am I not, then, for the Malecite to claim?"

"No, child." Evadine enclosed Ayin in tight embrace, resting her chin on the girl's head. "The Seraphile will never shun a soul such as yours." She continued to hold Ayin until her sobs abated, finally easing the girl back to tease the tear-dampened hair from her face. "Now then, your friend believes you are in the wrong place. Is he right?"

"No!" Ayin shook her head fiercely, although her eyes remained locked on Evadine's. "I will never be anywhere else, my lady."

"Just 'Captain' will do." Evadine smiled and tweaked Ayin's chin before guiding her to her feet. "You've been pestering me to find a page, Sergeant," she commented to Swain. "I believe I have."

Swain lowered his head in a respectful bow. "And a fine choice she is, Captain."

"My thanks, Alwyn Scribe," Evadine said to me. "Your concern for a fellow soldier does you credit."

My discomfort with what had just transpired made me hesitate before offering my own bow, realising as I did so that I had retreated several more steps. The desire to be gone from here was strong, as was the suspicion that, should she wish it, this woman could do to me what she had just done to Ayin.

"Come along," Evadine told Ayin, leading her by the hand to the two warhorses tethered nearby. "I have some new friends for you to meet."

Bobbing my head to the sergeant, I turned to go, then stopped as he muttered an order to wait.

"Sergeant?"

"Report to me after training tomorrow," he instructed. "The company books need attention. The fellow making the entries has a hand that looks like tracks left by a drunken beetle."

He turned and marched off without another word. Before hastening away, I spared a final glance at Ayin and Evadine. The girl laughed as she held a handful of oats to the muzzle of the grey warhorse while the black gently nuzzled her shoulder.

When we march, I decided, turning my back and striding away. *There'll be a chance to run off when we march.*

Chapter Twenty-Six

I t was another week before Crown Company marched away from Callintor. By then our sackcloth garb had been replaced by more hardy attire of woollen trews and shirts with jerkins of leather, all products of the Callintor artisans. Some of us had even been provided the accoutrements of war, after a fashion. The day before we marched, Sergeant Swain had handed me a sack full of pig-hide gloves with orders to share them out among my troop.

"Not a good notion to go into battle with bare hands," he sniffed. Since I hadn't detected more than a slight thaw in his regard for me, I deduced this to be a reward for my exemplary record keeping.

His description of the previous clerk's hand had, if anything, been overly generous. The ledgers recording the company's strength, equipment and, most interestingly, payroll had all been filled with an untidy, barely legible scrawl that offended my scribe's pride no end. So, without orders, I had copied all the existing books before embarking on recording fresh entries. This had the added benefit of revealing my predecessor's fraudulent accounting of the food stores, a decent portion of which had been surreptitiously sold off to the increasing stream of folk passing along the road. People fleeing war are often hungry and willing to pay excessive prices for basic fare.

Swain's treatment of the thieving clerk had, for the time being, blunted my interest in the payroll. Having stripped him fully naked, the sergeant bound him to a tree before delivering thirty strokes to his back and arse with a horsewhip. After that, the bleeding half-dead wretch was driven from camp still naked and the custodians at the Callintor gates instructed not to allow him entry. I assumed he had probably perished from exposure or blood loss by now.

"Better than nothing, I s'pose," Brewer said, flexing his hand after pulling on one of the thick gloves. "Still rather have a breastplate and helm, though. Or at least some mail."

"It's supposed to be waiting for us at the muster," I told him. "The captain received a letter from the council assuring her of such only yesterday."

My tone was only slightly sardonic, partly due to fatigue after a twelve-mile eastward march, also because it was the truth. The Lady Evadine kept up a constant, hectoring correspondence with the Luminants' Council. Her letters were filled with polite, but firm demands for more weapons, armour and, above all, recruits. So far, the only response had been a terse note confirming the consignment of armour had been dispatched and would be provided when the company rendezvoused with the king's host.

"You almost sound eager," Toria muttered. "Keen to get at the Pretender's vile horde, are we?"

"Why wouldn't he be?" Ayin enquired in the disapproving tone she adopted in rare moments of annoyance. It had become her habit to share the evening fire with us once her chores for the captain were complete. Since sinking to her knees before our anointed leader, Ayin's demeanour had become more consistent in its cheerfulness with only rare slips into vacant-eyed rambling. Whether she was now fully cleansed of her gelding habits, however, remained an open question.

"Captain Evadine says they're all evildoers and heretics," Ayin added, arching an eyebrow at Toria. "We shall be doing the Covenant a great service when we kill them all."

"Or," Toria countered with a caustic smile, "we'll be doing the crows a great service when they get to gobble up what's left of us when the Pretender's done."

"Victory is assured," Ayin shot back, her tone taking on a worrying heat. "The captain has foreseen it. She told me."

"Oh, foreseen my farting arse—"

"Toria," I snapped, catching her eye and shaking my head.

She flushed but fell silent, although her temper immediately began to boil again when Ayin added in a sullen huff, "Southern heretics shouldn't be allowed in this company, anyways."

"Let's take a walk!" I exclaimed, rising to bar Toria's path as she scrambled to her feet. Fortunately, she held to some measure of restraint, allowing me to lead her away.

We walked the dark lanes between the tents and the many huddled figures silhouetted by their night-time blazes. Although it was still late summer, the air felt chill, a feeling accentuated by the general absence of song in this camp. My criminal youth had led me through many a soldiers' bivouac and they were usually lively places, full of voices raised in ancient martial tunes or arguments over dice. With both gambling and drink forbidden in Covenant Company, our evenings were much quieter affairs.

Toria maintained a frigid silence for a time until our wanderings took us near the picket line. "Why exactly," she began in a controlled but angry tone, "do we have to share our fire with that fucking loon? I know she's pretty and all but you're not even tupping her, as far as I can tell."

"Last week I had exactly two friends in the whole world," I said with a shrug. "Now I have three."

"Because she cut some bastard's cock off? Is that all it takes?"

I had enlightened Toria and Brewer regarding the details of Erchel's demise, it being the principal reason for our presence in this company, although I knew Brewer would have volunteered in any case. I also doubted he would have little truck for what I was about to suggest.

"She's harmless, thanks to the good captain," I said. "Besides, I didn't drag you away to talk about her."

I halted, casting a deliberately slow eye over the picket line. The circle of sentries was a testament to Sergeant Swain's largely correct estimation of his soldiers. A third of the guards were veterans who had volunteered before the company's arrival at Callintor, all lay folk with long allegiance to the Covenant and experience of soldiering into the bargain. The rest were carefully selected from the most ardent recruits, and what they lacked in martial discipline they made up for in fervent devotion. In short, it would be a very difficult barrier to cross without bloodshed.

"You saw what Swain did to the clerk," Toria said, a needless reminder since the vision of the man's scored rump lived large in my mind. "And that was just for thieving. Desertion is a whole other business."

"Ever been in a battle?" I asked, still surveying the line of sentries.

"'Course not."

"Neither have I, and I'm very keen to maintain my ignorance of the experience, for I hear it's far from pleasant."

"All right." She gave a sigh and joined in my scrutiny of the pickets. "I take it you have a notion?" She let out a faint laugh before I could answer. "Of course you fucking do."

"I was hoping we could slip away on the march," I said, ignoring the jibe. "But Swain's posted outriders on the column and—" I nodded to the pickets "—we'd have to kill one of these to get clear, then we'd have to run even further and faster than we did from the Pit. Lord Eldurm's a dull-wit and still he damn near caught us. I'd wager Swain would chase us down in half the time."

"So?"

"So we wait. There's a good deal of road betwixt us and the king's host. Who's to say what trouble we'll find? A patrolling band of the Pretender's mob, maybe? Outlaws even? Either way, trouble creates a distraction which creates an opportunity. We just have to be ready for it."

"And if it doesn't? I recall sitting chained in a cart for days waiting for an opportunity that never came. Say we make it all the way to the muster, what then?"

"This company will join with the king's host. That's a lot of folk all mingled up in one place, and I doubt the churls all those nobles have scraped together will be so vigilant as this lot come nightfall."

"Brewer won't come, nor will your little friend. Our anointed captain's snared them too tight."

I met her eye with a steady gaze. "I know, and that's a shame."

She grunted, giving a small nod of satisfaction as we resumed our saunter. "Any notion of what we might do once we've put this mob behind us? And I don't want to hear any dung about Ascendant Sihlda's fucking testament."

I did indeed have plans for Sihlda's compiled wisdom but decided not to argue the point. Instead, I opted to voice a nebulous notion that had been worrying away at my thoughts with increasing persistence for days. "Ever hear of Lachlan's hoard?"

Toria stared at me, mouth quirking before she let out a laugh, loud and sharp in the gloom. Her mirth faded when she saw the seriousness of my expression. "You haven't bought a map, have you, Alwyn?" she enquired, brows knotted in bemused surprise. She patted her jerkin. "Wait, I think I have a Caerith spell charm that is certain to ward off all sickness. Only ten sheks and it's yours."

"Erchel spoke of it before he died," I said. "Didn't believe him at the time, but the more I ponder it, the more I wonder."

"A dying man will say anything if he thinks it gives him the slightest chance of catching another breath."

"He wasn't promising it. He had no notion of where it is, but he said Deckin did. It was how he was going to pay for his rebellion."

"So he said. I'm guessing Deckin never spoke of it to you."

"He wasn't the type to spill his secrets. Nor was he foolish enough to think he could seize the dukedom of the Shavine Marches with no war chest to pay those who followed him."

Toria shook her head again, but the light of a nearby fire caught the small, interested glimmer in her eye. "So, let's say, purely for argument's sake, that it's real. There truly is a great hoard of treasure out there. How would we ever find it?"

"Erchel spoke of the Shavine coast, but that's no surprise. Almost all the stories point to the coast as Lachlan's grave and most likely site of his loot."

"Not an easy place to search, I'd guess, else this hoard would've been found years ago, if it's there to find."

I recalled my sole sojourn to the coast. I had been with Deckin's band for two years when he ordered Klant to take me along on a message-running trip to a smuggling gang. Despite his limp, the result he claimed to be of a collision with a knight's warhorse during some battle or other – Klant was a spry, chatty fellow. All these years later I still feel a pang when I think of his eventual fate: caught and hanged by the sheriff's men the summer following our trip to the coast. It did, however, amply illustrate one of his favourite sayings: "Outlaws, boy, are always dangling from a fraying rope woven by their own misfortunes. One day, that rope becomes a noose for all of us."

What I recalled of the coast itself consisted of days of traipsing along windswept clifftops interspersed by repeated clambering up and down gullies of irksome depth. It was a wild place even in summer, beset by capricious tides and fierce gales prone to raising tall waves to lash against the innumerable crags and inlets. I remembered thinking it offered just as many places to hide as the forest, as long as you were willing to suffer the shivering dampness of it all.

"No," I agreed in a soft murmur. "Not an easy place to search. But, Deckin knew something of where to look, that much I'm content to believe."

"Why?"

Where the Hound laid his head . . . "Something he said once. Something Erchel repeated before he died. I know it's thin, but it's something."

"So, words but no map," Toria grunted. "Nothing more than another story, in truth."

"Except that it's real, for once. As for a map . . . " I trailed off, brow furrowing as thoughts churned within.

"Alwyn?" Toria prompted as my silence grew long.

"Sihlda once said that books are our guide to the future. A library is a map of the past, and to know where you're going you have to know where you've been. Deckin knew it too, but he couldn't read. Stories were his map. He loved them. Everywhere we went, every village, every tavern, he always called the storyteller to the fire and paid them well for their tales. I doubt he ever forgot a single one."

"Your plan is to rove the duchies of this realm seeking out story-tellers?"

"No, my plan is to seek out a well-stocked library, preferably one used to house tax records."

Toria's brow creased in puzzlement. "Why tax records?"

"Because to calculate tax with any accuracy you have to track the ownership of land and property over time. Sihlda always said tax farmers are by far the best historians."

Toria gave a dubious squint at this before shrugging. "There's a big old library in Couravel, also Athiltor. But I doubt they'd just throw their doors open to the likes of us."

"Since when has any door been a barrier to you?"

"True enough. But I'll need the right tools when the time comes . . ."

She trailed off as we came to a large cluster of seated soldiers, all listening in rapt fascination as Communicant Captain Evadine Courlain began her nightly sermon. She stood before a large bonfire, a tall silhouette somehow made more compelling by the inability to fully discern her features. I assumed the fire to be a deliberate piece of theatre; by concealing her face it transformed her into an ethereal figure, more than human.

Attendance at these gatherings was not compulsory but she never lacked for an audience. Glancing to my right, I saw Brewer and Ayin coming to join the throng. Ayin's features were bright with anticipation while Brewer's were stern, although his widened eyes indicated a hunger for the captain's lesson. I had begun to discern a discomfort in him in recent days, a sense that he saw his growing devotion to the Lady Evadine as a betrayal of Sihlda's legacy. If so, it was an inescapable betrayal, like a long-married man who can't resist the harlot's bed.

"Do you gather here in supplication to the Seraphile's grace and the Martyrs' example?" Evadine asked the assembly, receiving the customary response.

"We so gather."

At the commencement of most supplications these words were typically uttered in a habituated mumble, but here they rose as a fervent affirmation. During my first attendance at one of these sermons I had assumed that such enthusiasm resulted from the presence of Sergeant Swain and several other devout veterans. However, I now knew this zeal to be genuine and growing in volume each night.

It was also a typical feature of supplications for the presiding cleric to open with a passage from one of the Martyr Scrolls. The lazier the cleric the more lengthy the recitation for it spared them the effort of coming up with an original interpretation with which to enlighten their flock. Evadine, however, rarely quoted from the scrolls, and then only to illustrate a point. From start to finish, every lesson was hers alone and I never once heard her repeat a prior sermon.

"In recent days," she began, her voice strong but not strident, "I have heard some of you refer to me as 'anointed'. I must ask that you stop. Not for reasons of mere modesty, but because it is simply untrue. You see, my friends, I am not anointed by the Seraphile's grace; I am cursed."

She paused to allow the ripple of surprise ebb through her audience before raising a hand. "Not, you will be pleased to hear, by the Malecite, or—" her voice took on an amused edge "—by some trinket-waving Caerith mummer. No . . . " Her silhouette took on a sudden stillness and, even though her face remained in shadow, I and everyone else present felt as if she looked directly into our eyes. "My curse comes from the Seraphile, for it was into my eyes they chose to send their vision, a vision I would not wish upon the vilest, most wicked soul to walk this earth. The Seraphile, you see, showed me the Scourge. Not the Scourge that has been; not the great calamity that brought empires low and nearly wiped our race from the face of the world. No, they showed me the Scourge to come, the Second Scourge warned of in the Scrolls of Martyrs Stevanos, Athil and Hersephone. The coming great rising of the Malecite that our beloved Covenant was formed to prevent.

"I will not tell you all I saw, friends, for I do not wish to trouble your dreams with nightmares. But know this: I saw destruction. I saw violation. I saw agonies and torments it is beyond the wit of man to imagine. When you march tomorrow, look upon the beauty of nature.

Gaze at the simple wonder of trees, grass, river and sky. Then envision it all twisted, rotten, torn and sundered. See the sky turned deepest crimson. See each blade of grass turned to ash and every forest a blackened tangle. See every river and sea choked with poison and the blood of the slaughtered. And see the Malecite."

She faltered then, lowering her head, raising a hand to touch her brow as the congregation waited in desperate anticipation.

"It is not . . . " Evadine said, coughing to banish a catch in her throat " . . . not an easy thing to behold the true sight of the Malecite, when all their blandishments and deceits are stripped away. To look upon them is to look upon hate made flesh. And they hunger, friends. They hunger for our flesh and our souls. Our pain is their sustenance. Once they feasted and now they lust to feast again . . . Will you let them?"

"No!" It wasn't a shout at first, just an immediate, instinctive response, but no less fierce for its lack of volume. Of course, it didn't end there. "NO!" Their defiance rose in a discordant babble as they got to their feet, quickly taking on the cadence of a chant. "NO! NO! NO!" Fists were raised and weapons brandished. I saw both Brewer and Ayin on their feet, he thrusting a fist into the air while she jumped, face lit with joyous abandon.

It all stopped the instant Evadine raised her hand. Hushed stillness gripped the assembly as they waited for her word. If Ascendant Hilbert had been giving this sermon he would have sought to stoke their fervour to an even higher pitch, perhaps with a few choice aphorisms stolen from Sihlda's testament. But that, I knew, would be a mistake. Soon, these people would be required to fight. Sending them into too wild a frenzy at this time would inflame their spirits too early. This was just the first coal added to a fire that needed to burn white hot when battle dawned. I was undecided whether to admire or condemn the manipulation at play here, although I suspected the Lady Evadine might not be conscious of her own calculation. She believed, of that I had no doubt, and a believer will justify all acts in pursuit of their faith.

So, instead of imparting more of her vision, Evadine merely spoke the words that signified the sermon's end. "Will you go forth with hearts filled by the Seraphile's grace and steps guided by the Martyrs' example?"

Once again, the response was instant and shot through with conviction, but muted. "We will." I could sense their hunger, but also an acceptance arising from the knowledge that another ration of this addictive elixir would be doled out the following night.

Toria and I fell in alongside Brewer and Ayin and we joined the serene procession of mostly silent soldiers making their way back to their tents. To her credit, Toria maintained her silence until the crowd had dispersed before whispering to me, "She's fucking mad, y'know."

I glanced back at the bonfire still blazing beyond the dark angles of the surrounding tents. Like Toria, I had kept silent throughout it all: no fervent shouts or upraised fists for me. But still, although I pushed against the realisation, I knew Evadine's words had pierced the armour encasing my heart. She hadn't snared me, not yet. But compelling oratory spoken by a beautiful woman has a force all its own.

"Yes," I said. "She's mad all right."

CHAPTER TWENTY-SEVEN

To my dismay, our march to the muster produced no fortuitously distracting events. The company tramped its increasingly disciplined course along the road with no interruptions from the Pretender's scouts or obliging outlaws. It was a tiresome journey in many respects. We woke at first light to a breakfast of gruel then an hour of training under Supplicant Blade Ofihla's ever-critical eye. Then came the delightful prospect of eight hours on the road, the Supplicants hectoring our every step as they no longer tolerated untidy ranks or straggling. Evenings were taken up with pitching camp followed by a plain but admittedly hearty meal, then yet more drill before the captain's sermon.

While there were still no strictures enforcing attendance, every soldier would gather to hear the lesson, if lessons they could be called. As the days passed the sermons reminded me more and more of the times I had watched a blacksmith at work as a boy. Every word Evadine spoke was a precisely aimed hammer blow, shaping this cluster of one-time outlaws and villains into true swords of the Covenant.

Toria and I attended along with everyone else, for to do otherwise would attract notice. Each time I heard Evadine speak I felt another fractional piercing of my armour, although I still refused to join in the others' shouting gesticulations. There was a danger to this woman, a lure I knew I needed to resist as I had once needed to surrender to Sihlda's tutelage. Evadine did not teach; she inspired. Before concluding every supplication, she would ask a question, different each time but always leading us towards the ultimate goal.

"The Pretender fills his followers with lies," she told us that final night on the road. "He claims royal blood he does not have. He slakes their greed with plunder. He services their lusts with rape. He is a servant of the Malecite. This has been shown to me. Will you allow this creature his spoils? Will you let him cast open the gates to the Second Scourge?"

The clamour of "NO!" was complemented by an overlapping chorus of "NEVER!" The company was on their feet by then, raised up by the blossoming heat of Evadine's voice. I saw true rage on many faces alongside the wide, moist-eyed devotion. Ayin leapt in excitement, tears streaming down her laughing face while Brewer's features quivered with worshipful fury.

Sensing the fast-approaching moment when this congregation would transform into an unreasoning mob, I touched Toria's arm and we began to back away. Impending violence thrummed the air like the prickly oppression before the thunder roars, and I wanted no part of it. But, once again, Evadine calmed them by merely raising a hand.

"Tomorrow we join with the king's host," she said, her voice soft and intent but easily heard in the breathless silence. "Battle will surely follow. Know that I have the greatest pride in you. Know that I have witnessed more true devotion in your company than I ever saw in all my life. Know that I love you. We will speak again when battle dawns. Go now, friends, and rest."

Rest, however, eluded me that night. While Brewer snored, Toria fidgeted and Ayin lay curled in contented slumber, I stared up at the dense weave of our canvas roof. The sermon was loud among my thoughts but louder still were Sihlda's words spoken at the close of her testament, words I hadn't shared with Ascendant Hilbert.

I detest the notion that I am a victim, she told me as we huddled together in her alcove. I recalled the way the light of the candle stub played over one half of her face, catching the lines around her eyes and mouth. I thought her aged but made beautiful by wisdom.

My actions, she went on, *my sins remain my own and I'll not shirk the consequences, in this life or when I stand before the Seraphile to give my account and suffer their judgement. But, the fact remains that I am a victim, Alwyn. So are you. So is every member of this congregation and every unfortunate who labours in this Pit. We are the victims of a world made wrong, and its wrongness could be made right if only every victim saw the truth of it.*

Inevitably, I wondered what Sihlda would have made of Evadine. *Some are bestowed with the gift of snaring the souls of others with words alone*, she had said. Would she dismiss this visionary noblewoman as a mere rabble-rouser? Possessed of a voice and face sure to fire the souls of the ignorant or easily gulled? I doubted it. Sihlda's insight was always deeper, always pure in its precision.

Calculations, I thought, recalling how she would guide my thoughts towards conclusions she found obvious but eluded me. *Assemble the facts, find where they join, form conclusions.*

So, facts then: I served in a company recruited under Covenant auspices and captained by a noblewoman with visions of the Second Scourge. Adjacent fact: this was the same noblewoman upon whom Lord Eldurm had expended so much saccharine correspondence.

I knew from those many letters that her family were not merely noble, but so highborn that Evadine's grandfather had once served as adviser to King Tomas when he ascended to the throne as a boy of only nine years. Also, her family owned a goodly portion of the best land in Alberis. A beauty of such esteemed breeding and wealth would not have been wanting for suitors, and yet here she was commanding a few hundred supposedly redeemed villains as they trooped towards probable slaughter.

What is she doing here? I thought, grasping for a conclusion I couldn't find. *What does she want?*

The answer came with surprising swiftness and it was spoken in Sihlda's voice, the patient, measured tone I knew so well, loud and clear as if she lay next to me: *Her family will have shunned her for this, perhaps even disowned her. Such sacrifice comes only from a heartfelt desire for one thing: change, Alwyn. These visions she speaks of, assuming she believes them to be real, have birthed in her the same desire that possessed me. She wants what I wanted, what my testament was intended to produce. She wants to change it all, but not with words.*

Fatigue finally welled in me then, my eyelids drooping and the weave of the tent roof dissolving into blackness. As I slid towards slumber, Sihlda's wisdom followed me into the void: *And, like me, she'll need you to do it . . .*

The company arrived at the outer picket of the king's host around midday. We spent a short interval loitering while the captain and Sergeant Swain went off to consult with whatever noble luminaries held command. The company waited on the slope of a low hill affording a decent view of the entire host and I quickly lost count of the banners rising above the city of tents and corralled horses. The full extent of the encampment was partially occluded by a pall of mist, the accumulation of woodsmoke, sweat and the breath of so many folk and beasts. Even so, Toria and I managed to arrive at a decent estimation of the overall number which has been largely borne out by many a learned scholar since.

"Fifteen thousand," I opined.

"I'd say twenty," she countered. "You have to account for the camp followers and the gaggles of servants and arse-lickers the nobles drag around."

"A great and mighty army!" Ayin enthused, beaming once again. Her bright, white-toothed smile had become ever more frequent as the prospect of battle loomed closer. "We'll cut down the Pretender's filth like wheat before the scythe." Her eager tone caused me to reflect that Evadine may have done much to calm Ayin's mind, but she certainly hadn't mended it.

"That's an untidy picket line," Toria observed quietly, ignoring Ayin as was typical. "Seems most ragged to the south."

"We'll have to see where they put us," I murmured back. "Scrounge up some liquor from somewhere, make friends with the churls on guard. Maybe they'd appreciate a tot or two of brandy on a cold night."

"Drunken sentries." She gave a slight nod of approval. "My favourite kind."

Sadly, such clever scheming was frustrated when Sergeant Swain returned and issued orders for us to camp atop this very rise. His features were even more grim and forbidding than usual as he barked out the orders that had us scurrying to raise the tents and stack wood for the fires. I wondered at the significance of Swain returning without Evadine and concluded his darkened mood probably had something to do with it. So, it was with some trepidation that I heard him call my name.

"Scribe! Get over here!"

I dutifully trotted to his side, knuckling my brow and adopting the straight-backed, eyes-averted stance expected when addressing a Supplicant. My voice was flat, as I found it best when in his presence to maintain as neutral a tone and expression as possible. His suspicions of my character were far from quelled, despite my exemplary and honest bookkeeping.

"Fetch the company ledgers and take them to the captain," he instructed. "Bring ink and quill, also. You'll find her at the tent where the Covenant banner flies. Quick now!" he added in a growl when I hesitated a fraction too long.

It is my experience that armies can be counted on to produce three substances in abundance: mud, shit and blood, mostly the first two since many an army has marched hither and yon without spilling a drop of the red stuff. Those of you with a passing interest in recent history will know that this certainly wasn't the case with the host King Tomas gathered to face the Pretender's horde.

Navigating the camp was a messy and occasionally perilous business, burdened as I was by the sack containing the company ledgers. The atmosphere was heavy with a melange of smoke and horse dung, bringing an unpleasant itch to my nose and moisture to my eyes. Progress required much squelching of mud in between scrambling clear of carts and the horses of nobles or mounted men-at-arms.

Neither seemed to have much of a care for any wayward foot soldier who might happen into their path, some even letting out amused guffaws as they sent an unfortunate sprawling in the mud. I was surprised to find this camp such a disorderly place, the various clusters of tents having been pitched at random intervals with no attempt to create proper thoroughfares. This dirty disorganisation was reflected in the occupants, at least those I encountered as I searched for the Covenant banner.

"Got any leaf on ya?" one besmirched fellow called out to me from a cluster of particularly ill-favoured tents. The banner fluttering above them was unfamiliar, as was his accent, a sharp, halting grate I later learned hailed from the eastern extremity of the realm. He wore a leather jerkin studded with rusted iron and hadn't shaved in days. In Covenant Company, the Supplicants gave a man seven days to grow a beard then forced him to shave if he couldn't. I also had little doubt Supplicant Blade Ofihla would have beaten me bloody for going about with dried mud on my face.

"We're not allowed it in our company," I called back. "I've sheks for brandy, if you've got it."

"Oh piss off." He lost interest, waving a hand and turning away. "Not a bottle to be had in this whole shitting camp."

I moved on, trying to keep to the fringes of the muddy lanes as I scanned the forest of banners for the Covenant sigil. It was as I came to a small copse of trees that my gaze was distracted by a curious sight. For reasons unknown, there was a decent gap between these trees and the surrounding tents; however, beneath the branches of a tall birch a conical shelter sat alone.

It appeared to be fashioned from curved, intertwined branches, the gaps filled with a mix of moss and leaves. Alongside it a pot steamed over a small fire watched over by a slim figure in a cloak of earthy green. While the shelter was unusual, it was the sight of the woman sitting by the fire that captured my gaze, not lured by beauty, but by the sack of rough woven cloth she wore on her head. From the rear of the sack, long blonde hair cascaded down her back, but, as I saw when she turned to regard me, her face remained completely hidden.

The sack featured two small, diamond-shaped holes. What lay beyond was hidden in shadow, but I could sense the depth of scrutiny there. She had felt my gaze upon her, I was certain of that, but how remained a mystery. I felt a quickening of my heart as she continued to stare, rising from a small stool and turning to face me. The sack crinkled as she angled her head. It wasn't a particularly predatory gesture, but still it stirred an unease in me and a desire to be elsewhere. Yet I lingered, unable to look away from the black diamonds of her eyes. So commanding were they that I failed to hear the squelch of boots at my back.

"Got a stiff-stand for the Sack Witch, have you?" a familiar voice enquired. "I wouldn't. Way I hear it, the sight of what lies beneath that cloth is so foul to look upon it's like to drive all reason from a man's head."

Turning, I found myself confronted by a stocky man with grizzled features, clad in grey and black livery. His hand rested on the handle of the sword at his belt, his grip tight although his face remained affable.

"Sergeant Lebas," I said, eyes flicking to his left and right to confirm he wasn't alone. Two other guardsmen I recognised from the Pit stood at his back, their expressions far less benign.

It is at such times that I find fear diminishes. The outcome of this encounter was not in doubt, so the absence of uncertainty left no room for the kind of sweaty-palmed panic I might have felt had I merely glimpsed this man's face in the crowd.

"Alwyn Scribe," Lebas replied, inclining his head.

"Is she truly a witch?" I asked. I wasn't playing for time, just indulging my curiosity as I gestured to the woman with the sack-covered head.

"So they say." Lebas grinned and shrugged. "She's Caerith, y'see? Wherever there's a muster there she'll be with all manner of potions, for the right price. Cure anything from a drooping member to a poisoned gut. Haven't yet had need of her services, meself." A measure of the cheeriness slipped from his features as a hard glint shone in his eyes. "And I doubt you'll get the chance."

I returned his smile with one of my own. "Lord Eldurm sent you in answer to the king's muster, I take it?"

All pretence to amiability fell away then, Lebas's skin reddening and nostrils flaring. "The Pit is no longer the charge of the Gulatte family, thanks to you." His knuckles whitened on the sword's handle. "Just one escape after all those years and the king took away his lordship's charter, sold it off to another noble with a fatter purse. Now we're here so's Lord Eldurm can redeem his honour in the king's sight. In a day or so some of us'll be lying in the mud, thanks to you."

"Lot of folk lying by the gate every morning, as I recall."

"Worthless scum they were, just like you." His grin returned and he stepped closer, slipping the sword from its sheath. "Though, I should be thanking you. You're about to make me rich . . . "

There are many vagaries that decide the fate of a man at times like these. They can be something as simple as the course of the wind or the angle of the sun. Any number of factors now combined to decide whether I would survive this meeting, principally the fortuitous fact that Sergeant Lebas and his two friends were not truly soldiers; they were guards. It may be a subtle distinction, but it proved to be very important. Had he been a soldier rather than a man who had spent years intimidating and beating those with no chance to defend themselves, Lebas would have either been quicker in his approach, or more cautious. Instead, his attack was the charge of the lifelong bully surrendering to anger and therefore it gave him no chance to avoid the ledger-laden sack as I swung it to connect with the side of his head.

Before turning to sprint in the opposite direction, I caught the gratifying sight of blood exploding from the sergeant's mouth along with several teeth, his head jarred to a sharp angle as his stocky body fell. I heard the thud of his comrades' boots on the earth as I ran, heading for the copse of trees. I would dodge through them and make for the busiest part of the camp, hoping to lose the pursuit among the mass of tents and soldiers.

My course inevitably took me close to the Sack Witch. She stood still and unperturbed by the ruckus. Once again the black diamond holes that formed her eyes drew me in and time seemed to slow as I passed her. Just for a second I glimpsed a pinpoint of light gleaming on a deep blue orb.

Then I was beyond her, pounding hard, expecting to hear the whoosh of a sword blade at any instant. Instead I heard a sudden shout of alarm followed by the sound of a man falling to an untidy halt. Slowing a little, I glanced over my shoulder to see one of the pursuing guards on his knees, the other still standing but also halted. They both stared at the immobile form of the Sack Witch, their faces turned white in terror. I had no notion of what precisely had caused this sudden abandonment of the chase, but had no doubt it originated with her, even though her posture hadn't changed at all.

The kneeling man scrambled back from her, managing to regain his feet after a few faltering attempts before making a rapid retreat. His friend was more controlled, his gaze switching from the woman to me, flushing with dark frustration as he brandished his bared sword. He cursed, then cast a few insults at the Sack Witch, although was quick in walking away as he did so. My last sight of the pair was of them crouching to gather up Lebas's sagging form and drag him away.

I turned and kept running, feeling the Sack Witch's gaze on me until I disappeared into the city of tents.

I found the Covenant banner near the centre of the camp, pitched close to a well-guarded and multi-hued cluster of larger tents. The tallest banner of all rose above this colourful grouping, the flag emblazoned with three white horses on a black background. Heraldry had been a marginal part of Sihlda's tutelage, but she hadn't neglected it entirely and I was quick to recognise this as the banner of the Algathinet dynasty. Its size and the gold tassels fluttering from the corners identified this as the flag of King Tomas himself rather than some lesser vessel of the royal blood.

I found myself pausing to stare at it, my eyes sliding down the pole to the tents beneath. Despite the fact that I couldn't see a soul beyond the armoured, red-cloaked guards of Crown Company, I was still beset by the sheer novelty of being only a few dozen yards from the monarch of Albermaine.

Come to fight in person, after all, I mused. It appeared my assumption that the Court would decamp for safer climes during this crisis had been in error. This was decidedly at odds with everything I had heard or learned about the king and his noble cronies. *The king is a fool who loves the company of those yet more foolish* had been Sihlda's unvarnished description of the current occupant of the throne. *A foolish commoner is merely a danger to himself. A foolish king endangers all.*

"Over here, Scribe!"

Lady Evadine's voice banished my reverie instantly, coloured as it was by a previously unheard note of impatient ire. She stood beside a large cart, an old shaggy-footed dray horse tossing an unkempt mane in the withers. Beside Evadine stood a trim, neatly attired cleric, his thin, pale features drawn in a placid smile despite the captain's unconcealed frown of anger.

"Captain," I said, knuckling my forehead as I moved hastily to her side. "Sergeant Swain bid me—"

"Yes, yes," she cut in, nodding to the cleric. "Aspirant Arnabus requires sight of the ledgers."

The trim man's gaze flicked over me while I retrieved the leather-bound tomes from the sack. I saw only a brief interest in his small, near-black eyes as they passed across my face and garb before focusing on the ledgers. "Place them here, if you would, good soldier," he said, pointing to the cart's tailboard. He spoke with the same accent as Evadine, that of Alberis nobility, but with a smoother, more careful enunciation. "And be so kind as to direct me to the company inventory."

I did as he bid, leafing through the pages to the required entries, drawing a murmur of surprised approval from him in the process. "Very fine," he said, running a finger over the columns of numbers and letters. "Your work?"

I bobbed my head in confirmation. "It is, Aspirant."

"How fortunate your captain is to have found such a skilled hand." He revealed his teeth in a smile, teeth that seemed to possess an unnatural whiteness, resembling rows of small ivory beads. "Might I ask where you came by it?"

Thinking a fulsome explanation of my skills unwise, I opted for a concise response. "I worked in the scriptorium at the Shrine to Martyr Callin, Aspirant."

"Ah, that explains it. Tell me, does Master Arnild the Gilder still labour there?"

"He does, Aspirant. I count myself blessed to have received some of his teachings . . . "

I trailed off as Evadine let out a loud, pointed cough. I saw Aspirant Arnabus's eyes narrow and flick to her, although the increased breadth of his smile indicated a lack of annoyance, perhaps even satisfaction.

"Now," he said, returning to the ledger. "Let's have a look, shall we?"

He spent several minutes leafing through the pages, lips pursed and brow creased in apparently genuine interest. He asked occasional questions of Evadine, seemingly banal enquiries about minor details but, from her clipped, increasingly glowering responses, I divined a hidden barb in each one.

"Three letins a week expended on food alone," he commented with a raised eyebrow. "My researches indicate most companies of this size barely require two. Some noble captains, rightly keen to preserve the king's purse, make do with but one."

"And go into battle with starved soldiers barely capable of grasping a billhook," Evadine returned, keeping a steady, unblinking gaze on the Aspirant. "Rest assured, when they meet the Pretender's horde, those sworn to our banner will demonstrate fully the value of well-fed soldiery. Besides, Aspirant—" she gave him an entirely empty smile of her own " this company belongs to the Covenant, not the king."

"And the Covenant, much like the king, does not enjoy boundless wealth. Still—" the cleric's thin nose wrinkled in a sniff "—this all seems in order. Scribe." He gestured to me, slipping a scroll from the sleeve of his robe which he unfurled atop the open ledger. "Be so good as to enter these items into the inventory. I shall witness the accuracy of the record and you and the good captain can be on your way."

Receiving a nod from Evadine, I fished in the sack for my quill and ink and set to work. The Aspirant's scroll held a list of arms and armour,

CHAPTER TWENTY-EIGHT

We kept to the camp's southern precincts as we made our way back to the company. To my relief this course took us well clear of the copse where the Sack Witch made her home. I wasn't sure if I was more fearful of encountering Gulatte's men or the Caerith woman. The black diamonds of her eyes continued to linger in my mind, particularly the glimmer of light I had seen within. Just a fleeting glimpse gone in an instant, but I couldn't shake the sense of elusive significance.

Our course also had the good fortune to bring me within sight of another banner I recognised, this time due to familiarity rather than Sihlda's lessons. The banner of Duke Elbyn Blousset of the Shavine Marches stood tallest here, although not as tall as the king's, for such would be tantamount to treason. A silver hawk on a red background, it fluttered above a forest of sigils raised by the lesser houses of the duchy, all come in answer to the king's muster.

She's here, I thought, watching the banner ripple in the wind as the cart swayed over ruts and rises. *Unless the duke left his whore at home.* I thought this to be unlikely. Lorine would want to be among this accumulation of noble power. Surely, she would find the myriad opportunities presented here impossible to resist.

She'll be well guarded, I mused, searching the densely arrayed tents, neater than elsewhere and most likely home to more disciplined soldiers than the other slovens in this camp. *But not during the battle. When the battle starts she'll be alone, or at least only lightly guarded . . .*

My preoccupation with the Shavine encampment was such that I failed to notice immediately when Evadine reined her grey to a sudden halt. Luckily, the plodding old dray horse let out a warning snort before I steered her into the rump of the lady's mount. Dragging on the reins, I managed to bring the cart to a standstill in time, feeling a sudden lurch to the stomach when I looked to see what had caused the captain to stop.

Lord Eldurm Gulatte sat atop a fine stallion a dozen yards ahead, flanked on either side by mounted men-at-arms, a full score in number. His lordship's face had a flushed look to it, the expression of a man determined not to shirk a difficult but vital task.

"My lady," he greeted Evadine. He bowed but remained in the saddle. This I knew to be a breach of knightly etiquette, which normally required that a nobleman dismount and go to one knee before offering regards to a lady of equal or greater rank. I wondered if this might indicate a loss of regard for the object of his affections, but the sight of his face soon dispelled any such notion. As he gazed upon Evadine, his expression betrayed a mingling of lust and longing, the combination of emotions he had long mistaken for love. Thanks to my many hours spent helping him compose letters to this very woman, I knew what lay behind that expression was not love but hopeless obsession, the kind that could turn an otherwise amiable soul into a dangerous one.

"How it delights me to see you again," he added in tones that were strained and notable for their absence of delight.

"My lord," was the sum of Evadine's response, her tone flat and devoid of warmth. She continued to sit atop the grey with an air of light curiosity rather than concern.

"I heard tell of your . . . adventures," Lord Eldurm went on after a cough. "Very stirring and admirable. But I would, of course, expect nothing less. Though it grieves me to think of you in such proximity to danger—"

"My lord," Evadine cut in, her voice now possessed of a steely edge, "I believe our most recent correspondence marks the end of any and all association between us, except as allies in this noble cause. Now—" she took a tighter grip on the grey's reins "—unless you have martial business to discuss, I ask, with all due courtesy, that you make way. I have pressing business with my company."

I saw her words strike him with much the same power as a flight of arrows. He shrank in the saddle, his blocky, handsome features paling, a man borne down by a plummeting heart. Still, to his credit and my dismay, Eldurm rallied quickly. Drawing a deep breath, he straightened, forcing himself to meet Evadine's gaze with a resolute eye.

"I regret that I am not here on your account, my lady." His hard resolve shifted to grim anticipation as he switched his attention to me, extending an arm, finger pointed like a spearpoint. "I am here for him."

Evadine turned, regarding me with an upraised eyebrow to which I could only offer a weak smile.

"A villain of the worst character," his lordship continued. "A deceiver, a thief, a murderer, who no less than an hour ago assaulted one of my own men. By all rights under Crown law, he is mine to claim and I will see justice done."

Before she turned back to Eldurm, Evadine's mouth formed a curve. It was just a small expression of knowing humour but still somehow reassuring. "I don't care," she stated, speaking on with careful emphasis. "I know his tale. He remains my man, his oath sworn and accepted, under *Covenant* law."

"That churl-scum," Eldurm exploded, face reddening and horse fidgeting as it sensed its master's rage, "has pretended devotion to the Covenant before! You would be a fool to believe his lies. As I once was when I allowed him into my own chambers, allowed him to pen my letters . . . "

He faltered then, the redness of his pallor shifting to the pinker hue of embarrassment. Once again, however, he recovered his composure quickly, speaking on after a few calming breaths. "And I was not the only victim of his falsity. Ascendant Sihlda, once the most cherished voice of the Covenant, now lies forever entombed beneath rock and earth, lured into a hopeless escape by this man's perfidy. This betrayer who brought a tunnel down upon her head to secure his own escape."

"That's a fucking lie!"

My skin burned as I rose, spittle flying from my lips as I shouted out the denial. While no stranger to anger and its many hazards, I am usually capable of containing it, keeping it simmering away within for however long it takes before a chance at retribution dawns. The scale of this falsehood, however, was enough to strip away all such constraint, or deference to station. Had he been an outlaw, Gulatte would either have quailed and fled or reached for his knife. Instead, he cast a withering look of disgust over my snarling face before turning again to Evadine.

"You see how he addresses his betters, my lady?" he enquired in appalled repugnance. "How can you sully the Covenant's divine mission with one such as him?"

His recourse to deceit and casual dismissal stoked my rage to a deeper, unreasoning heat, though not completely stripping away my capacity for calculation. *Crossbows*, I recalled, twisting about to pull away the canvas sheet covering the cart's contents. *Each with a score of bolts.*

"Stay where you are, Scribe!"

The rapid bark of Evadine's command hit me like a slap, freezing my hands on the sheet's ties. Shuddering, I forced a measure of calm into my twitching hands, shifting to resume my seat and finding her gaze upon me once more. This time, her expression was far from amused.

"Sit still," she told me, speaking with hard, unambiguous deliberation. "Be quiet."

Her expression softened a fraction as she turned away, lowering her head. I sensed more reluctance than anger in her, the slump then abrupt rise of her shoulders conveying the impression of one summoning strength for a painful duty.

"The code of Covenant Company is clear," she said, addressing Lord Eldurm in formal tones. "As approved by the Luminants' Council and endorsed by the King's Seal. All previous crimes, no matter how heinous, are forgiven in return for diligent service. However . . . " she paused to reach for the longsword affixed to her saddle, drawing the blade free and resting it on her shoulder " . . . as a knight of this realm you hold the right of dispute."

She kicked her grey's flanks, spurring him to a trot that took her closer to Eldurm and his line of mounted men. Reining in a few yards short of him, she raised the sword in front of her face before lowering and raising the blade. It was the gesture of formal acknowledgement of an equal, one I had seen at the few tourneys I had attended. In order to fight, knights were required to temporarily set aside their disparities in rank or blood, so that no recriminations could fall upon the victor should the vanquished perish or suffer serious injury. Lady Evadine Courlain had, in effect, just challenged Lord Eldurm Gulatte to single combat.

"This man is mine," she told Eldurm in a voice that was all steel now; the voice of a captain, in fact. For the first time I realised fully that this woman was not some deluded noble beset by madness she mistook for visions. She was a warrior of the Covenant of Martyrs and would willingly die as such.

"If you want him," she went on, returning the sword to her shoulder, "you'll have to fight me."

Eldurm stared at her in rigid silence, his face now mostly bleached of colour. The longing from moments before was gone now, receded into forlorn defeat.

"We often fought as children, as I'm sure you recall," Evadine continued when Eldurm failed to answer. "You do remember all those years at court, don't you, Eld? You, Wilhum and I. How we fought, even though we were friends, the only friends we had, in fact. For the other children envied Wilhum, feared me and scorned you as the bumpkin son of the king's gaoler. Back then, you usually won. Perhaps you'll win now. Though I warn you, I've learned a great deal since."

Eldurm closed his eyes, just for a moment, but I knew he was

striving to contain what roiled within. My own anger dissipated somewhat at the sight of a strong man of some decent qualities rendered
pathetic by just a few words from the woman he thought he loved.

Opening his eyes, he straightened once more, the muscles of his
blocky face stark as he raised himself up to fix Evadine with a hard
glare. "Have a care on the field tomorrow, my lady," he said in a tight,
controlled voice. "It would grieve me greatly if you came to harm."

Some colour returned to his features as he shifted his gaze to me
one last time, calling out, "You'd best pray for death at the hands of
the Pretender, Scribe! This matter is not settled and you'll not find
me as merciful!"

He lowered his head to Evadine then hauled on his reins, turning
his mount, and galloped away, his men-at-arms following. Some
regarded Evadine with bemused glances as they rode off, though most
were more interested in casting dire looks or obscene gestures in my
direction.

"I thought the new hand in the ledgers looked familiar," Evadine
commented, sliding the sword back into its scabbard as I flicked the
reins to compel the horse into motion. We resumed our progress and
she guided her grey alongside, gaze lingering on my downcast features
in expectation as I fumbled for an answer.

"Your perception does you credit, Captain," I said finally, not
looking up.

"Also, his letters," she went on. "I discerned a considerable improvement in both style and grammar in that last flurry his lordship sent
me. Your influence, I assume?"

"He was . . . grateful for my advice. Then, at least."

She paused for a second, her tone shifting into something far more
serious. "What he said about Ascendant Sihlda . . . "

"A lie," I stated flatly, unable to keep the hard denial from my voice.
"The escape was her plan, something she had schemed for years. Her
demise . . . was not my doing."

"So, you did know her? That much is true?"

"I did. It was from her that I learned letters and the crafting of
them, and a great deal more besides."

"And do you think she was what some claim her to be?"

"And what is that, Captain?"

She voiced a short laugh. "Don't play the ignorant churl with me. It's a mask that doesn't fit you. There are those who contend that Ascendant Sihlda would have ascended to martyrdom upon her death, had she not been condemned for so vile an act. Did you find her so devout a soul as to warrant such claims?"

"I found her to be the finest soul I ever encountered, but not without flaws, like any other." I steeled myself and met her gaze, finding only genuine interest rather than the poorly concealed calculation of Ascendant Hilbert. "I had the honour of recording her testament shortly before her death," I said. "Although, if you've heard any of Ascendant Hilbert's sermons recently, you might find some of it familiar."

"I am discerning in my choice of sermon. Do you still have a copy of the testament? If so, I should greatly like to read it. In its uncorrupted form, of course."

I wondered if she might be intent on some theft of her own but discounted the thought. Having heard her speak every night on the march, I knew this woman had no need to steal another's words. "I do, Captain, and will be happy to provide you a copy."

"My thanks, Alwyn Scribe. But I doubt this fully settles the debt you owe me. Wouldn't you agree?"

I certainly couldn't argue this point. But for her intervention, I would at this juncture most likely have found myself swinging from a convenient tree branch, minus some bodily accoutrements. "I shall pay any price you require, Captain," I said, because she expected it and because, in that moment at least, I meant it.

"Then this is what I require to settle our debt." She paused, her expression taking on the same intent seriousness as when she had confronted Lord Eldurm, though I was grateful her tone was not so challenging. "Don't run off tonight as you and your friend were planning to."

I instinctively began to look away but something in her gaze held me. It also caged the pointless denial that bubbled to my lips. I could only stare in silence as she continued, "Sergeant Swain is well versed in sorting the runners from the fighters. You, he told me, are too clever not to be a runner. He tells me it's the smart ones who run when there's little chance of catching them, in the interval before battle is joined when captains draw in their pickets to form up companies. The less clever cowards wait until the battle's almost joined before taking to their heels."

I am not a coward, I wanted to say, but knew it to be an empty statement. Cowardice had always felt like a redundant concept to one born to a day-to-day struggle for mere survival. Some fights could be won; some could not. You fought when you had to or when you knew you could win. What shame was there in running from death? A deer felt none when it ran from a wolf.

"This war . . . " I began then stopped at the prospect of spilling unwise words. Evadine, however, was keen to hear them nonetheless.

"Speak," she instructed. "Without fear, for I'll not condemn a man for voicing his truth."

"This is not my war," I told her. "Nor my friends' war, though a few seem to think it is. A man I've never set eyes on claims his blood makes him worthy of taking the throne from another man I've never seen, and thousands have died for it. Perhaps the Pretender's a liar; perhaps he speaks the truth. I have no way of knowing. I do know our king and his nobles never did anything for me besides try to hang me. They are not worthy of my blood, low as it is. I'll not die for them."

I had expected more of her faithful invective, an appeal to my allegiance to the Covenant rather than the Crown. Instead, she sat back a little in the saddle, frowning as she considered a reply.

"Who would you die for?" she asked eventually. "Friends? Family? Ascendant Sihlda's memory? You've heard my sermons and I'm sure you have your doubts as to the truth of my words, as I would expect of a clever man, so I'll not appeal to your reason. In the end, all I can do is ask for your trust."

She leaned forward, eyes hard and unblinking as they stared into mine. "Trust my word, Alwyn Scribe, as you trusted the word of Ascendant Sihlda. You may think my visions mummery or madness . . . " She trailed off, her gaze unwavering but her face tightening, mouth twisting as unwelcome memories played through her mind. Taking a breath, she went on, "Again I ask for your trust when I tell you they are not. The Pretender brings only ruin for us all. Churl, outlaw and noble alike. This I have seen, though I would give anything to have been spared the sight."

She wasn't lying; I could tell that much. This woman truly believed she had been cursed by visions of the Second Scourge and her every act was now directed towards preventing them from coming true. Still, her truth did not make it real. Perhaps for Brewer, Ayin and the others. But not me. Ayin may have sunk to her knees and wept for Evadine's favour, but I would not. Even so, however illusory her visions might be, the weight of what I owed her remained real and undeniable. Also, the sight of Duke Rouphon's banner still loomed large in my mind. If I fled, it seemed unlikely I would ever find myself this close to Lorine again.

"I won't run," I told Evadine, forcing my gaze from hers and grasping the reins tighter. "In payment of our debt, Captain."

I was keen for this moment to end. This woman possessed a worrying capacity for perception. I sensed it wouldn't be long before she discerned another reason for my change of heart beyond simple obligation. I also found her directness and lack of noble condescension unnerving, or at least, that was what I told myself. Later, I would look deeper into that moment and know my discomfort came from something simpler, but far more frightening, something I wouldn't be prepared to acknowledge for a long time.

She sat in silent regard of my averted face and I felt the air thicken with the mutual knowledge of a conversation left unfinished. She expected more, I knew. Was it Ayin's unreasoning, tearful gratitude? Had Evadine Courlain, Anointed Communicant of the Covenant of Martyrs, become addicted to the adulation of her followers?

"On behalf of the Covenant, I thank you for your service, Scribe," she said before turning the grey and starting off at a canter. Watching her ride ahead, I wondered if I had in fact heard the injured tone in her voice. *Beauty turns the minds of men so easily*, I reminded myself as I snapped the reins and the old horse resumed her plodding. It was one of Sihlda's many lessons, provoked by an anecdote I had shared regarding my unwise and greatly regretted infatuation with Lorine. *Know this, Alwyn: no woman was ever unaware of her beauty, but many a man was unaware of being snared by it until far too late.*

There was no sermon that night, which surprised me, as did the curious jocularity prevalent in the camp. Talk and laughter abounded around the fires and songs were finally sung, mostly Covenant hymns but at least it was music of a sort. I even saw a few soldiers join arms in a dance or two. Apparently, the prospect of imminent battle raised their spirits no end.

Things were different at our fire. Ayin, of course, was cheerier than ever, dancing alone to the tune of a nearby flute, smiling face raised to the night sky and eyes closed in apparent blissful serenity. Toria, by contrast, sat hunched with her features set into a frozen scowl as she stared into the flames. He reaction to my decision to stay hadn't been pleasant to endure, however much I'd expected it. I had suggested she make her own escape, offering to distract the pickets so she could slink away through the tall grass covering the fields south of the camp. The torrent of profanity she directed at me in response was fouler than usual, albeit impressive in its inventiveness.

"Your brains are in your shit-crammed arse you fuckwitted, treacherous whoreson!"

Yet she stayed, her mood darker and more morose than during the worst times in the Pit. But still here, as trapped by her debt to me as I was by my debt to Evadine.

"Was there any scrap of this stuff that wasn't rusted?" Brewer muttered, scraping the tip of a dagger to a rivet on the breastplate he had been given.

The arms and armour I carted back to the company had been carefully shared out under Sergeant Swain's instruction. Pulling back the covering I had seen him conceal a grimace of professional disdain at the pile of assorted metal. Much of it gleamed dully in the sunlight, flecked in brown and red by rust and accumulated dirt. Still, the sergeant made a show of grunting approval as he handed various accoutrements and weapons to the waiting line of soldiers. The breast-plates and much of the mail went to the pikemen along with the falchions and swords. Pikes, we had been told many times by Supplicant Blade Ofihla, would inevitably be shattered or dropped after the first clash of arms, so it was important to have another weapon to reach for.

Swain had handed me a short-staved, crescent-bladed axe to go with my billhook. The half-moon blade was dark and rough from age and neglect, but an hour or so with a whetstone succeeded in putting a silvery edge to the crusted steel. The sergeant also handed me what at first appeared to be two squares of cracked leather with a row of loops into which some old iron rings had been fixed.

"Vambraces," he said. "They go on your forearms. The straps are frayed so you'll have to find a way to tie them on."

Fortunately, Ayin proved as deft with an awl and twine as she was with a skillet. Only a couple of hours' work, during which her normally animated features took on a stern frown of concentration, and she had fashioned sturdy straps and buckles to each vambrace. The fact that she hadn't been provided with either a weapon beyond the dagger she wore at her belt, or a single scrap of armour, didn't appear to concern her.

"The Seraphile's grace is the only safeguard I require," she told me when I enquired about her lack of protection. Upon expressing my concerns to Ofihla, I had been gruffly assured that Ayin would be ordered by the captain to remain with the baggage train for the duration of the battle. The Supplicant also regarded my entirely serious suggestion that the girl be chained to a cartwheel as a poor attempt at humour.

Toria's riches amounted to a mail shirt, the only one handed out to the dagger line as far as I could tell. Also, it had been pushed into her sullen grasp by Ofihla rather than Swain. It fitted Toria's wiry frame surprisingly well, almost as if it had been tailored for her. I also noted that the small interlinked iron rings that formed it held no sign of rust. Ofihla clearly intended for at least one of us to survive the coming day.

"But," Brewer went on, holding his breastplate up so it caught a faint sheen from the firelight, "I reckon it'll polish up nice enough if I can get hold of some oil."

"It's shit," Toria muttered, still staring into the flames. "All of it. Shit parcelled out to a gaggle of deluded scum following a madwoman's banner."

I glared a warning at her, shooting a glance in Ayin's direction. Luckily, she remained too lost in her dance to succumb to blasphemy-induced anger.

"Fuck off, Alwyn," Toria stated, very precisely.

I made no further attempt to ameliorate her mood, being somewhat preoccupied with my own undercurrent of dread. It hadn't built into outright fear as yet and perhaps it wouldn't. Much like the confrontation with Sergeant Lebas, panic did not assail me now there was no prospect of avoiding danger. But still, my lack of experience with what waited on the morrow inevitably birthed a hard discomfort in my gut that stubbornly refused to fade.

"You've done this before," I said to Brewer as he continued to polish his breastplate. "Been in battle, I mean to say."

"Twice," he confirmed, dabbing a cloth to his tongue before working the spit into the steel.

I fumbled over how to frame my next question, disliking the notion of unveiling my uncertainties. Toria, as usual, was less circumspect.

"Are we all going to die, d'you think?" The venom had leached from her voice and she spoke with a note of grim resignation.

Brewer left off from his polishing for a second, brows furrowed in consideration. "Some, certainly. Not all. Heart and fortitude count for as much in a battle as do discipline and skill at arms. This company, thanks to our anointed captain, has heart aplenty." He cast a sour glance at the many campfires beading the dark below the slope. "As for the rest, they seem a mixed bag to be sure. Too many churls who'd rather be elsewhere for my liking. Still, the king's gathered a big host. That's sure to count for something."

"The Pretender's lot are veterans," I pointed out. "Killers all, so they say."

"At the Red Drifts I saw men who'd fought a dozen battles drop their arms and flee." Brewer shrugged and returned to his task. "Courage is like rope: sooner or later it always runs out."

Feeling the weight of the stares Toria and I continued to direct at him, Brewer sighed and favoured us each with a steady glance of his single eye. "You two know how to brawl. That's something in your favour. Y'see, a battle, for all the guff the nobles spout about gallantry and such, is just a very large brawl, with weapons instead of fists. When the fury of it starts and the tidy ranks turn into a great mob of fighters, that's where the battle's lost or won. In the brawl. So—" he offered a rare smile "—brawl away and you'll have a fair chance of finding yourselves alive when it's done."

CHAPTER TWENTY-NINE

We were roused by the Supplicants just before dawn. It remains a marvel to me that I contrived to sleep through much of the night. More remarkable still is that it was an untroubled sleep. I was also able to wolf down the hearty breakfast of bread, milk and fresh fruit Sergeant Swain managed to procure from somewhere. The tight ball of dread in my guts hadn't faded but it couldn't negate a sudden ravenous hunger.

"Eat up!" Ofihla instructed a considerably less enthusiastic Toria, tossing her an apple from the half-emptied barrow. "Need your strength today."

Toria, pale of face and hollowed-eyed from a sleepless night, stared back expressionlessly. Nevertheless, as the Supplicant Blade lingered with an expectant frown, she consented to take an obedient bite of the fruit, quickly spitting it out once Ofihla moved on. "That cow's had it in for me since the first day I joined this bundle of fuckwits," Toria muttered.

"I really don't think that's the case," I told her, plucking the apple from her grasp since she seemed to have no use for it. I took a large bite, followed by several more as I offered Toria a grin. "Quite the opposite, in fact."

I expected a profane snarl or two in response, but instead Toria's narrow features assumed a grave sincerity. Stepping closer, she grasped my hand and met my eye, speaking with quiet but urgent solicitation: "Alwyn . . . I just want you to know. If I should die today . . . " the grip on my hand suddenly took on a painful, vice-like tightness as her eyes flashed, bright and savage " . . . it's your fucking fault!"

"Form up!" Sergeant Swain's voice cut through the chilled morning air, soon joined by the shouts of the Supplicants.

"I'll haunt you, y'bastard!" Toria promised in a farewell hiss before running to take her place in the troop.

"Marching order!" Ofihla called out, shoving her way through the throng. "Gather weapons and form ranks! Hurry now! You, Ayin, report to the captain. Don't dawdle, girl! Off with you!"

Ayin paused long enough to cast a bright smile at me and Brewer before scampering off towards Evadine's tent. I could only hope Ofihla had passed on my suggestion about chaining her up.

"Stand straight, Scourge take you!" The Supplicant moved along our line, pushing the slouches into place and cuffing the heads of laggards. Never a gentle soul, her demeanour now was even more forbidding, leaving none in any doubt as to the consequences of a slip in discipline.

"Scribe," she told me, glowering as she put her face close to mine, "get that hook on your shoulder like I showed you." Stepping back, she surveyed our ranks, chin jutting in grudging approval that didn't show in her voice. "You lot'll have a king's eyes on you this morn," she called out, "and I'll not have you shame the captain with your slovenly ways."

We waited in starchy immobility for what felt like a considerable interval, but in truth probably amounted to just a few minutes. I heard several bellies rumble, the drone of it punctuated by a wet fart or two. The notion of being sent off to war by such a malodorous chorus brought a laugh to my lips, one that spread throughout the troop. To my surprise, Ofihla let the mirth continue for a bit before snapping out a command to silence. I supposed she found some small encouragement in the sight of soldiers laughing in the face of imminent slaughter.

Finally, there came the bugle call that set us into motion, Ofihla leading the troop through the camp to join the company's marching column. By now, the hardness in my gut had begun to loosen into a nauseous, churning ball, one that lurched when I saw that our troop was last in line. We had trained as a full company a few times on the march, and each time the troop at the rear of the column always formed the right extremity of the battle line. Being on the right of any line, I had learned during my time with Klant, was never a good place to be.

It's all about turning flanks, y'see, lad, he'd told me one evening during our sojourn to the coast. *Or, more simply put, getting round the side so's you can have a go at your foe's arse. And, for reasons known only to the Seraphile, it's almost always the right flank they go for.*

So it was with sinking spirits that, as I marched dutifully along with all the others, I watched the rest of the company lining out to our left. My guts lurched with even greater energy as we formed our three ranks on their right, bridging a gap between the company and the river. Our troop was obliged to place half its number amid the tall rushes and bushes covering the bank. The ground beneath our feet was soft and soon rendered into mud by so many stamping boots. A snatched glance to my left revealed that not only was our troop at the end of the company's line; the company itself stood at the terminus of the entire army's battle order.

The site of what would become known as the Traitors' Field consisted of a three-acre stretch of recently grazed pasture, sloping gently from the river to the crest of a low rise. I made out the sight of the king's banner fluttering atop the rise. The space betwixt was filled with what seemed an inordinately thin line arrayed in varying degrees of tidiness. Knots of pikes bristled here and there but several stretches were occupied by just loosely arrayed churls bearing wood axes and scythes. Behind the line, armour-clad nobles and mounted men-at-arms cantered or walked their mounts, the beasts' breath steaming in the frigid morning air.

"Eyes front, Scribe!" Ofihla barked at me. She prowled the ground in front of our line, snapping out orders or delivering judicious blows to straighten it. Apparently satisfied, she then growled at us to remain in place and went to join the other Supplicants gathered around Evadine. The captain rode her black charger today, a more boisterous animal than the grey. It tossed its head continually, forehooves gouging the dew-damp sod. Evadine seemed unperturbed by her mount's fractiousness, her face betraying only affable approval as she exchanged words with the Supplicant Blades.

Sergeant Swain and several of the other Supplicants each carried one of the crossbows provided by Aspirant Arnabus, although Ofihla didn't. I wondered if this indicated some measure of disfavour but felt it more likely that she simply preferred the Lochaber axe she carried. This was a truly fearsome contrivance consisting of a yard-long steel cleaver fixed to a five-foot stave, resembling a billhook that had acquired some form of swelling disease. It seemed an unwieldy weapon to carry into battle but during practice I had seen Ofihla whirl it about as if it weighed no more than a slender length of willow. I decided that whatever transpired today, remaining somewhere in Ofihla's vicinity would likely serve me well.

The conference lasted only a short time before the sound of pealing trumpets rose from the crest of the rise. Despite the orders to keep facing front, all eyes soon tracked to the sight of a man riding a magnificent white stallion, closely followed by a large retinue of nobles in royal livery. One of the knights carried the royal banner, while trumpet-bearing outriders continued to proclaim his presence on the field.

"Silence in the ranks!" Ofihla shouted, quelling the rising murmur provoked by the sight of a man none of us had ever expected to clap eyes on in person. "Pay heed to the king!" Ofihla added taking up position to our front. I noted that, while she and the Supplicants had hurried back to their troops, Evadine remained where she was, regarding the king's retinue with an expression of only placid curiosity. It wasn't until the king reined his fine horse to a halt and the trumpeters blared out a final, somewhat discordant, note that our captain consented to dismount.

Seeing her fall to one knee, the entire company followed suit, as did the rest of the army. Behind the battle line, the nobles and mounted men-at-arms all climbed from their saddles to do the same. I felt the subsequent pause to be overly long as we waited for the king's word. Having witnessed more than my fair share of sermons, I knew an interval of silence before commencing a speech could be highly effective at commanding attention. However, this silence wore on to the point where the growing accumulation of snorting, impatient warhorses and coughing soldiers threatened to drown out any inspiring oratory.

As we waited, I risked a quick glance at the king. He had halted a good distance from our length of the line, making it hard to glean much from his appearance. However, my impression was not that of a striking figure of regal authority. The king was taller than most and his armour, burnished and shining bright in the burgeoning sunlight, was certainly impressive. Yet, my principal sense was of a man ill at ease with finding himself at the apex of his army's collective attention. My lack of awe was not helped by the sound of his voice when he finally consented to speak.

"Soldiers of the Crown!" he proclaimed in tones that were most charitably described as strained. A chronicler of less generous incli nations would later term it "a thin, reedy piping that resembled a child's flute for all the courage it inspired", and I find this an accurate account.

"This day we come not for war, but for justice!" the king went on, his volume dwindling with every word so that the rest of his speech was largely lost to our ears.

"What's he saying?" the pikeman next to Brewer whispered, his mottled features bunched in consternation.

"Not sure," Brewer whispered back. "He mentioned brothers, I think. Didn't know he had a brother."

"He doesn't," I said in low murmur. "That's the reason we're here, remember? His elder brother who died tupped a wench thirty years ago and now his bastard nephew wants the crown, if the Pretender even is his bastard nephew and not the most gifted trickster in history."

Hearing the king utter a few more unintelligible lines from a no doubt carefully crafted address, I turned a questioning glance on Toria, who had the best ears among us.

"Can't make out much," she reported after cocking her head in the king's direction. "Something about treason . . . Now something about the Covenant . . . Now it's something about his da."

My attention, however, quickly slipped from the distant voice of the king when my eye alighted on something beyond the bulky shoulder of Ofihla's kneeling form. At first, I thought it might be the swaying of tree branches jutting above the low hill some two hundred yards opposite, then it occurred to me that it was summer and these swaying branches were bare of leaves. Also, they were very narrow and spindly in appearance and seemed to be growing thicker by the second.

"Supplicant . . . " I hissed at Ofihla, drawing a furious glare.

"Silence, Scribe!"

Her fury swiftly transformed into stiff attentiveness when she followed my jabbing finger to take in the sight of the many pikes now jutting above the hill. From the ripple of unease that swept along the line, it was clear a large part of the host had also witnessed the approaching danger. King Tomas, however, had not.

While the knights in his retinue stirred and shifted, he continued to blithely chirp out his mostly unheard speech. I saw indecision reign among the knights, along with a good deal of whispered argument, until one figure spurred his mount to the king's side. A very tall figure with a helm bearing an iron spike, twisted and enamelled in red so that it resembled a flame.

I couldn't contain a palpable shudder at my first glimpse of Sir Ehlbert Bauldry, the King's Champion, finally revealed in full. His presence at the king's side was hardly surprising, but still I found it jarring to behold him in the flesh. I should have taken heart at the knowledge of being on his side during the coming tumult, for there never was a man so formidable. Instead, he birthed in me a knot of fear that was somehow deeper and more painful even than the nauseous roiling in my gut.

Sir Ehlbert paused for a moment at the king's side, leaning close to whisper something that brought the inspiring royal address, such as it was, to an abrupt halt. The knight then kicked his horse forwards, the great beast rearing as Sir Ehlbert drew his longsword and raised it high, calling out, "All hail King Tomas!" in a voice that no chronicler would ever describe as weak.

The response was far from immediate as the unease provoked by the unexpected sight of the enemy continued to ripple through the ranks. It wasn't until Evadine climbed onto her black charger and raised her own longsword, voice loud and strident in echoing the champion's call, that our company followed suit. Soon the cry went up all along the line, "Hail King Tomas! Hail King Tomas!" as noble and churl alike stabbed the air with their weapons. I cheered along with everyone else, although my attention remained primarily focused on the dark, jagged silhouette now cresting the opposite hill.

To his credit, the king did not ride off right away. Instead, he stayed for at least a full minute, sitting straight and poised on his fine white horse, gauntleted hand raised in acknowledgement of his host's praise. If the growing throng of his enemy only a few hundred paces away concerned him, he failed to show it. Watching him placidly absorb the adulation of his soldiers, I was forced to conclude that this man might not possess the voice of a hero, but neither did he have the heart of a coward.

As the cheer wore on, Sir Ehlbert spurred his mount alongside the king once more, head lowered to address him in unheard but evidently urgent tones. Whatever he said sufficed for the king to turn his mount and ride off, the retinue making for the centre of the line where an even taller royal banner fluttered.

"Stand up!" Evadine's steely voice snapped all eyes to her as she reined in her mount before Covenant Company. We rose as one and her hard, implacable gaze roved over each and every face, looking into every pair of eyes. I remember her as embodying purpose in that moment, as if resolve and unshakeable will had become fused into flesh and armour. We all knew with no shred of doubt that whatever the outcome on this field, our captain would never run from it. She had resolved to prevail today or die and, I knew, many if not most of those around me were content to share her fate.

Toria, naturally, proved an exception for she chose this moment to lean forward and vomit on my boots. "Serves you fucking right," she gasped, stepping back and wiping her mouth, the last word drowned by Evadine's strident proclamation.

"The time for doubt is over!"

My fellow soldiers stood taller as her words assailed us. Through the stink of Toria's spew I could smell a good deal of sweat and the acid tang of piss, but strangely I had no sense that any soul present was about to flee. Evadine's gaze and words held us in place as firmly as any shackle.

"You know what they call you in this army?" Evadine asked us, paying no heed to the long line of pikemen busily arranging themselves on the hill at her back. "Scum, villains," she went on. "The wretched dregs of the realm. That is what your comrades think of you. I will not ask if you agree, for I know they are wrong. I know that I would rather stand here with you than alongside the finest knight in all the Covenanted kingdoms of the earth. For I look upon true hearts and true souls. I look upon the true blades of the Covenant, blades the Pretender and his vile horde will learn to fear this day."

A harsh discordant blaring rose from the enemy host then, an accumulation of trumpets, bugles and the distinctly non-melodious bagpipes found in the mountainous regions of the Althiene duchy. It appeared the Pretender had a fair number of hill-clan savages among his ranks. This tuneless screeching was soon joined by a clamour of shouts and waving of weapons, the Pretender's horde resembling a storm-tossed thicket as they roared out their challenge. The shouting and gesticulating continued as the entire enemy line started forward, the thicket becoming a dark grey wave sweeping down the slope towards us. To my increasingly alarmed gaze it seemed both inexorable and irresistible, an impression made worse by the armoured knights I saw cantering behind their left flank.

"They seek to make you fear them!" Evadine told us, still not deigning to turn her gaze to the foe. "Do you?!" she demanded, longsword raised high. "DO YOU!?"

The reply erupted as a savage scream of "NO!" The shout continued as the company convulsed in a mingling of rage and eagerness, a sentiment to which only I and Toria remained immune. I could feel her face pressed against my back, repeating the same word in a soft whisper. "Fuck, fuck, fuck, fuck . . . "

"For the Covenant!" Evadine's strident call cut through the rageful tumult, the cry immediately echoed from every throat in the company. I also heard it taken up by the soldiers from the contingent to our left. They were a mixed bag of pressed churls and veterans from upper Cordwain under the command of a spindle-thin noble who couldn't have seen more than sixteen summers. Glancing over, I saw this child cheering along with his soldiers, visor raised to reveal pale, fragile features while he waved a mace I wouldn't have thought him capable of wielding.

"For the Covenant!"

The shout went up again and again, Evadine continuing to lead it as she guided her black charger to the very end of our line, standing tall amid the grassy bank.

"For the Covenant!"

I turned my gaze forwards, gloved hands taking a firmer grip on the stave of my billhook. The oncoming tide had swept to the nadir of the far slope, marching with a steady, measured cadence, the cacophony of their voices, pipes and trumpets failing to drown our own fervent chorus. Behind me, Toria's unending curses formed a faint counterpoint to it all.

"Fuck, fuck, fuck . . . "

"For the Covenant! For the Covenant!"

I could make out the faces of our enemy now, seeing a long row of mostly bearded men and a few women. It may have been a product of my fear, but I saw no callow youths among them; to my eyes these were all the fabled veteran killers who had followed the Pretender's trail of slaughter for years. Like us, they had their pike-bearers in front with sword- and axe-wielders behind. Also like us, they wore scant armour. I counted only a few helmeted heads and most bodies were clad in hardy woollen garb with hardly a breastplate or mail shirt to be seen.

"Fuck, fuck, fuck . . . " Toria cursed.

"For the Covenant! For the Covenant!" the company cried, their voices rising to a scream as the first rank of oncoming enemies came within twenty yards of our line, lowered their pikes and spurred to a run.

"For the Covenant!"

Our first rank took one forward step, jamming the butts of their pikes into the earth and lowering the long spears to the angle the Supplicants had drilled into them for so many days.

"FOR THE COVENANT!"

I have often reflected since that, at the moment the two lines of pikes first clattered together, I would have shit myself if I had remembered to do so. Instead, I stepped up close to Brewer's back as I had been taught, waited until the pike sliding past his own came within arm's reach whereupon I used my billhook to force it down, stamping my boot hard enough to snap the stave behind the iron spearpoint.

Apparently enraged by finding himself so disarmed, the pike's owner launched himself forwards, falchion in hand, a guttural cry of challenge emerging from his shaggy face. His charge was halted when he found himself jammed between Brewer and the mottle-faced fellow to the right.

This is murder, I knew as I raised my billhook above my head, bringing it down to split the trapped, snarling fellow's skull open.

And thus, dear reader, was battle joined.

Chapter Thirty

The bearded man didn't fall right away. Although plainly dead with a good deal of blood and other more greyish matter streaming down his shaggy face, the press of bodies contrived to keep him upright. Also, his eyes remained open. So, as the opposing lines shoved and jabbed at each other in an increasingly disorderly scrum, I was required to suffer the continual stare of the man I had just dispatched from this world. Feeling his gaze to possess an irksome, unblinking intensity, I experienced a sudden swelling of rage, so much so that I struck him again. Drawing the billhook back like a javelin, I stabbed the blade into his staring visage, sundering his face as the crudely hammered steel sank in and promptly became stuck.

"Oh, shit on it!" I hissed through clenched teeth, stepping forwards to push the impaled fellow clear. One of his companions, a wiry man with a beardless, weasel-like face, took the opportunity to stab at my outstretched arm with a long dirk. The narrow point jabbed painfully into my wrist but failed to penetrate my glove. It did, however, stoke my rage higher.

Keeping one hand on the billhook, still stuck fast in the corpse's head, I balled my free hand into a fist and drove it hard into the dirk wielder's face. With no room to dodge, he took the full force of the blow and slipped senseless to the churned mud. I assume he must have been trampled to death shortly after.

Grunting, I gripped the billhook with both hands and twisted it, glad that the cumulative shouts, grunts and screams drowned out the squelch and grind of metal working free of bone and flesh. This time, as the billhook came loose, the bearded man finally consented to fall thanks to a narrow gap having appeared between the opposing ranks. There came then the briefest of lulls, just long enough for all to drag breath into their lungs and allow for a survey of the dozen or so corpses or injured lying in the mud that separated us. Then, without benefit of command from the Supplicants, Covenant Company surged forwards.

Brewer and the more astute pikemen in the first rank had used the fleeting interval to raise the butts of their weapons above their heads, so that as they advanced the spearpoints stabbed down into the enemy. Many pikes bowed and snapped under the pressure, Brewer's among them. I saw him jab his splintered haft into the neck of an enemy, leaving the fellow on his knees with an arc of blood jetting from the wound. Kicking the stricken man aside, Brewer drew his falchion and began to hack at the press of bodies before him. He fought with a practised focus, his blows aimed at legs and overextended arms, leaving a short trail of maimed and screaming folk in his wake.

Alongside Brewer, the mottle-faced pikeman flailed away with a hatchet, displaying equal ferocity if markedly less expertise. Still apparently fuelled by Evadine's exhortation, the company assailed their foes with frenzied aggression, some still screaming out her invocation as they fought: "For the Covenant!"

I stumbled over flailing men to try to keep pace with Brewer, then halted at a high-pitched shout to my rear. Turning, I found Toria struggling with a man I had stepped over a second earlier. He had clearly been feigning death for a chance at easy prey. If so, he had chosen poorly. Having wrestled Toria to her knees, he tried to sink a dirk into her neck. Toria snapped her head forward, slamming her forehead into his nose. Taking advantage of his momentary confusion she drove her own dagger into his eye, sinking it in up to the hilt and holding it in place while he twitched and gibbered.

As I hurried towards her she looked up at me, eyes blazing in accusation from a face spattered in the red-brown paste of mingled gore and mud. Her enmity was such it took her a second before she responded to my shouted warning. "Get the fuck down!"

Luckily, she ducked just in time to avoid the slashing sword of the man who had reared up behind her. Before hacking him down, I took in the sight of his disordered face, one eye slashed to ruin and an ear hanging off, the flapping skin revealing the white bone of his skull beneath. I marvelled at the fortitude it must have taken to keep fighting. The Pretender, it seemed, could inspire just as much devotion as Evadine.

Taking heed from Brewer's example, I swung the billhook at the one-eyed man's legs rather than his body. Flesh sundered and bones broke as the heavy blade smashed into his thigh, sending him to the mud where Toria scrambled to finish him off. Her quick, wiry form reminded me of a ferret twisting to deliver the killing bite to a rabbit in the way she slashed the fellow's neck open.

I paused to glance around, my eyes greeted by an unexpectedly encouraging sight. Not only had Covenant Company succeeded in pushing the flank of the Pretender's line back a good forty yards but the Cordwainers to our left had also successfully beaten off their attackers. These were better armoured than the lot we faced but clearly less resolute in their cause. I assumed they must be a collection of hired swords drawn to the Pretender's banner by promise of pay or loot. In which case he had either not spent wisely or been insufficiently generous. I counted just ten bodies littering the ground to the Cordwainers' front and saw several of the retreating hirelings cast their weapons away in their haste to escape.

Beyond that, I could see little of the rest of the battlefield. The sweat and breath of so many men and horses in a relatively small space formed a mist through which I made out only a confused mass of shifting, struggling forms. Horses reared here and there among a roil of rising and falling blades, but it was impossible to say which side held the advantage.

"Come on," I said, hauling Toria to her feet. "Won't do to tarry."

I cast a meaningful glance at the Supplicants following along behind the main body of the company. Those with crossbows were either busy working the windlass or moving close to the struggle to discharge bolts directly into the faces of the enemy. I saw Swain among them but couldn't find Ofihla and assumed she was probably somewhere in the thick of the fight doing grim work with her axe.

Toria followed me back to the press of bodies where we closed up behind Brewer. To my relief I saw that a gap had once again opened up between the two sides, wider than before and those opposite now greatly reduced in number. Furthermore, in place of the savage determination from only moments ago, I could see fear in their faces. My relief deepened to grim delight when this decimated mob abruptly turned and fled. No order or bugle call sounded from their own leaders, but they all seemed to respond to the same unspoken command. I saw some weeping in shame or frustration as they ran, others pausing to voice curses in a dialect none of us could understand or raise their hands and form their fingers into what I assumed to be some form of insulting gesture. These lingerers, however, soon joined the runners when the Supplicants' crossbows dropped a few to the mud.

Another lull descended then, the wind swirling the battle haze around our disrupted ranks so that the company became like ghosts. Some, like me, leaned on their weapons, breath coming in ragged gasps. Others, like Brewer and the mottle-faced pikeman, raised their arms in triumph, their feral cries of victory mingling with the screams of the maimed not yet claimed by death. Toria sagged against my stooped-backed form, wiping the bloody dagger on my sleeve.

"Could've been worse," I told her, drawing a dark-eyed stare in response. Her face appeared to have aged years in the space of minutes and her gaze held such a depth of reproach I wondered if she would ever forgive me for having compelled her to this horror.

As I fumbled for another, assuredly resented, quip, Toria's narrow face bunched. "What's that?" she said, cocking an ear to the sky.

I heard it too late to react, a faint sibilant hiss that suddenly merged with a series of thuds and the percussive ping of colliding metal. In time I would come to know this sound well; the ugly song of an arrow storm meeting flesh and armour. But then, it was only when I saw an arrow impale the shoulder of the cheering mottle-faced pikeman that I realised the danger.

"Down!" I snapped, bearing Toria to the muddy earth. I gave a convulsive start as an arrow sank into the ground within a yard of my head, followed quickly by two more falling even closer. A short distance away a fellow billman, also having thrown himself down, took a shaft smack in the crown of his lowered head. Curiously, despite the arrowhead piercing his skull, he didn't die right away. Instead, rising to his knees, he frowned in apparent irritation, reaching up to scratch at the arrow as if it were nothing more than an offending louse. Blood seeped from his nose as his mouth tried to form words no one would ever comprehend. He lingered for another heartbeat or two then his eyes rolled back and he settled into a slump, still kneeling and somehow upright.

It occurred to me then, seeing three more comrades fall under the hail of arrows in as many seconds, that lying flat was not the best tactic in this circumstance.

"What the fuck are you doing?" Toria demanded, the words emerging in a furious rush as I got to my feet.

"We need a shield," I replied, dragging her along. I eschewed the relatively slight form of the kneeling billman, instead making for the far more impressively built, mottle-faced pikeman. Sheer good fortune saved us from the torrent of arrows as we darted towards the corpse.

"Get under," I said, gripping his mail shirt to drag him upright, grunting with the effort as I went to all fours, positioning the body on my back. Toria needed no further urging and quickly scrambled into the small space beneath my straining form.

It transpired that life had not yet fully departed the pikeman, for his body gave several violent shudders as it was repeatedly pierced. However, by the time the onslaught had abated a short while later, the corpse on my back had subsided into the slackness of death. Toria gave an irritated groan, squirming out from under me as I collapsed under the body's weight. I took some heart from the faint glimmer of gratitude in her gaze as she helped heave the multiple feathered pikeman off me, but the reproach and accusation were only partially dimmed.

"May the Scourge take all archers!"

The clenched exclamation snapped our gaze to Brewer's bulky form. He knelt a few paces away, besmirched face drawn in pain as he regarded the arrow impaling his right hand. The steel head jutted to a length several inches from the gap betwixt his thumb and forefinger, dripping blood and the scraps of his leather glove dangling from its barbs.

"Can't leave it in there," Toria advised, crouching to inspect the wound.

Swallowing, Brewer nodded and Toria drew her smaller, curve-bladed knife, placing the edge where the shaft emerged from the top of his hand. "Hold him," she told me curtly. I duly gripped his outstretched arm with both hands, holding it straight while Toria went about her work. Brewer hissed through gritted teeth as she sawed at the shaft. She made quick work of it although the energy of her labour surely added to Brewer's pains. With the shaft severed all the way through, she cast the fletched portion away and pulled the arrow-head free, tossing him the blood-smeared barb as she rose.

"Token for you." Her gaze soured as she turned to survey the surrounding carnage. "Though, I expect there'll be plenty more to gather this day."

"Form hedge!"

Ofihla's large silhouette resolved out of the haze a dozen yards away, her Lochaber axe, blade dark and wet, resting on her shoulder as she moved with a purposeful stride. "Gather up these pikes and form hedge! Move!"

"By the blood of all the Martyrs, isn't it done yet?" Toria asked in a bone-weary sigh.

The reason for the Supplicant's urgency became dreadfully clear as the drum of hooves sounded to our front. I felt a spasm of gratitude for all those tedious hours spent under Ofihla's harsh tutelage as the troop, reduced in number by about a third, assumed the required formation with reflexive speed. Unbroken pikes were retrieved and raised, the three ranks lined out alongside the neighbouring troops with seconds to spare before the knights came galloping from the haze to our front.

They numbered about fifty in all, a small contingent compared to the rest of the Pretender's host, one he had presumably held in reserve until now. These, I knew, were the so-called turncoat knights, those who had turned their backs on prior allegiance to the Algathinet line to throw their lot in with the Pretender. I had heard they were mostly the second or third sons of minor nobles, disappointed or overlooked youths willing to risk rebellion to win the acclaim and wealth they felt to be their due. Many had been disowned by enraged fathers as a consequence and the king had issued edicts stripping away lands and titles from those now condemned as traitorous wretches. However wretched their official status, to my eyes they still presented an impressive, bowel-loosening sight.

They galloped towards us at full pelt, lances levelled, breath steaming from their chargers' nostrils. The knights themselves were all clad in quality armour, no mismatched scavengings here. Their helms were crested with various motifs, their plate enamelled in blue or red, engraved with gold in places. The great wake of churned mud raised by their charge and the continuing fog of battle prevented the sun from catching on their armour as they drew ever closer. To me this made them appear more menacing, an unstoppable wall of noble steel and horseflesh sure to smash through this cluster of villainous churls.

If there was ever a time to run, this was it. And yet I didn't. I would tell myself later that it was Ofihla's presence and the sight of her gore-covered axe that kept me in place. This, and Sergeant Swain prowling behind the line with primed crossbow in hand, was reason enough for any coward to conquer their terror. However, I have since come to accept that it was not fear of the Supplicants that made me stand the appointed distance behind Brewer, billhook gripped and ready, staring into the eyes of the warhorse speeding towards me. I stayed because they, their captain and the friends I stood alongside had contrived to turn me into a soldier. In that moment, I could no more run than a mother could run from an imperilled child.

The apex of the knights' charge impacted on the section of our troop closest to the river, aimed with deliberate care to sunder our line and turn the whole army's flank. Although I had expected the line to dissolve under the blow, true to Ofihla's promise, the leading warhorses shied from the thicket of pikes at the last instant.

Screams and panicked whinnies sounded as spearpoints pierced necks and shoulders. One charger spilled its rider to the earth as it reared then fell, legs thrashing. I saw the knight abandon his lance and get to his feet, moving with surprising speed given the amount of plate he wore. He half-drew his sword and took one step towards our line then abruptly stiffened as a crossbow bolt punched through the mail covering the gap between helm and gorget. If that hadn't sealed his fate, the trampling hooves of the horse that came barrelling through next certainly did.

Unfortunately, this charger had its shoulders and neck covered by a thick quilted canvas. Its instinctive fear of the pikes caused it to slow as it neared the line, but it quickly rallied at the urgings of its rider, a large knight clad in red enamelled armour and a griffin-headed helm. Remarkably, the line held as the charger ploughed into it, although three pikemen were trampled before a frenzy of hacking, stabbing billhooks and a volley of crossbow bolts brought the warhorse down.

Once again, the knight tried to fight on, stumbling to his feet and laying about with a mace until Ofihla charged into the gap he had created in the first rank. She moved with bull-like speed and ferocity, keeping low and slamming her shoulder into the mace wielder's breastplate. The force of the blow was enough to send him sprawling, his attempted parry with the haft of the mace too feeble to deflect the overhead swing of her axe. The huge cleaver blade sundered the visor covering his face, birthing a brief but spectacular geyser of blood.

"Close up, you laggards!" she snarled at us, putting a foot on the knight's head to work the axe loose.

Another knight came at us as we hurried to comply, a tall black charger bearing a knight with armour coloured to match his mount. He resembled an obsidian statue brought to life as he loomed above us, his lance descending to spear an unlucky billman through the chest a few feet to my right. The weapon's point stuck in the billman's ribs, Ofihla cleaving the shaft in half with her axe before the knight could drag it clear. Brewer shifted to the Supplicant's side to jab his pike at the charger's mouth, another valuable trick she had drilled into us since few horses can abide damage to their maw. Blood joined the spittle flying from the animal's bared teeth and it turned, lashing out with its rear hooves. I saw another pikeman fall dead as an iron-shod hoof cracked his head open, but the warhorse's panic prevented his rider, or any of the other knights now crowding the ground to our front, from exploiting the gap.

Muffled curses emerged from the black-armoured knight's visor as he attempted to control his horse in between lashing at our line with a longsword. To his left and right, his comrades sought to guide their stalled mounts past, suffering a volley of crossbow bolts and viciously jabbing pikes all the while. Spotting a tear in the wayward horse's quilt covering, Brewer seized on the chance to sink his pike deep into the animal's flank. The beast screamed and reared, Brewer's pike snapping as the horse collapsed, spilling its rider into our first rank.

"Pull him in!" Ofihla shouted as I and another billman reached down to grab the knight by the rim of his helm. As soon as his greaves cleared the second rank, the dagger line descended on him like wolves swarming a lamed deer. Screams erupted from his visor as narrow blades stabbed into every gap in his plate. Having lost his sword, the knight flailed and punched at his tormentors, but to no avail. His struggles ended when Toria jammed her longest dagger into the slit in his visor, holding it in place while a wiry comrade pounded the pommel with a mallet until the hilt met steel.

Shifting my gaze from the ugly spectacle, I saw the knights had lost all momentum and were strung out along our line. As far as I could tell their aggressive efforts had been reduced to hacking at the hedge of pikes with their maces and swords. The Supplicants continued to methodically assail the knights with their crossbows, aiming for the horses rather than the riders. A half-dozen more fell while others reared and whinnied in protest at the torment and I saw that a gap had started to grow between these nobles and our unbroken company.

They're afraid, I realised, a surprised laugh escaping my lips. A half-trained mob of the worst miscreants in all Albermaine had taught fear to these noble turncoats. It was an unexpectedly sweet moment, but one that would be proven short-lived.

The trumpet sounded faint at first, a plaintive, almost comical wail rising above the tumult of combat. However, the message it conveyed was clearly understood by the Pretender's knights. Those who could easily disentangle themselves from the fray, about twenty in all, turned their mounts and rode towards the right of our line. A dozen or so were too lost in the frenzy of the fight or too fearful of turning their backs to heed the summoning trumpet. They lingered and fought on only to be brought down by the Supplicants' crossbows or the unrelenting pikes.

Once the last of them fell, both horse and rider feathered by several bolts and pierced by many spearpoints, I gained an unimpeded view of the reason for their comrades' sudden departure: a great mob of people advancing at a run close to the riverbank. There was little order to their ranks and scant sign of armour. As they ran, they shouted discordant exhortations and waved weapons above their heads, mainly scythes, pitchforks and axes. These were not soldiers, but churls, and at their head rode a man of impressive stature but unadorned armour. His visor was raised to reveal a long face of high cheekbones and a curved nose. Instead of a weapon he carried a banner, the great silken square flaring out behind his horse to reveal the winged, golden serpent of one Magnis Lochlain, self-proclaimed rightful king of Albermaine.

"Fuck me!" Toria breathed, gazing in unabashed wonder at the fast-approaching mob and their usurping leader. "Is that truly him?"

"I'd wager it is," I said, reaching up to touch gloved fingers to the wet trickle on my forehead. They came away bloody and I felt the sting of an open wound, one I had no memory of suffering. "Thought he'd be taller," I added, flicking the blood away.

"Dress those ranks!" came Ofihla's strident order. "Prepare to receive infantry!"

She and the other Supplicants dragged the dead and wounded behind the line while the company tidied itself. The pikemen raised then lowered their weapons to a lesser height, myself and the others in the second rank wiping the grime from our billhook hafts for a more secure grip. The sight of the oncoming mob, a true horde rather than the clan folk and knights we had already faced, it became increasingly plain that they outnumbered Crown Company by a considerable margin. Also, they advanced with a distinct and unnerving lack of hesitancy. If anything, the closer they came, the faster they ran, responding to the increased pace of their leader.

"Steady now!" Sergeant Swain's voice rang out – loudest of all among the Supplicants – as an uneasy mutter rippled through the company. "Remember what you fight for! Remember *who* you fight for!"

I watched the turncoat knights steer their mounts alongside the Pretender whereupon he raised his banner yet higher and they all spurred to full pelt towards the extreme end of our line where I saw Evadine Courlain sitting tall in the saddle. She wore no helm and I was close enough to read her expression as one of steady, unperturbed resolve. In an age when the word "fearless" has been cast at all manner of unworthy recipients, it must be said that she was the only truly fearless soul I ever met.

I heard Swain utter a muffled curse as it became clear that this charge had been carefully aimed at but one portion of our line rather than the company entire. The churlish mob was sprinting now, keeping in close if untidy order as it followed the Pretender's course. With the knights at their head, such a number was sure to overrun the line precisely where Evadine waited.

"Advance order!" Swain called out. The first rank duly raised their pikes, holding them horizontally in front of their chests while the rest of us straightened and shuffled into place. "Supplicants, the company will wheel to the right by troop!"

This was another tactic we had practised during the evenings on the march, though not with enough regularity to make the subsequent manoeuvre more than a messy parody of what the sergeant intended. The entire company was supposed to anchor itself on the right-most troop and swing around like a great door to take an enemy in the flank. Success depended on relative marching speed, those troops closest to the anchor point taking slow minimal strides while soldiers further out moved at a trot. With our numbers depleted and many soldiers beset by fatigue or the numbing confusion instilled by first exposure to battle, the resultant formation resembled more a bowed feather than a door. However, it did have the effect of forcing the churls and a few of the charging knights to turn and face us rather than continue their assault.

Off to our right there came the ugly thud and clatter of horseflesh and metal colliding as the Pretender and his knights slammed into the troop closest to the river. Before we closed on the churls, I caught sight of Evadine spurring her black charger forwards, longsword raised high, although what happened next was obscured by the Pretender's banner. A second later, the sting of a thrown stone rebounding from my head snapped my gaze forwards to be greeted by the image of a wall of screaming, besmirched faces and brandished blades.

The pikemen lowered their weapons level with their heads as the two sides met, but the raggedness of our formation ensured all order quickly dissolved. Within seconds Brewer's prediction was fully borne out as I found myself in the midst of the deadliest brawl I had ever known. I watched Brewer skewer an axe-wielding bear of a man with his pike before discarding the weapon and reaching for his falchion. As he did so, a stocky fellow with a crudely fashioned spear darted forwards, his rigid, crimson features that of a man intent on vengeance. I hacked him down as the spearpoint jabbed at Brewer's face, the bill-hook's blade sinking deep into the spearman's unprotected neck.

Hearing an enraged shout to my rear, I ducked and whirled, dragging the billhook clear and bringing it round to smash the knees of the churl who came at me with a scythe. He collapsed instantly, landing on his back and clutching at his ruined legs, his screams ending as Toria landed on his chest and sank her dagger into the hollow of his throat.

The screaming, rage-filled faces of the churls appeared to be all around us then and I saw the world take on a strange, crimson hue. My vision dimmed and narrowed with the focus born of an animalistic urge to survive. I hacked, stabbed, punched and gouged at every face that came within reach, only dimly aware of my body's aches. I have a memory of hacking a man's arm off at the elbow and another of holding a woman by the neck long enough for Toria to slash it open. But these are vague, the discordant glimpses of a nightmare best forgotten yet never fully faded from memory.

"Lay down, you heretic filth!"

Brewer's angry grunt brought me back to full sensibility, or as close to it as I could manage in that moment. Blinking as the red tinge faded from my eyes, I watched him slash his falchion across the thighs of a man who should by rights have already consented to die. He stumbled forwards with one hand clutching the snake-like mess spilling from a cut to his belly and the other clutching a blacksmith's hammer. His face was the gaunt, grey mask of a corpse and yet, even after Brewer's slash sent him to the mud, he continued to crawl towards us, still dragging his hammer.

"Martyrs preserve us." Brewer stamped a boot to the crawling man's head, continuing to pound it into the mud until blood erupted from the sundered skull. "There's some evil at work here," he said gravely. "The Anointed Captain spoke true. The Malecite have surely lent strength to this lot."

Looking around, I saw that the three of us stood in a clearing among the general mayhem. The company fought on in clusters, each assailed on all sides by the churls, the ground between littered by the dead or the crippled. Looking down, I found that I now held my axe rather than the billhook. The axe's crescent-shaped blade was dark and matted with gore but I couldn't recall losing one weapon and reaching for another.

Surveying the ongoing struggle, I found reason to doubt Brewer's claim of malign influence. It was true many churls continued to assail the company with frenzied energy and scant regard for danger, but, by my reckoning, the same number were now opting to keep clear of the fight. They knelt or staggered about, beset either by exhaustion or fear of risking further danger. Many wore the wide-eyed, pale faces of those who find the experience of true battle a jarring disappointment of glory-filled expectation. I felt no such sentiment; this day had been every morsel as dreadful as I'd imagined, except for the singular surprise of finding myself still alive.

I shuddered as the thrill of survival coursed through me, bringing a laugh to my lips.

"What's so fucking funny?" Toria demanded. Her eyes stared out from a face so covered in red and brown grime that it seemed she had donned a garish mask.

"Oh, nothing in particular," I replied, my mirth and renewed spirits dissipating as quickly as they had arrived. Fatigue clamped its heavy hand on me then, bringing a sag to my shoulders and threatening to buckle my legs. Every muscle I possessed ached and my head throbbed with a melange of recently witnessed horrors. The haft of my axe slipped through my fingers and I felt no inclination to prevent its fall until a fresh tumult erupted close by, banishing my exhaustion with a resurgence of panic mingled with now habitual aggression.

Some twenty paces distant, a cluster of knights were assailing each other, the swirling melee of clanging swords, maces and flailing hooves scattering the surrounding churls. As I watched, one knight fell from the saddle, brought down by an overhead swipe of a longsword that caved in the crest of his helm. As he tumbled to the mud, I glimpsed Evadine at the centre of the melee and realised that she was fighting the three remaining knights single-handed.

Such odds should have doomed her, but watching her parry a blow from a mace then immediately sway to avoid the jab of a longsword point, I wondered if her claims to divine guidance might have merit. She moved with such easy fluency it appeared to be more a rehearsed dance than a fight.

The captain cut down another knight with a perfectly placed thrust of her sword through his visor then hauled on the reins of her charger, making the animal rear and lash its hooves to the head of another knight's mount. The horse collapsed instantly, as if all tendons in its legs had been severed at once, the knight it bore also falling victim to the black charger. The iron-shod hooves descended like hammers, crumpling the fellow's breastplate as if it were fashioned from the thinnest copper.

The sole remaining knight, however, proved a resourceful soul and swung the spiked head of his mace into the rear leg of Evadine's charger. The warhorse screamed and reared, flailing about with such violence that Evadine was forced to relinquish the saddle. She landed hard on the muddy ground, the impact jarring the longsword from her grip. Fortunately, the struggles of the still-panicking black impeded the mace-wielding knight before he could close in to finish the captain. However, it was clear to me she had but seconds before his mount trampled the life from her.

I don't recall making a conscious decision to act, my response being immediate and void of thought. Sprinting forwards, I ducked to scoop up the blacksmith's hammer from the flaccid hand of its slain owner. The distance to the captain and her would-be killer had shrunk to about a dozen feet when I let fly with the implement, the implement impacting square in the centre of the knight's visor just as he had successfully pushed past the flailing black.

He toppled backwards and slipped over his horse's rump, one of his greaves catching in the stirrup as he fell. The animal, now apparently content to surrender to its fears with no master to hold its reins, immediately spurred to a full gallop, dragging its senseless rider away. Curiously, I have never discovered the fellow's identity or his fate. Perhaps he survived the day and lived on for many years to bore his grandchildren with a tale of unlikely deliverance. However, I find this doubtful, for the worst slaughter of that day was not yet upon us and it would be done with a conscientious dedication that spared few.

"Captain," I said, crouching to help Evadine to her feet while Brewer retrieved her sword.

"An impressive arm you have, Scribe," she told me, her face betraying a faint smile as she accepted my proffered hand and levered herself upright.

"Always better to throw than stab, if you can." This was another of Deckin's favourite lessons, the thought of him bringing an unexpected pang to my chest. *What would he have thought of seeing me here?* I wondered, although the answer was clear: he would have named me a fool and been right to do so.

I shook my head to clear the intrusive notion and the persistent throb. I ascribed the latter to either the stone that had struck me earlier, or a blow I didn't recall suffering. The fatigue had returned too, this time refusing to fade at the sight of the churls who were now turning their attention to the four lonely figures beside a dying horse. These were the stragglers and cravens unwilling to join their comrades in assailing what remained of Crown Company, but in us they had been presented with easier prey.

Evadine paid them scant heed, her attention captured by the plaintive whinnies of her stricken mount. The black's eyes were wide with terror as he tried vainly to rise from the mud, growing ever more viscous from the thick stream of blood pouring from the gash to his rear leg. Evadine's face tensed in sorrow as she laid a hand on his snout, the beast's struggles calming at her touch.

"Would you mind, good soldier?" she said, turning to Toria. "I don't think I can."

Toria gave a worried glare at the churls, now forming a tighter circle around us, then nodded and stepped closer to the charger, cutting knife raised. The slash was swift and carefully placed, opening the vein in his neck to birth a dark red gush. He huffed out a few more breaths, but somehow kept his head in place, unwilling to surrender Evadine's touch until at last his eyes rolled back and he settled onto his side.

"Captain," Brewer said, his voice rich in warning. Evadine raised her eyes from the fallen horse to regard the churls, edging closer now, faces set with renewed purpose.

"So many misguided souls," she said, hefting her longsword.

"Might I enquire, Captain," I ventured as the four of us drew closer together, "what became of the Pretender?"

"Oh, I fought him for a short time," she replied, her tone one of light regret. "But the melee drew us apart. Last I saw he was through our line, alone."

"And remains conspicuous by his absence," I noted, gesturing to the churls, not a noble among them and certainly no sign of a tall knight with a winged-serpent banner.

"He fled," Brewer stated. He let out a harsh, taunting laugh as he brandished his falchion at our foes. "You hear that, heretics? Your traitorous bastard has left you here to die!"

This had the unfortunate effect of stirring rather than negating the churls' anger. Obscenities and wordless growls rose as they edged nearer, axes, scythes and knives raised and twitching in anticipation, although they paused when Evadine's voice rang out.

"My friend speaks true!" she proclaimed. "The Pretender is gone from this field!"

I assumed it was her lack of fear that gave them pause, also the expression of pained, beseeching sorrow she wore as she stepped forwards, sword lowered and hand raised. Despite the madness of that day, I think they still managed to comprehend that this woman was not begging for her life but theirs.

"Please," she implored. "Give up this liar's cause, this false crusade. I see your hearts and know there is no evil there, only misplaced devotion."

Although I had seen the power of her rhetoric before, I still found myself astonished at the hesitancy these few words birthed in this murderous mob. Their advance halted, uncertain glances were exchanged, their raised weapons wavered. I heard Evadine take another breath, yet more transformative words about to spill from her mouth, but whatever they were, and what effect they might have had on our faltering enemy, would forever be lost to history.

From beyond the encircling churls there came a brief thunder of many hooves followed by the shouts and excited snorts of warhorses at the gallop. Next came the hard, overlapping thuds and screams of many living bodies being smashed aside at once. The knights surged into view a heartbeat later, a long line perhaps five hundred strong, maces and swords hacking as they tore through the commoners' disorderly ranks. My gaze was inevitably drawn to the tallest knight, his longsword describing a tireless series of crimson arcs as it scythed down a succession of fleeing churls. Sir Ehlbert Bauldry had evidently already done a good deal of bloody work this day, judging by the state of his armour, but he continued to slaughter with expert industriousness. I stopped counting his victims at ten and forced my morbidly fascinated, and increasingly fearful, gaze elsewhere.

The churls had scattered now, leaving the surrounding ground bare save for the dead or crawling wounded. I blinked in surprise at finding a good portion of Crown Company still standing in their tight clusters, many faces blank with incomprehension at their survival. Beside me, Evadine stiffened as a knight reined his horse to a halt a few paces away. He was a broad-shouldered fellow astride a charger with much the same colouring as Evadine's steel-grey mount. His helm was unusual in lacking a figurine crest, but his nobility was evident in the enamel motif on his shield: a black rose on a white background.

Behind him a young knight stumbled to his knees. He wore no helm and his face was caked in almost as much mud and gore as Toria's. Despite the dirt, I could still discern the visage of a handsome man, albeit a handsomeness currently drawn in abject misery. He wore a finely made suit of armour enamelled in sky blue but his gauntlets were gone, replaced by a thick, knotted rope that bound his wrists and trailed to the saddle of the mounted knight with the black-rose shield.

This noble's features were hidden by his visor but I could tell his gaze was focused entirely on Evadine. She returned it with an expression that, just for a moment, held a small glimmer of shame. It vanished quickly, however, and her features were expressionless as she went to one knee, head bowed.

"My lord," she said.

The knight spared her a short glance then reached to unfasten the rope from his saddle. A hard tug dragged the kneeling captive forwards to land face down in the mud before Evadine's kneeling form. She frowned then blinked as she took in his besmirched, downcast face.

"Wilhum?"

The mounted noble spoke then, the words emerging as a grating echo from the confines of his helm. "The king has decreed this a Traitors' Field. If you wish to preserve this wretch's neck, you don't have long."

Evadine bowed again and I noticed a quaver colouring the gratitude in her voice as she said, "Thank you, Father."

Sir Altheric Courlain, better known to scholars as the Black Rose of Couravel, straightened in the saddle, hidden eyes regarding his daughter for one more moment before he snapped his reins and rode off towards the riverbank. The knights' charge had driven the churls to the water's edge, the river roiling white as many desperately tried to swim to the far bank. The knights, unwilling to tolerate any escape from this field, spurred their mounts into the current and soon the waters were frothing red as well as white.

"An ill meeting on an ill day, Evie," the sprawled noble groaned. "Though the sight of you always brightens my heart, even now."

He raised himself up, white teeth showing among the grime as he regarded Evadine with a winning smile. Seeing it birthed a sudden spike of envy in my breast, for it was the kind of smile I had always tried to perfect but never quite managed, a smile that combined innate confidence with knowing rectitude. It appeared on this captive's lips with effortless ease but failed to win more than a sorrowful scowl from Evadine.

"You utter fool," she told him, voice hard but also tinged with grief.

"A pronouncement I find it hard to deny, at present." His smile faded and the misery from before returned in full, his eyes darkening into the inward gaze common to those contemplating imminent death.

Evadine stiffened and rose to her feet, turning to survey the scene from the continuing slaughter at the riverbank to the corpse-strewn ground to our rear. Now that combat had ended, the haze was fading. What had been a few acres of unremarkable pasture was now a great churned-up smear of black, brown and red. Riderless horses cantered among the dead and the dying while men-at-arms roved in small groups, pausing here and there to stab their halberds into the twitching or flailing bodies of the not-quite-dead. This was the fate of those who find themselves on the losing side when the king proclaims a

Traitors' Field. No nobles would be ransomed this day and no commoner granted mercy.

"Scribe," Evadine said, her eyes betraying a restrained flinch as they shifted to Crown Company. I reckoned about half were left, which itself seemed something of a miracle. I experienced an unexpected pulse of relief at seeing Ofihla still alive and apparently unwounded. She and Sergeant Swain were busy marshalling the survivors to gather up the wounded and the fallen weapons. There were many of both.

"I can't leave the company," the captain told me, "so must put this man in your charge." She nodded to the slumped form of the captive. "I ask that you get him clear of this field and secured in our camp. Will you do this?"

Does she ask treason of me? I wondered, taking note of the fact that she had framed this mission as a request and not an order. This man, this Wilhum of the handsome face and effortless smile, was plainly one of the turncoat knights. His life was forfeit, as mine would be if I were caught helping him evade the king's justice.

"I would consider it the greatest of favours," Evadine added, perceiving my hesitation.

"Might I ask, Captain," I said, turning a sour glance on the treacherous noble, "who this man is and why his life requires that you risk ours?"

I expected some form of rebuke, a curt reminder of our respective status, but she just gave a small grimace and replied in a soft reflective tone, "His name is Sir Wilhum Dornmahl. He was once . . . my betrothed, and I look to you to save him, Alwyn Scribe."

CHAPTER THIRTY-ONE

"I will never do this again," Toria informed me as we led Sir Wilhum towards our camp, passing a succession of horrors along the way. Nearby a man-at-arms was on his knees, both hands raised as he begged mercy from a trio of Crown Company halberdiers. "Are we not all soldiers?"

They let him scream himself hoarse before unleashing a frenzy of blows. Despite the wounds that laid him open, he still managed to keep screaming out his final appeal, as if it held some form of magical protection regardless of dreadful evidence to the contrary: "Are we not all soldiers! Are . . . we . . . "

"Not for her and not for you," Toria went on, wincing in mingled despair and annoyance as the unfortunate man-at-arms' cries dwindled into grating, agonised sobs. She didn't turn to look, however, addressing her words to me with harsh, insistent certainty. "You hear me, Alwyn? I'm done with playing soldiers."

"Played at it pretty well, from what I saw," Brewer muttered, wincing as he tugged the glove from his injured hand, revealing an ugly red and black hole.

"Supplicant Delric will see to it," I told him. "Bind it up till then."

"I would advise seeking aid sooner rather than later," our prisoner said, the first time he had spoken since we'd led him away. Sir Wilhum grimaced as he peered at Brewer's wound. "That has a decidedly ill look to it. An arrow, I assume?" He gave an apologetic shrug in response to Brewer's guarded nod. "Our Caustian bowmen were fond of smearing their arrowheads with all manner of foulness. A dreadful lot, to be sure, given to filthy manners and performing strange rites come nightfall."

"Shut yer arse crack, you!" Toria snapped with a livid glare, one she quickly turned on me. "It's not a quarter-hour since this fucker and his friends were doing their best to kill us. Remind me again why we're saving his hide?"

"Captain's orders," Brewer stated with a glower. "After today, can you ever doubt her? We march beneath a banner blessed by the Seraphile."

"I saw plenty die under that banner," she shot back. "Didn't do them much good, did it?"

"A realist and a fanatic in the same company," the young noble observed in muted amusement. "Which are you?" he added, raising an eyebrow at me as that effortless smile reappeared on his lips.

"Worse," I told him, stepping closer, his smile slipping as I placed the blade of my axe under his chin. "A cynic. Now—" I put a hand to his armoured shoulder and shoved, hard enough to send him stumbling "—be so good as to walk in silence, my lord."

We pressed on, averting our gaze from the murders that marked our progress. The preoccupation with scrupulously observing the king's edict spared us unwanted attention but, as the supply of victims grew thin, blood-drunk soldiers inevitably went in search of more.

"What's this one, then?" a beefy fellow enquired, mud squelching as he stumbled into our path. He carried a gore-matted hatchet in one hand and a bottle in the other. The unfocused cast to his eyes and stink of his breath told me he was drunk on more than just blood.

"Not one of our noble buggers, is he?" the beefy soldier observed, peering closer at Sir Wilhum, spattering red droplets onto the blue enamelled armour as he gestured with the hatchet. "I saw some bastard ride into our line wearing pretty coloured plate just like this . . . "

"Move on," Brewer instructed, stepping between our charge and the overly curious soldier. The fellow wasn't so drunk as to ignore a warning and duly stumbled off in the opposite direction, though not without casting an aggrieved glance or two over his shoulder.

"We're drawing too many eyes," I said, turning to his lordship and reaching for the straps on his vambrace. "Best get this plate off."

"This plate—" Sir Wilhum sniffed, snatching his arm away "—is worth more than every shek the three of you have earned in your entire lives."

"Do you want to die?" I asked, taking hold of the rim of his gorget and dragging him close. "Listen, you puffed-up, coddled fuckwit! The captain wants you alive and I'll do my best to see it happen. But, since I saved her life today, I doubt she'll hang me if I fail. So, do what you're told, or I'll dump your noble carcass at the feet of the next Crown Company man I see."

Espying the overlapping corpses of two warhorses a few paces off, I dragged him behind the fly-shrouded mound. His handsome features slumped once again into misery as we stripped off his armour, the pauldrons, greaves and sundry other bits consigned to a sack Toria had been saving for her promised loot.

"Reckon the captain'll let us keep it?" she asked. The armour clanked as she hefted the sack, giving Sir Wilhum an empty smile. "Since it's worth so much, and we're being denied our share of the spoils on this field." She inclined her head at the sight of a cluster of Cordwainers squabbling over the half-naked corpse of a fallen knight.

"A mob of beasts consumed by greed," the young noble sneered. "Just as the True King said you were."

"Funny that," Toria returned. "Our captain said much the same thing about your lot."

Shorn of his armour, Sir Wilhum was revealed as a young man of lean and athletic build clad in shirt and trews of thin cotton. He stood about my own height but without the broken nose and accumulated marks of a hard-lived life. At another time I was sure he would have made an impressive figure. But, shrunken in haggard self-pity and denied the trappings of wealth, he became pathetically human. He also still appeared to be every bit the captive.

"Here," I said, struggling free of my leather tunic. "Put this on. Anyone asks, you lost your billhook in the battle and we're off to see Supplicant Delric to get our cuts stitched."

We resumed our trudge, Brewer cursing as he shooed flies from his wounded hand while Toria soon gave up trying to carry the sack of armour and resorted to dragging it through the mud. Fortune smiled and we drew no more eyes, although, as we reached the firm green of untrammelled ground, we happened upon something that drew mine.

The silver-hawk banner of the Duke of the Shavine Marches fluttered atop a tall pole held by a man-at-arms of impressive stature. Next to him, a man of far less noteworthy bearing but much finer armour stood reading from an unfurled scroll. His words were addressed to a score of bound, kneeling captives cowering beneath the lowered halberds of men in the duke's livery. While most who met their end in the twilight of this battle were victims of haphazard murder, it appeared Duke Elbyn Blousset was keen to conduct matters on a more formal basis.

"For treason can inspire no mercy," he intoned in a voice I assumed was supposed to convey grave and implacable judgment. Instead, to my ears he resembled the nasal droning of an uninspired cleric to an empty shrine. "Neither testament nor contrition in word or payment may negate the traitor's crime and their only obligation is to suffer just punishment without unseemly complaint or cowardly display. So decreed by King Tomas Algathinet on this day in the sight of the Martyrs and in most humble gratitude for the Seraphile's grace."

He spoke on for a while longer, either keen to prolong the fears of his captives or due to love of his own voice. However, I paid scant heed, my full attention having been captured by the slender and finely attired figure standing a few paces to the right of the bannerman. Her hair was loosely bound and twisted in the breeze, its hue matching the fox-fur trimming of her cloak. Her face was pale and stiff, apparently taking no pleasure in what was about to unfold, but not opting to look away either. The years had not dimmed her looks; if anything, I found myself more captivated than ever.

"Alwyn!" Toria said, voice sharp and just loud enough to carry to the ears of the woman in the fox-fur cloak. Her head snapped around, gaze fixing on me in an instant. The rigid features slackened in shock and the pallor of her face abruptly shifted from pale to near white, eyes widening as she took an involuntary backwards step. While I was sure the years had not been so kind to my face, Lorine apparently had no difficulty in recognising it.

Another insistent call from Toria made me pause, and I realised I had taken a few involuntary steps of my own. I also had a firmer grip on my axe and, even though I didn't recall choosing to do so, had filled my free hand with the handle of my knife.

"Off with you, man!"

I blinked, finding my path barred by a wiry sergeant wearing the duke's colours. He waved a halberd at me, lean features hard with dismissal. "We don't need any more blades here and the loot's all spoken for. On your way."

I ignored him, looking past his shoulder to see Lorine swiftly regain her composure. She spared me a final, wide-eyed glance before turning her attention back to the doomed captives, her face once again serenely devoid of expression.

"And keep your eyes off the duchess," the sergeant warned, shifting to obstruct my view. "She's not to be gawped at by the likes of you."

"Duchess?" I asked. "Never heard her profession called that before."

"Watch your lip!" He crouched, halberd angled in readiness, which did nothing to cool the heat now raging in my chest. Looking him over, I saw how the blade of his weapon was comparatively free of gore and grime, his tunic being similarly lacking in the stains and rents that marked mine.

"You're awful clean-looking," I grated, jaw clenched as I started forwards. "Do any actual fighting today? I have."

"Alwyn!" Brewer's meaty hands clamped to my right arm and Toria's to my left. "We have a mission, remember?" Brewer hissed in my ear. I shuddered in frustration and mounting rage, finding I had to drag several breaths into my lungs before I consented to being pulled away.

The wiry sergeant, concealing evident relief behind a snarl, brandished his untarnished halberd again before striding back towards his men. I forced myself to turn as the blades began to fall. The sight of Lorine standing in placid observance of the slaughter would have rekindled my rage and I had already acted in a sufficiently stupid manner. *Shouldn't have let her see my face,* I berated myself as we led our prisoner towards the camp of Covenant Company. *Now she knows she'll have to kill me.*

Brewer's steps began to falter as we neared the camp, his skin showing an increasingly pale shade of grey beneath the covering of mud and dried blood. By the time Ayin came scampering to meet us at the picket line, his gaze had taken on an unfocused cast and his head lolled, words emerging as mumbled nonsense from his lips.

"Not yet . . . time . . . " he said, swiping at something only he could see. "Not yet time . . . "

"Brewer?" I asked, only for him to peer at me with blank incomprehension.

"Supper," he slurred. "It's not yet time for supper . . . " His words dwindled into gibberish before all sense fled his gaze and he fell. Toria and I rushed to catch him, though his bulk was such it bore us both to our knees.

"Is he drunk?" Ayin asked, cocking her head at Brewer's inert form before issuing a disdainful sniff. "I thought better of him. Who are you?" she added, casting a suspicious scowl at Sir Wilhum.

"Who he is doesn't matter," I grunted, attempting to heave Brewer upright. "Help us get this lump to Supplicant Delric. You too, my lord. Unless you feel assisting a mere churl to be beneath you."

"I swore an oath to the True King to do just that," Sir Wilhum replied, gesturing for Toria to stand aside so he could lay Brewer's arm across his shoulders.

I resisted the impulse to point out the numerous churlish corpses now twisting in the river's current as a result of his false king's promises and took hold of Brewer's other arm. Together the four of us managed to convey Brewer's utterly limp and insensate person to

Delric's tent where the healer was quick to identify the source of his malady.

"Poison," he said, long nose wrinkling as he sniffed at the blackened hole in Brewer's hand. "Not just filth. Acted too quickly."

"Do you have a . . . " I fumbled for the right word, the healing arts having been outside the scope of Sihlda's lessons. "A cure, a physic."

"Don't know what poison it is," Delric replied. His robe and face were liberally spattered with dried or recent blood, the tent crowded by a dozen soldiers in various states of injury. Outside, a line of twenty bodies lay under blankets awaiting rites and burial. These were those who had possessed enough strength to stagger here from the field where, I knew, many more lay still in the mud.

"No name for the poison, no cure," the Supplicant continued, reaching for a bowl of steaming water and a small knife. "I'll clean this," he said, nodding to Brewer's wound. "Nothing else to be done." Seeing the helpless concern evident on both Toria's face and mine, he added, "He's strong. Makes it through the night, he has a chance. Now leave."

"What was it like?" Ayin's face was bright with an excited curiosity that failed to dim in response to Toria's growling rebuke.

"Fucking horrible. What d'you think it was like?"

"Did the captain kill the Pretender?" Ayin went on blithely. "I heard she fought him. Did she kill him?"

"No," I said, casting a sidelong glance at Sir Wilhum sitting close to the fire in morose silence. "They say he fled like the worst of cowards."

The noble's features tensed in anger but he refused to rise to the taunt. The company had returned to the camp come dusk and there were too many soldiers and Supplicants about to risk an outburst. Sergeant Swain had been stern and unforgiving in resuming discipline, ordering all weapons cleaned and stacked before calling us into our troops to be counted. It transpired my estimate of our losses had been a trifle pessimistic. Instead of half, one-third had perished, though a good number of the survivors were wounded. Some had only minor cuts or broken bones that would heal in time. Others, like Brewer, would be lucky to see the morning.

"It's not all they're saying," Toria told me. She lowered her voice and looked around before stepping closer. "Took a turn around the rest of the camp earlier, heard some of the other companies talking, all manner of wild rumours. The usual nonsense spoken by folk who've seen too much too quick. But most of it was about the captain, how's she anointed and such. Blade of the Covenant, they're calling her."

"She held the line and won the day," I said, shrugging. "Every battle has its heroes."

"Hero," Toria corrected. "Just her. Not the king, not that monster champion of his. Anointed Lady Evadine, servant of the Covenant, not the Crown, and the nobles didn't like it. Saw a knight from Crown Company order a man flogged for speaking too loud about the greatness of the Holy Captain."

"What did he look like?" I asked, my interest piqued. "This knight?"

"Big, like most nobles who actually do the fighting, but not so big as the King's Champion. Had a brass hawk on his breastplate."

Althus Levalle, I concluded. It stood to reason he would be here somewhere. Roused by the knowledge that both the knight commander and Lorine were within a few hundred paces of where I now sat, my vengeance began whispering dangerous notions. *Could get it all done in one night. How hard would it be?*

I pulled my cloak about me, hunching in self-reproach. Lorine was well guarded and Sir Althus surrounded by kingsmen, not that either would be an easy kill. Lorine had always been a fine hand with a blade and, while my martial abilities had sufficed to ensure my survival this day, I knew I was no match for the knight commander. *Not when he's awake*, the dangerous voice inside whispered in awful temptation. *But a man can't fight when he's asleep . . .*

Toria's soft, worried gasp brought a welcome distraction. I followed her gaze to see Supplicant Delric outlined in the glow emanating from the healing tent, beckoning to us with a tired, impatient hand. The hope that flared in my chest as Toria and I hurried over died at the sight of his grave, fatigue-ridden face.

"He's got some hours left," he said, leading us to where Brewer lay on a narrow cot. He had been stripped to the waist and his thick-muscled frame had taken on the grey hue of dry slate, his skin slick with sweat that tainted the air and brought a sting to the nostrils. His wound was bandaged but the flesh surrounding it mottled in red and an ugly shade of purple. His chest rose and fell in sluggish heaves, head swaying and vacant eyes gleaming dull behind fluttering lids.

Next to me, Toria stiffened, arms wrapping tight around her chest. I suppressed the impulse to reach out a comforting hand. It wasn't her way.

"He would want to make testament," I told Delric, finding I had to cough away a catch in my throat to get the words out.

"Anything I used to rouse him will kill him before he could speak," the Supplicant replied. "If you talk, there's a chance he'll hear it."

With that, he gave a short nod and moved away to tend to another soul who might live to see the dawn.

"A fucking tainted arrow," Toria said, jaw clenching. She moved to Brewer's head, putting a hesitant hand to his sweat-covered brow. "Should've taken four men at least to bring him down."

"That it should." I watched Brewer's lips twitch, wondering if, somewhere within the fevered confusion of his mind, he might be trying to voice his testament after all. I thought it strange that throughout our years of captivity together I wouldn't have cared one whit about his death, yet after a few months of shared liberty here I was swallowing tears. There was also a small, shameful part of me that didn't relish the prospect of dragging his carcass to the grave come morning.

"Fetch the noble," I told Toria, gathering up a blanket and throwing it over Brewer's torso. "And that sack of plate."

"What for?" she asked with a puzzled squint.

Brewer gave a deep, rumbling groan as I swung his legs off the cot. "Payment," I said, grunting as I hauled him upright. "And not a word to the Supplicants or the captain. And especially not Ayin."

*

The Sack Witch's conical shelter still sat beneath the branches of the tall birch. As I brought the cart to a halt, smoke rose in wispy tendrils from a recently dampened fire close to the entrance. The shelter was sealed with some form of animal hide edged in yellow by the soft glow of a candle within. I had worried there might be a crowd of others seeking the Caerith woman's particular talents, but it seemed whatever custom she had enjoyed after the battle had dwindled come nightfall.

The old carthorse's irritated snorts joined with Brewer's increasingly pained groans as I climbed down from the cart, finding myself seized by uncertainty now the task lay at hand. *What is there to fear?* I asked myself, staring at the flickering outline of the entrance. *She can help him, or she can't.*

Still I dithered, thoughts of the chainsman looming large at the forefront of my mind. I also felt a mounting certainty that Evadine, should she hear of this, would take a decidedly dim view of seeking assistance from a Caerith witch.

"Are we doing this or not?" Toria enquired from the back of the cart. She had hold of one of Brewer's arms, his inert state having given way to much flailing about as the cart trundled its rickety course from the camp.

However, the decision was taken from my hands when the shelter's entrance parted and its occupant emerged. In the gloom, the two diamond-shaped holes in her sack were bottomless, her eyes catching no glimmer from the torch held by Sir Wilhum. He had come along willingly enough, I assumed in expectation of chancing an escape should the opportunity arise. So far, however, a journey marked by the presence of a good many soldiers, most in a state of aggressive drunkenness, had quelled any such notions.

The Sack Witch strode past me to glance over the cart's side at its stricken occupant, heedless of the halting greeting I offered.

"A poisoned arrow," I said as her anonymous gaze lingered. "We don't know what kind." I paused, watching the sack's shape alter as she angled her head and leaned closer to Brewer. I heard her make a few sniffs before she straightened, the black holes of her eyes turning to regard me.

"We can pay," I said, gesturing to Toria, who duly held up the sack containing Wilhum's armour. "Finest plate. Worth fifty full letins, according to its former owner here . . . "

The Sack Witch spoke then, her voice seeping through the weave in a wet rasp. The words were comprehensible but only just, the product of lips too malformed to utter them with any precision.

"I have no need of armour." She stepped closer and I found I had to suppress an instinctive desire to retreat. This woman exuded a curious earthy scent, like a forest kissed by the first rain of autumn. In truth, it was not altogether unpleasant, but it was unnerving. This was not how a person was supposed to smell.

"But," she went on, the sack pulsing with her words, "I will take payment."

"I . . . " My voice faltered and, as before, I found my gaze snared by the twin voids of her eyes. "I have some coin . . ."

"Your words, your . . . " she raised her hands, pale and strangely clean in the torchlight, miming a quill tracking over parchment " . . . skill. That will be your payment."

I nodded in agreement. "Whatever you require, I'll write it."

The eyeholes lingered in silent regard for a heartbeat longer. "Bring him," she said, returning to her shelter and disappearing inside, leaving the entrance open.

"How did she know you're a scribe?" Toria asked, as the three of us manoeuvred Brewer's feebly struggling bulk off the cart.

"She heard Gulatte's men say it," I said. In fact, during my confrontation with Sergeant Lebas, I hadn't thought the Sack Witch close enough to hear his words.

The Caerith had us set Brewer down at the entrance, displaying an unexpected, perhaps unnatural strength by dragging him the rest of the way herself. I took note of the bared forearms that emerged from her mildewed cloak as she did so, the flesh smooth and lean, lacking any sign of the malady that had ravaged her face.

"Wait," she told us in her malformed rasp before pulling the covering firmly back in place. I began to call out a query regarding how long this would take but stopped. Whatever was about to occur within was clearly not for me or anyone else to know.

"You know this is absurd, I assume?" Wilhum asked a short while later. We had scraped the damp ashes from the witch's fire and rekindled a blaze with what sticks we could gather. Toria, ever the scavenger, shared some dried beef she had purloined during her tour about the wider camp, even tossing a portion to the noble. He responded with a gracious bow and finely spoken words of thanks that set her lip curling.

"Caerith mummers tour this realm gulling folk with promise of cures, curses and charms," Wilhum persisted when I gave no answer. "Why is this one different?"

"Because the other soldiers in this camp are scared shitless of her," I replied. "I'm wagering that means something. Besides, what other option did we have? And, since we're bandying notions of absurdity, my lord, disinheriting yourself by swearing fealty to a man with no more claim to the throne than a chamber pot strikes me as particularly absurd."

I expected anger, or at least a caustic rejoinder, but the young noble merely sighed and chewed on more beef. Eventually, he murmured, voice quiet with sad reflection, "I was disinherited long before I ever heard tell of the True King. I went to him a pauper save for the armour I wore and the horse I rode. He accepted me with as much grace as if I had delivered him a hundred men-at-arms and a cart laden with treasure."

"Why'd your old man kick you out?" Toria enquired. "Lost too much at cards, was it? Got one wench too many up the stick?"

Once again, Wilhum confounded my expectations by smiling. It was not the winning wonder he had shown Evadine, rather just a slight, sorrowful bow to his lips. He had washed the grime from his face back at the camp and his flawless features made for a surreal image in the fire's glow, as if one of Master Arnild's illuminations from the Scroll of Martyr Stevanos had somehow come to life.

"In truth," he told Toria, "it was love that brought me to this pass, my dear. And yet, I find myself unable to regret it."

I felt my enmity for this man slip away then. The ingrained resentment of the low-born for the high, and the base jealousy he had provoked, suddenly felt like the petty indulgences of a child. He was right; he was as much a pauper as I. If anything, his plight was worse for his crime remained noteworthy and unforgivable, at least according to the king's edict.

"You should run," I told him, nodding to the gloom beyond the glow cast by our fire. "They're all sleeping it off now and I doubt the picket line will be well manned tonight."

"I thought your captain told you to keep me guarded?"

"She told us to get you to our camp, which we've done. Go. We won't stop you." Watching his wary indecision, I added, "However high her standing, and her blood, do you really think she'll be able to save you from a traitor's end when the king learns of your survival?"

"I owe her . . . " he paused, lowering his head and making no move to rise " . . . more than I can say. Since no sergeant appeared to shackle me, I assume she expects me to run. But doing so would put her at risk and that I'll not abide, even if it puts my neck beneath Sir Ehlbert's sword. In any case—" he let out a thin laugh "—where in all the world would I go?"

We all turned to regard the shelter as a low moaning emerged from within, a moan that soon rose to a panicked shout.

"What's she doing to him?" Toria said, getting to her feet. She started towards the shelter, snorting in anger when I moved to bar her path.

"Ever hear of a cure that was painless?" I asked, then grimaced as Brewer let out another shout. It was shorter than the last but richer in pain and followed by several more.

"You don't know the Caerith like my folk do," Toria told me. "When I was a girl the local shrine sent a missionary across the mountains to preach the Martyrs' example to those heathens. Next summer we found his rotted head impaled on a stake outside the shrine's door. They'd come a hundred miles or more to send a warning."

"Perhaps they just really hate visitors," Wilhum suggested. "My father certainly did."

Another voice rose from the shelter then, softer and far sweeter, a voice raised in song. It ascended to entwine itself with Brewer's shouts and for a time the two formed a discordant melody. Soon, however, the pained cries diminished as the soft singing continued. The words were alien but their cadence once again put me in mind of the chainsman; this was a Caerith song and, judging from the quietude it instilled in Brewer, possessed considerable calming power.

"That can't have been her," Toria breathed as the song faded, face tense with poorly concealed fear.

"If not, then who?" I asked.

"Something . . . else. Something she conjured." Her voice became a whisper, the firelight catching on her fear-widened eyes. "We shouldn't have done this, Alwyn."

"Perhaps," I admitted, glancing back at the now silent shelter. "But it's done, nonetheless."

CHAPTER THIRTY-TWO

The Sack Witch reappeared with the dawn, my bleary, misted eyes finding her standing a few paces off, wreathed in the smoke from our dying fire. Sleep had claimed us some time in the night when the strain of a day spent at slaughter finally took hold. It was the kind of sleep that only arises from exhaustion, a dreamless void for which I was grateful, for I knew my slumber in the days or even years to come would be less forgiving.

The Sack Witch beckoned with a pale hand and I rose on stiff legs, following her to find Brewer lying in our cart. He was still unconscious but the clammy greyness had faded from his skin. He remained pale but hints of pink showed in his face and his broad chest swelled with a regular, steady rhythm. Peering at his hand, I found it bandaged with clean muslin that concealed the wound. However, the ugly, mottled purple was gone from the surrounding flesh.

"I suppose," I said, swallowing away the tremor to my voice as I straightened to face the Sack Witch, "it would be best not to ask how this was done."

Her sack crinkled as she angled her head, conveying a sense of puzzlement. "His blood was riven with a blight," she rasped. "I took it away. Now his body heals itself."

I nodded, deciding further elaboration wasn't needed. I was keen to be gone from here before too many eyes witnessed our presence. "How long will he sleep?"

Her sack crinkled further. "Until he wakes."

I shrugged, voicing a thin laugh. "Of course. So, I assume you wish to conclude payment—"

"You should not fear me," she cut in and I found my words instantly stalled. It wasn't so much due to her interruption as her tone, for the malformed rasp was suddenly gone. Her voice now possessed an accented fluency that made it clear every word she had spoken up until now had been a performance. Her lips were as whole as mine, her voice possessed of a deep sincerity coloured by a faint note of regret.

Something about that voice, about the hurt I heard in it, drew an honest reply from my lips before I had chance to cage it. "I've known two of your people before. One an outlaw who worked charms. The other far worse. A very bad man, with a . . . worrisome ability. He also sang songs."

"Are there no bad men among your people?" she asked. "And, therefore, do you judge them all as evil?"

"Many." I gave a rueful, subdued grin. "But no, not all."

"Who was he? This man of evil?"

"A chainsman, a man who gathers captive outlaws and takes them to be sold for labour." I paused, again possessed of an urge to say more than I should. A lifetime of honing instincts geared towards survival left me in no doubt that this woman was dangerous, and yet I felt utterly secure in her presence. *Is this a spell she weaves?* I wondered. *Am I enchanted now?* Still, I spoke on and I know now it was not due to some form of unnatural compulsion. Rather it was out of recognition that, even though this woman's face remained hidden, she understood me in a way no other had.

"I think he wanted me for something," I told her. "After he sold me to the Pit, he tried to buy me back. I don't know why, but he had the look of a man who had made a grave error."

The sack shifted as the head within nodded. "I know of this man. And you are right to judge him evil, but he was made such. A heart twisted by the ills of the world and his own misjudgements. I also know why he wanted to buy you back, and you were fortunate he did not."

"Why? What did he want of me?"

"To kill you. His . . . ability is what your people term a curse. It enables him to glean coin from your nobles but also makes him forever an outcast. And it is fickle, as befits a curse intended to make its victim suffer. It plays tricks; it taunts; it leads him along paths best untravelled."

"Why?" I inched closer to her, taking in her scent once again and finding it transformed. Whereas the night before it had been off-putting in its strangeness, now I found it an intoxicating floral melange that brought forth memories of the Shavine Forest in summer. "Why would he kill me?"

"Because his curse told him, too late as is its wont, that one day you would kill him."

My face was so close to the sackcloth mask that I saw her eyes clearly, morning sunlight penetrating the weave to paint a glint on shadowed sapphires. I swallowed a sudden flood of drool, my heart pounding and sweat beading my forehead.

"So," she whispered in her flowing, raspless voice, "you came to me on a field of blood after all." Her tone was one of satisfaction coloured by sadness, as if she had received a long-promised gift and found it wanting.

"Enough," she murmured, stepping back. Instantly, the laboured throb of my heart calmed and the heat prickling my skin faded to a chill moistness. Also, the allure of her scent abruptly vanished, slipping into the autumnal musk from before.

Despite the sudden shift in sensation, I found I still had to suppress the urge to reach for her. There was more I wanted to say, more I wanted to know. About the chainsman's curse. About how she had taken the poison from Brewer's veins. But mostly I wanted to know about her.

"Do you have a name?" I asked.

"Yes," she replied with a brisk finality that told me it would not be forthcoming. "It is time for payment."

She reached into the folds of her mildewed cloak. For a second I entertained the absurd thought that she might be about to present me with a bill listing services rendered, but instead her hand emerged holding a book. It was old, the leather binding dark and cracked, the brass clasp tarnished and scratched. It bore no title on the cover or the spine, the aged leather engraved with complex whorls and interleaved patterns.

Holding it out, she maintained her silence until I consented to take it, undoing the clasp to look upon a page of dense but precisely inscribed text. Leafing through several pages I found the text interrupted by pictograms and illustrations, all rendered in simple ink rather than the gold and multi-hued dyes employed by Master Arnild. I found it instantly fascinating and confounding in equal measure for, learned as I was, I couldn't read a single word.

"What language is this?" I asked, glancing up at the Sack Witch.

"The language of my people. Or, more precisely, one of the many languages once spoken in the lands your folk call the Caerith Wastes."

I continued to thumb through the book, captivated and mystified. "And what does this book pertain to? Is it scripture?"

"Scripture?" Her tone held a faintly amused note. "My people have no equivalent of that word. But yes, I believe it has . . . sacred meaning."

"Believe?" I frowned at her. "You can't read this?"

The sack creased around her neck as she lowered her gaze. When she spoke again the humour had vanished from her voice. "Your people call it the Scourge. To my people it is *Ealthsar*: the Fall. Much was lost to us, our ancient stories and the knowledge to read them perhaps the most grievous loss of all, for it is in such things that the soul of a people lies."

"You think I can translate this?" I asked, looking again at the book. "This has no more meaning for me than a cluster of chicken scratchings."

"Meaning will come, in time. Unlike me, you can travel these lands unimpeded. There are places you will go that I cannot, places where the means of unlocking the knowledge in those words can be found."

"What places?"

"Places you were always going to go. Just as you and I were always going to find ourselves standing here at this moment. In time, we will find ourselves in another place, and there you will repay your debt."

She moved away from the cart, starting back towards her shelter, then pausing at my side. The pleasant scent of summer assailed me once again as she leaned close, whispering in her flowing, perfect voice, "The next service you require of me will entail a far greater debt. Be sure you're willing to pay it."

She said no more, even though I called after her, "How will I find you?" Crouching, she entered her shelter, sealing the entrance. The hide covering seemed a flimsy thing but I knew it was shut as tight as any dungeon door.

Brewer slept for all the following day and night, awakening come the morn with no recollection beyond our journey from the battlefield. Supplicant Delric insisted on spending several hours in close study of Brewer's person. He said little, as was customary, but his face betrayed evident mystification and no small measure of suspicion, neither of which was abated by my bland explication.

"He just got better, Supplicant." Delric continued to scowl wordlessly in the face of my smile as I added, "A miracle, you might say. Perhaps the Seraphile chose to reward one so faithful in his devotion to the Covenant."

The healer's gaze narrowed further but, for reasons unsaid, he made no further enquiry. Also, to my relief, neither Sergeant Swain nor Evadine appeared to be aware of this apparent miracle and so I was spared a barrage of potentially hazardous questions.

Much of the king's host had dispersed by then, the churls released back to their farms and the nobles to their castles. Covenant Company, however, lingered, for our now famed captain had volunteered to clear away the many bodies still littering the ground.

"The holy rites of the Covenant will not be denied to the fallen," she told us, "be they honoured friend or condemned foe."

In addition to the hacked, stiffened and rapidly putrefying remains suffering the attentions of the crows on the field, there were also dozens of corpses crowding the riverbank. Either slain by vengeful nobles or claimed by the river, they had been carried by the current to wash up on shore for over a mile downstream. Our troop was chosen to drag these unfortunates clear of the water so that they too might receive rites before being consigned to one of the half-dozen mass graves we had dug. In some ways it was almost as unpleasant a task as fighting in the battle itself, for water does vile things to a body while also carrying away much of the loot we might otherwise have garnered.

"Oh, Scourge take you, you dead bastard!" Toria's curses were muffled by the arm she clamped over her face as one particularly bloated corpse disgorged a miasma of truly noteworthy foulness from a gaping wound in its chest.

"Mind your tongue," Ofihla told her, though not with the curt snap she employed when rebuking the rest of us. "You heard the captain: respect the fallen."

"I'd respect these stinkers more if they had a single coin between them," Toria muttered as the Supplicant moved off.

"Here," Brewer grunted, dragging another body through the reeds fringing the bank. This one had been a hale fellow in life, long of limb and well muscled with it, not that his bulk troubled Brewer at all. Since waking he appeared to have acquired a limitless energy as well as a ready smile. "He's still got his purse."

"You don't want it?" Toria asked, squinting up at Brewer as she crouched at the corpse's side, hands busy on his belt.

"Wealth is frippery," Brewer said with a sniff, a quote from one of the sermons Evadine had given when we'd consigned another batch of dead to the earth. He raised his face to the sky, smiling as the sun played on his skin before wading back into the current, whistling a jaunty tune as he snagged another corpse.

"Much preferred him as a miserable sod," Toria said, her face souring further as she emptied the purse's contents into her palm. "Four sheks and a quartet of dice. My fortune is made."

She glanced up at me as I rifled the pockets of a far less impressive figure, rake thin, gapped of tooth and mean of garb. His hands were calloused from a life of fieldwork and it seemed unlikely he would provide any pickings of worth. Yet, when I dragged the thin leather shoe off his foot, a bright silver sovereign dropped into my hand, much to Toria's disgust.

"You lucky fuck." She frowned, watching me shrug and consign the sovereign to my own purse. "Could buy a horse with that and still have change, maybe two since there'll be plenty for sale after all this."

I said nothing. The suggestion in her words was obvious but not one I was willing to entertain.

"Brewer's turned cheerful and you've gone all misery-balls," Toria persisted, lowering her voice to a careful mutter. "Ever since we met that witch."

"Taking part in a slaughter is likely to change a man," I told her, though in truth I was aware of the reason for my reticence over the past couple of days. I'd spent what spare hours we'd had poring over the pages of the Sack Witch's book, finding nothing I understood but still scarcely able to take my eyes from it. Something about the curved elegance of the text and the enigma of the many baffling pictograms compelled me in a way books I could actually read did not.

"Do we still have a plan?" Toria pressed, leaning across the corpse that separated us, face hard and intent. "I meant what I said: I am not fighting another battle."

"I know," I said. "And yes, we still have a plan, but it requires us to stay soldiers, for a while at least." I thought for a second then reached for my purse, extracting the sovereign and tossing it to her. "Take some payment on account if it'll still your worries."

Her face bunched in consternation as she looked at the coin and then at me. "This buys a few months, but no more. You and I are fast running out of rope, Alwyn."

More placatory words might have come to my lips had we not been provided a welcome distraction in the form of a loud fracas further along the bank. Rising, I saw Wilhum delivering a hard shove to the chest of a wiry trooper named Tiler. The noble's face was hard with a forbidding mix of anger and grief.

"Get away from him, you filthy cur!" he snarled. Tiler, by far the weaker fellow, quailed for a moment before taking sudden heart as a group of comrades came to his side, lifting him from the mud.

"Got no rights to put hands on me!" Tiler shouted back, drawing an affirmative murmur from his helpers. "You're no fucking lord now!"

"Leave it," Toria cautioned as I started forward. "A beating might do the popinjay some good."

"I doubt this lot will stop at a beating," I returned. "And I didn't get him off that field to watch him die."

Tiler and his clutch of friends were edging forwards as I approached, he reaching for his dagger while the others balled their fists. My forcefully cheerful greeting caused them to pause but not retreat.

"What's this about, then?"

Tiler scowled at me while the others were more wary. I had been seen often enough in the captain's company to mark me out as holding a small measure of favour, but not actual authority.

"Piss off, Scribe," Tiler hissed. However, his voice was muted and his gaze averted. Evidently, he knew my type and I knew his. Like me, he had been one of those to swear to the company in Callintor, but the fact that I had only a vague recollection of his face marked him as a fellow who liked to keep to the shadows.

I regarded him for a silent second or two, seeing how he failed to meet my eye, before turning to Wilhum. The noble bore no arms but stood in readiness for combat, fists raised in a manner that indicated he knew how to use them. At his back, the body of a large man lay on the bank. Looking closer I saw the gleam of plate armour through the muck that covered it. A knight then. Something in the set of the man's slumped bearing stirred a sense of recognition and I moved closer, looking at the pale features pressed into the mud. Death will rob a face of much that makes it recognisable, so it took a moment of frowning concentration before I realised I knew these broad, blocky features.

"Sir Eldurm," I muttered. *So, he found his glory but not his reward.* I should have been relieved. This meant one less enemy at my back.

One less noose awaiting my neck. Instead, I could only think of all the hours spent with this man in his chamber, all that time composing letters to a woman who couldn't or wouldn't love him in the manner he craved. Even though Gulatte would have strung me up in a heartbeat, I felt he deserved a better end than drowning among rebels at the apex of a battle that had already been won.

Glancing over my shoulder, I fixed Tiler with the kind of stare he and I knew well: the promise of a final warning. "Fuck off," I told him with icy precision. He cast a glance at his supporters, but their prior aggression had now evaporated in favour of returning their attentions to rifling easier pickings among the other corpses. Tiler dared a final sour grimace in my direction before trudging away.

"The captain said you were friends," I commented to Wilhum as he turned back to Gulatte's body. "The three of you, when you were young."

Wilhum gave no reply beyond a stiff nod, his gaze fixed on the dead knight's bleached, dirt-spattered face.

"Well then," I said, moving to take hold of Gulatte's arms, teeth gritted as I dragged his feet clear of the water. "Let's get him seen to."

The task was done by noon the next day, Evadine calling the company together to hear her final sermon for the dead. In all, we had filled four mass graves with eight hundred and forty-three corpses, each one counted and entered in the company books by my own hand. The scant nobles among them were named along with a score of men-at-arms known to Sergeant Swain or the other Supplicants. Most were put into the earth with no record made beyond a tally mark in a ledger few eyes would ever see.

Sir Eldurm Gulatte was duly recorded as having died heroically in the final charge before being laid to rest in full armour, his gauntleted hands set atop the pommel of the sword placed upon his chest. Wilhum had taken great pains to clean and polish every scrap of his dead friend's plate, reacting with considerable harshness to Toria's suggestion that it and his sword would be worth a great deal to the right buyer. I thought it noteworthy that we found no sign of Sergeant

Lebas or any of Gulatte's men-at-arms among the dead. If they had survived the battle it seemed their loyalty didn't extend beyond their lord's demise. I assumed they were already off seeking employment elsewhere or heading back to the Pit Mines to beseech their new owner for a return to their prior roles.

Evadine had come to stand with Wilhum after we'd laid Gulatte to rest, the two joining hands as they stood vigil over their fallen friend until I heard Wilhum say in a strained murmur, "I always thought he would be the one to bury us, Evvie."

Her only reply was to squeeze Wilhum's hand before issuing an order to cover the bodies. With the last grave filled in she had the company form ranks to observe funeral rites. Her sermon was unusual in being a recitation from one of the Martyr Scrolls, the questions asked by Martyr Ahlianna of the heathen king who would subsequently execute her for spurning his offer of marriage.

"'Is it our blood that divides us, great king? No, for the blood in my veins is as red as yours, and, I assure you, runs just as hot. Is it our speech? No, for with time all tongues can be learned, and few are the souls not enlightened in the learning. It is faith that sets us apart. The faith that closes my heart to yours for I cannot love what is incapable of love. Only those who accept the Covenant between the Seraphile and the earthbound, in heart, body and soul, can know true love.'"

The captain paused, lowering her gaze to the freshly dug earth concealing the corpses beneath. The wind swept her hair from her face, revealing the unscarred, unspoilt beauty she remained. Despite crossing swords with the Pretender himself and her vicious melee with the turncoat knights, she hadn't suffered a single cut.

I saw her draw breath to say more but whatever it may have been was forever lost, for she turned towards the sound of approaching horses. A small party of knights crested the rise to the south, reining their mounts to a halt a hundred paces off, the king's banner rising from their midst.

"Our business here is concluded," Evadine told us. "Go now and spend the day at rest. Sergeant Swain, with me if you please."

The company began to disperse, wandering away to their tents or small amusements, but I lingered to watch as Evadine and the sergeant strode off towards the knights. They all wore the livery of Crown Company, my eye making out the brass eagle on the breastplate of the knight at the forefront of the party. I found it odd that Sir Althus and the other knights wore full armour. Surely there was no one left to fight.

As Evadine and Swain halted to greet him with a bow, Sir Althus raised his visor and unfurled a scroll. I saw how the sergeant tensed at the obvious insult of the knight commander failing to respond by dismounting to offer a bow of his own. Raising the scroll with formal stiffness, Sir Althus began to read, the words brief and too distant to make out. Upon finishing he leaned forward to proffer the document to Evadine, which she accepted, taking her time over reading it while the knight commander maintained what appeared to me an overly rigid composure. After reading the scroll, Evadine spoke. I could catch the inflection of a question but not the content. Whatever she had asked, it brought a hard frown to Sir Althus's brow and a series of clipped responses. Once again, the words were lost to me but not to Sergeant Swain, who exploded in anger.

"What worthless cur has spoken so?" he demanded, face dark with murderous intent as he started towards the knight commander, a hand on his sword. The rest of the king's knights instantly bridled, guiding their mounts to spread out, gauntleted hands reaching for swords and maces.

"Hold up!" I shouted, raising a hand and calling out to the company. "Look to the captain!"

Brewer, predictably, was the first to respond, drawing his falchion and letting out a loud growl, which was soon echoed throughout the ranks. The Supplicants shouted no orders and yet the company assembled itself into troops with unconscious automation, spreading to form a well-ordered line. The angry murmur built as they hefted their weapons. The Traitors' Field had provided little monetary wealth but had been rich in arms and armour. I had procured myself a well-made halberd in place of my billhook, as had many others, along with plenty of swords and axes.

The thicket of steel caught the midday sun as we faced the knights. I saw how they exchanged glances, picturing the nervous faces behind their visors. We had fought their kind now and knew them not to be invincible. Also, they were outnumbered by at least ten to one. But there would be no second battle on the Traitors' Field that day, much to my regret, for I felt it the best chance I would ever get to settle accounts with Sir Althus Levalle.

"Silence in the ranks!" Evadine's voice rang out, clear and sharp, with a note of angry reproach that quelled our ugly murmuring. She surveyed us with a forbidding glare, letting her gaze linger on several faces, my own included. Her ire was such that I found myself resisting the urge to bow in contrition. Instead, I met her gaze squarely, seeing it narrow in response before she turned back to the knight commander.

By some trick of the wind I managed to catch her reply as she furled the scroll she held and bowed. "My thanks, my lord. Please convey my deepest respects to the king and my gratitude for entrusting Covenant Company with this most vital mission."

Sir Althus straightened in the saddle, his gaze tracking over our ranks until, inevitably, it found me. As with Lorine, it would have been far smarter to have remained anonymous, but I had marked myself by calling out and further attracted his notice by virtue of Evadine's prolonged glare. In place of the instant shock of recognition I had seen on Lorine's face, Sir Althus's heavy features were drawn in confusion. He might have had difficulty in recalling my face, but I had none in remembering the man who had saved me from mutilation and hanging only to lock me in the pillory. I should have lowered my head and stepped back into the concealing crowd but found I couldn't. Vengeance exerted its perverse grip once again, keeping me in place to return his scrutiny in full until at last I saw the memory dawn. I wanted him to know I lived. I wanted him to know I had not forgotten.

Sir Althus made further contrast with Lorine by making no pretence of ignoring me once recollection dawned, a smile appearing on his lips as he inclined his head, the greeting a long-parted friend might offer another. I didn't return the gesture, which seemed to amuse him more.

"I'll fare you well then, my lady," he told Evadine with a laugh, finally consenting to bow but remaining in the saddle as he did so. "You might want to spend what funds the council gives you on furs. I hear it gets cold up there."

He laughed again, shooting a final glance in my direction, then wheeled his horse about and departed at the gallop. His no doubt relieved knights followed swiftly, apparently deaf to the catcalls and insults my more foolish comrades cast in their wake.

"Shut your yapping!" Swain snarled, his sergeant's voice effortlessly reaching the ears of all present and bringing an instant silence. "Break camp and prepare to march within the hour!" I had seen him angry many times, but the lividity of his face told of a previously unseen depth of rage. "And if any of you voices a single complaint, I'll see your backbone come nightfall!"

For the second time the company dispersed, but with far greater alacrity. I waited until most had cleared the field before daring to approach the sergeant. He stood watching Evadine mount her grey charger, his face less red but his lingering rage evident in the hard stare he turned on me. "What is it, Scribe?"

"Our destination, Supplicant Sergeant," I said. "For the company log. Upon commencement of a day's march the destination is to be recorded along with distance to be covered. It's stipulated in the company rules, as I'm sure you recall."

I was ready for a rebuke, possibly physical in nature, but Swain just let out a heavy sigh. It seemed my efforts on the field, including saving the captain's life, might have won me a measure of indulgence, but not particular regard.

"The world was made worse when you learned to read," he huffed, before straightening and turning to march away, casting a curt reply over his shoulder. "North, Scribe. We're marching north. Twenty miles before dusk. Laggards will not be tolerated."

When we marched out, within the hour as commanded, the company passed by the copse where the Sack Witch had built her shelter. It was just a tumble of disordered sticks now and, though I tried to deny it, it pained my heart greatly to find her gone.

PART III

"You ask how many died for my ambitions. Why do you assume my ambition was for me alone?"

From *The Testament of the Pretender Magnis Lochlain*,
as recorded by Sir Alwyn Scribe

CHAPTER THIRTY-THREE

"It's *fucking* freezing!" Toria's narrow face was a picture of red-nosed misery. She had muffled her ears with rags and wrapped her slim form in several layers of cloth, none of which appeared to afford any relief from the icy, seaborn winds that assailed us.

I was more preoccupied with containing the contents of my stomach than the cold. The helmsman seemed to possess an unerring gift for finding every gut-churning swell in these benighted grey waters. To my non-maritime eye our ship appeared no more than a tub of age-darkened timbers held together with fraying rope and old nails. She creaked, groaned and shuddered her way through the upper reaches of the Cronsheldt Sea. Worst of all, she heaved and bucked more than a horse with a brain full of maggots.

Boats I knew, having traversed many a river in my time with Deckin's band, some narrow, some wide with treacherous currents that could drown a man in seconds. But the sea, I had quickly discovered, was not a river. Three days out from the port of Farinsahl and my nausea had barely abated for more than a minute or two. Meals were forced down only to be forced up again in short order and sleep came in brief fits in between rolling around the stinking confines of the hold. There were forty of us crammed into this cog, which bore the entirely unfitting name of *Gracious Maid*, the rest of the company following in the seven other ships forming what had apparently been named the Northern Crown Fleet.

The object of our northwards march had not been explained until the Supplicants arrayed us in ranks along the Farinsahl quayside some six days after setting out from the Traitors' Field. Our ranks had been filled to a surprising degree while marching north, so much so that we numbered almost half again the strength we possessed during the march from Callintor. Some were villains scraped from various ducal gaols along the way, but most were willing recruits, all compelled to forsake their hamlets and towns by the growing legend of the Anointed Lady.

They were a curious mix of callow youth and older churl, all fired by the same zealous Covenant belief that made them trying company for us more jaded souls. As Evadine had reined her grey charger to a halt on the quayside, hooves clattering on the cobbles, these newcomers had stared at her as if she had just ridden from betwixt the Divine Portals. I could tell the pitch of awe on display among these new recruits sat uneasily on her shoulders. Although word had reached us that the Council of Luminants had elevated her in clerical rank from Communicant to Aspirant, she continued to mostly eschew any title beyond captain.

"The Covenant council and the king have seen fit to award us a singular honour," she proclaimed to the company without a trace of irony. "For it falls to us to extinguish the last remnant of the unholy Pretender's Revolt. To the north lies the Fjord Geld and the port of Olversahl, until recently a bastion of the usurper's vile cause, given over to him by the faithless Duke Huelvic, who now lies justly slain beneath the Traitors' Field. Word has reached us that the loyal towns-folk of Olversahl have overthrown their treacherous lords and restated their allegiance to King Tomas. They have petitioned the Crown for protection against the gangs of villains who linger in the wilds plotting to seize back their stolen spoils. We are the king's answer."

A cheer rose at this, although Evadine's tone hadn't possessed any particular exhortation. Such spontaneous acclaim had become typical during her night-time sermons, shouts of affirmation and occasionally unabashed adoration rising from the enraptured crowd in response to her lessons. I found it strange since, to my ears at least, her sermons sounded less fiery and more reflective in the aftermath of battle.

That day at the docks I had seen a weary annoyance pass across her brow before she'd put a placid smile on her lips and raised a hand for quiet. "The Fjord Geld is not your home," she said. "Many of the customs you will find there will seem strange to you. Remember that open displays of the Ascarlian gods are tradition in Olversahl and not an expression of heresy; therefore enforcement of the strictures in that regard is not required. However, it is true that those who swore themselves to the Pretender's cause did so in the hope of supplanting the Covenant with ancient and vile heresies. It is for this reason that our company was chosen for this task. We will secure King Tomas's rights over his property and restore the Covenant wherever it has been broken."

More cheers, another troubled crease to Evadine's brow before she turned and nodded to Swain. "Fall out by troop!" he shouted. "Stand ready to board when ordered. And watch your feet on the gangways, you clumsy sots! No one's fishing you out of the harbour if you fall."

"Try this," Wilhum said now, moving to Toria's side to proffer a small flask. We had positioned ourselves at the stern where the heaving seemed less acute, although that was surely just a comforting delusion. Like Toria, Wilhum appeared unaffected by seasickness. Although, whereas her immunity was the result of considerable prior acquaintance with seafaring, I suspected his had more to do with the copious amount of liquor he poured down his throat whenever opportunity arose.

"What's in it?" Toria asked, removing the flask's stopper to sniff the contents.

"Brandy, rum and . . . " Wilhum shrugged " . . . something else that tastes foul but has a nice warming effect. Traded one of the sailors a dagger for a quarter barrel of the stuff. Sadly, this is all I have left. But feel at liberty to sup away, my dear. I'll not have it said that I'm a miserly drinker."

Toria took a sip, smacking her lips before taking several more. "Had a lot worse," she said, offering the flask to me. Sadly, one whiff of the acrid contents was enough to double me over the rail once again.

"So," I gasped a moment or two later, wiping my sleeve across my mouth and turning a bleary eye on the noble, "care to enlighten us as to the truth behind this expedition, my lord?"

Wilhum favoured me with a tired grimace. "Are you ever going to stop calling me that?"

"Disinherited and shorn of titles or not—" I gave him a wan smile "—your nobility continues to shine through."

It was true that, in the eyes of the Crown, he was no longer a lord. During the march word had reached us that the king had rescinded the edict that saw so many captives slain on the Traitors' Field. The slaughter hadn't been confined to the battlefield and had in fact continued for several days afterwards as vengeful knights roved far in search of fleeing rebels. I assumed the king's mercy to be the result of petitioning by noble fathers either keen to save the necks of foolish sons or halt the culling of churls needed to till untended fields. In any case, Wilhum's life was no longer automatically forfeit though his status as a turncoat required loss of title and punishment via service in Crown Company. He no longer spoke of his cherished True King or expressed any reservations regarding his recently sworn oath to fight him if the need arose. If he was truly resigned to his fate, it was a morose, drunken resignation, one I had no confidence would continue should it be tested.

"You talk to her more than anyone," I added, grimacing as I swallowed bile. "And your insight benefits from a noble's perspective."

My desire for information was heightened by the dearth of it to be gleaned from the Supplicants or Evadine herself. As company scribe, I spent a short time with her every few days. However, although she set me to work copying the scroll given to her by Sir Althus, the document revealed little beyond what she had told the company in Farinsahl. Also, I detected a coolness in her regard for me now, a frosty reticence that, frankly, left me somewhat aggrieved. Hadn't I saved her anointed arse?

Wilhum rolled his eyes as Toria returned the flask, then proceeded to drain it in a few short gulps. "You recall the king's emissary, I assume?"

"Sir Althus Levalle," I said, which caused Wilhum to raise a curious eyebrow.

"You know him?"

"Only by repute. He brought the missive that set us on this course. I also recall he said something that got our beloved Supplicant sergeant mightily riled up."

"That he did. You see, this mission of ours is more an exile than a royal errand. Our captain's fame blossomed like a shooting star after the Traitors' Field, eclipsing even the king's renown, although it's said he pitched in bravely enough when the time came. Still, I suspect any man will find courage if he fights in the shadow of Sir Ehlbert Bauldry. But, fair is fair, and by rights it was the king's victory, not that you'd know it listening to the common folk. Tomas is, by all accounts, an affable fellow undaunted by injury to his pride, but his family and counsellors are a different matter.

"It's important to remember that King Tomas was the second son of his much-lamented father, Mathis the Fourth, strong of arm and wise of mind. It was his firstborn son who, everyone assumed, would one day ascend to become Arthin the Fifth. Sadly, the prince's horse had other ideas and Arthin the Fifth was destined to become Arthin the Broken-necked, leaving Albermaine with an heir who had barely tottered free of his wet nurse's tit. King Mathis sired him late in life, the son of his second, far younger queen. To be fair, Tomas rose well to the challenge, thanks, it's said, to the mentorship of his champion Sir Ehlbert Bauldry and the sage guidance of his elder sister Princess Leannor. But his reign has ever been dogged by the knowledge that he was the lesser son of a far mightier sire.

"Hence, the Algathinet family and their many sycophants remain watchful for any threat to Tomas's authority. Growing regard for the celebrant of the Traitors' Field, a warrior said to be anointed by the Seraphile's grace no less, was certain to rouse their fears. And who's to say they're wrong. Power is a fragile thing, after all."

"They sent Covenant Company to the Fjord Geld to get her out of the way," I said.

"Smart," Toria commented in a nasal sniffle. "Look at all those devout fools who threw themselves at her feet on the march north. A few more months and we'd have had an army, never mind a company."

"But that's not all, is it?" I asked Wilhum. "What tweaked the sergeant so that set him reaching for his sword?"

"Rumours," Wilhum said. He paused to upend the flask over his open mouth, letting the dregs drop onto his tongue. "She fought the Pretender and yet he lives, or at least no one's found his body. There are whispers at court that perhaps his escape was not accidental."

"That's absurd." I shook my head in amused disgust. "A clumsy attempt to impugn her reputation."

"Clumsy? Certainly, but even a poorly fashioned arrow can find the bullseye. Our Anointed Captain is not just being exiled; she is being tested. Olversahl is notorious as a nest of endlessly feuding merchant families and Ascarlian sympathisers, as is much of the Fjord Geld. They call Duke Huelvic a traitor, but in truth he was but one of five claimants to the duchy, all of whom are still drawing breath and you can wager they'll be even more keen to press their cause now he's dead. Olversahl is the largest port in the Geld and long considered the lynchpin upon which the whole duchy either topples or stands. Ensuring it doesn't fall into chaos will be no mean feat. Holding it for the king will be a triumph. But, if the Anointed Captain manages it, who then could gainsay her loyalty?"

"So's Olversahl's a bit of a shithole then?" Toria enquired. "Was hoping it'd be rich, at least in taverns and decent drink, I mean."

In pockets and merchants' locks worth picking, you mean, I surmised but didn't say, even though I doubted Wilhum gave a fart for our criminal inclinations.

"Actually, my dear," Wilhum said, "it's often referred to as the Jewel of the Geld. It's very old, you see, having changed hands between various kings and lords many times. The Sister Queens of Ascarlia held it for three centuries before King Tomas's great-grandfather wrested it from their grasp. There's a lot of old architecture to see, if you're so inclined. Some of it's said to even date back before the Scourge. The library is particularly interesting. The volume of books under its roof is quite remarkable, I must say. As are the statues of the Ascarlian gods hewn into the base of Mount Halthir, though perhaps don't let the Supplicants see you admiring them overmuch."

"There's a library there?" I asked.

"Yes, and fairly crammed with all manner of ancient tomes it is too. Fjord Gelders are a strange lot. They'll whip a man for murder but spare him the noose if he pays a blood tithe to his victim's family. But, should that man desecrate a book, they'll tie him to a tree and open his guts to provide carrion for the crows, and no amount of tithing will save him."

He upended the flask once again, a frustrated grimace marring his brow when no more drops consented to fall onto his tongue. His gaze took on the preoccupied, constantly roving cast that indicated his thirst had returned. I found I didn't like Wilhum sober; it made him far less talkative.

Grinning, I put an arm across his shoulder, guiding him away from the stern. "Why don't we go and find that sailor? I've got a few sheks to spare. Then you can tell me more about the contents of this library."

The port of Olversahl lay on the northern bank of an inlet known as Aeric's Fjord, positioned where the channel narrowed but remained deep enough to accommodate the draught of a ship. The port itself consisted of a dense mass of construction fringing the base of a huge mountainous slab of granite, the famed Mount Halthir Wilhum had spoken of. It ascended in grey, sheer-sided majesty to a height of at least a thousand feet. A single narrow road snaked around the mountain's southern flank, providing the only landward approach to the port. It also explained why the town itself lacked a protective wall, since only the most suicidal commander would attack along such a constricted avenue of approach and the harbour was too small to allow for a seaborne invasion.

"Really taken a liking to this soldiering shit, haven't you?" Toria commented after I pointed out this military reality.

"A man should educate himself in his profession," I replied. "Chosen or not."

Surveying the approaching town, I was struck by the novelty of a place so different from anything in the Shavine Marches. A parade of windmills, standing higher than any I had seen in the southern lands, lined a tall dyke that curved from the harbour all the way around to the northern flank of the mountain. Thanks to Wilhum's inebriated tutelage, I knew these and the harbour to be the twinned sources of the port's wealth. The Fjord Geld had plentiful fisheries and grazing land for goats and sheep, but little facility for growing crops, especially wheat. Grain was shipped in to be milled and then carted off to villages and towns who would pay for it with wool. This cargo would in turn fill the holds of ships ferrying it off to feed the looms of the southern duchies. It was a fruitful arrangement that had ensured Olversahl's unusual longevity, but also its status as a prize to be endlessly fought over.

However, it was not the mills that captured my attention, but the jumble of rooftops and towers beyond, particularly the large rectangular structure with a sloping roof. The Library of King Aeric, apparently some long-dead hero of Gelder legend, was the second-largest building in the port besides the much more recent and considerably taller spire that marked the Shrine to Martyr Athil.

"You think you'll find it there?" Toria asked, voice low and careful to avoid mention of the words "treasure" or "Lachlan". "The lore we'll need to find it, I mean?"

And a good deal more besides, I thought, feeling the weight of the Sack Witch's tome beneath my jerkin. I had concealed it in a leather pouch and bound it tight against my skin, away from the disapproving eyes of the Supplicants and safe from the depredations of rain and wind. In truth, though it shamed me, I guarded the Caerith book with even greater care than Sihlda's testament.

"Wilhum says it's better stocked than even the Covenant library at Athiltor," I murmured back. We crowded with the rest of our troop on the foredeck, Supplicant Ofihla among them, and it would be best if any important conversation didn't reach her oversharp ears.

"And once you've found it?" Toria's voice, though quiet, was loaded with meaning.

I gave her a reassuring smile. "Then it will be time for us to go in search of our just reward."

"Regardless of any other obligation?" She turned her weighty gaze towards Evadine. The captain stood at the prow of the ship, clad in her fine, unadorned armour, I assumed with the intent of making the appropriate impression when we landed. Watching the wind whip her hair into a dark flame, face serene and impassive despite the gusts of salt water the wind scraped from the sea, I felt certain this moment would be the one future illuminators and artists would choose when it came time to immortalise the Anointed Captain. I knew I was witnessing history today, the dawn of a new chapter in her story, for here she would find either triumph and glory, or defeat and disgrace. Perhaps even death. Despite her recent coolness towards me, the desire to keep witnessing her epic was strong, a compulsion to be part of something larger, something of inarguable importance. But it was her story, not mine.

"Regardless of everything," I said, shifting my gaze from the captain, although I found it difficult.

The company's arrival was greeted on the wharf by a dozen strong party of well-dressed folk and fifty men-at-arms clad in livery of silver grey and dark blue. I assumed these colours marked them as soldiers of the duke of the Fjord Geld, whoever he might be at this juncture. The well-dressed civilians were headed by a tall, broad-shouldered man with long ash-blond hair and a beard to match. The smile he offered at Evadine as she descended the gangway to the wharf made Wilhum's charm seem a paltry candle in comparison to a roaring blaze.

"Well met, my lady! Or is it Anointed Captain?" He let out a full, hearty laugh as he bowed, the other local luminaries arrayed at his back doing the same. "I, Elderman Maritz Fohlvast—" the blond man boomed on without waiting for a reply "—most loyal servant of Good King Tomas, bid you welcome to Olversahl."

Evadine returned his bow with a tight smile. "Aspirant Captain Evadine Courlain, my lord elderman."

"Not a lord, my lady," Fohlvast replied with another laugh. "Merely a humble merchant called to governance by my fellow citizens in these troubled times."

"No longer, my lord." Evadine presented my copy of Sir Althus's scroll. "Our most gracious king, in recognition of your tireless and courageous efforts in asserting his just rights over this duchy, has named you Sir Maritz Fohlvast, Knight of the Realm and Defender of the Mid-Fjord. You will find relevant grant of rights and lands listed here. I come with the king's warrant to submit my company to the defence of this port and its people."

In my experience, any man who ever called himself humble invariably proved to be the opposite, as the newly minted knight demonstrated when he took the scroll from Evadine's hand. He managed to not quite snatch it away but was quick in unfurling it. His eyes scanned the contents with a look I recognised full well: the bright, narrow focus unique to the truly greedy.

"I am honoured beyond measure," he told Evadine with a creditable attempt at putting a choke to his voice. "May the Martyrs guide my path to ensure my worthiness. Now—" Fohlvast straightened, extending a hand to the other civilians present "—allow me to introduce my fellow loyal eldermen, then we shall adjourn to the Hall of the Merchants' Council where a fine feast has been prepared in welcome—"

"I have no time for feasts, my lord," Evadine cut in, her tone polite but also clear in its refusal. "Nor introductions. Such things can wait until I have conducted a thorough inspection of the port's defences and seen to the disposition of my company. I trust suitable accommodation has been arranged?"

I saw the elderman's face twitch a little with the sting of recognising superior authority, never an easy thing for a man of his character. But he recovered well, summoning another hearty laugh and bowing once again. "Of course, Captain. As befits a true sword of the Covenant, eh? The Shrine to Martyr Athil has more than sufficient space for your fine soldiers since most of the clerics took it upon themselves to flee at the dawn of our recent disturbances. In fact, only one Supplicant and a few lay folk opted to stay and secure the shrine's relics."

Evadine's face darkened. "A very poor state of affairs. One that will not go unreported to the Luminants' Council. And the defences?"

Fohlvast laughed again, less hearty for possessing some genuine amusement. "Of course. We'll tour them now, if it please you. Though I should caution you, there really isn't much to see."

The locals called it the Gate Wall, a thick, sturdy construction of granite blocks stretching from the sheer face of the cliff at the base of Mount Halthir to the rocky shoreline, standing forty feet high and perhaps a hundred and fifty paces long. A battlement stretched along its top behind a series of crenellations on either side of a watchtower positioned above the only gate. The doors were fashioned from ancient oak buttressed by iron brackets, and further protected by a huge iron portcullis that could be raised or lowered as required. Beyond lay the road, curving away into the mist drifting in from the fjord. As we followed the elderman around the wall's meagre list of features, a few carts trundled through the gate but not so many as might be expected in such a famously bustling port.

"One hundred and eighty-six years ago," Fohlvast told Evadine with conspicuous pride. "That's the last time some fool attempted to assault this wall. An outcast bandit who styled himself a king. His army, such as it was, fled in short order and his head sat on a spike atop the tower for a year or more until it rotted away."

"Too thick and strong for even the mightiest siege engine to breach," Sergeant Swain commented, running an approving hand over the weathered granite of the battlement. He nodded to the road beyond. "And there's only enough ground to allow a single company to scale the walls at any given time. Five hundred troops could hold off ten times their number here."

"Which raises an important question, my lord," Evadine said, turning to the elderman. "What exactly is the strength of our enemy?"

"I regret that it's impossible to say with any accuracy." Fohlvast shrugged his impressive shoulders in apology. "The ducal companies numbered close to a thousand men-at-arms in better times, but they fractured according to their sympathies and blood ties when we seized the port for the Crown. We counted near a hundred dead in the streets once the fighting was over. The rest fled with the traitors who sold themselves like whores to the Pretender, Scourge take them. Currently there are three hundred or so loyal soldiers left to us."

Evadine's gaze slipped to me, receiving a fractional shake of the head in response. As per her instruction before we departed the ship, I had made a careful count of anyone bearing arms during our journey through the docks and the streets until we reached this wall. As my gaze sought out soldiery, it also tracked across more than a few sullen and resentful faces, albeit downcast and careful not to catch the elderman's eye. I also noted the many burnt-out houses and shops, clearly victims of recent vandalism. Olversahl was plainly a very troubled place. My count of those who could reasonably be described as soldiers amounted to one hundred and eight, making it unlikely there would be anything like Fohlvast's stated number in the town garrison. Perhaps his loyalist revolt hadn't been as popular with the ducal soldiery as he claimed.

"Our enemy will surely have more," he went on. "The rebel lords were all old blood with strong family connections among the folk in the deeper Geld. Many of them went off to join the Pretender's doomed march south, but far from all."

"But still no clear notion of their strength?" Evadine pressed. "Has any reconnaissance been conducted to ascertain their location, at least?"

"Any patrol that ventures more than a few miles beyond this wall is likely never to return." He gestured to the lone cart making its way towards the gate. "You see how paltry our trade has become. Those wool merchants who continue to bring us custom do so at considerable risk. Rebels haunt the roads and there are few among us with the knowledge of where in the wilds they make their dens. My people know the sea and the coast. The deeper Geld, however, is another matter."

"How fortunate then that there is one in my company who possesses just such knowledge." Evadine's lips formed a faint smile as she turned to regard Wilhum. "Do you not, Trooper Dornmahl?"

I had wondered why she'd ordered him to accompany us during this inspection. Now it became clear as Wilhum gave a very small grin in response. "It's been some years, Captain," he said. "But I suppose I know the Geld as well as any southerner could claim to."

"Trooper Dornmahl's mother hailed from the Mid-Geld, you see?" Evadine told Fohlvast. "He spent a good deal of his youth here before familial duty called him back to the duchies. He will conduct our reconnaissance." Her smile faded as she turned to me, birthing a dispiriting plummet to the guts when I divined her next order. "And our scribe shall accompany him, since he possesses the keenest eye for numbers in our ranks."

She held my gaze for a fraction longer than I felt necessary, all humour gone from her bearing. I discerned that some form of punishment was being administered but couldn't identify a crime worthy of such chastisement. She certainly hadn't liked it when I'd called on the company to back her against Althus's knights; that much had been clear. But, while it might explain her recent mood, did it merit risking my hide in this manner? It seemed poor reward for her saviour. Or was the fact that I had saved her life at the heart of this, the resentment of a burdensome debt?

"I trust you have some suitable mounts?" Evadine enquired of Fohlvast. "Fleet but sturdy?"

"My personal stable is at your disposal, Captain," he assured her, inclining his head.

"Excellent." She turned back to Wilhum and me. "Set off as soon as you're able, and don't tarry over the task. I need to know what we're facing here."

"If I may, Captain," I said as she began to turn away, receiving a stern stare in response that brought a cough to my throat. "I . . . can't ride. Not with any skill, that is."

She pursed her lips, then nodded to Wilhum. "Trooper Dornmahl will teach you. It shouldn't take more than a day or two. Then you can set off." Her eyes narrowed and her voice grew hard. "Unless you would care to wait and seek out a Caerith witch to cast a protective spell or somesuch?"

The acid tone with which she uttered the word "witch" made me swallow any further protest and lower my head in acquiescence. So, that was it. Some overly inquisitive eye had seen us at the Sack Witch's camp. Or Supplicant Delric had correctly deduced the true reason for Brewer's recovery.

"See to it," she snapped, jerking her head at the stairs before turning her attention back to the elderman. "Now, my lord, with your permission, I should like to inspect the garrison. Then we shall proceed to the stores."

CHAPTER THIRTY-FOUR

Wilhum described the horse he chose for me as a hunter rather than a charger, though to my novice eye it possessed more than enough bulk to make a warhorse. He was a handsome, black-coated beast with a placid nature according to Wilhum's expert judgement, though that didn't prevent him from casting me off his back when the opportunity arose.

"Holding the reins too tight," Wilhum said after one particularly bruising encounter with the ground. My lessons in horsemanship took place in the small paddock alongside Elderman Fohlvast's stables. It hadn't surprised me to find he possessed the largest house in Olversahl, positioned as close to the centre of the town as the grounds of the shrine and the library would allow. It was a recent construction of red brick rather than the locally quarried granite, each brick imported at considerable expense according to the aged stable master.

"Old saying in this town," he told us, his much-wrinkled face creasing further as he gave a conspiratorial wink. "No Fohlvast ever spent a shek where a sovereign would do."

"Loosen your grip," Wilhum added as I got to my feet. "You wouldn't like someone continually tugging at a bit shoved into your mouth and neither does he. And try to relax. You're too stiff. It makes him nervous."

"Not everyone grew up in a castle with tutors in the knightly arts," I grumbled. As I hauled myself back into the saddle, the stallion, who the stable master had named Karnic, after the Ascarlian god of the hunt, let out a resigned huff. Two days spent at this and I had succeeded in walking him back and forth across the paddock. My slip had been the result of attempting my first trot.

"You wouldn't have liked my tutor," Wilhum told me. His eyes bore the reddened look of one suffering the effects of a night's drinking while the way he worked his mouth told of an undiminished thirst for more. Liquor clearly had a hold on him now and I wondered if our mission might be Evadine's attempt to spare him further unhealthy indulgence, at least for a while.

"Redmaine, his name was," he went on with an air of nostalgic remembrance. "He was too low-born to ever gain a title, but he'd spent half his life at war or tourney and the rest of it teaching what he knew to upstart whelps, as he liked to call his students. If you fell from your horse under his eye it would have meant a birched arse doused in salt water. Worse if you dropped your sword."

"Your father let a commoner beat you?"

"Of course. It's how such things are done. Knights are made, Master Scribe, not born. My father had his arse birched more than a few times as a lad, so why spare mine? Come." He turned his own mount about, displaying what I now recognised as enviable skill in the way the beast seemed to dance at his touch. "Let's try it again."

In all, it required five days of bruising lessons before I could be counted on to ride a horse for any length of time. I took some comfort from Evadine's forbearance in allowing the lessons to proceed for so long, concluding that she didn't want me to perish in the wilds of the Geld. However, her treatment of me remained one of curt authority and I was permitted in her presence only as long as it took to approve the relevant entries in the company ledgers. At first, I had borne her coldness with a cheerful demeanour and assiduous attention to my scribing duties. But, as the days wore on and her mood failed to warm, I couldn't help but nurture a growing ball of resentment. Our scales were balanced now, so what did I owe her?

In addition to the basics of riding, Wilhum also took it upon himself to school me in the knightly form of combat. "You can't wield a halberd from the saddle," he said, tossing me a sheathed longsword I had seen Supplicant Ofihla wearing on her back after the Traitors' Field. Our fighting clerics took no part in looting the corpses for coin or trinkets, but their restraint didn't extend to fallen weaponry. For reasons unknown she had apparently consented to giving up her prize, which surprised me for even I could tell it was a finely made blade.

"I've never used a sword in my life," I told Wilhum, casting an admiring but doubtful eye over the steel as I drew it from the scabbard. The metal was clean and bright for the most part, marred here and there by cloudy patches, the edge possessed of the slight unevenness that came from grinding away the depredations of combat. Its unfortunate noble owner had evidently been a man of some experience, and wealthy with it.

"That's to the good," Wilhum replied. "Means I won't have to cure you of any bad habits."

So, each day before taking to the saddle he would tutor me in swordplay, a more complicated business than might be expected. The sword, I learned quickly, was more than just an elongated cleaver. Using it well required a marriage of skill and strength rather than the mix of viciousness and brute force that had served me so well in my only battle. Much of my initial education was spent developing the particular concordance of muscle and sinew required to swing it around as I attempted to copy the various strokes Wilhum demonstrated. The reason for his athletic frame became obvious as he used his own longsword to describe a series of elegant arcs with seemingly effortless fluency. My efforts to do the same left me sweating and aching in previously untaxed muscles.

"Wield it with one hand in the saddle and two on the ground. And never forget the value of a thick glove." Wilhum demonstrated his meaning by extending his sword, holding it out laterally across his chest, one mail-covered hand on the handle, the other grasping the blade. "Whereupon, what was a sword becomes a quarterstaff." He extended one leg, raising the blade above his head in a parry. "Now a spear." He shifted his hips, bringing up the swordpoint to jab within an inch of my face. "Then a mace." Stepping forward, he levered the weapon, bringing the brass cylinder that formed the pommel round, halting it just before it would have smashed into my jaw.

He smiled as I flinched, stepping back. "You try. Then we'll see if you can draw it while in the saddle."

Due to my training in horsemanship and swordplay, all this equestrian nonsense meant that it wasn't until the afternoon before our intended journey that I managed to visit King Aeric's Library, only to be denied access to the riches within.

"This is not your place, southlander," the larger of the two guards on the doors told me. He and his companion made a contrast to the other soldiers in this town by being both properly attired and well armed. Their livery was also different to the ducal men-at-arms, featuring a white sash embroidered with the angular script that adorned so many buildings and statues here. They held themselves with accustomed readiness and one look at each stern, resolute face told me any attempt at bribery would be pointless. It appeared that this town put great stock in protecting its books.

"Only townsfolk of good standing and scholars bearing a pass signed by the elderman's council are permitted access," the larger guard told me in response to a polite request as to why I couldn't enter. He narrowed his eyes in a doubtful scowl. "You a scholar, are you?"

"A scribe," I replied. "Company scribe to Aspirant Captain Evadine Courlain, in point of fact."

His scowl lessened at this, but only a little. "Still can't come in," he said, putting a meaningful hand on his sword. "Now, get you gone and stick to the shrine precincts in future. Not everyone's as welcoming as us."

Never one to pursue a hopeless cause, I inclined my head in civil acceptance and turned to descend the broad steps that led to the library's doors. These had either been crafted by masons with little regard for comfortable proportions or were the product of an age when folk were considerably taller, for they required a good deal of concentration to navigate without falling on one's posterior. My pre-occupation with making a successful descent was such that I failed to notice when a slender figure paused nearby.

"I thought you had no use for old words on old paper."

I stopped, turning to regard a young woman with the blonde, pleated hair typical of most females here. Her eyes were a piercing blue that shone with a mix of amusement and recognition as she looked me over. She wore a plain brown dress under a grey shawl, but, like the library guards, also bore an embroidered white sash across her chest.

"Cheated the hangman, I see," she went on. "And now you follow an Anointed Captain, no less. A strange fate for one who once mocked the beliefs of a naive girl."

It was the mention of the hangman and the twinkle of amused reproach in her gaze that banished my puzzlement with the requisite memory. That night in the forest after Deckin killed the Ascarlian with the sword, the night I had come between Erchel and his prey. "Berrine," I said.

"You remember." Her smile broadened and she descended one of the overlarge steps to come closer, peering at my face. "Not quite sure how I remembered you. Your nose was a good deal straighter then, I think."

"That it was." I gave a formal bow. "Alwyn Scribe, of Covenant Company."

"A scribe and a soldier both? You were odd back then. Seems you're odder still. What happened to your leader, the big fellow with the beard? I always had a sense I would be hearing more of him."

His name was Deckin. I watched him die for his ambitions. "No longer among the living," I said. "And his legend lives on in the south, after a fashion."

She moved her slim shoulders in an affable shrug. "Skeinweld got the fame he wanted too, after our return to the Geld. My former comrades spun such a tale of his bravery and death at the hands of a southern monster. I found it all too sickening to endure. When they began their recent insurrection, I wanted no part of it."

"No more *Skard-ryken* then?" I asked. "No more Altvar?"

"There comes a point in life where childish notions must be abandoned, or one is condemned to a fool's existence. Either that, or end up cast into the fjord lashed to a boulder, which is where you'll find the *Skard-ryken* these days."

She paused, her gaze shifting from me to the library entrance. "Told you to get lost, did they?"

"I'm just a poor scribe seeking to better his mind. Sadly, that appears to be insufficient reason to grant me entry." I looked closer at her sash and the strange lettering stitched into the fabric. "I take it this is some mark of distinction?"

"The Ribbon of Learning signifies that I am a trusted servant of the elderman's council and the treasured Library of King Aeric, which is their most sacred charge. I work here, most days anyways, when I'm not checking the accounts of various merchants to ensure they're paying their due in taxes."

"A tax collector?" I winced again. "In the Shavine Marches, such folk are often less popular than outlaws or heretics."

"It's a trade with certain advantages. Besides, I merely count what is owed. The actual collecting is left to the eldermen and their guards." She glanced again at the library doors before stepping closer. "Forgive me my suspicions, Alwyn Scribe of Covenant Company, but I'd wager you're after more from this place than just an improved mind."

I gave a tight smile and retreated a step, deciding it was time to leave. This woman was a far less closed and resentful version of her younger self, not to mention highly pleasing to the eye, but her irksome gift for insight remained as sharp as ever. "I've detained you long enough . . ."

"I can get you in." She angled her head, mouth bowed in a faintly amused curve as her keen, unblinking eyes gauged my reaction. "If you would like."

I paused, letting what little I knew of her churn in my mind, weighing danger against reward with accustomed swiftness. *She's far too friendly. And if coin is her object, a soul so clever would have little trouble fleecing the merchants of this place in return for a smaller tax bill.* So, what she wanted I couldn't say, but what I wanted was so near at hand and, I reckoned, worth a risk or two.

"Such an offer is both generous and welcome," I said. "But a favour done raises the question of what might be expected in return."

"Just an honest answer to a single question." Her smile returned as she stepped back, giving a very slight incline of her head towards the library's west-facing wall. "There's a set of steps leading down to a small door. Be there one hour past the midnight bell."

"And your question?" I asked as she resumed her ascent of the oversized steps.

"Isn't it obvious?" She laughed, striding upward with practised ease. "I want to know what you're looking for."

CHAPTER THIRTY-FIVE

It was Ayin's habit to sing as she cooked, her voice high but far from grating. Her songs were sometimes pleasing renditions of old staples like "The Ballad of the Hawk, the Hound and the Lady", but more often than not consisted of her own compositions. These ranged from wordless melodies to more cryptic verse forged from phrases pushed into concordance for no other reason than that they rhymed.

"The Gelder-man raised his axe," she sang, as she chopped onions for the stewpot, "And the weaver woman twisted flax. A man rose high in a sailing boat, While a huntsman skinned a fine old goat . . . "

She had taken on the cooking duties for our troop during the march to Farinsahl, a chore I had performed for a time until popular opinion saw me usurped in favour of Ayin's more flavoursome concoctions. Her songs tended to summon smiles among the audience of hungry soldiers awaiting their evening feed, although there was always one exception.

"It was her," Toria said, brow heavy and eyes dark as she stared at Ayin. "In case you were wondering."

"Her?" I enquired, although I had a fair notion of what she meant.

"She followed us." Toria's brow creased as her frown deepened. "That night we took Brewer to the Sack Witch. Simply can't keep her mouth shut around the Anointed Captain. Now you're in the shit and getting packed off to the wilds and she's singing songs."

"Thought as much." My offhand tone drew Toria's dark gaze to me.

"Squealers don't deserve second chances. Leastways, not where I'm from."

I watched Ayin consign the onions to the pot before turning her attention to the meat, a large side of pork, the fat running from its slashed sides hissing as it fell into the fire in a slick cascade. Her song became wordless as she turned the spit and sprinkled a mix of salt and sage onto its upper side, the resultant aroma bringing an appreciative growl from the stomachs of all present.

"She's better than she was," I said. "Her mind is less busy with the urge to do . . . what she used to do. Instead, it's filled with love, or worship depending on how you look at it. Of course she told the captain. Can't blame a believer for saying prayers, can you?" Seeing no softening in Toria's features, I added, "Leave her alone. I mean it. If I return from tomorrow's excursion and find any harm's come to her, we're done, Toria."

I could have said more, added a reminder about my weakness for nurturing unresolved grudges, but the threat of ending our friendship seemed to suffice. "Was only going to suggest a beating," Toria grumped, turning away.

No, you weren't. I left it unsaid. With Toria, it was always better not to poke at a cooling fire. Also, she'd made a relevant point. Ayin, for all her confusion of mind, remained a disturbingly observant person.

"You still got any of that stuff the sailor sold us?" I asked. "Not the rum and brandy; the elixir he said was good for calming the guts."

In truth, the elixir had little effect when it came to alleviating my seasickness, but it did result in several hours of blissfully oblivious sleep. So much so that Ofihla had had to kick me awake the morning after I took a small, experimental sip.

"Still got most of it," Toria said, fishing in her bundle for the bottle. "Didn't like the way it made me feel."

"Then you'd best eat elsewhere tonight."

I waited until Ayin began to sing a more familiar song, "The Ferryman's Wake", a lively, jocular tune that never failed to rouse the rest of the troop to join in. The shared laughter that followed provided distraction enough for me to tip the entire contents of Toria's bottle into the stewpot without drawing undue notice.

When all the eating and merriment were done, we drifted back to our billets in the Shrine to Martyr Athil. Although young by the standards of most local architecture, the shrine had the chilly atmosphere common to old buildings, its generally unwelcoming ambience heightened by the fact that it hadn't been constructed as a barracks. For the most part, Covenant Company bedded down beneath the vaulted, echoing roof of the main chapel. Thanks to our unannounced but now customary role as guards to the Anointed Captain, Ofihla's troop was consigned to the rooms adjoining the Aspirant's chambers where she had established her private quarters. The shrine's sole remaining cleric, a stoop-backed old Supplicant, who I suspected had stayed when the others fled because he reasoned it unlikely he would have survived the voyage, had insisted Evadine take the largest room by dint of her seniority in clerical ranking.

Having surreptitiously grabbed a meal from one of the neighbouring troops, I lay in my bunk without suffering the effects of the sailor's sleep-inducing elixir. Toria had ignored my advice and slipped immediately into slumber, quickly followed by the rest of the troop. Even so, after counting off the minutes following the chime of the midnight bell, I was careful to ensure Ayin was truly and soundly asleep before making a soft-footed exit. The shrine was guarded but, as is ever the case with sentries, their gaze was focused outward and it wasn't too difficult to slip away unnoticed.

Once clear of the shrine, I found a shadowed corner and paused to pull on my boots. I made hurried progress to the library, keeping to the gloomiest alleyways for fear of encountering the elderman's patrols. For a fellow who claimed to embody the will of his townsfolk, Fohlvast appeared greatly concerned with watching them closely, especially after dark. I was obliged to hide from three separate patrols during a relatively short journey.

Finding the required descending steps and small door was not difficult, although I discovered it to be firmly locked when testing the handle. Suspecting a trap, I crouched at the base of the steps, a hand on my knife. *She was far too friendly.* However, the soft clatter of a carefully worked lock quelled my suspicions and I quickly sheathed the blade as the door opened to reveal Berrine. She wore much the same half-amused smile from before, her eyes catching a yellow gleam from the small lantern she carried.

"Come on, then," she told me in a cheerful whisper, stepping aside and inclining her head. "No dawdling. If you're caught in here, it'll be a gut-opening for both of us."

The prospect of such a fate seemed to amuse her further, a soft laugh escaping her lips as I hurried into the gloomy interior. Old instincts made me flatten myself against the wall of the passage inside, eyes searching the shadows that danced in the wayward light from Berrine's lantern as she locked the door.

"Don't worry," she said in a mock-dramatic whisper. "We're quite alone, I assure you."

"No guards on the main door?" I asked, following her silhouette along the passage to a spiral staircase.

"Two, as always. But they're accustomed to me working the late hours. I often sleep here as well. It pays to be known as a diligent soul, don't you find?"

Her tone held the taunting note of a joke shared between those of the same profession. I had already marked her as a practised deceiver, but was she a thief too?

I followed as she ascended, the confines of the stairwell abruptly giving way to a cavernous space in which the glow of her lantern appeared little more than an ember. Straight, tall shadows rose on all sides, ascending from floor to distant ceiling in monolithic grandeur. As Berrine led me towards the nearest monolith I recognised it as a huge stack of shelves, her light playing over a long row of leather-bound books. Looking up I saw that what at first appeared to be a complex web woven by some form of giant spider was in fact a network of ladders and walkways stretching between each of the vast shelf stacks.

"Welcome to the Library of King Aeric," Berinne said. Her tone had changed, losing much of its humour and her gaze was shrewd and appraising as it studied my rapt, wonderstruck features. "I can see we share a common interest," she added.

"How many?" I breathed. Even in the meagre light, the array of books seemed endless.

"In truth, an exact count is impossible." Berrine stooped a little to play her lantern's glow over the lowest tier of the nearest stack. The binding it revealed was ancient and flaking, the degraded skin of a dying book. "Old books wither and new ones are added. We copy the oldest, of course, but inevitably some have been lost over the years. Others languish in our vaults awaiting resurrection that may never come. It is the way with any archive. Like memory, a measure of it will always fade."

She straightened and stepped closer to me, causing me to blink in alarm as she put the lantern close to my face. Her humour had all but gone now, however the shrewd insight blazed bright in her eyes. "Which brings me to my singular question, Alwyn Scribe. What are you looking for here? And please do not insult me with a lie. Not if you want my help, that is."

My gaze flicked up at the dark bulk of the stack towering above. Just one of many in this place, a maze of knowledge impossible to navigate without expert assistance.

"Yes," Berrine murmured, reading my thoughts with apparent ease. "You'll never find it, whatever it may be, without me. I have climbed these shelves since childhood. It was here that I learned the older, darker legends of the Altvar, also the truth of our history rather than the nonsense spouted by the likes of Elderman Fohlvast. My parents were merchants, loyalists who followed the Covenant and cast me out when I took up with the *Skard-ryken*, but I never felt any love from them in any case. They grubbed for money while I always thirsted for knowledge. These books are my true parents and if you want their help, you'll need to be honest."

I met her gaze again, knowing lies would not suffice for one so sharp of insight. "Lachlan's hoard," I said.

Berrine blinked and let out a faintly disgusted sigh before stepping back, the sudden removal of the lantern's glow leaving me in a void until I caught sight of her retreating silhouette. "How utterly mundane," she said. "Just another treasure seeker."

"I have sound reason to believe it real," I said, hurrying to catch up. "Deckin had a notion of where to find it, and he was not a man given to fancy."

"A claim made by gullible idiots the world over." Berrine's voice echoed loud as she moved with a purposeful stride, leading me down one channel between the stacks before turning to traverse another. "Do you imagine you're the first deluded soul to turn up here convinced he's found a clue to the location of some long-hidden treasure or other? If it's not Lachlan's hoard it's King Thaelric's golden axe. Don't you think, after the passage of so many centuries, that if such things could be found they would have by now?"

"Things get lost. You said so yourself."

She sighed again and came to an abrupt halt beside a wrought-iron ladder ascending a cliff-like stack. "That I did. I also promised you access in return for answering my question, which you have done, disappointing though your answer is. Three tiers up—" she inclined her head at the stairs "—twenty paces to the right. Every book, map, scroll or letter in this library that ever made mention of Lachlan's hoard. We compiled it decades ago, in return for a considerable fee, at the behest of a southland duke convinced he could find the fabled hoard that had eluded so many others." She gave me an empty smile. "He failed. Have at it as you will, Alwyn Scribe." She set her lantern down and turned to go. "I can only give you until dusk, so work fast."

I spared only a brief glance of consternation for the ladder, knowing that a scant few hours would be grossly insufficient for any meaningful research, before picking up the lantern and hurrying after her. "I can promise a share in the spoils . . . "

"So does every gold-maddened fool who fetches up here. If you'll excuse me, I have a rather fascinating account from the First Reign of the Sister Queens to transcribe." She turned another corner, causing me to collide with a stone buttress as I attempted to follow.

I swallowed a curse, rubbing a bruised arm and calling after her rapidly retreating shadow, "There's something else." Berrine slowed a little but only consented to halt when I added, "Something even more fascinating, I think you'll find."

Berrine's footsteps were slow and her face drawn in a sceptical grimace as she emerged from the shadow. "What something might that be?"

I found I had to quell a spasm of reluctance as I reached into my jerkin. Revealing it to another felt like a betrayal, also a danger. But what choice was there?

A soft hiss escaped her lips as I drew the book free of the fabric binding it to my side, smothering the urge to snatch it back when she took it from my hand. Her fingers traced over the swirling abstract pattern of the binding before opening it, her sibilant breath becoming a soft laugh of delight as her eyes grew wide, drinking in the revealed text.

"Caerith script," she murmured. "The archaic form, no less." Her eyes flicked up at me. "Where did you get this?"

"From a witch," I said, seeing little point in deceit now. "Can you read it?"

"A few symbols, a couple of phrases. See here." She proffered the book, her finger tracing along a particular line of text. "'And in a grain of sand may you find a world entire.'"

I frowned. "What does it mean?"

"It's one of the more commonly inscribed phrases to be found in old Caerith. As to its meaning, no one has ever been entirely sure, except the Caerith themselves, of course, and they have always displayed a violent dislike of visiting scholars. Those who travel beyond the borders of their wastes are a tight-lipped bunch to be sure, unless you have coin to trade for enchanted trinkets."

Berrine closed the book with a snap, placing it back into my hands, her smile fully returned. It was far warmer now, less amused but lit with something I hadn't seen in a woman's face for a very long time. "Why seek treasure when you already have one?" she asked, finger tracing over the book's cover before finding my hand, where it lingered.

"It may surprise you to hear," I said, "that my recruitment into Covenant Company was not exactly willing. I've seen one battle and will be glad to never see another. Lachlan's hoard, if it can be found, will be my passage to a far more peaceful life."

Berrine arched an eyebrow, pursing her lips in consideration. "You'll trade this for a chance at some fabled pile of loot?"

"No." My voice was sharp with refusal and I forced a calmer note into it as I went on. "But I'll let you copy it, perhaps use what knowledge resides here to translate it, if you can."

In truth, I was asking for two favours rather than a trade. My debt to the Sack Witch required I unlock the knowledge in this book, not that Berrine knew that. Her hunger for it was plain and I suspected she would have paid a considerable sum to own it. Would she settle for the chance to make a copy?

"I assume," Berrine said, "this man you spoke of, the one not given to fancy, had some notion of where to look for the hoard?"

"The Shavine coast, so I'm told."

"That's more of a clue than your fellow treasure seekers possess, at least. Come on." Her finger slipped from my hand as she brushed past me. "I've gained enough insight over the years to sort the fanciful from the promising."

Climbing the ladder felt like a perilous business in the gloom, although Berrine ascended with the unconscious rapidity of one who could navigate this entire library blindfolded. She held the lantern at a helpful angle as I nervously clambered from the ladder to the metal scaffold that stretched along the third tier, then turned its glow upon the requisite tomes.

"Although Lachlan's story has been greatly embellished over time," she told me, her voice reminding me a good deal of Sihlda's tutoring tone, "there's no doubt he actually existed. Here—" she played the lantern over a row of tall but narrow books bound in red leather "—we have copies of the sheriff's records dating from his most active periods of thievery and murder. The spelling of his name varies and it's clear he employed several aliases, but his habit of collecting rather than spending his spoils is frequently mentioned. However, there are only two contemporary sources that make mention of his famed hoard."

She passed the light to me and stood on tiptoe to retrieve a wooden scroll tube, twisting the lid free to extract the contents. "A letter from the Duke of the Shavine Marches to King Arthin the Third," she said, holding up a document consisting of one page and a few lines of text. "It's dated shortly after Lachlan's disappearance and refers to a lost missive from the king enquiring as to the whereabouts of the outlaw's hoard. It appears Lachlan stole a good deal of tax revenue over the years and the king was keen for its return. Sadly, the duke clearly had no notion of where it might be."

Berrine sifted through the parchment and held up another document, this one consisting of several pages. "A fulsome account from one Sir Dalric Strethmohr, then Champion to the King, prepared two years after Lachlan's demise. It appears King Arthin dispatched his most trusted knight on an errand to find the outlaw's treasure. The poor man spent months scouring the Marches and beyond for any clue that might reveal its whereabouts. He lists over three dozen of Lachlan's former associates put under torture 'to compel honest testimony in place of churlish lies'. All without success, although before the rack snapped his spine, one did make mention of a smuggler of Lachlan's acquaintance."

"A smuggler," I said. "One who would know well the hiding places on the Shavine coast."

"Quite so. Unfortunately, it seems the fellow was inconsiderate enough to die before he could cough up the name of said smuggler." She waved the pages at the other books on the shelf. "The rest of this consists of various researches and musings on the possible location of the hoard, some of it scholarly, most of it nonsense. Wealthy folk have beggared themselves searching for it, spending their lives in hopeless pursuit of something that may well not exist."

I surveyed the other books, some thick, most small and all dusty with neglect. "There's no other mention of the mysterious smuggler among all this?"

"A great deal of conjecture only. Smuggling was even more rife in those days and there are plenty of candidates among those who rose high in the trade. But, as is often the case with outlaws, parsing fact from rumour and legend to identify a real person is often impossible."

I grunted in disappointment but little surprise. Finding the hoard had always been an overindulged fantasy, something to keep Toria at my side more than a true ambition. Still, as the months passed I had begun to wonder. "So," I said, playing a finger across the dusted row of books, "no clue here to where the Hound laid his head."

"Hound?" Berrine stepped closer, her brow furrowing with renewed interest.

"Something Deckin said, and another who also had some knowledge of this. That fellow I threw the stone at, in fact. He's dead too, by the way."

"But they spoke of the Hound in regard to Lachlan?"

"Erchel did. Deckin was far more circumspect. I assumed it was just another name for Lachlan. Perhaps folk called him the Hound of the Shavine Forest, or somesuch."

"No." Berrine's frown deepened. "There are no accounts that refer to him as such. He was called a dog many times, but never the Hound."

For a second her eyes took on the unfocused cast of a busy mind then she abruptly turned about and strode away, the iron platform thrumming with her purposeful steps. I followed at a less hasty pace, the way this metal scaffold squealed and shuddered making me wonder just how old it might be. She led me to another ladder, scaling it with her unconscious ease and scant regard for the lack of illumination she afforded her companion. Consequently, I was obliged to grope my way up the ladder, finding her on her knees, hands busy as she extracted and replaced one book after another.

"Where is it?" she muttered. Reading her expression, set in the concentration of an expert at work, I stayed silent, deciding she wouldn't appreciate any distracting questions. After some more rummaging she let out a triumphant gasp and got to her feet, book in hand.

"The lettering is somewhat outmoded," she said, holding it out to me. "But a scribe should be able to read it."

Taking the book, I squinted at the words embossed onto its cracked leather cover. They were formed of overly elaborate Albermainish script, the characters flaked with specks of gold. It was not something I knew how to craft, although not altogether alien for I had seen Master Arnild doodle something similar on spare scraps of parchment.

"'*The Sea Hound*'," I read, peering closer at the denser words below the main title. "'*A Chronicle of Piracy in the First Tri-Reign*'." The First Tri-Reign, I knew, referred to the period of Albermaine history under the first three kings of the Algathinet dynasty. It was often considered something of a golden age by modern scholars, a time when the realm was young and the royal bloodline remained pure. Sihlda had been dismissive of such notions, calling them "the chauvinism of the nostalgia addict".

"The Sea Hound," Berrine told me in hushed excitement, "was a notorious pirate chieftain during the time of Kings Arthin the Second and Third. He menaced the realm's coast from the Fjord Geld to the Bay of Shalvis. It's not known where he was born but it is clear that his home port was not in the duchies."

She took the book from my hands and thumbed through the first few pages, revealing a map I recognised as depicting the seas off Albermaine's western coast. Berrine's finger stabbed at a small cluster of islets a good distance out in the midst of the Cronsheldt Sea. "'The Iron Maze', they call it. A notorious graveyard for ships, said to be unnavigable by all save the Sea Hound. A handy place to stow treasure, wouldn't you say?"

"This seems something of a stretched thread," I said. "You think Lachlan and the Sea Hound were allies?"

"Perhaps. We do know they were contemporaries. It's not stretching the thread too much to imagine the foremost outlaw of the Shavine Forest and the greatest pirate of the age forming some kind of association. But, until now, no one has suggested such a link. Folk have been looking for a smuggler this whole time when they should have been looking for a pirate."

Seeing doubt linger on my face, she laughed, leaning closer. "It will require further research, of course. But there are far more accounts of the Sea Hound's exploits in this library than there are of Lachlan's. Fjord Gelders love sea stories, after all. Give me time and perhaps I can point to a particular spot on more detailed map."

"How much time?"

"Time enough—" her voice grew soft as she leaned closer still, reaching into my jerkin where I had consigned the witch's book "—to translate a portion of this, for I sense it's your principal object, is it not? The treasure is but a trifle compared to this."

Her lips were close enough to brush my cheek, summoning an automatic response I surprised myself by resisting. *Far, far too friendly.* However, such resistance dissolved when Berrine's arms encircled my shoulders, breath hot against my ear.

"When the Ascarlians laid down the foundations for this library," she whispered, "King Aeric fucked his favourite slave on the keystone for all to see then cut her throat to bathe it in her blood. It was how they invited the gods' blessing in those days . . . "

Her words died as I smothered her mouth with mine, crushing her body against me and rejoicing at the feel of female flesh. The movement summoned a fresh judder to the scaffold of sufficient violence to make me stop, breaking the kiss to glance nervously around.

"How sturdy is this?" I asked to which Berrine responded with a laugh that echoed long and loud in this ancient place.

"Sturdy enough," she said, reaching to gather up her skirts. The sight of her legs, long, pale and golden in the lamplight, was enough to banish all other concerns and I pulled her close once again. Fortunately for the longevity of this tale, most cherished reader, she was proven right about the sturdiness of the scaffold.

CHAPTER THIRTY-SIX

The trinket was old and pitted, but the gleam of real silver shone bright as I turned it in my fingers. The metal had been shaped by skilled hands into a perfect semblance of a rope twisted into a complex knot. The weave of the rope and slight bulge where it pressed against itself were all crafted with a precision that brought a smile to my lips.

"Take it," Berrine had said in the small hours of the morning. We lay together in the chamber where she slept most evenings, having forsaken the distractingly creaky scaffold after our first somewhat energetic encounter. The next couple of hours left us sweaty and spent, tangled in contented lethargy on her narrow bed. She had made a gift of the silver knot she wore on a chain beneath her robe when I told her of my intended patrol into the wilds that day.

"You may get to keep that book," I commented with a flippancy I didn't feel. "Since I'd be a liar if I said I was sure of coming back."

"It's just a lucky charm, of sorts," she told me as I regarded the token with a puzzled frown. "Don't worry," she sighed, resting her head on my chest. "It doesn't mean we're bound in eternal union. Such notions are the delusions of your Covenant-infested lands where women are enslaved as whores under the name of 'wife'."

Had my mind been less addled by post-carnal torpor, the venom with which she spoke of the Covenant would have roused me to question her further. Instead, I was content to lie with her a while longer, my gaze roving the many sheets pinned to the walls of her chamber. They were a mix of drawings and writings, often intertwined.

"My own researches," she said, seeing my interest.

"Into what?"

"Oh, whatever snares my eye. It varies over time."

Surveying the notes and sketches, I noted how Berrine wrote with a messy, near feverish speed while her drawings bespoke a measured and careful attention to detail. She was evidently a better artist than a scribe, though I felt it best not to say so. I also saw that, while much of the notes were set down in Albermainish script, a good many were rendered in the angular lettering etched into many a window and doorway in this town.

"Ascarlian runic," she explained when I asked what it might be called. "The archaic form rather than the more standardised text used today. I've been trying to master it for years but it's tricky. Meaning can be altered with just a small change to the spacing between the characters."

One particular cluster of sheets drew my attention more than the others. They were all in runic and positioned in a chaotic mass around a sketch of the statues carved into the base of Mount Halthir. I hadn't yet managed to view these up close, catching only glimpses of the mighty gods of the Altvar rearing above the rooftops.

"The bases of the statues are liberally inscribed," Berrine said when my gaze lingered on this patch of wall. "And not all have been translated. The master librarian is content for me to work on it when time allows. If I manage to compile a complete translation, he promised I will have a book of my own to place on these shelves."

There was a guarded note to her voice, one she tried to hide, but I knew a lie when I heard it. There was more to these notes than just the promise of a book with her name on it, however laudable such an ambition might be. I debated pressing her on the matter but, with daylight creeping around the edges of her small shuttered window, I thought it best to take my leave.

"Five days," she said as I dressed. "I think I should have some answers then."

The sight of her propped on one elbow, flaxen hair cascading over her shoulders and the bedsheets only half covering her nakedness, brought a severe temptation to stay. However, Sergeant Swain's reaction should he feel compelled to seek me out, as he surely would if I failed to appear at the allotted hour, was enough to have me pulling on my trews and reaching for my boots.

"And the Caerith book?" I asked.

"That will take longer, as I think you know. Still, I'd hazard that your company will be here a good while, don't you? I'll find you there when you return. Best if you don't risk coming here again." A regretful pout passed across her lips before she lay back, placing a forearm over her eyes and smothering a yawn. "Diverting as this was, we would've been lucky to get away with just a flogging if they found you here."

Feeling another swell of temptation, I tore my gaze from her breasts and made for the door.

"Reconnaissance only," Evadine told Wilhum and me when we led our mounts to the Gate Wall. "No fighting unless you have to. I'll expect you back in three days. After five, I'll assume you dead." She had the good grace to put a regretful frown on her face as she said this, although the coldness I still saw in her eyes as she looked me over raised doubt as to its sincerity.

The captain paused to clasp hands with Wilhum. They said nothing but the look that passed between them told of a lifelong affection. I had the sense of a farewell in the way she swallowed and lowered her head a fraction before stepping back and moving to me. Her face was guarded, and voice clipped to near a whisper as she said, "If he chooses to run, let him go."

I glanced at Wilhum, watching him climb into the saddle and tease a hand through his horse's mane. I could tell he'd had a gutful of drink the night before and he wore the expression I'd seen on plenty of men, the blank-eyed, partly ironic mask of those who consider themselves lost.

"He won't do that, Captain," I replied in a similarly quiet murmur. "Only cowards run from those they love. And he is no coward."

Evadine's mouth twitched with controlled emotion and she looked away. "Even so," she said in a tone of curt instruction. "Remember my order."

I hauled myself into the saddle, drawing a snort from Karnic who at least consented not to toss his head in protest this morning.

"Here." I looked down at the sound of Swain's gruff rasp, seeing him strapping a crossbow and quiver of bolts to the rear of my saddle. It was a stirrup crossbow, lacking a windlass so not as likely to fell a man with a single bolt, but much faster to recharge. "Know how to use one, I trust?" Swain enquired, stepping back.

I grinned, knuckling my forehead with expected servility. "That I do, Supplicant Sergeant."

"Good. Lose it and the cost will come out of your pay. And mind what the captain said; five days and you're dead."

A mile or two from the fjord, the perennial mist it breathed over the shore dissipated to reveal a landscape of steep-sided valleys bordering rolling, forest-clad hills. The trees also lay in a thick green blanket over the lower reaches of the slopes and the sparse open ground was riven with many streams and rivers of varying depth and breadth.

I was accustomed to places mostly untouched by human hand, but only in the depths of the Shavine Forest, where even the duke's foresters feared to tread. Much more familiar were the outer fringes of the forest thinned by constantly felling and charcoal burning while beyond lay the hedged fields where the churls toiled. The innards of the Fjord Geld had no hedges, or any stone walls that I saw. It was truly a wild place, and cold with it.

"This is late summer," Wilhum told me with a laugh when I complained of the chill. "If you think this is bad, you should see a winter in the Geld. When the nights grow longest you can't venture outside for more than a moment or two without sucking tiny shards of frozen air into your lungs."

We rode at a sedate walk, Wilhum seeming to pay little heed to our course except to maintain a vaguely eastward direction. My enquiries as to our intended destination met with only a muttered "Wherever the enemy may be found, I suppose." I found it lacking in reassurance.

"Did it occur to you that you're being tested?" I asked. My mood, already sour, had been worsened by the experience of fording a particularly energetic stream, its current churning over loose rock, which set Karnic to stomping in annoyance once we cleared the bank. My boots were filled with icy water and I worried my feet might freeze come nightfall. "You've turned your coat twice now, after all," I went on. "It seems odd our Anointed Captain would entrust command of this oh-so-important mission to you."

"It does," Wilhum agreed with a mild shrug. "But then, she expects me to run, does she not?" His gaze settled on my face, still drawn in weary resignation but with a knowing steadiness. "Did she tell you to kill me? Is that what the crossbow's for? Perhaps we're both being tested, Master Scribe. Or punished. Me for disloyalty, you for your sacrilegious visit to a practitioner of heathen arts."

We were halted now, alone in the wilds, well beyond the sight of the port or any other set of human eyes. I was suddenly reminded of the skills I had seen Wilhum display in his attempts to teach me the sword. The gap between us was short, leaving little time for me to reach for, load and loose the crossbow. I could draw my own sword, but I had little doubt as to what would result if I did.

"I need to empty my boots," I said, climbing down from the saddle. I sat on Karnic's reins to stop him wandering off and unbuckled each boot in turn, Wilhum sitting in placid observance as I tipped the water out.

"She told me to let you go," I said finally when his lingering stare became irksome. "My test, I suspect, is to actually return with some useful intelligence. You're not supposed to return at all." I glanced up at him with an empty smile. "Looks like it pays to have been raised among nobility. Even one so wedded to her faith as our captain will cast aside her principles to save a childhood friend. Her former betrothed, in fact. Was the engagement broken due to her piety? She preferred the Martyrs to you. That must have been galling."

"You think you know her," Wilhum said. "You think she is, what? Both a fanatic and a hypocrite?" He shook his head. "You have no notion of what made her as she is."

"Visions given unto her by the Seraphile." I peeled the socks from my feet and wrung them out, flicking the moisture away. "So she claims."

"Visions, yes. And real or not, they are real to her. I know only this, Master Scribe: she is the best of us. Not just the best of nobles, all of us. You, me, every miserable denizen of our miserable kingdom. She rises above it all, for she is the only true heart I have ever met."

"What about the Pretender? Was his heart not so true?"

Wilhum's face darkened, the placidity for once giving way to a flicker of anger. "No king's heart can ever be completely true," he said, tugging his reins to resume the eastward trek. "Hurry up or I'll leave you behind. This is not a place to journey alone."

Wilhum's demeanour became more alert when we reached the wooded hills, I suspected due to a warrior's ingrained instinct for danger rather than sudden observance of duty. My own inherent nose for unseen threats reasserted itself as the forest's shade enclosed us. The trees were mostly pine interspersed with the occasional beech or ash, tall and close packed. They created a dark, uneven wall rich in shadows, any of which might harbour a rebel with a bow or axe poised for throwing. Wilhum refused to take the easier course offered by the channels between the hills, forcing us to repeatedly dismount and lead the horses up a succession of slopes. It made for tedious progress but I felt no urge to complain; each gully and ravine was a ready-made trap.

We kept on until dusk, making camp atop the rocky crest of the steepest hill we had yet encountered. Tethering the horses at the base, we ascended to find a summit that resembled a miniature natural fortress, the rocks forming the crenellations of a battlement. I divined from the way Wilhum moved about the hilltop that he had been here before, a suspicion confirmed when he crouched to scrape a patch of moss from one of the stones, revealing a crude but readable inscription chiselled into the rock.

"'Wilhum and Aldric's Mount'," I read aloud. "Aldric being . . ."

He traced his fingers over the letters, voice barely a whisper. "Just a friend of old." He rose, nodding to the eastern slope. "Any visitors are likely to come from that direction. All the other approaches are barred by the river. We'll eat, then I'll take the first watch."

I sat down to retrieve the salted pork from my saddlebags. I didn't bother asking about the possibility of lighting a fire since it would betray our presence.

"In my darker and less enlightened days," I said, "I mean to say, before being called to service as a soldier of the Covenant, our band would always know within the space of an hour when strangers had ventured into our patch. I take it the Fjord Gelders we seek are unlikely to be any less observant."

"You do have a gift for employing ten words when one will do, Scribe." Wilhum perched himself on a rock and drew his sword, pulling a whetstone from the pouch on his belt to hone the edge. "If you mean, 'do they know we're here?' The answer is: probably but not definitely. Anticipating your next question: yes, they will certainly attempt to kill us should they find us."

"And will you fight them if they do?"

He didn't look up from his task, the stone drawing a long hiss from the blade as he worked it all the way to the point. "I'm keeping my steel sharp, aren't I?" he asked, a ghost of his old winning smile on his lips.

He shook me awake a few hours past midnight, not that I required much rousing. My sleep had been shallow, but sadly, not so as to forbid dreams. The Traitors' Field had been a regular night-time visitor since my equally troubled slumber aboard the *Gracious Maid*. The dream was typically an unnerving melange of frenzied violence and discordant screams, but now and then the face of the first man I had killed that day would loom out of the chaos in garish splendour. Sometimes he would just stare in vacant regard, features slack and grey save for the blood that ran in thick rivulets from the billhook embedded in his forehead. Other times he was more vocal, his lips squirming like worms as they sang songs, recited scripture or, most aggravating of all, asked questions in a convivial tone of light curiosity.

"Don't you ever wonder," he enquired shortly before Wilhum shook me awake for my turn on watch, "why your whore mother didn't strangle you at birth? Or leave you out for the foxes or wolves? What possessed her to preserve one such as you?"

Consequently, I spent the hours before sunrise untroubled by the lure of sleep, for I had no desire to face more of the corpse's questions. I kept Swain's crossbow close at hand. The longsword I left sheathed so its steel wouldn't catch a betraying gleam, but I drew my knife, concealing the blade beneath my cloak. Fortunately, no rebels came to trouble us that night, but the experience left me with the nagging sense of lingering peril when we broke camp and moved on at first light. It wasn't quite the itch that told of being observed by unseen eyes, more the prickle to the skin that warned I was now traversing dangerous ground. When we set off, I kept the crossbow tied to the pommel of my saddle, a bolt tucked into each boot.

It was close to noon when the smell reached me, mostly composed of woodsmoke but laced with the sharper sting of shit. Wilhum sensed it too and immediately drew his sword, pressing his thumb to the blade as it slid free of the scabbard to muffle the betraying scrape of metal. I moved with similar caution to prime the crossbow and we turned our horses into the wind, keeping to a slow walk.

When we caught sight of some wispy smoke rising through the trees, Wilhum halted his mount and raised his arm. We dismounted, tethering the horses to branches and moving forward in a crouch. My ears strained for the sound of voices, hearing only the creak of trees and the occasional flutter of birds on the wing. I stopped when I saw the man and touched a hand to Wilhum's arm in warning. The stranger stood part wreathed in smoke from a dwindled fire. His posture was odd, standing with both arms outstretched and head slumped forward. As we crept closer, I realised that his arms had been fixed by ropes to two saplings. Also, he was very dead.

"Well, that's a new one," I observed softly.

The body was stood in the centre of a small clearing. He had been stripped naked and propped amid the remains of a well-rummaged camp. The man's back had been opened with two deep vertical cuts, the ribs, obscenely clean and white among the gore, broken and spread open. Flies buzzed around the reddish-black organs that had been drawn out and laid over his shoulders. I was grateful now for the chilly climate as warmer weather would have attracted a great deal more bugs.

"The Crimson Hawk," Wilhum said, features drawn in grim recognition. He gestured at the offal resting on the man's shoulders. "The lungs are supposed to resemble wings, you see."

I shifted my gaze from the gruesome sight to inspect what was left of the camp. "Pleasant customs these Fjord Gelders have."

"This isn't the work of the Geld folk. It's an Ascarlian blood rite, only ever performed by a Tielwald of high rank."

"Tielwald?"

"A mix of warrior and priest. Besides the Sister Queens, they're the closest thing the Ascarlians have to nobility." Wilhum's gaze grew wary as he scanned the surrounding forest. "And they don't travel alone. This poor fellow was caught by a warband."

"Cart tracks here," I said, kicking churned mud at the edge of two narrow furrows in the ground. They led off to the east, disappearing into the woods after a dozen paces. "He must've been a wool merchant on his way to Olversahl. Desperate too if he was willing to risk travelling unprotected in times like these."

"If the fishing's bad the crofters go hungry. Wool is all they have to trade." Wilhum drew his dagger and moved to take hold of the dead man's wrist, setting the blade to the rope that bound it. "A good man will risk all to feed his children."

"Be better if you left him as he is," I warned. "Cut him down and they'll know others have passed this way."

"I intend for them to know me full well before long." He flicked his dagger, severing the bond before moving to the other.

"We don't have the time to bury him," I said, watching Wilhum set the corpse down.

"Fjord Gelder's don't bury their dead. They say their prayers and leave them to feed the creatures of the wild and succour the earth with the marrow of their bones. So in death we give life." He knelt and closed his eyes, murmuring an unfamiliar cant in archaic dialect. I recognised it as aligning with the Covenant in its mention of the Martyrs and the Seraphile, but much of it was meaningless to my ear.

When done, he got to his feet, moving towards his horse with a purposeful stride.

"You know what this means," I said, hastening to catch up. "An Ascarlian warband within the borders of the realm is no small thing. The captain should know of this."

"Then go and tell her." He climbed into the saddle and aligned his mount with the cart tracks. "Though I don't think it wise for you to return without an accurate count of their number."

He kicked his horse into a trot before I could voice another protest. I stood watching him fade into the forest's shadow, seized by indecision. *Just tell her he died,* my weary inner critic drawled. *The Ascarlian savages killed him and you barely got away. As for the warband, fifty sounds about right. Sixty if you want to appear brave.*

"She'll know," I grated, hurrying to mount Karnic and setting off in pursuit. "She always knows."

CHAPTER THIRTY-SEVEN

Wilhum, being a considerably better horseman, soon drew so far ahead I had no hope of catching him before he found his quarry. Still I kept on, drawn by the sound of pounding hooves as he spurred to a canter whenever the trees thinned. I found it best to give Karnic his head, his hunter's instincts finding the most efficient course through the trees as he sought out his stablemate. I knew this was folly, an unwise surrender to urges I would once have ignored. *If he runs, let him go.* Here he was, running, albeit set on a punitive excursion that would most likely see us both dead before long. If I were to ride off in the opposite direction, would I not be simply following orders?

I have often pondered my failure to succumb to common sense at this juncture. Typically, I ascribe it to the odd, near-inexplicable web of familiarity, habit and mutual reliance that binds one soldier to another. Or, it may have just been due to the fact that, for all his noble pretensions and enviable charm, I liked Wilhum Dornmahl and would rather he didn't die. Sentiment is always the deadliest toxin.

Still, as one mile of pursuit became two, then three, the nagging sense of peril that had bedevilled me since entering this forest grew into a bone-deep certainty of imminent doom. Why should I not trust it? Had it not been fear that had kept me alive for so long?

Finally, as terror-born nausea summoned a lurch to my gut and a near retch to my throat, I hauled on Karnic's reins and brought him to a halt. He huffed and stamped in protest, still intent on finding his friend, but I was having none of it.

"Shut up, you!" I snapped, provoking a loud snort as I turned his head west. *Seventy*, I decided. *There were at least seventy, Captain. Huge, blond-haired savages, they were. Each with a freshly severed head impaled on their swords . . .*

Luck, however, decided to take flight at that very moment, for, echoing through the trees, came the loud scream of a horse suffering great injury. It was enough for Karnic to forget all bonds of obedience and whirl about, spurring unbidden into a gallop. I could only gasp out a few profane curses and hang on as he sped onwards. I ducked some branches and suffered scratches to my crown from others, coming close to tipping from the saddle several times when Karnic rounded the more substantial trees, barely slowing in the process. The ride was so alarming I began to entertain the notion of drawing my dagger and sinking it into the beast's neck if he didn't consent to halt soon.

We burst free of the trees in a cloud of displaced pine needles and leaves to be instantly blinded by a pall of thick black smoke. I coughed, blinking stinging eyes as Karnic bore me through it until a shift in the wind brought a sudden glare of sunlight. Smoke-born tears cleared from my eyes to afford only a brief glance of the scene ahead. The pall came from a tall stack of blazing wood, the column of dark fog it birthed rising high into the air. It was positioned where a stretch of rocky ground met the edge of a steep cliff, beyond which lay a broad stretch of blue sea.

I glimpsed Wilhum on the far side of the fire, whirling his long-sword with furious energy in the midst of what appeared to be no fewer than six armed assailants. They were all uniformly bulky in appearance, clad in a mix of furs, leather and armour. A couple wore helms of iron but the others were bareheaded, their braids whipping about as they fought.

Wilhum's hunter was down, the stallion's legs flailing as crimson foam frothed from its mouth and blood streamed from the large wound in his flank. I also saw two fur-clad bodies on the ground, indicating Wilhum had at least managed to claim some recompense for the unfortunate wool merchant before ensuring his own imminent demise.

More concerning, however, was the realisation that Karnic was galloping towards the clifftop without any indication of stopping. As we neared the edge, another figure sprang up from the rocks to our front, drawn bow in hand. He had been aiming at Wilhum but, hearing the thunder of Karnic's hooves, instantly turned his arrow upon us. For all his swiftness, he wasn't quite quick enough, Karnic riding him down without pause, the bow sending the arrow wide and its owner's cries choking off into a short-lived scream accompanied by a welter of cracking bones.

At last recognising the danger, Karnic began to rear, skidding over the earth and colliding with a large boulder with sufficient force to dislodge me from the saddle. I landed on my side, fortunately on a patch of soft earth rather than rock. I also had no weapon to hand beyond the knife at my belt and the crossbow bolts tucked into each boot. It was not the best state with which to land in the midst of a furious skirmish. Hearing a shout close by, I resisted the impulse to scramble upright, lying still and letting out a pained groan. I continued to feign injury until my half-closed eyes glimpsed a pair of boots, then snatched the knife from my belt.

I was lucky that the fellow's boots were fashioned from soft leather, the blade cutting through both just above the ankle with relative ease. Their owner let out a yell that was a combination of both scream and roar as I rolled clear, his sword slicing into the earth rather than my neck. My next action was the result of long-ingrained skill and outlaw's intuition. Wilhum was a master of the longsword but I had been killing people with knives since childhood.

Shifting my legs under me I launched myself at the swordsman, wrapping one arm around his neck and twisting us both into a ragged pirouette. I feinted a jab at his eyes, causing him to raise his elbow, then drove the blade deep under his arm, finding a gap between his furs and leathers. I bore him down as the blade bit home, feeling the hot rush of blood on my knife hand. A hardy fellow, he continued to roar and struggle despite what was surely a mortal wound, attempting to shift his sword to his other arm. I raised myself up and brought my forehead snapping down into his nose. It stunned him for only a brief second, but it was enough for me to pull the knife free and stab him in the throat.

I reached across his twitching form for the sword he still clutched in his part-slackened hand, but quickly abandoned the attempt at the sound of more feet to my rear. Another swordsman had forsaken the fight with Wilhum for easier meat, this one with a stout iron helm on his head and bearing an oaken shield. Beyond him, Wilhum still battled his attackers, now reduced to three in number meaning another life claimed to balance the wool merchant's murder. However, I could tell he was tiring.

A shout from the shield-bearing swordsman snapped my gaze back to more immediate concerns. His face was set in a mask of furious challenge and, before I turned and ran in the opposite direction, I made out the angular web of blue ink tattooed into the flesh beneath his beard. It is my honest duty, dear reader, to inform you that, if Karnic had not blundered into my path at that moment, I would most likely have fled into the woods. But blunder he did, and in doing so swung Sergeant Swain's crossbow, still tied to the pommel of his saddle, comfortably within reach of my arm.

I tore it free and ducked, rolling under Karnic and sprinting forwards, hearing the mingled shouts of horse and shield-bearer to my rear as the fellow attempted to clear the horse's path. I ran for the tallest boulder I could see, leaping atop it and jamming my foot into the crossbow's stirrup. I forced myself not to look up as I drew the cord back into the lock, snatched a bolt from my boot, laid it into the groove along the stock, raised and loosed it without pause.

My pursuer had made the unwise decision of leaping in order to swing his sword at my chest, lowering his shield in the process. As a consequence, there was nothing to prevent the bolt from finding his cheek just to the left of the iron guard covering his nose. The stirrup crossbow lacked the power of its windlass cousin, but at so close a range it had no difficulty in driving a bolt clear through the muscle and bone of a man's face and into the brain beyond. The shield-bearer was dead before he hit the ground.

I lost no time in recharging the crossbow, setting the second bolt in place and levelling it at the trio of warriors still assailing Wilhum. All notion of fleeing the scene had gone now, as is often the way when the fight takes hold, banishing rational thought and leaving just the compulsion to do further injury.

Instinct guided my aim to the tallest of the three, an axe-wielding bear of a man who also wore a helm but no armour to protect his legs. He staggered as the bolt sank into the rear of his thigh, Wilhum taking swift advantage of the distraction to lunge forwards and spit the axe wielder through the neck. Wilhum kept his sword in place, grabbing the spasming warrior's shoulder and turning him to deflect another charge from one of his surviving assailants. He continued to use the dying man as a shield, heaving him to and fro to ward off further attacks.

I ran for Karnic, hoping to retrieve the quiver of bolts, but his fractious mood persisted. Wilhum's mount had ceased its death struggles and Karnic's herd-born instinct had seemingly died with it. He turned as I got near, preventing me from grabbing the quiver but briefly presenting the handle of my longsword. I managed to catch hold of the pommel, drawing the blade clear of the scabbard before Karnic reeled away, eyes wide in panic as he sped off.

"Fucking coward," I muttered, hefting the sword and turning towards the three battling men. Wilhum still kept his near-dead makeshift shield upright while the two attackers constantly sought to flank him, however I could tell the former noble's strength was close to its last ebb. The pair of swordsmen evidently saw it too, leaving off their assaults to draw back a little, one circling left, the other right. As soon as Wilhum allowed their spitted companion to fall his end would be swift in coming.

Noting the easy familiarity with which both men twirled their swords in anticipation, I deduced charging headlong into this fight would be too great a challenge for my still-meagre sword skills. Instead, I hurried to gather up the shield of the man who had fallen to my crossbow. It was a heavy contrivance, the oak planks that formed it daubed with a design in red and blue paint that spiralled out from an iron boss in its centre. However, with my body stoked by the heat of combat, it felt light enough as I fixed the straps over my forearm.

I chose the attacker to Wilhum's right, since he seemed most preoccupied with his flagging prey. I crouched as I charged straight at the fellow, positioning the shield so it covered me from nose to crotch, and quelling the urge to voice a challenging shout. Due to this, or simple good fortune, he failed to turn until I was almost upon him. He did manage a swipe at my head, but I ducked in time and the blade only shaved splinters from the shield before the boss struck him in the chest.

He rebounded a few feet, shifting his stance so he didn't fall, but the impact of the blow left him sluggish. He succeeded in parrying the thrust I aimed at his gut, but not in arresting the blade's momentum, so that it slid down his own and bit deep into his hip. He fell, letting out a shout of mingled frustration and pain, snarling at me as I closed in for the killing blow. Before I could thrust, his companion forced me to duck again with an overhead swing of his sword. I caught it with the shield and replied with an ineffectual riposte, the fellow nimbly sidestepping the arcing blade and drawing his own back for another go, murderous intent writ large in his glaring features. His next blow never came, for at that juncture Wilhum's longsword sliced off the top portion of the fellow's golden-haired skull.

Seeing a human brain exposed in such a way is a morbidly fascinating sight. I stared transfixed at the revealed organ in all its glistening and partially mashed pinkness as the warrior tottered about, still clinging to life by some strange working of his soon-to-be-lifeless body. His lips mangled out what may have been a last word or two, but I doubted they made sense even in his own tongue. When he at last consented to topple over, I found all urges to further violence abruptly slip away to be replaced by a wave of deep, nauseous weariness that had me leaning on my sword, drawing in laboured breaths.

The wounded man lurched across the ground towards me, jabbing his sword at my legs, but it was a weak gesture. The cut I had dealt him had evidently nicked an important vein for a red torrent flowed thick down his legs. His eyes were hot coals of hatred amid rapidly paling features, teeth white as he bared them to cast out what I assumed to be a curse in a tongue I had never heard.

"'Godless son of a whore'," Wilhum said by way of translation. He stood with his longsword resting on his shoulder, regarding the stricken warrior with a grimly satisfied frown. The Crimson Hawk hadn't been forgiven. "At least I think so," he added. "My Ascarlian is a little rusty."

"Can't say he's altogether wrong," I replied, raising my face to the sky as sweat caught a chill kiss from the seaward wind.

"I must say, you surprised me, Scribe." Wilhum's tone was mostly reflective but also tinged with a measure of gratitude. "I'm shamed to say I assumed you'd be halfway back to Olversahl by now."

Any sardonic reply I might have dreamt up was forgotten when the wounded Ascarlian suddenly launched into song. It was a discordant tune to my ear but presumably more melodious to his, or perhaps he was just a very poor singer. He tipped his head back as he sang, casting the words out to the sky. His voice was strong at first, but soon began to dwindle as his face grew ever paler.

"What was that?" I asked Wilhum when the song finally faded. The Ascarlian slumped onto his back, chest rising and falling with renewed energy as his body tried to stave off the inevitable end.

"His death ode." Wilhum angled his head to watch the warrior's final seconds play out. "He implores Ulthnir, Father of the Altvar, to recognise a warrior fallen in battle and accept his shade into the Halls of Aevnir, where the feast and the fight never end."

Seeing the Ascarlian shudder out his last ragged breath, twitch a bit and lie still, I grunted, "I'd rather have the feast than the fight."

"They're the same thing."

Wilhum was the first to react to the new voice, whirling about with his longsword poised for a thrust. My continuing fatigue was such that I responded with far less alacrity, grimacing at the shield's suddenly irksome weight as I shifted it higher and rested my long-sword atop the rim.

I had deduced already that Ascarlians were a tall breed, but the man standing a dozen paces off was of even more imposing stature than those we had just sent off to their mythic hall. I fancied he stood closer to seven feet than six, broad of shoulder and thick of limb. The fact that a man of such bulk had contrived to make a soundless approach was disturbingly impressive. A black bearskin lay over his shoulders, contrasting sharply with his unconstrained mass of steel-grey hair. A glance at the deeply lined and weathered visage above his equally grey beard, the skin marked by a complex mass of tattoos in faded blue ink, confirmed this was not a young man. Still, his age didn't prevent him from easily hefting the huge axe in his hands. In addition to its size, the weapon was made even more disconcerting by virtue of its twin blades, fashioned from stone rather than steel.

The thought of another bout of combat was dispiriting enough, but fighting this monster surely meant doom. In any case, the notion became even less appealing at the sight of a score more Ascarlians spreading out on the slope behind him. Most carried swords and axes but there were also some archers among them, arrows notched to the strings of their longbows. However, it was the appearance of the two wolves that banished any thought of further battle from my mind.

They appeared on either side of the hulking Ascarlian, one with fur of purest white, the other deep black, and both were massive. Wolves were a common enough sight in the Shavine Forest and, despite the many fear-filled tales spun about them, posed little danger as long as they were treated with careful respect. Shavine wolves were typically grey pelted and, while usually far larger than any dog, could not compete in size with this pair, both standing at least four feet at the shoulder. They settled placidly enough at the Ascarlian's side, but the steady, unblinking gaze of their yellow eyes told me they possessed none of the fear of man instilled in their southern cousins.

I gave a hopeless laugh and lowered the shield while Wilhum bridled, bringing his longsword up so it was level with his eyes, the point aimed at the grey-haired giant. He snarled something in Ascarlian then and, although I never did learn what it was, it brought forth a hearty if derisive chorus of laughter from our foes. The two wolves sank a little lower, lips trembling in a burgeoning snarl. However, they calmed when the hulking axeman winced and said, "You sound like a vomiting cat."

The Ascarlian's voice was heavily accented but his Albermainish flowed with precisely spoken ease. "Please, insult my tongue no further."

Wilhum said nothing but kept his sword where it was, not that this seemed to concern the Ascarlian overmuch. His gaze changed as it shifted to me, taking on a surprisingly expectant cast. I might have taken it for recognition but for there being no earthly chance either of us had ever clapped eyes on the other before this moment.

"This, I take it," I said to Wilhum, "is the Tielwald you spoke of."

The giant laughed before Wilhum could answer, bowing a little, albeit with a stiffness that indicated it was an unfamiliar gesture. "That I am. Margnus Gruinskard. It means Margnus of the Stoneaxe in your tongue." His gaze roved briefly over the bodies surrounding us, displaying thoughtful admiration rather than anger. "And you, my brave and skilful friends?"

"Alwyn Scribe," I said, returning the bow. "It means . . . Alwyn the scribe." I glanced at Wilhum, finding his features taking on a worryingly reddened hue. "This is Wilhum Dornmahl. I don't know what his name means. You'll have to forgive his rudeness, but what you did to the wool merchant we found in the woods has stirred his chivalric nature."

"Ah." Margnus Gruinskard settled a steady gaze on Wilhum. "The Crimson Hawk is a just punishment for those who break oaths made to the Altvar. All the farmers of this land swore to sell no more wool to Olversahl. The man in the woods proved himself a liar and paid for it."

"Was his oath freely given?" Wilhum demanded. "I doubt it. And are you going to feed his children now there is no one to fish the fjords and work the land?"

The Ascarlian stiffened a little, a faintly offended tone colouring his response. "Children do not go hungry in the realm of the Sister Queens. We are a people of few laws, but that is one we hold to."

"This land does not belong to the Sister Queens," I pointed out, adopting a far milder tone than Wilhum. "In fact, you are trespassing on the lawful domain of King Tomas Algathinet and I would thank you to remove yourself with all dispatch."

The Tielwald's face creased in puzzlement for a second before he let out a hearty chuckle, one that was swiftly echoed by his fellow warriors. The two wolves, however, merely yawned.

"You speak with flowers in your voice," Margnus Gruinskard observed before nodding at Wilhum. "Yet this one's voice is cleaner. He is, what is the term, 'high born'? And you are low. Yes?"

"There is no distinction between high and low in Covenant Company," Wilhum replied. "We are all equal in our devotion to the Seraphile's grace and the Martyrs' example."

"Covenant Company." The Tielwald repeated the words with evident distaste, shaking his head. "Still, after all these years, your people enslave themselves to lies. Is that why you are here? This is a—" his distaste turned to amusement "—grand crusade against the heathen?"

"We merely come to protect what is rightfully ours," Wilhum said. "And has been so for centuries."

The Ascarlian laughed again, but this time it was more of a short, bitter grunt. "When I was a boy, I stole a piglet from my neighbour, kept it hidden in the forest and raised it up into fine boar. We slaughtered and roasted him to honour the Altvar on my fifteenth birthday when, drunk and loose of tongue, I confessed to my father what I had done years before. He leathered my rump until it bled, then made me work a full winter on my neighbour's farm in recompense. What is stolen remains so, regardless of time."

Without warning he hefted his axe and started forwards. Wilhum tensed for an attack while I resisted the urge to raise the shield. Fighting was pointless now. I began to formulate some last witticism that might divert the coming slaughter but stilled my tongue when the giant kept clear of us, striding past to regard the body of the fellow whose shield I held. The Tielwald's expression was one of impassive scrutiny but his tone sombre when he glanced at me once again, nodding to the shield.

"That is not yours to keep," he said.

Eager for the chance to win any measure of favour, I unhooked the thick wooden circle from my arm and set it down. Margnus Gruinskard acknowledged the gesture with a fractional nod before resuming his scrutiny of the fallen warrior.

"This is Tahlwild, my nephew," he said. "A fool and a braggart, it must be said, and his woman won't mourn him, or his children if truth be told. But never let it be said that he failed to honour the Altvar, slacked at his oar, or turned his back to a bared blade. Now I have to carry his shield home to his mother. My sister's tongue, when sharpened by grief, is not an easy thing to bear."

I was pondering the wisdom of offering some form of apology when Wilhum burst out, "No one invited your kind here, Ascarlian. A pox on your nephew and your warband of cravens."

I glared at him in exasperated reproach, seeing only anger and hunger for yet more blood in the stare he shot back. I realised then that he hadn't sought out these interlopers to administer justice. This was to be his glorious end, the turncoat knight finding ultimate redemption in a hopeless but brave stand against the heathen northmen.

"Die if you want," I hissed at him. "But don't expect me to join you. I'm done saving your noble arse today."

"I didn't ask you to, Scribe," he returned evenly. "She told you to let me run, didn't she?"

My profanity-laden rejoinder was stilled at the sound of a loud cough from Margnus Gruinskard. When I turned to face him he had closed the distance between us by a considerable margin. I now stood well within the sweep of his axe while he was still clear of the reach of my sword.

"Fear me not," he said and once again I saw the same expectant cast to his gaze. It turned to muted consternation when I replied with only a baffled grin that I'm sure bore more resemblance to a fearful grimace.

"Our fight is not ordained for today," he went on, his hand moving to pluck a trinket from beneath his furs. It hung from his neck on a leather cord, a small nugget of silver fashioned by expert hands to resemble a knotted rope. As he worked it between thumb and fore-finger I felt a pulse of heat beneath my jerkin. I would spend many hours later convincing myself it had been an illusion, some product of my near-panicked mind, but felt it I did. It was a small thing, no more than the warmth of a taper as it brushes your skin, but it was there, and it came from the token Berrine had given me. The token that was identical to the one now held by this Tielwald, a man who was both warrior and priest.

"Besides," he added, "I have a request to make of you. I should be grateful if you would carry a message back to the captain of your company." He let the silver knot fall from his fingers and raised his hand to point over my shoulder.

Still unnerved by the heated trinket and not altogether sure I wasn't about to receive the full force of his stone axe between my shoulder blades, I turned to follow his outstretched finger. It pointed to the blue expanse of sea beyond the clifftop. The sun was high in a mostly cloudless sky and the haze was low and thin. Consequently, it wasn't long before I discerned a line of dark smudges on the horizon. I counted a dozen at first, then a dozen more, the smudges resolving into broad square sails. As they drew ever nearer, I made out the oars dipping and rising as the ships ploughed a course for this very stretch of shore, guided, no doubt, by the blazing beacon fire on the clifftop. I counted close to a hundred before the Tielwald spoke again.

"You are wrong to say we were not invited here." I turned to find him crouching to retrieve his nephew's shield. He gave a grim, almost apologetic smile as he rose, slinging it over his shoulder. "Go back to Olversahl and report what you saw. I would consider it a special favour if you would tell that dog Fohlvast personally. When we take the port, I'll spare you long enough to hear you describe the look on his face."

He hefted his axe and gestured towards the forest. "Now, my friends, it is time for you to go. I have a funeral feast to officiate and, while I appreciate your company, I regret to say your presence would not be welcomed by the Altvar."

CHAPTER THIRTY-EIGHT

Elderman Fohlvast's expression upon hearing our report was certainly a sight worth seeing. He was unable to conceal the flare of utter terror that rose in his eyes, or the sudden, sweaty paling of his skin. I have seen many a man confront his worst fears and it is often mundane in its uniformity. Fohlvast's bowels and bladder, I knew, were presently loosening while his heart drove rapid hammer blows against his chest. It wouldn't have surprised me to see a pool of piss spread across the floor around his boots. Still, ever the actor, he made a valiant effort to master himself, coughing and trying to keep his features impassive as Evadine merely sighed and turned her gaze to the map unfurled on the large table in her quarters.

Wilhum and I had arrived beneath the Gate Wall barely an hour before, bedraggled and hollow-eyed from a forced march across rough country. Cowardly Karnic failed to make a reappearance until we were within sight of the port, even then he trotted on ahead without deigning to come close enough to be mounted. We maintained a cold silence for much of the journey, Wilhum walking with a sullen but determined cast to his face while my thoughts were equally distracted. The sight of the Ascarlian fleet loomed large but mostly it was the pulse of heat from the silver token beneath my jerkin that set my mind to worried pondering. *Merely a product of fear*, I told myself.

Or some heathen trick, an illusion. Still, I dwelt on it with reluctant obsession, stirred by similarly baffling memories of the Sack Witch and the chainsman.

The only meaningful words to pass between us came during a brief pause for rest in the forest. By unspoken agreement we made no effort to encamp for the night and struggled on despite the darkness. Margnus Gruinskard might have called us friends and let us go, but he remained a heathen savage with a grudge to settle and who was to say his mercy wasn't some sadistic jape?

"You could still have died back there," I said, propping myself against a tree and resisting the urge to slump to the ground. If I sat down, I knew I would sleep. "Charged the Tielwald or his fellows. A final act of valour. They might even have let me live to carry the tale back to Olversahl. So why didn't you? Death was your object, was it not?"

Wilhum had sunk to his haunches by a stream, dipping his hands in the current to wash away the dried blood. "You saw their fleet," he said. "She'll need every sword now."

"Here, you say?" Evadine asked him now, pointing to a cove on the northern coast of the long tongue of land that lay between Aeric's Fjord and the open sea.

"As best as I can judge," Wilhum confirmed. "It's a good choice. High ground to cover the approaches and plenty of timber for fire-wood and repairs to their longships."

"Was two hundred the full count?" Sergeant Swain asked, looking to me.

"Just the most I counted before we were sent off," I said, shaking my head. "I'd guess this Margnus of the Stoneaxe didn't want us to see the full size of their fleet."

I darted a glance at Fohlvast as I spoke the Tielwald's name, enjoying again the same spasm of fear as when I first described an Ascarlian of such impressive stature. It was plain that the elderman had heard the name before and didn't relish the chance of meeting him in person.

"Ascarlian longships vary greatly in size," Wilhum said. "But even the smallest can carry at least twenty warriors. We should reckon on a force five thousand strong."

"There will be more," Fohlvast said, speaking with a forcefulness that didn't quite smother the quaver in his tone. "Margnus Gruinskard is no mere Tielwald. He is the First Sworn to the Sister Queens, their greatest living warrior and their most respected priest. At his call, all the warriors in Ascarlia will muster. His presence in the Fjord Geld means open war. At long last, they have come to seize this land."

Seize it back, you mean, I thought, recalling the Tielwald's tale of the stolen piglet.

"How many warriors can he bring against us?" Evadine asked Fohlvast.

"A full count of the populace in the lands of the Sister Queens has never been made." The elderman folded his arms and stroked his chin in what I assumed to be an effort to convey calm reflection. I doubt the captain found it any more convincing than I did. "They are a people that despise formality and restrict writing to the recording of their heretic sagas and battle deeds. However, King Aeric's Library holds an account of their last invasion of the Fjord Geld a hundred years ago. It puts the size of their army at twenty thousand. Given the passage of time we may be facing a force of even greater size."

"Historical accounts tend to exaggerate numbers," I said, my interjection drawing a sharp glance from Fohlvast. Evidently, he was a fellow who expected a common soldier to keep his place in fine company. I displayed my lack of shits to give by meeting his gaze squarely, drawing forth another blossom of fear by adding, "Besides, I don't think the Tielwald intends to rely on numbers alone. He said the Ascarlians had been invited into the Fjord Geld."

Fohlvast's face flushed and I allowed myself a small grin as he floundered for a swift reply. However, it was Evadine who spoke. "Your meaning?"

"I've known schemers all my life," I said. "Gruinskard is a schemer, not just a mindless brute with a big axe. He has a plan and, I suspect, friends within these walls to help carry it out."

The elderman's discomfort boiled into anger as he swung his gaze to Evadine. "Must you allow this churl to cast calumny on my people so, Captain?"

"Your people," I returned, broadening my grin, "love you so much you have to patrol the streets at night to stop them conspiring to stick a knife in your back—"

"Enough, Scribe!" Evadine snapped. She fixed me with a warning glare, holding it until I consented to knuckle my forehead and step back from the table. "You have both done well," she said, voice softening as she shifted her gaze between Wilhum and me. "Go now and rest."

We bowed and made our exit, I contriving to linger at the door long enough to hear Swain's observation before it swung closed. "Even with twenty thousand men, getting over that wall is impossible. And there's no landing place for a fleet save the harbour, which is easily blocked . . ."

I slept for a time but it was short and troubled despite my fatigue. The rest of the company was at drill and Wilhum had taken himself off somewhere, I assumed in search of drink. For the most part I lay awake in my bunk, working the silver knot between thumb and forefinger, still pondering its mysteries. The trinket was just cold metal now, still ordinary save for its craftsmanship, and yet I knew it contained a meaning that eluded me.

Finally, still tired from the trek but unable to resume slumber, I rose and made my way to the statues at the base of the mountain. Walking the streets, I sensed a new tension among the townsfolk, their glances yet more guarded and windows shuttered even in daytime. Mothers herded children indoors and shops that had been open for business only days before were now firmly shut. Although Wilhum and I had been sworn to strictest secrecy, I couldn't help but connect this shift in mood to our return. Gossip and rumour move at remarkable speed, especially in towns. The arrival of two men on foot who had left mounted days before would surely have been remarked upon. It was also possible that the taut atmosphere had more to do with the increase in local soldiery on the streets. They were mostly Fohlvast's men, town militia rather than ducal men-at-arms, and their demeanour was far from cheerful, faces hard and eyes busy beneath their helms. My general impression was that Olversahl was a place poised in expectation, but of what?

Thanks to the pervasive grimness of mood, there were few people about when I reached the statues, allowing me to enjoy an uninterrupted tour of the impressive spectacle they represented. They all stood close to fifty feet high, carved in a manner that recalled the angular, near caricature style of the many wooden figures chiselled into doors and posts throughout the city. There was none of the fine, if weathered, anatomical precision found in the usually incomplete examples of pre-Scourge statuary I had encountered over the years. However, the sheer size and majesty of these stone gods overcame any sense that they were born of a lesser culture. This parade of divine beings was the product of decades of labour by skilled hands, hands that had somehow crafted the illusion they had been grown from the very substance of the mountain rather than brought forth through the tireless pounding of countless chisels.

I couldn't name them save for the tallest, a bearded warrior of grave aspect clutching a sword in one hand and a hammer in the other. This, I knew, must be Ulthnir, Father of the Altvar. As for the names of the two female figures that flanked him, I had no notion, but Berrine, of course, knew them well.

"Aerldun and Nerlfeya," she said, appearing at my side. "Lovers to Ulthnir the Worldsmith, the mothers of the lesser gods."

I turned to find her regarding me with a smile that seemed to hold a measure of actual relief, if not a creditable facsimile of such. I wondered if it reflected poorly on me to nurse such suspicion for a woman who I had coupled with so enthusiastically only days before, but the old outlaw's nose for duplicity was not to be ignored. Nor was the silver knot about my neck.

"You're not dead," she observed, arching an impressed eyebrow. "Well done."

"You don't sound so surprised as you might," I replied, keeping my tone light but neutral.

"A man such as you has a knack for survival." She came closer, darting her head forward to peck a kiss to my nose and laughing as she drew back. "Perhaps that's why I like you so much."

Pleased as she appeared to be by my return, I sensed an additional guardedness to her, a business to her eyes and stiffness to her bearing that I recognised as controlled fear.

"Were you followed?" I asked, surveying the mostly empty streets nearby. "I know your elderman is ever a suspicious fellow."

"No one followed me. If I appear . . . disconcerted it's for another reason." She reached into the satchel she carried on her shoulder, extracting the Caerith book I had given her.

"You're finished already?" I asked in surprise.

"No." I saw how her throat worked and the small tremble to her hand as she held the book out to me. "Nor will I be, Alwyn. I want no part of this."

"Part of what?"

She didn't answer right away, instead continuing to hold the book out until I consented to take it. "I marked the page I reached before I . . decided to abandon my studies."

I thumbed my way to the relevant scrap of parchment, finding a small sheet of scribbled notes between two pages. "My translation," Berrine said. "Read it."

Frowning, I extracted the sheet and held it up to the light, reading the untidy script aloud. "'I'll take some more information as payment. If you're offering.'" I gave a faint sigh of bemusement as I looked again at Berrine. "What is this?"

"Keep reading," she said, her face completely serious now.

Shrugging, I returned my gaze to the words on the sheet. "'Ascarlian blood runs in my veins,'" I read, "'as it does in all true Fjord Gelders, regardless of the southern kings we are forced to bow to' . . . " My voice dwindled to silence as the memory rose from the recesses of my mind.

"It's us," Berrine said in a soft, fearful murmur. "You and me that night in the forest. There are five pages and they record every word exchanged between us, words I scarce remember speaking." She laughed, a short shrill gasp devoid of amusement. "I thought at first you had played some grand jape on me, until I realised the impossibility of it. But what is written in that book is no more possible. There they are, clear as day, our words set down in Caerith script in a book that must be centuries old."

I closed the book, my hand suddenly just as unsteady as hers. Thoughts of the Sack Witch raced through my head as I searched for meaning, finding only more mystery. *So, you came to me on a field of blood after all*, she had said. It was clear to me now that our meeting on the Traitors' Field had been foretold. If so, had she read it in this book? Was all her talk of lost knowledge just mummery so she could place this in my hands? Why?

"Is it all like this?" I asked.

"I don't know." Berrine gave a smile that was more of a wince. "The first few pages are all fragmentary conversations between a young outlaw and a man who appears to be his mentor. Once I realised I was translating my own words, I stopped. I fancy myself a woman not lacking for courage, but . . . " A thin sigh escaped her lips. "Some knowledge is best left unlocked, at least by me."

Her hand dipped into her satchel once more, emerging with another book. I judged it as newly made from the cleanliness of the binding. When I opened it, I found clean pages filled by Berrine's untidy but readable hand.

"*A Guide to Translating Ancient Caerith*, by Berrine Jurest," she said. "My first authored work, just for you. With this, you should be able to complete your own translation. Though, and it pains my librarian's heart to say it, I suggest you throw that thing in the nearest fire."

I found it hard to argue that she was wrong; the book was unnatural, the product of vile heathen practices. However, I knew I could no more cast it into a fire than I could myself.

"And the treasure?" I asked, keen to shift the conversation to less worrisome matters. "Did you find the Sea Hound's lair?"

She straightened, a measure of her previous surety returning as she nodded at the new book I held. "The last page."

Opening her text once again I found a map rendered with a clarity that confirmed to me her hand was better suited to drawing than writing. I recognised it as a more refined and detailed depiction of the islets in the midst of the Cronsheldt Sea from the chronicle of piracy describing the Sea Hound's exploits. "The Iron Maze," I said, my eye alighting upon a small circle surrounding one of the smaller islets. "It's here?"

"I unearthed an account from a sailor who served aboard a merchantman captured by the Sea Hound," Berrine said. "He described being taken to a vast cave beneath the smallest islet in the chain. There was no mention of the fabled treasure, but what better hiding place could the Hound wish for?"

I looked up to find her smiling warmly once again. "Part of me wishes I could go with you," she said with a note of regret.

"Then do." I meant the offer. For all her evident duplicity, she was an interesting companion and the prospect of renewing our carnal adventures held considerable appeal.

"I can't leave the library." She sighed and hunched her shoulders in resignation. "With so much trouble brewing, she'll need a true guardian in days to come."

"Trouble is indeed brewing," I repeated. "In truth, I'm not sure how much longer it'll be safe for me and my comrades to remain in this port. An early departure would be very welcome."

"There's a sea captain of my acquaintance, a man open to secluding an extra passenger aboard his ship, for the right price."

"Two extra passengers. I have a partner."

"As you wish. Captain Din Faud is the man you want, skipper of the *Morning Star*. It's an old cog, but fast. And he's an old rogue but trustworthy once hands are shook on a deal. Mention my name when you seek him out; otherwise he's likely to get tetchy. I happen to know the *Morning Star* is due back in six days."

"I begin to suspect there is little that occurs in this port that you don't know." I held up the books before consigning them to the folds of my tunic. "We haven't discussed your price for this."

"Oh," Berrine said, turning to go, "I think you already paid me in full, Alwyn Scribe."

"You didn't ask why," I said, causing her to pause.

She turned back with an arched eyebrow. "Why?"

"Why it's not going to be safe here. Nor did you ask about my recent adventure. Aren't you curious as to what I found out there in the wilds?"

She said nothing, continuing to regard me with only mild curiosity as I gestured to the mighty statue looming above. "As it happens," I said, "I met a man out there who reminded me a great deal of Ulthnir here, except he carried an axe. A great stone axe."

"And yet you seem to have suffered no injury." Berrine angled her head, smiling. "Not all southerners who meet an Ascarlian can count themselves so fortunate."

"I didn't say he was Ascarlian."

This brought a faintly sheepish twitch to her mouth, but no sign of particular concern.

"We came upon him shortly after he tortured a man to death," I went on, which at least had the effect of shifting her expression into something far more serious. "The Crimson Hawk. Have you heard of it? Inflicted upon a man who had committed the apparently grievous crime of carting wool for sale in this town so he could feed his family."

"An act to be greatly regretted," Berrine returned. "But then, so are many in war."

I moved closer, tugging the cord about my neck to reveal her gift. "He also had one of these." I dangled the silver knot in front of her eyes. "Curious, wouldn't you say?"

Berrine's gaze lingered on the trinket for a brief second before she stepped away, raising her face to regard Ulthnir's impassive stone visage far above. "The Altvar-Rendi," she said, "tells of how Ulthnir, Overlord of the Far Realms, fought a great battle against the Heltvar, vile beasts of the Anguished Pit. Having vanquished them, and keen to cleanse his domain of their corpses, he wove them all into a new realm, this earth upon which we stand. Hence, when the world was born the very soil was seeded with evil. It was from this evil that all the wrongs of man and nature arose. Shamed by his error, Ulthnir vowed to protect his creation and the mortal beings that dwelt upon it, swearing all his children and grandchildren to this task. He made himself the guardian of the Halls of Aevnir, so that even beyond the veil of death, the most worthy would receive just reward. Such is Ulthnir's devotion to his creation and such is the debt we mortals owe him. What are you devoted to, Alwyn?"

I doubted she expected an answer, so I gave none. Berrine's eyes tracked from Ulthnir's grimly resolute features to the base of his statue, a square plinth richly inscribed in runes. To this day I don't know if she deliberately allowed her gaze to linger on one particular set of characters or if it was simply an unconscious reflex born of years of study. Out of sentiment, I choose to believe the former.

"It was good to see you again," she said before walking away, her stride brisk.

I waited until she had disappeared into the maze of streets before approaching the plinth. The runic characters that had attracted her focus were at the very end of the inscription and, naturally, meant nothing to me. Taking a charcoal stub and parchment from my pocket I very carefully copied them down. Somewhere in this soon-to-be-besieged port there was bound to be at least one soul who knew their meaning.

CHAPTER THIRTY-NINE

"Redmaine called it the trickster's jab," Wilhum explained, tapping the pommel of his longsword against the lower rim of my visor. We were tangled together in a clinch in the centre of Fohlvast's stableyard. He was once again clad in his fine blue armour, me in a mismatched but serviceable collection of battlefield scavengings bought or purloined from my fellow soldiers. With little else to occupy us save tedious drill or walking the short span of the wall, we had sought and obtained the captain's permission to continue my lessons in the knightly arts.

I was gratified to find the former noble a mostly patient tutor. Also, judging by the new keenness of his gaze and lack of liquor on his breath, he was now entirely sober. He would guide me through the various sword scales with careful advice rather than the scorn or punishment that I knew had coloured much of his own education. Sparring with him after the first few days, it was easy to fool myself that I had begun to match his skills. However, every now and then he would display a sudden ferocity or wickedly devious tactic that illustrated in stark terms just how much his inferior I remained.

"All knightly helms have a weak point," he went on, pressing the pommel hard against my visor and craning my neck to a painful angle. He had contrived to snare me in this position by a blurringly fast reverse of his sword that trapped my own blade against his armoured side. Too quick to follow, he then looped his left arm around my right and pulled me close. I could have swung a punch at his head, but it was clear his pommel would have done its work before it landed.

"Hit it hard enough," he went on, "and the visor will come loose, maybe even snap your opponent's neck in the process." He released me and stepped back. "You try."

"All these tricks don't seem particularly chivalrous," I commented as he slowly demonstrated the required set of movements. He had already shown me all the various gaps in knightly armour through which a dagger could be thrust, a particular favourite being the unprotected patch behind the knee. One good stab at that and any knight would find himself lamed.

"War is always a trick," he replied. "Or so Master Redmaine was fond of saying. Churls are tricked into following their lord's banner on promise of loot, or the threat of a flogging which they could avoid if they just stood as one and told him to piss off. Nobles trick themselves with notions of glory or a king's boon. And chivalry—" Wilhum let out a short, bitter laugh "—is the worst trick of all, for it fools us with the illusion that war is anything but a chaos of slaughter and suffering."

"A cheery fellow, then."

"No, he was a miserable, sadistic swine of the worst kind. But he had his moments of insight."

Shortly after, we sparred with quarterstaffs which Wilhum used in lieu of a better simulacrum for the length and weight of a longsword. I quickly became aware that he had gone easy on me over the first couple of days, a concession he was abandoning with increasing violence as my lessons continued. Thanks to my brawler's acumen, I could hold my own for the first few blows, but he invariably found a way to put me on my arse before long. Still, I knew my skills were improving and the longsword was no longer the unwieldy length of iron it had once been. With enough time I reckoned I might actually come close to matching Wilhum, or at least have a chance of surviving a real encounter with a knight of similar ability. But time was against us. In three days I would seek out Berrine's sea captain and purchase my passage out of this company and its precarious situation.

I considered inviting Wilhum to accompany Toria and me when the time came but knew it would be a wasted effort. He and Evadine spent most evenings conversing in seclusion now, often in counsel with Sergeant Swain. No doubt they were planning their defence of this port, meaning Wilhum was now effectively part of the command of this company. He continued to hold no more rank than I did, yet could speak his mind to Evadine and the Supplicants without fear of chastisement. Nor was he expected to knuckle his forehead in their company.

I hadn't noticed any particular thawing in Evadine's regard since returning from our reconnaissance, her gaze remaining bright with reproachful accusation. However, she hadn't felt the need for any further life-endangering punishments, which was something. Also, her willingness to allow me to forgo the routines of soldiery in order to receive Wilhum's tutelage spoke of a largesse not extended to my comrades. Perhaps I had been forgiven, or at least deemed worthy of possible redemption for my indulgence of heathen ways. Not that it mattered now, or so I imagined up until the moment one of Fohlvast's servants came running past us with his voice raised to panicked shrillness.

"They've come, my lord!" he screeched, arms flapping in a way that I would normally have found comical. He stumbled to a halt beneath Fohlvast's window, casting out a plaintive, desperate call. "The northern monsters are here!"

"Three hundred and forty-eight," I reported, unable to keep the doleful disappointment from my voice as I handed the spyglass to Evadine. The Ascarlian fleet had appeared out of the mist some three miles off the harbour mouth, the multiple splash of their anchors announcing their presence better than any pealing of trumpets.

"As Trooper Dornmahl said," I went on, "some are bigger than others, but they're all sitting low in the water."

"Fully laden then," Sergeant Swain surmised, squinting as he surveyed the fleet. "The elderman was right: they've brought at least twenty thousand swords against us. And it appears they aren't going to oblige us by assaulting the wall."

"And yet there is nowhere for them to land," Evadine mused. She didn't appear especially troubled, her brow creased with puzzlement rather than concern. "The outer dykes are protected by a sea wall and too steep for a ship to beach on even at high tide. They could assault the harbour directly but with the mouth blocked they would have to scale the mole, and that's just as easy to defend as the wall."

"It could be they see no reason for an attack," Wilhum put in. "As long as they remain in the fjord no trade will leave or enter this city. Nor will any fishing craft put to sea."

Swain gave a soft grunt of agreement. "A blockade then. This Tielwald of theirs intends to starve us into submission."

"Which raises the question of stocks, my lord Fohlvast," Evadine said, turning to the elderman.

He appeared more composed today, standing straighter with a look of calm assurance on his handsome features. However, I judged his pallor to be a shade paler than normal and his expression the result of extensive practice in front of a mirror glass.

"We have enough grain, preserved meat and other sundries to last through the summer and into winter," he said, his tone just as studied as his expression. "Longer even, if properly rationed. If the Sister Queens' pet dog thinks he can beggar my city, he shall find himself disappointed." He sniffed, stiffening his back and casting a dismissive hand at the Ascarlian ships. "I think more likely that it is they who shall starve, Captain. Let them sit there stewing in their heathen stink. In winter, Aeric's Fjord becomes a channel for bergs sloughed off the glaciers to the east. Only the worst fool would remain at anchor then. If their grumbling bellies haven't convinced them to depart, the prospect of shattered hulls surely will."

"Months on end of just sitting here bodes ill, Captain," Swain said. "We have boats aplenty in the harbour. Let me take a dozen or so, scurry out in the dead of night and set some fires in those hulls. It would certainly inspire the company."

Evadine considered for a short interval before inclining her head in agreement. "Very well, Sergeant. Volunteers only, mind." Any notion that she might have been harbouring warmer feelings towards me vanished as her eyes slipped from the sergeant to mine. "How about it, Scribe?" she enquired, eyebrows raised and a faint smile of expectation on her lips. "Fancy another chance at the heathen?"

Does she think me a traitor? I thought, wondering if my safe return hadn't aroused some suspicions in her mind. But then, Wilhum had also returned unmolested and she harboured no apparent odium towards him. *Just spite then*, I decided, jaw aching as I clenched it and bowed, knuckle pressed to my forehead once again.

"As the Covenant requires, Captain," I said.

Swain's volunteers consisted of thirty souls in all. Brewer and Toria couldn't be dissuaded from stepping forwards once they learned I was to be part of this mad folly. Wilhum joined us too and, to my surprise, Ayin was also permitted to volunteer.

"She's keen to prove her courage and her devotion to the Covenant," the captain said when I made a clipped but determined objection. "Who am I to deny her?"

The party was assembling on the wharf close by, clad in only the lightest scraps of armour. Every blade and face was darkened with smeared soot and only dimmed lanterns were allowed. Ayin certainly appeared keen and nimble as she hopped into one of the three long-boats that would carry us from the harbour. I watched her position herself at the prow, turning to wave happily at where Evadine and I stood on the quay.

"She's still mad," I said. "Less mad than she was, to be sure, but her mind remains broken. I doubt battle will mend it."

"You should have more faith in your comrades." Evadine's tone was quiet but possessed of a now familiar hardness. "In fact, Scribe, I find your faith lacking in many respects."

The heated response of *Fuck my faith!* rose to my lips but I managed to cage it in time. "I can understand your desire to punish me, Captain,"

I said, speaking with a controlled terseness. "But my friends should not be part of it."

"Why do you assume this to be a punishment?" She fixed me with a look of bland enquiry. "What could you have done to merit such treatment?"

More unwise words boiled up to be contained once again, though only barely. "I'll not apologise for saving Brewer's life," I said. "By heathen means or any other."

"And what of his soul? Do you imagine the Seraphile will allow him through the Portals now it has been so besmirched?"

"Scripture speaks of the Seraphile's grace as being boundless in its compassion. Perhaps it is you who should have more faith in them, Captain."

Anger had pushed me to stray far beyond my bounds and I expected a harsh command to mind my place, possibly even a call for Swain to clap me in irons. Instead, Evadine's anger was only momentary. Her brow creased then smoothed as she lowered her head, eyes closed as she drew in a slow breath.

"I know why you did what you did," she said, opening her eyes. I was taken aback to find them fearful rather than angry. "And, in their wisdom, the Seraphile have seen fit to show much of what you will do, Alwyn Scribe. So, know that this—" she gestured to the boats "—is not a punishment."

Her gaze settled on my face, shining with a scrutiny I found more off-putting than her fear. Unusually, I couldn't think of a thing to say, staring in dumb silence when she stepped closer, narrowed eyes peering into mine. "What they show me is often . . . confused, even contradictory. I saw both triumph and defeat on the Traitors' Field. I saw the Council of Luminants both laugh and bless me when I sought permission to raise this company. Now the Seraphile send visions of you . . . and me." She raised a hand, extending it towards my face. "Sometimes we are—"

A soft cough from Swain froze the passage of her hand. Evadine blinked and withdrew it, stepping back and turning to the sergeant with a brisk smile. "Ready for the off then, Supplicant Sergeant?"

"Boats loaded and all keen to get at the heathen, Captain."

I wasn't sure whether to be more troubled by the squint of bemused suspicion Swain struggled to keep from his face or the complete lack of irony in his voice.

"Very well," Evadine said. "I'll muster the full company on the dockside should the Ascarlians be foolish enough to come in pursuit once you've done your work."

She gave me a final glance before she strode off, her face taut. However, the mingling of fear and doubt in her eyes caused me to track her departure, my unease deepening into abject fear. Something was very wrong this night, something far worse than the prospect of rowing out in the dark to confront thousands of Ascarlians.

"Stop gawping and get aboard, Scribe," Swain snapped when the captain's tall form faded into the gloom beyond the lanterns.

It would have been a comparatively easy task to extend a swift jab at his chest with my sheathed longsword as I passed him by. Watching him flail and sputter in the harbour waters may well have been worth the dire consequences. But I didn't. Intuition told me I would be grateful for the sergeant's abilities before this night was out.

In Aeric's Fjord the tide ebbs just after midnight, creating a slow shift in current that enables a boat to drift free of the harbour without benefit of oars. Of course, we had oars loaded. They would be slotted into the rowlocks to be hauled with frenzied energy during the return journey, but our approach was made in tense, protracted silence save for the swish and slap of water against the hulls. The moon was a thin crescent behind drifting clouds, meaning the boats resembled just a trio of shadows amid the darkened chaos of the fjord's shifting waters.

We all lay prone beneath black cloaks, blades sheathed until they were needed. Those of us in the lead boat had been given a dozen clay pots each, all filled with lamp oil. When the hull of the first longship came within throwing range, we would dash the pots against the timbers, the boats behind would light torches and soon a decent-sized inferno would rage among the outer fringe of their fleet. With luck and a favourable wind, it might even spread to the other ships.

I had to admit this was a clever scheme, as such things went. Whatever our fate, a victory of sorts would be scored tonight. What concerned me wasn't the likelihood of successfully setting a few ships ablaze; it was the unlikelihood of making it back to the harbour once the Ascarlians had been fully roused. I knew Swain saw our lives as fair exchange for ensuring the port's survival, but I did not.

Consequently, as we neared the outermost line of ships, I raised my cloak to gain a better view. It was my hope that I should espy or be espied by a vigilant warrior appointed sentry for the night. Upon catching sight of said fellow it was my full intention to do everything to snare his attention thereby raising a commotion of shouts which would force us to abandon this suicidal enterprise. Sadly, no keen-eyed Ascarlian obliged me and the curving rail of the nearest longship remained conspicuously vacant. Neither had the irksomely negligent crew taken the simple precaution of posting lit torches fore and aft. In fact, as far as I could tell, the entire Ascarlian fleet was shrouded in darkness unbroken by a single torch.

"Make ready," Swain whispered and there rose a shuffling in the boat as my comrades readied their pots. "Wait for the order."

Jutting from the ship's prow was a garishly coloured carving of some snarling bird of prey. As the gaping beak loomed above and our boat made loud contact with the longship's hull, the curious absence of any alarm sounded a deeper warning in my mind. Not only was there no one on watch and no torches, there was barely a sound from the ship beyond the creak of timbers and faint rasp of rope.

"Don't," I said, turning to Swain as he opened his mouth to voice the command to throw. "Something's not right."

"Just ready your arm, Scribe," he hissed back. "The captain may indulge your indiscipline, but I won't . . ."

I turned away from him and stood, casting off the cloak and calling out to the ship. "Anyone there?"

Instead of a line of hastily armed warriors rushing to the rail, I was confronted by the sight of a lone, small pale face. It bobbed up to blink two wide, scared eyes at us before disappearing followed by the faint urgent whisper of two youthful voices.

"Scourge take you, Scribe!" Swain erupted as I jumped from the boat and latched my hands to the rail. I scrambled over to tumble to the deck beyond, crouching with one hand reaching for the hilt of my longsword. I began to draw it then stopped at the sight of two boys standing a few paces away.

They had the blond, braided locks common to other Ascarlians I had seen, but little of their ferocity. I reckoned the smallest at about ten years old, the other twelve at most. It was the oldest who reacted first, after a moment in which he and his companion exchanged indecisive glances. Drawing a small knife from his belt, the boy let out a creditable attempt at a challenging roar and launched himself at me, stabbing overhand with more enthusiasm than skill.

"That's enough of that," I said, catching his wrist and hauling him up. The knife fell as I tightened my grip before turning to survey the otherwise empty deck. "Where's your kin?" I asked, receiving an eyeful of defiant spit in return. Blinking, I shifted my gaze to the ship anchored barely a dozen yards to port. Its deck was also bare of all crew save a trio of small figures. A glance at the other nearby ships confirmed the same state of affairs with each.

With the boy still dangling in my grasp, I turned and called over the rail, "Something's afoot, Sergeant! The ships are all empty save for whelps like him!"

The sergeant's no doubt anger-filled response was drowned by a loud, bear-like yell from the ship's stern. Looming out of the shadows came a far larger figure. At first I thought it might actually be a bear, the shaggy head and fur-covered bulk conveying a distinctly animalistic impression, but then I saw the battleaxe it held.

Casting the boy aside, I stepped clear of the rail, drawing my longsword. The charging axeman altered his course to match, raising his weapon high. He continued to yell out his challenge, voice hoarse but strong until it ended in an abrupt shout of surprise as Brewer vaulted the rail and drove his boots into the axeman's back. He landed face down on the deck, the axe jarred from his grip. Grunting with the effort, he tried to rise only to be forced down when Brewer pressed a knee to his neck, dagger poised to stab into his temple.

"Don't kill him yet," I said.

"What is this?" Sergeant Swain demanded, clambering onto the ship. His wrath had been obviated somewhat by the unfolding mystery, but still he regarded me with a baleful intensity that told of imminent retribution.

"Nary a warrior to be had," I said, moving to tap the toe of my boot to the pinioned axeman's head. I saw for the first time how grey his hair was, and the depth of the wrinkles surrounding the eye he strained to glare up at me. "Apart from him, and he's at least a grandfather by my reckoning."

I saw the sergeant's anger vie with his duty as he scanned the ship's deck and the surrounding fleet. Ayin and Toria had also made their way on board, the former compelled by basic curiosity and the latter, I assumed, in search of loot. Wilhum followed shortly after, taking in the scene with a frown of understanding rather than bafflement. Crouching, he peered at a gap between the deck boards, letting out a grunt of confirmation.

"The hull's filled with recently cut timber," he said, face grim. "That's why they sat so low in the water. If their warriors aren't here, it's plain they'll have purpose elsewhere."

I found myself momentarily distracted by the sight of Ayin skipping towards the two Ascarlian boys. They huddled together at the base of the main mast, eyes bright with terror.

"Hello," Ayin greeted them with her customary fondness for pups. "What's your name?" Her face formed an aggrieved pout when they responded only with puzzled suspicion. "Don't be mean," she said, extending a hand to pet the head of the youngest. "My name's Ayin—"

Her voice ended when Toria lunged towards her, catching her about the waist and bearing her to the deck just as a volley of arrows whipped through the air. There were only a few dozen shafts, not especially well aimed but still sufficing to force us all to seek cover. I ducked down behind a barrel, flinching as an arrow careened off the iron rim in a flower of sparks. Raising my head a little, I saw another grey-haired fellow on the neighbouring ship raising a longbow. Beyond him several more grandfatherly types were doing the same. Few in number and too old for battle they may have been, but they were apparently determined to put up some sort of fight.

Just then a loud but completely unfamiliar sound came echoing across the fjord from the port. My gaze snapped towards the town, seeing a large blossoming of dust at the base of Mount Halthir, precisely where the statues of the Ascarlian pantheon stood. The sound resembled the rushing of a waterfall, but harsher, accompanied by numerous overlapping thuds that told of heavy objects impacting on the cobbled streets. The dust was thick and only partly illuminated by the lights of the town, but through its billowing clouds I discerned the sight of a very large shape toppling.

"Ulthnir's statue," I breathed.

"What in the name of all the Martyrs is happening?" Sergeant Swain half rose from the coil of rope he had been crouching behind. His features were suddenly rendered near unrecognisable by a mingling of bewilderment and fear. I, however, felt a growing realisation as the statue completed its fall, birthing a thunderous boom of such volume it shook the ship.

Reaching into my pocket, I hurried to where Brewer still had the captive Ascarlian pinned. Luckily, it appeared the aged archers on the other ships were just as stunned by the statue's collapse, for they failed to cast any arrows at me as I traversed the deck. "What does this say?" I demanded, unfolding the scrap of parchment before the Ascarlian's eyes. They narrowed in obvious understanding upon surveying the runic characters, but his face remained stony and lips firmly closed.

"Wilhum!" I shouted, keeping my gaze locked on the captive's while I pointed at the two boys still cowering at the main mast. "Explain to this old fuck that if he doesn't tell me what this says he can watch us cut these brats' throats."

The fellow apparently knew enough Albermainish to understand my words, letting out a rageful growl as he tried vainly to rise. "Craven southern scum!" he grated, spittle flying from between clenched teeth. "Making war on children!"

I grabbed a fistful of his hair and held the parchment closer to his face. "Tell me what it says and I won't have to."

The old warrior's nostrils flared as he drew in some ragged, furious breaths, although I did detect some smugness in the reply he grunted out: "'Ulthnir falls so that the Ascar may rise.' That's what it says, you pox-ridden son of a whore."

"I don't have the pox," I muttered in response. Releasing him, I returned my gaze to the town. The dust had covered most of the buildings in a grey pall from which arose a multitude of shouts and screams. In the streets closest to the mountain an orange glow flared, probably the result of fire catching in the ruins of shattered houses. But my thoughts were filled with the many drawings and scribblings fixed to the wall of Berrine's bedchamber. Also, the way her gaze had lingered on these words inscribed into the base of Ulthnir's statue. *Ulthnir falls so that the Ascar may rise.*

"Sergeant Swain!"

Eyes drawn by the familiar sound of Supplicant Ofihla's voice raised in a shout, I saw a score of longboats swiftly approaching the fleet from the direction of the harbour. Ofihla stood at the prow of the leading vessel, hands cupped about her mouth.

"The captain sends orders!" she called. "We are to seize what ships we can and sail for home!"

"Where is she?" Swain called back.

"Still ashore! She said she'll follow when ready and we're not to tarry!"

"You left her?"

I saw Ofihla's bulky shoulders move in a helpless shrug. "It was her command!"

"She told me she had a vision," I said, causing Swain's eyes to meet mine. I could tell from the twitch in his otherwise rigid features that this was a man engaged in asserting all the self-control he could muster.

"Vision of what?" he asked.

I shook my head. "She was . . . vague on the details." I broke the stare to survey the port once again. The screams rising from the billowing dust were louder now. There is a unique pitch to the clamour that arises from those facing slaughter and, once heard, is unmistakable. I knew with sudden certainty that fire was not the only danger within those clouds.

Know that this is not a punishment, Evadine had said.

"I think she expects to die here," I told Swain. "She's trying to spare us her fate."

I saw Swain master himself then, lowering his head momentarily while his back straightened and all impression of uncertainty vanished. When he raised his face, the twitch was gone and he gave voice to the only profanity I ever heard him speak: "Well, that's not fucking going to happen, is it?"

CHAPTER FORTY

We found the harbour in chaos. A panicked crowd of townsfolk thronged the quayside, all struggling to get aboard one of the ships or fishing boats anchored along the wharf. The foreign merchantmen were equally keen on pushing off and sailing away, their crews beating back the crowd with clubs and boathooks, sending a constant trickle of yelling people tumbling into the water. The fisher-folk were more welcoming. Several boats passed us as we rowed through the harbour mouth, their decks heaving with townsfolk clutching bundles containing what valuables they could gather before fleeing what was now a doomed port.

"Ascarlians came out of the mountain!" one fisherman called in reply to Swain's shouted question. "Thousands of the bastards! They're killing all they can find!"

His words caused the pace of our oars to quicken without the need for any command from Swain. He had ordered Ofihla to take two-thirds of the company and set about the task of seizing ships, once the annoyance of the aged archers had been dealt with. There were a few former sailors among the ranks who would be set to work readying the vessels for departure.

"If we don't return by dawn—" Swain began only for Ofihla to stiffen and snap out a rare interruption.

"Then we shall come ashore and find you, Supplicant Sergeant. We are not leaving without the captain."

We had about a hundred company soldiers crammed into five boats, a meagre force to contend with thousands of blood-crazed northern savages, but we all heaved our way towards the wharf with undaunted energy. I had surely settled my debt to Evadine Courlain on the Traitors' Field, and I still harboured a kernel of resentment for ordering me on that near-fatal reconnaissance. Even so, I worked my own oar with the same zeal as the others, for I found the prospect of staying behind simply unthinkable.

Toria, by contrast, had been quick to make herself scarce as soon as Swain's intent became apparent. She shot me a despairing, disgusted look before dragging Ayin off towards the stack of barrels at the ship's stern, ignoring her plaintive wails.

"But I want to help get the captain—"

"Shut up, you mad bitch!"

The crush of people on the quay was so thick Swain had to order us to fight our way ashore. Brewer was at the apex of the brief struggle as he led a group of soldiers who reversed their halberds and thrashed the crowd until it thinned. Even in their panic, the fleeing townsfolk possessed enough sense to stay clear of us after that.

Swain ordered a score of soldiers to stand guard on the boats before pausing to peer at the smoke-shrouded streets beyond the docks. "Form spearhead!" he barked.

This was a more novel formation than we were accustomed to, one the company had learned on the march north. It consisted of a narrow triangle of halberdiers preceding a base formed of two ranks of sword- and dagger-men. It was designed to puncture an enemy's line of battle with a swift, concentrated charge, the swords and daggers completing the assault by doing their deadly work amid the subsequent chaotic scrum. Brewer placed himself at the head of the spear while Wilhum and I fell in alongside Swain in the base, longswords drawn.

"How do we find her in all this?" Wilhum asked, nodding to the flickering smoke ahead. We could see little beyond running shadows but the constant chorus of screams told the story well enough. It was also punctuated by the occasional tumult of combat. Someone was still fighting.

"We go where the fight is thickest," Swain told him before raising his voice to a sergeant's bark once again. "At the quick march, advance!"

The smoke enveloped us instantly, making it impossible to discern more than a few feet in front of our noses. Still the formation kept together through a mix of determination and harshly instilled discipline. Townsfolk flitted past all the while, some blundering into our ranks in their terror only to be shoved aside. Others assailed us with desperate pleas for help or protection. I saw one fellow, a merchant of good standing judging by his ermine cloak and fine clothes, follow along with us for a time, an open purse clutched in his outstretched hand. Tears streamed down his fleshy face as he gabbled out promises of wealth in return for safe passage from the town. We paid him no more heed than we did the shoeless woman a few streets on who held up her wailing babe and cursed us as cowards when we ignored her pleas.

The sense of having stepped into a realm of nightmare increased at the sight of the bodies. I stopped counting the corpses when I reached a dozen. They lay on blood-slicked cobbles, cut down without regard for age or gender. Some bore the gaping wounds that told of axe work; others lacked obvious injury but still bled in fulsome torrents. I had often thought tales of blood running in the streets when a town suffers a sacking to be a product of lurid exaggeration, but I saw it that night.

We came upon our first Ascarlians when Swain ordered us down one of the broader streets fringing the merchants' quarter. He had been following the din of battle, a course that I saw, with scant surprise, drew us ever closer to the base of Mount Halthir. Rounding a corner, we found about a dozen Ascarlian warriors busily hacking away at a pile of bodies that appeared to be composed of mostly townsfolk with a few of the local soldiery. Seeing us, the northmen left off their slaughter and stared in apparent stupefaction as we approached at a steady march. Seeing how they failed to either attack or flee, I wondered if they were drunk on blood, or simply drunk. It was clear that our appearance was unexpected – remarkably so, for it wasn't until we closed to within the last few paces that the Ascarlians let out a collective war cry and charged our formation.

Their ferocity was impressive, as was their lack of care for their own lives, but they were facing true soldiers now, not Fohlvast's hirelings or defenceless civilians. Also, they were considerably outnumbered. The halberdiers cut them all down without undue difficulty, suffering a few minor wounds before the spearhead swept on. Naturally, successive encounters were not so quickly overcome as more and more Ascarlians became aware of our intrusion into their happy butchery.

A trio of axe wielders came roaring out of an alley and succeeded in hacking down two halberdiers before falling to the stabbing blades of their comrades' weapons. Wiser enemies were content to loose arrows at us from the rooftops, claiming several more lives before we cleared the merchants' quarter and beheld a scene of utter devastation. The streets closest to the parade of statues lay in ruin, their stones and timbers transformed into piles of rubble, the ugly mounds seeded by corpses and speckled in flame. The granite monolith that had been Ulthnir lay among the destruction, shattered into five huge pieces.

Swain brought the troop to a halt a dozen paces short of Ulthnir's great stone head, the huge eyes regarding us with what I felt to be mocking satisfaction. Beyond him I could see a huge crack in the fabric of the mountain where he had stood less than an hour before, a black jagged triangle through which Ascarlians streamed by the dozen. The opening was narrow and the tunnel within presumably extended all the way through to the mountain's northern flank. I had wrongly assumed the full strength had already invested the city, but now I understood it to be a mere vanguard. The bulk of their force was only now joining the fray.

To the front of the tunnel mouth, a fierce struggle raged atop the largest mound of rubble where a hundred or so ducal men-at-arms battled the invaders. The northmen seemingly had little use for the niceties of well-ordered ranks, throwing themselves with frenzied abandon against the cordon the duchy men had formed up on the slopes of the mound, in the centre of which stood a tall, armoured figure with a longsword.

"To the captain, double quick!" Swain barked, sending the troop into the fastest pace it could adopt while still maintaining order. The distance to the mound, where the struggle grew more ferocious by the second, was at least a hundred paces. The piled rubble and frequent gusts of smoke also made for delayed progress, as did the burgeoning number of Ascarlians seeking to bar our path.

The first few attackers were smashed aside without much difficulty but resistance soon thickened into something that resembled an actual formation. Two ragged ranks of highly vocal warriors strung out before us, many with shields, forcing Swain to shout out the order for a charge.

As one, the spearhead accelerated into a run, the point striking the centre of the Ascarlian line. The momentum and weight of numbers sufficed to break their ranks but, as we had been trained to expect, ensured the struggle immediately dissolved into a free-for-all.

"To the captain!" Swain yelled, sidestepping the thrust of an Ascarlian's sword before felling the warrior with a swift blow from his mace. He rushed on, crushing the skull of another northman who stumbled into his path. "To the captain!"

Swain's words were soon taken up by the rest of the troop, echoing loud in my ears as I followed Wilhum in the sergeant's wake. Knowing the folly of allowing myself to become snared in any prolonged fracas, I kept running and slashed my longsword at any warrior who came close. Through the drifting smoke and struggling figures I could see Evadine's tall form, her longsword moving with unceasing energy, a succession of Ascarlians seeming to wither around her like wheat before the scythe. Then my gaze discerned the rise of a far larger figure cresting the mound at her back, a shaggy-haired giant bearing an axe that caught only a speckled sheen from the fire's glow, as might a stone.

"Captain!" I called out, the warning lost amid the tumult of combat. Rushing forwards, I ducked the sweep of a sword and dodged a descending axe before a shield-bearing Ascarlian stepped into my path. In no mood to be halted, I leapt, planting a foot on the fellow's upraised shield and vaulting over him. I felt a rush of air as he chased me with his sword, feeling a small sting on the back of my neck. I ignored it and pressed on towards Evadine, calling out another warning. Both Swain and Wilhum had been compelled to halt and fend off attackers, while I had a clear path through to her.

Whether she heard my warning or not, I couldn't tell, but she did turn in time to avoid the first blow of Margnus Gruinskard's axe. Rubble shattered into powder as the massive stone blade descended, the Tielwald drawing it back for another try as if it weighed no more than a fly switch. It seemed incredible to the point of impossibility that a man of such age and stature could move so quickly, but Evadine was equally quick.

Instead of delivering another blow, Margnus was forced to raise the haft of his axe to ward off the thrust Evadine jabbed at his throat, then again as she whirled, slashing at his face. The Tielwald succeeded in blocking the strike, but Evadine displayed even greater swiftness, ducking low and darting forwards so that she closed the gap between them, rising at the last instant to drive the point of her longsword into the flesh below the Ascarlian's chin. Had she succeeded in pushing home, it would surely have spitted his head and deprived the northmen of their general. Whether this might have saved Olversahl for the king is another question, although many a historian will tell you so. Personally, I've always had my doubts. Even with their Tielwald slain, the Ascarlians now had sufficient numbers to sack the port several times over and their blood was fully stoked for carnage. Olversahl, and most of its people, was always destined to perish that night.

In any event, such speculation is entirely academic, for Margnus Gruinskard did not die in that moment. In fact, all these years later, I receive occasional reports that the mysterious old bastard somehow contrives to draw breath to this day. If so, he draws it through deformed lips and I certainly hope his missing eye pains him a great deal.

Once again moving with his age-defying swiftness, the Tielwald jerked his head aside just as the point of Evadine's sword touched his flesh. It scored its way up his face, slicing through both lips and his left eye before leaving a deep channel in the maze of creases covering his forehead. But, grievous injury though it surely was, it didn't kill him.

Reeling away with a roar of pain and fury, the Tielwald swung his axe in a wide arc, Evadine ducking low to evade it, her sword poised for another thrust. With Gruinskard off balance and wounded, it may well have been this blow that struck him down, but it was one the Anointed Lady never got the chance to deliver.

The two wolves bounded over the crest of the mound, the black leaping high, the white low. Evadine pivoted in time to slash her sword deep into the side of the white wolf, but not before it clamped its jaws on her leg. The black angled its huge head to fix its maw on Evadine's chest. I was close enough now to see her breastplate buckle under the pressure and blood spurt as teeth bit through steel.

Evadine's sword spun free of her hand as the wolves brought her down in an untidy tangle, jaws still locked and heads shaking with furious violence. The blood gushing from the white's side failed to distract it from joining its brother in attempting to rend Evadine apart. So fixated were they on their victim, they failed to notice my charge. The black was nearest so I stabbed it first, putting all my weight behind my longsword and driving it deep into the beast's back. I had aimed to sever its spine but the brute shifted at the last instant and my blade pierced its ribs instead.

Releasing its hold on Evadine's chest, the wolf arched its body to snap at me, the teeth closing within an inch of my face. I felt my fear return at the hot blast of the beast's breath on my skin, my nostrils filling with the rank stench of its breath. Faced with such raw ferocity, my body shuddered with the urge to let go of my sword and run, but the brawler's instinct told me that would be a mistake. A glimpse of the wolf's glaring, hate-filled eyes made it clear it was now intent upon my death. Wounded though it was, if I ran I would cover no more than a few steps before it brought me down.

So I fought instead, slamming a punch into the wolf's eye then clamping both hands to my sword, heaving and twisting the blade then driving it deeper towards where I hoped its heart lay. Fortune favoured me, for the wolf abruptly stiffened and let out a sound that mingled a growl with a piteous whimper. Twitching and vomiting blood, the black-coated monster collapsed.

I began to drag the longsword clear then felt a massive weight on both my shoulders. Rubble cracked beneath my back as the white wolf's paws pressed down, gaping mouth rearing to deliver a killing bite. A loud crunching thud and my vision turned instantly red. Instead of the expected explosion of pain followed by, I hoped, swift oblivion, I felt a hot wetness cover my face.

"Get up, Scribe!" Sergeant Swain instructed. I blinked then wiped warm gore from my eyes to see him grunting with the effort of heaving the white wolf's corpse aside. Blood dripped from his mace and I caught sight of brains spilling from the shattered skull of the beast as it tumbled down the rubble slope.

"See to the captain!" Swain shouted and a group of company soldiers rushed past. I staggered to my feet, watching them gather Evadine up and finding my gaze transfixed by her bleached, sagging features. Her eyes were open but possessed only the dullest gleam and her face tensed repeatedly with pain.

A loud bellowing drew my sight to where a line of soldiers was holding off a mob of Ascarlians. Wilhum stood in the centre, his longsword rising and falling with expert and deadly skill. The bellowing, louder even than the shouts and screams of the combatants, came from beyond the melee. Through the haze I made out Margnus Gruinskard's bulky form surrounded by a brace of struggling northmen. For one mad instant I thought he had turned on his own kind then realised they were pulling him from the fray.

"Form crescent!" Swain barked and the troop quickly assumed the half-moon formation favoured for an orderly withdrawal. The ranks were joined by a dozen or so surviving ducal men-at-arms, but a quick count of numbers made it clear we had lost near half our strength getting to the captain's side.

Fortunately, the troop's initial charge had possessed enough ferocity to kill or discourage most of the northmen in the immediate vicinity. A few more stalwart or battle-maddened souls were unwilling to see us leave this gathering so soon and threw themselves against the arcing line as we retreated. Wilhum cut down two in rapid succession while the halberdiers accounted for the rest. More forceful attacks would surely have followed, perhaps eventually turning our withdrawal to the harbour into a rout, then a massacre. But fortune was to smile on us once more in the shape of a thick, choking pall of ember-rich smoke that swept in from the centre of the town. It enveloped us in an instant, stinging eyes and birthing a chorus of coughs.

"Grab the shoulder of the man next to you!" Swain called out, voice hoarse but still strong. "Stay together!"

I reached out my left hand, finding no convenient shoulder within reach, while the hand that touched mine failed to gain purchase on my gore-covered pauldron. Blinded by the smoke, I jostled and stumbled along, trying to stay within the formation until my feet found an inconveniently placed corpse.

"Martyrs' guts!" I cursed, landing hard on wet cobbles. I tried to scramble to my feet only for the bloodied ground to trip me once more. A blast of hot air accompanied by the crack and roar of tumbling timber had me huddling with an arm thrown over my head. When the heat abated, I blinked wet eyes to find the smoke had thinned and I was now alone in a corpse-strewn street. The route to the docks had been blocked by the collapsed, burning remnants of a house.

Regaining my feet, I ran, letting my senses guide me away from the heat. Landmarks were swallowed by the smoke which stung my eyes every time I dared open them. Also, every breath felt like swallowing a cloud of hot needles, forcing me into repeated bouts of coughing, some violent enough to send me to my knees. Finally, a turn in the wind brought some relief and I found myself standing amid the familiar broad stretch of cobbles that surrounded the library.

My panicked mind quickly fixated on the great stone building as a possible refuge. However, as I stumbled towards it, I found stark evidence that the Ascarlians did not share the Fjord Gelders' sacred convictions regarding books.

The library's walls were stone, but the roof was ancient and dry timber. Whether those aged beams had caught an ember, or the conflagration that now engulfed the heart of the building was the result of deliberate vandalism, remains a matter of much scholarly conjecture. Whatever the truth of it, the result was the near complete destruction of an archive that had existed for at least a thousand years. Fed by countless pieces of parchment and vellum, the flames that had consumed the roof and what lay within burned bright and hot, licking up at the sky like the myriad tongues of some ethereal ravenous spirit. For a scribe it was an ugly thing to behold, almost as ugly as the corpses littering the streets. For a librarian, of course, it was far worse.

I saw her slim form outlined against the flames, standing too close to the blaze than was safe but she didn't appear to care about the embers swarming around like angry wasps. Berrine remained a statue as I approached, an unmoving witness to the destruction of the place that was more than her work, more than her home.

I will confess that I thought of killing her then, finding no shame in the prospect of hacking down a defenceless woman before she had the chance to even turn around. But I didn't. *All born killers are outlaws, but not all outlaws are born killers.* Deckin's words from long ago. A long dead, betrayed fool he may have been, but he had known my heart with unerring clarity.

So, instead of hacking her neck through with my longsword, I coughed and summoned enough spit to say, "Ulthnir falls so that the Ascar may rise."

She consented to turn then, revealing a face that was as rigid as her body. Tears had scored pale channels through the soot covering her cheeks, but it appeared she had wept herself dry now. The eyes that stared into mine were not quite those of a madwoman, but neither were they fully sane. Guilt and hatred put a very particular sheen to the eye, and I saw both in hers. But I doubted her hatred was for me.

"They built it when the city was young," she told me. Her voice possessed a disturbing calmness, the words flowing without any smoke-born catch to her throat. "When they honoured this place with the statues of the Altvar. What better place to craft an escape route should they ever need it?"

"An escape?" I gave a bitter laugh and saw her face twitch with the cruelty of it. I didn't care. I wouldn't kill her but neither would I spare her. "No one else knew, did they?" I asked, shouting above the roar of the flames. "Only you with your unique insight into this library and all its many secrets. Only you could have unearthed so priceless a treasure. You must have felt very special. What did the Tielwald promise you in return for the key to this port?"

A bright, unblinking stare was her only reply but I knew the answer. "They were all going to be yours, weren't they?" I stabbed a finger at the blackened shell of the library. "All the books. No more senior librarians to get in the way. This would be your kingdom. Look at it now."

She continued to stare so I lunged for her, grasping her shoulders and forcing her to face the inferno. "Look at it!"

"Will you . . . " Berrine's slim form shuddered in my grasp, her voice finally betraying some emotion as she faltered, desperate entreaty colouring the words she gasped out. "Will you . . . please, kill me . . . Alwyn?"

The anger leached from me then, a thunderous rumble of collapsing timbers from the library and another shift in the wind reminding me that my time in this place was over. I released her and stepped away, then stopped. I don't know why I spoke my next words – that old serpent sentiment perhaps, or just obligation born of recent intimacy.

"We've seized some ships," I grunted. "There's a place on board if you want it." I let out another laugh, this one more wry than cruel. "Plenty more books in the southlands."

Before Berrine lowered her head, I like to think there was some measure of gratitude there, but it may have been the shifting glow of the fire playing over her face. "Why do you imagine I have a choice where I go?" she asked. She reached for her collar and drew out a small trinket on a leather cord. I wasn't shocked by the fact that it was another silver knot, but the fact that it was shimmering with a bright yellow glow was highly disconcerting.

"He's calling for me," she said. "And for you, Alwyn."

A sudden flare of warmth over my breastbone had me reaching for my own token. Pulling it out I saw that it too had begun to glow. It wasn't as bright as Berrine's and the colour was red rather than yellow. At another time it might have transfixed me with wonder, stirred my ever-curious mind to stay and demand answers. But in that moment, I felt only repulsion at the sheer impossibility of it.

"It seems he likes you," Berrine observed. "But also, you appear to have made him angry. What did you do?"

I killed one of his wolves, I thought, not understanding how I knew that, but knowing it with utter certainty nonetheless. I began to back away, the silver knot pulsing brighter with every step.

"There'll be a price to pay," Berrine warned. "But you'll live, and his rewards will be great, if you stay. After all, what is there for you in the southlands?"

Her voice was a shout now, harsh with admonition, so unlike her own and I wondered if it were truly her speaking. My fear soared to new heights at the notion, the urge to survive reasserting itself with implacable force. I took one last look at Berrine's stern, demanding features, threw the silver knot at her feet, then turned and ran.

CHAPTER FORTY-ONE

"Is she dying?"

Evadine's eyes were closed, her skin pale as a marble statue. Supplicant Delric had bound her torso with bandages and forced a succession of different medicinal concoctions down her throat, but none of it had summoned more than a faint groan from her lips. Delric changed the bandages every few hours, but the blood that stained them seemed darker each time.

He gave no answer to my question beyond a short, angry glance, one mirrored in the faces of Swain and Wilhum. It was clear they, and the rest of Covenant Company, had no desire to confront what increasingly appeared to be a dire inevitability – not yet in any case.

Evadine had been placed beneath the awning at the stern of our stolen Ascarlian longship. Their shipwrights didn't appear to trouble themselves with such niceties as cabins so shelter on deck consisted of what could be improvised from cloaks and unused sails. Still, I felt it to be a more seaworthy craft than the gut-roiling bucket that had carried us north.

Shifting my gaze from Evadine's unresponsive features, I surveyed the twenty ships and several dozen townsfolk-laden fishing craft that comprised our newly created fleet. Supplicant Ofihla had been typically efficient in seizing enough craft to carry the entire company.

The feat hadn't been accomplished without loss, for the boys and old men left behind to crew them were disinclined to surrender without a struggle. Even so, by the time Swain returned with the stricken Evadine, resistance had mostly been quelled and many of the surplus vessels put to the torch. Most of the old ones had had to be cut down but the boys were generally spared. Ofihla had them pushed into rowboats and set adrift. A few Ascarlian craft managed to scramble enough hands together to row themselves clear of danger, but it was plain this victory had cost the Sister Queens dear, in ships if not lives.

My own escape from Olversahl had not been easy, involving much avoidance of falling buildings and fighting my way through a growing horde of fleeing townsfolk. It wasn't surprising to find that my comrades had opted not to await my arrival, although Wilhum later assured me the decision to cast off had been a difficult one, if swiftly taken. Finding the quay bare of ships and the few remaining fishing boats already under way, I made for the mole. On the seaward side I discovered a cluster of small boats, their occupants busily attempting to row away with varying degrees of success. I chose the largest boat I could see and eschewed descending one of the iron ladders for simply jumping into the midst of the merchant family who had somehow gained possession of it. The husband was initially disinclined to allow me to join their crew, but a bared dagger convinced him otherwise and soon we were rowing for the ships.

One day out from Olversahl and the smoke of its destruction still rose above the northern horizon. I would learn later of the many foul deeds that marked its fall. The incineration of the library is the principal crime remembered by scholars when they depict this event, which tends to overlook the massacre and wanton destruction that accompanied it, including the desecration of the Shrine to Martyr Athil. One more lurid tale has it that the old Supplicant knelt before the relic altar and his lips continued to intone the Martyr for deliverance even after an Ascarlian warrior hacked his head from his shoulders.

The story of Lord Elderman Fohlvast is far more believable. Having been discovered hiding under a dung heap in his stables he was promptly dragged out to suffer the Crimson Hawk under the stern, one-eyed gaze of Margnus Gruinskard. It transpired that, prior to seizing Olversahl for the Crown, the elderman had entered into negotiations with the Sister Queens to surrender it to them for the right price. When they failed to meet his demands he promptly rediscovered his loyalty to King Tomas. While I have occasion to regret many things that transpired in that unfortunate port, the demise of Maritz Fohlvast is not among them.

Watching the smoke rise, I pondered Berrine's fate and the frightful impossibilities I had witnessed. The Caerith book was once again strapped to my side together with her guide to translating the ancient text it held. When I found the leisure to set myself to that particular task I had little doubt I would find a fulsome description of our parting. It was not a discovery I relished making, but knew I would make it nonetheless. The book was even more irresistible now, the promise in its pages both terrifying and alluring. It appeared I had gained possession of the maps to two treasures: one the long-sought-after hoard of a long dead outlaw, the other my own future. The very obvious dilemma presented by the latter did occur to me, of course, but not with the import it should have: *If it has already been written down, can I still change it?*

"Delric won't say it, but I can read his answer in his eyes."

I turned to find Wilhum coming to my side, his own gaze also fixed on the distant column of smoke. "She's dying." His voice caught as he said it and I spared him further discomfort by looking away from the tears welling in his eyes. Glancing at Evadine's pale, hollow-cheeked face, I found the sight of it clutched at my heart with a forcefulness I didn't like.

Then she'll be the Martyr Sihlda wasn't, I thought, trying to summon a bitter cynicism I didn't feel. *They'll give her a shrine. Pickle her organs and bones and set them on an altar for desperate fools to grovel at for centuries to come. Martyr Evadine, the Anointed Lady, Sword of the Covenant, slain by heathen treachery. Think of the tithes she'll bring.*

I said none of this to Wilhum, suspecting he might kill me for it. "The seas are calm," I told him, opting to employ forced optimism for want of anything else. "We'll have a swift passage to Farinsahl where there are healers more skilful even than Delric."

Wilhum wiped his eyes, his grief giving way to a grimace of deep foreboding. "And a Crown agent who will lose no time reporting our failure to King Tomas. We lost the jewel of the Fjord Geld to the Ascarlians, and with it the duchy."

"We also destroyed most of their fleet and captured several prizes, escaping with most of the company intact. That has to be worth something."

"It won't be enough. You know the enemies she has ranged against her. Mortally wounded or not, dead or not, they cannot allow the legend of the Anointed Lady to prosper." Wilhum grasped my forearm, his grip and features hard with insistence. "She'll need us. To guard her legacy if not her life. Promise me, Scribe, you'll not abandon her."

I wondered why he set so much store in the oath of a low-born outlaw, but the fierceness of his demand bespoke a genuine regard, or at least a recognition of my usefulness in fraught circumstances.

"I've been a constant thief," I told him. "A frequent liar, an occasional fraud and, according to need or rage, a murderer. But—" I tugged my arm free of his grip "—I've never yet abandoned a friend." I gave him a thin, lopsided smile, my bruises aching with it. "I have so few, you see? So it rarely becomes an issue."

Our arrival at Farinsahl was greeted with weather of an appropriately miserable cast. The port, never an especially picturesque sight, huddled under low clouds of grey and black that spilled recurrent showers on the maze of narrow streets. Evadine, thanks to calm seas and Delric's assiduous care, still drew breath, albeit in shallow, painful groans. She had regained consciousness a few times during the voyage but only briefly. Swain, Wilhum and I took turns to sit with her when Delric was forced to sleep and it had been my misfortune to witness her first awakening.

I had expected bafflement or pain to be the principal expression to colour her face if she ever awoke, but instead I found myself regarding the dark, glowering visage of an enraged soul.

"I . . ." she gasped at me, teeth bared as her hands balled into fists. "I . . . told you . . . to leave!"

Although she had disconcerted me on many occasions, this was the first time I truly feared her. Mortally stricken, weak and barely able to draw breath, still the depth of resentment and anger in her gaze contrived to stir much the same fear Deckin once had. Her eyes, now somehow rendered as black as the legends would later claim, fixed on mine with unblinking, implacable accusation. The sense of being seen as a traitor after having saved her life for the second time stoked enough anger to banish my fear.

"We couldn't," I told her, my tone harsher than one might typically adopt when addressing a dying woman. "If your visions tell you so much, I would have thought they'd have told you that too."

Her eyes dulled then, showing a small measure of contrition, but mostly just weary regret. "They showed me . . . " she murmured, head lolling on her pillow as unconsciousness reasserted its grip " . . . what would happen . . . if you failed . . . to . . . let me die."

We were met at the end of the long jetty that dominates Farinsahl harbour by a small and somewhat bemused delegation of local officials. The only personage of note was the lord of exchange, his status as de facto overseer of this town arising from the fact that he was an appointed Crown agent and therefore beholden to the king rather than Duke Elbyn. He was, in truth, little more than a glorified tax farmer, but such men can rise high in busy ports if they keep their graft small and ensure the king gets his due.

Swain instructed Wilhum to take care of the necessary formalities, reckoning that his noble tones would suit the occasion better. The lord of exchange, a man of advanced years but undiminished faculties, reacted to the news of Olversahl's seizure with unconcealed shock. His concern for our wounded captain was less notable, but he did undertake to summon the most able among the local healers. Evadine was duly carried off to his house while Covenant Company were permitted to billet in the dockside sheds normally given over to the wool trade but now standing empty.

"Messengers will be sent to the king and the duke forthwith," the lord of exchange advised Wilhum in ominous tones. "Know, young sir, that I expect a Crown delegation will arrive as soon as they are able. When they do, prepare yourself and your fellows to provide a full and unexpurgated account of this calamity."

The fact that he made no mention of Evadine providing such an account said much for what he thought of her chances. It did, however, rouse Wilhum to an unwise pitch of anger. "This company answers only to its captain, my lord," he replied, the words spoken with precise terseness any noble would surely take as an insult. "*She* answers only to the Martyrs and the Seraphile."

I saw recognition in the old tax farmer's gaze as he bridled. He knew Wilhum's story and was no doubt about to voice a rebuke and an insult that would escalate this confrontation to unnecessary heights. Stepping between them, I bowed low and spoke in the most obsequious tones I could summon.

"There are many beggared folk among us, my lord. Poor but loyal souls who have forsaken their ancient home to seek the king's mercy. On their behalf, I beg for shelter and provisions."

"The king's mercy is famed," his lordship said, evidently glad to seize on the chance to display both importance and largesse, a habit to which such men are often prone. "Bring them ashore so that they may know the goodness of King Tomas while I adjourn to gather alms for their succour."

He gave the most cursory of bows and strode away, barking out instructions to a clerk who hurried in his wake. "Be sure to note every name, and list a full accounting of valuables in their possession . . . "

"Robbing bastard," I muttered, knowing that any charity afforded the survivors of Olversahl would likely come at a hefty price.

As befits one who spent much of his days scouring a busy port for every spare coin owed the king, the home of the lord of exchange resembled more a fortress than a house. It had begun life as a gatehouse in the town's west-facing wall, but successive owners had expanded it to the dimensions of a minor castle, complete with battlements and a defensive ditch. I found it noteworthy that the ditch covered the approaches from the town and didn't extend beyond the outer walls.

Evadine was placed in a large bedchamber normally given over to visitors of importance who, apparently, once included King Tomas's famous father during one of his tours of the kingdom. Consequently, his lordship had been permitted to emblazon the chamber wall with a large, garishly coloured rendering of the Algathinet coat of arms. I felt sure Evadine would have preferred to be domiciled in the Shrine to Martyr Ihlander, the largest Covenant structure in the city, but the lord of exchange wouldn't hear of it. Also, Delric agreed the shrine was far too draughty a place to be conducive to the captain's recovery.

"Recovery?" I asked him, keeping my voice quiet. I stood at his side in a corner of the room where he busied himself mixing curatives on a small table. Throughout the day the town's most able healers had all come to peer and prod at Evadine. They formed a parade of mostly aged men and women who all shared the creditable trait of refusing to give false hope to the hopeful. The general consensus was that she might last a week, though one stoop-backed old woman insisted she would endure for two.

"Got the Martyrs' blessing on her," she informed us with a confident sniff. "See it plain as day. Ain't the only one, neither."

This was certainly true. People had begun to gather the evening after our arrival. At first it was just a score of the port's most ardent Covenanters, maintaining a silent vigil on the stretch of bare ground beyond the ditch. Come the dawn, they had grown to a hundred souls with more arriving by the hour. I could see them through the half-open shutters on the windows. Some clustered around lay preachers or Supplicants from the shrine, heads bowed as they listened to endlessly recited scripture and murmured their affirmations. Reports had also come of more travelling here from the surrounding villages as word of the Anointed Lady's return spread, moving faster, it seemed, than a fire through a sun-dried forest.

"'And though his wounds were grievous and the sand grew dark with his blood, Athil did raise his face to the sky and smile,'" Delric said. It was the only quotation I had heard from his lips, and the most words he had spoken in a single sentence during our acquaintance. I knew this one well, as did every soul with even the most basic education in Covenant lore.

"'"Why do you smile, teacher?" his followers asked him,'" I said, completing the passage, "'"for is not death upon you?" "No, my beloved," he said. "For there is beauty in all life, and life is never lost to a faithful soul, regardless of what wounds may afflict the body."'"

It was the closest Delric had come to acknowledging Evadine's impending demise, and I could see from the tension in his jaw how it had cost him.

"What you did after the Traitors' Field," he said. He didn't look at me, his strong hands busy with a mortar and pestle as he concocted another blending of herbs and mysterious powder.

"What of it?" I asked after a careful glance at Ayin. She hadn't strayed far from Evadine throughout the voyage and now refused to be excluded from the room. When not called upon to change bandages or see to the captain's bodily needs, Ayin spent her time in agitated pacing or sitting and staring in forlorn desperation at Evadine's wan features. Still, however preoccupied Ayin might have appeared, who could say what she might hear and blithely gabble out later?

Delric's hands didn't cease their labour, the veins standing out in stark relief as they worked the pestle. When he spoke, his voice was soft enough to be part muffled by the grind of stone on stone. "Can it be done again?"

"You know what you ask of me?" I murmured back, deciding not to elaborate with any talk of heathen practices.

The pestle ceased its grind and he turned to me, gaze hard and intent. "I do. So do Sergeant Swain and Lord Wilhum."

Then we'll all burn together, I thought, unable to keep a hollow laugh from my lips. "He's not a lord any longer," I said, my humour fading quickly in the face of his stony visage. "I don't know," I added with a sigh of honest despair. "I would have to find . . . her. If she can be found."

"Two weeks is . . . optimistic." Delric's eyes slipped to Evadine, once so vital and tall, now made small by the largeness of the bed she lay in and the encroaching reach of death. "But, not impossible."

Wherever there's a muster, there she'll be. At least according to Sergeant Lebas, who could be lying at the bottom of the Shalewell River for all I knew. It was a thin thread but I had no others to follow. Besides, her final words that night after she healed Brewer afforded some reason to believe that this might not be a hopeless mission, albeit one I didn't relish. *The next service you require of me will entail a far greater debt. Be sure you're willing to pay it.*

"I'll need a horse," I said. "And coin. A good deal of coin."

They all wanted to come with me – Toria, Swain, Wilhum and Brewer. I suspected the entire company would have marched out in search of the Sack Witch had they been asked. All save Ayin, of course, who found the thought of shifting from Evadine's side unthinkable. I refused them all. Something warned me that seeking out the Caerith woman could only be done alone; the bargain I would need to strike was between the two of us and no other.

Wilhum had used company funds to purchase the swiftest mount he could find, a piebald mare with mercifully kinder manners than Karnic the craven. When I mounted up, Swain handed me a purse bulging with letins and a few silver sovereigns.

"The company payroll," he said. The fact that he felt no reluctance in placing such a fortune in my hands said a great deal about his current priorities. "Promise more if you have to."

In truth, I had no great faith that the Sack Witch had any more interest in coin than she had in Wilhum's armour. But it couldn't hurt to have funds at hand if need arose.

"Where will you look?" Wilhum asked.

"There's talk of Duke Elbyn's sheriff hiring fighters for a sweep of the woods," I said. "A village ten miles north or so. It's the only muster of any size I could glean gossip of. A place to start, at least."

Wilhum forced a smile and slapped a hand to the piebald's rump. "Ride swiftly, Scribe."

*

I had a decent knowledge of the roads around Farinsahl, having done some thieving here years ago. Keeping to the east road, I turned north at the crossroads two miles from the port as it afforded the most direct route to the upper marches. My piebald mare was bred for speed and soon grew fractious at being kept to a mere canter. She spurred happily to a gallop at the first brush of my heels to her flanks, maintaining it for an impressive passage of time until the sky began to dim.

And so, cherished reader, began the fabled, perilous quest of Alwyn Scribe as he went in search of the Sack Witch. Many were the miles he rode through the dark forest. Frequent were the dangers he faced. Mighty were the foes he slew, until, finally, near dead from his travails, he found her. Or, at least that's the tale many a storyteller will spin you in exchange for a meal and a place by the fire.

The true story is that my quest lasted barely a few hours from the gates of Farinsahl. It would have been prudent to force the mare to a walk then make camp when the night became truly dark. However, I remained a novice rider and, preoccupied with the task of remaining in the saddle, failed to notice the rope stretched across the road until an instant before the mare's forelegs collided with it.

I heard bones snap as I flew from her back, the mare letting out a shrill whinny of agonised distress. I landed hard, without benefit of the cushioned armour that made such tumbles easier to bear. I had left my armour behind when I'd set out, not without regret for I nurtured a peculiar fondness for the mismatched collection the more I wore it. My regret deepened to despair as I lay stunned on the verge, mouth gaping in an attempt to fill suddenly emptied lungs.

"She said you would be too clever for this trick." A soft laugh somewhere beyond my sight, the voice accented and, despite the intervening years, immediately and dreadfully familiar. "She was wrong."

I couldn't see his face as he loomed above, but the shape of him was unmistakable, the shaggy mane of his hair as he leaned closer adding to the impression of a dire spectre summoned from a night-mare.

"Hit a man just a gentle tap and he can still die," the chainsman said, something small and shiny gleaming in his hand. "And she wants you breathing and whole. So no hitting for you. Cutting comes later . . . "

Hard fingers gripped my face, a knee pressing into my chest to stop me rising. I got a good look at the shiny thing as the chainsman tipped it, his iron-like fingers forcing my jaw open. It was a small bottle, dripping a thick and foul liquid into my mouth. I was fortunate enough to faint before I tasted the concoction in full, but recalling even that brief tinge still makes me shudder. If death had a taste, that was surely it.

CHAPTER FORTY-TWO

I awoke to the tuneless dirge I recalled from the cart that had carried me to the Pit Mines, quickly coming to the doleful conclusion that the chainsman's voice hadn't improved over the years. As my eyes regained focus, the sense of unwelcome familiarity increased at the sight of manacles encasing my wrists. Also, a thick chain encircled my chest and the hard, rough bulk of a tree trunk pressed into my back. A crack of burning wood snapped my gaze to a bulky, fur-clad silhouette crouching at a fire.

His song faded and he straightened a little but didn't turn. Clearly, he still took great delight in showing his back to his captives. "So, you are awake," he said with the same accented precision. "You are stronger now. The boy has become a man, eh?" This evidently amused him for he gave one of the shrill, if muted, giggles I remembered so well.

I said nothing, raising my gaze to the sky. It was still dark but the fading moon told me we were nearing the onset of dusk. Lowering my head, I surveyed our surroundings, seeing just an anonymous clearing that could have been anywhere in the Shavine Forest. Despite this, I reasoned it couldn't be more than a few hours since my capture, putting us only a couple of miles from the road.

"Still much given to calculation, I see." The chainsman glanced over his shoulder to partially reveal his mottled, flame-marked face, one eye glittering. "It did not help you then. It will not help you now."

I stared into that eye. The intervening years had given me ample time to ponder this man and, while I would have been a fool not to fear him, the principal emotion that rose in me then was not terror, but hate-filled anger.

"She said you were cursed," I told him. "She said whatever your heathen ability is, it lies to you, leads you along paths best untravelled—"

He moved with a speed that I would have thought impossible for one of his bulk. The fur-clad silhouette vanishing from the fire in a blur, my words choking off a second later as his hand closed on my throat. My vision dimmed as he leaned closer and I heard a sharp intake of breath above the sudden pounding in my ears.

"The *Doenlisch*," he hissed, voice quivering with a mix of hunger and barely suppressed terror. Despite the pain, I felt a perverse sense of triumph mingled with recognition as he spoke these words, the same words he had spoken to Raith before he'd murdered him. It appeared I had at least secured one answer this night, not that it aided me at this juncture.

"I smell her on you." His hand tightened on my throat. "Is she near? Does she follow you?"

Still my own fear failed to blossom in full and I found the fortitude to afford him a glaring sneer, keeping my jaw firmly closed. The chainsman squeezed tighter still, then stopped, his hand trembling on my neck before he snatched it away.

He muttered something in his own tongue, stepping back, his hands stroking his fur cloak in a way that put me in mind of a child seeking reassurance. His gaze roved the irregular shadows of the surrounding trees, eyes bright in wary expectation.

"*Doenlisch*," I rasped after a bout of painful coughing. "I don't know this word." Raising my head, I arched an eyebrow at him. "What does it mean?"

He stared back at me, the pale portions of his face standing out stark and near white in the dark. In that moment I saw him not as the spectre drawn from a nightmare. Now he was merely a man rendered pathetic by fears he had nurtured for a very long time. But all moments are fleeting, and so it proved with the chainsman. The flame mask of his face grew dark with rage, his fists bunching. I suspect he would surely have beaten me to death then, had not necessity kept him check.

"You thought her," he said, voice filled with scorn, "a witch? A healer, perhaps? You *Aeschlin* are all the same. So ignorant. So easily gulled. The *Doenlisch* is beyond your understanding." He edged closer and I understood for the first time that much of his fear arose from me. Chained and helpless though I was, his fear kept him from laying hands on me again, at least for now.

"You think me cursed, boy?" he asked, head tilted and eyes unblinking. "I will not deny it. I walk through a world of the dead, and they whisper their truths to me. My song keeps their whispers from driving me beyond the bounds of reason, but I am obliged to let them speak when need arises. Most of the wretches I chain have at least one, a wronged soul willing to share their secrets. Yours is the man you murdered to escape Moss Mill. He whispered your plans when you rode in my cart. He talked of what you did and what you would do. For it is the way with the dead. They are removed from this plane just enough to see not only the paths they walked in life, but the paths of those that wronged them. But—" a spasm of anger passed across his features and he edged an inch closer, fists clenching and unclenching "—they delight in lies. They take pleasure from tormenting me, these sundered, bitter souls. That day at the Pit he waited until I sold you before telling me you would one day contrive to bring about my death. But, here you sit, a bound hog waiting for the butcher, while I—" he unclenched a fist to paw at his chest "—I will see the dawn, boy, and a thousand more. If fortune smiles, I will even get to see the *Doenlisch* burn. Will that not be a fine sight?"

He paused, breathing deep as he gathered strength, then lunged for me, both hands clamping onto my head, his thick thumbs digging into my eyes. "But you will not be there," he grunted as I vainly tried to wrest my skull from his grip, "no matter what that lying corpse says—"

"That's enough!" A new voice, sharp with command. A female voice and, despite its noble inflection, familiar.

The chainsman stopped, hands quivering, my vision flashing red and white as his thumbs maintained their pressure for a second longer. Then, with a shout of frustration, he removed his grip. Tears streamed from my eyes as I blinked furiously, the liquid blur clearing to reveal a vague, slender shape beyond the fire.

"You are truly the cursed one."

I shifted my gaze to find the chainsman had retreated a few paces, once again regarding me with the same mix of fear and frustrated anger. But there was also malice in his gaze as he spoke on. "The curse of a *Doenlisch* is worse than all others. She bound you tighter than I ever could—"

"I said, that's enough." The slender figure came closer. A cowl covered her face but a few tendrils of hair twisted in the slight forest breeze. I felt little surprise at the hue of those tresses, painted a deep red in the firelight.

"Our arrangement . . . " the chainsman began then faltered, voice clipped in a manner that told me he feared this woman almost as much as he feared me. "I was promised—"

"You got what you were promised." The woman came closer still, obliging me to crane my neck to stare up into the black void of her cowl. "And," she added, "if you wish to ever ply your trade in this duchy again, you'll shut your heathen mouth until I give you leave to speak."

A small laugh bubbled to my lips at this; outer sweetness and inner steel had always been her way.

"My compliments on the voice," I told her. "Did it take long to master?"

"I was an actress once," she reminded me. "Voices are just another tool in my bag."

She crouched before me, revealing long, crimson polished nails as she raised her hands to draw back the cowl. Lorine's smile was far warmer than I'd expected but failed to stir any sense of reassurance. While I could only summon hate and rage for the chainsman, Lorine had no difficulty in stirring fear into the mix.

"You look . . . well," I offered. "Nobility suits you."

Her smile slipped a little. "It always did," she said. "You look . . . " she reached out a long-nailed hand to tease the hair back from my forehead, fingertips soft as they played over my brow " . . . changed, Alwyn." Her fingers traced over my face, touching old scars and new, caressing the uneven slab of my nose. "I'm sorry for that."

A spasm of anger had me jerking my head away, spittle flying as I let loose a snarl. "I don't want your fucking pity!"

Lorine grimaced and withdrew her hand, voicing a deep sigh. "I can see you have a story to tell. Or is it one you've been telling yourself these past years? The Tale of Lorine the Great Betrayer. The treacherous whore who sold out Deckin Scarl and made herself a duchess into the bargain."

"It wasn't just Deckin," I reminded her.

"No." Another grimace, her eyes clouding with sorrow that was either real or more evidence of her acting skills. "Did you know we're all that's left? Just us. All the others are gone. Erchel was the only other member of our legendary band still drawing breath, until recently. I heard tell of what happened to him in Callintor. Seemed a little excessive for you, but I assume life in the Pit Mines will do that."

"That and more." A roiling in my gut and increased thump of my heart warned me that my fear was close to overwhelming my anger. I forced myself to meet Lorine's gaze, hoping hate would keep it at bay, but even hate was proving fickle now. I wanted her to taunt me. I wanted the laughing torment of a well-satisfied victor. It was how this was supposed to end. But all I beheld was a very sad woman burdened by a great deal of regret.

Lorine shifted, gathering her cloak beneath her to sit alongside me, peering into my eyes with keen scrutiny. "Did you ever reflect on your remarkable good fortune as a child?" she asked. "Left to wander the woods without food or shelter only to be rescued by the great

Outlaw King himself. Didn't that strike you as a little convenient, Alwyn?"

I avoided her gaze, saying nothing and still trying to stoke my hate, to little avail.

"Deckin had an arrangement with the whoremaster," Lorine went on. "Feed up the whores' most likely whelps and leave them in the forest when they were old enough to be useful, and he found a great deal of use in you, didn't he? The other bastards were just tools to be used and discarded as need arose, but not you. In you he saw the chance to play the father. Sometimes he liked to opine that you might actually be the issue of his loins, so much did he see himself in you. He was a frequent visitor to that particular whorehouse, so it is possible. Personally, I doubt it. You've grown big, but not as big as him. I'd fancy you're a good deal smarter too, and you're not mad, as he grew to be." She leaned closer, a hard insistence colouring her tone. "And he was fully mad at the end. You know that, Alwyn."

"I know," I grated, straining to put my face close to hers, "that his head ended up on a spike because of you. I know that Gerthe took a bolt to the chest and Justan and Yelk and all the others were slaughtered, because of you. I know that I had to slit Hostler's throat . . ." I stuttered to a halt and looked away. I had been playing this game of vengeance for years now, and faced with defeat, I found the prospect both wearying and, despite my increasing terror, oddly satisfying. Only one of us could win, after all.

"Just get it done," I told her in a groan. "Unless you've come to talk me to death. In truth I think I'd prefer a knife to your tongue."

"You didn't always think so." Hearing the smile in her voice, I looked up to find her laughing, the warmth once again shining in her eyes. "I have missed you, Alwyn. The others too . . . well, most of them." She paused, angling her head, features entirely serious now. "What did Erchel tell you before you cut his balls off?"

I shrugged, or rather attempted to in the confines of the chain. "What does it matter?"

"Indulge my curiosity. I am a duchess and some measure of civility would seem appropriate."

Another laugh escaped me, short and bitter, but still a laugh. "It was after he lost his balls," I said. "And, in truth, it was another hand that did the cutting, so he didn't have long. He told me about Lachlan's hoard, about the promises you made him and his kin. Told me about how you had them all slaughtered too."

"Lachlan's hoard." Lorine's voice grew wistful. "Deckin's favourite piece of madness. He truly thought he'd found it, you know? Unearthed the secret from the tangle of all those stories he collected. Supposedly, there's a great cavern dug under the Grey Cliffs on the Shavine coast, and therein lies an ancient, abandoned city from the days before the Scourge. Lachlan, by means unknown, happened upon it and used it to store his fabled treasure. A couple of years ago, I had my dear husband send a party to find this city beneath the earth. They came back with nothing. No cavern, no city, no treasure. It was as much a figment of Deckin's mind as his dreams of making himself a duke. As for slaughter, I'll happily confess to removing Erchel's pestilent kin from this world, but Deckin and the others were not my doing. I'm afraid, Alwyn, you've been hunting the wrong fox all this time."

She reached out to me again, grasping my chin and turning my face so our eyes met. Her gaze was steady and her voice intent, keen for me to hear the truth she told.

"The Mill was Todman's scheme," she said. "I wouldn't have thought him capable, but it transpired he'd been hiding a good deal of wit behind that brute's mask of a face. I'd suspected he was up to some manner of mischief when we made our way to Leffold Glade; too many unexplained absences, too much snooping where he shouldn't. I assumed he was just planning to make off with some loot, maybe sell us out to the sheriff, even though it would have been too late to stop us reaching Castle Duhbos in time to prevent Deckin massacring the duke's household. But the elaborate trap he set was the work of weeks and bespeaks a mind of remarkable cunning. Todman must have gone to Crown Company just after the old duke lost his head, struck his deal and sneaked back to camp without anyone noticing. He told Erchel it was my notion, of course, and that's what the little rat told his kin. That night at the Mill . . . "

Lorine's eyes clouded and she lowered her face. "Todman pulled me into a stable just before Crown Company's bowmen loosed their first volley. 'You're mine now,' he said. 'The forest, all of it. It's mine. The duke and the king have ordered it.' I struggled, tried to get free of him, but he was a strong fellow. 'He would've killed us all, Lorine,' he told me and I knew he was right. I had tried so many times to steer Deckin from his mad course, but he was set on it. Losing that noble filth he called his father broke him, I knew it, but still I followed. For that is what we do for those we love, is it not? That's why this heathen fuck knew you would be riding this road all alone at that particular hour. You rode off to save a madwoman who thinks she receives visions from the Seraphile. I dutifully followed a madman who thought he was a duke. We are both made fools by love.

"I killed Todman that night. Wasn't so difficult. For all his hidden wit, he was a man driven by lust. A moment of acting the grateful slattern and he relaxed his grip long enough for me to slit him from cock to chops. An ugly death, but I'm of the opinion he died too quickly. Part of his agreement was that I would be spared along with him. He'd told them I was a collaborator in his plot so all I need do was play along. Even so, that bastard Levalle still wanted to string me up with the others, but the King's Champion wouldn't hear of it, nor would the new duke who took a very swift liking to me. He liked me even more when he heard the wisdom of my counsel, but it was only when I came up with a scheme to rid the woods of all remaining outlaws that I think he fell in love with me. What I did to Erchel's kin was revenge, Alwyn, not betrayal, and I'll go to my grave insisting the world is improved by their absence."

Her lips twitched then, eyes blinking tears as she smoothed a hand over my brow and rose. "But not yours. Your absence is a necessity, not a pleasure. I can see you still blame me, still cling to your hate. I can't leave you at my back. Not now." Her hands moved to her cloak, drawing it aside to reveal the swollen bulge of her belly. I reckoned she was four or five months along.

"So you're about to give the duke an heir." My guts roiled again with treacherous fear but I managed to gather enough fortitude to grin up at her. "Is it his? Or did you fuck your way through his men-at-arms until you found one with seed foul enough to make purchase on your pestilent womb?"

A hard punch to my jaw flooded my mouth with the iron sting of blood and scattered stars across my eyes. Painful to be sure, but also a surprise. The old Lorine would have knifed me in an instant.

"All you have endured and you are still a spite-tongued child," she breathed, stepping back from me. "I had thought you might be reached, that I could pierce the hate you cloak yourself in. I could have found you a place at my side. This duchy is now mine in all but name. The things we could have done . . . " She trailed off in the face of the glower I showed her, breath hissing from her lips in resignation.

"I can see there's only one way to end this," she said, closing her eyes and straightening her back as she gathered her resolve. Then, without glancing at me again, she turned to the chainsman and nodded.

Fear finally won out over hate as I watched him approach, his eyes aglitter with anticipation. Many desperate hopes flitted through my mind. Swain and the others would appear out of the shadows at the last instant. A crossbow bolt would come whistling out of the darkness to strike the vile Caerith monster dead. Toria would fall on him like a ravening fox. None of that happened.

The chainsman laid a hand on my head and I felt my bowels loosen at his touch. I fought down the pitiful pleas rising from within, but knew that once he got to work I would beg. In the end, I was no different from all those others I had watched weep, implore and promise their way through their final agonies.

"What else did the *Doenlisch* tell you?" the chainsman enquired, his fingers tightening on my skull. "Be truthful and I will make it quick."

I took in a shuddering breath, fully intending to use it to advise him to find a large branch with which to fuck himself. However, the words that babbled from my lips were these: "She had a book. A book of prophecy."

His fingers froze and I looked up to see the flame-like mask of his face had become the transfixed visage of a man both amazed and terrified. "A . . ." he said in a small, childlike voice " . . . boo—?"

The point of Lorine's knife dislodged a few teeth before slicing through his lips. It was her signature killing blow: a single strike to the base of the skull delivered with enough force to push the blade all the way through. He convulsed and coughed one of his teeth onto my upturned face, followed by a thick cascade of blood that ended when Lorine jerked the blade free and let him fall.

She gave me a hard, reproachful stare as she crouched beside his corpse, wiping the blade on his furs. "Pestilent womb?"

I had the good sense to reply in as neutral a tone as I could manage. "I was fairly sure you were about to let him kill me."

Lorine huffed and rummaged through the chainsman's clothes, her hands emerging with a ring of keys. "I trust," she said, crouching beside me once again, "this balances things betwixt us."

I looked hungrily at the keys in her hand, my heart still thrumming from recent peril. However, still I hesitated. I had nurtured my vengeance for so long that letting it go was harder than expected, like severing a part of my soul, diseased and deceitful though it might be. I paused long enough for Lorine to deliver another blow to my head, a slap rather than a punch. "Wake up, Alwyn! I told the truth, and I know you heard it."

She was right, of course. Fine actress that she was, it was possible she had sold me a lie. But why bother? If my long-harboured suspicions had been true she would have stood in silence and watched the chainsman end me, or not troubled herself to witness this affair at all. Why would a duchess concern herself with the removal of an old, best-forgotten enemy?

"Did he know?" I asked her. "Deckin. Did he die thinking you had betrayed him?"

Lorine's face tightened and her throat constricted, lips forming a hard line. Evidently, describing the fate of the man she had surely loved was not easy. But I had loved him too, in my way, and I wanted to know.

"I saw him only once before they dragged him off," she said. "He'd heard me bear out the unfortunate Todman's story, make my claim to be the engineer of this fine trap. I looked over at him as they bundled him onto the cart, all chained and bloody. He smiled at me, Alwyn. Just for a second, but he was always a man who could say a great deal with just a smile." She pushed the ring of keys into my hand. "He knew."

She lingered for a moment, the hardness of her face once again shifting into a warm smile before she pressed a kiss to my forehead. "The mad bitch is going to die," she told me in a soft murmur. "One way or another. Let her lie and get yourself far away from this realm."

She rose and walked away, a slender, cloaked shadow in the gathering dawn mist, soon swallowed by the shadows of the forest.

Chapter Forty-Three

Fiddling the right key into the manacles was a difficult task, requiring more dexterity than my bruised and recently terror-ised self possessed. Consequently, I fumbled my first attempt, causing the whole bundle of keys to slip from my grasp. The protracted stream of profanity that emerged from my lips was loud, echoing through the trees to a considerable distance and raising a hope that Lorine might hear it. If she did, it didn't compel her to return.

I slumped in my bonds, body shuddering with exertion and the strain of recent events. The chainsman lay at my feet, blood welling in his mouth and regarding me with sightless but bright eyes. I wondered if the spirits that plagued him in life still lingered nearby or if his demise had released them.

"Are you here, Hostler?" I asked in a tired groan, resting my head against the rough bark of the tree. "If so, I'm sorry. For all of it. Not just the killing you bit, but you having to suffer this bastard's company for so long." I delivered a hard kick to the chainsman's corpse, which had the beneficial effect of causing his staring face to loll to one side, spilling the pooled blood in a thick cascade.

"You have to admit, though," I went on, a faint smile creeping over my lips, "it's all somewhat ironic. I mean, you spent your life grovel-ling to the Martyrs and the Seraphile expecting they would let you walk straight through the Portals when the time came. Instead, for years your soul ends up shackled to an evil fucker like him."

The thought summoned a laugh to my lips, one that continued for far longer than it should considering my plight. When it finally faded and I blinked mirth-moistened eyes, I found that the first gleam of dawn had caught the web of branches above.

"Sorry," I told Hostler again. "Never could resist taunting you, could I?"

"Who are you talking to?"

She stood wreathed in the wispy tendrils of the chainsman's fire, a slim, green-cloaked figure, sack-covered head tilted at a curious angle. Her voice was formed of the clean, lightly accented tones I recalled from when she allowed her artifice to slip after healing Brewer.

"An old friend," I told her. "He's dead."

"Oh." She came closer, pausing only briefly to spare a glance for the chainsman's corpse. As she passed from view, my senses were assailed by the floral scents of summer I remembered from our last meeting. It was enough to convince me she was truly here and not the conjuration of my desperately hopeful mind.

The keys jangled and I felt the brush of her fingers on my wrists before the chains fell away. I slumped forwards, groaning in relief at the sudden absence of constriction, my deep breaths bringing an ache to my chest. When I looked up the Sack Witch had taken a seat beside the extinguished fire. The small, black diamonds of her eyes were fixed on the dead man at my feet and the voice that emerged from her sack was faint with reflection.

"He had been looking for me these past few years. Strange to think he only had to sit here and wait."

"*Doenlisch*," I said, which had the effect of drawing her gaze to me. "That's your name, isn't it? Your true name."

The question appeared to arouse only the faintest interest and her cloak barely shifted at her shrug. "It is *a* name. I have several, as do you."

"It sounded more like a title," I persisted, teeth gritted as I rubbed at chafed wrists. "What does it mean?"

"You will find its meaning in the book I gave you." I detected a very small note of humour in her voice and knew there must be a smile behind the weave of her sack. "Didn't you think to look?"

"I've been busy," I replied with sullen gruffness, grunting as I used the tree trunk to lever myself upright.

She watched me move away from the chainsman's body, humour once again showing in her tone when she said, "They're all gone, the spirits that assailed him in life."

"You could see them too?"

"No, but I would know if they were here."

I nodded, meeting her blank eyes. "It's good to see you again," I said, surprised that I meant it. "I've also been looking for you, in fact."

The sack creased a little, but she continued to sit in silent observance of my fumbling attempts to frame my request. Fortunately, the Sack Witch spared me the effort.

"You have something for me," she stated.

Of course, I knew what she meant. The Caerith book was a hard, uncomfortable bulk at my side, one the chainsman had missed in his hunger to secure my end. But, for all the irritation it had caused me, the thought of parting with it summoned an unaccustomed depth of reluctance. While I had spent a good deal of my life in pursuit of other people's possessions, I had never truly treasured any of my own. The loss of what few keepsakes I had collected pained me not at all, given the ill luck they seemed to bring. This book was very different, for its value was incalculable.

"So," I said. "This is the price you spoke of."

"No. It is payment for the task I already performed, as we agreed. The price to come will be far higher, it being equal to the task you require of me."

"And what is that?"

The diamond eyes narrowed as she leaned forward. "Stop attempting to distract me." She extended a hand, palm open and expectant. "Give me the book and the means to decipher it or I will leave, and we shall never set eyes on one another again."

I would be a liar if I said I gave it over with no hesitation. That I reached into my jerkin and tore the book free, kneeling as I proffered it to the Sack Witch, promising I would give her anything she asked if she would only save Evadine's life. But I did not.

I stood with my face set in a mask of poorly suppressed anger, thoughts churning with all manner of justifications that would permit me to walk away from this meeting. I would journey to a different port, find a ship and sail away, seek out a nice, quiet corner of some far-off land where I would compose my own translation. Thus armed with a map to the course of my life, a long one given the denseness of the text, I imagined in my youthful folly that I had naught but years of ease ahead of me. Evadine would soon perish, but did she not lust for martyrdom? Had her punitive commands not already brought me to the grave's edge?

My anger arose not just from pique at losing the book, but also a severe depth of self-reproach that I hadn't yet deciphered a single word of it. I told myself it was due to lack of time during the voyage from Olversahl, and the days since had been equally fraught. But these were lies. Since learning of its true nature, I had hardly touched the book except to strap it to my side. Although I couldn't admit it, the prospect of discovering what had been set down on those pages scared me. In time I may have summoned the nerve to open it, but time was gone now.

"Did you know?" I asked the Sack Witch, voice curt as I tugged the book free of its bindings. Berrine's guide to translation was affixed to it with a cord and I saw how the Sack Witch's fingers played over it as I placed both volumes in her hands. I couldn't tell if it was due to fear or nervous delight. "What it is," I pressed as she consigned the books to her satchel. "Did you know?"

"I knew it would have great value for you, and for me. That is how it must be if the balance is to be shifted from death to life. The . . . nature of what I do has a structure, a web you could say, one that cannot be reordered by such mundanities as material wealth. To alter it requires something *real*, something of the soul and the heart."

"You're in those pages too, aren't you? And not just today, or when we met before. That's why you want it. The next time we meet all the advantages will be yours."

"The next time we meet . . . " Her voice dwindled then abruptly rose in a laugh, so loud and unexpected it made me start. "You still think like a thief. Weighing advantage and disadvantage as if this is some manner of game." She laughed again, the sound smaller now, and considerably more bitter. "If so, then we are two very minor pieces on the board."

More mystery to ponder, but I felt no great urge to question her further. I knew she had no answers to give, not now at any rate. Also, I found the book's sudden absence from my side brought a sense of lightness and urgency rather than resentment at its loss. Still, I couldn't keep one more question from my lips, for some just have to be asked.

"Why me?" I asked. "Why did an unknown Caerith scribe from ages past see fit to set down a prophecy of my life? I am just a whore's bastard made a thief and a murderer because there was no other place for me in this land. I am a pariah to be shunned by churl and noble alike. This land and its people have no use for me, save to earn an ugly death and an unmarked grave fighting their wars."

"The life of a pariah can be as meaningful as that of a king," she replied, her voice softer now and I discerned a weariness in the way her shoulders slumped. "Every life is significant, but some are . . . more so. You, it transpires, were the key to unlocking the secrets of this book, and with that key my people will unlock further secrets. We have so many books, all unread since the Fall. Now the precious knowledge they contain will belong to us once more. You should be proud."

She straightened, the sackcloth covering her mouth thrumming as she drew in a deep breath. "So, to the task at hand," she said, getting to her feet.

I didn't bother asking how she already knew what I required of her, nor enquire as to the nature of the dire price it entailed. As Raith had said, some paths have to be walked.

"It's a fair distance," I warned. "Take us the rest of the day to reach the port, I'd reckon. And we'll need to steal a cart along the way. Something to hide you in so we can smuggle you into the lord of exchange's house. There's a big crowd of faithful fools sitting vigil for the captain's recovery. It would be best if they didn't see . . ."

I trailed to dumbfounded silence as she reached up to grip the hem of her sack, drawing it up with a careful slowness. The breeze twisted her hair as the sack came free, concealing her face for a second until it parted to reveal her features in full.

I could spend the next few pages waxing poetic about the woman I beheld, but it will suffice to say that she was beautiful in a manner I knew to be dangerous. It was the kind of beauty that drives men, and I'd hazard many women, to see another as something to possess, a precious object to be owned and never shared. One glance was enough to convince me she had been wise to wear that sack for so long. Unlike Raith and the chainsman, her face had no pattern of birthmarks. Instead, there was one small red mark in the centre of her brows, resembling a ruby in the way it contrasted with the pale smoothness of her skin.

"When I first began to travel these lands," she said, sweeping her tangled tresses back, "I soon realised that your people put far too much stock in appearance. Shall we go?"

Swain found her a maid's gown to wear before we led her into the house, completing the disguise with a basket of laundry. Inevitably, she drew more than a few glances from the lord of exchange's guards and the town watchmen on the gate, but none saw fit to do more than leer. Once through the servants' entrance, Brewer distracted the other menials with loud demands for clean water for the Anointed Lady while we quickly ushered our visitor up the winding stairs to the bedchamber.

Ayin greeted our entrance with frowning suspicion. Although normally transfixed by the sight of pretty things, she exhibited no such enchantment upon catching sight of this blonde newcomer.

"Who's that?" she demanded, stepping protectively between the stranger and the captain.

"A friend, Ayin," I said, gently easing her aside. "Come to help."

Ayin's features, rarely mature at the best of times, bunched into childish disdain and she consented to move only with stiff reluctance. "She smells . . . strange," she whispered as I guided her to the window.

Delric, who had been dozing in a chair beside the bed, snapped to instant wakefulness and proved far more willing to step aside for the Sack Witch. He stared long at the Caerith's face, though I saw no lust in that gaze, only fear.

"Can you . . . ?" he began, faltering when the Sack Witch placed a hand on Evadine's brow. She had fallen to slumber again, the hollows beneath her cheeks darker than ever and her skin grey rather than bleached white.

The Sack Witch's lips made a tight line and I saw doubt pass across her features before she withdrew her hand and straightened. "Get out," she said with a sharp glance at Delric and Ayin. "You," she added, catching my eye as I ushered a still-truculent Ayin from the room, "need to stay."

Remaining in this room, which had abruptly contrived to become a notch or two colder even though the fire still blazed merrily in the hearth, was perhaps the last thing I wanted to do at this juncture. The sense of being at the precipice of a very long drop was strong, but so was the knowledge that as far as any Covenant tribunal would care, all of us had already stained our souls far beyond cleansing.

Still, I duly pushed Ayin into the hall and closed the door on her scowling face and Delric's sombre frown. Turning, I found the Sack Witch sloughing off her maid's garb. She had left her satchel and cloak downstairs in Brewer's care and wore only a loose shift of cotton. The material was thin enough to reveal much of the body beneath, a sight that would have been arousing but for my increasing pitch of fear. She carried no implements, wore no charms and held no bottles containing marvellous elixirs. Apparently, what would be done here required only her, or so I assumed until she turned and extended a hand to me.

"A price equal to the task," she said. "Be sure you're willing to pay it."

I stared at her outstretched hand, my fear rapidly shifting to terror. The fire blazed on but the sudden sweat beading my skin brought a shiver. In that moment I was a child again, as lost and frantic as I had been the day Deckin found me wandering the woods.

"What . . . " I began, finding I had to swallow and cough before I could get the words out. "What will you do?"

"Remake the web that binds this woman to life. Many of the threads have been broken and must be woven anew." She gave an insistent flex of her fingers. "But they cannot be woven from nothing. For life to be restored, it must be taken."

I shuddered, my eyes flicking to the door although my feet had apparently become as one with the floor. I wondered if she had cast some spell to compel me to stillness, but knew this indecision, this cowardice, was mine alone.

"You didn't do this with Brewer," I pointed out in a hoarse, desperate rasp.

"Remaking his web required that I kill the poison in his veins. This is different."

"Will it . . . kill me?"

"No."

"Will it hurt?"

"Yes." Her fingers flexed again. "If you do not pay this price she will die before the sun rises."

The words forced my gaze towards Evadine's shrunken, wasted face. Another death to witness. Another killing in truth, for by refusing I would surely kill her. How many had it been now? I had never allowed myself to count them all, but neither could I forget them. The soldier with the Martyr charm that had nearly doomed me. Hostler who had saved me with his lessons but couldn't save himself. That poor bastard at the Traitors' Field with my billhook jammed into his face . . . So many others. What was one more?

Let the pious noble bitch die! a savage voice chimed in my head, sharp and jagged. *Without me she would've died twice already. This witch talks of prices to be paid. What price am I owed? And who will ever pay me?*

"I suppose," I said, a weak smile twisting my lips, "there's no chance you'll let me see that book again? I'm sure there's a page or two relating what I do now."

Her lips formed a smile of their own, one that mixed both sadness and sympathy. "You already know what you do. And you know why."

Finding I had no more words and my well of resistance had run dry,

I stepped forward and took her hand. Her skin was smooth and warm against my rough, calloused palm, a brief and pleasant sensation before her hand gripped mine, the strength of it enough to make me gasp.

I have attempted many times to recall in detail what happened next, but my mind consents to provide only a few fragments. I remember a numbness creeping along my outstretched arm. Also, although I remained still, the sense of being pulled was strong. My vision blurred as the numbness reached my shoulder and began to spread to my neck and chest. Through the shifting haze I saw the Sack Witch reach out her free hand and clasp it to Evadine's pale, limp forearm. Then came the pain.

The years since I have wondered many times whether I would have agreed to her price if the Sack Witch had been more fulsome in describing its nature. Pain is too meagre and piffling a word to describe what I endured in the few thudding beats of my heart before I collapsed into oblivion. Agony and torture are similarly inadequate. In fact, to equate it to any other form of physical distress is in many ways redundant. This went beyond the merely physical. I knew even as I fainted that something had been wrenched from the core of my being, something vital. *For life to be restored, it must be taken.* To perform her task, the Sack Witch had taken something from me that I would never recover. It was only much later that I would fully understand what she had wrought.

"Alwyn Scribe."

I awoke to the sting of grit in my eyes and the feel of dried tears on my face. For a second I experienced the bliss that arises from an absence of pain, but it was brief for my body soon let its grievances be known. It seemed most of my muscles and sinews had been strained to near their limit, my spine being an especially busy nest of fiery cramps. I spent a moment engaged in unmanly shuddering and whimpering until fresh tears cleared the grit from my eyes.

"Are you hurt?"

Evadine's brow, pale but healthy once again, furrowed as she stared down at me. I could only gape at her, distracted by the twin realisations that she stood unaided and was, apart from her bandages, completely naked.

Her eyebrow arched in judgement as I continued to gape. "You weren't drinking last night were you?"

I blinked and managed to paw the tears away with a jerky hand, my gaze roving the bedchamber. "Where is she?"

"She?"

"The . . ." I began before good sense forced its way through my befuddled mind to close my mouth. From Evadine's baffled face it was clear she had no notion of what had transpired the previous night and I found I had not the courage to tell her. *Leave it to Swain, or Wilhum. They're brave.*

"Ayin," I croaked. "She was here . . . before."

"Perhaps she went to get help when you collapsed." Evadine turned away and moved to the window, throwing the shutters wide without a care for any inquisitive eyes beyond. Sunlight outlined her form in white gold as she arched her back, letting out a groan of delight. "Such a glorious day."

She stiffened a little then, her hand going to the bandage covering her chest. "Did I dream it, or was I bitten by a wolf?"

"Two wolves," I groaned, climbing to my feet. The room reeled for a moment before consenting to settle. "I killed one. Sergeant Swain the other."

She glanced at me over her shoulder, a faintly impish grin on her lips. "Then my debt to you grows ever higher," she said.

Yes, it does, I thought, concealing a wince at the memory of what I had endured on her behalf. "Debts between soldiers are repaid with every battle," I said. I wasn't sure where this particular gem came from. I had probably picked it up from a drunken man-at-arms in a tavern somewhere, but Evadine appeared satisfied with it.

"Quite so. Where are we, incidentally?"

"Farinsahl. The lord of exchange was kind enough to provide a room for your care."

"So Olversahl is lost." The smile slipped from her lips and she looked away, head slumping.

"I doubt there was ever a chance of saving it," I said. "I also suspect that is the very reason you were sent there." I paused, forcing myself to straighten my back despite my aches. "Captain, it is likely the king's agents are already on their way here. I know you cannot be deaf to the voices that whisper against you . . . "

"A lie is a lie whether it's whispered or shouted." Evadine raised her head, voice soft with reflection. "It makes no difference in the end. For I have no lies to speak."

Hearing a rising murmur from beyond the window, I moved to the shutters. "It might be best if we closed these."

Evadine frowned, noticing the crowd for the first time. "Who are they?"

"Townsfolk, villagers and such. All faithful Covenanters come to beseech the Martyrs and the Seraphile for your recovery."

I pulled the shutters closed as an upsurge of commotion from the crowd signalled many had caught sight of the naked woman in the window.

"Then it is to them I owe this," Evadine said, hands caressing her bandage before beginning to tear it away. I found myself unable to avert my eyes as she revealed herself in full. The flesh beneath her breasts had been a mass of red and purple, darkening to black where the wolf's teeth had punctured her skin. Now it was once again her usual paleness, albeit marked by two arcing lines of small, button-shaped scars.

"I had a vision as I slept, Alwyn," she told me, her voice a tremulous murmur, eyes wide and unblinking. "So different from all the others. Before, when the Seraphile came to me I felt their presence, but never did they consent to show me their face. This time . . . " A smile ghosted across her lips. "I had thought them beyond such mundanities as gender, for they are so far above us. They transcend these prisons we call bodies. But the Seraphile who came to me was a woman, and so beautiful." She spread her fingers as they explored her scars. "With such compassion. I am restored by the Seraphile's grace this day."

The blank wonder on her face abruptly shifted to determination, her eyes narrowing in decision. "People must know of this. I cannot deny them such knowledge."

"The king's agents—" I began, only for her to cut me off.

"The king stands no higher than any other in the Seraphile's sight."

This calm statement of heretical treason was enough to still my tongue. Even Sihlda at her most radical had never spoken something so transgressive. I thought about voicing a reminder of the edicts of the Luminants' Council regarding the exalted status of royal blood and the special blessing it enjoyed, but her steady resolve and still-unblinking eyes told me it would find no purchase on her resolve.

"We should muster the company," I said, deciding a more practical tack might bear fruit. "March out from here."

She finally consented to blink, fixing me with a bemused stare. "To where?"

"Somewhere the king's agents will find hard to follow . . . "

She let out a faintly caustic laugh, shaking her head. "I will not scurry about this realm like hunted vermin."

"There are other realms where the Covenant holds sway. Other kings who would welcome your service, especially with a full company of veteran soldiers under your banner."

"No. My mission is here. I see it now." Her gaze softened and I contained a spasm of discomfort when she came towards me, reaching out to grasp my hands in hers. We were of about equal height and her gaze was level with mine, lit by a strange mix of kindness and commanding intensity.

"I know you see it too," she said. "The Seraphile who came to me, in her grace and wisdom, showed me a great deal. I know what resides in your heart, Alwyn Scribe, despite the lies you use as a shield. I know what you have suffered, and I know what you have done to preserve my life."

She leaned closer, lowering her head so our foreheads touched. Such proximity to so beautiful a woman, naked no less, should have been intoxicating. I should have pulled her close, crushed her too me, pressed my lips to hers. But there was no lust in that moment. I found myself frozen while within churned a welter of bewilderment and fear. She was healed but she was also changed. Her previous ardency had been a mere candle to this flame, and I knew now that if I stayed with her it would surely burn me.

My absence of lust, however, didn't appear to be matched in Evadine for she shifted closer still. "There are many things," she said, breath hot on my face, "that I have denied myself. I felt it necessary. To serve the Covenant in the manner required of me I had to shun the temptations that snare so many others. Now, I wonder . . . "

Many things might have happened next and would undoubtedly have altered much of what follows in this narrative. But it is the way with moments of great import that their outcome can be transformed by the smallest thing. In this case, it came in the form of a light, tentative knock at the door followed by an uncomfortable cough. It said much of the distinctiveness of Swain's voice that I could recognise even a wordless clearing of his throat.

Evadine sighed out a laugh, squeezing my hands and stepping back from me. "You were right," she said, moving to the bed. "About mustering the company, although we won't be marching anywhere. Be so good as to relay the order to the sergeant and ask Ayin to bring me a robe of some description. And food, if she would be so kind. I find I'm quite famished."

I found Toria playing dice with some sailors in a dockside tavern. She was losing, as was typical since her many talents didn't extend to success in games of chance. Consequently, they tended to make her mood sour and her throat thirsty. So, when I pulled her from the circle, she was a little dulled of focus but sharper than ever of tongue.

"Get off, you lying gobbler of donkey cocks," she snapped, pulling her arm from my grasp.

"Are you sober enough to listen?" I enquired. "Or do I need to dunk you in a horse trough?"

She scowled, the inner debate of whether to hit me or voice more profane insults playing out on her face. "Where's your witch?" she asked, casting a pointed glance to either side. "Buggered off and left you, has she?"

"Yes." A bland confirmation that masked a good deal of regret. The Sack Witch's disappearance from the house of the lord of exchange hadn't been witnessed by anyone, yet she was very definitely gone from this port. The cloak and satchel she'd left in Brewer's care had also vanished and the watchmen on the gate claimed not to have witnessed the departure of an unusually beauteous blonde woman.

Toria made only a token effort to conceal a triumphant smirk. "And the captain?"

"Fully healed and more determined on martyrdom than ever."

Toria's smirk became a weary grimace. "Meaning you'll be equally keen to march off and get yourself killed at her side, I s'pose?"

I stepped closer, lowering my voice. "Meaning it's time for us to get the fuck away from here. Do you still have that sovereign?"

CHAPTER FORTY-FOUR

"Berrine Jurest, eh?" Captain Brahim Din Faud bared an impressively white wall of teeth in a wide smile. Although the darkness of his skin betrayed foreign origins, he spoke Albermainish with the broad vowels of the southern coast, complete with overly expressive contortions to his weathered and bearded face.

"Now, there's a tidy piece," he reflected, brows twisting to form something that was part leer and part fond recollection. "Free of spirit and generous to boot, especially if I had books to bestow. How is she?"

"Grieving the loss of her library," I said. "Last I saw."

"Ah yes." Din Faud's mouth dipped in sorrow. "I heard about that business up north. Always bad for trade, you know, war and such. And, for a folk who proclaim to love freedom, Ascarlians are even harsher with their taxes than your lot. It'll be a good long while before I take my dearest anywhere near Olversahl, mark me well."

By his "dearest", I divined in our short association, he meant his ship. She was named the *Sea Crow* and the hue of her timbers and sails matched her name. Narrow of hull but with plentiful rigging she had plainly been built with an eye for speed. Her colouring, which her captain claimed to be the natural shade of the very special breed of oak that formed her hull, would also greatly benefit a ship engaged in the smuggling trade.

"But," Din Faud added with a laboured wink that made me doubt he had ever studied a mirror when practising these mannerisms, "that ain't where you two lovebirds want to go, is it now?"

"We're not fucking lovebirds," Toria told him.

"So—" Din Faud's brows resembled a coiling snake as he attempted to convey contemplation "—brother and sister, then?"

"Who we are doesn't matter," I said. "What matters is where we want to go and whether we have coin to pay for it. Or am I mistaken?"

Din Faud's chair creaked as he reclined a little, studying us with a gaze that was too blank not to be genuine appraisal. Our tour of the varied and many taverns ringing the Dornmahl docks had unearthed a few possibilities but each captain had been given to excessive inquisitiveness. A chance hearing of Din Faud's name had led us to this dingy rum palace on one of the narrower streets. The many hard glances and much inching of hands towards knives when we entered had convinced me we were in the right place.

"You're young," Din Faud observed and I noticed his accent had shifted to something more precise and less familiar. "But also wise in ways you need to be when venturing into a pit like this, eh? Hands never stray far from your weapons. You sit with your backs to the wall. She watches the room while you watch the door, and I doubt you even know you're doing it."

"Is that a problem?" I asked.

"All problems are solvable for the right price." He leaned forwards, face still mostly lacking expression as he continued to study us. "But you are right; we only really have two questions to discuss: where and how much? The answer to the second, you will understand, depends very much on the answer to the first."

I exchanged a brief glance with Toria, receiving a short nod in response. We both had ample experience of men like Din Faud. While the chance of betrayal was always present, he was of a sort that could generally be counted on to stick to a deal.

"Across the Cronsheldt," I told him. "To the Iron Maze."

His face twitched, something I judged to be the result of containing a dubious frown. "A place of wayward currents and great slabs of jagged rock," he said. "I've seen ships founder there and it's not a pretty sight. The risk will be reflected in the price." He lapsed into silence. Not asking why we wanted to go there was, of course, the final test of this particular transaction and he passed it.

Toria's sovereign made an ugly scraping noise as she pushed it across the table's surface, placing it to the side of Din Faud's tankard. "Just for taking us there," she said.

The captain regarded the coin for a second before picking it up. He didn't insult us by testing it with his teeth, but he did hold it up to the light streaming through the window. "From the reign of the last Arthin to sit the throne," he said, baring his teeth once again. "A fine thing, worth twice the value of a sovereign bearing King Tomas's head." The coin spun as he flicked it back at Toria, her hands snatching it out of the air.

"Not enough." Din Faud's southern burr and fondness for exaggerated expression returned, his brows forming a steep arch. "And, since it seems ye've nothing else to offer—" he began to rise from his chair "—I'll bid you young darlings good day."

"There'll be more," I said, voice forceful enough to make him pause. I moderated my tone before speaking on, alert to the danger of being overhead in this place. "But only when we reach our destination. Consider the sovereign an advance on future earnings."

"They'd need to be considerable," the captain warned. "The Iron Maze is far out of my way for I've a yen to sail for the southern trade routes, things being so troubled in these northern climes. And I've a crew to think of, free men and women who swore to my mast in expectation of decent reward. Can't see them tolerating such a risky venture just on the word of two Covenant Company deserters. No offence."

Toria and I exchanged another glance. Reading my intention, her eyes widened in warning but I saw little option. "You may not trust my word," I said. "What about Berrine's?"

Din Faud shrugged. "She ain't here to vouch, my lad. As far as I know you never even met her, just cobbled together a story from gossip."

"I met her. She showed me the library. Did she ever show you?"

He angled his head, a less exaggerated smile on his lips. "Mayhap she did. What of it?"

"Then you'll know how skilled she was in rummaging all those many books, digging through all that parchment to unearth treasure." I spoke the last word with a soft emphasis, but the captain heard it.

I saw his eyes narrow with interest even as he let out a small, derisive grunt. "Been a sailor for forty-odd years now. I've heard tales of treasure from here to the Ivory Horn and back again. Chasing after them is folly."

"Not if you have a map. A map drawn by Berrine's very own hand."

Another grunt, this one more amused than contemptuous. "Going to sell it to me, are you?"

"That would be hard. I burnt it." I punctuated this lie with a tap to my forehead. "It's all up here." I leaned forward, lowering my voice to just above a whisper. "Lachlan's hoard. It's real, and I know where to find it."

"And Berrine just gave this to you? It must have been a very special visit to the library."

"I . . . did her a service." The cloud of regret that passed across my features must have made some impression, for much of the doubt slipped from the captain's gaze. His own attempts to convey emotion might be cack-handed and entirely false, but it seemed he had the gift of reading genuine feeling in others.

Letting out a sigh, Din Faud shook his head. "I'm an old fool, it must be said. But there's a lure to this tale I'll not deny." Looking at each of us in turn, his voice hardened as he added, "But should it turn out to be false, the Iron Maze will have two more sets of bones to litter its rocks."

Rising, he took a final swig from his tankard. "We sail with the next moon; I have business to attend to in the meantime. Secrete yourselves on board before the evening tide six days hence. If your fellow soldiers come to drag you off for a hanging before we weigh anchor, don't expect me or mine to fight for you. That sovereign buys passage, and that is all. We'll talk more of prices if this . . . " he paused for a cautious glance at our fellow patrons " . . . promise of yours bears fruit."

Toria watched him leave before rounding on me, voice quiet but fierce. "Stuck on a ship with a bunch of smugglers who are likely to slit our throats the moment they catch sight of . . . it. Such a great bargainer you are."

"Do you have another ship handy?" I enquired. "And would you know how to sail it if you did?"

"I've sailed plenty." She huffed and turned away, muttering, "Not single-handed though."

"Well, there it sits. We either stay and take our chances with the Anointed Lady or we cast our die with the good captain." Gauging the indecision in her face, I added, "You know those faithful loons are already calling her a Risen Martyr. They truly think she died and was returned to life by the Seraphile. Word will no doubt soon reach the Luminants' Council and the king that the first new Martyr in centuries has not only been acclaimed but also still draws breath. Do you really want to be here once they realise the full import of that?"

She remained sullen but I saw the uncertainty fade from her eyes. "Brewer?" she asked.

"He'll never leave her, not now."

The same was undoubtedly true of Ayin and Wilhum, not that I would have risked asking them to join our impending adventure. However, I didn't like the notion of leaving them behind to face what I knew would be a very ugly storm. There are times when an educated mind can be a curse, for I could see how it would all play out. While the ever curious scholar in me wanted to witness what would soon be a transformative moment in the history of this realm, the outlaw wanted no part of the resultant chaos. In defeat, Evadine Courlain had become far more powerful than she could ever have in victory. Such is the paradox of martyrdom, although she would be unique in being alive to witness the fruits of her sacrifice. The entwined pillars of Crown and Covenant could not tolerate so powerful an agent of change. While Evadine gave sermons, Crown Company would be mustering and the Covenant's senior clerics preparing their condemnations.

I took some comfort from the distance betwixt Dornmahl and the capital – a good two weeks' ride even for the fastest horse. Still, I knew the next six days would feel very long indeed.

*

By the third day following Evadine's supposed resurrection, the crowd encamped about the house of the lord of exchange had grown to at least a thousand. The next day it had tripled, for it was on the third day that she gave her first sermon. Before, they had been drawn merely by the chance they might catch a glimpse of the Anointed Lady, now transformed into a Risen Martyr. However, the reaction when she began to speak made me conclude that my dire predictions may have been somewhat optimistic.

"Why have you come?" she asked them in a voice that had lost none of its ability to command attention. If anything, it had strengthened, reaching all ears present with no difficulty. In addition to the devoted horde clustered about the house, many townsfolk thronged the surrounding streets or hung out of windows, all unable to resist the new Martyr's sermon. I stood with Toria at the edge of the house's defensive ditch, arranged with the rest of the company into a cordon to guard against any agitation from the crowd. Scanning the array of rapt faces, I glimpsed a Supplicant from the shrine busily scribbling down Evadine's words, as were several local scribes. I didn't bother reaching for my own pen and parchment, knowing there was very little chance I would forget this speech, and so it has proven.

"Do you seek guidance?" Evadine went on. She stood on the balcony outside her bedchamber, clad in a plain white shift that seemed to shimmer in the midday sun. "Do you think I have wisdom and insight beyond your own?" She paused to voice a faint laugh, kind rather than judgemental. "Be assured, friends, I know little about the Covenant that you do not. You know what the Seraphile require of us. You know the import of the Martyrs' example. You know that should we fail in these obligations the Divine Portals will be sealed against us and the Second Scourge will consume this world. And yet—" she raised her hands, palms open as she gestured to the assembly "—here you stand, expecting to be told what you have always known. Why should that be?"

I watched the Supplicant's pen pause. His face was a stern, focused contrast to the wonderstruck gapers that surrounded him. When Evadine answered her own question, I was unsurprised to see the cleric's face grow several shades darker.

"Long have I pondered this, friends." Remarkably, Evadine's voice managed to increase in volume, a ripple of tension thrumming through her audience as it became apparent something of considerable import was about to be said. "But, as ever, it was only with the aid of the Seraphile themselves that I discerned the answer: you have been failed. You have been betrayed. You have been denied truth and sold lies. This . . . uncertainty, this doubt that brings you to my door is no fault of yours. It is mine. It is theirs." Her arm shot out, pointing straight at the spire of the Shrine to Martyr Ihlander. "It is the crime shared by all of us who joined with the Covenant, for I see now that it has been corrupted and no longer speaks for the Martyrs."

I took amused if grim satisfaction in watching the Supplicant's pen trail an ugly ink splotch over his parchment. He gaped along with the others now, but it was the open-mouthed stare of a shocked and fearful man. Evadine Courlain, Risen Martyr, had just spoken heresy to an audience of thousands, and she wasn't done.

"How often have you known hunger, friends?" she asked, voice now coloured by a mounting anger. "And in your hunger, as you listened to your children cry for the emptiness of their bellies, did you look upon your Supplicant and find them hungry too? How often have you watched your young folk dragged away to wars not of their making and heard the Supplicant bless the slaughter to come? How often have you counted out coin for tithes in return for empty promises of good fortune or healing?"

She paused for a brief second, letting the stoked passions of the crowd simmer before proclaiming in a voice that I fancied carried all the way to the docks, "I TELL YOU THIS IS NOT THE WAY!"

The sound that erupted from the crowd was a mix of snarl and cheer. Fists punched the air and discordant acclamation soon coalesced into a chant. "The Martyr speaks! The Martyr speaks!"

As the tumult continued, I watched the Supplicant's shock turn first to anger then fear as his neighbours took note of his robe. Jeers and spit quickly transformed into jostling then shoving until the unfortunate cleric found himself on his knees, his pen and parchment trampled into the mud. I knew he was in for a kicking at the least, possibly a knifing too if their anger continued to build. I'll admit to considering making a quick foray into the crowd to rescue him, then decided placing myself in the heart of a raging mob was an unwise notion. So I stood and winced in sympathy as a burly fisherman was the first to drive a boot into the Supplicant's side, which naturally became a signal for every other enraged loon to join in. The first public sermon of the Risen Martyr may well have been marked by the death of a Supplicant if Evadine hadn't noticed the commotion.

"STOP THAT!"

It seemed her voice had instantly conjured an invisible wall of ice around the kneeling, bloody unfortunate, so quickly did the crowd abandon their beating.

A hush descended as the Supplicant huddled on the ground, shuddering in pain and coughing out piteous sobs. I watched Swain glance up at the captain and, receiving a nod in response, quickly organise a trio of soldiers to retrieve the fallen cleric.

"Get him to Supplicant Delric," he snapped as they dragged him towards the house, the words swallowed as Evadine spoke again.

"I come to restore what was broken," she told her audience which had once again shifted into a congregation rather than a mob. "Not to destroy. There has been war enough in these lands. Judge your neighbour as you judge yourself and know that we are all guilty. This sin is shared among us in equal measure, from the highest lord to the lowest churl. For we have shunned the Martyrs' example too long. Where they laboured we have been indolent. Where they sacrificed we have been greedy. Where they spoke hard truths we have cloaked ourselves in comforting lies. No longer!"

Another ripple in the throng, this time the result of the assembly flinching from the controlled fury they heard in the voice of Martyr Evadine. When I glanced up at her once more, I saw her eyes had closed and a semblance of serenity returning to her features. Drawing a deep breath, she opened her eyes and spoke in tones of earnest entreaty.

"In a few days I will set out from this place, for it has been revealed to me that this knowledge I impart to you must be shared. In every corner of this realm and in the furthest reaches of all that lies beyond, all souls must know these truths, for, my good friends, the Second Scourge draws nearer with every passing day. As we descend further into deceit and delusion so the Malecite rise. We must prepare. We must arm ourselves with the shield of the Seraphile's grace and the sword of the Martyrs' example."

She raised her arms again, head thrown back as she cast out her final question: "WILL YOU ARM? WILL YOU TAKE UP THE SHIELD AND THE SWORD!"

The collective choices of crowds are a strange thing, for they happen with remarkable speed and a complete absence of discussion. So it was after only a short interval of discordant shouting that what would soon become known as Martyr Evadine's Cant arose from the multitude.

"SHIELD AND SWORD! SHIELD AND SWORD! SHIELD AND SWORD!"

Watching them chant, all faces red with passion as they cried it out with rhythmic precision, it occurred to me for the first time that the Crown and the Covenant had more to fear from this woman than she had to fear from them. The notion might have reawakened my scholarly instincts, but for the crowd. Inflamed by devotion and peerless oratory they were a stark contrast to the sanctuary seekers at Callintor who had sat in rapt observance of Sihlda's wisdom. These were more like the baying mob that tormented me in the pillory: ordinary folk inflicting cruelty on a helpless youth purely because they had been given licence to do so. What licence had Evadine just given this lot? What passions would she stoke in others when she began her Martyr's progress across this realm? A badly beaten Supplicant was only the beginning and I wanted no part of what came next.

CHAPTER FORTY-FIVE

I said my goodbyes over the course of the next two days, not that any of my soon-to-be-absent friends knew it. I drew sentry duty with Brewer the night after Evadine's sermon and we spent a few lively hours keeping the adoring faithful at bay. They still clustered in large numbers beyond the ditch but the more ardent, and resourceful, weren't content to remain at a remove from their beloved Martyr.

"But I have a message of great import for Martyr Evadine!" one fellow squealed in protest after Brewer dragged him from a sewer grate. A man of small dimensions, he must have crawled for hours through layers of shit to attempt a personal introduction.

"She's likely to condemn you to the Scourge for stinking the place up so," Brewer advised, grimacing in distaste as he hauled the fellow towards the ditch.

"She would never do that!" the diminutive ardent insisted, staining Brewer's gloves with ordure as he clutched at his wrist. "Her heart is too kind. Please, good soldier! She must hear my warning!"

Brewer raised a questioning eyebrow at me and, receiving a shrug, set the small man on his feet at the edge of the ditch. "All right," he said. "Warning of what exactly?"

The interloper's dung-smeared brow crinkled as he glanced around before responding in a whisper. "I must be careful, lest *they* overhear."

Brewer pursed his lips and leaned closer, matching the fellow's whisper. "And who are *they*?"

"The Malecite, of course." Another cautious glace to either side, his whisper becoming a hiss. "They think I don't see them, but I do. They infest every corner of this port and have for years. Now Martyr Evadine is here I fear what they will do."

Brewer nodded gravely. "But only you can see them?"

"I see their true faces, the ones they keep hidden behind their stolen masks of flesh." The man's eyes slid to the upper windows of the house. "The lord of exchange, he is one."

"Really?" Brewer's brows rose in apparent shock. "Who else?"

"Master Eckuld, the baker on Crossmark Street. His wife too, and that fat little shit of a son they spawned. Also, the tallyman on the tenth wharf and that thieving scribe on Middlereach Lane—"

"Quite a list," Brewer said, straightening and spinning the fellow around. "Best go home and write it all down."

"I don't know letters . . . "

His words trailed into a dismayed exclamation as Brewer's boot connected with his arse, sending him into the ditch. "Then piss off and learn."

The small man spent a time flailing about the ditch and gabbling out a stream of denunciations that seemed to include every shopkeeper or person of importance he had ever encountered. He finally fell to silence when some of the faithful beyond the ditch grew tired of his ranting and began throwing litter. Climbing clear of the ditch, he cast an aggrieved glare back at Brewer, no doubt adding him to his list of flesh-masked evildoers, then stomped off into the gloom.

"Earlier there was a woman claiming to be the Anointed Lady's mother," Brewer said. "When I pointed out they looked to be about the same age she said the birth had come about through union with one of the Seraphile which had kept her young ever since. For the mother of a Risen Martyr, she had a tongue foul enough to put Toria to shame."

"Do you ever wonder what Ascendant Sihlda would have made of this?" I asked, nodding to the crowd beyond the ditch. They had thinned since the sermon, but hundreds continued to linger, grouped around their fires in communal devotion. Every now and then chants of "Shield and sword!" and "Heed the Risen Martyr!" would spring up. I found it annoying and troubling in equal measure.

"That can never be known," Brewer replied, though the discomfort I saw in his gaze made me conclude this was a question he had pondered more than once. "You wrote her testament," he pointed out. "Don't you know?"

"She foresaw a good many things, but never this." I shifted my gaze to Evadine's window, shuttered now but a bright light burning within. "Never her."

"And yet here she is, a true living Martyr, as real as you or me." His broad, craggy face formed the tight but genuine smile of a man content with where life had placed him. Although I had known asking him to sail off with Toria and me would be a pointless proposition, now I understood it to be dangerous too.

"I think the Ascendant would have been . . . gratified to see your faith rewarded," I told him, which brought a bemused creasing to his forehead. It was true we were friends, of a sort, but it was not a friendship that accommodated expressions of regard or kindness.

"You been at the grog?" he asked, causing me to ponder the fact that I hadn't partaken of a drop of liquor since Olversahl, and even then it hadn't been near enough to get me drunk.

"No," I said. "A failing I'll need to rectify soon."

My last practice sessions with Wilhum took place the next morning. He was always keen to follow the routine set down by the unpleasant Master Redmaine, requiring much early rising and dunking in troughs of cold water. After this, I would attempt to follow his movements as he went through a series of sword scales. I had thought these absurdly complex when he began to teach me, but now understood those first exercises to be the equivalent of a dance taught to children. To my surprise, I found I could match his moves most of the time, not with the same fluency and speed, but neither was I the slow, clumsy oaf I had been when we'd started. However, while he appeared satisfied with my progress in the swordly arts, he was not so impressed with my motley armour.

"Worthless scrap," he said, flicking a hand to my elbow cop, a dented and discoloured contrivance I'd got for two sheks from another soldier after the Traitors' Field. It refused to shine regardless of how much time I spent polishing it. "I'll ask the captain for funds to have a suit made for you," Wilhum added. "Since she seems keen to have escorts of knightly appearance at her side when she starts her progress."

I noted she was always "the captain" when he spoke of her now, never "Evadine". But never "Martyr Evadine" either. Also, I had discerned a guardedness to his gaze when in her presence and he addressed her with a clipped formality in place of their prior familiarity. I knew it to be partly due to her suddenly exalted status, but ascribed this change in demeanour to guilt most of all.

"You haven't told her, have you?" I said. "About the Sack Witch."

He tightened the strap on my elbow cop then moved to deliver an uncomfortable heave to my breastplate. "Neither have you. Neither has Sergeant Swain nor Supplicant Delric, by mutual agreement. Best if we keep it that way, don't you think?"

I think she believes a Seraphile descended from the Realm of Endless Grace to restore her to life. I think she's about to set out on a journey that will transform these lands for ever, perhaps bathe them in blood from end to end, all on the basis of a lie. I said none of this, for, despite his strength, courage and skills, I knew Wilhum to be a fragile soul in many ways and had no desire to cause him pain at this, our last meeting.

"You don't like lying to her, do you?" I asked. "This deceit weighs on you. Against the knightly code or somesuch?"

"The knightly code is a collection of meaningless doggerel cobbled together by hypocrites. Master Redmaine knew that, and tried to teach me the truth of it, though I was too young and lost in my self-regard to hear him."

He moved to prop his longsword against one of the fence posts ringing the paddock where we practised, taking up the pair of wooden replicas. He paused for a second, eyes distant with remembrance. "They killed him, you know. Master Redmaine. Hung him for treason. He had been wounded in battle just days before, one of the later skirmishes of the Duchy Wars. As befits a man who sells his skills for money, he had pledged his sword to the duke with the fattest purse, but also the worst judgement. They dragged him from his bed, wounds still bleeding, and hung him from the scaffold alongside a dozen others. My father, a lord he had served for years, was the one to put the rope around his neck. Before he died, Redmaine begged his former lord to have a care for his wife and son, they having been beggared by the confiscation of all his chattels. Always keen to appear gracious, at least in public, my father took them in, made the wife a maid and the boy my page." An ugly, bitter smile twisted Wilhum's lips. "A rare act of kindness I'm sure he regrets to this day."

The smile slipped away as he met my gaze, tossing one of the wooden swords to me. "I told you love brought me down, did I not?" He raised his ash blade in the formal salute as he advanced towards me, moving with a disconcertingly purposeful stride. "It was love for a page who became a man-at-arms."

He didn't wait for me to return the salute before launching his attack, feinting an overhead swing then jabbing a thrust at my midriff. I managed to parry it and twist aside in time avoid the follow-up swipe at my legs.

"A man-at-arms who had learned everything his father could teach him." Wilhum's voice grew harsh and ragged as he launched into another assault, driving me back as he wielded the wooden sword with two hands, my feet raising dust as I scrambled back.

"A mere commoner who could best any knight, save perhaps Sir Ehlbert Bauldry and even then I fancy it would have been a close-run thing."

I ducked a slash to the head and attempted a thrust at his belly which he turned aside with a casual flick of his wrist.

"Watching him at tourney was like watching one of the fabled heroes of old, or one of the Ascarlian warrior gods. A son of Ulthnir made flesh." He stepped closer, too quick to dodge, trapping my sword arm with his gauntleted fist, grating his words into my face as he held me tight. "What it is to love a god, Alwyn. And what a fate to be loved in return."

The bitter smile flickered across his lips once again before he pivoted, bending at the waist to throw me to the ground. The impact was enough to jar my wooden sword from my hand, but I knew better than to chase after it. Rising to one knee, I reached up in time to grab hold of his forearms as he brought his sword down with the kind of force that might well have cracked my skull.

"Father didn't like it, of course." Wilhum grunted as he swung his left leg, driving an armour-clad foot into the centre of my breastplate. The force sufficed to dislodge my grip and I was obliged to roll across the dirt to avoid his next flurry of blows. "'Suck all the cocks you like,' he told me. 'But do you have to shame me with this cow-eyed devotion to a commoner?'"

I quelled the instinct to keep evading his blows and rolled onto my back, jerking my head aside as he drove a thrust towards it. The wooden blade splintered as it connected with the ground, sending a loud crack into my ear. Wincing, I delivered a kick of my own, hard enough to dent Wilhum's breastplate and force him back a few steps.

"So," he went on, tossing his ruined weapon aside and raising his fists as I surged to my feet, nimbly sidestepping my first punch, "when my young god told me he had a yen to go off and swear his sword to the Pretender, how could I not follow?"

He jabbed at my nose and I batted his fist aside, metal ringing as our gauntlets met. "Aldric," I said. "That was his name."

"That it was. We travelled far and wide together, to the Fjord Geld and back." Wilhum blocked the right hook I aimed at his jaw and replied with one of his own. I managed to avoid the worst of it, but the edge of his gauntlet left a bloody scrape on my scalp.

"Nice to know you were paying attention. But—" he lowered his head and charged me, arms encircling my waist and bearing me down "—you always are, aren't you? Nothing's ever beneath the notice of Alwyn Scribe."

I raised my vambraces to cover my head as he rained down a series of blows. "Such an observant churl! And so skilled with the pen! So worthy of the Anointed Lady's favour!"

I suffered the blows and waited for the inevitable pause as he tired. It took longer than I would have liked and I was sure my arms would show numerous bruises when I removed my armour. Finally, he slackened a little, faltering just enough for me to latch a hand to his wrist, drawing the dagger from my belt and flicking at his eye. Although angered by his assault and my stinging bruises, I possessed enough good sense to halt the blade before it sank home, angling it to press the edge to his partially exposed neck.

"I never asked for her fucking favour!" I spat.

Fear remained absent from Wilhum's eyes as the blade pressed against his flesh. "And yet she gives it," he observed, his voice cold. "You see her clearly, but she doesn't really see you. Not any more. She doesn't see the man who's about to run."

His eyes flicked down and I followed them, finding his own dagger poised above the gap between two of the taces that covered my waist. Wilhum held it there for what felt like a very long time, then let out heavy breath and I felt the desire for conflict seep out of him.

I drew back my own dagger and we rolled apart, lying on our backs, panting at the sky as sweat cooled on our skin.

"What happened to him?" I asked when my heart had calmed. "Aldric."

Wilhum placed an arm over his eyes to shield them from the sun, his answer coming after a long pause. "He fell and broke his neck. We were escorting the True King through the Althiene hill country, recruiting clansmen to join his cause. Most of the clans were receptive, steeped in grievances against the Algathinet dynasty that cowed them long ago. But not all. The clans love to war with each other more than they do the Crown, and an alliance with one will earn you the enmity of another.

"They came at us in a great rush, hundreds of them streaming down the slopes of the glen, screaming loud enough to make Aldric's horse rear. It was a young stallion and untrained for war, his capering so sudden and fierce it tipped Aldric from the saddle before he had chance to calm him. I heard Aldric's neck break, despite the screaming hill folk and the clashing blades. I heard it and I knew he was gone. I sat there and stared at his broken body while the struggle raged around me. Death would come for me too; I knew that. And I welcomed it. However, the True King did not. He fought his way to my side and cut the head from a clansman just as he was about to stick his spear in my face.

"Joining his great crusade had always been Aldric's passion, not mine. But after that day, I felt I owed the True King a debt, so I stayed. Besides, I fully planned to get myself killed at the first opportunity. Even managed to mess that up thanks to Evadine's father. If Aldric had been at the Traitors' Field . . . "

He voiced a rueful sigh that became a groan as he sat up. "Well, I feel sure you would now be addressing Lord Chamberlain Wilhum Dornmahl, a fellow who stands high in the court of King Magnis the First."

"No," I said, righting myself. "I'd be dead. So would everyone else in this company, including *her*."

He didn't argue the point, it being so blatantly true. "I won't be coming with you," he said, climbing to his feet. "In case you were thinking of asking."

"I wasn't."

Wilhum laughed, stooping to offer his hand. "You're getting better," he said, hauling me upright. "Quite a lot better, in fact. Wherever you fetch up, you would do well to find another teacher, preferably one who knows horses. You still ride like a fat-arsed sow perched on a donkey."

"Are you going to tell her?" I asked as he began to walk away. "That I'm leaving."

"I already did. She laughed at me. Apparently, you leaving her now is contrary to her vision, so it simply won't happen." Wilhum Dornmahl bowed low to me, the first time I could recall any noble doing so. "Fare you well, Alwyn Scribe. When you write of me, and I'm sure you will, make me . . . " he straightened, frowning in consideration " . . . handsome. A man worthy of having been loved by a god. I think I should like that."

"She says you're to teach me letters and numbers," Ayin informed me, pausing as she bounced down the stairs to Evadine's chamber. "Says you'll be too busy to manage the company books so I'll be doing it now."

"Busy doing what?" I enquired, moving past her.

"Oh, war and such, I expect. She says there's hard times ahead and I should prepare myself to meet them." A line appeared on her smooth brow. "I don't like it when she talks like that."

"No, neither do I, Ayin," I added as she turned to resume her bouncing descent. Looking upon her open, guileless expression, I found I had no words to offer, none she would find meaningful at any rate. Of all the souls I would miss, she was the one that stirred the most guilt. As dangerous as she was, in her own way she was as fragile as the infant creatures she fawned over.

"She's right," I said finally. "When the company marches out there'll be bad men on the road. Keep your knife sharp, and close, eh?"

She shrugged. "Always do. And the letters?"

I turned and resumed my climb, wary of letting the lie show in my eyes. "Tomorrow," I said, putting a gruffness to my tone to mask the sudden catch in my throat. "Find me after morning drill."

After knocking and receiving leave to enter, I found Evadine already had a visitor. The lord of exchange kept his head at a low angle as he addressed her, hands clasped together across his waist. My estimation of his intelligence was confirmed by the whiteness of his knuckles and the strict control he exerted over his voice, formal and polite without slipping into servility. Harbouring a Risen Martyr who had recently proclaimed heresy, and arguably treason, from atop his very own balcony placed him in a position that was far beyond mere embarrassment. This man would know that. He would also know asking her to leave was an equally risky proposition, surrounded as she was by loyal soldiers and a still-growing congregation.

He paused as I entered, eyes flicking towards me but, seeing no one of particular note, instantly resuming their downcast state. "I believe it would do much to calm the current mood in the town, my lady," he said. "Reaffirm your belief in the Covenant's core teachings."

"Perhaps so, my lord," Evadine said. She sat by the window, clad in the hardy travelling clothes she wore on the march, her sword propped within easy reach beside the fireplace. I wondered if it was significant that she didn't correct the noble in addressing her as a lady rather than a captain. "However," she went on briskly, "I would normally expect a request to stand at the altar during supplications, on a Martyr's feast day no less, to come from the shrine's principal cleric."

"The Ascendant is reluctant to venture forth at the moment." The lord of exchange's trim form shifted in restrained discomfort. "Given what happened to one of his Supplicants during your sermon, his caution is understandable. I have also been obliged to station guards around the shrine. There has been some . . . misguided vandalism of late. If you were to attend supplications tonight, many would see it as your blessing on the Covenant in this port. Hopefully, they would then realise their frustrations were better directed elsewhere."

"If by frustrations you mean justified outrage and renewed devotion, I take your point." Evadine got to her feet, inclining her head. "Please inform the Ascendant I shall be happy to attend. Also, I should like to thank you for your hospitality. My company will muster and depart on the morrow and I do not consider any formality is required to mark the occasion."

I was impressed by the way the lord of exchange managed to keep the immensity of his relief from his voice and posture as he bowed. "It has been my pleasure and honour, my lady." He backed towards the door and contrived to leave without appearing to scurry.

"I was pondering the notion of emptying his vaults before we leave," Evadine said when I closed the door. "Funds stolen from these people would be put to better use in our hands, don't you think?"

"I think the king's friendship won't be won if you start stealing his taxes." I paused to offer her a bow of my own. "Captain."

She raised an eyebrow at the baldness of my statement, but her mouth quirked in a smile. "Why should the king's friendship concern me?" she asked.

"Because, like it or no, winning this realm to your cause will require Crown approval. Or—" I glanced at the door and lowered my voice "—a different head to wear it."

We held each other's gaze then and I knew that the disparity in our status mattered little now. Within this room, and whenever we found ourselves alone in future, we would be as close to equal as we could ever be. The realisation might have made me consider abandoning my scheme, but instead I used it to fuel my determination. *I will die in short order if I stay at your side.*

"I can see our course will be steered by your counsel," she said, her lips forming a tight line. "Counsel I welcome, Alwyn. I hope you know that."

"I do. In fact—" I reached into my jerkin, extracting a thick sheaf of parchment bound in a black ribbon "—I come to offer yet more, but not my own."

Evadine's gaze warmed as she accepted the bundle from me, murmuring aloud the words inscribed, with considerable artistry I might say, on the topmost page: "'The Testament of Ascendant Sihlda Doisselle'."

"I should have liked to have had it properly bound," I said. "Perhaps illuminated, but there is no time. It's the full testament, including a good deal more of her wisdom than the copy in possession of Ascendant Hilbert in Callintor. Also, it contains a . . . certain piece of information I think sure to aid any negotiations you might enter into with the Crown."

The warmth in her eyes dimmed, her features taking on a shrewd calculation I had rarely seen before her healing. "How so?"

"You'll understand when you read it. Some will surely claim it counts for nothing, just ink scratched onto parchment, for any scribe or disgraced cleric can lie. But when spoken by a Risen Martyr, the truth of this testament will be far harder to deny."

Her hand smoothed over the title page in much the same way a woman might caress a bejewelled gift from a lover. "Then I shall read it with interest," she assured me in a hushed murmur.

I bowed and turned to go, coming to an abrupt halt as she added in far from hushed tones, "This is not a parting gift, Alwyn."

Turning, I found her expression more sad than commanding, almost apologetic in fact. "Although," she went on, "I know you imagine it to be. I'll not begrudge you your fear, for only a fool would look upon the task set to us without it. But it is our task, fear or no. It is given unto us and whatever schemes you have hatched will come to nothing. We are bound now. So have the Seraphile ordained."

I nearly told her then, my lips parting to cast out the truth rising from within, demanding to be set free. *Your vision is a lie! The Seraphile ordain nothing for you or me! This is all the contrivance of a heathen, Caerith witch!*

Despite all the countless doubts and questions that have beset me in the years since, never once have I pondered how different it all would have been if I had set the truth free in that moment. How many lives would have been saved? How much of this realm and those beyond spared destruction? It cannot be doubted that I have much to atone for, but failing to speak then is not one of my crimes, for I know with no shred of doubt that it would have altered nothing. Her faith was hardened now, hammered into something stronger than steel.

"I . . . " I stammered, then coughed, then backed away, shying from her steady but sorrowful gaze as it tracked me to the door. I wondered if she might call for Swain, have me clapped in chains so she could keep me at her side like a dog. But she didn't, for she knew she had no need of chains where I was concerned.

"By your leave, Captain," I said upon reaching the door, knuckling my forehead with all due respect before turning to make a hasty descent of the stairs.

CHAPTER FORTY-SIX

The night air was windless and the waters of the harbour becalmed beneath a cloudless sky, the bright disc of a full moon shining amid the many ships at anchor. Din Faud had advised Toria and me to wait in the lee of a piled consignment of timber close to his mooring. It would have been wiser to seek a shadowy notch among the stacked planks and sit out the interminable hours before the tide shifted, but I found I couldn't stop pacing. I started at every sound, expecting Swain or Ofihla to come striding out of the gloom flanked by a dozen Covenant troopers, manacles in hand. Instead, my gaze alighted only on the whipping tails of scurrying rats.

"Will you fucking settle?" Toria said. She had perched herself atop the tallest pile of timber to keep watch on the docks and was as close to cheerful as I had ever seen her. The tense hunch I had thought to be her natural posture was gone, as was the habitual scowl. The reason wasn't difficult to divine; after years a prisoner she finally felt herself free. I, on the other hand, felt more trapped than ever.

My gaze roved from one shadowed corner of the wharf to another in between continual glances at the water's edge as I vainly tried to gauge the progress of the tide. *How much longer?* After all my careful planning, it still seemed incredible that it should be this easy. I was about to desert the Covenant Company of Risen Martyr Evadine Courlain and, it appeared, no one was inclined to stop me. The notion might have irked my pride if I hadn't been so keen to be gone from this port.

I looked up as Toria shifted on her perch, seeing her sharp features pointed to the dark bulk of the *Sea Crow*. A single lamp glowed at the stern and I could make out shadowy forms manoeuvring a gangplank into place.

"Ready?" Toria asked, landing at my side. I caught a flash of steel as she drew a knife, reversing her grip so the blade was concealed by her forearm. "Best to be careful," she said with a shrug. "The captain seems trustworthy, right enough, but he's still an outlaw."

"Just like us," I said, setting off with my eyes still roaming the stacks of cargo littering the quayside.

"Right." Toria let out a quiet laugh as she followed a few paces behind, the sound peculiar in its light, airy quality. "Just like us."

She's who she wants to be again, I realised, feeling a sharp pang of envy for her absence of doubt.

A pair of sailors waited at the foot of the gangplank, greeting us with the suspicious stare common to the criminally inclined. I took comfort from their unfriendliness; smiles and proffered hands were indicators of deceit and betrayal in such moments. Glancing up, I saw Din Faud's bulky form on the *Sea Crow*'s deck. Like me, he was busy surveying the docks for any sign of trouble; another good sign.

"Wasting time," one of the sailors said, a dark-skinned woman with a scimitar strapped across her back.

I nodded, stepping onto the gangplank and that's when it struck me. At first I assumed we must have been betrayed after all, so harsh was the blow that felled me. But, I quickly realised it had come from within, not without. I staggered as a fist clutched my chest, my heart suddenly pounding and vision swimming. For a second I was back in Evadine's bedchamber clutching hands with the Sack Witch, the same unique brand of pain searing its way through my core. I reeled away from the ship, eyes dragged by an unseen but irresistible hand towards the town.

At first I saw nothing, but I did hear it. The sound was dulled by distance and the maze of interweaving streets, but my ears were well attuned to the tumult of folk engaged in conflict. Brief but loud shouts, a few screams, then the flicker of torchlight, shifting yellow and red shadows playing over the tall spire of the Shrine to Martyr Ihlander.

My pulse calmed somewhat and the pain receded, but a heavy weight of foreboding lingered. The flickering torchlight shifted, slipping from the walls of the shrine to play over the roofs of nearby houses, moving rapidly towards the port's eastern wall.

"Trouble at the shrine," Toria said, her voice now a hoarse contrast to the lightness from seconds before. Turning to meet her gaze, I saw that she understood fully what would happen next. Her eyes were wet in the moonlight, cheeks hollowed by the clenching of her jaw. "You think she . . . loves you?" she asked, the words barely escaping the cage of her teeth. "You're the worst of fools, Alwyn."

I wanted to embrace her, but feared the knife she held. "It should be easy enough to follow," I said, taking the scrolled map from my pocket and holding it out. "Perhaps you'll have a mind to throw some coin at an old fool one day."

She snatched the map from my hand without hesitation and started up the gangplank without a backward glance.

"Anything happens to her," I told the woman with the scimitar, "and there's nowhere in this world you can hide from me. Tell your captain."

I didn't wait for the inevitable insult-laden argument and ran towards the shrine as fast as I could.

I had to fight my way through a thickening crowd of congregants to get to the shrine's door, feeling scant optimism for what I would discover inside. Still, the amount of blood slicking the aisle was a grim surprise. A dead man in a Supplicant's robe lay close to the door. Pausing to glance at his features I saw no one I recognised, but I did glimpse the mail shirt through a rent in his robe.

Hearing an overlapping chaos of shouts and pleading from the altar, I shouldered past a pair of company soldiers, both bloody from wounds to the face and arms, coming to a halt at the sight that assailed me. The shrine's clerics lay dead on the steps to the altar, the Ascendant among them. Most of the noise came from the throat of the lord of exchange. He was on his knees, held in place by Ofihla's gauntleted hand while she used the other to level a sword at his neck.

"I didn't know . . ." the noble choked out repeatedly. "By all the Martyrs I didn't know . . . "

The sound of weeping drew my gaze from the begging noble to Ayin, her slender, shuddering form pressed against Brewer's broad chest. He lay at the foot of the altar steps, face slack and utterly still. Moving closer, I saw Ayin clutching at the trio of crossbow bolts that had pierced his breastplate.

"Get up," Ayin told him through a veil of tears and snot. "She's gone and you have to go and get her . . . "

Crouching, I pressed a hand to Brewer's brow, the flesh cool and soft, lacking all life. He was beyond even the Sack Witch's skills now.

"She didn't want swords in the shrine," Ofihla told me, swordpoint still pressed against the scrawny neck of the lord of exchange. "Only let Brewer escort her in. We came running when we heard the noise." Her heavy jaw worked as she bit down on a curse. "They had a dozen swordsmen seeded in the crowd and a few others posing as Supplicants. Held us off while they took her out the back." Her eyes flicked to meet mine, bafflement vying with fury. "She didn't even fight, Scribe."

"Sergeant Swain?" I asked. "Wilhum?"

"They went off in pursuit. The sergeant ordered me to get what I could out of this one." She dug her armoured fingers hard into the lord of exchange's shoulder, drawing forth a pained gasp.

"The Ascendant," he said in a plaintive sob. "It was his request that she attend. I know nothing!"

"He's dead," Ofihla pointed out. "You're not, yet."

I rose and moved to one of the slain clerics. Like the dead man at the door, his mail was revealed by the deep slashes that had opened his robe. However, I judged from the crumpled, gory ruin of his head he had been felled by a blow from a brass candlestick. *Brewer's work,* I concluded with a spasm of grief. The dead man's features were obscured by blood, but I felt a dull pulse of recognition as I peered closer. Stooping to grasp the slick mass of his hair, I raised the dripping face from the tiles, finding the lean features of a wiry fellow I had seen some months before. *He was cleaner then*, I reflected, letting the wiry sergeant's head fall to the tiles with a wet smack.

The mad bitch is going to die, one way or another. Lorine's words from the forest, now given additional meaning.

"This is one of Duke Rouphon's men," I said, moving to Ofihla's side. "It's my guess they'll be taking the captain to Castle Ambris. Assassinating a Risen Martyr in a shrine simply wouldn't do. They need a speedy trial, but at a defensible place with a good-size audience to witness it." I stared down into the twitching eyes of the lord of exchange. "Do I have it right, my lord? And I caution you, I have a very keen ear for lies."

A feverish calculation played out on the noble's face before a hard jerk of Ofihla's hand forced a reply from his lips. "They had a Crown warrant!" he blurted. "And a letter with the duke's seal. What choice did I have?"

I stepped back, watching Ofihla wrestle with the prospect of murder, a bead of blood swelling on the point of her sword as it pressed yet harder against the noble's pallid flesh.

"You faithless wretch!" she grunted, sound judgement overcoming rage as she cast the noble away. Killing so senior a Crown agent would be a disastrous act, even now when all seemed lost in any case. Ayin, however, was never one for judgement, sound or otherwise.

As his lordship sagged in relief, she fell on him, feral and ferocious, her knife hand blurring. Blood rose in a thickening spray as she drove the lord of exchange down, the knife stabbing his face, neck and eyes, rendering him unrecognisable in a scant few seconds. I felt no inclination to intervene and Ofihla's good sense also prevented her from attempting to drag Ayin off before she was done.

"Bad men . . ." she gasped, rising from the noble's mutilated corpse, sniffing as she palmed the dripping gore from her nose. "Bad men everywhere." She turned to me, baring red-stained teeth and wearily brandishing her knife. "Kept it close."

I replied with a smile of my own before turning and striding for the door.

"Where are you going, Scribe?" Ofihla demanded.

"Castle Ambris," I told her. "Where the fuck else? Are you coming?"

The watch sergeant on the eastern gate was disinclined to surrender his horse, then disinclined to argue the point when he found himself on his arse nursing a recently punched nose. My stolen mount was a sturdy, shaggy-footed mare bred for strength rather than speed, but I'd managed to get a fair gallop out of her.

My desire to get to Castle Ambris was a feverish need when I set out but cooled as the journey wore on and the mare slowed to a canter then a walk. The reduced pace gave me time to reflect on what precisely I intended to do when I reached my destination. I knew the duke and any Crown agents involved in this enterprise would want the deed done quickly. The sooner Evadine was condemned as a heretic and all suggestion of her martyrdom suppressed, the better it would be for king and Covenant. In all likelihood, I would be fortunate to arrive in time to witness Evadine's execution, never mind prevent it.

My pondering faded when I noticed the bodies lying on the verge ahead. I halted my mount, resting a hand on my sword, eyes scanning the trees on either side of the road. A glance at the corpses revealed a trio of men-at-arms in Shavine ducal livery, bearing wounds that told of recent and frenzied combat. One, however, was unarmoured, clad in the light garments that bespoke a messenger rather than a man-at-arms

"He was bearing missives for the king."

I jerked at the sound of Swain's voice. He stood at the edge of the forest, bloody mace in hand and face drawn in a suspicious glare. Hanging from his belt was a leather tube that I assumed contained the unfortunate messenger's cargo. "Where've you been, Scribe?" he asked in a tone that indicated he'd expected me sooner.

"I've known grandmothers who could run faster than this nag," I said, dismounting. I led the horse from the road, nodding to the messenger's tube. "I assume you would like help reading that?"

Swain's features tensed a little in offence, but he duly tossed the tube into my hands. He could read, and write a little, but not particularly well. "Come on," he said, turning. "We're camped nearby."

"It's an account of her trial," I told Swain and Wilhum a while later before reading aloud the contents of the single sheet of parchment. It had been the only document in the messenger's care and bore the irregular, sprawling text that told of an unskilled scribe writing in haste.

"'His Gracious Majesty is hereby informed that Evadine Courlain, formerly known as the Lady of Leshalle and Aspirant of the Covenant of Martyrs, was today found by lawful assembly of noble and cleric to have engaged in the vilest forms of treason and heresy. To wit: the connivance with agents of the Sister Queens of Ascarlia to deliver the port of Olversahl into their hands and the heretical and patently false claim of martyrdom and resurrection by virtue of the Seraphile's intervention. Sentence of death is proclaimed under the laws of both Crown and Covenant and will be carried out within two days. Should His Majesty deign to grant mercy to this vile traitor, his wishes will be fully respected.'"

"Lying bastards!" Wilhum said. His injured arm was confined by a sling and he paced back and forth, though his pallor and the stains that discoloured his bandage indicated he would be better off at rest. He and Swain had engaged in a headlong gallop towards Castle Ambris, blundering into the messenger's party with no time to lay an ambush. Wilhum's haste and rage had made him uncharacteristically clumsy, falling victim to a blow from the third man-at-arms after quickly dispatching the other two. Luckily, Swain's mace had accounted for the final soldier before he could finish the job. The messenger had taken the unwise if admirable decision to try to flee rather than surrender his charge, suffering a thrown mace to the skull for his pains.

"It's signed by Duke Elbyn," I said, lowering the missive, "and a long list of clerics and nobles, only one of whom matters." I extended the parchment to Wilhum, pointing out the relevant signature.

"Sir Althus Levalle," he said, his face taking on some colour as his anger deepened. "So, the Crown has a hand in this."

"Crown Company, at least," Swain said. "As for the king, the fact that he's not here may mean something. And why delay for two days? The deed will be done before the message even reaches the capital."

"Appearances." Wilhum winced and adjusted the fit of his sling, fury and pain vying for control of his features. "Should the commons be angered by this, he can claim he wasn't told of it in time to intervene, so remains blameless. I'd wager the two-day interval is so they can raise the scaffold and gather an audience. Simply killing her within the castle walls with no mob to stand witness makes it murder, regardless of any farcical trial they might have held. They're afraid. That's something."

"Afraid or not," Swain mused, running a hand over his chin, "they've got Crown Company and the duke's full complement of men-at-arms. Even with the full company, fighting our way through to her would be next to impossible."

"Two days from Farinsahl is a hard march," I said. "But not impossible for soldiers committed to their cause. I'd be surprised if Supplicant Ofihla hasn't already put the whole company on the road."

Swain gave a helpless grunt, shaking his head. "Still won't be enough. Numbers favour them, and no amount of devotion can sway a battle when the odds are so uneven."

"Devotion . . . " I repeated, voice faint as his words struck a chord in my head.

"Scribe?" Swain's expression was one of reluctant insistence. He still harboured doubts about me, as well he might, but seemed to have acquired some modicum of regard for my cunning.

"You and Wilhum should retrace the road," I told him. "Find the company and speed their march as best you can. As for numbers, I doubt that will be an issue."

"It'll be close," Wilhum warned. "Executions are always carried out in the morning."

"Then we'll need to force a further delay. If they want this to be a proper legal proceeding, then they'll have to observe the required forms. Which offers an opportunity."

"For what?"

Considering the stratagem I was about to suggest, the absence of a nauseous churn in my guts was remarkable. *The curse of a* Doenlisch *is worse than all others*, the chainsman had said. *She bound you tighter than I ever could . . .*

"I don't suppose," I said, "you brought my armour with you?"

CHAPTER FORTY-SEVEN

"Look upon this traitor!"

The formal denunciation had already begun by the time I began to push my way through the crowd, an unseen but commanding voice calling out from the scaffold. The thickness of the gathering, far more numerous than the few score that had come to gawp at the demise of Duke Rouphon, obscured my view but I could make a fair guess of who would be present on the scaffold. The speaker's voice, however, was one I couldn't place.

"This most dire blasphemer of the Covenant's truths! Behold her shame and her guilt!"

Despite the fact that dawn had broken only a few hours before, some of those who had gathered or been compelled to witness this ugly spectacle were already drunk and reluctant to shift without a hard shove. Those roused to anger by my aggression forsook their snarling threats when they took full measure of my appearance. My armour was still in Farinsahl, but Wilhum had been wearing his when he accompanied Evadine to the Shrine of Martyr Ihlander. It all fitted me quite well and some hard work with cloth and spit had burnished the blue enamelled plate to a fair shine. So, to the eyes of the sober folk who scrambled aside, and the quailing drunkards, I appeared a knight. More than a few even bowed and knuckled their foreheads as they cleared a path.

"Do not be fooled by her face, good people! For it is but a mask! A veneer that covers unspeakable maleficence!"

"What's that mean?" I heard one churl mutter to another, drawing an equally baffled response.

"Dunno. What's 'veneer' mean?"

I was close enough to make out a portion of the dignitaries arrayed on the scaffold now, finding scant surprise at the sight of Duke Elbyn. I had caught only a partial glimpse of him at the Traitors' Field and I found him an unedifying figure, distinguished mainly by the sour impatience of his expression. He was flanked by a number of retainers but Lorine was absent from his side. I greatly doubted he had any inkling where his wife had been a week before, or any other night for that matter.

"Not content with selling one of the beloved jewels of this realm to our hated heathen adversaries in the north, this vile deceiver has also dared to award herself the mantle of Martyr! Is there no terminus to her well of depravity?"

The speaker had a fine, strong voice that would have been commanding but for his choice of words. Evadine always knew not only how to reach the ears of her audience, but how to capture their souls with words they understood. This was the voice of a man in love with his own eloquence who, I suspected, couldn't care a quarter-shek for the opinion of this mob. I slowed as I neared the front of the crowd, the speaker finally coming into view, finding that I knew him after all.

"And so good people," Aspirant Arnabus proclaimed, "I ask you for the last time to behold the traitor." His arm shot out to cast an unwavering finger at the woman in the white shift standing a few paces to his side. Arnabus's narrow face, which had seemed unusually pale that day at the king's encampment, was now florid and beaded with sweat. I couldn't tell if it was due to fear or relish.

Evadine's features were, by marked contrast, placid to the point of near indifference. Always pale, her skin seemed as white as the shift she wore and there was something statue-like in her placidity. Her wrists had been bound with rope but her expression betrayed no pain.

Rather it was one of patient expectation, the face of a woman suffering through a tedious conversation she was too polite to curtail. Of fear, I saw no sign at all.

She was flanked by two kingsmen of Crown Company and, standing close to the edge of the scaffold, a large knight in full armour, his breastplate emblazoned with a brass eagle. Not finding the King's Champion here had been a gamble, but a calculated one. By all accounts Sir Ehlbert Bauldry had taken on the role of the old duke's executioner only with extreme reluctance. Much to my relief, it seemed he had refused to besmirch his knightly honour with any part of this liars' farce. Sir Althus Levalle, however, indulged no such scruples.

"I ask you to bear witness to her just execution and harden your hearts against pity." My gaze snapped back to Aspirant Arnabus as his voice grew in volume. "I ask that you, as loyal subjects of King Tomas, take heed of what you see this day. And finally, I ask, having heard all the charges against her proven, will any come forth to bear arms in this traitor's defence?"

"I WILL!"

I allowed no pause between question and answer, making sure to roar the words out as loud as my throat would allow as I pushed my way through the last few churls. A line of ducal men-at-arms stood to the front of the scaffold and reacted to my appearance with predictable alarm. The closest levelled halberds and scrambled to form an arc around me.

"I come to bear arms in defence of one unjustly charged!" I called out, raising my longsword above my head and drawing it from the scabbard. The sky was partially overcast that morning but I was lucky in catching a decent gleam as I held the bared blade aloft. "As is my right! The right of all subjects of Albermaine under the laws set down in the first Tri-Reign!"

I turned as I spoke, keeping the sword raised and casting my words to the crowd. "A subject of any station may make this challenge, be he churl, knight or beggar! Will you honour it, or let this proceeding be seen for the charade it is?!"

My gaze swung back to the platform, finding a parade of shocked faces, with three notable exceptions. While the duke and his retainers engaged in a good deal of excited muttering, Aspirant Arnabus regarded me with upraised brows but no special sense of unease or grievance. I fancied I saw his lips curve a little and, if anything, his face resembled that of a child presented with a new and unexpectedly delightful toy.

Evadine also smiled, bright and welcoming, but displayed none of the cleric's surprise. I understood in the short interval during which our eyes met that she had harboured no doubt that I would come.

Sir Althus Levalle didn't smile exactly, his broad features forming something that was more a satisfied grimace that made me wonder if he too had anticipated my appearance.

"Who is this man?"

Duke Elbyn got to his feet, striding to the edge of the platform to regard me with all the agitation and anger so lacking in Aspirant Arnabus. When presiding over impending slaughter at the Traitors' Field the duke's voice had at least contained an attempt at nobility. Now I found it so peevish and childlike I wondered how Lorine had managed to stomach his company for so long, never mind conceive his heir. He addressed his question to Arnabus, flapping a hand for emphasis. "Who is he to interrupt this . . . important occasion?"

"A fellow who knows the law, apparently," Arnabus replied mildly before calling out to me. "And, being such, will also know that he is required to state his name when making a formal challenge contesting the verdict of our court."

"My name is Alwyn Scribe," I called back, raising my voice and half turning to the now rapt throng as I spoke on. "Soldier in the Covenant Company and servant of the Risen Martyr Evadine Courlain, blessed is she by the Grace of the Seraphile!"

"Lies!" The duke flapped his hand at me. "Lies and heresy! You!" His fluttering hand shifted to the cordon of ducal soldiers. "Bind this man! He too will face justice—"

"HOLD!"

Sir Althus's voice had lost none of its facility for command over the years. Although they weren't under his banner, the duke's soldiers came to a rigid halt. The knight commander moved to the scaffold steps with a slow, measured stride, his helm under his arm and hand resting on his sword's pommel. His eyes stayed on me as he walked, not shifting when Duke Elbyn reached for his arm, muttering fierce words I couldn't hear. However, I did hear Sir Althus's reply: "Shut your prattle, you feckless turd."

He descended the steps with the same unhurried stride, barking out a series of orders that had a score of kingsmen hurrying to push the crowd back. After creating a decent gap, they established a cordon around us, poleaxes held level to keep the now keenly interested assemblage at bay.

"Nice plate," Sir Althus commented, coming to a halt a dozen paces from me. "Where'd you steal it?"

He wore a humourless smile which I returned in full. "It was a gift."

"Then I'll be sorry to besmirch it." He donned his helm and began to fasten the straps. "So, revenge is it?" he asked. "For the pillory and the Pits, I assume."

"I'm not here for you." I donned my own helm, the only part of my armour not provided by Wilhum. His helm had proven to be too small for my skull so I had been obliged to make do with a less fine replacement scavenged from the Traitors' Field by Swain. It was sturdy enough but lacked a full visor, facial protection being afforded by a grate of four iron tines.

"Her then?" Sir Althus nodded to Evadine as he unbuckled his sword, drawing the blade free of the scabbard. "You really imagine she is what she claims?"

"I imagine her to be worth saving." I levelled my sword at him, not troubling myself with the customary salute. I knew it wouldn't be returned. Besides, I felt no inclination towards honouring this man. "As I know you are worth killing."

A tic of amusement passed across his features, but his eyes grew hard. "There'll be no sparing you this time, boy. My obligation to Deckin is paid, and I owe nothing to you."

"On the contrary, my lord." I gripped my sword in two hands, adopting the half-crouch Wilhum had taught me. "You owe blood, and not just to me."

"Well," Sir Althus sighed as he tossed his empty scabbard away and lowered his visor, "that gets it said."

He attacked with no further preamble, or any careful circling as he searched for an opening, just raised his sword level with his shoulders and charged. Thanks to Wilhum's lessons, I knew this as a tactic often employed against novice knights on the tourney field. The natural instinct was to parry the thrust of the sword, thereby laying oneself open to a knee to the groin or a hard kick to the shin. Wilhum had felled me several times with this trick before I learned the lesson so, instead of sweeping the knight commander's sword aside, I stepped to the left and thrust my own at his visor.

He ducked before the tip could find the slit, the steel leaving a scratch on his plate. I brought my sword up and down in a swift chop at his shoulder, but he was too quick, swaying back and keeping me at bay with an arcing slash at my legs.

"Had a little education, eh?" he said, voice emerging as a metallic taunt from behind his visor. "In a dozen years or so you might actually make a decent knight, lad. As of now, though, you're still just a child in a man's armour."

He attacked again, wielding his sword two-handed to deliver a series of blows at my head. I managed to parry them all but had to back away in the process, my feet not quite matching the rapid light step Wilhum performed so easily. I tripped after the first few paces, just a small stumble but enough for Sir Althus to get a blow past my guard. I turned my head as the blade hit, but not enough to avoid the sting of sparks and flecked metal as it sundered one of my helm's tines.

Feeling the first wet kiss of blood on my skin, I staggered, apparently stunned, sword drooping in my grasp. I reasoned the knight commander's overconfidence would make him careless, and so it proved. He lunged too soon and too quick, trying to drive his sword-point into my part-exposed face, but putting himself off balance as he did so. Lowering my head to let his blade slide over the top of my

helm, I drove a shoulder into the centre of his chest, denting the plate
and sending him careering back. He recovered quickly, bringing his
sword back to guard, but not in time to stop the blow I delivered to
his right leg.

I had hoped to break it, but Sir Althus contrived to deflect enough
of the force to prevent that. However, I did succeed in two important
respects. First, the blow was strong enough to dislodge the cuisse
protecting his thigh and leave behind a livid and no doubt painful
bruise. Second, I had made him angry.

"You shit-grubbing churlish fuck!" his tinny, enraged voice sputtered behind the visor.

Anger makes a man incautious, but it also makes him fast. Wilhum
might have been able to dodge his next swipe at my head, but not I.
A flash of lightning blinded me as the earth tipped beneath my feet,
a myriad of colours swimming before my eyes. A strange, sudden
weariness filled me from head to foot as I fell, the soft, dew-kissed
ground feeling very much like the blankets of a warmed bed.

It was the jarring impact of my helm on the earth that saved me,
the flash of pain and choke of my throat as the straps bit into my
flesh banishing the weariness in an instant. Reaching for the straps,
I tore the helm free, gasping for air and trying to rise.

"No," Sir Althus advised, planting an armoured foot on my chest
and forcing me back down. "I think I'd rather you stay there."

I slashed at him with the sword that I'd somehow contrived to keep
hold of, but he simply raised an arm, allowing the weak blow to land,
then trapping the blade. "Seems a fitting end for you," Sir Althus
grunted, drawing his foot back and aiming the pointed tip at my face.
"Being kicked to death in the mud."

Realising I still had my helm in hand, I swiftly brought it down
into the path of his foot. The pointed toe stabbed through the metal
but failed to find my flesh. Snarling, I twisted, abandoning the grip
on my sword and snatching the dagger from my belt. Seeing the
danger, Sir Althus attempted to draw his foot back, but I pressed the
helm harder, keeping it entangled just long enough to drive the dagger
into the unarmoured gap behind his knee. The dagger didn't do the

damage I wanted, Sir Althus having worn thick quilted trews beneath his armour, but I had the satisfaction of feeling the hot rush of fresh blood as I drove it in.

Roaring, he drove a gauntleted fist at my head. Another flash of lightning behind the eyes, more swirling colours, but no accompanying weariness this time. I was fully in this scrap now, for scrap it was. All knightly pretensions were forgotten. Now we were two outlaws fighting to the death, something I had done before.

Keeping hold of the knife, I twisted it deeper to increase his pain, forcing him to reach for it and thereby freeing my sword. By sheer good fortune it fell smack into my hand and I lost no time in swinging it with all the energy I could muster. The blade connected with his helm at the visor's weak point, sending it spinning away along with a spray of blood and spit.

I drove a kick at the knight commander's groin, causing him to reel back and allow me to regain my feet. I wanted very badly to rush him and finish it, but now the immediate threat had gone, my body forced a delay. I leaned on my sword, chest heaving while Sir Althus recovered a few paces off. This time, when he raised his sword, he began to circle, albeit with a notable limp. His face had become the narrow-eyed mask of a craftsman setting himself to a difficult task.

"Not so much of a child, eh?" I asked him.

"I'm always happy to kill a man too," he spat back, forcing me to raise my sword as he thrust at my midriff. One of the taces protecting my gut had come loose in the struggle, providing a tempting opening. Steel rang as I parried the thrust, replying with a side swipe at his injured leg which he avoided with ease.

"And a woman?" I enquired as we continued to circle one another.

"She's fucking mad, boy." Blood seeped from Althus's split lips as he sneered. "And this realm doesn't need another Martyr."

"Not her," I said, coming to a halt, fixing his gaze with mine. "Sihlda."

I saw the name strike home with the force of a punch, the sneer vanishing from the knight commander's face as he blinked in shock.

"You must have thought she'd died in the Pit Mines years ago." I said, eyes still fixed on his. "She didn't. She lived long enough to teach me letters so that I could write her testament. She told me all of it, my lord. Do you think these people would like to hear the tale?"

"Shut your mouth." The instruction emerged as a hoarse whisper, Althus's face pale and quivering now. I had imagined a soul as black as his to be immune to guilt, but it appeared I was wrong.

"She told me," I went on, inching closer, "about the two youthful knights who escorted a pregnant noblewoman to her shrine. One was a commoner raised to knighthood, the other destined to become the greatest knight of his day."

"Shut up!" Althus lunged, fast but clumsy with rage, the lancing blade easily turned. I made no riposte, speaking on as I continued to circle him.

"She told me how trust and friendship blossomed between her and this commoner knight, how they would spend hours talking. In time, trust and friendship became love. But, when the noblewoman's child, a son, was born he followed his sworn duty and left with her and his brother knight, who, it transpired, was the child's father. And his mother was a queen."

Althus swung his sword high, an incoherent howl of rage erupting from his throat as he brought it down. Instead of dodging aside, I crouched and charged closer. As our steel-clad bodies collided, I tried to jam my swordpoint into the gap between his gorget and breastplate. But I judged the angle badly, the blade sliding up to slice across his cheek and ear instead. Luckily, the force of my charge was enough to bring him down, air whooshing from him as I landed on his chest. He swung a punch to dislodge me, but I snapped my forehead into his face before it landed, leaving him stunned beneath me.

"She loved you." Bloody spittle flew as I hissed into his face. "She trusted you. When you returned years later she thought it was for her. But you murdered a Supplicant and blamed it on her so you could stick her in that shithole!"

I raised myself up, reversing the grip on my sword, the point poised to stab down into his mouth. "Tomas Algathinet is a bastard with no more right to sit the throne than I do!" I shouted the words, hoping all ears present could hear them, but fate is ever fickle.

At that precise moment a great commotion seized the throng, raising a confusion of voices loud enough to drown my words. Hesitating, I turned to see the crowd convulsing beyond the cordon of kingsmen, then surging against it as those behind began a panicked rush. The soldiers attempted to hold them back, first with shoves and threats, then blades. But the weight of numbers was too great to hold the throng despite the blood that began to fly as the halberds rose and fell.

A second outburst drew my gaze to the scaffold where another disturbance had broken out, but before I could discern its nature, Sir Althus, a man well attuned to grasping an advantage, recovered enough strength to slam his sword pommel into the side of my head.

Once again the earth greeted me with a welcoming embrace, although it felt a good deal colder this time. A swirling red mist filled my eyes, making crimson shadows of the world as I tried vainly to work suddenly enfeebled limbs. I was aware of being shoved onto my back, of a large shape looming above and might well have met my end in this welter of confusion if Sir Althus hadn't wanted me to hear his farewell.

"Hear me, boy!" A hard slap of a mailed palm to my cheek brought enough pain to summon clarity, but sadly not strength. I blinked at the knight commander's bleeding, besmirched features as he leaned close, eyes lit with the kind of rage-filled hate I knew so well; the hate for one who has hurt you in soul rather than body, cut you deeper than any blade could ever cut. Staring into his wide, maddened eyes, I knew I had pierced the armour he had wrapped around his heart all these many years. Whatever tales he had told himself to justify consigning the woman he once loved to the worst of prisons were now revealed as shameful lies. It's never an easy thing to hear the truth of what we are, and Sir Althus clearly found it so painful he had to summon more lies.

"It was for duty I did it," he grated at me. "For it is duty that binds this realm, Scribe. The duty of men like me is what preserves us, keeps chaos at bay, defeats the schemes and intrigues of scum like you."

I regret to record that this was one of the few occasions in life when I found I had nothing to say. Much as I have been tempted to compose a rejoinder of supreme wit and insight to fit this particular occasion, the truth is that the only answer I could conjure in the moment was to spit a thick wad of blood into the face of Sir Althus Levalle, Knight Commander of Crown Company and as disgraced a soul as I ever encountered.

When he reared, snarling, arm raised for the killing blow, I could only flail ineffectually at his breastplate. As he brought his sword down, a second blade flickered at the edge of my vision, expertly aimed to drive his sword aside before sweeping on to cut deep into his unprotected skull. I watched the knight commander's eyes roll up and his brows form a curious squint, as if he had been asked a particularly troublesome question. But it was one he would never answer.

The puzzled frown remained frozen on his face when it slumped to the earth an inch from mine. I was momentarily fascinated by his expression until the sight of the sword blade being jerked from his skull brought me back to a semblance of awareness.

"Can you walk, Alwyn Scribe?"

Evadine's wrists were still bound and she clutched the sword between two hands. Her shift clung to her body where it was dampened by blood, and it was very damp. I gaped at her until the familiar shout of a charging soldier tore my gaze away. One of the kingsmen came at us, halberd levelled at me. Had he been a wiser fellow it would surely have been aimed at Evadine. A swirl of white and red, the scrape of steel on steel and the charging soldier lay dead alongside his knight commander.

"Alwyn!" Evadine said, voice sharp with impatience. She upended the sword she held and stabbed it into the earth then began sawing the rope binding her wrists along the edge. Beyond her I saw the scaffold was now a chaos of struggling figures, ducal men-at-arms vainly trying to stave off the rush of the crowd. As I expected, many were the congregants who had gathered outside the lord of exchange's house in Farinsahl. The long march from the port didn't appear to have tired them for they threw themselves into the fray with animalistic ferocity. Some carried staffs or axes but most lacked any arms at all and simply clawed at the rapidly withering line of soldiers.

Looking around I saw similar carnage everywhere. Isolated kingsmen laid about with their halberds only to be overwhelmed and beaten into the dirt. Not all assailants were congregants; many were townsfolk from Ambriside and churls from the surrounding fields. Despite having only glimpsed the Risen Martyr this very morn, still they had been roused to her defence.

I saw a few dozen kingsmen form up into a defensive circle and succeed in holding their ranks for a time. However, their attempt to fight their way clear ended when they were set upon by Covenant Company. I took a perverse pride in watching them envelop the veteran kingsmen, the swiftness of their victory owing much to weight of numbers, but still, it was finely done.

"Up!" Evadine looped an arm under mine and tried to drag me upright. After a few seconds' grunting effort, I succeeded in gaining my feet, though the constant sway of the ground and sky meant I had to hold onto her for support.

"Captain!"

Swain's unmistakable rasp cut through the general tumult and I saw him lead a contingent of company soldiers towards us. "The duke has gained the castle and is mustering the full garrison," he reported. "Folk here say there's two more companies in the keep."

"Then we take it," Wilhum said, appearing at my side. Looking me over, he winced before putting my arm over his shoulders. "This lot seem fit to take on the whole world."

I cast a bleary gaze at Evadine as she surveyed the field. All the kingsmen were slain or had fled while the duke had contrived to escape along with a decent number of retainers and men-at-arms. Many congregants and townsfolk were streaming towards the castle in an untidy mob but I doubted their chances against a barred gate and staunchly held walls, as did Evadine.

"No," she said. "There's been enough blood today. Sergeant, spread the word as best you can. Tell these people Martyr Evadine thanks them for their courage and devotion and asks that they return to their homes."

"Then where do we go?" Wilhum asked. "Back to Farinsahl?"

Evadine shook her head. "I'll not subject innocents to a siege on my account."

"Then where?"

"Forest," I muttered, feeling a desire to help. My head lolled as I turned to Evadine. "Lots of places to hide in the forest . . . "

"Alwyn?"

Wilhum's voice dwindled to a vague, distant murmur as many colours returned to swirl in my eyes. For a time, those twisting hues were all I saw and when they faded I found myself staring up at passing clouds. My heart beat slower than it should, growing slower by the second, and I possessed enough reason to know what that meant. I was dimly aware of being carried, of voices continually speaking my name but it was very far away. Soon the clouds were riven by a dark web of branches and the air took on a familiar coolness.

"Trees . . . " I murmured, feeling a smile creep across my lips. "It always . . . calms me to regard . . . the trees . . . "

And so, into the woods I was borne, made an outlaw once again.

The story continues in . . .

Book Two of The Covenant of Steel

ACKNOWLEDGEMENTS

Thanks to my agent, Paul Lucas, and to my UK and US editors, James Long and Bradley Englert, for their encouragement and hard work in bringing the tale of Alwyn Scribe to life.

extras

orbit

meet the author

Photo Credit: Ellie Grace Photography

ANTHONY RYAN lives in London and is the *New York Times* best-selling author of the Raven's Shadow and Draconis Memoria series. He previously worked in a variety of roles for the UK government, but now writes full time. His interests include art, science and the unending quest for the perfect pint of real ale.

Find out more about Anthony Ryan and other Orbit authors by registering for the Orbit newsletter at orbitbooks.net.

if you enjoyed
THE PARIAH

look out for

SON OF THE STORM

Book One of
The Nameless Republic

by

Suyi Davies Okungbowa

From one of the most exciting new storytellers in epic fantasy, the first book in the Nameless Republic trilogy is a sweeping tale of violent conquest and forbidden magic, set in a world inspired by the precolonial empires of West Africa.

In the thriving city of Bassa, Danso is a clever but disillusioned scholar who longs for a life beyond the rigid family and political obligations expected of the city's elite. A way out presents itself when Lilong, a skinchanging warrior, shows up wounded in his barn. She comes from the Nameless Islands, which, according to Bassa lore, don't exist. And neither should the mythical magic of ibor she wields.

Now swept into a conspiracy far beyond his understanding, Danso will set out on a journey with Lilong that reveals histories violently suppressed and magics found only in lore.

Prologue

Oke

The Weary Sojourner Caravansary stood at the corner of three worlds.

For a multitude of seasons before Oke was born, the travelhouse had offered food, wine, board, and music—and for those who had been on the road too long, companionship—to many a traveller across the Savanna Belt. Its patronage consisted solely of those who lugged loads of gold, bronze, nuts, produce, textile, and craftwork from Bassa into the Savanna Belt or, for the even more daring, to the Idjama desert across Lake Vezha. On their way back, they would stop at the caravansary again, the banana and yam and rice loads on their camels gone and now replaced with tablets of salt, wool, and beaded ornaments.

But there was another set of people for whom the caravansary stood, those whose sights were set on discovering the storied isthmus that connected the Savanna Belt to the yet-to-be-sighted seven islands of the archipelago. For people like these, the Weary Sojourner stood as something else: a vantage point. And for people like Oke who had a leg in all three worlds, walking into the Weary Sojourner called for an intensified level of alertness.

Especially when the fate of the three worlds could be determined by the very meeting she was going to have.

She swung open the curtain. She did not push back her cloak.

Like many public houses in the Savanna Belt, the Weary Sojourner operated in darkness, despite it being late morning. During her time in the desertlands, Oke had learned that this was a practice carried over from the time of the Leopard Emperor when liquor was banned in its desert protectorates, and secret houses were operated under the cover of darkness. Even though that period of despotism was thankfully over, habitual practices were difficult to shake off. People still preferred to drink and smoke and fuck in the dark.

Which made this the perfect place for Oke's meeting.

She took a seat at the back and surveyed the room. It was at once obvious that her contact wasn't around. There were exactly three people here, all men who had clearly just arrived from the same caravan. Their clothes gave them away: definitely Bassai, in brightly coloured cotton wrappers, bronze jewellery—no sensible person travelled with gold jewellery—over some velvet, wool, and leatherskin boots for the desert's cold. Senior members of the merchantry guild, looking at that velvet. Definitely members of the Idu, the mainland's noble caste. Guild aside, their complexions also gave that away—high-black skin, as dark as the darkest of humuses, just the way Bassa liked it. It was the kind of complexion she hadn't seen in a long time.

Oke swept aside a nearby curtain and looked outside. Sure enough, there was their caravan, parked behind the establishment, guarded by a few private Bassai hunthands. Beside them, travelhands—hired desert immigrants to the mainland judging by their complexions, what the Bassai would refer to as *low-brown* for how light and lowly it was—unpacking busily for an overnight stay and unsaddling the camels so they could drink. There were no layers of dust on anyone yet, so clearly they were northbound.

"A drink, maa?"

Oke looked up at the housekeep, who had come over, wringing his hands in a rag. She could see little of his face, but she had been here twice before, and knew enough of what he looked like.

"Palm wine and jackalberry with ginger," she said, hiding her hands.

The housekeep stopped short. "Interesting choice of drink." He peered closer. "Have you been here before?" He enunciated the words in Savanna Common in a way that betrayed his border origins.

Oke's eyes scanned him and decided he was asking this innocently. "Why do you ask?"

"You remember things, as a housekeep," he said, leaning back on a nearby counter. "Especially drink combinations that join lands that have no place joining."

"Consider it an acquired taste," Oke said, and looked away, signalling the end of the discussion. But to her surprise, the man nodded at the group far away and asked, in clear Mainland Common: "You with them?"

Oke froze. He had seen her complexion, then, and knew enough to know she had mainland origins. What had always been a curse for Oke back when she was a mainlander—*Too light, is she punished by Menai?* people would ask her daa—had become a gift in self-exile over the border. But there were a few people with keen eyes and ears who would, every now and then, recognise a lilt in her Savanna Common or note how her hair curled a bit too tightly for a desertlander or how she carried herself with a smidgen of mainlander confidence. There was only one way to react to that, as she always did whenever this came up.

"What?" She frowned. "Sorry, I don't understand that language."

The housekeep eyed her for another moment, then went away.

Oke breathed a sigh of relief. It was of the utmost importance that no one knew who she was and what she was doing here, living in the Savanna Belt. Because the history of the Savanna Belt was what it was, a tiny enough number of people who originated from this side of the Soke border looked just a bit like she did. Passing as one was easier once she perfected the languages. Thank moons she had studied them as a scholar in Bassa.

She drank slowly once the housekeep brought her order, and she put forward some cowries, making sure to add a few pieces to clearly signal she wanted to be left alone.

Halfway through her drink, she realised her contact was running late. She looked outside again. The sky had gone cloudy, and the sun was missing for a while. She went back to her drink and nursed it some more.

The men in the room rose and went up to be shown to their rooms. Oke peeked out of the curtain again. The travelhands were gone. One hunthand stood and guarded the caravan. One stood at the back door to the caravansary. The camels still stood there, lapping water.

Oke ordered another drink and waited. The sun came back out. It was past an hour now. She looked out again. The camels had stopped drinking and now lay in the dust, snoozing.

Something was wrong.

Oke got up without touching her new drink, put down some more cowries on the counter in front of the housekeep, and walked to the front door of the caravansary. On second thought, she turned and went back to the housekeep.

"Your alternate exit. Show me."

The man pointed without looking at her. Oke took it and went around the building, evading both the men and the animals. She eventually showed up to where she had left her own animal—a kwaga, a striped beauty with tiny horns. She untied and patted it. It snorted in return. Then she slapped its hindquarters and set it off on a run, barking as it went.

She waited for a moment or two, then dashed away herself.

Going through a secluded route on foot, while trying to stay as nondescript as possible, took a long time. Oke had to take double the usual precautions, as banditry had increased so much on the trade routes that one was more likely to get robbed and murdered than not. Back when Bassa was Bassa—not now with its heavily diluted population and generally weakening influence—no one would dare attack a Bassai caravan anywhere on the continent for fear of retaliation. These days, every caravan had to travel with private security. The Bassai Upper Council was well known for being toothless and only concerned with enriching themselves.

The clouds from earlier had disappeared, and the sun beat mercilessly on her, causing her to sweat rivers beneath her cloak, but Oke knew she had done the right thing. It was as they had agreed: If either of them got even a whiff of something off, they were to make a getaway as swiftly as possible. She was then to head straight for the place nicknamed the Forest of the Mist, the thick, uncharted woodland with often heavy fog that was storied to house secret passages to an isthmus that connected the Savanna Belt to the seven islands of the eastern archipelago.

It didn't matter any longer if that bit of desertland myth was true or not. Whether the archipelago even still existed was moot at this point. The yet undiscovered knowledge she had gleaned from her clandestine exploits in the library at the University of Bassa, coupled with the artifacts her contact was bringing her—if either made it into the wrong hands, the whole continent of Oon would pay for it. Oke wasn't ready to drop the fate of the continent in the dust just yet.

Two hours later, Oke looked back and saw in the sky the grey tip of what she knew came from thick, black smoke. Not the kind of smoke that came from a nearby kitchen, but the kind that said something far away had been destroyed. Something big.

She took a detour in her journey and headed for the closest high point she knew. She chose one that overlooked a decent portion of the savanna but also kept her on the way to the Forest of the Mist. It took a while to ascend to the top, but she soon got to a good enough vantage point to look across and see the caravansary.

The Weary Sojourner stuck out like an anthill, the one establishment for a distance where the road from the border branched into the Savanna Belt. The caravansary was up in flames. It was too far for her to see the people and animals, but she knew what those things scattering from the raging inferno were. The body language of disaster was the same everywhere.

Oke began to descend fast, her chest weightless. The Forest of the Mist was the only place on this continent where she would be safe now, and she needed to get there *immediately*. Whoever set that fire to the Weary Sojourner knew who she and her contact were. Her contact may or may not have made it out alive. It was up to her now to ensure that the continent's biggest secret was kept that way.

The alternative was simply too grave to consider.

1

Danso

The rumours broke slowly but spread fast, like bushfire from a rain-cloud. Bassa's central market sparked and sizzled, as word jumped from lip to ear, lip to ear, speculating. The people responded minimally at first: a shift of the shoulders, a retying of wrappers. Then murmurs rose, until they matured into a buzzing that swept through the city, swinging from stranger to stranger and stall to stall, everyone opening conversation with whispers of *Is it true? Has the Soke Pass really been shut down?*

Danso waded through the clumps of gossipers, sweating, cursing his decision to go through the central market rather than the mainway. He darted between throngs of oblivious citizens huddled around vendors and spilling into the pathway.

"Leave way, leave way," he called, irritated, as he shouldered through bodies. He crouched, wriggling his lean frame underneath a large table that reeked of pepper seeds and fowl shit. The ground, paved with baked earth, was not supposed to be wet, since harmattan season was soon to begin. But some fool had dumped water in the wrong place, and red mud eventually found a way into Danso's sandals. Someone else had abandoned a huge stack of yam sacks right in the middle of the pathway and gone off to do moons knew what, so that Danso was forced to clamber over yet another obstacle. He found a large brown stain on his wrappers thereafter. He wiped at the spot with his elbow, but the stain only spread.

Great. Now not only was he going to be the late jali novitiate, he was going to be the dirty one, too.

If only he could've ridden a kwaga through the market, Danso thought. But markets were foot traffic only, so even though jalis or their novitiates rarely moved on foot, he had to in this instance. On this day, when he needed to get to the centre of town as quickly as possible while raising zero eyebrows, he needed to brave the shortest path from home to city square, which meant going through Bassa's most motley crowd. This was the price he had to pay for missing the city crier's call three whole times, therefore setting himself up for yet another late arrival at a mandatory event—in this case, a Great Dome announcement.

Missing this impromptu meeting would be his third infraction, which could mean expulsion from the university. He'd already been given two strikes: first, for repeatedly arguing with Elder Jalis and trying to prove his superior intelligence; then more recently, for being caught poring over a restricted manuscript that was supposed to be for only two sets of eyes: emperors, back when Bassa still had them, and the archivist scholars who didn't even get to read them except while scribing. At this rate, all they needed was a reason to send him away. Expulsion would definitely lose him favour with Esheme, and if anything happened to their intended-ship as a result, he could consider his life in this city officially over. He would end up exactly like his daa—a disgraced outcast—and Habba would die first before that happened.

The end of the market pathway came within sight. Danso burst out into mainway one, the smack middle of Bassa's thirty mainways that crisscrossed one another and split the city perpendicular to the Soke mountains. The midday sun shone brighter here. Though shoddy, the market's thatch roofing had saved him from some of the tropical sun, and now out of it, the humid heat came down on him unbearably. He shaded his eyes.

In the distance, the capital square stood at the end of the mainway. The Great Dome nestled prettily in its centre, against a backdrop of Bassai rounded-corner mudbrick architecture, like a god surrounded by its worshippers. Behind it, the Soke mountains stuck their raggedy heads so high into the clouds that they could be seen from every spot in Bassa, hunching protectively over the mainland's shining crown.

What took his attention, though, was the crowd in the mainway, leading up to the Great Dome. The wide street was packed full of mainlanders, from where Danso stood to the gates of the courtyard in the distance. The only times he'd seen this much of a gathering were when, every once in a while, troublemakers who called themselves the Coalition for New Bassa staged protests that mostly ended in pockets of riots and skirmishes with Bassai civic guards. This, however, seemed quite nonviolent, but that did nothing for the air of tension that permeated the crowd.

The civic guards at the gates weren't letting anyone in, obviously—only the ruling councils; government officials and ward leaders; members of select guilds, like the jali guild he belonged to; and civic guards themselves were allowed into the city centre. It was these select people who then took whatever news was disseminated back to their various wards. Only during a mooncrossing festival were regular citizens allowed into the courtyard.

Danso watched the crowd for a while to make a quick decision. The thrumming vibe was clearly one of anger, perplexity, and anxiety. He spotted a few people wailing and rolling in the dusty red earth, calling the names of their loved ones—those stuck outside the Pass, he surmised from their cries. Since First Ward was the largest commercial ward in Bassa, businesses at the sides of the mainway were hubbubs of hissed conversation, questions circulating under breaths. Danso caught some of the whispers, squeaky with tension: *The drawbridges over the moats? Rolled up. The border gates? Sealed, iron barriers driven into the earth. Only a ten-person team of earthworkers and ironworkers can open it.* The pace of their speech was frantic, fast, faster, everyone wondering what was true and what wasn't.

Danso cut back into a side street that opened up from the walls along the mainway, then cut into the corridors between private yards. Up here in First Ward, the corridors were clean, the ground was of polished earth, and beggars and rats did not populate here as they did in the outer wards. Yet they were still dark and largely unlit, so that Danso had to squint and sometimes reach out to feel before him. Navigation, however, wasn't a problem. This wasn't his first dance in the mazy corridors of Bassa, and this wasn't the first time he was taking a shortcut to the Great Dome.

Some househands passed by him on their way to errands, blending into the poor light, their red immigrant anklets clacking as they went. These narrow walkways built into the spaces between courtyards were natural terrain for their caste—Yelekuté, the lower of Bassa's two indentured immigrant castes. The nation didn't really fancy anything undesirable showing up in all the important places, including the low-brown complexion that, among other things, easily signified desertlanders. The more desired high-brown Potokin were the chosen desertlanders allowed on the mainways, but only in company of their employers.

Ordinarily, they wouldn't pay him much attention. It wasn't a rare sight to spot people of other castes dallying in one backyard escapade or another. But today, hurrying past and dripping sweat, they glanced at Danso as he went, taking in his yellow-and-maroon tie-and-dye wrappers and the fat, single plait of hair in the middle of his head, the two signs that indicated he was a jali novitiate at the university. They considered his complexion—not dark enough to be wearing that dress in the first place; hair not curled tightly enough to be pure mainlander—and concluded, *decided*, that he was not Bassai enough.

This assessment they carried out in a heartbeat, but Danso was so used to seeing the whole process happen on people's faces that he knew what they were doing even before they did. And as always, then came the next part, where they tried to put two and two together to decide what caste he belonged to. Their confused faces told the story of his life. His clothes and hair plait said *jali novitiate*, that he was a scholar-historian enrolled at the University of Bassa, and therefore had to be an Idu, the only caste allowed to attend said university. But his too-light complexion said *Shashi caste*, said he was of a poisoned union between a mainlander and an outlander and that even if the moons intervened, he would always be a disgrace to the mainland, an outcast who didn't even deserve to stand there and exist.

Perhaps it was this confusion that led the househands to go past him without offering the requisite greeting for Idu caste members. Danso snickered to himself. If belonging to both the highest and lowest castes in the land at the same time taught one anything, it was that when people had to choose where to place a person, they would always choose a spot beneath them.

He went past more househands who offered the same response, but he paid little heed, spatially mapping out where he could emerge closest to the city square. He finally found the exit he was looking for. Glad to be away from the darkness, he veered into the nearest street and followed the crowd back to the mainway.

The city square had five iron pedestrian gates, all guarded. To his luck, Danso emerged just close to one, manned by four typical civic guards: tall, snarling, and bloodshot-eyed. He made for it gleefully and pushed to go in.

The nearest civic guard held the gate firmly and frowned down at Danso.

"Where you think you're going?" he asked.

"The announcement," Danso said. "Obviously."

The civic guard looked Danso over, his chest rising and falling, his low-black skin shiny with sweat in the afternoon heat. Civic guards were Emuru, the lower of the pure mainlander caste, but they still wielded a lot of power. As the caste directly below the Idu, they could be brutal if given the space, especially if one belonged to any of the castes below them.

"And you're going as what?"

Danso lifted an eyebrow. "Excuse me?"

The guard looked at him again, then shoved Danso hard, so hard that he almost fell back into the group of people standing there.

"Ah!" Danso said. "Are you okay?"

"Get away. This resemble place for ruffians?" His Mainland Common was so poor he might have been better off speaking Mainland Pidgin, but that was the curse of working within proximity of so many Idu: Speaking Mainland Pidgin around them was almost as good as a crime. Here in the inner wards, High Bassai was accepted, Mainland Common was tolerated, and Mainland Pidgin was punished.

"Look," Danso said. "Can you not see I'm a jali novi—"

"I cannot see anything," the guard said, waving him away. "How can you be novitiate? I mean, look at you."

Danso looked over himself and suddenly realised what the man meant. His tie-and-dye wrappers didn't, in fact, look like they belonged to any respectable jali novitiate. Not only had he forgotten to give them to Zaq to wash after his last guild class, the market run had only made them worse. His feet were dusty and unwashed; his arms, and probably face, were crackled, dry, and smeared with harmattan dust. One of his sandal straps had pulled off. He ran a hand over his head and sighed. Experience should have taught him by now that his sparser hair, much of it inherited from his maternal Ajabo-islander side, never stayed long in the Bassai plait, which was designed for hair that curled tighter naturally. Running around without a firm new plait had produced unintended results: Half of it had come undone, which made him look unprepared, disrespectful, and not at all like any jali anyone knew.

And of course, there had been no time to take a bath, and he had not put on any sort of decent facepaint either. He'd also arrived without a kwaga. What manner of jali novitiate *walked* to an impromptu announcement such as this, and without a Second in tow for that matter?

He should really have listened for the city crier's ring.

"Okay, wait, listen," Danso said, desperate. "I was late. So I took the corridors. But I'm really a jali novitiate."

"I will close my eye," the civic guard said. "Before I open it, I no want to see you here."

"But I'm supposed to be here." Danso's voice was suddenly squeaky, guilty. "I *have* to go in there."

"Rubbish," the man spat. "You even steal that cloth or what?"

Danso's words got stuck in his throat, panic suddenly gripping him. Not because this civic guard was an idiot—oh, no, just wait until Danso reported him—but because so many things were going to go wrong if he didn't get in there immediately.

First, there was Esheme, waiting for him in there. He could already imagine her fuming, her lips set, frown stuck in place. It was unheard of for intendeds to attend any capital square gathering alone, and it was worse that they were both novitiates—he of the scholar-historians, she of the counsel guild of mainland law. His absence would be easily noticed. She had probably already sat through most of the meeting craning her neck to glance at the entrance, hoping he would come in and ensure that she didn't have to suffer that embarrassment. He imagined Nem, her maa, and how she would cast him the same dissatisfied look as when she sometimes told Esheme, *You're really too good for that boy.* If there was anything his daa hated, it was disappointing someone as influential as Nem in any way. He might be of guild age, but his daa would readily come for him with a guava stick just for that, and his triplet uncles would be like a choir behind him going *Ehen, ehen, yes, teach him well, Habba.*

His DaaHabba name wouldn't save him this time. He could be prevented from taking guild finals, and his whole life—and that of his family—could be ruined.

"I will tell you one last time," the civic guard said, taking a step toward Danso so that he could almost smell the dirt of the man's loincloth. "If you no leave here now, I will arrest you for trying to be novitiate."

He was so tall that his chest armour was right in Danso's face, the branded official emblem of the Nation of Great Bassa—the five ragged peaks of the Soke mountains with a warrior atop each, holding a spear and runku—staring back at him.

He really couldn't leave. He'd be over, done. So instead, Danso did the first thing that came to mind. He tried to slip past the civic guard.

It was almost as if the civic guard had expected it, as if it was behaviour he'd seen often. He didn't even move his body. He just stretched out a massive arm and caught Danso's clothes. He swung him around, and Danso crumpled into a heap at the man's feet.

The other guards laughed, as did the small group of people by the gate, but the civic guard wasn't done. He feinted, like he was about to lunge and hit Danso. Danso flinched, anticipating, protecting his head. Everyone laughed even louder, boisterous.

"Ei Shashi," another civic guard said, "you miss yo way? Is over there." He pointed west, toward Whudasha, toward the coast and the bight and the seas beyond them, and everyone laughed at the joke.

Every peal was another sting in Danso's chest as the word pricked him all over his body. *Shashi. Shashi. Shashi.*

It shouldn't have gotten to him. Not on this day, at least. Danso had been Shashi all his life, one of an almost nonexistent pinch in Bassa. He was the first Shashi to make it into a top guild since the Second Great War. Unlike every other Shashi sequestered away in Whudasha, he was allowed to sit side by side with other Idu, walk the nation's roads, go to its university, have a Second for himself, and even be joined to one of its citizens. But every day he was always reminded, in case he had forgotten, of what he really was—never enough. Almost there, but never complete. That lump should have been easy to get past his throat by now.

And yet, something hot and prideful rose in his chest at this laughter, and he picked himself up, slowly.

As the leader turned away, Danso aimed his words at the man, like arrows.

"Calling me Shashi," Danso said, "yet you *want* to be me. But you will always be less than bastards in this city. You can never be better than me."

What happened next was difficult for Danso to explain. First, the civic guard turned. Then he moved his hand to his waist where his runku, the large wooden club with a blob at one end, hung. He unclipped its buckle with a click, then moved so fast that Danso had no time to react.

There was a shout. Something hit Danso in the head. There was light, and then there was darkness.

if you enjoyed
THE PARIAH
look out for

THE JASMINE THRONE
Book One of
The Burning Kingdoms

by

Tasha Suri

Tasha Suri's The Jasmine Throne *begins the powerful Burning Kingdoms trilogy, in which two women—a long-imprisoned princess and a maidservant in possession of forbidden magic—come together to rewrite the fate of an empire.*

Exiled by her despotic brother when he claimed their father's kingdom, Malini spends her days trapped in the Hirana, an ancient, cliffside temple that was once the source of the magical deathless waters but is now little more than a decaying ruin.

A servant in the regent's household, Priya makes the treacherous climb to the top of the Hirana every night to clean Malini's chambers. She is happy to play the role of a drudge so long as it keeps anyone from discovering her ties to the temple and the dark secret of her past.

*One is a vengeful princess seeking to steal a throne. The other
is a powerful priestess seeking to save her family. Their destinies
will become irrevocably tangled.*

And together, they will set an empire ablaze.

PROLOGUE

In the court of the imperial mahal, the pyre was being built.

The fragrance of the gardens drifted in through the high
windows—sweet roses, and even sweeter imperial needle-flower,
pale and fragile, growing in such thick profusion that it poured in
through the lattice, its white petals unfurled against the sandstone
walls. The priests flung petals on the pyre, murmuring prayers as
the servants carried in wood and arranged it carefully, applying
camphor and ghee, scattering drops of perfumed oil.

On his throne, Emperor Chandra murmured along with his
priests. In his hands, he held a string of prayer stones, each an acorn
seeded with the name of a mother of flame: Divyanshi, Ahamara,
Nanvishi, Suhana, Meenakshi. As he recited, his courtiers—the
kings of Parijatdvipa's city-states, their princely sons, their bravest
warriors—recited along with him. Only the king of Alor and his
brood of nameless sons were notably, pointedly, silent.

Emperor Chandra's sister was brought into the court.

Her ladies-in-waiting stood on either side of her. To her left,
a nameless princess of Alor, commonly referred to only as Alori;
to her right, a high-blooded lady, Narina, daughter of a notable
mathematician from Srugna and a highborn Parijati mother. The
ladies-in-waiting wore red, bloody and bridal. In their hair, they
wore crowns of kindling, bound with thread to mimic stars. As

they entered the room, the watching men bowed, pressing their faces to the floor, their palms flat on the marble. The women had been dressed with reverence, marked with blessed water, prayed over for a day and a night until dawn had touched the sky. They were as holy as women could be.

Chandra did not bow his head. He watched his sister.

She wore no crown. Her hair was loose—tangled, trailing across her shoulders. He had sent maids to prepare her, but she had denied them all, gnashing her teeth and weeping. He had sent her a sari of crimson, embroidered in the finest Dwarali gold, scented with needle-flower and perfume. She had refused it, choosing instead to wear palest mourning white. He had ordered the cooks to lace her food with opium, but she had refused to eat. She had not been blessed. She stood in the court, her head unadorned and her hair wild, like a living curse.

His sister was a fool and a petulant child. They would not be here, he reminded himself, if she had not proven herself thoroughly unwomanly. If she had not tried to ruin it all.

The head priest kissed the nameless princess upon the forehead. He did the same to Lady Narina. When he reached for Chandra's sister, she flinched, turning her cheek.

The priest stepped back. His gaze—and his voice—was tranquil.

"You may rise," he said. "Rise, and become mothers of flame."

His sister took her ladies' hands. She clasped them tight. They stood, the three of them, for a long moment, simply holding one another. Then his sister released them.

The ladies walked to the pyre and rose to its zenith. They kneeled.

His sister remained where she was. She stood with her head raised. A breeze blew needle-flower into her hair—white upon deepest black.

"Princess Malini," said the head priest. "You may rise."

She shook her head wordlessly.

Rise, Chandra thought. *I have been more merciful than you deserve, and we both know it.*

Rise, sister.

"It is your choice," the priest said. "We will not compel you. Will you forsake immortality, or will you rise?"

The offer was a straightforward one. But she did not move. She shook her head once more. She was weeping, silently, her face otherwise devoid of feeling.

The priest nodded.

"Then we begin," he said.

Chandra stood. The prayer stones clinked as he released them.

Of course it had come to this.

He stepped down from his throne. He crossed the court, before a sea of bowing men. He took his sister by the shoulders, ever so gentle.

"Do not be afraid," he told her. "You are proving your purity. You are saving your name. Your honor. Now. *Rise.*"

One of the priests had lit a torch. The scent of burning and camphor filled the court. The priests began to sing, a low song that filled the air, swelled within it. They would not wait for his sister.

But there was still time. The pyre had not yet been lit.

As his sister shook her head once more, he grasped her by the skull, raising her face up.

He did not hold her tight. He did not harm her. He was not a monster.

"Remember," he said, voice low, nearly drowned out by the sonorous song, "that you have brought this upon yourself. Remember that you have betrayed your family and denied your name. If you do not rise... sister, remember that you have chosen to ruin yourself, and I have done all in my power to help you. Remember that."

The priest touched his torch to the pyre. The wood, slowly, began to burn.

Firelight reflected in her eyes. She looked at him with a face like a mirror: blank of feeling, reflecting nothing back at him but their shared dark eyes and serious brows. Their shared blood and shared bone.

"My brother," she said. "I will not forget."

1

PRIYA

Someone important must have been killed in the night.

Priya was sure of it the minute she heard the thud of hooves on the road behind her. She stepped to the roadside as a group of guards clad in Parijati white and gold raced past her on their horses, their sabers clinking against their embossed belts. She drew her pallu over her face—partly because they would expect such a gesture of respect from a common woman, and partly to avoid the risk that one of them would recognize her—and watched them through the gap between her fingers and the cloth.

When they were out of sight, she didn't run. But she did start walking very, very fast. The sky was already transforming from milky gray to the pearly blue of dawn, and she still had a long way to go.

The Old Bazaar was on the outskirts of the city. It was far enough from the regent's mahal that Priya had a vague hope it wouldn't have been shut yet. And today, she was lucky. As she arrived, breathless, sweat dampening the back of her blouse, she could see that the streets were still seething with people: parents tugging along small children; traders carrying large sacks of flour or rice on their heads; gaunt beggars, skirting the edges of the market with their alms bowls in hand; and women like Priya, plain ordinary women in even plainer saris, stubbornly shoving their way through the crowd in search of stalls with fresh vegetables and reasonable prices.

If anything, there seemed to be even *more* people at the bazaar than usual—and there was a distinct sour note of panic in the air.

News of the patrols had clearly passed from household to household with its usual speed.

People were afraid.

Three months ago, an important Parijati merchant had been murdered in his bed, his throat slit, his body dumped in front of the temple of the mothers of flame just before the dawn prayers. For an entire two weeks after that, the regent's men had patrolled the streets on foot and on horseback, beating or arresting Ahiranyi suspected of rebellious activity and destroying any market stalls that had tried to remain open in defiance of the regent's strict orders.

The Parijatdvipan merchants had refused to supply Hiranaprastha with rice and grain in the weeks that followed. Ahiranyi had starved.

Now it looked as though it was happening again. It was natural for people to remember and fear; remember, and scramble to buy what supplies they could before the markets were forcibly closed once more.

Priya wondered who had been murdered this time, listening for any names as she dove into the mass of people, toward the green banner on staves in the distance that marked the apothecary's stall. She passed tables groaning under stacks of vegetables and sweet fruit, bolts of silky cloth and gracefully carved idols of the yaksa for family shrines, vats of golden oil and ghee. Even in the faint early-morning light, the market was vibrant with color and noise.

The press of people grew more painful.

She was nearly to the stall, caught in a sea of heaving, sweating bodies, when a man behind her cursed and pushed her out of the way. He shoved her hard with his full body weight, his palm heavy on her arm, unbalancing her entirely. Three people around her were knocked back. In the sudden release of pressure, she tumbled down onto the ground, feet skidding in the wet soil.

The bazaar was open to the air, and the dirt had been churned into a froth by feet and carts and the night's monsoon rainfall. She felt the wetness seep in through her sari, from hem to thigh, soaking through draped cotton to the petticoat underneath. The man who had shoved her stumbled into her; if she hadn't snatched her calf swiftly back, the pressure of his boot on her leg would have been agonizing. He glanced down at her—blank, dismissive, a faint sneer to his mouth—and looked away again.

Her mind went quiet.

In the silence, a single voice whispered, *You could make him regret that.*

There were gaps in Priya's childhood memories, spaces big enough to stick a fist through. But whenever pain was inflicted on her—the humiliation of a blow, a man's careless shove, a fellow servant's cruel laughter—she felt the knowledge of how to cause equal suffering unfurl in her mind. Ghostly whispers, in her brother's patient voice.

This is how you pinch a nerve hard enough to break a handhold. This is how you snap a bone. This is how you gouge an eye. Watch carefully, Priya. Just like this.

This is how you stab someone through the heart.

She carried a knife at her waist. It was a very good knife, practical, with a plain sheath and hilt, and she kept its edge finely honed for kitchen work. With nothing but her little knife and a careful slide of her finger and thumb, she could leave the insides of anything—vegetables, unskinned meat, fruits newly harvested from the regent's orchard—swiftly bared, the outer rind a smooth, coiled husk in her palm.

She looked back up at the man and carefully let the thought of her knife drift away. She unclenched her trembling fingers.

You're lucky, she thought, *that I am not what I was raised to be.*

The crowd behind her and in front of her was growing thicker. Priya couldn't even see the green banner of the apothecary's stall any longer. She rocked back on the balls of her feet, then rose swiftly. Without looking at the man again, she angled herself and slipped between two strangers in front of her, putting her small stature to good use and shoving her way to the front of the throng. A judicious application of her elbows and knees and some wriggling finally brought her near enough to the stall to see the apothecary's face, puckered with sweat and irritation.

The stall was a mess, vials turned on their sides, clay pots upended. The apothecary was packing away his wares as fast as he could. Behind her, around her, she could hear the rumbling noise of the crowd grow more tense.

"Please," she said loudly. "Uncle, *please*. If you've got any beads of sacred wood to spare, I'll buy them from you."

A stranger to her left snorted audibly. "You think he's got any left? Brother, if you do, I'll pay double whatever she offers."

"My grandmother's sick," a girl shouted, three people deep behind them. "So if you could help me out, uncle—"

Priya felt the wood of the stall begin to peel beneath the hard pressure of her nails.

"Please," she said, her voice pitched low to cut across the din.

But the apothecary's attention was raised toward the back of the crowd. Priya didn't have to turn her own head to know he'd caught sight of the white-and-gold uniforms of the regent's men, finally here to close the bazaar.

"I'm closed up," he shouted out. "There's nothing more for any of you. Get lost!" He slammed his hand down, then shoved the last of his wares away with a shake of his head.

The crowd began to disperse slowly. A few people stayed, still pleading for the apothecary's aid, but Priya didn't join them. She knew she would get nothing here.

She turned and threaded her way back out of the crowd, stopping only to buy a small bag of kachoris from a tired-eyed vendor. Her sodden petticoat stuck heavily to her legs. She plucked the cloth, pulling it from her thighs, and strode in the opposite direction of the soldiers.

orbit

Follow us:

f /orbitbooksUS

/orbitbooks

/orbitbooks

Join our mailing list
to receive alerts on our
latest releases and deals.

orbitbooks.net

Enter our monthly
giveaway for the chance
to win some epic prizes.

orbitloot.com